AMERICAN SHORT STORY MASTERPIECES

AMERICAN SHORT STORY MASTERPIECES

EDITED BY

Raymond Carver and Tom Jenks

DELACORTE PRESS / NEW YORK

Published by
Delacorte Press
1 Dag Hammarskjold Plaza
New York, N.Y. 10017

Manufactured in the United States of America

First printing

Library of Congress Cataloging in Publication Data

American short story masterpieces.

1. Short stories, American. 2. American fiction—
20th century. I. Carver, Raymond. II. Jenks, Tom.
PS648.S5A49   1987   813'.01'09   86-19964
ISBN 0-385-29524-3

AMG

MAY 1 9 1987

Alfred A. Knopf, Inc.: "Water Liars" by Barry Hannah, from *Airships*. First published in *Esquire*. Copyright 1978 by Barry Hannah.

Delacorte Press/Seymour Lawrence: "Letters from the *Samantha*" by Mark Helprin, from *Ellis Island and Other Stories*. First published in *The New Yorker*. Copyright 1976 by Mark Helprin.

Harper & Row, Inc.: "Ile Forest" by Ursula K. Le Guin, from *Orsinian Tales*. Copyright 1976 by Ursula K. Le Guin.

Farrar, Straus & Giroux, Inc.: "The Magic Barrel" by Bernard Malamud, from *The Magic Barrel*. Copyright 1954, 1958 by Bernard Malamud.

Harper & Row, Inc.: "Shiloh" by Bobbie Ann Mason, from *Shiloh and Other Stories*. First published in *The New Yorker*. Copyright 1982 by Bobbie Ann Mason.

Little, Brown and Co.: "The Story of a Scar" by James Alan McPherson, from *Elbow Room*. First published in *The Atlantic*. Copyright 1973 by James Alan McPherson.

Farrar, Straus & Giroux, Inc.: "Murderers" by Leonard Michaels, from *I Would Have Saved Them If I Could*. First published in *Quarry*. Copyright 1971, 1975 by Leonard Michaels.

International Creative Management: "The Misfits" by Arthur Miller, from *The Misfits & Other Stories* (Scribners Signature). Copyright 1957 by Arthur Miller.

Vanguard Press, Inc.: "Where Are You Going, Where Have You Been?" by Joyce Carol Oates, from *The Wheel of Love*. First published in *Epoch*. Copyright 1965, 1966, 1967, 1968, 1969, 1970 by Joyce Carol Oates.

Harcourt Brace Jovanovich, Inc.: "A Good Man Is Hard to Find" by Flannery O'Connor, from *A Good Man Is Hard to Find and Other Stories*. Copyright 1953 by Flannery O'Connor.

Elaine Markson Literary Agency, Inc.: "The Used-Boy Raisers" by Grace Paley, from *The Little Disturbances of Man*. Copyright 1959 by Grace Paley.

Delacorte Press/Seymour Lawrence: "The Heavenly Animal" by Jayne Anne Phillips, from *Black Tickets*. First published in *Fiction International*. Copyright 1975, 1976, 1978, 1979 by Jayne Anne Phillips.

David Quammen: "Walking Out" by David Quammen. First published in *Tri-Quarterly*. Copyright 1980 by David Quammen.

Houghton Mifflin Co.: "The Conversion of the Jews" by Philip Roth, from *Goodbye, Columbus*. First published in *The Paris Review*. Copyright 1959 by Philip Roth.

James Salter: "Akhnilo" by James Salter. First published in *Grand Street*. Copyright 1981 by James Salter.

Alfred A. Knopf, Inc.: "The Christian Roommates" by John Updike, from *The Music School*. First published in *The New Yorker*. Copyright 1964 by John Updike.

Random House, Inc.: "The Wedding" by Joy Williams, from *Taking Care*. Copyright 1982 by Joy Williams.

The Ecco Press: "The Liar" by Tobias Wolff, from *In the Garden of the North American Martyrs*. First published in *The Atlantic*. Copyright 1981 by Tobias Wolff.

Additional thanks to Noy Holland for research and to Sara London for editorial assistance.

CONTENTS

viii   *Contents*

CHRONOLOGICAL TABLE OF CONTENTS

ABOUT THE EDITORS

RAYMOND CARVER is the founding editor of *Quarry West* magazine and the author of three short story collections, *Will You Please Be Quiet, Please?*, *What We Talk About When We Talk About Love*, and *Cathedral*. His poems have been collected in three volumes, *Where Water Comes Together With Other Water*, *Ultramarine*, and in *Fires*, which also includes short stories, an interview, and personal essays.

TOM JENKS is a senior editor at Charles Scribner's Sons, an editor of *The Paris Review* and of *EQUATOR* magazine, and a former fiction editor of *Esquire*. He is also the editor of *Soldiers & Civilians*, an anthology of contemporary American short stories that reflect the influence of military values in our lives.

INTRODUCTION

> The excellent becomes the permanent.
> ARISTOTLE

When we began the work of assembling short stories for this book, one of our criteria—unspoken, but there nonetheless—was that a story's narrative interest would be one of the deciding factors in our selections. We also felt that we were not out to be democratic in our selections, or even representative. There was only so much space in the anthology after all, and a limit to the number of stories we could include. Decisions had to be made that were not always easy. But aside from this, however, we were simply not interested in putting before the reader further samples of what some have called "postmodern" or "innovative" fiction, and others have hailed as "the new fiction"—self-reflexive, fabulist, magical realist, as well as all mutations, offshoots, and fringe movements thereof. We were interested in stories that had not only a strong narrative drive, with characters we could respond to as human beings, but stories where the effects of language, situation, and insight were intense and total—short stories which on occasion had the ambition of enlarging our view of ourselves and the world.

A tall order, indeed. But isn't it true that with any great, or even really good short story (or any other singular work of literary art), just something like this does often happen? We think the thirty-six short stories included herein are ample evidence that it *is* possible for stories to produce such salutary effects; and in our selections we aimed for work that aspired to nothing less—stories of consequence that in some important way bear witness to our own lives. In any event, in light of our sensibilities and according to our criteria, time and again we found ourselves moved and exhilarated as we read and selected the work that follows.

It's our view, and one not held lightly, certainly not defensively, that the best short stories of the past thirty years can stand alongside the best of those of earlier generations—the several generations of writers represented, say, in *Short Story Masterpieces*, that excellent book edited by Robert Penn Warren and Albert Erskine. In its way, this present collection may be seen as a companion volume to that earlier book. Most important in this regard, the bias of this collection, as in the other, is toward the lifelike—that is to say, toward realistically fashioned stories that may even in some cases approximate the outlines of our own lives. Or, if not our own, at least the lives of fellow human beings—grown-up men and women engaged in the ordinary but sometimes remarkable business of living and, like ourselves, in full awareness of their mortality.

In the last thirty years there was, on the part of many writers, a radical turning away from the concerns and techniques of realism—a turning away from the "manners and morals" that Lionel Trilling correctly saw as the best subject matter for fiction. In place of realism, a number of writers—writers of considerable skill and stature, some of them—substituted the surreal and the fantastic. A smaller and less-talented group mixed the weird and the far-out with a relentless and sometimes disquieting nihilism. Now it seems that the wheel has rolled forward again and fiction that approximates life—replete with recognizable people, and motive, and plot, and drama—fiction of *occurrence* and *consequence* (the two are inseparable), has reasserted itself with a reading public that has grown tired of the fragmentary, or bizarre. Fiction that asks that the reader give up too much—in some cases deny what reason, common sense, the emotions, and a sense of right and wrong tell him—is seemingly in retreat these days.

No one should be surprised then at the resurgence, not to say new dominance, of realistic fiction, that most ancient of storytelling modes. This book might be seen as a celebration of, and a tribute to, the lasting power of narrative short fiction. We further feel we have gathered together some of the best stories recently produced by this oldest of literary traditions, work that we like to think has as good a chance as any, and better than most, of withstanding "the tooth of time."

A notable difference between *Short Story Masterpieces* and this book is that fully a third of the thirty-six stories in the earlier collection are by writers from England and Ireland. When we were establishing some ground rules to determine how we planned to go about selecting stories for this anthology, we decided early on to include works by American writers only. There was, we felt, plenty of significant work on this side of the Atlantic from which to choose. We also decided not to include stories by writers who were already included in *Short Story Masterpieces*. Thus, Peter Taylor, Eudora Welty, and John Cheever, some of whose best work was published after 1954 (the year *Short Story Masterpieces* appeared) were reluctantly left out.

In one respect, at least, it would seem that life was simpler in the literary world of the early 1950s: Warren and Erskine didn't have to talk about "postmodernism" or any of the other "isms"—including "realism." They didn't find it necessary to explain the reasons that lay behind their choices, or articulate their taste and methodology. They simply discussed good and great stories—masterpieces, by their definition— and masters of the form. The word *masterpiece* meant something in those days and signaled a benchmark of excellence that most readers (and writers) could agree on. No one had to debate the concept itself, or the wisdom of applying such a term to select examples of serious, imaginative writing. The editors found two dozen stories by American writers, spanning fifty years or more of American life and literary endeavor, and they put these stories alongside a dozen stories by their English and Irish counterparts of roughly the same period. They had their book. We limited ourselves to American writers only, as has been noted, and our selections cover thirty-three years—1953 to 1986, to be exact—surely the most climactic, and traumatic, period in American literary history. Traumatic, in part, because it has been a time during which the currency of narrative fiction has fluctuated wildly and been variously assailed from several quarters. Now is as good a time as any, perhaps, to try to reestablish the term *masterpiece* as it applies to singular stories with a narrative durability, within a discernible *narrative* tradition.

As we considered the merits of each story, we asked ourselves at how deep a level of feeling and insight the writer was operating. How compelling, and coherent, was the writer's *sincerity* (Tolstoy's word, and one of his criteria for excellence) toward his material? Great fiction—good fiction—is, as any serious reader knows, intellectually and emotionally significant. And the best fiction ought to have, for want of a better word, *heft* to it. (The Romans used the word *gravitas* when talking about work of substance.) But whatever one wants to call it (it doesn't even need naming), everyone recognizes it when it declares itself. When a reader finishes a wonderful story and lays it aside, he should have to pause for a minute and collect himself. At this moment, if the writer has succeeded, there ought to be a unity of feeling and understanding. Or, if not a unity, at least a sense that the disparities of a crucial situation have been made available in a new light, and we can go from there. The best fiction, the kind of fiction we're talking about, should bring about this kind of response. It should make such an impression that the work, as Hemingway suggested, becomes a part of the reader's experience. Or else, and we're serious, why should people be asked to read it? Further—why write it? In great fiction (and this *is* true, and we mustn't fool ourselves that it's otherwise), there is always the "shock of recognition" as the human significance of the work is revealed and made manifest. When, in Joyce's words, the soul of the story, its "whatness leaps to us from the vestment of its appearance."

In his "Introduction to the Works of Guy de Maupassant," Tolstoy wrote that talent is "the capacity to direct intense concentrated attention on the subject . . . a gift of seeing what others have not seen." We think the writers included in these pages have done this, have directed "intense concentration" on their subject, seeing clearly and forcefully what others have not seen. On the other hand, considering some of these stories and their insistence on depicting the "familiar," we think something else is just as often at work—another definition of "talent," perhaps. We'd like to suggest that talent, even genius, is also *the gift of seeing what everyone else has seen, but seeing it more clearly, from all sides.* Art in either case.

The writers in this book have talent, and they have it in abundance. But they have something else as well: They can all tell a good story, and good stories, as everyone knows, have always been in demand. In the words of Sean O'Faolain, a contributor to the earlier book, the stories that follow have "a bright destination." We hope readers will be affected by more than a few of these and will perhaps find occasion to laugh, shudder, marvel—in short, be *moved,* and maybe even a little haunted by some of the lives represented here.

—Raymond Carver and Tom Jenks

AMERICAN
SHORT STORY
MASTERPIECES

JAMES BALDWIN

Sonny's Blues

I read about it in the paper, in the subway, on my way to work. I read it, and I couldn't believe it, and I read it again. Then perhaps I just stared at it, at the newsprint spelling out his name, spelling out the story. I stared at it in the swinging lights of the subway car, and in the faces and bodies of the people, and in my own face, trapped in the darkness which roared outside.

It was not to be believed and I kept telling myself that, as I walked from the subway station to the high school. And at the same time I couldn't doubt it. I was scared, scared for Sonny. He became real to me again. A great block of ice got settled in my belly and kept melting there slowly all day long, while I taught my classes algebra. It was a special kind of ice. It kept melting, sending trickles of ice water all up and down my veins, but it never got less. Sometimes it hardened and seemed to expand until I felt my guts were going to come spilling out or that I was going to choke or scream. This would always be at a moment when I was remembering some specific thing Sonny had once said or done.

When he was about as old as the boys in my classes his face had been bright and open, there was a lot of copper in it; and he'd had wonderfully direct brown eyes, and great gentleness and privacy. I wondered what he looked like now. He had been picked up, the evening before, in a raid on an apartment downtown, for peddling and using heroin.

I couldn't believe it: but what I mean by that is that I couldn't find any room for it anywhere inside me. I had kept it outside me for a long time. I hadn't wanted to know. I had had suspicions, but I didn't name them, I kept putting them away. I told myself that Sonny was wild, but he wasn't crazy. And he'd always been a good boy, he hadn't ever turned hard or evil or disrespectful, the way kids can, so quick, so quick, especially in Harlem. I didn't want to believe that I'd ever see my brother going down, coming to nothing, all that light in his face gone out, in the condition I'd already seen so many others. Yet it had happened and here I was, talking about algebra to a lot of boys who might, every one of them for all I knew, be popping off needles every time they went to the head. Maybe it did more for them than algebra could.

I was sure that the first time Sonny had ever had horse, he couldn't have been much older than these boys were now. These boys, now, were living as we'd been living then, they were growing up with a rush and their heads bumped abruptly against the low ceiling of their actual possibilities. They were filled with rage. All they really knew were two darknesses, the darkness of their lives, which was now closing in on them, and the darkness of the movies, which had blinded them to that other darkness, and in which they now, vindictively, dreamed, at once more together than they were at any other time, and more alone.

When the last bell rang, the last class ended, I let out my breath. It seemed I'd been holding it for all that time. My clothes were wet—I may have looked as though I'd been sitting in a steam bath, all dressed up, all afternoon. I sat alone in the classroom a long time. I listened to the boys outside, downstairs, shouting and cursing and laughing. Their laughter struck me for perhaps the first time. It was not the joyous laughter which—God knows why—one associates with children. It was mocking and insular, its intent to denigrate. It was disenchanted, and in this, also, lay the authority of their curses. Perhaps I was listening to them because I was thinking about my brother and in them I heard my brother. And myself.

One boy was whistling a tune, at once very complicated and very simple, it seemed to be pouring out of him as though he were a bird, and it sounded very cool and moving through all that harsh, bright air, only just holding its own through all those other sounds.

I stood up and walked over to the window and looked down into the courtyard. It was the beginning of the spring and the sap was rising in the boys. A teacher passed through them every now and again, quickly, as though he or she couldn't wait to get out of that courtyard, to get those boys out of their sight and off their minds. I started collecting my stuff. I thought I'd better get home and talk to Isabel.

The courtyard was almost deserted by the time I got downstairs. I saw this boy standing in the shadow of a doorway, looking just like Sonny. I almost called his name. Then I saw that it wasn't Sonny, but somebody we used to know, a boy from around our block. He'd been Sonny's friend. He'd never been mine, having been too young for me, and, anyway, I'd never liked him. And now, even though he was a grown-up man, he still hung around that block, still spent hours on the street corners, was always high and raggy. I used to run into him from time to time and he'd often work around to asking me for a quarter or fifty cents. He always had some real good excuse, too, and I always gave it to him, I don't know why.

But now, abruptly, I hated him. I couldn't stand the way he looked at me, partly like a dog, partly like a cunning child. I wanted to ask him what the hell he was doing in the school courtyard.

He sort of shuffled over to me, and he said, "I see you got the papers. So you already know about it."

"You mean about Sonny? Yes, I already know about it. How come they didn't get you?"

He grinned. It made him repulsive and it also brought to mind what he'd looked like as a kid. "I wasn't there. I stay away from them people."

"Good for you." I offered him a cigarette and I watched him through the smoke. "You come all the way down here just to tell me about Sonny?"

"That's right." He was sort of shaking his head and his eyes looked strange, as though they were about to cross. The bright sun deadened his damp dark brown skin and it made his eyes look yellow and showed up the dirt in his kinked hair. He smelled funky. I moved a little away from him and I said, "Well, thanks. But I already know about it and I got to get home."

"I'll walk you a little ways," he said. We started walking. There were a couple of kids still loitering in the courtyard and one of them said good night to me and looked strangely at the boy beside me.

"What're you going to do?" he asked me. "I mean, about Sonny?"

"Look. I haven't seen Sonny for over a year, I'm not sure I'm going to do anything. Anyway, what the hell *can* I do?"

"That's right," he said quickly, "ain't nothing you can do. Can't much help old Sonny no more, I guess."

It was what I was thinking and so it seemed to me he had no right to say it.

"I'm surprised at Sonny, though," he went on—he had a funny way of talking, he looked straight ahead as though he were talking to himself— "I thought Sonny was a smart boy, I thought he was too smart to get hung."

"I guess he thought so too," I said sharply, "and that's how he got hung. And how about you? You're pretty goddamn smart, I bet."

Then he looked directly at me, just for a minute. "I ain't smart," he said. "If I was smart, I'd have reached for a pistol a long time ago."

"Look. Don't tell *me* your sad story, if it was up to me, I'd give you one." Then I felt guilty—guilty, probably, for never having supposed that the poor bastard *had* a story of his own, much less a sad one, and I asked, quickly, "What's going to happen to him now?"

He didn't answer this. He was off by himself some place. "Funny thing," he said, and from his tone we might have been discussing the quickest way to get to Brooklyn, "when I saw the papers this morning, the first thing I asked myself was if I had anything to do with it. I felt sort of responsible."

I began to listen more carefully. The subway station was on the corner, just before us, and I stopped. He stopped, too. We were in front of a bar and he ducked slightly, peering in, but whoever he was looking for didn't seem to be there. The jukebox was blasting away with something black and bouncy and I half watched the barmaid as she danced her way from the jukebox to her place behind the bar. And I watched her face as she laughingly responded to something someone said to her, still keeping time to the music. When she smiled one saw the little girl, one sensed the doomed, still-struggling woman beneath the battered face of the semi-whore.

"I never *give* Sonny nothing," the boy said finally, "but a long time ago I come to school high and Sonny asked me how it felt." He paused, I couldn't bear to watch him, I watched the barmaid, and I listened to the music which seemed to be causing the pavement to shake. "I told him it felt great." The music stopped, the barmaid paused and watched the jukebox until the music began again. "It did."

All this was carrying me some place I didn't want to go. I certainly didn't want to know how it felt. It filled everything, the people, the houses, the music, the dark, quicksilver barmaid, with menace; and this menace was their reality.

"What's going to happen to him now?" I asked again.

"They'll send him away some place and they'll try to cure him." He shook his head. "Maybe he'll even think he's kicked the habit. Then they'll let him loose"—he gestured, throwing his cigarette into the gutter. "That's all."

"What do you mean, that's *all*?"

But I knew what he meant.

"I *mean*, that's *all*." He turned his head and looked at me, pulling down the corners of his mouth. "Don't you know what I mean?" he asked, softly.

"How the hell *would* I know what you mean?" I almost whispered it, I don't know why.

"That's right," he said to the air, "how would *he* know what I mean?" He turned toward me again, patient and calm, and yet I somehow felt him shaking, shaking as though he were going to fall apart. I felt that ice in my guts again, the dread I'd felt all afternoon; and again I watched the barmaid, moving about the bar, washing glasses, and singing. "Listen. They'll let him out and then it'll just start all over again. That's what I mean."

"You mean—they'll let him out. And then he'll just start working his way back in again. You mean he'll never kick the habit. Is that what you mean?"

"That's right," he said, cheerfully. "*You* see what I mean."

"Tell me," I said at last, "why does he want to die? He must want to die, he's killing himself, why does he want to die?"

He looked at me in surprise. He licked his lips. "He don't want to die. He wants to live. Don't nobody want to die, ever."

Then I wanted to ask him—too many things. He could not have answered, or if he had, I could not have borne the answers. I started walking. "Well, I guess it's none of my business."

"It's going to be rough on old Sonny," he said. We reached the subway station. "This is your station?" he asked. I nodded. I took one step down. "Damn!" he said, suddenly. I looked up at him. He grinned again. "Damn it if I didn't leave all my money home. You ain't got a dollar on you, have you? Just for a couple of days, is all."

All at once something inside gave and threatened to come pouring out of me. I didn't hate him anymore. I felt that in another moment I'd start crying like a child.

"Sure," I said. "Don't sweat." I looked in my wallet and didn't have a dollar, I only had a five. "Here," I said. "That hold you?"

He didn't look at it—he didn't want to look at it. A terrible closed look came over his face, as though he were keeping the number on the bill a secret from him and me. "Thanks," he said, and now he was dying to see me go. "Don't worry about Sonny. Maybe I'll write him or something."

"Sure," I said. "You do that. So long."

"Be seeing you," he said. I went on down the steps.

And I didn't write Sonny or send him anything for a long time. When I finally did, it was just after my little girl died, he wrote me back a letter which made me feel like a bastard.

Here's what he said:

> Dear brother,
>
> You don't know how much I needed to hear from you. I wanted to write you many a time but I dug how much I must have hurt you and so I didn't write. But now I feel like a man who's been trying to climb up out of some deep, real deep and funky hole and just saw the sun up there, outside. I got to get outside.
>
> I can't tell you much about how I got here. I mean I don't know how to tell you. I guess I was afraid of something or I was trying to escape from something and you know I have never been very strong in the head (smile). I'm glad Mama and Daddy are dead and can't see what's happened to their son and I swear if I'd known what I was doing I would never have hurt you so, you and a lot of other fine people who were nice to me and who believed in me.
>
> I don't want you to think it had anything to do with me being a musician. It's more than that. Or maybe less than that. I can't get anything straight in my head down here and I try not to think about what's going to happen to me when I get outside again. Sometime I think I'm going to flip and *never* get outside and sometime I think

I'll come straight back. I tell you one thing, though, I'd rather blow my brains out than go through this again. But that's what they all say, so they tell me. If I tell you when I'm coming to New York and if you could meet me, I sure would appreciate it. Give my love to Isabel and the kids and I was sure sorry to hear about little Gracie. I wish I could be like Mama and say the Lord's will be done, but I don't know it seems to me that trouble is the one thing that never does get stopped and I don't know what good it does to blame it on the Lord. But maybe it does some good if you believe it.

Your brother,
Sonny

Then I kept in constant touch with him and I sent him whatever I could and I went to meet him when he came back to New York. When I saw him many things I thought I had forgotten came flooding back to me. This was because I had begun, finally, to wonder about Sonny, about the life that Sonny lived inside. This life, whatever it was, had made him older and thinner and it had deepened the distant stillness in which he had always moved. He looked very unlike my baby brother. Yet, when he smiled, when we shook hands, the baby brother I'd never known looked out from the depths of his private life, like an animal waiting to be coaxed into the light.

"How you been keeping?" he asked me.

"All right. And you?"

"Just fine." He was smiling all over his face. "It's good to see you again."

"It's good to see you."

The seven years' difference in our ages lay between us like a chasm: I wondered if these years would ever operate between us as a bridge. I was remembering, and it made it hard to catch my breath, that I had been there when he was born; and I had heard the first words he had ever spoken. When he started to walk, he walked from our mother straight to me. I caught him just before he fell when he took the first steps he ever took in this world.

"How's Isabel?"

"Just fine. She's dying to see you."

"And the boys?"

"They're fine, too. They're anxious to see their uncle."

"Oh, come on. You know they don't remember me."

"Are you kidding? Of course they remember you."

He grinned again. We got into a taxi. We had a lot to say to each other, far too much to know how to begin.

As the taxi began to move, I asked, "You still want to go to India?"

He laughed. "You still remember that. Hell, no. This place is Indian enough for me."

"It used to belong to them," I said.

And he laughed again. "They damn sure knew what they were doing when they got rid of it."

Years ago, when he was around fourteen, he'd been all hipped on the idea of going to India. He read books about people sitting on rocks, naked, in all kinds of weather, but mostly bad, naturally, and walking barefoot through hot coals and arriving at wisdom. I used to say that it sounded to me as though they were getting away from wisdom as fast as they could. I think he sort of looked down on me for that.

"Do you mind," he asked, "if we have the driver drive alongside the park? On the west side—I haven't seen the city in so long."

"Of course not," I said. I was afraid that I might sound as though I were humoring him, but I hoped he wouldn't take it that way.

So we drove along, between the green of the park and the stony, lifeless elegance of hotels and apartment buildings, toward the vivid, killing streets of our childhood. These streets hadn't changed, though housing projects jutted up out of them now like rocks in the middle of a boiling sea. Most of the houses in which we had grown up had vanished, as had the stores from which we had stolen, the basements in which we had first tried sex, the rooftops from which we had hurled tin cans and bricks. But houses exactly like the houses of our past yet dominated the landscape, boys exactly like the boys we once had been found themselves smothering in these houses, came down into the streets for light and air and found themselves encircled by disaster. Some escaped the trap, most didn't. Those who got out always left something of themselves behind, as some animals amputate a leg and leave it in the trap. It might be said, perhaps, that I had escaped, after all, I was a school teacher; or that Sonny had, he hadn't lived in Harlem for years. Yet, as the cab moved uptown through streets which seemed, with a rush, to darken with dark people, and as I covertly studied Sonny's face, it came to me that what we both were seeking through our separate cab windows was that part of ourselves which had been left behind. It's always at the hour of trouble and confrontation that the missing member aches.

We hit 110th Street and started rolling up Lenox Avenue. And I'd known this avenue all my life, but it seemed to me again, as it had seemed on the day I'd first heard about Sonny's trouble, filled with a hidden menace which was its very breath of life.

"We almost there," said Sonny.

"Almost." We were both too nervous to say anything more.

We live in a housing project. It hasn't been up long. A few days after it was up it seemed uninhabitably new, now, of course, it's already run-down. It looks like a parody of the good, clean, faceless life—God knows the people who live in it do their best to make it a parody. The beat-looking grass lying around isn't enough to make their lives green, the hedges will never hold out the streets, and they know it. The big windows fool no one, they aren't big enough to make space out of no space. They don't bother with the windows, they watch the TV screen instead. The playground is most popular with the children who don't play at jacks, or skip rope, or roller skate, or swing, and they can be found in it after dark. We moved in partly because it's not too far from where I teach, and partly for the kids; but it's really just like the houses in which Sonny and I grew up. The same things happen, they'll have the same things to remember. The moment Sonny and I started into the house I had the feeling that I was simply bringing him back into the danger he had almost died trying to escape.

Sonny has never been talkative. So I don't know why I was sure he'd be dying to talk to me when supper was over the first night. Everything went fine, the oldest boy remembered him, and the youngest boy liked him, and Sonny had remembered to bring something for each of them; and Isabel, who is really much nicer than I am, more open and giving, had gone to a lot of trouble about dinner and was genuinely glad to see him. And she's always been able to tease Sonny in a way that I haven't. It was nice to see her face so vivid again and to hear her laugh and watch her make Sonny laugh. She wasn't, or, anyway, she didn't seem to be, at all uneasy or embarrassed. She chatted as though there were no subject which had to be avoided and she got Sonny past his first, faint stiffness. And thank God she was there, for I was filled with that icy dread again. Everything I did seemed awkward to me, and everything I said sounded freighted with hidden meaning. I was trying to remember everything I'd heard about dope addiction and I couldn't help watching Sonny for signs. I wasn't doing it out of malice. I was trying to find out something about my brother. I was dying to hear him tell me he was safe.

"Safe!" my father grunted, whenever Mama suggested trying to move to a neighborhood which might be safer for children. "Safe, hell! Ain't no place safe for kids, nor nobody."

He always went on like this, but he wasn't, ever, really as bad as he sounded, not even on weekends, when he got drunk. As a matter of fact, he was always on the lookout for "something a little better," but he died before he found it. He died suddenly, during a drunken weekend in the middle of the war, when Sonny was fifteen. He and Sonny hadn't ever got on too well. And this was partly because Sonny was the apple of his father's eye. It was because he loved Sonny so much and was frightened for him, that he was always fighting with him. It doesn't do any good to fight with Sonny. Sonny just moves back, inside himself, where he can't be reached. But the principal reason that they never hit it off is that they were so much alike. Daddy was big and rough and loud-talking, just the opposite of Sonny, but they both had—that same privacy.

Mama tried to tell me something about this, just after Daddy died. I was home on leave from the army.

This was the last time I ever saw my mother alive. Just the same, this picture gets all mixed up in my mind with pictures I had of her when she was younger. The way I always see her is the way she used to be on a Sunday afternoon, say, when the old folks were talking after the big Sunday dinner. I always see her wearing pale blue. She'd be sitting on the sofa. And my father would be sitting in the easy chair, not far from her. And the living room would be full of church folks and relatives. There they sit, in chairs all around the living room, and the night is creeping up outside, but nobody knows it yet. You can see the darkness growing against the windowpanes and you hear the street noises every now and again, or maybe the jangling beat of a tambourine from one of the churches close by, but it's real quiet in the room. For a moment nobody's talking, but every face looks darkening, like the sky outside. And my mother rocks a little from the waist, and my father's eyes are closed. Everyone is looking at something a child can't see. For a minute they've forgotten the children. Maybe a kid is lying on the rug, half asleep. Maybe somebody's got a kid in his lap and is absentmindedly stroking the kid's head. Maybe there's a kid, quiet and big-eyed, curled up in a big chair in the corner. The silence, the darkness coming, and the darkness in the faces frightens the child obscurely. He hopes that the hand which strokes his forehead will never stop—will never die. He hopes that there will never come a time when the old folks won't be sitting around the living room, talking about where they've come from, and what they've seen, and what's happened to them and their kinfolk.

But something deep and watchful in the child knows that this is bound to end, is already ending. In a moment someone will get up and turn on the light. Then the old folks will remember the children and they won't talk anymore that day. And when light fills the room, the child is filled with darkness. He knows that everytime this happens he's moved just a little closer to that darkness outside. The darkness outside is what the old folks have been talking about. It's what they've come from. It's what they endure. The child knows that they won't talk anymore because if he knows too much about what's happened to *them*, he'll know too much too soon, about what's going to happen to *him*.

The last time I talked to my mother, I remember I was restless. I wanted to get out and see Isabel. We weren't married then and we had a lot to straighten out between us.

There Mama sat, in black, by the window. She was humming an old church song, *Lord, you brought me from a long ways off.* Sonny was out somewhere. Mama kept watching the streets.

"I don't know," she said, "if I'll ever see you again, after you go off from here. But I hope you'll remember the things I tried to teach you."

"Don't talk like that," I said, and smiled. "You'll be here a long time yet."

She smiled, too, but she said nothing. She was quiet for a long time. And I said, "Mama, don't you worry about nothing. I'll be writing all the time, and you be getting the checks. . . ."

"I want to talk to you about your brother," she said, suddenly. "If anything happens to me he ain't going to have nobody to look out for him."

"Mama," I said, "ain't nothing going to happen to you *or* Sonny. Sonny's all right. He's a good boy and he's got good sense."

"It ain't a question of his being a good boy," Mama said, "nor of his having good sense. It ain't only the bad ones, nor yet the dumb ones that gets sucked under." She stopped, looking at me. "Your Daddy once had a brother," she said, and she smiled in a way that made me feel she was in pain. "You didn't never know that, did you?"

"No," I said, "I never knew that," and I watched her face.

"Oh, yes," she said, "your Daddy had a brother." She looked out of the window again. "I know you never saw your Daddy cry. But *I* did— many a time, through all these years."

I asked her, "What happened to his brother? How come nobody's ever talked about him?"

This was the first time I ever saw my mother look old.

"His brother got killed," she said, "when he was just a little younger than you are now. I knew him. He was a fine boy. He was maybe a little full of the devil, but he didn't mean nobody no harm."

Then she stopped and the room was silent, exactly as it had sometimes been on those Sunday afternoons. Mama kept looking out into the streets.

"He used to have a job in the mill," she said, "and, like all young folks, he just liked to perform on Saturday nights. Saturday nights, him and your father would drift around to different places, go to dances and things like that, or just sit around with people they knew, and your father's brother would sing, he had a fine voice, and play along with himself on his guitar. Well, this particular Saturday night, him and your father was coming home from some place, and they were both a little drunk and there was a moon that night, it was bright like day. Your father's brother was feeling kind of good, and he was whistling to himself, and he had his guitar slung over his shoulder. They was coming down a hill and beneath them was a road that turned off from the highway. Well, your father's brother, being always kind of frisky, decided to run down this hill, and he did, with that guitar banging and clanging behind him, and he ran across the road, and he was making water behind a tree. And your father was sort of amused at him and he was still coming down the hill, kind of slow. Then he heard a car motor and that same minute his brother stepped from behind the tree, into the road, in the moonlight. And he started to cross the road. And your father started to run down the hill, he says he don't know why. This car was full of white men. They was all drunk, and when they seen your father's brother they let out a great whoop and holler and they aimed the car straight at him. They was having fun, they just wanted to scare him, the way they do sometimes, you know. But they was drunk. And I guess the boy, being drunk, too, and scared, kind of lost his head. By the time he jumped it was too late. Your father says he heard his brother scream when the car rolled over him, and he heard the wood of that guitar when it give, and he heard them strings go flying, and he heard them white men shouting, and the car kept on a-going and it ain't stopped till this day. And, time your father got down the hill, his brother weren't nothing but blood and pulp."

Tears were gleaming on my mother's face. There wasn't anything I could say.

"He never mentioned it," she said, "because I never let him mention it before you children. Your Daddy was like a crazy man that night and for many a night thereafter. He says he never in his life seen anything as dark as that road after the lights of that car had gone away. Weren't nothing, weren't nobody on that road, just your Daddy and his brother and that busted guitar. Oh, yes. Your Daddy never did really get right again. Till the day he died he weren't sure but that every white man he saw was the man that killed his brother."

She stopped and took out her handkerchief and dried her eyes and looked at me.

"I ain't telling you all this," she said, "to make you scared or bitter or to make you hate nobody. I'm telling you this because you got a brother. And the world ain't changed."

I guess I didn't want to believe this. I guess she saw this in my face. She turned away from me, toward the window again, searching those streets.

"But I praise my Redeemer," she said at last, "that He called your Daddy home before me. I ain't saying it to throw no flowers at myself, but, I declare, it keeps me from feeling too cast down to know I helped your father get safely through this world. Your father always acted like he was the roughest, strongest man on earth. And everybody took him to be like that. But if he hadn't had *me* there—to see his tears!"

She was crying again. Still, I couldn't move. I said, "Lord, Lord, Mama, I didn't know it was like that."

"Oh, honey," she said, "there's a lot that you don't know. But you are going to find it out." She stood up from the window and came over to me. "You got to hold on to your brother," she said, "and don't let him fall, no matter what it looks like is happening to him and no matter how evil you gets with him. You going to be evil with him many a time. But don't you forget what I told you, you hear?"

"I won't forget," I said. "Don't you worry, I won't forget. I won't let nothing happen to Sonny."

My mother smiled as though she were amused at something she saw in my face. Then, "You may not be able to stop nothing from happening. But you got to let him know you's *there.*"

Two days later I was married, and then I was gone. And I had a lot of things on my mind and I pretty well forgot my promise to Mama until I got shipped home on a special furlough for her funeral.

And, after the funeral, with just Sonny and me alone in the empty kitchen, I tried to find out something about him.

"What do you want to do?" I asked him.

"I'm going to be a musician," he said.

For he had graduated, in the time I had been away, from dancing to the jukebox to finding out who was playing what, and what they were doing with it, and he had bought himself a set of drums.

"You mean, you want to be a drummer?" I somehow had the feeling that being a drummer might be all right for other people but not for my brother Sonny.

"I don't think," he said, looking at me very gravely, "that I'll ever be a good drummer. But I think I can play a piano."

I frowned. I'd never played the role of the older brother quite so seriously before, had scarcely ever, in fact, *asked* Sonny a damn thing. I sensed myself in the presence of something I didn't really know how to handle, didn't understand. So I made my frown a little deeper as I asked: "What kind of musician do you want to be?"

He grinned. "How many kinds do you think there are?"

"Be *serious,*" I said.

He laughed, throwing his head back, and then looked at me. "I *am* serious."

"Well, then, for Christ's sake, stop kidding around and answer a serious question. I mean, do you want to be a concert pianist, you want to play classical music and all that, or—or what?" Long before I finished he was laughing again. "For Christ's *sake*, Sonny!"

He sobered, but with difficulty. "I'm sorry. But you sound so— *scared!*" and he was off again.

"Well, you may think it's funny now, baby, but it's not going to be so funny when you have to make your living at it, let me tell you *that.*" I was furious because I knew he was laughing at me and I didn't know why.

"No," he said, very sober now, and afraid, perhaps, that he'd hurt me, "I don't want to be a classical pianist. That isn't what interests me. I mean"—he paused, looking hard at me, as though his eyes would help me to understand, and then gestured helplessly, as though perhaps his hand would help—"I mean, I'll have a lot of studying to do, and I'll have

to study *everything,* but, I mean, I want to play *with*—jazz musicians."
He stopped. "I want to play jazz," he said.

Well, the word had never before sounded as heavy, as real, as it
sounded that afternoon in Sonny's mouth. I just looked at him and I was
probably frowning a real frown by this time. I simply couldn't see why
on earth he'd want to spend his time hanging around nightclubs, clowning around on bandstands, while people pushed each other around a
dance floor. It seemed—beneath him, somehow. I had never thought
about it before, had never been forced to, but I suppose I had always put
jazz musicians in a class with what Daddy called "good-time people."

"Are you *serious?*"

"Hell, *yes,* I'm serious."

He looked more helpless than ever, and annoyed, and deeply hurt.
I suggested, helpfully: "You mean—like Louis Armstrong?"

His face closed as though I'd struck him. "No. I'm not talking about
none of that old-time, down home crap."

"Well, look, Sonny, I'm sorry, don't get mad. I just don't altogether get
it, that's all. Name somebody—you know, a jazz musician you admire."

"Bird."

"Who?"

"Bird! Charlie Parker! Don't they teach you nothing in the goddamn
army?"

I lit a cigarette. I was surprised and then a little amused to discover
that I was trembling. "I've been out of touch," I said. "You'll have to be
patient with me. Now. Who's this Parker character?"

"He's just one of the greatest jazz musicians alive," said Sonny, sullenly, his hands in his pockets, his back to me. "Maybe *the* greatest," he
added, bitterly, "that's probably why *you* never heard of him."

"All right," I said, "I'm ignorant. I'm sorry. I'll go out and buy all the
cat's records right away, all right?"

"It don't," said Sonny, with dignity, "make any difference to me. I
don't care what you listen to. Don't do me no favors."

I was beginning to realize that I'd never seen him so upset before.
With another part of my mind I was thinking that this would probably
turn out to be one of those things kids go through and that I shouldn't
make it seem important by pushing it too hard. Still, I didn't think it
would do any harm to ask: "Doesn't all this take a lot of time? Can you
make a living at it?"

He turned back to me and half leaned, half sat, on the kitchen table.
"Everything takes time," he said, "and—well, yes, sure, I can make a
living at it. But what I don't seem to be able to make you understand is
that it's the only thing I want to do."

"Well, Sonny," I said, gently, "you know people can't always do exactly what they *want* to do—"

"No, I don't know that," said Sonny, surprising me. "I think people *ought* to do what they want to do, what else are they alive for?"

"You getting to be a big boy," I said desperately, "it's time you started thinking about your future."

"I'm thinking about my future," said Sonny, grimly. "I think about it all the time."

I gave up. I decided, if he didn't change his mind, that we could always talk about it later. "In the meantime," I said, "you got to finish school." We had already decided that he'd have to move in with Isabel and her folks. I knew this wasn't the ideal arrangement because Isabel's folks are inclined to be dicty and they hadn't especially wanted Isabel to marry me. But I didn't know what else to do. "And we have to get you fixed up at Isabel's."

There was a long silence. He moved from the kitchen table to the window. "That's a terrible idea. You know it yourself."

"Do you have a *better* idea?"

He just walked up and down the kitchen for a minute. He was as tall as I was. He had started to shave. I suddenly had the feeling that I didn't know him at all.

He stopped at the kitchen table and picked up my cigarettes. Looking at me with a kind of mocking, amused defiance, he put one between his lips. "You mind?"

"You smoking already?"

He lit the cigarette and nodded, watching me through the smoke. "I just wanted to see if I'd have the courage to smoke in front of you." He grinned and blew a great cloud of smoke to the ceiling. "It was easy." He looked at my face. "Come on, now. I bet you was smoking at my age, tell the truth."

I didn't say anything but the truth was on my face, and he laughed. But now there was something very strained in his laugh. "Sure. And I bet that ain't all you was doing."

He was frightening me a little. "Cut the crap," I said. "We already decided that you was going to go and live at Isabel's. Now what's got into you all of a sudden?"

"You decided it," he pointed out. *"I* didn't decide nothing." He stopped in front of me, leaning against the stove, arms loosely folded. "Look, brother. I don't want to stay in Harlem no more, I really don't." He was very earnest. He looked at me, then over toward the kitchen window. There was something in his eyes I'd never seen before, some thoughtfulness, some worry all his own. He rubbed the muscle of one arm. "It's time I was getting out of here."

"Where do you want to *go*, Sonny?"

"I want to join the army. Or the navy, I don't care. If I say I'm old enough, they'll believe me."

Then I got mad. It was because I was so scared. "You must be crazy.

You goddamn fool, what the hell do you want to go and join the *army* for?"

"I just told you. To get out of Harlem."

"Sonny, you haven't even finished *school*. And if you really want to be a musician, how do you expect to study if you're in the *army?*"

He looked at me, trapped, and in anguish. "There's ways. I might be able to work out some kind of deal. Anyway, I'll have the G.I. Bill when I come out."

"*If* you come out." We stared at each other. "Sonny, please. Be reasonable. I know the setup is far from perfect. But we got to do the best we can."

"I ain't learning nothing in school," he said. "Even when I go." He turned away from me and opened the window and threw his cigarette out into the narrow alley. I watched his back. "At least, I ain't learning nothing you'd want me to learn." He slammed the window so hard I thought the glass would fly out, and turned back to me. "And I'm sick of the stink of these garbage cans!"

"Sonny," I said, "I know how you feel. But if you don't finish school now, you're going to be sorry later that you didn't." I grabbed him by the shoulders. "And you only got another year. It ain't so bad. And I'll come back and I swear I'll help you do *whatever* you want to do. Just try to put up with it till I come back. Will you please do that? For me?"

He didn't answer and he wouldn't look at me.

"Sonny. You hear me?"

He pulled away. "I hear you. But you never hear anything *I* say."

I didn't know what to say to that. He looked out of the window and then back at me. "OK," he said, and sighed. "I'll try."

Then I said, trying to cheer him up a little, "They got a piano at Isabel's. You can practice on it."

And as a matter of fact, it did cheer him up for a minute. "That's right," he said to himself. "I forgot that." His face relaxed a little. But the worry, the thoughtfulness, played on it still, the way shadows play on a face which is staring into the fire.

But I thought I'd never hear the end of that piano. At first, Isabel would write me, saying how nice it was that Sonny was so serious about his music and how, as soon as he came in from school, or wherever he had been when he was supposed to be at school, he went straight to that piano and stayed there until suppertime. And, after supper, he went back to that piano and stayed there until everybody went to bed. He was at the piano all day Saturday and all day Sunday. Then he bought a record player and started playing records. He'd play one record over and over again, all day long sometimes, and he'd improvise along with it on the piano. Or he'd play one section of the record, one chord, one change, one progression, then he'd do it on the piano. Then back to the record. Then back to the piano.

Well, I really don't know how they stood it. Isabel finally confessed that it wasn't like living with a person at all, it was like living with sound. And the sound didn't make any sense to her, didn't make any sense to any of them—naturally. They began, in a way, to be afflicted by this presence that was living in their home. It was as though Sonny was some sort of god, or monster. He moved in an atmosphere which wasn't like theirs at all. They fed him and he ate, he washed himself, he walked in and out of their door; he certainly wasn't nasty or unpleasant or rude, Sonny isn't any of those things; but it was as though he were all wrapped up in some cloud, some fire, some vision all his own; and there wasn't any way to reach him.

At the same time, he wasn't really a man yet, he was still a child, and they had to watch out for him in all kinds of ways. They certainly couldn't throw him out. Neither did they dare to make a great scene about that piano because even they dimly sensed, as I sensed, from so many thousands of miles away, that Sonny was at that piano playing for his life.

But he hadn't been going to school. One day a letter came from the school board and Isabel's mother got it—there had, apparently, been other letters but Sonny had torn them up. This day, when Sonny came in, Isabel's mother showed him the letter and asked where he'd been spending his time. And she finally got it out of him that he'd been down in Greenwich Village, with musicians and other characters, in a white girl's apartment. And this scared her and she started to scream at him and what came up, once she began—though she denies it to this day— was what sacrifices they were making to give Sonny a decent home and how little he appreciated it.

Sonny didn't play the piano that day. By evening, Isabel's mother had calmed down but then there was the old man to deal with, and Isabel herself. Isabel says she did her best to be calm but she broke down and started crying. She says she just watched Sonny's face. She could tell, by watching him, what was happening with him. And what was happening was that they penetrated his cloud, they had reached him. Even if their fingers had been a thousand times more gentle than human fingers ever are, he could hardly help feeling that they had stripped him naked and were spitting on that nakedness. For he also had to see that his presence, that music, which was life or death to him, had been torture for them and that they had endured it, not at all for his sake, but only for mine. And Sonny couldn't take that. He can take it a little better today than he could then but he's still not very good at it and, frankly, I don't know anybody who is.

The silence of the next few days must have been louder than the sound of all the music ever played since time began. One morning, before she went to work, Isabel was in his room for something and she suddenly realized that all of his records were gone. And she knew for certain that he was gone. And he was. He went as far as the navy would carry him. He finally sent me a postcard from some place in Greece and that was the first I knew that Sonny was still alive. I didn't see him anymore until we were both back in New York and the war had long been over.

He was a man by then, of course, but I wasn't willing to see it. He came by the house from time to time, but we fought almost every time we met. I didn't like the way he carried himself, loose and dreamlike all the time, and I didn't like his friends, and his music seemed to be merely an excuse for the life he led. It sounded just that weird and disordered.

Then we had a fight, a pretty awful fight, and I didn't see him for months. By and by I looked him up, where he was living, in a furnished room in the Village, and I tried to make it up. But there were lots of people in the room and Sonny just lay on his bed, and he wouldn't come downstairs with me, and he treated these other people as though they were his family and I weren't. So I got mad and then he got mad, and then I told him that he might just as well be dead as live the way he was living. Then he stood up and he told me not to worry about him any-more in life, that he *was* dead as far as I was concerned. Then he pushed me to the door and the other people looked on as though nothing were happening, and he slammed the door behind me. I stood in the hallway, staring at the door. I heard somebody laugh in the room and then the tears came to my eyes. I started down the steps, whistling to keep from crying, I kept whistling to myself, *You going to need me, baby, one of these cold, rainy days.*

I read about Sonny's trouble in the spring. Little Grace died in the fall. She was a beautiful little girl. But she only lived a little over two years. She died of polio and she suffered. She had a slight fever for a couple of days, but it didn't seem like anything and we just kept her in bed. And we would certainly have called the doctor, but the fever dropped, she seemed to be all right. So we thought it had just been a cold. Then, one day, she was up, playing, Isabel was in the kitchen fixing lunch for the two boys when they'd come in from school, and she heard Grace fall down in the living room. When you have a lot of children you don't always start running when one of them falls, unless they start screaming or something. And, this time, Grace was quiet. Yet, Isabel says that when she heard that *thump* and then that silence, something happened in her to make her afraid. And she ran to the living room and there was little Grace on the floor, all twisted up, and the reason she hadn't screamed was that she couldn't get her breath. And when she did scream, it was the worst sound, Isabel says, that she'd ever heard in all her life, and she still hears it sometimes in her dreams. Isabel will sometimes wake me

up with a low, moaning, strangled sound and I have to be quick to
awaken her and hold her to me and where Isabel is weeping against me
seems a mortal wound.

I think I may have written Sonny the very day that little Grace was
buried. I was sitting in the living room in the dark, by myself, and I
suddenly thought of Sonny. My trouble made his real.

One Saturday afternoon, when Sonny had been living with us, or,
anyway, been in our house, for nearly two weeks, I found myself wandering aimlessly about the living room, drinking from a can of beer, and
trying to work up the courage to search Sonny's room. He was out, he
was usually out whenever I was home, and Isabel had taken the children
to see their grandparents. Suddenly I was standing still in front of the
living room window, watching Seventh Avenue. The idea of searching
Sonny's room made me still. I scarcely dared to admit to myself what I'd
be searching for. I didn't know what I'd do if I found it. Or if I didn't.

On the sidewalk across from me, near the entrance to a barbecue
joint, some people were holding an old-fashioned revival meeting. The
barbecue cook, wearing a dirty white apron, his conked hair reddish
and metallic in the pale sun, and a cigarette between his lips, stood in
the doorway, watching them. Kids and older people paused in their
errands and stood there, along with some older men and a couple of
very tough-looking women who watched everything that happened on
the avenue, as though they owned it, or were maybe owned by it. Well,
they were watching this, too. The revival was being carried on by three
sisters in black, and a brother. All they had were their voices and their
Bibles and a tambourine. The brother was testifying and while he testi-
fied two of the sisters stood together, seeming to say, amen, and the
third sister walked around with the tambourine outstretched and a
couple of people dropped coins into it. Then the brother's testimony
ended and the sister who had been taking up the collection dumped the
coins into her palm and transferred them to the pocket of her long black
robe. Then she raised both hands, striking the tambourine against the
air, and then against one hand, and she started to sing. And the two
other sisters and the brother joined in.

It was strange, suddenly, to watch, though I had been seeing these
street meetings all my life. So, of course, had everybody else down
there. Yet, they paused and watched and listened and I stood still at the
window. *"Tis the old ship of Zion,"* they sang, and the sister with the
tambourine kept a steady, jangling beat, *"it has rescued many a thousand!"* Not a soul under the sound of their voices was hearing this song
for the first time, not one of them had been rescued. Nor had they seen
much in the way of rescue work being done around them. Neither did
they especially believe in the holiness of the three sisters and the
brother, they knew too much about them, knew where they lived, and
how. The woman with the tambourine, whose voice dominated the air,

whose face was bright with joy, was divided by very little from the woman who stood watching her, a cigarette between her heavy, chapped lips, her hair a cuckoo's nest, her face scarred and swollen from many beatings, and her black eyes glittering like coal. Perhaps they both knew this, which was why, when, as rarely, they addressed each other, they addressed each other as Sister. As the singing filled the air the watching, listening faces underwent a change, the eyes focusing on something within; the music seemed to soothe a poison out of them; and time seemed, nearly, to fall away from the sullen, belligerent, battered faces, as though they were fleeing back to their first condition, while dreaming of their last. The barbecue cook half shook his head and smiled, and dropped his cigarette and disappeared into his joint. A man fumbled in his pockets for change and stood holding it in his hand impatiently, as though he had just remembered a pressing appointment further up the avenue. He looked furious. Then I saw Sonny, standing on the edge of the crowd. He was carrying a wide, flat notebook with a green cover, and it made him look, from where I was standing, almost like a schoolboy. The coppery sun brought out the copper in his skin, he was very faintly smiling, standing very still. Then the singing stopped, the tambourine turned into a collection plate again. The furious man dropped in his coins and vanished, so did a couple of the women, and Sonny dropped some change in the plate, looking directly at the woman with a little smile. He started across the avenue, toward the house. He has a slow, loping walk, something like the way Harlem hipsters walk, only he's imposed on this his own half-beat. I had never really noticed it before.

I stayed at the window, both relieved and apprehensive. As Sonny disappeared from my sight, they began singing again. And they were still singing when his key turned in the lock.

"Hey," he said.

"Hey, yourself. You want some beer?"

"No. Well, maybe." But he came up to the window and stood beside me, looking out. "What a warm voice," he said.

They were singing *If I could only hear my mother pray again!*

"Yes," I said, "and she can sure beat that tambourine."

"But what a terrible song," he said, and laughed. He dropped his notebook on the sofa and disappeared into the kitchen. "Where's Isabel and the kids?"

"I think they went to see their grandparents. You hungry?"

"No." He came back into the living room with his can of beer. "You want to come some place with me tonight?"

I sensed, I don't know how, that I couldn't possibly say no. "Sure. Where?"

He sat down on the sofa and picked up his notebook and started leafing through it. "I'm going to sit in with some fellows in a joint in the Village."

"You mean, you're going to play, tonight?"

"That's right." He took a swallow of his beer and moved back to the window. He gave me a sidelong look. "If you can stand it."

"I'll try," I said.

He smiled to himself and we both watched as the meeting across the way broke up. The three sisters and the brother, heads bowed, were singing *God be with you till we meet again.* The faces around them were very quiet. Then the song ended. The small crowd dispersed. We watched the three women and the lone man walk slowly up the avenue.

"When she was singing before," said Sonny, abruptly, "her voice reminded me for a minute of what heroin feels like sometimes—when it's in your veins. It makes you feel sort of warm and cool at the same time. And distant. And—and sure." He sipped his beer, very deliberately not looking at me. I watched his face. "It makes you feel—in control. Sometimes you've got to have that feeling."

"Do you?" I sat down slowly in the easy chair.

"Sometimes." He went to the sofa and picked up his notebook again. "Some people do."

"In order," I asked, "to play?" And my voice was very ugly, full of contempt and anger.

"Well"—he looked at me with great, troubled eyes, as though, in fact, he hoped his eyes would tell me things he could never otherwise say—"they *think* so. And *if* they think so—!"

"And what do *you* think?" I asked.

He sat on the sofa and put his can of beer on the floor. "I don't know," he said, and I couldn't be sure if he were answering my question or pursuing his thoughts. His face didn't tell me. "It's not so much to *play.* It's to *stand* it, to be able to make it at all. On any level." He frowned and smiled: "In order to keep from shaking to pieces."

"But these friends of yours," I said, "they seem to shake themselves to pieces pretty goddamn fast."

"Maybe." He played with the notebook. And something told me that I should curb my tongue, that Sonny was doing his best to talk, that I should listen. "But of course you only know the ones that've gone to pieces. Some don't—or at least they haven't *yet* and that's just about all *any* of us can say." He paused. "And then there are some who just live, really, in hell, and they know it and they see what's happening and they go right on. I don't know." He sighed, dropped the notebook, folded his arms. "Some guys, you can tell from the way they play, they on something *all* the time. And you can see that, well, it makes something real for them. But of course," he picked up his beer from the floor and sipped it and put the can down again, "they *want* to, too, you've got to see that. Even some of them that say they don't—*some,* not all."

"And what about you?" I asked—I couldn't help it. "What about you? Do *you* want to?"

He stood up and walked to the window and remained silent for a long time. Then he sighed. "Me," he said. Then: "While I was downstairs before, on my way here, listening to that woman sing, it struck me all of a sudden how much suffering she must have had to go through—to sing like that. It's *repulsive* to think you have to suffer that much."

I said: "But there's no way not to suffer—is there, Sonny?"

"I believe not," he said and smiled, "but that's never stopped anyone from trying." He looked at me. "Has it?" I realized, with this mocking look, that there stood between us, forever, beyond the power of time or forgiveness, the fact that I had held silence—so long!—when he had needed human speech to help him. He turned back to the window. "No, there's no way not to suffer. But you try all kinds of ways to keep from drowning in it, to keep on top of it, and to make it seem—well, like *you*. Like you did something, all right, and now you're suffering for it. You know?" I said nothing. "Well, you know," he said, impatiently, "why *do* people suffer? Maybe it's better to do something to give it a reason, *any* reason."

"But we just agreed," I said, "that there's no way not to suffer. Isn't it better, then, just to—take it?"

"But nobody just takes it," Sonny cried, "that's what I'm telling you! *Everybody* tries not to. You're just hung up on the *way* some people try —it's not *your* way!"

The hair on my face began to itch, my face felt wet. "That's not true," I said, "that's not true. I don't give a damn what other people do, I don't even care how they suffer. I just care how *you* suffer." And he looked at me. "Please believe me," I said, "I don't want to see you—die—trying not to suffer."

"I won't," he said, flatly, "die trying not to suffer. At least, not any faster than anybody else."

"But there's no need," I said, trying to laugh, "is there? in killing yourself."

I wanted to say more, but I couldn't. I wanted to talk about willpower and how life could be—well, beautiful. I wanted to say that it was all within; but was it? or, rather, wasn't that exactly the trouble? And I wanted to promise that I would never fail him again. But it would all have sounded—empty words and lies.

So I made the promise to myself and prayed that I would keep it.

"It's terrible sometimes, inside," he said, "that's what's the trouble. You walk these streets, black and funky and cold, and there's not really a living ass to talk to, and there's nothing shaking, and there's no way of getting it out—that storm inside. You can't talk it and you can't make love with it, and when you finally try to get with it and play it, you realize *nobody's* listening. So *you've* got to listen. You got to find a way to listen."

And then he walked away from the window and sat on the sofa again, as though all the wind had suddenly been knocked out of him. "Sometimes you'll do *anything* to play, even cut your mother's throat." He laughed and looked at me. "Or your brother's." Then he sobered. "Or your own." Then: "Don't worry. I'm all right now and I think I'll *be* all right. But I can't forget—where I've been. I don't mean just the physical place I've been, I mean where I've *been*. And *what* I've been."

"What have you been, Sonny?" I asked.

He smiled—but sat sideways on the sofa, his elbow resting on the back, his fingers playing with his mouth and chin, not looking at me. "I've been something I didn't recognize, didn't know I could be. Didn't know anybody could be." He stopped, looking inward, looking helplessly young, looking old. "I'm not talking about it now because I feel *guilty* or anything like that—maybe it would be better if I did, I don't know. Anyway, I can't really talk about it. Not to you, not to anybody," and now he turned and faced me. "Sometimes, you know, and it was actually when I was most *out* of the world, I felt that I was in it, that I was *with* it, really, and I could play or I didn't really have to *play*, it just came out of me, it was there. And I don't know how I played, thinking about it now, but I know I did awful things, those times, sometimes, to people. Or it wasn't that I *did* anything to them—it was that they weren't real." He picked up the beer can; it was empty; he rolled it between his palms: "And other times—well, I needed a fix, I needed to find a place to lean, I needed to clear a space to *listen*—and I couldn't find it, and I—went crazy, I did terrible things to *me*, I was terrible *for* me." He began pressing the beer can between his hands, I watched the metal begin to give. It glittered, as he played with it, like a knife, and I was afraid he would cut himself, but I said nothing. "Oh well. I can never tell you. I was all by myself at the bottom of something, stinking and sweating and crying and shaking, and I smelled it, you know? *my* stink, and I thought I'd die if I couldn't get away from it and yet, all the same, I knew that everything I was doing was just locking me in with it. And I didn't know," he paused, still flattening the beer can, "I didn't know, I still *don't* know, something kept telling me that maybe it was good to smell your own stink, but I didn't think that *that* was what I'd been trying to do—and—who can stand it?" and he abruptly dropped the ruined beer can, looking at me with a small, still smile, and then rose, walking to the window as though it were the lodestone rock. I watched his face, he watched the avenue. "I couldn't tell you when Mama died—but the reason I wanted to leave Harlem so bad was to get away from drugs. And then, when I ran away, that's what I was running from—really. When I came back, nothing had changed, *I* hadn't changed, I was just—older." And he stopped, drumming with his fingers

on the windowpane. The sun had vanished, soon darkness would fall. I
watched his face. "It can come again," he said, almost as though speaking to himself. Then he turned to me. "It can come again," he repeated.
"I just want you to know that."

"All right," I said, at last. "So it can come again. All right."

He smiled, but the smile was sorrowful. "I had to try to tell you," he
said.

"Yes," I said. "I understand that."

"You're my brother," he said, looking straight at me, and not smiling
at all.

"Yes," I repeated, "yes. I understand that."

He turned back to the window, looking out. "All that hatred down
there," he said, "all that hatred and misery and love. It's a wonder it
doesn't blow the avenue apart."

We went to the only nightclub on a short, dark street, downtown. We
squeezed through the narrow, chattering, jam-packed bar to the entrance of the big room, where the bandstand was. And we stood there
for a moment, for the lights were very dim in this room and we couldn't
see. Then, "Hello, boy," said a voice and an enormous black man, much
older than Sonny or myself, erupted out of all that atmospheric lighting
and put an arm around Sonny's shoulder. "I been sitting right here," he
said, "waiting for you."

He had a big voice, too, and heads in the darkness turned toward us.

Sonny grinned and pulled a little away, and said, "Creole, this is my
brother. I told you about him."

Creole shook my hand. "I'm glad to meet you, son," he said, and it was
clear that he was glad to meet me *there*, for Sonny's sake. And he smiled,
"You got a real musician in *your* family," and he took his arm from
Sonny's shoulder and slapped him, lightly, affectionately, with the back
of his hand.

"Well. Now I've heard it all," said a voice behind us. This was another
musician, and a friend of Sonny's, a coal-black, cheerful-looking man,
built close to the ground. He immediately began confiding to me, at the
top of his lungs, the most terrible things about Sonny, his teeth gleaming like a lighthouse and his laugh coming up out of him like the
beginning of an earthquake. And it turned out that everyone at the bar
knew Sonny, or almost everyone; some were musicians, working there,
or nearby, or not working, some were simply hangers-on, and some
were there to hear Sonny play. I was introduced to all of them and they
were all very polite to me. Yet, it was clear that, for them, I was only
Sonny's brother. Here, I was in Sonny's world. Or, rather: his kingdom.
Here, it was not even a question that his veins bore royal blood.

They were going to play soon and Creole installed me, by myself, at a
table in a dark corner. Then I watched them, Creole, and the little black

man, and Sonny, and the others, while they horsed around, standing just below the bandstand. The light from the bandstand spilled just a little short of them and, watching them laughing and gesturing and moving about, I had the feeling that they, nevertheless, were being most careful not to step into that circle of light too suddenly: that if they moved into the light too suddenly, without thinking, they would perish in flame. Then, while I watched, one of them, the small, black man, moved into the light and crossed the bandstand and started fooling around with his drums. Then—being funny and being, also, extremely ceremonious—Creole took Sonny by the arm and led him to the piano. A woman's voice called Sonny's name and a few hands started clapping. And Sonny, also being funny and being ceremonious, and so touched, I think, that he could have cried, but neither hiding it nor showing it, riding it like a man, grinned, and put both hands to his heart and bowed from the waist.

Creole then went to the bass fiddle and a lean, very bright-skinned brown man jumped up on the bandstand and picked up his horn. So there they were, and the atmosphere on the bandstand and in the room began to change and tighten. Someone stepped up to the microphone and announced them. Then there were all kinds of murmurs. Some people at the bar shushed others. The waitress ran around, frantically getting in the last orders, guys and chicks got closer to each other, and the lights on the bandstand, on the quartet, turned to a kind of indigo. Then they all looked different there. Creole looked about him for the last time, as though he were making certain that all his chickens were in the coop, and then he—jumped and struck the fiddle. And there they were.

All I know about music is that not many people ever really hear it. And even then, on the rare occasions when something opens within, and the music enters, what we mainly hear, or hear corroborated, are personal, private, vanishing evocations. But the man who creates the music is hearing something else, is dealing with the roar rising from the void and imposing order on it as it hits the air. What is evoked in him, then, is of another order, more terrible because it has no words, and triumphant, too, for that same reason. And his triumph, when he triumphs, is ours. I just watched Sonny's face. His face was troubled, he was working hard, but he wasn't with it. And I had the feeling that, in a way, everyone on the bandstand was waiting for him, both waiting for him and pushing him along. But as I began to watch Creole, I realized that it was Creole who held them all back. He had them on a short rein. Up there, keeping the beat with his whole body, wailing on the fiddle, with his eyes half closed, he was listening to everything, but he was listening to Sonny. He was having a dialogue with Sonny. He wanted Sonny to leave the shoreline and strike out for the deep water. He was Sonny's witness that deep water and drowning were not the same thing

—he had been there, and he knew. And he wanted Sonny to know. He was waiting for Sonny to do the things on the keys which would let Creole know that Sonny was in the water.

And, while Creole listened, Sonny moved, deep within, exactly like someone in torment. I had never before thought of how awful the relationship must be between the musician and his instrument. He has to fill it, this instrument, with the breath of life, his own. He has to make it do what he wants it to do. And a piano is just a piano. It's made out of so much wood and wires and little hammers and big ones, and ivory. While there's only so much you can do with it, the only way to find this out is to try; to try and make it do everything.

And Sonny hadn't been near a piano for over a year. And he wasn't on much better terms with his life, not the life that stretched before him now. He and the piano stammered, started one way, got scared, stopped; started another way, panicked, marked time, started again; then seemed to have found a direction, panicked again, got stuck. And the face I saw on Sonny I'd never seen before. Everything had been burned out of it, and, at the same time, things usually hidden were being burned in, by the fire and fury of the battle which was occurring in him up there.

Yet, watching Creole's face as they neared the end of the first set, I had the feeling that something had happened, something I hadn't heard. Then they finished, there was scattered applause, and then, without an instant's warning, Creole started into something else, it was almost sardonic, it was *Am I Blue*. And, as though he commanded, Sonny began to play. Something began to happen. And Creole let out the reins. The dry, low, black man said something awful on the drums, Creole answered, and the drums talked back. Then the horn insisted, sweet and high, slightly detached perhaps, and Creole listened, commenting now and then, dry, and driving, beautiful and calm and old. Then they all came together again, and Sonny was part of the family again. I could tell this from his face. He seemed to have found, right there beneath his fingers, a damn brand-new piano. It seemed that he couldn't get over it. Then, for a while, just being happy with Sonny, they seemed to be agreeing with him that brand-new pianos certainly were a gas.

Then Creole stepped forward to remind them that what they were playing was the blues. He hit something in all of them, he hit something in me, myself, and the music tightened and deepened, apprehension began to beat the air. Creole began to tell us what the blues were all about. They were not about anything very new. He and his boys up there were keeping it new, at the risk of ruin, destruction, madness, and death, in order to find new ways to make us listen. For, while the tale of how we suffer, and how we are delighted, and how we may triumph is never new, it always must be heard. There isn't any other tale to tell, it's the only light we've got in all this darkness.

And this tale, according to that face, that body, those strong hands on those strings, has another aspect in every country, and a new depth in every generation. Listen, Creole seemed to be saying, listen. Now these are Sonny's blues. He made the little black man on the drums know it, and the bright, brown man on the horn. Creole wasn't trying any longer to get Sonny in the water. He was wishing him Godspeed. Then he stepped back, very slowly, filling the air with the immense suggestion that Sonny speak for himself.

Then they all gathered around Sonny and Sonny played. Every now and again one of them seemed to say, amen. Sonny's fingers filled the air with life, his life. But that life contained so many others. And Sonny went all the way back, he really began with the spare, flat statement of the opening phrase of the song. Then he began to make it his. It was very beautiful because it wasn't hurried and it was no longer a lament. I seemed to hear with what burning he had made it his, with what burning we had yet to make it ours, how we could cease lamenting. Freedom lurked around us and I understood, at last, that he could help us to be free if we would listen, that he would never be free until we did. Yet, there was no battle in his face now. I heard what he had gone through, and would continue to go through until he came to rest in earth. He had made it his: that long line, of which we knew only Mama and Daddy. And he was giving it back, as everything must be given back, so that, passing through death, it can live forever. I saw my mother's face again, and felt, for the first time, how the stones of the road she had walked on must have bruised her feet. I saw the moonlit road where my father's brother died. And it brought something else back to me, and carried me past it. I saw my little girl again and felt Isabel's tears again, and I felt my own tears begin to rise. And I was yet aware that this was only a moment, that the world waited outside, as hungry as a tiger, and that trouble stretched above us, longer than the sky.

Then it was over. Creole and Sonny let out their breath, both soaking wet, and grinning. There was a lot of applause and some of it was real. In the dark, the girl came by and I asked her to take drinks to the band-stand. There was a long pause, while they talked up there in the indigo light and after a while I saw the girl put a Scotch and milk on top of the piano for Sonny. He didn't seem to notice it, but just before they started playing again, he sipped from it and looked toward me, and nodded. Then he put it back on top of the piano. For me, then, as they began to play again, it glowed and shook above my brother's head like the very cup of trembling.

ANN BEATTIE

Weekend

On Saturday morning Lenore is up before the others. She carries her baby into the living room and puts him in George's favorite chair, which tilts because its back legs are missing, and covers him with a blanket. Then she lights a fire in the fireplace, putting fresh logs on a few embers that are still glowing from the night before. She sits down on the floor beside the chair and checks the baby, who has already gone back to sleep—a good thing, because there are guests in the house. George, the man she lives with, is very hospitable and impetuous; he extends invitations whenever old friends call, urging them to come spend the weekend. Most of the callers are his former students—he used to be an English professor—and when they come it seems to make things much worse. It makes *him* much worse, because he falls into smoking too much and drinking and not eating, and then his ulcer bothers him. When the guests leave, when the weekend is over, she has to cook bland food: applesauce, oatmeal, puddings. And his drinking does not taper off easily anymore; in the past he would stop cold when the guests left, but lately he only tapers down from Scotch to wine, and drinks wine well into the week—a lot of wine, perhaps a whole bottle with his meal—until his stomach is much worse. He is hard to live with. Once when a former student, a woman named Ruth, visited them—a lover, she suspected—she overheard George talking to her in his study, where he had taken her to see a photograph of their house before he began repairing it. George had told Ruth that she, Lenore, stayed with him because she was simple. It hurt her badly, made her actually dizzy with surprise and shame, and since then, no matter who the guests are, she never feels quite at ease on the weekends. In the past she enjoyed some of the things she and George did with their guests, but since overhearing what he said to Ruth she feels that all their visitors have been secretly told the same thing about her. To her, though, George is usually kind. But she is sure that is the reason he has not married her, and when he recently remarked on their daughter's intelligence (she is five years old, a girl named Maria) she found that she could no longer respond with simple pride; now she feels spite as well, feels that Maria exists as proof of her own good genes. She has begun to expect perfection of the child. She knows this is wrong, and she has tried hard not to communicate her anxiety to Maria, who is already, as her kindergarten teacher says, "untypical."

At first Lenore loved George because he was untypical, although after she had moved in with him and lived with him for a while she began to see that he was not exceptional but a variation on a type. She is proud of observing that, and she harbors the discovery—her silent response to his low opinion of her. She does not know why he found her attractive—in the beginning he did—because she does not resemble the pretty, articulate young women he likes to invite, with their lovers or girlfriends, to their house for the weekend. None of these young women have husbands; when they bring a man with them at all they bring a lover, and they seem happy not to be married. Lenore, too, is happy to be single—not out of conviction that marriage is wrong but because she knows that it would be wrong to be married to George if he thinks she is simple. She thought at first to confront him with what she had overheard, to demand an explanation. But he can weasel out of any corner. At best, she can mildly fluster him, and later he will only blame it on Scotch. Of course she might ask why he has all these women come to visit, why he devotes so little time to her or the children. To that he would say that it was the quality of the time they spent together that mattered, not the quantity. He has already said that, in fact, without being asked. He says things over and over so that she will accept them as truths. And eventually she does. She does not like to think long and hard, and when there is an answer—even his answer—it is usually easier to accept it and go on with things. She goes on with what she has always done: tending the house and the children and George, when he needs her. She likes to bake and she collects art postcards. She is proud of their house, which was bought cheaply and improved by George when he was still interested in that kind of work, and she is happy to have visitors come there, even if she does not admire them or even like them.

Except for teaching a night course in photography at a junior college once a week, George has not worked since he left the university two years ago, after he was denied tenure. She cannot really tell if he is unhappy working so little, because he keeps busy in other ways. He listens to classical music in the morning, slowly sipping herbal teas, and on fair afternoons he lies outdoors in the sun, no matter how cold the day. He takes photographs, and walks alone in the woods. He does errands for her if they need to be done. Sometimes at night he goes to the library or goes to visit friends; he tells her that these people often ask her to come too, but he says she would not like them. This is true— she would not like them. Recently he has done some late-night cooking.

He has always kept a journal, and he is a great letter writer. An aunt left him most of her estate, ten thousand dollars, and said in her will that he was the only one who really cared, who took the time, again and again, to write. He had not seen his aunt for five years before she died, but he wrote regularly. Sometimes Lenore would find notes that he has left for her. Once, on the refrigerator, there was a long note suggesting clever Christmas presents for her family that he had thought of while she was out. Last week he Scotch-taped a slip of paper to a casserole dish that contained leftover veal stew, saying: "This was delicious." He does not compliment her verbally, but he likes to let her know that he is pleased.

A few nights ago—the same night they got a call from Julie and Sarah, saying they were coming for a visit—she told him that she wished he would talk more, that he would confide in her.

"Confide what?" he said.

"You always take that attitude," she said. "You pretend that you have no thoughts. Why does there have to be so much silence?"

"I'm not a professor anymore," he said. "I don't have to spend every minute *thinking.*"

But he loves to talk to the young women. He will talk to them on the phone for as much as an hour; he walks with them through the woods for most of the day when they visit. The lovers the young women bring with them always seem to fall behind; they give up and return to the house to sit and talk to her, or to help with the preparation of the meal, or to play with the children. The young woman and George come back refreshed, ready for another round of conversation at dinner.

A few weeks ago one of the young men said to her, "Why do you let it go on?" They had been talking lightly before that—about the weather, the children—and then, in the kitchen, where he was sitting shelling peas, he put his head on the table and said, barely audibly, "Why do you let it go on?" He did not raise his head, and she stared at him, thinking that she must have imagined his speaking. She was surprised—surprised to have heard it, and surprised that he had said nothing after that, which made her doubt that he had spoken.

"Why do I let what go on?" she said.

There was a long silence. "Whatever this sick game is, I don't want to get involved in it," he said at last. "It was none of my business to ask. I understand that you don't want to talk about it."

"But it's really cold out there," she said. "What could happen when it's freezing out?"

He shook his head, the way George did, to indicate that she was beyond understanding. But she wasn't stupid, and she knew what might be going on. She had said the right thing, had been on the right track, but she had to say what she felt, which was that nothing very serious could be happening at that moment because they were walking in the woods. There wasn't even a barn on the property. She knew perfectly well that they were talking.

When George and the young woman had come back, he fixed hot apple juice, into which he trickled rum. Lenore was pleasant, because she was sure of what had not happened; the young man was not, because he did not think as she did. Still at the kitchen table, he ran his thumb across a pea pod as though it were a knife.

This weekend Sarah and Julie are visiting. They came on Friday evening. Sarah was one of George's students—the one who led the fight to have him rehired. She does not look like a troublemaker; she is pale and pretty, with freckles on her cheeks. She talks too much about the past, and this upsets him, disrupts the peace he has made with himself. She tells him that they fired him because he was "in touch" with everything, that they were afraid of him because he was so in touch. The more she tells him the more he remembers, and then it is necessary for Sarah to say the same things again and again; once she reminds him, he seems to need reassurance—needs to have her voice, to hear her bitterness against the members of the tenure committee. By evening they will both be drunk. Sarah will seem both agitating and consoling, Lenore and Julie and the children will be upstairs, in bed. Lenore suspects that she will not be the only one awake listening to them. She thinks that in spite of Julie's glazed look she is really very attentive. The night before, when they were all sitting around the fireplace talking, Sarah made a gesture and almost upset her wineglass, but Julie reached for it and stopped it from toppling over. George and Sarah were talking so energetically that they did not notice. Lenore's eyes met Julie's as Julie's hand shot out. Lenore feels that she is like Julie: Julie's face doesn't betray emotion, even when she is interested, even when she cares deeply. Being the same kind of person, Lenore can recognize this.

Before Sarah and Julie arrived Friday evening, Lenore asked George if Sarah was his lover.

"Don't be ridiculous," he said. "You think every student is my lover? Is Julie my lover?"

She said, "That wasn't what I said."

"Well, if you're going to be preposterous, go ahead and say that," he said. "If you think about it long enough, it would make a lot of sense, wouldn't it?"

He would not answer her question about Sarah. He kept throwing Julie's name into it. Some other woman might then think that he was protesting too strongly—that Julie really was his lover. She thought no such thing. She also stopped suspecting Sarah, because he wanted that, and it was her habit to oblige him.

He is twenty-one years older than Lenore. On his last birthday he was fifty-five. His daughter from his first marriage (his *only* marriage; she keeps reminding herself that they are not married, because it often seems that they might as well be) sent him an Irish country hat. The present made him irritable. He kept putting it on and putting it down hard on his head. "She wants to make me a laughable old man," he said. "She wants me to put this on and go around like a fool." He wore the hat all morning, complaining about it, frightening the children. Eventually, to calm him, she said, "She intended *nothing."* She said it with finality, her tone so insistent that he listened to her. But having lost his reason for bitterness, he said, "Just because you don't think doesn't mean others don't think." Is he getting old? She does not want to think of him getting old. In spite of his ulcer, his body is hard. He is tall and hand-some, with a thick mustache and a thin black goatee, and there is very little gray in his kinky black hair. He dresses in tight-fitting blue jeans and black turtleneck sweaters in the winter, and old white shirts with the sleeves rolled up in the summer. He pretends not to care about his looks, but he does. He shaves carefully, scraping slowly down each side of his goatee. He orders his soft leather shoes from a store in California. After taking one of his long walks—even if he does it twice a day—he invariably takes a shower. He always looks refreshed, and very rarely admits any insecurity. A few times, at night in bed, he has asked, "Am I still the man of your dreams?" And, when she says yes he always laughs, turning it into a joke, as if he didn't care. She knows he does. He pretends to have no feeling for clothing, but actually he cares so strongly about his turtlenecks and shirts (a few are Italian silk) and shoes that he will have no others. She has noticed that the young women who visit are always vain. When Sarah arrived, she was wearing a beautiful silk scarf, pale as conch shells.

Sitting on the floor on Saturday morning, Lenore watches the fire she has just lit. The baby, tucked in George's chair, smiles in his sleep, and Lenore thinks what a good companion he would be if only he were an adult. She gets up and goes into the kitchen and tears open a package of yeast and dissolves it, with sugar and salt, in hot water, slushing her fingers through it and shivering because it is so cold in the kitchen. She will bake bread for dinner—there is always a big meal in the early evening when they have guests. But what will she do for the rest of the day? George told the girls the night before that on Saturday they would walk in the woods, but she does not really enjoy hiking, and George will be irritated because of the discussion the night before, and she does not want to aggravate him. "You are unwilling to challenge anyone," her brother wrote her in a letter that came a few days ago. He has written her for years—all the years she has been with George—asking when she is going to end the relationship. She rarely writes back because she knows that her answers sound too simple. She has a comfortable house. She cooks. She keeps busy and she loves her two children. "It seems unkind to say *but,*" her brother writes, "but . . ." It is true; she likes simple things. Her brother, who is a lawyer in Cambridge, cannot understand that.

Lenore rubs her hand down the side of her face and says good morning to Julie and Sarah, who have come downstairs. Sarah does not want orange juice; she already looks refreshed and ready for the day. Lenore pours a glass for Julie. George calls from the hallway, "Ready to roll?" Lenore is surprised that he wants to leave so early. She goes into the living room. George is wearing a denim jacket, his hands in the pockets.

"Morning," he says to Lenore. "You're not up for a hike, are you?"

Lenore looks at him, but does not answer. As she stands there, Sarah walks around her and joins George in the hallway and he holds the door open for her. "Let's walk to the store and get Hershey bars to give us energy for a long hike," George says to Sarah. They are gone. Lenore finds Julie still in the kitchen, waiting for the water to boil. Julie says that she had a bad night and she is happy not to be going with George and Sarah. Lenore fixes tea for them. Maria sits next to her on the sofa, sipping orange juice. The baby likes company, but Maria is a very private child; she would rather that she and her mother were always alone. She has given up being possessive about her father. Now she gets out a cardboard box and takes out her mother's collection of postcards, which she arranges on the floor in careful groups. Whenever she looks up, Julie smiles nervously at her; Maria does not smile, and Lenore doesn't prod her. Lenore goes into the kitchen to punch down the bread, and Maria follows. Maria has recently gotten over chicken pox, and there is a small new scar in the center of her forehead. Instead of looking at Maria's blue eyes, Lenore lately has found herself focusing on the imperfection.

As Lenore is stretching the loaves onto the cornmeal-covered baking sheet, she hears the rain start. It hits hard on the garage roof.

After a few minutes Julie comes into the kitchen. "They're caught in this downpour," Julie says. "If Sarah had left the car keys, I could go get them."

"Take my car and pick them up," Lenore says, pointing with her elbow to the keys hanging on a nail near the door.

"But I don't know where the store is."

"You must have passed it driving to our house last night. Just go out of the driveway and turn right. It's along the main road."

Julie gets her purple sweater and takes the car keys. "I'll be right back," she says.

Lenore can sense that she is glad to escape from the house, that she is happy the rain began.

In the living room Lenore turns the pages of a magazine, and Maria mutters a refrain of "Blue, blue, dark blue, green blue," noticing the color every time it appears. Lenore sips her tea. She puts a Michael

Hurley record on George's stereo. Michael Hurley is good rainy-day music. George has hundreds of records. His students used to love to paw through them. Cleverly, he has never made any attempt to keep up with what is currently popular. Everything is jazz or eclectic: Michael Hurley, Keith Jarrett, Ry Cooder.

Julie comes back. "I couldn't find them," she says. She looks as if she expects to be punished.

Lenore is surprised. She is about to say something like "You certainly didn't try very hard, did you?" but she catches Julie's eye. She looks young and afraid, and perhaps even a little crazy.

"Well, we tried," Lenore says.

Julie stands in front of the fire, with her back to Lenore. Lenore knows she is thinking that she is dense—that she does not recognize the implications.

"They might have walked through the woods instead of along the road," Lenore says. "That's possible."

"But they would have gone out to the road to thumb when the rain began, wouldn't they?"

Perhaps she misunderstood what Julie was thinking. Perhaps it has never occurred to Julie until now what might be going on.

"Maybe they got lost," Julie says. "Maybe something happened to them."

"Nothing happened to them," Lenore says. Julie turns around and Lenore catches that small point of light in her eye again. "Maybe they took shelter under a tree," she says. "Maybe they're screwing. How should I know?"

It is not a word Lenore often uses. She usually tries not to think about that at all, but she can sense that Julie is very upset.

"Really?" Julie says. "Don't you care, Mrs. Anderson?"

Lenore is amused. There's a switch. All the students call her husband George and her Lenore; now one of them wants to think there's a real adult here to explain all this to her.

"What am I going to do?" Lenore says. She shrugs.

Julie does not answer.

"Would you like me to pour you tea?" Lenore asks.

"Yes," Julie says. "Please."

George and Sarah return in the middle of the afternoon. George says that they decided to go on a spree to the big city—it is really a small town he is talking about, but calling it the big city gives him an opportunity to speak ironically. They sat in a restaurant bar, waiting for the rain to stop, George says, and then they thumbed a ride home. "But I'm completely sober," George says, turning for the first time to Sarah. "What about you?" He is all smiles. Sarah lets him down. She looks embarrassed. Her eyes meet Lenore's quickly, and jump to Julie. The two girls stare at each other, and Lenore, left with only George to look at, looks at the fire and then gets up to pile on another log.

Gradually it becomes clear that they are trapped together by the rain. Maria undresses her paper doll and deliberately rips a feather off its hat. Then she takes the pieces to Lenore, almost in tears. The baby cries, and Lenore takes him off the sofa, where he has been sleeping under his yellow blanket, and props him in the space between her legs as she leans back on her elbows to watch the fire. It's her fire, and she has the excuse of presiding over it.

"How's my boy?" George says. The baby looks, and looks away.

It gets dark early, because of the rain. At four-thirty George uncorks a bottle of Beaujolais and brings it into the living room, with four glasses pressed against his chest with his free arm. Julie rises nervously to extract the glasses, thanking him too profusely for the wine. She gives a glass to Sarah without looking at her.

They sit in a semicircle in front of the fire and drink the wine. Julie leafs through magazines—*New Times, National Geographic*—and Sarah holds a small white dish painted with gray-green leaves that she has taken from the coffee table; the dish contains a few shells and some acorn caps, a polished stone or two, and Sarah lets these objects run through her fingers. There are several such dishes in the house, assembled by George. He and Lenore gathered the shells long ago, the first time they went away together, at a beach in North Carolina. But the acorn caps, the shiny turquoise and amethyst stones—those are there, she knows, because George likes the effect they have on visitors; it is an expected unconventionality, really. He has also acquired a few small framed pictures, which he points out to guests who are more important than worshipful students—tiny oil paintings of fruit, prints with small details from the unicorn tapestries. He pretends to like small, elegant things. Actually, when they visit museums in New York he goes first to El Grecos and big Mark Rothko canvases. She could never get him to admit that what he said or did was sometimes false. Once, long ago, when he asked if he was still the man of her dreams, she said, "We don't get along well anymore." "Don't talk about it," he said—no denial, no protest. At best, she could say things and get away with them; she could never get him to continue such a conversation.

At the dinner table, lit with white candles burning in empty wine bottles, they eat off his grandmother's small flowery plates. Lenore looks out a window and sees, very faintly in the dark, their huge oak tree. The rain has stopped. A few stars have come out, and there are glints on the wet branches. The oak tree grows very close to the window. George loved it when her brother once suggested that some of the bushes and trees should be pruned away from the house so it would not always be so dark inside; it gave him a chance to rave about the beauty of nature, to say that he would never tamper with it. "It's like a tomb in here all day," her brother had said. Since moving here, George has learned the names of almost all the things growing on the land: he can point out abelia bushes, spirea, laurels. He subscribes to *National Geographic* (although she rarely sees him looking at it). He is at last in touch, he says, being in the country puts him in touch. He is saying it now to Sarah, who has put down her ivory-handled fork to listen to him. He gets up to change the record. Side two of the Telemann record begins softly.

Sarah is still very much on guard with Lenore; she makes polite conversation with her quickly when George is out of the room. "You people are so wonderful," she says. "I wish my parents could be like you."

"George would be pleased to hear that," Lenore says, lifting a small piece of pasta to her lips.

When George is seated again, Sarah, anxious to please, tells him, "If only my father could be like you."

"Your father," George says. "I won't have that analogy." He says it pleasantly, but barely disguises his dismay at the comparison.

"I mean, he cares about nothing but business," the girl stumbles on.

The music, in contrast, grows lovelier.

Lenore goes into the kitchen to get the salad and hears George say, "I simply won't let you girls leave. Nobody leaves on a Saturday."

There are polite protests, there are compliments to Lenore on the meal—there is too much talk. Lenore has trouble caring about what's going on. The food is warm and delicious. She pours more wine and lets them talk.

"Godard, yes, I know . . . panning that row of honking cars *so* slowly, that long line of cars stretching on and on."

She has picked up the end of George's conversation. His arm slowly waves out over the table, indicating the line of motionless cars in the movie.

"That's a lovely plant," Julie says to Lenore.

"It's Peruvian ivy," Lenore says. She smiles. She is supposed to smile. She will not offer to hack shoots off her plant for these girls.

Sarah asks for a Dylan record when the Telemann finishes playing. White wax drips onto the wood table. George waits for it to solidify slightly, then scrapes up the little circles and with thumb and index finger flicks them gently toward Sarah. He explains (although she asked for no particular Dylan record) that he has only Dylan before he went electric. And "Planet Waves"—"because it's so romantic. That's silly of me, but true." Sarah smiles at him. Julie smiles at Lenore. Julie is being polite, taking her cues from Sarah, really not understanding what's going on. Lenore does not smile back. She has done enough to put them at ease. She is tired now, brought down by the music, a full stomach, and again the sounds of rain outside. For dessert there is homemade vanilla ice cream, made by George, with small black vanilla-bean flecks in it. He is still drinking wine, though; another bottle has been opened. He sips wine and then taps his spoon on his ice cream, looking at Sarah. Sarah smiles, letting them all see the smile, then sucks the ice cream off her spoon. Julie is missing more and more of what's going on. Lenore watches as Julie strokes her hand absently on her napkin. She is wearing a thin silver choker and—Lenore notices for the first time—a thin silver ring on the third finger of her right hand.

"It's just terrible about Anna," George says, finishing his wine, his ice cream melting, looking at no one in particular, although Sarah was the one who brought up Anna the night before, when they had been in the house only a short time—Anna dead, hit by a car, hardly an accident at all. Anna was also a student of his. The driver of the car was drunk, but for some reason charges were not pressed. (Sarah and George have talked about this before, but Lenore blocks it out. What can she do about it? She met Anna once: a beautiful girl, with tiny, childlike hands, her hair thin and curly—wary, as beautiful people are wary.) Now the driver has been flipping out, Julie says, and calling Anna's parents, wanting to talk to them to find out why it has happened.

The baby begins to cry. Lenore goes upstairs, pulls up more covers, talks to him for a minute. He settles for this. She goes downstairs. The wine must have affected her more than she realizes; otherwise, why is she counting the number of steps?

In the candlelit dining room, Julie sits alone at the table. The girl has been left alone again; George and Sarah took the umbrellas, decided to go for a walk in the rain.

It is eight o'clock. Since helping Lenore load the dishes into the dishwasher, when she said what a beautiful house Lenore had, Julie has said very little. Lenore is tired, and does not want to make conversation. They sit in the living room and drink wine.

"Sarah is my best friend," Julie says. She seems apologetic about it. "I was so out of it when I came back to college. I was in Italy, with my husband, and suddenly I was back in the States. I couldn't make friends. But Sarah wasn't like the other people. She cared enough to be nice to me."

"How long have you been friends?"

"For two years. She's really the best friend I've ever had. We understand things—we don't always have to talk about them."

"Like her relationship with George," Lenore says.

Too direct. Too unexpected. Julie has no answer.

"You act as if you're to blame," Lenore says.

"I feel strange because you're such a nice lady."

A nice lady! What an odd way to speak. Has she been reading Henry

James? Lenore has never known what to think of herself, but she certainly thinks of herself as being more complicated than a "lady."

"Why do you look that way?" Julie asks. "You *are* nice. I think you've been very nice to us. You've given up your whole weekend."

"I always give up my weekends. Weekends are the only time we socialize, really. In a way, it's good to have something to do."

"But to have it turn out like this . . ." Julie says. "I think I feel so strange because when my own marriage broke up I didn't even suspect. I mean, I couldn't act the way you do, anyway, but I—"

"For all I know, nothing's going on," Lenore says. "For all I know, your friend is flattering herself, and George is trying to make me jealous." She puts two more logs on the fire. When these are gone, she will either have to walk to the woodshed or give up and go to bed. "Is there something . . . *major* going on?" she asks.

Julie is sitting on the rug, by the fire, twirling her hair with her finger. "I didn't know it when I came out here," she says. "Sarah's put me in a very awkward position."

"But do you know how far it has gone?" Lenore asks, genuinely curious now.

"No," Julie says.

No way to know if she's telling the truth. Would Julie speak the truth to a lady? Probably not.

"Anyway," Lenore says with a shrug, "I don't want to think about it all the time."

"I'd never have the courage to live with a man and not marry," Julie says. "I mean, I wish I had, that we hadn't gotten married, but I just don't have that kind of . . . I'm not secure enough."

"You have to live somewhere," Lenore says.

Julie is looking at her as if she does not believe that she is sincere. Am I? Lenore wonders. She has lived with George for six years, and sometimes she thinks she has caught his way of playing games, along with his colds, his bad moods.

"I'll show you something," Lenore says. She gets up, and Julie follows. Lenore puts on the light in George's study, and they walk through it to a bathroom he has converted to a darkroom. Under a table, in a box behind another box, there is a stack of pictures. Lenore takes them out and hands them to Julie. They are pictures that Lenore found in his darkroom last summer; they were left out by mistake, no doubt, and she found them when she went in with some contact prints he had left in their bedroom. They are high-contrast photographs of George's face. In all of them he looks very serious and very sad; in some of them his eyes seem to be narrowed in pain. In one, his mouth is open. It is an excellent photograph of a man in agony, a man about to scream.

"What are they?" Julie whispers.

"Pictures he took of himself," Lenore says. She shrugs. "So I stay," she says.

Julie nods. Lenore nods, taking the pictures back. Lenore has not thought until this minute that this may be why she stays. In fact, it is not the only reason. It is just a very demonstrable, impressive reason. When she first saw the pictures, her own face had become as distorted as George's. She had simply not known what to do. She had been frightened and ashamed. Finally she put them in an empty box, and put the box behind another box. She did not even want him to see the horrible pictures again. She does not know if he has ever found them, pushed back against the wall in that other box. As George says, there can be too much communication between people.

Later, Sarah and George come back to the house. It is still raining. It turns out that they took a bottle of brandy with them, and they are both drenched and drunk. He holds Sarah's finger with one of his. Sarah, seeing Lenore, lets his finger go. But then he turns—they have not even said hello yet—and grabs her up, spins her around, stumbling into the living room, and says, "I am in love."

Julie and Lenore watch them in silence.

"See no evil," George says, gesturing with the empty brandy bottle to Julie. "Hear no evil," George says, pointing to Lenore. He hugs Sarah closer. "I speak no evil. I speak the truth. I am in love!"

Sarah squirms away from him, runs from the room and up the stairs in the dark.

George looks blankly after her, then sinks to the floor and smiles. He is going to pass it off as a joke. Julie looks at him in horror, and from upstairs Sarah can be heard sobbing. Her crying awakens the baby.

"Excuse me," Lenore says. She climbs the stairs and goes into her son's room, and picks him up. She talks gently to him, soothing him with lies. He is too sleepy to be alarmed for long. In a few minutes he is asleep again, and she puts him back in his crib. In the next room Sarah is crying more quietly now. Her crying is so awful that Lenore almost joins in, but instead she pats her son. She stands in the dark by the crib and then at last goes out and down the hallway to her bedroom. She takes off her clothes and gets into the cold bed. She concentrates on breathing normally. With the door closed and Sarah's door closed, she can hardly hear her. Someone taps lightly on her door.

"Mrs. Anderson," Julie whispers. "Is this your room?"

"Yes," Lenore says. She does not ask her in.

"We're going to leave. I'm going to get Sarah and leave. I didn't want to just walk out without saying anything."

Lenore just cannot think how to respond. It was really very kind of Julie to say something. She is very close to tears, so she says nothing.

"Okay," Julie says, to reassure herself. "Good night. We're going."

There is no more crying. Footsteps. Miraculously, the baby does not wake up again, and Maria has slept through all of it. She has always slept well. Lenore herself sleeps worse and worse, and she knows that George walks much of the night, most nights. She hasn't said anything about it. If he thinks she's simple, what good would her simple wisdom do him?

The oak tree scrapes against the window in the wind and rain. Here on the second floor, under the roof, the tinny tapping is very loud. If Sarah and Julie say anything to George before they leave, she doesn't hear them. She hears the car start, then die out. It starts again—she is praying for the car to go—and after conking out once more it rolls slowly away, crunching gravel. The bed is no warmer; she shivers. She tries hard to fall asleep. The effort keeps her awake. She squints her eyes in concentration instead of closing them. The only sound in the house is the electric clock, humming by her bed. It is not even midnight.

She gets up, and without turning on the light, walks downstairs. George is still in the living room. The fire is nothing but ashes and glowing bits of wood. It is as cold there as it was in the bed.

"That damn bitch," George says. "I should have known she was a stupid little girl."

"You went too far," Lenore says. "I'm the only one you can go too far with."

"Damn it," he says, and pokes the fire. A few sparks shoot up. "Damn it," he repeats under his breath.

His sweater is still wet. His shoes are muddy and ruined. Sitting on the floor by the fire, his hair matted down on his head, he looks ugly, older, unfamiliar.

She thinks of another time, when it was warm. They were walking on the beach together, shortly after they met, gathering shells. Little waves were rolling in. The sun went behind the clouds and there was a momentary illusion that the clouds were still and the sun was racing ahead of them. "Catch me," he said, breaking away from her. They had been talking quietly, gathering shells. She was so surprised at him for breaking away that she ran with all her energy and did catch him, putting her hand out and taking hold of the band of his swimming trunks as he veered into the water. If she hadn't stopped him, would he really have run far out into the water, until she couldn't follow anymore? He turned on her, just as abruptly as he had run away, and grabbed her and hugged her hard, lifted her high. She had clung to him, held him close. He had tried the same thing when he came back from the walk with Sarah, and it hadn't worked.

"I wouldn't care if their car went off the road," he says bitterly.

"Don't say that," she says.

They sit in silence, listening to the rain. She slides over closer to him, puts her hand on his shoulder and leans her head there, as if he could protect her from the awful things he has wished into being.

GINA BERRIAULT

The Bystander

The room on Vernal Street in Los Angeles was the last room my father rented for us. In that old green three-storied house with pigeons and gables and fire escape, he went over the line and his decline wasn't anymore a matter between father and son. For he assaulted a woman in that house, the woman he had liked the most and spent some nights with. It was a Saturday twilight and I had been reading on the bed up in our room and had thought the noise nothing unusual. Outbursts of voices came at any hour from the rooms below us, and along the hallways after two in the morning the homing tenants bungled and cursed. But someone leaped up the stairs and threw open the door and shouted at me to grab a blanket or a coat or *something for crissakes* and wrap your old man up. He had run out of the house with nothing on but the soap from the bath he'd been taking in the woman's rooms.

Under a date palm in the yellow dirt and yellow grass of the steep front yard of another rooming house half a block away, he stood shouting threats at the woman he'd left lying on the floor; and roomers watched from porches and from windows, and across the street men and women from the bar stood under the red neon goblet, laughing. He was marble white in the twilight, and the sour bar smell of his breath mingled with the fragrance of the soap. When I tried to cover him, he struck me away with his elbow, sharp in my ribs as a crowbar, but when the police came, when he heard the siren, he allowed me to throw the blanket around him.

The ward was located in the old hospital, as it was called, a rambling place of red brick curtained by ivy, and a block west of the new many-storied structure of concrete. I brought his suitcase, as the young man social worker had told me in some huge loft of hundreds of desks and social workers in an agency building somewhere else in the city. It contained his suit of navy blue worsted; his one white shirt and striped tie; his gray work shirt and white work socks, and his dry, bumpy, carpenter's work shoes. And over my arm I carried his raincoat and in my pocket his wallet, containing, under celluloid, a snapshot of my mother taken the year before she died—a dark-haired girl in a short, flowered dress—and a snapshot of myself at the age of five, standing high in the bowl of a drinking fountain.

The bald fellow in shirtsleeves in an office on the first floor told me, as he accepted the personal property across the counter, that my father had shown enough improvement in the past week to permit him among the more tractable patients on the second floor and that yesterday he had been moved up from the basement quarters. He told me, also, that my father had been examined by staff psychiatrists and the institution they'd chosen for him was Camarillo, in the coastal hills near Ventura. I was leaning my elbow on the counter, smoking a cigarette, demonstrating with that pose my reasonable nature. If the father was unreasonable it did not follow that the son was, also; the son, said the leaning elbow, said the cigarette in hand, might profit in wisdom by the father's breakdown in a six weeks' ordeal in hotel and housekeeping rooms. Though it did not matter to this clerk whether I approved or disapproved of their taking my father off my hands. In this old brick building of ramps and ivy and barred windows, the personal element was extraneous; it was a place run by public taxation and the public was protecting itself. The thousands of the city who had never heard of him and never would hear of him were afraid of him, and his confinement and classification was a matter between him and them. When the police rushed him up to our room for his clothes and down the stairs again, the tenants' fear and contempt had seemed to shove him out of the house forever—the dazed, quaking man in soiled trousers and unbuttoned shirt. Climbing the rubber-carpeted ramp to the second floor and crossing the hallway, I pressed the bell to the side of double doors.

"Lewis Lisle," I said to the orderly unlocking the doors. "He's my father," and jarringly discovered that the name I was saying was that of a mentally incompetent person confined in these quarters that the orderly guarded. Before, I had thought that a name was like a mentor, even determining the person's physical peculiarities; now, I found that a name followed after, an echoing of a person.

The room I entered was long and furnished as a living room with many wicker chairs and three wicker sofas with flat and faded cretonne cushions. The patients here were males, dressed in pajama-like, gray, cotton-flannel trousers and shirts, and on their feet were gray canvas slippers. Some sat with relatives and some sat by themselves, and one lay upon a sofa with his back outward. A group of them were conversing at the wide door to the sleeping room, and he was among them, his hands clasped behind him, his head tilted by a smug, lonely amusement with the peculiar reasoning of the others. The impact of his presence in this alien place made my throat swell, and I went up to him quickly and laid my hand upon his back but could not say the word, could not recall the name of what he was to me.

At first I thought my hand was unfelt, he responded so slowly to it, but then I saw in the slow, annoyed turn of his eyes that he mistook me for a fellow inmate, bothering him with some crazy kind of confidence. He said my name "Arty," and the smell of oranges was on his breath. That was good, I thought; if he had eaten an orange then he was comparatively content.

"Did you have an orange?" I asked him.

"A visitor brought them to one of the boys," he said, and these were the first words exchanged between us in five days, the calmness of our voices recalling the shouting.

We sat down together on a wicker sofa, and the stun of exile was in his eyes and in his joints. He had lost more weight and his hair had grown longer and seemed grayer, an iron gray that was the heavy color of an ending; in spite of the orange, his lips were dry, rimmed by a white dust in the cracks. He sat with legs crossed, his troubled hands clasped on the upper knee.

"What you been doing with yourself, Arty?" he asked.

"Oh, I had a cold for a couple of days," I said.

"What did you do for it?"

"I did what you always said, I sweated it out."

But he was embarrassed by the absence of one front tooth, lost a few weeks before, the night he got into a brawl in a cafe. His tongue hissed a little in the gap.

Beyond the door to the sleeping room were two rows of cots, several of them occupied. The men lay fully clothed atop the blankets, each enwrapped in his delusions as in a mummy winding, and one turned over with a great lethargic wrench, pushing with his elbows. At a table by a window in the sleeping room two patients were playing cards, one of the players a Negro, and his wife sat by him, feeding him pink ice cream from a pint carton with a little wooden spoon. In the room with us a young patient was playing the upright piano with meticulous discordancy, and among the relatives and patients and piano notes wandered an elderly man who recalled Caesar, anciently Roman, and yet would not have come to his prototype's shoulder. With warning flashes of his small black eyes he struck into being everyone he glanced at. A woman's bathrobe was tied smartly about his stocky body, a dark robe patterned with flowers.

"I want you to stay and meet my son," he said to me, laying his hand on my shoulder.

"Go on, beat it, go on," my father said to him, the jerking of his elbow establishing his brotherhood with the rest.

"He's a bastard, my son," the Caesar said.

The orderly, lounging in a wicker chair at the far end of the piano, laid his *Argosy* down upon his thigh and watched, and the old man, seeing my eyes darting to the place behind him where he knew the orderly sat, lifted his hand from me and went into the sleeping room where he stood with his back to us, watching the cardplayers.

"A son of a bitch himself," my father said, shifting position sprawl-ingly. "The loony tried to murder his own son. This guy is always talking about how his son and his son's wife were figuring to dig up some three thousand bucks he's got buried somewhere. What the hell he thinks three thousand bucks is? I made that much in overtime the couple years I worked at Douglas Aircraft during the war. That's what it amounts to —nothing. A down payment on a Ford, a funeral, a loan to your uncle, a week for you and me at Catalina, and it was gone. And this guy thinks it's enough to kill his son about. A loony."

The long living room was like Sunday—the inmate curled on the sofa, the visitors, the scent of oranges; the only thing missing was the comic papers. Over by a closed door to somewhere, a middle-aged woman in a black dress and a black straw hat with red cherries that had ripened before I was born sat on one side of a gray-clad patient and her middle-aged sister sat on the other side of him—a middle-aged brother whom sunlight hadn't touched in a long while—a man who had sat all day on an army cot in a screened porch. Now, out in the world, he sat as stooped and as deaf, watching me with fear in his pale eyes. I saw him rise and stroll away, feeling more cornered by my glance than by the women who pressed him in between them. They continued to talk across him, not missing him, but I was interested in my effect upon him and sought him out wherever he had wandered, glancing into the sleeping room and finding him standing sideways, ten feet away, still as a stone, waiting for me to meet his eyes.

"What do you think they'll do to me, Arty?" my father was asking petulantly. He slid down, resting his elbow on the arm of the sofa and with his hands forming an arch to hide his face from the orderly, and his dominance over me and his dependency sprang across the week of our separation and we were as before. "I'd like to get rid of this cough," he said. "My chest has been bothering me from the coughing. They had me in the basement for a while, and the cold came up from the floor. Ah, Jesus, it was miserable down there, like a menagerie in the hold of a ship. The croakings and cryings."

"They do anything for your cough?"

"Nothing. The hell with them. Maybe they like you to come in with lung cancer or TB or whatever it is I got. Maybe they want you to die as soon as you can, conditions in bughouses being as crowded as they are."

"They got these places to cure people," I said.

He laughed explosively, folding up with the coughing laugh and then unfolding so far that his legs stretched straight out and his back arched out from the sofa's back. The patient on the next sofa turned over and, his head hanging over the edge, watched my father with the unblinking eyes of a mild and curious animal.

"They give us hot chocolate before we go to bed," my father said, "and a little cookie, star-shaped. You see how far man has progressed? They never did that in Bedlam, Arty, you tell that to any cynic you meet. You tell them in the psycho ward they give your father hot chocolate and a little cookie."

We were sitting facing the double doors to the hallway, and through the screen saw an orderly come up the ramp pushing a food conveyance and wait in the hallway, ringing for admittance. He pushed the metal cart through the living room and to the closed door, and the door was left open after he had passed through and I saw that the room beyond was a dining room. Two women attendants were setting the long, dark table, and beyond that room was a kitchen with cabinets and a sink; and the sound of plate on plate from those rooms was a reassuring sound, and it seemed, though I knew it was impossible, that a wood fire had been lighted behind a screen somewhere in that room where the women set the table. The noises of the plates and silver prophesied for me the meals that I would spend in company of persons whose existence I did not know of, in houses I did not know of, as I had not known of this locked living room with the gray inmates and the wicker chairs.

Over on the sofa by the dining room door the sisters wound the straps of their purses around their right wrists, set their black oxfords heavily on the floor, and went to the sleeping room to find their brother and say good-bye. The Negro woman, tall and with the composure of a civil service clerk, drew on her coat over her high shoulders.

"They make everybody leave at suppertime, I guess," I said.

"Where you going to eat?" my father asked.

"I don't know," I said, not wanting to eat anywhere.

"There's a Chinese dump around the corner from Vernal," he said. "You seen it. They got chicken giblet chop suey and they don't leave the liver out—most gyp joints save the liver for something fancy—and they got those peas cooked in the pod, you know how they do." And disgusted by his detailing of trivia, he set his palms over his eyes. Under his blindfold, his mouth asked me, "You still at that place on Vernal?"

"Yes," I said.

"You going back to your Aunt Glorie's?"

"I guess I won't," I said.

"You going back to San Diego at all?"

"No, I guess I won't." We were talking lower for the other visitors were moving past us to the door, and the inmate lying on the next couch was awake on his back, his arms under his head.

"What you going to write to her then?"

"What you want me to write to her?"

He thought about it a minute as if he had not thought about it every day of his confinement. "Well, I'd like her to keep my tools intact," he said. "I got the key to my toolbox with me, or maybe you got it now, but that don't mean anything if she wants to sell them. I got some London spring steel saws in there I'd hate to lose. I'm afraid if you tell her where they got me, she'll sell my tools, she'll think I'm never coming back to live there anymore and hoping I won't. So you tell her not to sell my tools and that's all. Just write it in a letter and don't say anything else." He removed his hands to see if I was nodding.

"All right." I nodded.

"You could get a job in this lousy town. I was working in a laundry when I was eighteen."

We stood up, then, to be with the rest of the visitors gathering by the double doors, waiting for the orderly. The cardplayer, a heavyset fellow with a shaven head, came out to his wife, but the army cot patient did not come out with his sisters. Caesar in his flowered robe stood by the sofa we had vacated, muttering his chagrin with his son's failure to show up even at the last moment. The orderly in his white uniform strode from the dining room, jangling his keys playfully under the visitors' noses, and the visitors, stuporous from the afternoon's confinement, smiled servilely.

My father shook hands with me, it was the thing to do in public. In the corners of his eyes were white dots of weariness, and there was a sickly smell of anxiety upon him; I felt the sweat of it in the palm of his hand.

"The clerk says I can take the Greyhound bus, it'll get me there, or almost. Then I take a jitney that runs from the town to the hospital," I told him.

"They got a private bus for us patients," my father said, loudly so the orderly could hear his joking. "I hear it's a nice ride, see the ocean, see the hills, go past them mansions of the movie stars in Malibu."

The orderly, his *Argosy* folded in his hip pocket, smiled as he turned the key. There was no hanging back after that, the atmosphere of the ward became unbreathable at the final moment when the door was opened to the outer air, and I followed the three women down the ramp, out through the swinging glass doors, and down the concrete steps with the metal rail that the sisters held on to.

As I went along by the high wire fence, ivy-woven, I glanced up to the second floor, not expecting at all to locate that particular ward and was surprised to find myself looking into the windows of the sleeping room. I saw the bent heads of the cardplayers and the back of the chair that the wife had sat in. By another window in that room the army cot inmate was standing in his gray garments, watching me go. For a second I thought he was my father, and I knew then, meeting eyes with the man, that I was guilty of something and he was accusing me of it, and it was the guilt of sight. For the man *was* my father and was also the father in the flowered robe who was probably still facing the locked doors. He was the parent who breaks down under the eyes of his child, the parent in the last years when all the circumstances of his life have got him trussed and dying, while the child stands and watches the end of the struggle and then walks away to catch a streetcar.

VANCE BOURJAILY

The Amish Farmer

A couple of weeks ago in class, I told the Amish farmer story again. I hadn't thought I would and never planned at all to write it down. I guess this was because I used to think it a simple story, which I understood so well that, with any further telling, my own interest in it would be used up. But this particular class had people in it whom I liked, we had an hour of open time, and the Amish farmer story had got people into lively discussions in the past.

The class is a workshop in writing fiction; I got my storytelling energy up for them. Often it helps to pick a particular student, from whom my teaching ego happens to crave a little response, and then to think in terms of summoning energy for him or for her. On this day, the student I held in mind and with whom I had eye contact as I started talking was one we call Katie Jay; she is smart, searching, scathing sometimes, very talented, a leader though not without enemies, cool, almost elegant in her blond slimness. Is Katie Jay. It is because of her that I am writing the story now.

"Listen to this," I said. "What I'm going to try to illustrate is the remarkable power of point of view. I'm going to tell you a story in which I think you'll recognize the kind of material a writer might decide to use. I'll tell it pretty much as it came to me, and then let's talk about how it would change in tone, mood, meaning—in the basic kind of piece it would make—just from changing the point of view from which it's told from that of one character in it to that of another."

Katie Jay smiled and nodded at me slightly; I smiled back and started catching other eyes.

On a spring morning (I said) about ten years ago, I got a call from a friend and student named Noel Butler, asking if he could come to the house. He sounded upset.

"Come along," I said. "You in trouble, Noel?"

"I think somebody just tried to kill me," Noel said.

I stepped outside, onto the lawn, to wait for him. The temperature was up around 60. The dirt glittered and steamed where it showed, wet and black beneath the grass plants. I didn't have much doubt that the situation had to do with Noel's wife.

At that time I had seen Dawn Butler only twice, and four months earlier, but she was vivid to me as she was to all men.

Let me explain that Noel had come to Indiana from Boston to start graduate school the previous September without Dawn and nervous about it. He was someone we'd recruited for the graduate program, an engaging, articulate young writer with a couple of publications, a year of prep school teaching, and a year in publishing. We'd offered him an assistantship, something we rarely do for first-year students; he was going to start right in teaching core lit to sophomores, as well as taking his graduate hours.

It seemed plain from the first look at Noel that we'd made a good move. He was poised, talkative, nice-looking in a horn-rimmed, wavy-haired, Brooks Brothers way. He probably looked archaic to some of his peers, but he looked just right to me; and if his flow of persuasive speech was a little glib at times, he was still a pleasure to have in class. He kept things moving. We heard that his undergraduate students doted on him from the first "Good morning, people."

I was just starting to get to know Noel. It wasn't really quite appropriate yet for intimate matters to come up between us, but he just couldn't keep himself from telling me about Dawn: she was beautiful and wild, and he loved her desperately, and he might even have to leave us if she kept on refusing to join him here in our midwestern city, which she supposed must be pretty dull. He said that at first Dawn had promised to come along as soon as he found them a decent place to live; he had a place located, but she kept delaying. He also told me that she had a child, a boy, born illegitimately when she was seventeen, the son of a celebrated choreographer whose protégée Dawn had been. She'd been scared of the man, who was also a celebrated bisexual and capable of violence, had run away from him, given up dancing, and had the child. But that was only part of it, Noel said. I'd have to see Dawn to believe her.

Midway through October he got himself excused from classes for a week, got friends to cover his core lit meetings, and flew to Boston. He phoned me excitedly from there to ask me to check on his academic arrangements but really to say, triumphantly, that she'd agreed to come. I reminded him that the director of our program was giving a cocktail party Friday for the staff and teaching assistants, and Noel said proudly that he'd be there with Mrs. Butler.

So. It was in the rather formal living room at the director's house that I first saw Dawn. I can almost say, without a sense of exaggeration, that I felt her. She had that kind of insistent sexual presence that men think they perceive as a wave of heat. It makes your cheeks tingle and the hair bristle at the back of your neck. I'd met a few women with that brute magnetism before, but none who had more of it than Dawn Butler and only one, an actress, who combined it, as Dawn did, with more physical beauty than seemed fair.

I remember that I guessed which room she'd be in before I saw her, because every other man at the party was in that room already.

Dawn had dark hair, which she wore brushed back in long, soft waves down to below her shoulder blades. Her face was round and her brown, protruding eyes so large they made the other features seem more delicate than they probably were, and the skin paler. Her mouth, on second look, and one certainly did look twice, was actually quite wide. It was also very mobile, open much of the time, with the small, conspicuously white teeth parted. She had an unsettling way of flicking her tongue forward so that you were aware of the tip of it striking the upper front teeth.

She was not quite tall, but willowy, which gave an impression of height. Her arms were rather short, her shoulders quite square, and she stood dancer-style with her feet spread and toed out, which brought her pelvis forward and her head back and up, there in the director's living room. She had the look of a woman standing her ground and at the same time enticing you to share it with her.

She was wearing black with a silver belt. The dress bared her neck and collarbones but was not cut low. Instead it was slit, down to the diaphragm, and under it she must have been wearing one of those wire brassieres that create a look of nudity down the center of the chest while providing a slightly unnatural amount of breast separation. It was provocative enough.

She also grabbed my hand with both of hers when we were introduced, not quite pulling me toward her, and exhaled a small sound of some sort. Noel stood beaming at her side.

Say she was overdoing, if you like; that form of greeting wasn't used on me alone, I'd better add. As the evening went on, she was conducting public dalliance simultaneously with as many of us as could crowd around, four or five at a time.

"I don't know if I can get to like it here," she said. "Noel has us at that Holiday Inn so far, up on the hill. It makes me apprehensive, looking down at your lights, not knowing what to expect." Suddenly she showed us her right palm, ran the fingertips of her left hand over it. "Damp. That's how lie detectors work, isn't it? I couldn't fool a lie detector."

Then she touched the damp palm to her cheek, smiled, flicked her tongue, and wiped the hand on her hip lightly. I remember being both smitten, as were all the other men, and struck by the thought that there was something wrong, something consonant with the overdone greeting. It was what was missing from the voice—a young, light, reasonably

well educated, Eastern-city voice. It didn't have, in spite of the smiles
and the flicking tongue, much fun in it.

Generally a good coquette, doing her magic publicly, will spurt, shim-
mer, and sparkle with a kind of laughter, now open, now repressed, a
laughter both at the men for being gulled and at herself for spending all
that gorgeous candlepower on gulling them. Brilliance, raillery, self-
mockery, all of it in fun: Dawn Butler's performance didn't have those
qualities. It was as if she had already passed on, with each man who
listened to her, beyond flirtation, to some further stage in a relationship
already intimate, about to be serious, even dangerous.

The next thing would almost have to be a note, folded very small,
pressed into your hand, to be read urgently, secretly, and the note
would say, "Where is your car parked?" or even "Save me."

I have splendid resistance to people who dramatize themselves. So
when Dawn said, to someone offering her a whiskey, "Oh, but I only
drink wine," I collided with the director in the living room doorway,
both of us rushing to the kitchen, where I'd left a bottle of wine and he
had several on the shelf. Dawn was twenty-two years old.

The other time I saw her that fall was the next evening; she was more
relaxed. She and Noel were with some of his student friends, drinking
beer at Hickey's Tavern. They asked me to join them, and I did for a few
minutes, sitting down by Dawn, asking her about the place Noel had
found for them to live in. She replied by taking my wrist between her
thumb and forefinger, looking into my eyes, holding on for a couple of
beats, and then squeezing quite hard. But her voice, when she let go,
was sultry and amused: "Don't you know? Don't you really know? I'm
being taken out to a farm, miles away. I'll never see you again."

She came close to being right about that, but before I go on I want to
be fair to Dawn. She did display, there with the student group, a little
gaiety. It wasn't sparkling, perhaps, but it wasn't stagy, either—a sort of
sweet naughtiness that was quite engaging and that had the student
males riding around no-hands and standing on their heads, at about the
same junior high school level to which she'd reduced the staff the night
before.

Then she was gone. Noel did take her far from this city, more than
twenty miles, but not just in distance. He came as close as you can to
taking her away in time as well, about three centuries.

He took her to an Amish farm, where he had rented the small, spare
house intended for the parents when the inheriting son took the place
in charge. I will have to tell you a little more about the Amish in a
moment. They are, of course, the people who call themselves "plain,"
the lace-capped women and bearded men who drive buggies and still
farm with horses.

"Are you surprised Dawn was willing to go down there?" Noel asked me, visiting one day soon afterward in my office. "I admit I didn't give her much choice."

I said something dumb, like "It should be an interesting experience for both of you."

"We've had enough interesting experiences," Noel said, and then, not very smooth for once: "Dawn agrees. She does now. After Boston—well, look. Otherwise I wouldn't have brought her and Jimmer out here in spite of missing her so much. I told her."

Jimmer, I remembered, was her little boy, but I didn't actually see him until spring.

And now you've got to hear about the winter, and more about the Amish, too.

The winter that Dawn and Noel Butler, and Dawn's son—strange changeling child of a passionate adolescent girl and a perverse, creative man, much older—never mind. That winter was a bitch.

It snowed early, got cold, stayed cold. The country roads were often impassable, and it was a struggle for Noel to get back and forth to meet his classes. But he would tell me, from time to time, that it was worth it to him, and I understood him to mean that he and Dawn were happy and cozy and trusting.

About the Amish I'll try not to tell you any more than you need to know. They include several conservative splinter groups from the Mennonite Church, and of them all the most conservative are the Old Order Amish. Like all Mennonites, they are pacifist, believe in nonresistance, refuse to take oaths, and are very strict in matters of recreation and self-indulgence. The Old Order Amish, in addition, try to live just as the first of their faith did in 1650—wearing similar clothing, hairstyles, and face-hair styles, farming by the same methods, without the use of engines or electricity. They are a God-and-family-centered people, and their way of life endures, in its enclaves in Indiana, Pennsylvania, Iowa, and Oregon, because of its tight structure in which the children are brought up believing that they are, like their parents, among the chosen very, very few. They are not quaint; they are proud. They own excellent small farms, farm them well, and pass them along carefully through the generations.

They maintain their own schools, which go only through the eighth grade. They take a distant, not altogether unworldly, interest in us, whom they must meet in bargaining situations, and a very intense interest in one another. Community is hardly less important to them than family.

On the Old Order Amish farm where Dawn, Noel, and Dawn's child spent the winter, there was a patriarch as head of the household, a widower in his late sixties. His older sons were established with families on farms of their own, which he'd helped buy; the youngest son, of whom, Noel said, the old man was particularly proud, was heir designate to the family farm. This heir was called Daniel.

Daniel was thirty-two, with a wife and seven children. Noel found him a scrupulous landlord. Though Daniel worked an extremely long, hard day, he would always take time to make sure Dawn and Noel's cottage was snug and in repair. But though he had provided the cottage with electricity, as well as a telephone, when he and his father had decided to rent it, he would not use power tools nor himself turn off or on a light.

"Strong arms, bright blue eyes, and a reddish-brown beard," Noel said. "With that upper lip shaved clean the way they do. He's always so solemn when we see him, and he won't let his wife or any of the kids come in our door."

That was as much as I knew about the family when Noel arrived at my house, just before noon on a spring day, to say that Daniel, the Amish farmer, had tried to kill him.

Every story has its relatives. This one is some sort of cousin, in my mind, to a play I saw as a boy, called *Rain*. In the play, as I remember it, a missionary and a loose woman are trapped in a hotel in the tropics by incessant rain, which becomes her ally in the temptation and seduction of the man. Dawn's allies were cold, wind, snow, and ice, perhaps, but I don't want to push the comparison with the old play too far: Dawn, after all, was still quite girlish, and Daniel's rectitude was of a personal, not a missionary, kind.

Noel said that as a matter of fact, Dawn first reacted to Daniel with some awe. Noel couldn't say just when Dawn had started regarding Daniel as either an interesting possibility or an actual attraction. Noel admitted quite abjectly his own stupidity. He and the winter had made Dawn and Daniel the only man and woman in the world.

My guess is that she was simply, in the beginning, unable to keep from making just a very slight test of Daniel, a little test of herself as well, with no serious motive except curiosity—I'm willing to see it as innocent curiosity, if it wasn't actually unconscious—just to see if he'd respond to her at all. And once he'd responded just a little—was it with a stammer, or a blush, or a clumsy pressing back against a pressing hand? —then it may suddenly have been too late for both of them.

She had to go on with it. The ice and snow insisted, and her imprisonment. Daniel, I imagine, fought and prayed—and came back for another press of the hand, and one day a hug, and—how much later?—something that was barely the first kiss.

It would all have been very gradual, very difficult, very absorbing to the two imaginations, in a rhythm deliberate as seasons changing. I thought of Dawn, passing her winter days that way, moving toward him, guardedly, the excitement allowed to grow very slowly, having to keep the embraces, as they intensified little by little, out of sight of her child, her husband, the Amish family. The potential lovers were as hemmed in, as hard put to find times of privacy, as any couple could be.

"I know when it finally happened," Noel said. It clearly hurt him to tell me, but he had to. "The first time. Dawn and I drove into Yodertown one afternoon to shop and didn't start back until after dark. It was storming by then, a wet, wild, late-winter storm, with ruts and mud frozen on the surface, soft and treacherous underneath, and the wind howling and freezing and the snow blowing. We got to within about three miles of the place before the windshield wouldn't clear anymore and I ran off the road and got us stuck in the ditch.

"I was wearing boots and outdoor clothing, though not really enough of it. Dawn would never dress for winter when we were going somewhere in a heated car. Her shoes were thin and even had heels on them. She was wearing a kind of high-fashion wool cloak that looked romantic as hell, but nothing to keep the wind out. I'd have given her my hat and jacket, but there was no way to beat the shoe problem.

"We had most of a tank of gas. I might have stayed with her, but Jimmer was home and hungry and the night was scary. The car'd be twice as hard to get out in the morning, when I had to get to school. We decided I'd better go for help. Dawn was to run the motor periodically for heat and to turn on the headlights for half a minute out of every five, to show where she was. So I left.

"God, it was a terrible walk. It kept getting colder. The wind got higher, and the snowfall was the heaviest I've ever been out in. I could hardly see. Luckily, it was coming at my back, but I still stumbled and struggled in the bad footing, and once I got so far off the road I ran into barbed-wire fence. It probably took me an hour to go three miles. I was going to phone . . ." Noel hesitated. "As a matter of fact, Vance, I was going to phone you, because I knew you had a four-wheel-drive truck. I hoped when the storm let up, you could find the place and wouldn't mind coming after me so we could get Dawn and try to pull the car out."

I nodded.

"When I finally got there, the phone was out. The lights, too. Jimmer was terrified. I didn't know what to do. I lit candles and tried to comfort the boy. The stove worked all right, so I fixed him some soup. I remember standing there, stirring it, with my teeth chattering. I couldn't get warm.

"I thought of putting Jimmer to bed under blankets, taking Dawn's winter boots and jacket, and walking back, but I wasn't too sure I could make it, going against that wind, or that she could, coming back. I decided I was going to have to get Daniel's help and advice. I should be able to say that some damn warning voice told me not to, but it isn't so. Whatever'd been happening, they'd concealed it very well.

"Anyway, I didn't know if his team of horses and the closed carriage— a sort of van they use in the winter—could go through the weather. I was wondering about that when he knocked at the door. He'd seen the candlelight. He knew the car hadn't come in. He came to check up, and I explained.

"When he learned that Dawn was out there alone, Daniel got quite upset. Especially, I suppose, because, not being familiar with cars, he couldn't believe that she was safe and comfortable.

"I asked if his team could go out, and he said no.

"I asked what he thought we should do, and he said, 'Likely I'll take tractor to pull out. Sure.' I was almost shocked. There was this monstrous, big old iron-wheeled tractor in the barn. One of Daniel's older brothers had bought it years before, when some of the Old Order people argued that a tractor was permissible on the farm so long as it didn't have rubber tires. Instead, these tractors had lugs, almost spikes, and they tore up the country roads so bad the Secondary Roads Department banned them. Daniel himself didn't use the tractor, but he'd learned to drive it as a boy—an act of rebellion, I suppose, if not real wickedness. A couple of times a year the older brother would come over and start the thing up and do maintenance on it.

"I asked if I should ride along. Daniel didn't even answer. I was in no shape to go out again, anyway. The night was getting worse. Jimmer was there. I gave Daniel Dawn's boots and things to take along, and out he went in his coat and overalls. They're not allowed to use buttons. Their clothes are held together with safety pins. He had a scarf and a black, broadbrimmed hat, knit gloves and galoshes. After a while I heard the big old machine start, and then I heard it lumber past our little house. It didn't have any lights."

Here I paused, as Noel had paused. I looked around the class and seemed to have their attention; but it was hard to tell about Katie Jay, my smart student. Her eyes were down and away, studying her tabletop.

Wouldn't Daniel's father and the Amish family (I asked the class) have heard that tractor moving out? They might have taken it for the county snowplow passing on the road.

The rest is much too easy to imagine: Daniel on his iron tractor seat, laboring against the unfamiliar steering wheel, turning into the wind, chugging through the night. Snow and dark, forces of nature storming in his face, trying to turn him back; the scarf tight, facial skin around his beard getting numb, hands and feet freezing as the slow machine gripped and bumped. But after a time he'd have started to see the faint glimmering of the headlights at long intervals, calling him to her. I don't know whether in his own mind he was damned before he got there; but the great, clanking, spike-wheeled thing he rode was an engine of sin, no question. And it failed him, going into the ditch itself a hundred yards before he reached the car, so that he finished getting there on foot.

Imagine Daniel knocking, then, on the deeply frosted window, and Dawn opening the door to what must have looked like a man of ice.

"Is it Daniel?"

"Are you all right, missus?"

"Daniel, get in. Get in. You'll die out there."

"But it's you worries me."

"Please. Get in."

He does. The door closes. And they are trapped together in the night. There is a nearly frozen man to thaw. She holds him. She croons to him. She wipes his hair and beard with her cloak. I think that an embrace develops out of this, gets almost violent before, perhaps with a sob, he pulls away. And the wind howls, the snow blows and piles. Dawn waits. Perhaps she touches him, and, with another sob, he hurls himself at her again and is, after how many engagements, received into a warmth like no other.

That this happened, Noel was quite sure—whatever guilts and indecisions followed, whatever withdrawals and renewals—because of what took place the next night. It was clear and extremely cold, and in the morning there was a curious frozen smudge in the center of one of the panes of glass in their bedroom window. Jimmer said someone had looked in, very late. Dawn said it was the boy's imagination. But Noel felt sure that the smudge was made, and others like it as other nights came and went, by the Amish farmer pressing his cheek against the cold glass that separated him from the woman he loved.

"God, how we've fought since then," Noel said. "I knew. Dawn has a crazy-lady act that goes with having an affair. I'd seen it before. So I accused her.

" 'Oh, what fun, Noel darling, who?'

" 'Daniel,' I said, and she almost had hysterics laughing at me. She pulled a handful of her hair around and held it to her chin for a beard, and ran around being Daniel, getting drunk on carrot juice and pinching pumpkins on the fanny. . . . I said to cut it out, that I knew for sure, and she said oh, then she'd run and get Daniel so I could tell him all about it.

"Yesterday I got home an hour before she expected me. I saw Daniel leave the house. I went in, and Jimmer was napping. Dawn said Daniel was getting the sink unclogged. This morning I looked, and then I showed her, there's no way that sink could clog up because the drain's so big. You couldn't stop it up with a sweater.

"So she grabbed a sweater of mine and started stuffing it into the drain, and I told her to go to hell, I was leaving. I got out a suitcase and started to pack it. She grabbed the clothes out of it and ran out the door, screaming and dropping my stuff all over the yard. I was furious. I ran out after her, and there was Daniel, over by the barn, working on that monstrous tractor with a wrench as long as your arm.

"Dawn ran over and got behind him, pointing at me, and right away Daniel started for me with that wrench. First I couldn't believe it. Then I ran. I ran to the car with Daniel after me, and he pounded the car with the wrench as I drove away. You can see the dents, Vance. Look."

Well (I said to the class), Noel needed his clothes and his books. He was afraid to go back. I said I'd go, and my phone rang.

"Is Noel there?" It was Dawn.

"Yes."

"Will he talk to me?"

I asked. Noel shook his head. "I'm sorry," I said.

"Tell him Daniel has to see him."

I did. Noel turned pale and whispered, "Oh, my God."

I covered the mouthpiece and said, "Noel, I don't know the man, but I'll bet you anything he wants to beg your pardon."

"Ask Dawn," Noel said, and I did.

"Daniel's in an agony of shame," Dawn said. "I think he wants to get down on his knees to Noel."

I passed that along. "She's such a liar," Noel said, but he agreed to a meeting with Daniel. I went too. It took place in a local filling station, owned by a backslid uncle of Daniel's. The young farmer was pretty close to tears, if not quite on his knees. He wanted Noel to forgive him and to pray for him, but afterward Noel still felt wary about going for his stuff. I went, after all, and saw Dawn again.

Her appearance was strained—we none of us come out of the winters here looking terrific—but her manner was curiously relaxed. I found her, this time, easy to talk to. She seemed to be waiting, without any great anxiety, to see what would happen. None of the Amish family was in sight when I drove in, nor were they when I drove out again.

Noel graduated and left eight years ago. But Dawn and Jimmer are still in Indiana, as far as I know, living between Gary and Michigan City, by the shore of the big lake. They went there with Daniel. He gave it all up, his God, his inheritance, his family, his community. He's working up there as a truck driver, I understand.

I paused and said, "Okay. True story." Then I looked toward Katie Jay, the bright student I spoke of, who often asserts the privilege of first comment; but her eyes were on her hands and her hands were still on the table in front of her. "Who wants to pick a point-of-view character for it?"

Dave, who is fast and sedulous, said, "Yours. I don't see anything wrong with the way you told it."

"But it stays a raconteur's story," I said. "A pastime. What happens if you use one of the characters?"

"The raconteur could be more involved," Dave said. "Something could happen to him, as a consequence. Or he could be more of a commentator, more cynical or more compassionate or more open about drawing a moral."

"Let's drop him, anyway," I said. "And tell it from Noel's point of view. What happens?"

Ernie's hand went up—but let me summarize rather than try to quote our discussion.

No acceptable serious story could be told from Noel's point of view, the class felt, because he would be weak and a loser, just one more sensitive young man betrayed and asking for our pity. But there were comic possibilities—a mean, ironic one if Noel were the kind of flawed narrator who, thinking he has the reader's sympathy, shows that he really drove Dawn straight into Daniel's arms. Or, said someone, give Noel enough perspective to be aware of that himself now and it could be a farce, about the smart guy who outsmarts himself but comes out a winner anyway because he's free of an impossible situation.

The talk of flawed narrators led to some discussion of having the story seen and heard through the eyes and ears of Jimmer, the child, whose understanding of certain things might be precocious and exceed the reader's, the reader in turn seeing other things of which Jimmer would be unaware. Several in the class saw that solution as being too literary and as taking away a certain harsh dignity the story might have if it were Daniel's.

From Daniel's point of view, we'd have a serious psychological melodrama to write, full of guilt, struggle, and prayer. We would have to decide whether to regard him as a victim or not, and the piece could be pretty heavy going. What about doing it as Dawn would see it?

"A sappy romance," someone said, a male.

"Depends on Dawn," said one of the women. "It could be a sophisticated romance if she's sophisticated. It could even be another kind of comedy, you know, if you make her able to deal with his religion thing."

Again I looked at Katie Jay. I really wanted to hear her get going on Dawn Butler. I expected a strong, funny attack. This was because Katie Jay had once explained to me, when we were speaking about a very cool man-woman piece she'd written, that sex was something she could not take seriously. When she was fifteen, Katie Jay said, and had her first boyfriend, her mother had simply put an extra pillow on the bed. That was all sex meant to slim-necked, caustic Katie Jay, with her shiny blond head and sharp tongue: the essence of no big deal.

When she had nothing to say, I asked my final question: "Is there any way this story could be written as a serious tragedy?" Then I answered myself: Yes, again as a function of choosing a particular point of view. Recently, I explained, I have come to know a very old Amish farmer, a fine, thoughtful man in his seventies. He is, although he interests himself a little in worldly matters, essentially and attractively an innocent man, if not naive. His name is Aaron, and I can admire if not quite envy him. He has lived that life structured for him by fanatical Dutch peasants three centuries ago, and has been fulfilled by it.

"Suppose," I said, "we think of Daniel's father as a man like Aaron, which he must have been. A man who, if only because of his years, is aware before the rest, before Daniel even, of what might happen, yet too appalled to think it really will. He is a man who can truly and simply use a word like *Jezebel* and feel the damnation in it. And he's a patriarch, waiting to be consulted and obeyed, but he will hesitate a long time, too long, to acknowledge so great a sin as actual. Suppose we saw through Aaron's eyes not just the loss, day by day, of his finest son, but the way in which it foretells the whole structure breaking down, the wearing away of order in the world—wouldn't that point of view give you a chance to build some tragic power?"

The class couldn't disagree, because I wouldn't let them. It was one of those days when I felt like having the last word, and it was time to dismiss them anyway. But as they went out, free and clamorous, Katie Jay was still sitting as she had been, not jumping up in her usual way to cry out sharply to her friends, proclaim where they were to go to have a beer. She sat there, uncharacteristically still, but finally she did look up at me.

I went around the table to her and smiled. Katie Jay's hand moved up and took my arm above the elbow, and the grip, between thumb and forefinger, reminded me of another's grip, ten years before, on my wrist.

"Yes, Katie?"

She continued looking at me for a moment. Then her eyes went away, her face turned back toward the table, and she released my arm.

"Katie Jay?"

She shook her head. She gathered up her books and stood. I moved aside, concerned, confused, a little cross, and watched her walk to the door of the classroom where she turned back to look at me again.

"I need him," Katie Jay said, and there was nothing cool, nothing detached, nothing even very smart about her voice. "Oh, I need that Amish farmer. Don't you see?"

RICHARD BRAUTIGAN

1/3, 1/3, 1/3

It was all to be done in thirds. I was to get 1/3 for doing the typing, and she was to get 1/3 for doing the editing, and he was to get 1/3 for writing the novel.

We were going to divide the royalties three ways. We all shook hands on the deal, each knowing what we were supposed to do, the path before us, the gate at the end.

I was made a 1/3 partner because I had the typewriter.

I lived in a cardboard-lined shack of my own building across the street from the rundown old house the Welfare rented for her and her nine-year-old son Freddy.

The novelist lived in a trailer a mile away beside a sawmill pond where he was the watchman for the mill.

I was about seventeen and made lonely and strange by that Pacific Northwest of so many years ago, that dark, rainy land of 1952. I'm thirty-one now and I still can't figure out what I meant by living the way I did in those days.

She was one of those eternally fragile women in their late thirties and once very pretty and the object of much attention in the roadhouses and beer parlors, who are now on Welfare and their entire lives rotate around that one day a month when they get their Welfare checks.

The word "check" is the one religious word in their lives, so they always manage to use it at least three or four times in every conversation. It doesn't matter what you are talking about.

The novelist was in his late forties, tall, reddish, and looked as if life had given him an endless stream of two-timing girlfriends, five-day drunks and cars with bad transmissions.

He was writing the novel because he wanted to tell a story that had happened to him years before when he was working in the woods.

He also wanted to make some money: 1/3.

My entrance into the thing came about this way: One day I was

standing in front of my shack, eating an apple and staring at a black
ragged toothache sky that was about to rain.

What I was doing was like an occupation for me. I was that involved in
looking at the sky and eating the apple. You would have thought that I
had been hired to do it with a good salary and a pension if I stared at the
sky long enough.

"HEY, YOU!" I heard somebody yell.

I looked across the mud puddle and it was the woman. She was
wearing a kind of green mackinaw that she wore all the time, except
when she had to visit the Welfare people downtown. Then she put on a
shapeless duck-gray coat.

We lived in a poor part of town where the streets weren't paved. The
street was nothing more than a big mud puddle that you had to walk
around. The street was of no use to cars anymore. They traveled on a
different frequency where asphalt and gravel were more sympathetic.

She was wearing a pair of white rubber boots that she always had on
in the winter, a pair of boots that gave her a kind of childlike appearance. She was so fragile and firmly indebted to the Welfare Department
that she often looked like a child twelve years old.

"What do you want?" I said.

"You have a typewriter, don't you?" she said. "I've walked by your
shack and heard you typing. You type a lot at night."

"Yeah, I have a typewriter," I said.

"You a good typist?" she said.

"I'm all right."

"We don't have a typewriter. How would you like to go in with us?"
she yelled across the mud puddle. She looked a perfect twelve years old,
standing there in her white boots, the sweetheart and darling of all mud
puddles.

"What's 'go in' mean?"

"Well, he's writing a novel," she said. "He's good. I'm editing it. I've
read a lot of pocketbooks and the *Reader's Digest*. We need somebody
who has a typewriter to type it up. You'll get 1/3. How does that sound?"

"I'd like to see the novel," I said. I didn't know what was happening. I
knew she had three or four boyfriends that were always visiting her.

"Sure!" she yelled. "You have to see it to type it. Come on around.
Let's go out to his place right now and you can meet him and have a look
at the novel. He's a good guy. It's a wonderful book."

"OK," I said, and walked around the mud puddle to where she was
standing in front of her evil dentist house, twelve years old, and approxi-
mately two miles from the Welfare office.

"Let's go," she said.

We walked over to the highway and down the highway past mud puddles and sawmill ponds and fields flooded with rain until we came to a

road that went across the railroad tracks and turned down past half a
dozen small sawmill ponds that were filled with black winter logs.

We talked very little and that was only about her check that was two
days late and she had called the Welfare and they said they mailed the
check and it should be there tomorrow, but call again tomorrow if it's
not there and we'll prepare an emergency money order for you.

"Well, I hope it's there tomorrow," I said.

"So do I or I'll have to go downtown," she said.

Next to the last sawmill pond was a yellow old trailer up on blocks of
wood. One look at that trailer showed that it was never going anywhere
again, that the highway was in distant heaven, only to be prayed to. It
was really sad with a cemeterylike chimney swirling jagged dead smoke
in the air above it.

A kind of half-dog, half-cat creature was sitting on a rough plank
porch that was in front of the door. The creature half-barked and half-
meowed at us, "Arfeow!" and darted under the trailer, looking out at us
from behind a block.

"This is it," the woman said.

The door to the trailer opened and a man stepped out onto the porch.
There was a pile of firewood stacked on the porch and it was covered
with a black tarp.

The man held his hand above his eyes, shielding his eyes from a bright
imaginary sun, though everything had turned dark in anticipation of
the rain.

"Hello, there," he said.

"Hi," I said.

"Hello, honey," she said.

He shook my hand and welcomed me to his trailer, then he gave her a
little kiss on the mouth before we all went inside.

The place was small and muddy and smelled like stale rain and had a
large unmade bed that looked as if it had been a partner to some of the
saddest lovemaking this side of The Cross.

There was a green bushy half-table with a couple of insectlike chairs
and a little sink and a small stove that was used for cooking and heating.

There were some dirty dishes in the little sink. The dishes looked as if
they had always been dirty: born dirty to last forever.

I could hear a radio playing western music someplace in the trailer,
but I couldn't find it. I looked all over but it was nowhere in sight. It was
probably under a shirt or something.

"He's the kid with the typewriter," she said. "He'll get 1/3 for typing
it."

"That sounds fair," he said. "We need somebody to type it. I've never
done anything like this before."

"Why don't you show it to him?" she said. "He'd like to take a look at
it."

"OK. But it isn't too carefully written," he said to me. "I only went to the fourth grade, so she's going to edit it, straighten out the grammar and commas and stuff."

There was a notebook lying on the table, next to an ashtray that probably had 600 cigarette butts in it. The notebook had a color photograph of Hopalong Cassidy on the cover.

Hopalong looked tired, as if he had spent the previous night chasing starlets all over Hollywood and barely had enough strength to get back in the saddle.

There were about twenty-five or thirty pages of writing in the notebook. It was written in a large grammar school sprawl: an unhappy marriage between printing and longhand.

"It's not finished yet," he said.

"You'll type it. I'll edit it. He'll write it," she said.

It was a story about a young logger falling in love with a waitress. The novel began in 1935 in a cafe in North Bend, Oregon.

The young logger was sitting at a table and the waitress was taking his order. She was very pretty with blond hair and rosy cheeks. The young logger was ordering veal cutlets with mashed potatoes and country gravy.

"Yeah, I'll do the editing. You can type it, can't you? It's not too bad, is it?" she said in a twelve-year-old voice with the Welfare peeking over her shoulder.

"No," I said. "It will be easy."

Suddenly the rain started to come down hard outside, without any warning, just suddenly great drops of rain that almost shook the trailer.

You sur lik veel cutlets dont you Maybell said she was holding holding her pensil up her mowth that was preti and red like an apl!

Onli wen you tak my oder Carl said he was a kind of bassful loger but big and strong lik his dead who ownd the starmill!

Ill mak sur you get plenti of gravi!

Just ten the caf door opend and in cam Rins Adams he was hansom and meen, everi bodi in thos parts was afrad of him but not Carl and his dead dad they wasnt afrad of him no sur!

Maybell shifard wen she saw him standing ther in his blac macinaw he smild at her and Carl felt his blod run hot lik scallding cofee and fiting mad!

Howdi ther Rins said Maybell blushed like a flower flouar while we were all sitting there in that rainy trailer, pounding at the gates of American literature.

HAROLD BRODKEY

Verona: A Young Woman Speaks

I know a lot! I know about happiness! I don't mean the love of God, either: I mean I know the human happiness with the crimes in it.

Even the happiness of childhood.

I think of it now as a cruel, middle-class happiness.

Let me describe one time—one day, one night.

I was quite young, and my parents and I—there were just the three of us—were traveling from Rome to Salzburg, journeying across a quarter of Europe to be in Salzburg for Christmas, for the music and the snow. We went by train because planes were erratic, and my father wanted us to stop in half a dozen Italian towns and see paintings and buy things. It was absurd, but we were all three drunk with this; it was very strange: we woke every morning in a strange hotel, in a strange city. I would be the first one to wake; and I would go to the window and see some tower or palace; and then I would wake my mother and be justified in my sense of wildness and belief and adventure by the way she acted, her sense of romance at being in a city as strange as I had thought it was when I had looked out the window and seen the palace or the tower.

We had to change trains in Verona, a darkish, smallish city at the edge of the Alps. By the time we got there, we'd bought and bought our way up the Italian peninsula: I was dizzy with shopping and new possessions: I hardly knew who I was, I owned so many new things: my reflection in any mirror or shopwindow was resplendently fresh and new, disguised even, glittering, I thought. I was seven or eight years old. It seemed to me we were almost in a movie or in the pages of a book: only the simplest and most light-filled words and images can suggest what I thought we were then. We went around shiningly: we shone every-where. *Those clothes.* It's easy to buy a child. I had a new dress, knitted, blue and red, expensive as hell, I think; leggings, also red; a red loden-cloth coat with a hood and a knitted cap for under the hood; marvelous lined gloves; fur-lined boots and a fur purse or carryall, and a tartan skirt

—and shirts and a scarf, and there was even more: a watch, a bracelet: more and more.

On the trains we had private rooms, and Momma carried games in her purse and things to eat, and Daddy sang carols off-key to me; and sometimes I became so intent on my happiness I would suddenly be in real danger of wetting myself; and Momma, who understood such emergencies, would catch the urgency in my voice and see my twisted face; and she—a large, good-looking woman—would whisk me to a toilet with amazing competence and unstoppability, murmuring to me, "Just hold on for a while," and she would hold my hand while I did it.

So we came to Verona, where it was snowing, and the people had stern, sad faces, beautiful, unlaughing faces. But if they looked at me, those serious faces would lighten, they would smile at me in my splendor. Strangers offered me candy, sometimes with the most excruciating sadness, kneeling or stooping to look directly into my face, into my eyes; and Momma or Papa would judge them, the people, and say in Italian we were late, we had to hurry, or pause, and let the stranger touch me, talk to me, look into my face for a while. I would see myself in the eyes of some strange man or woman; sometimes they stared so gently I would want to touch their eyelashes, stroke those strange, large, glistening eyes. I knew I decorated life. I took my duties with great seriousness. An Italian count in Siena said I had the manners of an English princess —at times—and then he laughed because it was true I would be quite lurid: I ran shouting in his *galleria,* a long room, hung with pictures, and with a frescoed ceiling: and I sat on his lap and wriggled: I was a wicked child, and I liked myself very much; and almost everywhere, almost every day, there was someone new to love me, briefly, while we traveled.

I understood I was special. I understood it *then.*

I knew that what we were doing, everything we did, involved money. I did not know if it involved mind or not, or style. But I knew about money somehow, checks and traveler's checks and the clink of coins. Daddy was a fountain of money: he said it was a spree; he meant for us to be amazed; he had saved money—we weren't really rich but we were to be for this trip. I remember a conservatory in a large house outside Florence and orange trees in tubs; and I ran there too. A servant, a man dressed in black, a very old man, mean-faced—he did not like being a servant anymore after the days of servants were over—and he scowled but he smiled at me, and at my mother, and even once at my father: we were clearly so separate from the griefs and wearinesses and cruelties of the world. We were at play, we were at our joys, and Momma was glad, with a terrible and naïve inner gladness, and she relied on Daddy to make it work: oh, she worked too, but she didn't know the secret of such —unreality: is that what I want to say? Of such a game, of such an extraordinary game.

There was a picture in Verona Daddy wanted to see; a painting; I remember the painter because the name Pisanello reminded me I had to go to the bathroom when we were in the museum, which was an old castle, Guelf or Ghibelline, I don't remember which; and I also remember the painting because it showed the hind end of the horse, and I thought that was not nice and rather funny, but Daddy was admiring; and so I said nothing.

He held my hand and told me a story so I wouldn't be bored as we walked from room to room in the museum/castle, and then we went outside into the snow, into the soft light when it snows, light coming through snow; and I was dressed in red and had on boots, and my parents were young and pretty and had on boots too; and we could stay out in the snow if we wanted; and we did. We went to a square, a piazza —the Scaligera, I think; I don't remember—and just as we got there, the snowing began to bellow and then subside, to fall heavily and then sparsely, and then it stopped: and it was very cold, and there were pigeons everywhere in the piazza, on every cornice and roof, and all over the snow on the ground, leaving little tracks as they walked, while the air trembled in its just-after-snow and just-before-snow weight and thickness and gray seriousness of purpose. I had never seen so many pigeons or such a private and haunted place as that piazza, me in my new coat at the far rim of the world, the far rim of who knew what story, the rim of foreign beauty and Daddy's games, the edge, the white border of a season.

I was half mad with pleasure, anyway, and now Daddy brought five or six cones made of newspaper, wrapped, twisted; and they held grains of something like corn, yellow and white kernels of something; and he poured some on my hand and told me to hold my hand out; and then he backed away.

At first there was nothing, but I trusted him and I waited; and then the pigeons came. On heavy wings. Clumsy pigeony bodies. And red, unreal bird's feet. They flew at me, slowing at the last minute; they lit on my arm and fed from my hand. I wanted to flinch, but I didn't. I closed my eyes and held my arm stiffly; and felt them peck and eat—from my hand, these free creatures, these flying things. I liked that moment. I liked my happiness. If I was mistaken about life and pigeons and my own nature, it didn't matter *then*.

The piazza was very silent, with snow; and Daddy poured grains on both my hands and then on the sleeves of my coat and on the shoulders of the coat, and I was entranced with yet more stillness, with this idea of his. The pigeons fluttered heavily in the heavy air, more and more of them, and sat on my arms and on my shoulders; and I looked at Momma and then at my father and then at the birds on me.

Oh, I'm sick of everything as I talk. There is happiness. It always makes me slightly ill. I lose my balance because of it.

The heavy birds, and the strange buildings, and Momma near, and Daddy too: Momma is pleased that I am happy and she is a little jealous; she is jealous of everything Daddy does; she is a woman of enormous spirit; life is hardly big enough for her; she is drenched in wastefulness and prettiness. She knows things. She gets inflexible, though, and foolish at times, and temperamental; but she is a somebody, and she gets away with a lot, and if she is near, you can feel her, you can't escape her, she's that important, that echoing, her spirit is that powerful in the space around her.

If she weren't restrained by Daddy, if she weren't in love with him, there is no knowing what she might do: she does not know. But she manages almost to be gentle because of him; he is incredibly watchful and changeable and he gets tired; he talks and charms people; sometimes, then, Momma and I stand nearby, like moons; we brighten and wane; and after a while, he comes to us, to the moons, the big one, and the little one, and we welcome him, and he is always, to my surprise, he is always surprised, as if he didn't deserve to be loved, as if it were time he was found out.

Daddy is very tall, and Momma is watching us, and Daddy anoints me again and again with the grain. I cannot bear it much longer. I feel joy or amusement or I don't know what; it is all through me, like a nausea—I am ready to scream and laugh, that laughter that comes out like magical, drunken, awful and yet pure spit or vomit or God knows what, that makes me a child mad with laughter. I become brilliant, gleaming, soft: an angel, a great bird-child of laughter.

I am ready to be like that, but I hold myself back.

There are more and more birds near me. They march around my feet and peck at falling and fallen grains. One is on my head. Of those on my arms, some move their wings, fluff those frail, feather-loaded wings, stretch them. I cannot bear it, they are so frail, and I am, at the moment, the kindness of the world that feeds them in the snow.

All at once, I let out a splurt of laughter: I can't stop myself and the birds fly away but not far; they circle around me, above me; some wheel high in the air and drop as they return; they all returned, some in clouds and clusters driftingly, some alone and angry, pecking at others; some with a blind, animal-strutting abruptness. They gripped my coat and fed themselves. It started to snow again.

I was there in my kindness, in that piazza, within reach of my mother and father.

Oh, how will the world continue? Daddy suddenly understood I'd had enough, I was at the end of my strength—Christ, he was alert—and he picked me up, and I went limp, my arm around his neck, and the snow fell. Momma came near and pulled the hood lower and said there were snowflakes in my eyelashes. She knew he had understood, and she wasn't sure she had; she wasn't sure he ever watched her so carefully. She became slightly unhappy, and so she walked like a clumsy boy beside us, but she was so pretty: she had powers, anyway.

We went to a restaurant, and I behaved very well, but I couldn't eat, and then we went to the train and people looked at us, but I couldn't smile; I was too dignified, too sated; some leftover—pleasure, let's call it—made my dignity very deep, I could not stop remembering the pigeons, or that Daddy loved me in a way he did not love Momma; and Daddy was alert, watching the luggage, watching strangers for assassination attempts or whatever; he was on duty; and Momma was pretty and alone and *happy*, defiant in that way.

And then, you see, what she did was wake me in the middle of the night when the train was chugging up a very steep mountainside; and outside the window, visible because our compartment was dark and the sky was clear and there was a full moon, were mountains, a landscape of mountains everywhere, big mountains, huge ones, impossible, all slanted and pointed and white with snow, and absurd, sticking up into an ink-blue sky and down into blue, blue shadows, miraculously deep. I don't know how to say what it was like: they were not like anything I knew: they were high things: and we were up high in the train and we were climbing higher, and it was not at all true, but it was, you see. I put my hands on the window and stared at the wild, slanting, unlikely marvels, whiteness and dizziness and moonlight and shadows cast by moonlight, not real, not familiar, not pigeons, but a clean world.

We sat a long time, Momma and I, and stared, and then Daddy woke up and came and looked too. "It's pretty," he said, but he didn't really understand. Only Momma and I did. She said to him, "When I was a child, I was bored all the time, my love—I thought nothing would ever happen to me—and now these things are happening—and you have happened." I think he was flabbergasted by her love in the middle of the night; he smiled at her, oh, so swiftly that I was jealous, but I stayed quiet, and after a while, in his silence and amazement at her, at us, he began to seem different from us, from Momma and me; and then he fell asleep again; Momma and I didn't; we sat at the window and watched all night, watched the mountains and the moon, the clean world. We watched together.

Momma was the winner.

We were silent, and in silence we spoke of how we loved men and how dangerous men were and how they stole everything from you no matter how much you gave—but we didn't say it aloud.

We looked at mountains until dawn, and then when dawn came, it was too pretty for me—there was pink and blue and gold, in the sky, and on icy places, brilliant pink and gold flashes, and the snow was colored too, and I said, "Oh," and sighed; and each moment was more beautiful than the one before; and I said, "I love you, Momma." Then I fell asleep in her arms.

That was happiness then.

CAROL BLY

Talk of Heroes

Two women, one with hair gone gray, wearing a woolen dress and carrying a raincoat, and the other only twenty-four, gathering the velvet lapels of her dressing gown around her throat, stood a moment on a low hill overlooking White Bear Lake. A thick evening mist lolled upward from the lake surface itself, so that all the dockside equipment —the polyurethane floats, the white boat lifts, the bobbing milk cartons chained to great weights far below—all the bright playthings of American Midwest lakefronts were hidden. The evening mist suggested much greater, more classic waters than a suburban lake.

Emily Anderson had meant to pause alone for a second before jumping into her car and driving to St. Paul to introduce a speaker, but her daughter, Sandra Anderson-Keefer, had ambled out of the house after her. Sandra began to tell an odd dream she had had when she fell asleep in the late afternoon. It was not exactly to do with Bruce, her husband, but somehow she felt it had to do with a vague semblance of him. Not like a ghost exactly, she told Emily, but something unclear and generalized. Emily shifted the raincoat on her arm and started energetically across the cold grass for the car, with Sandra following, trying to explain the dream sequence.

Emily was feeling the elation of conscientious hosts when they can temporarily escape a ubiquitous houseguest. No matter that Sandra was her daughter, and a humorous and kindly-inclined girl, home to get it, as she put it, all together for a few days—the fact was, Sandra talked a lot and Emily wasn't used to it.

She had not yet given up the silent house on its rise over the lake, the oak trees' dripping, the autumn fogs in the morning and evening. She was used to standing outside for her early morning coffee. She was used to moving about her work, from room to room, without conversation. In the past four days, however, Sandra had followed her from her book-packing in the library to her cleaning of the downstairs closets. Sandra generally left her alone when she made off to her study, saying, "Oh—

you're going to work! I won't invade," and wandered into the living room for an afternoon nap. Like many people in personal turmoil, she rose late, didn't dress other than to cloak herself in her dressing gown, and she fell asleep easily throughout the day. For a few hours, late after dinner, she would talk in a jerking, high-pitched voice, about her married life. Her young face gleaming nervously, she would repeat for Emily what Bruce, her husband, had said and then what she had replied. She was trained as a group therapist, so she tended to use phrases like "thinking through her options"—but the griefs of men and women, getting along, not getting along, were there, recognizable despite her sporty jargon.

Emily hid her own relief at escaping for an evening by crying once more as they neared the car, "You're absolutely sure you don't want to come with me to the Tusend Hjem program? Old Mr. Elvekrog—poor dear—would be happy to see you! He'd welcome any member your age —probably with open arms!"

"I bet!" Sandra said.

"And wasn't Chuck Iversen an old friend of yours? He still comes, for his dad's sake no doubt—but he does try to brighten things up."

Sandra said with a laugh, "I made the Tusend Hjem scene with you and Dad for fifteen, sixteen years, and it ruined one evening of every single Christmas vacation, too! Don't you try to talk me into it, Mama! I couldn't hoke up the slightest enthusiasm in Norwegian-American culture now if you gave me a million dollars." Sandra paused. "Seriously, Mama—if you were the speaker you know I wouldn't miss it for anything! But you're introducing—so what we're looking at is a first-quality, four-minute introduction and then a half-hour of horrible speech and a half-hour of horrible slideshow. . . ."

"Movie!" said Emily, laughing.

"Horrible movie, complete instructions in how to knit Norwegian socks! Then another horrible hour of cookies and coffee with enough caffeine and sugar intake to o.d. Norway itself for a week! And then the awful singing of the Norwegian national anthem, with everyone pretending they still understand the words and care two cents for what they mean! No, Mama—sorry! I think *you're* awfully good to do it, but Tusend Hjem is definitely not one of my priorities."

Emily gave her briefcase a cheerful toss into the back seat. "The movie isn't Norwegian knitting," she said. "That's what they were going to have—Mrs. Thorstad talking about Norwegian knitting. But apparently the national office in Brooklyn called up and changed the program. The movie is about World War Two."

"Oh my God," Sandra said, smiling in through the open car window. "But I can see why you're interested. You and Dad knew someone, whoever it was, who was in it, didn't you? But it's not my war, Mama. And I know too much about human relationships now to pretend to have feelings I haven't got." She added, with a small lift of chin, "I have kind of a sense of my own war, sort of."

Emily told her, "I will be back as fast as I can leave."

Sandra looked chilled and uncertain; her dressing gown at this late time of day suggested a patient in a hospital rather than a grown woman trying with any bravado to decide whether or not to leave a husband. Emily felt sorry for her, but also at odds: her own mood was public and practical. She was geared simply to do a job. Sandra was thinking of passion only, wandering through her own personal situation all these days. Emily felt the superior edge of administrators who feel superior to expressive talkers—simply because the talkers happen not to be doing any particular work at the moment.

She drove gladly into the gloomy evening. It was only twenty minutes into St. Paul, to West Seventh Street, where Tusend Hjem leased the entire upper story of a very old, well-made brick building. Tusend Hjem was chartered in 1897 as the Minnesota chapter of the national organization of Norwegian-American immigrants. In the old days, there had been triweekly gymnastics classes, and everyone had spoken Norwegian, and had known the anthem from which the name, *tusend hjem*, or thousand homes, was taken.

Even now, Mr. Elvekrog's program committee made sure there was a meeting once a month, with some sort of cultural offering. And even when the program content itself left something to be desired (like the films occasionally sent out from the national office), the people could still count on the Norwegian-style boiled coffee, brought up three times with an egg—and the homemade cookies. Mrs. Iversen's committee kept the great gloomy hall absolutely clean; the chipped tiles in the kitchen and bathrooms were scrubbed regularly. Everyone wished they could reach the great west window to wash it.

It was a huge Roman arch, with radiating pie-sections of glass and blackened lead-soldering. It looked like a window meant to light genuinely serious human affairs, like the window of an old science laboratory where honest discoveries were made, or the window of a major embassy where people argued late at night about affairs later described in the papers. In the summertime the sun would just be failing as Tusend Hjem started its meetings, and a smeary, kindly light fell through the dusty glass arch, showing the gym ropes still knotted neatly and the rows of auditorium chairs. Along the high, plastered walls hung photographs of 1920s and 1930s gym classes; the men's knees, jutted out toward the photographer, must by now be full of creaks and aches, if not in many cases put to rest.

Emily closed the heavy street-door of the building, with its clanking nightchains. She started up the clean, wooden stairs. Above her head, she heard the committee members scurrying between kitchen and the

great hall. They would be unpacking nine-by-seventeen trays of chocolate bars and paper plates of krullers and fattigmenn, in their little
prisons of Saran Wrap. The women did not let the men simply stand
around, either. "Here—you, Merv!" Mrs. Thorstad cried, just as Emily
came to the landing, "Take this!" Then, Mrs. Iversen, hearing Mrs.
Thorstad's remark, looked about for her Chuck. He was lounging under
a framed illustrated print of the Lord's Prayer in Norwegian, joking
with Bernt Nielsen. "You can make yourself useful, too!" his mother
cried. "They'll be coming in another fifteen minutes now!" Chuck Iversen was regarded as the clown of Tusend Hjem, so now he made some
witty rejoinder and then caught sight of Emily. "Oh boy!" he shouted,
laughing, at her. "Good thing you got here!" He began separating dozens of Styrofoam coffee cups. "Old Elvekrog is climbing the walls in
there worrying—'Will Emily show up OK?' he asks everyone!"

Emily said with a smile, "He knows perfectly well I'll show up."

Chuck told her, "Yes, but he doesn't know about that so-called famous
speaker from Norway that's coming—the one you're supposed to introduce!" Chuck waved his head back to a partitioned corner of the hall. It
was an eight-foot-high enclosure, making a little office, something like
the little offices put into great factory spaces—islands isolated off from
the general noise and work. "You'd better go in there and cheer him
up," Chuck said.

Mr. Elvekrog leapt up from his seat the moment she went in the
doorway of his office. He came round the desk to give her a brief, limp
handshake. "Sometimes I just don't know what to do about National!"
he cried.

"What have they done?" Emily asked. She sat down with her raincoat
in her lap. Above the flimsy plywood and two-by-four construction of
the office, she could see the huge ceiling of the main hall, and part of the
steel and glass window. Immediately next to her was a little table covered with thick, artificial velvet of silver-green: on it, in a neat semicircle, stood propped-up small photographs of Ibsen, Björnstjerne
Björnsen, Hamsun, and Haakon VII. There was also a very bright
Kodacolor picture of fourteen or fifteen middle-aged American women
stuffed into Hardanger national costumes. Their permanents and wing-
shaped eyeglasses were heartbreaking, over the blouses of openwork
embroidery. Opposite the table stood a file case in which all Tusend
Hjem members had file folders. As they died, their folders were moved
from the upper drawer to the lower one. Last August, when Emily's
husband's file was moved, Mr. Elvekrog had kindly sent her the ribbon
awarded her husband for fifty years of Tusend Hjem membership.

Now Mr. Elvekrog, looking very old and nervous, said, "Well! I
wanted to talk to you in here—but of course it doesn't give much
privacy!"

Everyone who passed the office looked in. Women went by with mason jars in which orange sticks bearing tiny Norwegian flags were arranged in a circle, with some Kleenex stuffed in the center to keep them in position. Chuck Iversen and Bernt Nielsen passed, listening to Mrs. Thorstad, who was talking loudly about knitting.

"National needn't act so high-handed with me!" said Mr. Elvekrog. "They aren't such fine folk! I was there once, Emily—I wonder if I told you? Right in their office, there, at National. Their office—now—why, it's not even in New York City. It's in Brooklyn and I had a terrible time just to find the place. You have to know to take the BMT subway to the Forty-sixth Street stop. But Emily—I don't have to tell you—you and your husband must have been there, when you went through on your way to Norway that time, at least! The time I was there, I had called ahead to say I was coming—but do you think anyone met me? Not a soul! All there was was a janitor is all, someone just hired, too—not a genuine Tusend Hjem volunteer—not a real member. And this janitor kept vacuuming around my feet. I kept thinking that the hired coordi-nator—that's the kind of things they go in for these days—a hired coordinator—would come greet me. Finally, the janitor said, would I move my feet. That did it, Emily! I told him straight out, 'You bet I will! I will just move them right out of here, too!' I have always wondered if the janitor told the rest of them how quick I talked right up to him! Emily, when they call you from National, you would think they were calling from the gates of heaven for the tone they put on! This hired coordinator that called two weeks ago, she made me cancel the evening we had all planned for tonight—all because of this famous Norwegian war hero who was doing a tour across the country anyway!"

"Willi Varig," Emily said.

"Yes, this Willi Varig," Mr. Elvekrog said. He went on in his bitter tone: "I had already asked Mrs. Thorstad would she do her knitting patterns for us. You see, for all these past six weeks we have had an announcement up that Mrs. Thorstad would be showing us the Norwe-gian knitting patterns which she brought back from Bergen last sum-mer. In the original Norwegian language, too, but with her own transla-tions into English measure. And afterwards, Mrs. Iversen was going to serve her homemade krullers. I try to keep that bulletin board up to date, you know—and then suddenly, National calls up and says we have to have this war hero. Well, Emily—in my book, that war was a long time ago and we all want to forget it. I told them I am sorry we can't accommodate you eking out this so-called war hero's lecture schedule across the United States—which is all they really cared about, I bet. 'We have our own program already planned, thank you,' I told them. They just came back as cool as cats and said, 'Cancel whatever you have and fit this Varig in because he is famous.' Well, Emily, I for one never heard of him! And then they said that this Willi Varig had mentioned to their lecture series manager that he knew you, back in the 1950s, in Oslo, and

National asked that you introduce him! I was so surprised! Then they said, well, he would be showing a movie about Norwegian heroes during the war and we were to provide a sixteen-millimeter movie projector. Then I saw my way out, Emily! I told them, without mincing any words, that the projector had been lent to the Tomah, Wisconsin, Chapter of Tusend Hjem, and they hadn't returned it yet because it was broken and they wanted to get it fixed before they sent it back. Then National got sassy with me and said there were millions of people in St. Paul and Minneapolis and didn't we know anyone who would trust us with a projector? The upshot of it was, Tomah did finally send our projector back, and you were nice enough to say you *would* introduce this Varig—so we have to just hope it is all fixed up OK. But I can tell you, Emily, without fear of its going any further, that Mrs. Thorstad was really hurt when I had to explain to her that we wouldn't want her knitting program for tonight. But anyway, I am glad it is you doing the introducing, Emily. You two were always such good Tusend Hjem members. And I guess we ought to be grateful to have this famous speaker. Apparently he is talking to all kinds of groups, not just Tusend Hjem chapters, but the American Legion and VFW posts and goodness knows what all else. So finally all I said was, OK—but you make sure he gets here on time and that he is sober, too! The last speaker they sent us had had a good deal to drink. Everyone noticed it. Now they promised this one would be here no later than 7:30 and it is already twenty to eight and he isn't here that I can see!" Mr. Elvekrog looked closely into Emily's eyes. "Emily, does he drink as far as you know?" he asked in a low voice.

"It is a long time since I knew Willi," Emily told him. "In 1955. But National is right about at least one thing," she went on in an encouraging tone. "He really was a very great hero in the war." She forbore to tell Mr. Elvekrog that she had never once, during the whole winter when she and her husband had known Willi, seen the hero sober or even middling-sober. It had always been the same: They would be eating cod and boiled potatoes in the smoky, workmen's restaurant above some shops in Drammensveien, while Willi and any one of his various vivid girlfriends would tell stories. Then Willi would leave them to go out into the town. He would drink his way down past Karl Johansgate until he got to the railroad station or the harbor. Much later the police brought him home, to the flat of whoever the girlfriend of the moment was. However, Willi, like Emily herself, was much older now— he might even be sixty. Perhaps he was changed.

"If that speaker doesn't show up, I won't know what to think!" cried Mr. Elvekrog.

Emily said, "If he doesn't show up, I will tell the group what he did during the war and then Mrs. Thorstad can show us the Norwegian knitting patterns if she brought them, or we can ask her questions at least."

Now it was eight o'clock. The hall had filled, and Tusend Hjem members kept turning their heads about from the seats to see if the speaker had come. Mr. Elvekrog flitted back and forth between the projector, which he wouldn't trust anyone else with, and the speaker's microphone on the podium. He pretended to check the silver-taping of the wires along the aisle. Little slips on which he had jotted the announcements kept fluttering from his fingers. Chuck Iversen, the club wit, would rescue them and make jokes to everyone. "Mr. Elvekrog? Mr. Elvekrog? Did you drop this?" he would call, waving a slip over people's heads. He pretended to be making out difficult handwriting. "It says here," he shouted, "that Mrs. Thorstad has promised to send five boxes of fattigmenn to every member of the United States Congress? Can that be right, Mrs. Thorstad?" Everyone laughed and clapped and Mrs. Thorstad grew pink and her eyes got shy as a girl's. People settled to enjoying Chuck's sideshow effects. If their speaker was some big shot too important to bother to show up at their chapter on time, then they darned well, they told each other with grins, had their own people to amuse them, and their own jokes that the speaker wouldn't understand anyway. The older members began passing around the smeary purple-dittoed copies of the Norwegian national anthem, and young people concentrated, biting their lips, some of them, trying to think up good jokes to call out, the way Chuck Iversen did.

At last, they all heard the heavy door open on the first floor. It slammed shut with a rattle of night chains. A male voice made a sharp remark; there was an equally sharp return in a higher, feminine voice, and feet started up the staircase. Definitely, then, two people were coming—very slowly considering how late they were.

It was Willi Varig. At the top of the staircase, he hung onto the handrail newel for a moment, staring round with a red, burly face. Emily recognized him despite the twenty-five years and she went lightly along a side aisle to shake hands with him. At his side stood a woman of thirty or less, who appeared to be supporting him with one arm. She reminded Emily of all of Willi's women in Oslo; it was the same startlingly pretty, rather impatient sort of girl, who would fling herself down to join them at dinner, toss off her SAS jacket and immediately regale them all with a story of what some idiot had done at Fornebu Airport or on an Air France newspaper-delivery flight.

Willi had always had a cynical cast to his nature: he liked a story told with exasperation. He would slam the girl an affectionate blow on the shoulder blade and cry, "A woman deserves a drink when she has been through what you have been through!"

Now he smiled rather unpleasantly into Emily's face and shook her hand very hard, with single jerk, in the Norwegian way. He gave a laugh. "All these years! And you have not changed a little!" he said. "I would recognize you anywhere! You do not mind if I shake your hand, I hope?" He introduced the two women, getting their names eventually. In a raucous tone, in loud English, he remarked to the Norwegian girl, "Now this is an American woman that you shake hands with! You do not dare to give her a kiss—not this one! Oh no! No, you do not do that with this one! She would explain to you that she was married already! She would not hit you across the face—she wouldn't do that! She would tell you that she admired you—Oh yes! All that wonderful admiration! But no kisses—not even for old times' sake! So we shake hands!"

The Norwegian woman brought out the bland, stewardess smile which serves a million cold situations. Emily saw Mr. Elvekrog approaching, with his desperate, creased forehead. She introduced him in Norwegian to the two visitors and told him *sotto voce* that she would introduce Willi in two minutes, not four, and that she felt he ought not to try giving the announcements before the anthem. If Willi stayed on his feet another five minutes, she thought, he would just be able to give a three-minute talk. Then he could capsize all he liked, because Mr. Elvekrog could order the lights out and start the film without him.

Supported a little by the girl, Willi began hobbling forward. The two of them tried to pass the projector in the aisle at the same time. Mr. Elvekrog's chair went over and Willi's hip gave the projector itself a smash, but Mr. Elvekrog leapt to the other side and kept it from going over onto the floor. The room was utterly silent. At the podium, waiting until Mr. Elvekrog should have settled the Norwegians in two reserved seats in the center of the first row, Emily decided she would further shorten her introduction, from the look of things—and she would not bet two cents on Willi's being able to carry off a discussion period after the film at all.

Then she smiled to the audience and said, "Good evening! I think we will sing the anthem and have the announcements after the speaker tonight, instead of in our usual order. Before I introduce the speaker, though, I *would* like to make one very important announcement. Mrs. Thorstad *will* be showing Tusend Hjem her Norwegian knitting patterns next meeting: we will not get beat out of that!"

Emily then said it was an honor to present a speaker who was a genuine hero. "We haven't a great many real heroes," she told them. "But Willi Varig is one." She told them that Willi had belonged to a group of four Underground agents who sent information back to England from Lofthus, Hardanger, on the west coast of Norway. Willi was caught by the Germans in May of 1944. They questioned him about the names of his colleagues so that they could gather them in as well. Willi's World War II, Emily told them, was fought alone in a cellar which held two other people, both of whom were members of the enemy. They were Gestapo officers who were skilled in making people give them the information they needed. Now," Emily continued, "the only reason I have told you even this much—when I know that you want to hear the speaker himself—is that I am afraid he won't tell you that he was an extraordinarily brave man. It is an honor to present to you Willi Varig."

Emily took a seat which Mrs. Thorstad, all smiles, energetically pointed out to her, next to herself. Willi made it to the microphone. He turned a belligerent face to Emily and spoke so closely into the mike that his words racketed: "Well then!" he shouted. "I didn't know I was such a hero then! I feel as if I were attending my own funeral sermon!" He gave a rough, very loud laugh, looking about between the rims of his eyelids, expecting the audience to laugh with him. Emily was one of theirs, however, and in any case, they didn't understand his sardonic tone. Most important of all, he was visibly drunk. He looked as if his knees were about to give way.

"It is an honor to address you!" he went on, "since we fought on the same side of the war. I know that the American Legion represents the very bravest of America's veterans!"

Willi's girlfriend leaned forward as if to correct him. But then she sighed, crossed her arms, and leaned back. Mr. Elvekrog half-stood at the projector, and called in his quavering tone, "Herr Varig? This is the Minnesota Chapter of Tusend Hjem!"

Willi pounded his fist on the podium, as if to make a salient point, and then said, only, in a kind of snarl: "I think we will now have the film, please, if you will close the lights."

In the sudden, grateful darkness, the people could hear their speaker stumbling back toward his seat. The screen lighted up.

"Norsk Film A/S," the screen told them in white print on black. Then white, typed credits appeared in jerks over clips of a young woman tapping wireless messages under the speckled shade of camouflage; three figures sneaked up under a bridge on which a German-helmeted soldier was slowly walking, occasionally glancing overside; two Norwegian girls smiled widely at two Gestapo officers leaving a wooden hut. But the instant the door was shut, one girl crouched at it, listening, while the other quickly lifted a *dynetrekk* and folded it back, revealing a radio set. She put on a pair of earphones and immediately began sending.

Then, all of a sudden, the projector clattered. Mr. Elvekrog gave an exclamation, the screen whitened with lightning and tortured patterns, the aisle area began to reek of burnt celluloid. In the next instant, Mr. Elvekrog called sharply, "Someone turn the lights on please!" Other, younger, more resonant men's voices added, "Yes—someone get the lights back there!"

People rubbed their eyes in the brightness. They turned to Mr. Elvekrog, who sat beside the projector with curls and curls of movie-tape bunched and falling about his lap and legs. With his bleak expression, he looked like a provincial actor who has just removed an elaborate Louis XVI wig.

Chuck Iversen cried out, "Well, I see that the Tomah Chapter didn't repair the projector too good! So much for lending things to the neighbors is what I say!"

People tittered. They were not a club that relished documentaries anyway. They had been resigned to the film, because they knew that at least coffee and krullers would follow sooner or later. Now it would be sooner, they saw, and they cheered up. With the projector broken, and the fellows beginning to act up, there might be some fun.

Here and there, men stood up and put their hands into their pockets. They wandered back to the cleared area behind all the auditorium seating, away from the women and the others who passively waited in their seats. Meanwhile, Mr. Elvekrog bent over the film feeder. The teeth had somehow shredded some film edge and left celluloid about like auger tailings on the floor. He said in anguish to Emily, who had come back to see if she could help: "National is going to raise a fuss about this! I just know they are!"

Minutes passed. At last, Chuck Iversen shouted to everyone generally, "So what is wrong with singing *Ja, vi elsker dette landet* and having the coffee and cookies? History lessons or cookies, give me cookies every time!"

Someone in the rear, from the knot of men who were changing their weight from foot to foot, shouted, "You don't have any culture, Chuck, is what your trouble is!"

Chuck shouted back, when people stopped laughing: "Oh, to get my hands on the fellow that got off *that* remark!"

The moment was passing into the hands of the people.

"Willi has completely passed out," Emily whispered to Mr. Elvekrog, bending over him while handling film as if she were helping him with the mechanics of repair. "Do you want me to go up and explain very fast exactly what he did during the war and then announce the anthem and you can do the announcements and we will have the lunch?"

"Oh, would you?" cried the program committee chairman.

Up at the podium, Emily waited for silence, glancing over at the Norwegian speaker. He lay oddly twisted on the woman's lap, his left hand hung down between the thighs of her expensive trousers, his face buried in her stomach as her hand patted his shoulder.

Emily said into the PA system, "If we can all somehow get Chuck Iversen to shut up for a second!"

This brought her the laugh she needed.

Then she went on, fast: "Here is what we will do. I am going to tell you very briefly what Willi Varig did. I will keep it down to a few minutes—and then we will do the anthem and announcements and have our coffee. Is that OK with all of you?"

There were nods, almost everywhere in the room, and the scattered muttering directed not to one another in the rows but directly from individual people to her, which Emily knew meant the people were relieved—a leader is taking over and it will all get solved.

Emily told the group about the German invasion of Norway, in April 1940. She told them how the Norwegian Underground kept in touch with the RAF and British Intelligence through air drops, radio, telegraph—and when things were very wrong, through escape via small boats across the North Sea.

"When I first knew Willi Varig, however," Emily said, "it was ten years after the war. My husband and I lived in Oslo on a Fulbright—and German tourists were just beginning to come into Norway again. Willi used to be drunk nearly every night. We would have dinner with him, in a small students' dining room in Drammensveien, which I am sure many of you have walked in during your summer visits to Norway. Then, after dinner, Willi would wander down to the Ostbanestasjonen by himself." Emily paused to let the Norwegian-Americans proudly whisper back and forth to one another, "Ostbanestasjonen—the East railway station!"

"Willi would wander along close behind the groups of tourists getting off the train, deliberately listening to their talk of getting porters, finding hotels, and so on. He paid no attention to the younger ones with their rucksacks and knee socks. They weren't what he wanted. He followed those of about thirty or more. When he had determined they were Germans he would catch up with whichever man appeared to be the father or the leader and say, in his perfect schoolboy German, 'I beg your pardon, sir, but is the Herr visiting Norway for the first time?' The polite German would get over his surprise at being addressed by a stranger. In the next moment, he would be charmed by this Norwegian in his good shirt and tie and sports jacket—and sometimes Willi even went down to the train in his dinner coat—and the German would smile and say, 'Well—no, actually, it *isn't* my first time! I have seen Norway before! And I told myself then, that when I married, the first thing I would do is bring my wife back to this so beautiful country and I would show her the wonderful mountains! I especially think the Hardanger plateau is beautiful! But of course, your city, Oslo, is beautiful as well!' Then, Willi, smiling, would say, 'Ah, then, the Herr was in Norway a long time ago and is returning with pleasure? I can understand that!' and the German, poor sap, would respond, 'Not a *long* time ago—I was stationed here during the war in fact—and grew very much to love this country!' That, of course, is what Willi was waiting for, so then he would put a heavy hand to the German's shoulder, bringing him to a stop. They had been walking along, with the baggage man and his cart ahead of them. When Willi stopped the German, the baggage man stopped at the same moment, before even looking around. Still smiling now, Willi would say, 'And would the Herr have any idea that when people love a thing—a person or their own country—they do not like to have it taken away?' and before the German could see the turn the conversation had taken, Willi would have struck him as hard as he could manage in the man's face. The German generally fell down, unless Willi was so drunk he missed his mark. People stood around waiting for the man to rise. Norwegian railway officials went through the motions of linking their arms around Willi's elbows. The baggage man turned forward again and pulled the cart as if nothing had happened. Soon you would hear the Oslo two-toned police sound. Everyone made a little way for the police. 'Right, Willi!' they said briskly, 'In you go!' and they popped him into their car. Dozens of people knew the routine perfectly well. Back at the station, the policemen would give Willi some coffee and drive him sedately back up Karl Johansgate, past the castle, up Drammensveien, and deliver him to his woman of the moment."

Emily went on, "That was eleven years after Willi's war was over. He had been laying a flare path near Stavali, on the Hardanger plateau, in preparation for an RAF equipment drop. He was caught by the Germans. Willi noticed, with satisfaction, that, when the patrol arrested him, his friends, who were two men and a woman, had vanished. That meant they knew that he had been taken and that they had not been seen: that was important. Once anyone was taken prisoner, the others had to use the preplanned flight to the sea. Anyone captured would talk, sooner or later, so you simply had to run either east to Sweden or west and south to England. Willi's group kept a shabby fishing boat at Lofthus, with its dinghy shoved under what looked like an abandoned dock. It was arranged that a fisherman take their sailboat out nearly every other day, letting himself be seen on deck, making small repairs, running her sail up and down, trying different engine richnesses. The German coast patrols had trained their glasses on the man for so long they knew his figure by heart—the thick white sweater he wore even on the hottest days when he must have sweltered, and even on the coldest days when he would have been better off with a stormcoat like the other fishermen.

"The Germans took Willi to the nearest office," Emily explained. "A pleasant-spoken young Gestapo officer told Willi that all they really needed were the names of his immediate colleagues and a few practical details. These details would be useful to them, the man explained, with a rueful tone, who had to go on fighting the tiresome war, but not to Willi since he would be able to relax now, in prison. They needed to know his radio frequencies, and the summer's drop plans. At least for now, they told him, that was all they needed. Willi felt he had an hour before he would be made to talk. The German officer would be willing to spend an hour in establishing a trust relationship; beyond that, he would know that Willi was stalling. But up to an hour, he might feel that Willi saw reason and would tell him what he needed for his report. An hour would take Willi's friends from the flare site to Stavali, and another two hours would get them down the steep mountainside to Lofthus. The hour passed as if it were two minutes. The German went out a moment and brought back in with him a colleague whom he politely introduced by name. The colleague knelt by Willi's chair and proceeded to loosen Willi's right kneecap with a screw. Then the colleague, or someone, splashed water on Willi, and when he came to they began again. The second time he came to, he found only the original officer in the room with him. 'You know, Willi, if I may call you by your first name? In a few years' time, perhaps in only one year, the war will be over, and I will go back to Germany and be married and raise a family. I would like my son to go to Berlin—the University. And the same for you, Willi. You will return to your Oslo and marry and have a family— you will watch your children waving flags on May 17th with all the other children—and later, you will watch them strolling around in their student caps. And we will both get old, but gradually, easily—in the leisure of time, Willi! You in your beautiful country, Willi, and I in mine! And there is not a soul on earth who will remember what was said or done, in this room, today. What is a single spring day in 1944 when it has gotten to be 1970, 1980, or perhaps even 1990?' He paused. 'If you tell me what I have to know simply because it is my job, I will arrange for you to live, Willi. If you make us *make* you tell us, you will probably die—but in any case, we would shoot you. And you know better than to think you won't talk! Everyone talks! How is your knee now? You know, Willi, when my colleague comes in again, he will not stick only to the right knee. Next time it will be the other knee. I can check on it—but I am pretty sure that is how they do it. They pretty much follow the same routine each time . . . first the one, then the other. Then after the war I will go back to Germany and marry and raise my family—and my wife will never know that I spent today making a prisoner talk in this room. And of course you will be dead, so you will never have a wife.' Here the intelligence officer paused, and then he added, making the only mistake he had made: 'Willi, everyone talks! . . . *sooner or later.*' "

Emily paused herself and then went on. "The German's mistake was in saying 'sooner or later.' This reminded Willi that talking sooner was not at all the same as talking several hours later. What he had to do was wipe out of his mind's eye the picture of 1970, 1980, 1990, which the German had kept painting for him—the picture of the gentle future when all would be peaceful and wonderful for those still alive to enjoy it. He needed to put some other picture into his mind's eye—and keep it there—for one hour, for two hours if he could. He needed to imagine his friends, the two Underground men and the woman, who would, if Willi did not talk right away, scramble down the rocky path behind Lofthus, shove the dinghy out from under its rotten boarding, and row out to the fishing boat which always stood at its mooring. He had to force this image into his mind, over and over—and what helped him to do it was the German's saying 'sooner or later.' So now he said to himself, 'If I last ten minutes more, they have reached the dock. I wonder if dark is coming on now—but I mustn't trust to that, because it is getting on for Sankthansaften and the days are extraordinarily long. If I last,' Willi thought—for now the second German had returned to the cellar room and was kneeling at the other side of Willi's chair, 'if I last another ten minutes, they are all in the dinghy now and they are saying, "Good old Willi! He must not have talked yet!" Now I think I will not last a whole another ten minutes but I could do five, I think, because the fjord is quiet and the motor started right up without any trouble. And now my friend has put on that filthy white sweater which was left right where it was supposed to be and he has the tiller and the others hidden below are sending on the wireless; they are already asking for help now! Thank God then, the motor started up all right for them! And now the Germans are looking at the boat quietly going out the main fjord and saying, "Oh—there's that idiot in the white sweater and that wreck of a boat again!" ' Then Willi told himself, 'I do not remember my friends' names anyway. I do not know how many there were of them. I do not remember them. There may have been five, there may have been six. And soon they will be out to sea, and the man in the white sweater will be joined by the people who now can come topside out of hiding. They have sent their wireless call for help, and someone in England or on the Sea and in the Channel has heard, and someone in turn rang up Air/Sea Rescue and they had better have got her mainsail up now—in just this last minute I think they did get their mainsail up all right!' Then when he had passed out again and the enemy had brought him to again, Willi said to himself, 'I should say they have picked up a several-force wind out there, but it is from the North so they are running southward to England, south by west, and there is not much difficulty with the waves because they are running with them, but it is rough and the sea is chopped up by the wind.' When Willi woke up the next time he saw in his mind's eye that at last it was night. A submarine rose, shedding a white robing of sea from its bilges, and even after her captain appeared at the conning tower, water slid gently and uniformly off her deck and bilges. The captain was a young Englishman and he shouted at the crew of a Norwegian fishing vessel. The Norwegians brought their boat about so she shuddered now into the wind, and the Englishmen sent over two sailors in a rubber boat. At the submarine, the Norwegian woman handed up a canvas bag and said, 'Will you be so kind as to sink our boat, please, as she may give away information?' The Englishman and his guncrew and the Norwegians watched, their jaws shaking with cold, as the bullets struck the little fishing boat at the waterline. Then the English captain cried, 'Right! Now! Down below with all of you!' The three Underground agents went gingerly below, their feet now gone so cold they felt nothing at the knees and below. They sank gingerly down the rungs and into the oddly motherly, smelly warmth of the sub. Then Willi made the picture in his mind of the submarine's smooth round side frothing and slipping below the huge waves of the North Sea. It moved with its electric ease, far under the tortured waves.

"Then Willi talked. He told the Gestapo officer the names of the two men and the woman. But you see," Emily said heavily to the Tusend Hjem members, "he talked later, not sooner. His partners did make it to England. Then, Germans being Germans, they repaired Willi's knees fairly well. As you all noticed tonight, Willi doesn't walk perfectly, but he does walk.

"And now I am done talking," Emily told them, "but for one thing. If you will please all look over to where Willi is now."

Those sitting near Willi and his girlfriend had already been peeping, anyhow. The girl, with Willi's hand still dangling between her legs, glared at no one in particular with her composed, inimical expression. People toward the rear stood up and peered over heads. People whispered. "Now what I am asking of Tusend Hjem is," Emily said, "that we choose. We can keep a kind of mental picture of this Willi here, the one you are looking at right now—or, you can imagine him in your mind's eye, strapped in a chair, with the German intelligence officers. The one who spoke so pleasantly, and the one with the screws. You can remember that scene."

Then Mr. Elvekrog came forward, wiping something from the projector off his hands. He gave the announcements, he led them in the Norwegian anthem. Presently, Emily was able to drive the twenty minutes home to White Bear Lake. Mist still rose, more strongly than before, from all the hollows alongside I-35 E. She felt peaceful and absentminded, and hoped that her daughter would be in bed and the house would be dark and still.

She brought the car very slowly into the drive, so as not to wake Sandra in case she was asleep. Then she crept out and decided to have a look over the lake in the dark. But impressions from the house would creep in, and disturb her mood. She could not help thinking how unhappy her daughter was—how something either major or minor was wrong with Sandra's marriage. She felt, with what she hoped was mistaken intuition, that her daughter was interested in someone other than her husband.

The mist over White Bear Lake was absolutely solid now. The water itself was invisible in the mist and the night, but she felt its presence, so full and rich with rainwater it was nearly rounded upward.

She thought, again, of the Norwegian Underground agents. Neither she nor Willi nor anyone else would ever have the slightest notion what the three people whom Willi had saved had done with their lives. There was nothing to guarantee they had not wasted them. They may never have done anything lovely at all. Emily tried to picture the woman of that Underground team. If she was still alive, she would be old by now. Perhaps she had married for love—but perhaps she had then met someone else, later, who stirred her somehow as she had never imagined possible, but perhaps she did not marry this other person, but stayed with the husband. But then, Emily thought, so many years have passed —likely one or both of the men are dead now. Or perhaps they are utterly dull.

Still, Emily felt herself growing elated, as she stood there staring out over the fog. She did not really have in her mind's eye a picture of aged, paunchy, or lonely old Norwegians. What she really had in mind was the little sailing boat in the North Sea, with its crew young and beautiful; the sea had misted crystal into their hand-knitted caps and sweaters; their hands had chilled on the sheets and stays and tiller; their knees ably took the sea's heave—and all the time, the three of them kept looking and looking, hoping and half-knowing a powerful friend would emerge from the deep, and come up alongside, and save them.

RAYMOND CARVER

Fever

Carlyle was in a spot. He'd been in a spot all summer, since early June when his wife had left him. But up until a little while ago, just a few days before he had to start meeting his classes at the high school, Carlyle hadn't needed a sitter. He'd been the sitter. Every day and every night he'd attended to the children. Their mother, he told them, was away on a long trip.

Debbie, the first sitter he contacted, was a fat girl, nineteen years old, who told Carlyle she came from a big family. Kids loved her, she said. She offered a couple of names for reference. She penciled them on a piece of notebook paper. Carlyle took the names, folded the piece of paper, and put it in his shirt pocket. He told her he had meetings the next day. He said she could start to work for him the next morning. She said, "Okay."

He understood that his life was entering a new period. Eileen had left while Carlyle was still filling out his grade reports. She'd said she was going to Southern California to begin a new life for herself there. She'd gone with Richard Hoopes, one of Carlyle's colleagues at the high school. Hoopes was a drama teacher and glass-blowing instructor who'd apparently turned his grades in on time, taken his things, and left town in a hurry with Eileen. Now, the long and painful summer nearly behind him, and his classes about to resume, Carlyle had finally turned his attention to this matter of finding a baby-sitter. His first efforts had not been successful. In his desperation to find someone—anyone—he'd taken Debbie on.

In the beginning, he was grateful to have this girl turn up in response to his call. He'd yielded up the house and children to her as if she were a relative. So he had no one to blame but himself, his own carelessness, he was convinced, when he came home early from school one day that first week and pulled into the drive next to a car that had a big pair of flannel dice hanging from the rearview mirror. To his astonishment, he saw his children in the front yard, their clothes filthy, playing with a dog big enough to bite off their hands. His son, Keith, had the hiccups and had been crying. Sarah, his daughter, began to cry when she saw him get out of the car. They were sitting on the grass, and the dog was licking their hands and faces. The dog growled at him and then moved off a little as Carlyle made for his children. He picked up Keith and then he picked up Sarah. One child under each arm, he made for his front door. Inside the house, the phonograph was turned up so high the front windows vibrated.

In the living room, three teenaged boys jumped to their feet from where they'd been sitting around the coffee table. Beer bottles stood on the table and cigarettes burned in the ashtray. Rod Stewart screamed from the stereo. On the sofa, Debbie, the fat girl, sat with another teenaged boy. She stared at Carlyle with dumb disbelief as he entered the living room. The fat girl's blouse was unbuttoned. She had her legs drawn under her, and she was smoking a cigarette. The living room was filled with smoke and music. The fat girl and her friend got off the sofa in a hurry.

"Mr. Carlyle, wait a minute," Debbie said. "I can explain."

"Don't explain," Carlyle said. "Get the hell out of here. All of you. Before I throw you out." He tightened his grip on the children.

"You owe me for four days," the fat girl said, as she tried to button her blouse. She still had the cigarette between her fingers. Ashes fell from the cigarette as she tried to button up. "Forget today. You don't owe me for today. Mr. Carlyle, it's not what it looks like. They dropped by to listen to this record."

"I understand, Debbie," he said. He let the children down onto the carpet. But they stayed close to his legs and watched the people in the living room. Debbie looked at them and shook her head slowly, as if she'd never laid eyes on them before. "Goddamn it, get out!" Carlyle said. "Now. Get going. All of you."

He went over and opened the front door. The boys acted as if they were in no real hurry. They picked up their beer and started slowly for the door. The Rod Stewart record was still playing. One of them said, "That's my record."

"Get it," Carlyle said. He took a step toward the boy and then stopped.

"Don't touch me, okay? Just don't touch me," the boy said. He went over to the phonograph, picked up the arm, swung it back, and took his record off while the turntable was still spinning.

Carlyle's hands were shaking. "If that car's not out of the drive in one minute—one minute—I'm calling the police." He felt sick and dizzy with his anger. He saw, really saw, spots dance in front of his eyes.

"Hey, listen, we're on our way, all right? We're going," the boy said.

They filed out of the house. Outside, the fat girl stumbled a little. She weaved as she moved toward the car. Carlyle saw her stop and bring her hands up to her face. She stood like that in the drive for a minute. Then one of the boys pushed her from behind and said her name. She dropped her hands and got into the back seat of the car.

"Daddy will get you into some clean clothes," Carlyle told his children, trying to keep his voice steady. "I'll give you a bath, and put you into some clean clothes. Then we'll go out for some pizza. How does pizza sound to you?"

"Where's Debbie?" Sarah asked him.

"She's gone," Carlyle said.

That evening, after he'd put the children to bed, he called Carol, the woman from school he'd been seeing for the past month. He told her what had happened with his sitter.

"My kids were out in the yard with this big dog," he said. "The dog was as big as a wolf. The baby-sitter was in the house with a bunch of her hoodlum boyfriends. They had Rod Stewart going full blast, and they were tying one on while my kids were outside playing with this strange dog." He brought his fingers to his temples and held them there while he talked.

"My God," Carol said. "Poor sweetie, I'm so sorry." Her voice sounded indistinct. He pictured her letting the receiver slide down to her chin, as she was in the habit of doing while talking on the phone. He'd seen her do it before. It was a habit of hers he found vaguely irritating. Did he want her to come over to his place? she asked. She would. She thought maybe she'd better do that. She'd call her sitter. Then she'd drive to his place. She wanted to. He shouldn't be afraid to say when he needed affection, she said. Carol was one of the secretaries in the principal's office at the high school where Carlyle taught art classes. She was divorced and had one child, a neurotic ten-year-old the father had named Dodge, after his automobile.

"No, that's all right," Carlyle said. "But thanks. *Thanks*, Carol. The kids are in bed, but I think I'd feel a little funny, you know, having company tonight."

She didn't offer again. "Sweetie, I'm sorry about what happened. But I understand your wanting to be alone tonight. I respect that. I'll see you at school tomorrow."

He could hear her waiting for him to say something else. "That's two baby-sitters in less than a week," he said. "I'm going out of my tree with this."

"Honey, don't let it get you down," she said. "Something will turn up. I'll help you find somebody this weekend. It'll be all right, you'll see."

"Thanks again for being there when I need you," he said. "You're one in a million, you know."

" 'Night, Carlyle," she said.

After he'd hung up, he wished he could have thought of something else to say to her instead of what he'd just said. He'd never talked that way before in his life. They weren't having a love affair, he wouldn't call it that, but he liked her. She knew it was a hard time for him, and she didn't make demands.

After Eileen had left for California, Carlyle had spent every waking minute for the first month with his children. He supposed the shock of her going had caused this, but he didn't want to let the children out of his sight. He'd certainly not been interested in seeing other women, and for a time he didn't think he ever would be. He felt as if he were in mourning. His days and nights were passed in the company of his children. He cooked for them—he had no appetite himself—washed and ironed their clothes, drove them into the country, where they picked flowers and ate sandwiches wrapped up in waxed paper. He took them to the supermarket and let them pick out what they liked. And every few days they went to the park, or else to the library, or the zoo. They took old bread to the zoo so they could feed the ducks. At night, before tucking them in, Carlyle read to them—Aesop, Hans Christian Andersen, the Brothers Grimm.

"When is Mama coming back?" one of them might ask him in the middle of a fairy tale.

"Soon," he'd say. "One of these days. Now listen to this." Then he'd read the tale to its conclusion, kiss them, and turn off the light.

And while they'd slept, he had wandered the rooms of his house with a glass in his hand, telling himself that, yes, sooner or later, Eileen would come back. In the next breath, he would say, "I never want to see your face again. I'll never forgive you for this, you crazy bitch." Then, a minute later, "Come back, sweetheart, please. I love you and need you. The kids need you, too." Some nights that summer he fell asleep in front of the TV and woke up with the set still going and the screen filled with snow. This was the period when he didn't think he would be seeing any women for a long time, if ever. At night, sitting in front of the TV with an unopened book or magazine next to him on the sofa, he often thought of Eileen. When he did, he might remember her sweet laugh, or else her hand rubbing his neck if he complained of a soreness there. It was at these times that he thought he could weep. He thought, You hear about stuff like this happening to other people.

Just before the incident with Debbie, when some of the shock and grief had worn off, he'd phoned an employment service to tell them something of his predicament and his requirements. Someone took down the information and said they would get back to him. Not many people wanted to do housework *and* baby-sit, they said, but they'd find somebody. A few days before he had to be at the high school for meetings and registration, he called again and was told there'd be somebody at his house first thing the next morning.

That person was a thirty-five-year-old woman with hairy arms and run-over shoes. She shook hands with him and listened to him talk without asking a single question about the children—not even their names. When he took her into the back of the house where the children were playing, she simply stared at them for a minute without saying anything. When she finally smiled, Carlyle noticed for the first time that she had a tooth missing. Sarah left her crayons and got up to come over and stand next to him. She took Carlyle's hand and stared at the woman. Keith stared at her, too. Then he went back to his coloring. Carlyle thanked the woman for her time and said he would be in touch.

That afternoon he took down a number from an index card tacked to the bulletin board at the supermarket. Someone was offering baby-sitting services. References furnished on request. Carlyle called the number and got Debbie, the fat girl.

Over the summer, Eileen had sent a few cards, letters, and photographs of herself to the children, and some pen-and-ink drawings of her own that she'd done since she'd gone away. She also sent Carlyle long, rambling letters in which she asked for his understanding in this matter —*this matter*—but told him that she was happy. Happy. As if, Carlyle thought, happiness was all there was to life. She told him that if he really loved her, as he said he did, and as she really believed—she loved him, too, don't forget—then he would understand and accept things as they were. She wrote, "That which is truly bonded can never become un-bonded." Carlyle didn't know if she was talking about their own rela-tionship or her way of life out in California. He hated the word *bonded*. What did it have to do with the two of them? Did she think they were a corporation? He thought Eileen must be losing her mind to talk like that. He read that part again and then crumpled the letter.

But a few hours later he retrieved the letter from the trash can where he'd thrown it, and put it with her other cards and letters in a box on the shelf in his closet. In one of the envelopes, there was a photograph of her in a big, floppy hat, wearing a bathing suit. And there was a pencil drawing on heavy paper of a woman on a riverbank in a filmy gown, her hands covering her eyes, her shoulders slumped. It was, Carlyle as-sumed, Eileen showing her heartbreak over the situation. In college, she had majored in art, and even though she'd agreed to marry him, she said she intended to do something with her talent. Carlyle said he wouldn't have it any other way. She owed it to herself, he said. She owed it to both of them. They had loved each other in those days. He knew they had. He couldn't imagine ever loving anyone again the way he'd loved her. And he'd felt loved, too. Then, after eight years of being married to him, Eileen had pulled out. She was, she said in her letter, "going for it."

After talking to Carol, he looked in on the children, who were asleep. Then he went into the kitchen and made himself a drink. He thought of calling Eileen to talk to her about the baby-sitting crisis, but decided against it. He had her phone number and her address out there, of course. But he'd only called once and, so far, had not written a letter. This was partly out of a feeling of bewilderment with the situation, partly out of anger and humiliation. Once, earlier in the summer, after a few drinks, he'd chanced humiliation and called. Richard Hoopes answered the phone. Richard had said, "Hey, Carlyle," as if he were still Carlyle's friend. And then, as if remembering something, he said, "Just a minute, all right?"

Eileen had come on the line and said, "Carlyle, how are you? How are the kids? Tell me about yourself." He told her the kids were fine. But before he could say anything else, she interrupted him to say, "I know *they're* fine. What about *you?*" Then she went on to tell him that her head was in the right place for the first time in a long time. Next she wanted to talk about his head and his karma. She'd looked into his karma. It was going to improve any time now, she said. Carlyle listened, hardly able to believe his ears. Then he said, "I have to go now, Eileen." And he hung up. The phone rang a minute or so later, but he let it ring. When it stopped ringing, he took the phone off the hook and left it off until he was ready for bed.

He wanted to call her now, but he was afraid to call. He still missed her and wanted to confide in her. He longed to hear her voice—sweet, steady, not manic as it had been for months now—but if he dialed her number, Richard Hoopes might answer the telephone. Carlyle knew he didn't want to hear that man's voice again. Richard had been a colleague for three years and, Carlyle supposed, a kind of friend. At least he was someone Carlyle ate lunch with in the faculty dining room, someone who talked about Tennessee Williams and the photographs of Ansel Adams. But even if Eileen answered the telephone, she might launch into something about his karma.

While he was sitting there with the glass in his hand, trying to remember what it had felt like to be married and intimate with someone, the phone rang. He picked up the receiver, heard a trace of static on the line, and knew, even before she'd said his name, that it was Eileen.

"I was just thinking about you," Carlyle said, and at once regretted saying it.

"See! I knew I was on your mind, Carlyle. Well, I was thinking about you, too. That's why I called." He drew a breath. She *was* losing her mind. That much was clear to him. She kept talking. "Now listen," she said. "The big reason I called is that I know things are in kind of a mess out there right now. Don't ask me how, but I know. I'm sorry, Carlyle. But here's the thing. You're still in need of a good housekeeper and sitter combined, right? Well, she's practically right there in the neighborhood! Oh, you may have found someone already, and that's good, if that's the case. If so, it's supposed to be that way. But see, just in case you're having trouble in that area, there's this woman who used to work for Richard's mother. I told Richard about the potential problem, and he put himself to work on it. You want to know what he did? Are you listening? He called his mother, who used to have this woman who kept house for her. The woman's name is Mrs. Webster. She looked after things for Richard's mother before his aunt and her daughter moved in there. Richard was able to get a number through his mother. He talked to Mrs. Webster today. Richard did. Mrs. Webster is going to call you tonight. Or else maybe she'll call you in the morning. One or the other. Anyway, she's going to volunteer her services, if you need her. You might, you never can tell. Even if your situation is okay right now, which I hope it is. But some time or another you might need her. You know what I'm saying? If not this minute, some other time. Okay? How are the kids? What are they up to?"

"The children are fine, Eileen. They're asleep now," he said. Maybe he should tell her they cried themselves to sleep every night. He wondered if he should tell her the truth—that they hadn't asked about her even once in the last couple of weeks. He decided not to say anything.

"I called earlier, but the line was busy. I told Richard you were probably talking to your girlfriend," Eileen said and laughed. "Think positive thoughts. You sound depressed," she said.

"I have to go, Eileen." He started to hang up, and he took the receiver from his ear. But she was still talking.

"Tell Keith and Sarah I love them. Tell them I'm sending some more pictures. Tell them that. I don't want them to forget their mother is an artist. Maybe not a great artist yet, that's not important. But, you know, an artist. It's important they shouldn't forget that."

Carlyle said, "I'll tell them."

"Richard says hello."

Carlyle didn't say anything. He said the word to himself—*hello*. What could the man possibly mean by this? Then he said, "Thanks for calling. Thanks for talking to that woman."

"Mrs. Webster!"

"Yes. I'd better get off the phone now. I don't want to run up your nickel."

Eileen laughed. "It's only money. Money's not important except as a necessary medium of exchange. There are more important things than money. But then you already know that."

He held the receiver out in front of him. He looked at the instrument from which her voice was issuing.

"Carlyle, things are going to get better for you. I *know* they are. You may think I'm crazy or something," she said. "But just remember."

Remember what? Carlyle wondered in alarm, thinking he must have missed something she'd said. He brought the receiver in close. "Eileen, thanks for calling," he said.

"We have to stay in touch," Eileen said. "We have to keep all lines of communication open. I think the worst is over. For both of us. I've suffered, too. But we're going to get what we're supposed to get out of this life, both of us, and we're going to be made *stronger* for it in the long run."

"Good night," he said. He put the receiver back. Then he looked at the phone. He waited. It didn't ring again. But an hour later it did ring. He answered it.

"Mr. Carlyle." It was an old woman's voice. "You don't know me, but my name is Mrs. Jim Webster. I was supposed to get in touch."

"Mrs. Webster. Yes," he said. Eileen's mention of the woman came back to him. "Mrs. Webster, can you come to my house in the morning? Early. Say seven o'clock?"

"I can do that easily," the old woman said. "Seven o'clock. Give me your address."

"I'd like to be able to count on you," Carlyle said.

"You can count on me," she said.

"I can't tell you how important it is," Carlyle said.

"Don't you worry," the old woman said.

The next morning, when the alarm went off, he wanted to keep his eyes closed and keep on with the dream he was having. Something about a farmhouse. And there was a waterfall in there, too. Someone, he didn't know who, was walking along the road carrying something. Maybe it was a picnic hamper. He was not made uneasy by the dream. In the dream, there seemed to exist a sense of well-being.

Finally, he rolled over and pushed something to stop the buzzing. He lay in bed awhile longer. Then he got up, put his feet into his slippers, and went out to the kitchen to start the coffee.

He shaved and dressed for the day. Then he sat down at the kitchen table with coffee and a cigarette. The children were still in bed. But in five minutes or so he planned to put boxes of cereal on the table and lay out bowls and spoons, then go in to wake them for breakfast. He really couldn't believe that the old woman who'd phoned him last night would show up this morning, as she'd said she would. He decided he'd wait until five minutes after seven o'clock, and then he'd call in, take the day off, and make every effort in the book to locate someone reliable. He brought the cup of coffee to his lips.

It was then that he heard a rumbling sound out in the street. He left his cup and got up from the table to look out the window. A pickup truck had pulled over to the curb in front of his house. The pickup cab shook as the engine idled. Carlyle went to the front door, opened it, and waved. An old woman waved back and then let herself out of the vehicle. Carlyle saw the driver lean over and disappear under the dash. The truck gasped, shook itself once more, and fell still.

"Mr. Carlyle?" the old woman said, as she came slowly up his walk carrying a large purse.

"Mrs. Webster," he said. "Come on inside. Is that your husband? Ask him in. I just made coffee."

"It's okay," she said. "He has his Thermos."

Carlyle shrugged. He held the door for her. She stepped inside and they shook hands. Mrs. Webster smiled. Carlyle nodded. They moved out to the kitchen. "Did you want me today, then?" she asked.

"Let me get the children up," he said. "I'd like them to meet you before I leave for school."

"That'd be good," she said. She looked around his kitchen. She put her purse on the drainboard.

"Why don't I get the children?" he said. "I'll just be a minute or two."

In a little while, he brought the children out and introduced them. They were still in their pajamas. Sarah was rubbing her eyes. Keith was wide awake. "This is Keith," Carlyle said. "And this one here, this is my Sarah." He held on to Sarah's hand and turned to Mrs. Webster. "They need someone, you see. We need someone we can count on. I guess that's our problem."

Mrs. Webster moved over to the children. She fastened the top button of Keith's pajamas. She moved the hair away from Sarah's face. They let her do it. "Don't you kids worry, now," she said to them. "Mr. Carlyle, it'll be all right. We're going to be fine. Give us a day or two to get to know each other, that's all. But if I'm going to stay, why don't you give Mr. Webster the all-clear sign? Just wave at him through the window," she said, and then she gave her attention back to the children.

Carlyle stepped to the bay window and drew the curtain. An old man was watching the house from the cab of the truck. He was just bringing a Thermos cup to his lips. Carlyle waved to him, and with his free hand the man waved back. Carlyle watched him roll down the truck window and throw out what was left in his cup. Then he bent down under the dash again—Carlyle imagined him touching some wires together—and in a minute the truck started and began to shake. The old man put the truck in gear and pulled away from the curb.

Carlyle turned from the window. "Mrs. Webster," he said, "I'm glad you're here."

"Likewise, Mr. Carlyle," she said. "Now you go on about your business before you're late. Don't worry about anything. We're going to be fine. Aren't we, kids?"

The children nodded their heads. Keith held on to her dress with one hand. He put the thumb of his other hand into his mouth.

"Thank you," Carlyle said. "I feel, I really feel a hundred percent better." He shook his head and grinned. He felt a welling in his chest as he kissed each of his children good-bye. He told Mrs. Webster what time she could expect him home, put on his coat, said good-bye once more, and went out of the house. For the first time in months, it seemed, he felt his burden had lifted a little. Driving to school, he listened to some music on the radio.

During first-period art-history class, he lingered over slides of Byzantine paintings. He patiently explained the nuances of detail and motif. He pointed out the emotional power and fitness of the work. But he took so long trying to place the anonymous artists in their social milieu that some of his students began to scrape their shoes on the floor, or else clear their throats. They covered only a third of the lesson plan that day. He was still talking when the bell rang.

In his next class, watercolor painting, he felt unusually calm and insightful. "Like this, like this," he said, guiding their hands. "Delicately. Like a breath of air on the paper. Just a touch. Like so. See?" he'd say and felt on the edge of discovery himself. "*Suggestion* is what it's all about," he said, holding lightly to Sue Colvin's fingers as he guided her brush. "You've got to work with your mistakes until they look intended. Understand?"

As he moved down the lunch line in the faculty dining room, he saw Carol a few places ahead of him. She paid for her food. He waited impatiently while his own bill was being rung up. Carol was halfway across the room by the time he caught up with her. He slipped his hand under her elbow and guided her to an empty table near the window.

"God, Carlyle," she said after they'd seated themselves. She picked up her glass of iced tea. Her face was flushed. "Did you see the look Mrs. Storr gave us? What's wrong with you? Everybody will know." She sipped from her iced tea and put the glass down.

"The hell with Mrs. Storr," Carlyle said. "Hey, let me tell you something. Honey, I feel light-years better than I did this time yesterday. Jesus," he said.

"What's happened?" Carol said. "Carlyle, tell me." She moved her fruit cup to one side of her tray and shook cheese over her spaghetti. But she didn't eat anything. She waited for him to go on. "Tell me what it is."

He told her about Mrs. Webster. He even told her about Mr. Webster. How the man'd had to hot-wire the truck in order to start it. Carlyle ate his tapioca while he talked. Then he ate the garlic bread. He drank Carol's iced tea down before he realized he was doing it.

"You're nuts, Carlyle," she said, nodding at the spaghetti in his plate that he hadn't touched.

He shook his head. "My *God*, Carol. God, I feel good, you know? I feel better than I have all summer." He lowered his voice. "Come over tonight, will you?"

He reached under the table and put his hand on her knee. She turned red again. She raised her eyes and looked around the dining room. But no one was paying any attention to them. She nodded quickly. Then she reached under the table and touched his hand.

That afternoon he arrived home to find his house neat and orderly and his children in clean clothes. In the kitchen, Keith and Sarah stood on chairs, helping Mrs. Webster with gingerbread cookies. Sarah's hair was out of her face and held back with a barrette.

"Daddy!" his children cried, happy, when they saw him.

"Keith, Sarah," he said. "Mrs. Webster, I—" But she didn't let him finish.

"We've had a fine day, Mr. Carlyle," Mrs. Webster said quickly. She wiped her fingers on the apron she was wearing. It was an old apron with blue windmills on it and it had belonged to Eileen. "Such beautiful children. They're a treasure. Just a treasure."

"I don't know what to say." Carlyle stood by the drainboard and watched Sarah press out some dough. He could smell the spice. He took off his coat and sat down at the kitchen table. He loosened his tie.

"Today was a get-acquainted day," Mrs. Webster said. "Tomorrow we have some other plans. I thought we'd walk to the park. We ought to take advantage of this good weather."

"That's a fine idea," Carlyle said. "That's just fine. Good. Good for you, Mrs. Webster."

"I'll finish putting these cookies in the oven, and by that time Mr. Webster should be here. You said four o'clock? I told him to come at four."

Carlyle nodded, his heart full.

"You had a call today," she said as she went over to the sink with the mixing bowl. "Mrs. Carlyle called."

"Mrs. Carlyle," he said. He waited for whatever it was Mrs. Webster might say next.

"Yes. I identified myself, but she didn't seem surprised to find me here. She said a few words to each of the children."

Carlyle glanced at Keith and Sarah, but they weren't paying any attention. They were lining up cookies on another baking sheet.

Mrs. Webster continued. "She left a message. Let me see, I wrote it down, but I think I can remember it. She said, 'Tell him'—that is, tell you—'what goes around, comes around.' I think that's right. She said you'd understand."

Carlyle stared at her. He heard Mr. Webster's truck outside.

"That's Mr. Webster," she said and took off the apron.

Carlyle nodded.

"Seven o'clock in the morning?" she asked.

"That will be fine," he said. "And thank you again."

That evening he bathed each of the children, got them into their pajamas, and then read to them. He listened to their prayers, tucked in their
covers, and turned out the light. It was nearly nine o'clock. He made
himself a drink and watched something on TV until he heard Carol's car
pull into the drive.

Around ten, while they were in bed together, the phone rang. He
swore, but he didn't get up to answer it. It kept ringing.

"It might be important," Carol said, sitting up. "It might be my sitter.
She has this number."

"It's my wife," Carlyle said. "I know it's her. She's losing her mind.
She's going crazy. I'm not going to answer it."

"I have to go pretty soon anyway," Carol said. "It was real sweet
tonight, honey." She touched his face.

It was the middle of the fall term. Mrs. Webster had been with him for
nearly six weeks. During this time, Carlyle's life had undergone a number of changes. For one thing, he was becoming reconciled to the fact
that Eileen was gone and, as far as he could understand it, had no
intention of coming back. He had stopped imagining that this might
change. It was only late at night, on the nights he was not with Carol,
that he wished for an end to the love he still had for Eileen and felt
tormented as to why all of this had happened. But for the most part he
and the children were happy; they thrived under Mrs. Webster's atten-
tions. Lately, she'd gotten into the routine of making their dinner and
keeping it in the oven, warming, until his arrival home from school.
He'd walk in the door to the smell of something good coming from the
kitchen and find Keith and Sarah helping to set the dining-room table.
Now and again he asked Mrs. Webster if she would care for overtime
work on Saturdays. She agreed, as long as it wouldn't entail her being at
his house before noon. Saturday mornings, she said, she had things to do
for Mr. Webster and herself. On these days, Carol would leave Dodge
with Carlyle's children, all of them under Mrs. Webster's care, and Carol
and he would drive to a restaurant out in the country for dinner. He
believed his life was beginning again. Though he hadn't heard from
Eileen since that call six weeks ago, he found himself able to think about
her now without either being angry or else feeling close to tears.

At school, they were just leaving the medieval period and about to
enter the Gothic. The Renaissance was still some time off, at least not
until after the Christmas recess. It was during this time that Carlyle got
sick. Overnight, it seemed, his chest tightened and his head began to
hurt. The joints of his body became stiff. He felt dizzy when he moved
around. The headache got worse. He woke up with it on a Sunday and
thought of calling Mrs. Webster to ask her to come and take the children
somewhere. They'd been sweet to him, bringing him glasses of juice
and some soda pop. But he couldn't take care of them. On the second

morning of his illness, he was just able to get to the phone to call in sick. He gave his name, his school, department, and the nature of his illness to the person who answered the number. Then he recommended Mel Fisher as his substitute. Fisher was a man who painted abstract oils three or four days a week, sixteen hours a day, but who didn't sell or even show his work. He was a friend of Carlyle's. "Get Mel Fisher," Carlyle told the woman on the other end of the line. "Fisher," he whispered.

He made it back to his bed, got under the covers, and went to sleep. In his sleep, he heard the pickup engine running outside, and then the backfire it made as the engine was turned off. Sometime later he heard Mrs. Webster's voice outside the bedroom door.

"Mr. Carlyle?"

"Yes, Mrs. Webster." His voice sounded strange to him. He kept his eyes shut. "I'm sick today. I called the school. I'm going to stay in bed today."

"I see. Don't worry, then," she said. "I'll look after things at this end."

He shut his eyes. Directly, still in a state between sleeping and waking, he thought he heard his front door open and close. He listened. Out in the kitchen, he heard a man say something in a low voice, and a chair being pulled away from the table. Pretty soon he heard the voices of the children. Sometime later—he wasn't sure how much time had passed—he heard Mrs. Webster outside his door.

"Mr. Carlyle, should I call the doctor?"

"No, that's all right," he said. "I think it's just a bad cold. But I feel hot all over. I think I have too many covers. And it's too warm in the house. Maybe you'll turn down the furnace." Then he felt himself drift back into sleep.

In a little while, he heard the children talking to Mrs. Webster in the living room. Were they coming inside or going out? Carlyle wondered. Could it be the next day already?

He went back to sleep. But then he was aware of his door opening. Mrs. Webster appeared beside his bed. She put her hand on his forehead.

"You're burning up," she said. "You have a fever."

"I'll be all right," Carlyle said. "I just need to sleep a little longer. And maybe you could turn the furnace down. Please, I'd appreciate it if you could get me some aspirin. I have an awful headache."

Mrs. Webster left the room. But his door stood open. Carlyle could hear the TV going out there. "Keep it down, Jim," he heard her say, and the volume was lowered at once. Carlyle fell asleep again.

But he couldn't have slept more than a minute, because Mrs. Webster was suddenly back in his room with a tray. She sat down on the side of his bed. He roused himself and tried to sit up. She put a pillow behind his back.

"Take these," she said and gave him some tablets. "Drink this." She held a glass of juice for him. "I also brought you some Cream of Wheat. I want you to eat it. It'll be good for you."

He took the aspirin and drank the juice. He nodded. But he shut his eyes once more. He was going back to sleep.

"Mr. Carlyle," she said.

He opened his eyes. "I'm awake," he said. "I'm sorry." He sat up a little. "I'm too warm, that's all. What time is it? Is it eight thirty yet?"

"It's a little after nine thirty," she said.

"Nine thirty," he said.

"Now I'm going to feed this cereal to you. And you're going to open up and eat it. Six bites, that's all. Here, here's the first bite. Open," she said. "You're going to feel better after you eat this. Then I'll let you go back to sleep. You eat this, and then you can sleep all you want."

He ate the cereal she spooned to him and asked for more juice. He drank the juice, and then he pulled down in the bed again. Just as he was going off to sleep, he felt her covering him with another blanket.

The next time he awoke, it was afternoon. He could tell it was afternoon by the pale light that came through his window. He reached up and pulled the curtain back. He could see that it was overcast outside; the wintry sun was behind the clouds. He got out of bed slowly, found his slippers, and put on his robe. He went into the bathroom and looked at himself in the mirror. Then he washed his face and took some more aspirin. He used the towel and then went out to the living room.

On the dining-room table, Mrs. Webster had spread some newspaper, and she and the children were pinching clay figures together. They had already made some things that had long necks and bulging eyes, things that resembled giraffes, or else dinosaurs. Mrs. Webster looked up as he walked by the table.

"How are you feeling?" Mrs. Webster asked him as he settled onto the sofa. He could see into the dining-room area, where Mrs. Webster and the children sat at the table.

"Better, thanks. A little better," he said. "I still have a headache, and I feel a little warm." He brought the back of his hand up to his forehead. "But I'm better. Yes, I'm better. Thanks for your help this morning."

"Can I get you anything now?" Mrs. Webster said. "Some more juice or some tea? I don't think coffee would hurt, but I think tea would be better. Some juice would be best of all."

"No, no thanks," he said. "I'll just sit here for a while. It's good to be out of bed. I feel a little weak is all. Mrs. Webster?"

She looked at him and waited.

"Did I hear Mr. Webster in the house this morning? It's fine, of course. I'm just sorry I didn't get a chance to meet him and say hello."

"It was him," she said. "He wanted to meet you, too. I asked him to come in. He just picked the wrong morning, what with you being sick and all. I'd wanted to tell you something about our plans, Mr. Webster's and mine, but this morning wasn't a good time for it."

"Tell me what?" he said, alert, fear plucking at his heart.

She shook her head. "It's all right," she said. "It can wait."

"Tell him what?" Sarah said. "Tell him what?"

"What, what?" Keith picked it up. The children stopped what they were doing.

"Just a minute, you two," Mrs. Webster said as she got to her feet.

"Mrs. Webster, Mrs. Webster!" Keith cried.

"Now see here, little man," Mrs. Webster said. "I need to talk to your father. Your father is sick today. You just take it easy. You go on and play with your clay. If you don't watch it, your sister is going to get ahead of you with these creatures."

Just as she began to move toward the living room, the phone rang. Carlyle reached over to the end table and picked up the receiver.

As before, he heard faint singing in the wire and knew that it was Eileen. "Yes," he said. "What is it?"

"Carlyle," his wife said, "I know, don't ask me how, that things are not going so well right now. You're sick, aren't you? Richard's been sick, too. It's something going around. He can't keep anything on his stomach. He's already missed a week of rehearsal for this play he's doing. I've had to go down myself and help block out scenes with his assistant. But I didn't call to tell you that. Tell me how things are out there."

"Nothing to tell," Carlyle said. "I'm sick, that's all. A touch of the flu. But I'm getting better."

"Are you still writing in your journal?" she asked. It caught him by surprise. Several years before, he'd told her that he was keeping a journal. Not a diary, he'd said, a journal—as if that explained something. But he'd never shown it to her, and he hadn't written in it for over a year. He'd forgotten about it.

"Because," she said, "you ought to write something in the journal during this period. How you feel and what you're thinking. You know, where your head is at during this period of sickness. Remember, sickness is a message about your health and your well-being. It's telling you things. Keep a record. You know what I mean? When you're well, you can look back and see what the message was. You can read it later, after the fact. Colette did that," Eileen said. "When she had a fever this one time."

"Who?" Carlyle said. "What did you say?"

"Colette," Eileen answered. "The French writer. You know who I'm talking about. We had a book of hers around the house. *Gigi* or something. I didn't read *that* book, but I've been reading her since I've been out here. Richard turned me on to her. She wrote a little book about what it was like, about what she was thinking and feeling the whole time she had this fever. Sometimes her temperature was a hundred and

two. Sometimes it was lower. Maybe it went higher than a hundred and
two. But a hundred and two was the highest she ever took her temperature and wrote, too, when she had the fever. Anyway, she wrote about
it. That's what I'm saying. Try writing about what it's like. Something
might come of it," Eileen said and, inexplicably, it seemed to Carlyle,
she laughed. "At least later on you'd have an hour-by-hour account of
your sickness. To look back at. At least you'd have that to show for it.
Right now you've just got this discomfort. You've got to translate that
into something usable."

He pressed his fingertips against his temple and shut his eyes. But she
was still on the line, waiting for him to say something. What could he
say? It was clear to him that she was insane.

"Jesus," he said. "Jesus, Eileen. I don't know what to say to that. I
really don't. I have to go now. Thanks for calling," he said.

"It's all right," she said. "We have to be able to communicate. Kiss the
kids for me. Tell them I love them. And Richard sends his hellos to you.
Even though he's flat on his back."

"Good-bye," Carlyle said and hung up. Then he brought his hands to
his face. He remembered, for some reason, seeing the fat girl make the
same gesture that time as she moved toward the car. He lowered his
hands and looked at Mrs. Webster, who was watching him.

"Not bad news, I hope," she said. The old woman had moved a chair
near to where he sat on the sofa.

Carlyle shook his head.

"Good," Mrs. Webster said. "That's good. Now, Mr. Carlyle, this may
not be the best time in the world to talk about this." She glanced out to
the dining room. At the table, the children had their heads bent over
the clay. "But since it has to be talked about sometime soon, and since it
concerns you and the children, and you're up now, I have something to
tell you. Jim and I, we're getting on. The thing is, we need something
more than we have at the present. Do you know what I'm saying? This is
hard for me," she said and shook her head. Carlyle nodded slowly. He
knew that she was going to tell him she had to leave. He wiped his face
on his sleeve. "Jim's son by a former marriage, Bob—the man is forty
years old—called yesterday to invite us to go out to Oregon and help
him with his mink ranch. Jim would be doing whatever they do with
minks, and I'd cook, buy the groceries, clean house, and do anything
else that needed doing. It's a chance for both of us. And it's board and
room and then some. Jim and I won't have to worry anymore about
what's going to happen to us. You know what I'm saying. Right now, Jim
doesn't have anything," she said. "He was sixty-two last week. He hasn't
had anything for some time. He came in this morning to tell you about it
himself, because I was going to have to give notice, you see. We thought
—*I* thought—it would help if Jim was here when I told you." She waited
for Carlyle to say something. When he didn't, she went on. "I'll finish

out the week, and I could stay on a couple of days next week, if need be. But then, you know, for sure, we really have to leave, and you'll have to wish us luck. I mean, can you imagine—all the way out there to Oregon in that old rattletrap of ours? But I'm going to miss these little kids. They're so precious."

After a time, when he still hadn't moved to answer her, she got up from her chair and went to sit on the cushion next to his. She touched the sleeve of his robe. "Mr. Carlyle?"

"I understand," he said. "I want you to know your being here has made a big difference to me and the children." His head ached so much that he had to squint his eyes. "This headache," he said. "This headache is killing me."

Mrs. Webster reached over and laid the back of her hand against his forehead. "You still have some fever," she told him. "I'll get more aspirin. That'll help bring it down. I'm still on the case here," she said. "I'm still the doctor."

"My wife thinks I should write down what this feels like," Carlyle said. "She thinks it might be a good idea to describe what the fever is like. So I can look back later and get the message." He laughed. Some tears came to his eyes. He wiped them away with the heel of his hand.

"I think I'll get your aspirin and juice and then go out there with the kids," Mrs. Webster said. "Looks to me like they've about worn out their interest with that clay."

Carlyle was afraid she'd move into the other room and leave him alone. He wanted to talk to her. He cleared his throat. "Mrs. Webster, there's something I want you to know. For a long time, my wife and I loved each other more than anything or anybody in the world. And that includes those children. We thought, well, we *knew* that we'd grow old together. And we knew we'd do all the things in the world that we wanted to do, and do them together." He shook his head. That seemed the saddest thing of all to him now—that whatever they did from now on, each would do it without the other.

"There, it's all right," Mrs. Webster said. She patted his hand. He sat forward and began to talk again. After a time, the children came out to the living room. Mrs. Webster caught their attention and held a finger to her lips. Carlyle looked at them and went on talking. Let them listen, he thought. It concerns them, too. The children seemed to understand they had to remain quiet, even pretend some interest, so they sat down next to Mrs. Webster's legs. Then they got down on their stomachs on the carpet and started to giggle. But Mrs. Webster looked sternly in their direction, and that stopped it.

Carlyle went on talking. At first, his head still ached, and he felt awkward to be in his pajamas on the sofa with this old woman beside him, waiting patiently for him to go on to the next thing. But then his headache went away. And soon he stopped feeling awkward and forgot how he was supposed to feel. He had begun his story somewhere in the middle, after the children were born. But then he backed up and started at the beginning, back when Eileen was eighteen and he was nineteen, a boy and girl in love, burning with it.

He stopped to wipe his forehead. He moistened his lips.

"Go on," Mrs. Webster said. "I know what you're saying. You just keep talking, Mr. Carlyle. Sometimes it's good to talk about it. Sometimes it has to be talked about. Besides, I want to hear it. And you're going to feel better afterwards. Something just like it happened to me once, something like what you're describing. Love. That's what it is."

The children fell asleep on the carpet. Keith had his thumb in his mouth. Carlyle was still talking when Mr. Webster came to the door, knocked, and then stepped inside to collect Mrs. Webster.

"Sit down, Jim," Mrs. Webster said. "There's no hurry. Go on with what you were saying, Mr. Carlyle."

Carlyle nodded at the old man, and the old man nodded back, then got himself one of the dining-room chairs and carried it into the living room. He brought the chair close to the sofa and sat down on it with a sigh. Then he took off his cap and wearily lifted one leg over the other. When Carlyle began talking again, the old man put both feet on the floor. The children woke up. They sat up on the carpet and rolled their heads back and forth. But by then Carlyle had said all he knew to say, so he stopped talking.

"Good. Good for you," Mrs. Webster said when she saw he had finished. "You're made out of good stuff. And so is she—so is Mrs. Carlyle. And don't you forget it. You're both going to be okay after this is over." She got up and took off the apron she'd been wearing. Mr. Webster got up, too, and put his cap back on.

At the door, Carlyle shook hands with both of the Websters.

"So long," Jim Webster said. He touched the bill of his cap.

"Good luck to you," Carlyle said.

Mrs. Webster said she'd see him in the morning then, bright and early as always.

As if something important had been settled, Carlyle said, "Right!"

The old couple went carefully along the walk and got into their truck. Jim Webster bent down under the dashboard. Mrs. Webster looked at Carlyle and waved. It was then, as he stood at the window, that he felt something come to an end. It had to do with Eileen and the life before this. Had he ever waved at her? He must have, of course, he knew he had, yet he could not remember just now. But he understood it was over, and he felt able to let her go. He was sure their life together had happened in the way he said it had. But it was something that had passed. And that passing—though it had seemed impossible and he'd fought against it—would become a part of him now, too, as surely as anything else he'd left behind.

As the pickup lurched forward, he lifted his arm once more. He saw the old couple lean toward him briefly as they drove away. Then he brought his arm down and turned to his children.

EVAN S. CONNELL

The Fisherman
from Chihuahua

Santa Cruz is at the top of Monterey Bay, which is about a hundred
miles below San Francisco, and in the winter there are not many people
in Santa Cruz. The boardwalk concessions are shuttered except for one
counter-and-booth restaurant, the Ferris-wheel seats are hooded with
olive green canvas and the powerhouse padlocked, and the rococo
doors of the carousel are boarded over and if one peers through a
knothole into its gloom the horses which buck and plunge through
summer prosperity seem like animals touched by a magic wand that
they may never move again. Dust dims the gilt of their saddles and sifts
through cracks into their bold nostrils. About the only sounds to be
heard around the waterfront in Santa Cruz during winter are the voices
of Italian fishermen hidden by mist as they work against the long pier,
and the slap of waves against the pilings of the cement dance pavilion
when tide runs high, or the squeak of a gull, or once in a long time
bootsteps on the slippery boards as some person comes quite alone and
usually slowly to the edge of the gray and fogbound ocean.

The restaurant is Pendleton's and white brush strokes on the glass
announce *tacos, frijoles,* and *enchiladas* as house specialties, these being mostly greens and beans and fried meat made arrogant with pep-
per. Smaller letters in pseudo-Gothic script say *Se Habla Español* but
this is not true; it was the man who owned the place before Pendleton
who could speak Spanish. From him, though, Pendleton did learn how
to make the food and this is the reason a short fat Mexican who worked
as a mechanic at Ace Dillon's Texaco station continued eating his sup-
pers there. He came in every night just after eight o'clock and sat at the
counter, ate an astounding amount of this food, which he first splattered
with Tabasco sauce as casually as though it were ketchup, and then
washed it farther down with beer. After that he would feel a little drunk
and would spend two or three dollars playing the pinball machine and
the great nickelodeon and dancing by himself, but inoffensively, contentedly, just snapping his fingers and shuffling across the warped

boards often until Pendleton began pulling in the shutters. Then, having had a suitable evening, he would half-dance his way home, or at least back in the direction of town. He was a squat little man who waddled like a duck full of eggs and he had a face like a blunt arrowhead or a Toltec idol, and he was about the color of hot sand. His fingers were much too thick for their length, seemingly without joints, only creases where it was necessary for them to bend. He smelled principally of cold grease and of urine as though his pants needed some air, but Pendleton who did not smell very good himself did not mind and besides there were not many customers during these winter months.

So every evening shortly after dark he entered for his food and some amusement, and as he appeared to contain all God's world within his own self Pendleton was not disinterested when another Mexican came in directly behind him like a long shadow. This new man was tall, very tall, six feet or more, and much darker, almost black in the manner of a sweat-stained saddle. He was handsome, silent, and perhaps forty years of age. Also he was something of a dandy; his trousers, which were long and quite tight, revealed the fact that he was bowlegged, as befits certain types of men, and made one think of him easily riding a large fast horse, not necessarily toward a woman but in the direction of something more remote and mysterious—bearing a significant message or something like that. Exceedingly short black boots of finest leather took in the cuffs of his narrow trousers. For a shirt he wore long-sleeved white silk unbuttoned to below the level of his nipples which themselves were vaguely visible. The hair of his chest was so luxuriant that an enameled crucifix there did not even rest on the skin.

These two men sat at the counter side by side. The tall one lifted off his sombrero as if afraid of mussing his hair and he placed it on the third stool. His hair was deeply oiled, and comb tracks went all the way from his temples to the back of his thin black neck, and he reeked of green perfume. He had a mustache that consisted of nothing but two black strings hanging across the corners of his unforgiving mouth, ending in soft points about an inch below his chin. He seemed to think himself alone in the restaurant because, after slowly licking his lips and interlacing his fingers, he just sat looking somberly ahead. The small man ordered for them both.

After they had eaten supper the little one played the pinball machine while this strange man took from his shirt pocket a cigarillo only a little bigger than his mustache and smoked it with care; that is, he would take it from his mouth between his thumb and one finger as if he were afraid of crushing it, and after releasing the smoke he would replace it with the same care in the exact center of his mouth. It never dangled or rolled; he respected it. Nor was it a cheap piece of tobacco; the smoke ascended heavily, moist and sweet.

Suddenly the fat Mexican kicked the pinball game and with a surly expression walked over to drop a coin into the nickelodeon. The tall man had remained all this time at the counter with his long savage eyes half-shut, smoking and smoking the fragrant cigarillo. Now he did not turn around—in fact all he did was remove the stump from his lips—but clearly he was disturbed. When the music ended he sat motionless for several minutes. Then he lifted his head and his throat began to swell like that of a mating pigeon.

Pendleton, sponging an ashtray, staggered as if a knife had plunged through his ribs.

The Mexican's eyes were squeezed shut. His lips had peeled away from his teeth like those of a jaguar tearing meat, and the veins of his neck looked ready to pop. In the shrill screams bursting from his throat was a memory of Moors, the ching of Arab cymbals, of rags and of running feet through all the marketplaces of the East.

His song had no beginning; it had no end. All at once he was simply sitting on the stool looking miserably ahead.

After a while the small fat Mexican said to Pendleton "Be seeing you, man," and waddled out the door. A few seconds later the tall one's stool creaked. He put on the high steepled sombrero as though it were a crown and followed his friend through the door.

The next night there happened to be a pair of tourists eating in the back booth when the Mexicans entered. They were dressed as before except that the big one's shirt was lime green, and Pendleton noticed his wristwatch—fastened not to his wrist but on the green shirtsleeve where it bulged like an oily bubble. They took the same stools and ate fried beans, tacos, and enchiladas for half an hour, after which the short one who looked like his Toltec ancestors gently belched, smiled in a benign way, and moved over to his machine. Failing to win anything he cursed it and kicked it before selecting some records.

This time Pendleton was alert; as the music ended he got ready for the first shriek. The tourists, caught unaware, thought their time had come. When they recovered from the shock they looked over the top of the booth and then the woman stood up in order to see better. After the black Mexican's song was finished they all could hear the incoming tide, washing softly around the pillars of the pavilion.

Presently the two men paid their bill and went out, the short one leading, into the dirty yellow fog and the diving, squeaking gulls.

"Why, that's terrible," the woman laughed. "It wasn't musical." Anyone who looked at her would know she was still shuddering from the force of the ominous man.

Her husband too was frightened and laughed. "Somebody should play a little drum behind that fellow." Unaware of what a peculiar statement he had made he formed a circle of his thumb and forefinger to show how big the drum should be.

She was watching the door, trying to frown compassionately. "I wonder what's the matter with that poor man. Some woman must have hurt him dreadfully."

Pendleton began to wipe beer bracelets and splats of Tabasco sauce from the lacquered plywood counter where the men had been eating.

"We're from Iowa City," the woman said with a smile.

Pendleton had never been to Iowa City or anywhere near it even on a train, so he asked if they would like more coffee.

"Those two fellows," her husband said, "do they come here every night?"

Pendleton was seized with contempt for this domestic little man, though he did not know why. He walked stiffly away from their booth and stood with both hairy hands on his hips while he listened to the sea thrashing and rolling in the night.

"Who?" he demanded. "Them two?"

The couple, overpowered by his manner, looked at each other uneasily.

On the third night when the Mexicans sat down at the counter Pendleton said to the one who spoke English, "Tell your buddy no more yowling."

"Tell him yourself," the Toltec replied. "Eight tacos, four beers, and a lot of beans, man."

"What do you think this is, buster, some damn concert hall?"

For a moment the little Mexican became eloquent with his eyebrows; then both he and Pendleton turned their attention to the silent one who was staring somberly at the case of pies.

Pendleton leaned on his hands so that his shoulders bulged. "Now looky, Pablo, give him the word and do it quick. Tell him to cut out that noise."

This enraged the small man whose voice rose to a snarl. "Pablo yourself. Don't give me that stuff."

Pendleton was not angry but set about cleaving greens for their tacos as though he were furious. While the blade chunked into the wood beside his thumb he thought about the situation. He did not have anything particular in mind when all at once he slammed down the cleaver and with his teeth clenched he began bending his eyes toward the two.

"No debe cantar," said the little one hurriedly, waggling a negative finger at his companion. *"No más."*

"All right, by God," Pendleton muttered as though he understood. He wished to say something in Spanish but he knew only *mañana, adiós,* and *señorita,* and none of these seemed to fit. He resumed work, but doubtfully, not certain if the silent one had heard either of them. Without turning around he explained his attitude: "People come here to eat supper."

Abel W. Sharpe, who had once been county sheriff and who now lived in a retirement home, came through the door alone but arguing harshly. He took a stool beside the tall Mexican, looked up at him twice, and then ordered hot milk and a waffle. While he was pouring syrup into the milk the nickelodeon music stopped and the black Mexican did it again.

At the first note the old man jumped off his stool and crouched several feet away, a spoon in one hand and his cup of sweet milk in the other. "Can't hear nothing," he said angrily to Pendleton. "The bastard deefened me."

The Toltec, who was playing pinball, paid not the least attention because he had lighted four pretty girls which meant he probably would win several games. His friend, now motionless, sat on the stool and gazed ahead as though he could see clear into some grief-stricken time.

Not until the eighth or ninth night did Pendleton realize that the restaurant was drawing more customers; there would be half-a-dozen or so extra for dinner, maybe more.

Then there came a night when the Toltec waddled in as usual but no one followed. That night the restaurant was uneasy. Things spilled, and while cleaning up a table Pendleton discovered a menu burned through and through with cigarette holes. By ten thirty the place was deserted.

Pendleton said, "Hey, Pablo."

The Toltec gave him a furious look.

"All right," Pendleton apologized, "what's your name?"

"What's yours?" he replied. He was insulted.

"Where's your buddy?"

"He's no friend of mine."

Pendleton walked down the counter behind a damp rag, wrung it over the sink, and then very casually did something he never even thought of doing: he opened a bottle of beer and indicated to the Mexican that it was free.

Toltec, though still aggrieved, quickly accepted this gift, saying, "I just met the guy. He asked me where to get some decent food."

Pendleton wiped a table and for a while appeared to be idly picking his teeth. When he judged enough time had gone by he said, "Got tired of my grub, I guess."

"No, tonight he's drunk. Man, he's out of his skull."

Pendleton waited a couple of minutes before saying, "He looks like a bullfighter I saw once in Tijuana called Victoriano Posada."

This proved to be a shrewd inquiry because after drinking some more of the free beer the fat Mexican remarked, "He calls himself Damaso."

Pendleton, wondering if some other information would follow, pretended to stretch and to yawn and smacked his chops mightily. He thought that tomorrow, when the tall man arrived, he would call him by name.

"Know what? He goes and stands by himself on the sea wall a lot of times. Maybe he's getting ready to knock himself off."

"Tell him not to do it in front of my place," Pendleton answered.

Through the screen door could be seen a roll of silvery yellow fog with the moon just above it, but the sea was hidden.

"These Santa Cruz winters," Pendleton said. Opening the icebox he chose a beer for himself and leaned against the counter, far enough away that his guest might not feel the friendship was being forced. Peeling off the wet label he rolled it into a soggy gray ball which he dropped into a bucket. "Singers make plenty money, I guess."

The Mexican looked at him slyly. "What are you talking about?"

Pendleton, after scratching his head, yawned again. "Huh? Oh. I was just thinking about what's-his-name. That fellow you come in here with."

"I know it," the Mexican said, laughing.

For a while Pendleton studied his beer and listened to the combers, each of which sounded as if it would smash the door. "Feels like something standing up in the ocean tonight," he said. "I could use a little summer."

"You want the town full of tourists? Those sausages? You're crazy. You're off the rocks."

Pendleton judged that the Mexican was about to insult the summer people still more, so he manipulated the conversation once again. "Somebody told me your friend got himself a singing job at that night spot near Capitola."

"Look," said the Toltec, patient, but irritated, "I just met the guy a couple of weeks ago."

"He never said where he's from, I guess."

"Chihuahua, he says. That's one rough town. And full of sand. That Chihuahua—it's noplace."

Breakers continued sounding just beyond the door and the fog now stood against the screen like a person.

"What does he do?"

The Mexican lifted both fat little shoulders.

"Just traveling through?"

The Mexican lifted both hands.

"Where is he going?"

"All I know is he's got a pretty good voice."

"He howls like a goddamn crazy wolf," Pendleton said, "howling for the moon."

"Yah, he's pretty good. Long time ago I saw a murder down south in the mountains and a woman screamed just like that."

Pendleton opened the icebox for two more beers. The Mexican accepted one as though in payment for service. For some seconds they had been able to hear footsteps approaching, audible after every tunnel of water caved in. The footsteps went past the door but no one could be seen.

"Know what? There was an old man washed up on the beach the other day."

"That so?" said Pendleton. "Everything gets to the beach sooner or later."

The Mexican nodded. Somewhere far out on the bay a little boat sounded again and again. "What a night," he said.

Pendleton murmured and scratched.

"Know something, mister? That Damaso, he ain't no Mexicano."

"I didn't think so," Pendleton lied.

"No, because he's got old blood. You know what I mean? I think he's a Gypsy from Spain, or wherever those guys come from. He's dark in the wrong way. He just don't *feel* Mexicano to me. There's something about him, and besides he speaks a little Castellano."

Both of them considered this.

"What's he howling about?" Pendleton asked. "Some girl?"

"No, nothing like that."

"Then why the hell does he do it?"

But here the little Mexican lost interest; he revolved on the stool, from which only his toes could reach to the floor, hopped off, and hurried across to the nickelodeon. Having pushed a nickel through the slit he studied the wonderful colors and followed the bubbles which fluttered up the tubes to vanish; next, he dialed *"Tuxedo Junction"* and began shuffling around the floor, snapping his fingers and undulating so that in certain positions he looked about five months pregnant.

"Who knows?" he asked of no one in particular while he danced.

The next night he again came in alone. When Pendleton mentioned this he replied that the dark one was still drunk.

And the next night when asked if the drunk was going into its third day he replied that Damaso was no longer drunk, just sick from being so, that he was at present lying on the wet cement having vomited on his boots, that probably by sunrise he would be all right. This turned out to be correct because both of them came in for supper the following night. Toltec, smiling and tugging at his crotch, was rumpled as usual and smelled human while his tall companion was oiled and groomed and wearing the white silk again. A good many people were loitering about the restaurant—every booth was full—because this thing had come to be expected, and though all of them were eating or drinking or spending money in some way to justify themselves, and although not everybody looked up at the entrance of the two Mexicans, there could be no doubt about the situation. Only these two men seemed not to notice anything; they ate voraciously and drank quite a few beers after which the Toltec began playing pinball and Damaso remained on the stool with his long arms crossed on the counter.

Later the nickelodeon lighted up. When at last its music died away there was not a sound in the restaurant. People watched the head of the dark man bow down until it was hidden in his arms. The crucifix disentangled itself and dropped out the top of his gaucho shirt where it began to swing to and fro, glittering as it twisted on the end of its golden chain. He remained like that for quite some time, finally raised his head to look at the ticket, counted out enough money, and with the sombrero loosely in one hand he stumbled through the door.

The other Mexican paid no attention; he called for more beer, which he drank all at once in an attempt to interest a young girl with silver slippers and breasts like pears who was eating supper with her parents, but, failing to win anything at this or again at the machine, he suddenly grew bored with the evening and walked out.

The next night he entered alone. When asked if his companion had started another drunk he said Damaso was gone.

Pendleton asked late in the evening, "How do you know?"

"I feel it," he said.

Then for a while Pendleton stood listening to the advancing tide which had begun to pat the pillars like someone gently slapping a dead drum. After taking off his apron he rolled it up, as he always did, and put it beneath the counter. He untied the sweaty handkerchief from around his neck and folded it over the apron, but there his routine altered; before pulling in the shutters he stopped at the screen door and looked out and listened, but of course did not see or hear any more than he expected.

Sharply the Toltec said, "I like to dance." And he began to do so. "Next summer I'm really going to cut it up. Nothing's going to catch me." He read Pendleton's face while dancing by himself to the odd and clumsy little step he was inventing, and counseled, "Jesus Christ, he's gone. Forget about it, man."

FRANK CONROY

Midair

A sunny, windy day on the Lower East Side of New York. The year is 1942. Sean, aged six, is being more or less pulled along the sidewalk by his father, who has shown up from nowhere to take him home from school. Sean tries to keep the pace, although he does not remember the last time he has seen this big, exuberant man, nor is he altogether sure that he trusts him. Mary, on the other side, is nine. Her legs are longer, and she seems happy, skipping every now and then, shouting into the wind, calling him Daddy. Sean cannot hear what they're saying except in fragments—the wind tears at the words. His hand, wrist, and part of his forearm are enclosed in his father's fist. The big man strides along, red-faced, chin jutting forward proudly, his whole carriage suggesting the eagerness and confidence of a soldier marching forward to receive some important, hard-won medal.

He is not a soldier, as Sean's mother has recently explained. He is not in the Army (although a war is going on) but in something called a rest home, where people go in order to rest. He does not seem tired, Sean thinks.

"It'll be a different story now, by God," his father says as they turn the corner onto Seventh Street. "A completely different story." Energy seems to radiate from the man like an electrical charge. His body carries a pale-blue corona, and when he speaks his white teeth give off white lightning. "What a day!" He lets go of the children's hands and makes a sweeping gesture. "An absolute pip of a day. Look at that blue sky! The clouds! Seventh Street! Look how vivid the colors are!"

Sean cannot look. He is preoccupied with the unnatural force of his father's enthusiasm. It is as if all that has been pointed out is too far away to be seen. The boy's awareness is focused on the small bubble of space immediately surrounding himself, his father, and his sister. Within that area he sees clearly—as if his life depended on it—and there is no part of him left over to see anything else.

They reach the tenement building and climb the stoop. His father hesitates at the door.

"The key," he says.

"Mother has it," Mary says.

"You haven't got it?" He rolls his head in exasperation.

"I'm sorry." Mary is afraid she has failed him. "I'm sorry, Daddy."

Sean is uneasy with her use of the word "Daddy." It sounds strange, since they never use it. It is not part of their domestic vocabulary. On those extremely rare occasions when Sean, Mary, and their mother ever mention the man, the word they have always used is "Father."

Mrs. Rosenblum, second floor rear, emerges from the house.

"Good morning," his father says, smiling, catching the door. "In you go, children."

Mrs. Rosenblum has never seen this big man before but recognizes, from his expensive clothes and confident manner, that he is a gentleman, and the father of the children. A quick glance at Mary, smiling as he touches her head, confirms everything.

"Nice," Mrs. Rosenblum says. "Very nice."

Inside, Sean's father takes the steps two at a time. The children follow up to the top floor—the fourth—and find him standing at the door to the apartment, trying the knob.

"No key here, either, I suppose."

"It's the same one," Mary says.

He gives the door a hard push, as if testing. Then he steps back, looks around, and notices the iron ladder leading up to the hatch and the roof.

"Aha! More than one way to skin a cat." He strides over to the ladder and begins to climb. "Follow me, buckos. Up the mainmast!"

"Daddy, what are you doing?" Mary cries.

"We'll use the fire escape." He pushes up the hatch and sunlight pours down. "Come on. It's fun!"

Sean can hear the wind whistling up there as his father climbs through. Mary hesitates an instant and then mounts the ladder. As she approaches the top, Sean follows her. He ascends into the sunshine and the wind.

The big man moves rapidly across the tarred roof to the rear of the building and the twin hoops of the fire-escape railing. He shouts back at the children, but his words are lost. He beckons, turns, and grabs the railings. His feet go over the edge and he begins to descend. Then he stops—his head and shoulders visible—and shouts again. Mary moves forward, the big man sinks out of sight, and Sean follows.

The boy steps to the edge and looks over. His father is ten feet below, on the fire-escape landing, red face up-turned.

"Come on!" The white teeth flash. "The window's open."

The wind whips Mary's skirt around her knees as she goes over. She has to stop and push the hair out of her eyes. When she reaches the landing below, Sean grabs the hoops. Five floors down, a sheet of news-paper flutters across the cement at the bottom of the airshaft. It seems no bigger than a page from a book. He climbs down. Pigeons rise from the airshaft and scatter. On the landing, he sees his father, already inside, lifting Mary through the kitchen window. He follows quickly on his own.

The kitchen, although entirely familiar in every detail, seems slightly odd in its totality. The abruptness of the entry—without the usual prep-aration of the other rooms—tinges the scene with unreality. Sean fol-lows his father and sister through the kitchen, into the hall, and to the doorway of his mother's room. His father does not enter but simply stops and looks.

"Have you been here before?" Sean asks.

"Of course he has, silly," Mary says rapidly.

His father turns. "Don't you remember?"

"I don't think so," Sean says.

As they pass the main door to the apartment, toward the front of the hall, his father pauses to slip on the chain lock.

For more than a hour they have been rearranging the books on the living-room shelves, putting them in alphabetical order by author. Sean's father stops every now and then, with some favorite book, to do a dramatic reading. The readings become more and more dramatic. He leans down to the children to emphasize the dialogue, shouting in different voices, gesticulating with his free arm in the air, making faces. But then, abruptly, his mood changes.

"The windows are filthy," he says angrily, striding back and forth from one to another, peering at the glass. The books are forgotten now as he goes to the kitchen. Mary quickly pushes them over to the foot of the bookcase. Sean helps. While doing this, they look very quickly, almost furtively, into each other's eyes. It takes a fraction of a second, but Sean understands. He is aware that his father's unexplained aban-donment of an activity in which he had appeared to be so deeply involved has frightened Mary. His own feelings are complex—he is gratified that she is scared, since in his opinion she should have been scared all along, while at the same time his own fear, because of hers, escalates a notch.

"What's going to happen?" Sean asks quietly.

"Nothing. It's OK." She pretends not to be afraid.

"Get Mother." The sound of water running in the kitchen.

Mary considers this. "It's OK. She'll come home from work the way she always does."

"That's a long time. That's too long."

The big man returns with a bucket and some rags. His face seems even more flushed. "We'll do it ourselves. Wait till you see the difference." He moves to the central window, and they are drawn in his wake. Sean recognizes a shift in the atmosphere: before, with the books, there was at least a pretense of the three of them doing something together—a game they might all enjoy—but now his father's attention has narrowed and intensified onto the question of the windows. He seems barely aware of the children.

He washes the panes with rapid, sweeping movements. Then he opens the lower frame, bends through, turns, and sits on the sill to do the outside. Sean can see his father's face, concentrated, frowning, eyes searching the glass for streaks.

Sean begins to move backward.

"No," Mary says quickly. "We have to stay."

The boy stops beside the rocking chair where his mother sits after dinner.

The big man reenters, and steps back to regard the results of his work. "Much better. Much, much better." He moves on to the next window. "Fresh water, Mary. Take the bucket."

Mary obeys, and goes back to the kitchen.

The big man stares down at the street. Sean stays by the rocking chair.

"You don't remember," the big man says. "Well, that's all right. Time is different for children. In any case, the past is behind us now. What counts is the future." He gives a short, barking laugh. "Another cliché rediscovered! But that's the way it is. You have to penetrate the clichés, you have to live them out to find out how true they are. What a joke!"

Mary brings the bucket of water to his side. Suddenly he moves closer to the window. He has seen something on the street.

"God damn." He moves back rapidly. He turns and runs down the hall to the kitchen. Sean and Mary can see him closing and locking the rear windows. "Bastards!" he shouts.

Mary moves sideways to glance through the window to the street.

"What is it?" Sean asks.

"An ambulance." Her voice is beginning to quaver. "It must be that ambulance."

Now he comes back into the living room and paces. Then he rushes to the newly washed window, opens it, and tears the gauzy curtains from the rod and throws them aside. Sean can see Mary flinch as the curtains are torn. The big man moves from one window to the next, opening them and tearing away the curtains. Wind rushes through the room. Torn curtains rise from the floor and swirl about.

He gathers the children and sits down on the couch, his arms around their shoulders. Sean feels crushed and tries to adjust his position, but his father only tightens his grip. The big man is breathing fast, staring into the hall, at the door.

"Daddy," Mary says. "It hurts."

A slight release of pressure, but Sean is still held so tightly to the man's side he can barely move.

"Oh, the bastards," his father says. "The tricky bastards."

The buzzer sounds. Then, after a moment, a knock on the door. The big man's grip tightens.

Another knock. The sound of a key. Sean watches the door open a few inches until the chain pulls it short. He sees the glint of an eye.

"Mr. Kennedy? This is Dr. Silverman. Would you open the door, please?"

"Alone, are you, Doctor?" An almost lighthearted tone.

A moment's pause. "No. I have Bob and James here with me." A calm voice, reassuring to Sean. "Please let us in."

"The goon squad," his father says.

"Bob in particular is very concerned. And so am I."

"Bob is a Judas."

"Mr. Kennedy. Be reasonable. We've been through this before, after all."

"No, no." As if correcting a slow student. "This is different. I'm through with you people. I'm through with all of that. I've come home, I'm here with my children, and I'm going to stay."

A pause. "Yes. I can see the children."

"We've been having a fine time. We've been washing the windows, Doctor." An almost inaudible chuckle.

"Mr. Kennedy, I implore you to open the door. We simply must come in. We must discuss your plans."

"I'm not going to open the door. And neither are you. What we have here, Doctor, is a Mexican standoff. Do you get my meaning?"

"I'm very sorry to hear you say that." Another pause—longer this time. "Bob would like a word with you."

"Mr. Kennedy? This is Bob." A younger voice.

"I'm not coming back, Bob. Don't try any crap with me. I know why you're here."

"I'm worried about you. You're flying. You know that."

"Got the little white jacket, eh, Bob? The one with the funny sleeves?"

"Look, if you don't come back they'll assign me to Mr. Farnsworth. You wouldn't do that to me. Please."

"Cut the crap, Bob."

"Listen. I'm with you. You know that. I mean, how many times have we talked about your—"

A tremendous crash as the door is kicked in, the frame splintering where the chain has come away. Sean is aware that things are happening very fast now, and yet he can see it all with remarkable clarity. Wood chips drift lazily through the air. Three men rush through the door—two in white uniforms, one in ordinary clothes. He knows they are running toward the couch as fast as they can—their faces frozen masks of strain—but time itself seems to have slowed down.

Still clamped to his father's side, Sean feels himself rise up into the air. He sees his father's other hand make a grab for Mary, who is trying to escape. He gets hold of her hair, but she twists away with a yell. Sean feels betrayed that she has gotten away. She was the one calling him Daddy. The wind roars as the big man rushes to the window and climbs out on the sill.

"Stop where you are!" he shouts back at the men.

Sean cannot see, but he senses that the men have stopped. He can hear Mary crying, hear the wind, and hear the sound of his father's heart racing under the rough tweed of his jacket. He stares down at the street, at the cracks in the sidewalk. With the very limited motion available to his arms, he finds his father's belt and hangs on with both fists.

"You bastards," his father shouts. "What you don't realize is I can do anything. Anything!"

Something akin to sleepiness comes over Sean. As time passes he realizes—a message from a distant outpost—that he has soiled himself. Finally, they are pulled back in, with great speed and strength, and fall to the floor. His father screams as the men cover him.

In college, his father long dead, and all memory of his father's visit in 1942 completely buried, Sean looks for a wife. He is convinced that if he doesn't find someone before he graduates, he will have missed his chance for all time. The idea of living alone terrifies him, although he is not aware that it terrifies him. He lives as if he did not have a past, and so there is a great deal about himself of which he is not aware. He is entirely ignorant of his lack of awareness, and believes himself to be in full control of his existence. He zeroes in on a bright, rather guarded girl he meets in Humanities 301, and devotes himself to winning her hand. It is a long campaign, and the odds are against him—her family disapproves vehemently, for reasons that are never made clear, and she is more intelligent than Sean, and ambitious, in a way he is not, for power in some as yet unnamed career. She is older than he is. She is not afraid of living alone. Yet in the end his tenacity prevails. Graduate school provides no route for her ambition, she drifts for a bit, and finally capitulates over the telephone. Sean is exultant.

They are married by a judge in her parents' midtown brownstone. Sean is six feet two inches tall, weighs a hundred and thirty-three pounds, and appears, with his Irish, slightly acned face, to be all of seventeen. (He is actually twenty-two.) His wife is struck by the irony of the fact that more than half of the relatives watching the event are divorced. Sean is impressed by the activity outside the window during the ceremony. The New York Foundling Hospital is being torn down—

the wrecker's ball exploding walls even as the absurdly short judge drones on. For both of them—in a moment of lucidity whose importance they are too young to recognize—the ceremony is anticlimactic, and faintly ridiculous.

Four years pass, and nothing happens. They both have a small monthly income from trust funds. She dabbles in an occasional project or temporary job but always retreats in mysterious frustration to the safety of their apartment. He writes a book, but it contains nothing, since he knows very little about people, or himself. He remains a boy; the marriage that was to launch him into maturity serves instead to extend his boyhood. Husband and wife, they remain children. They live together in good will, oddly sealed off from one another, and from the world. He dreams of people jumping out of windows, holding hands, in eerie accord. He has no idea what the dreams mean, or where they come from. She confesses that she has never believed in romantic love. They are both frightened of the outside, but they respond differently. She feels that what is out there is too dangerous to fool with. He feels that, however dangerous, it is only out there that strength can be found. In some vague, inchoate way, he knows he needs strength.

Privately, without telling him, she decides to have children. Philip is born. John is born. Sean is exultant.

A summer night in 1966. Sean drives down from Harlem, where he has gotten drunk in a jazz club. The bouncer, an old acquaintance, has sold him an ounce of marijuana. Sean carries it in a sealed envelope in his back pocket. He turns off the Henry Hudson Parkway at Ninety-sixth Street, slips along Riverside Drive for a couple of blocks, turns, and pulls up in front of Judy's house. It's a strange little building—five floors with a turret up the side, a dormer window on her top-floor apartment, bits of crenellation and decoration, like some miniature castle. A Rapunzel house.

He had met her on the sidelines during a soccer game. Kneeling on the grass, he had turned his head to follow the fullback's kick, and found himself looking instead at the slender, blue-jeaned thigh of the girl standing next to him. Perhaps it was the suddenness, the abrupt nearness of the splendid curve of her backside, the images sinking into him before he had time to protect himself. The lust he felt was so pure it seemed, for all its power, magically innocent, and he got to his feet and began talking to her. (She was eventually to disappear into medical school, but never, as it turned out, from his memory.)

He stares up at the dark window. Behind the window is a room, and in the room a bed, in which for a year he has been making love to Judy. She is gone now, away for a month, driving around France in a *deux-chevaux* Citroën leased by him as a gift. The room is dark and empty, and yet he has to go in. He does not question the urge. He simply gets out of the car and approaches the building. Once he is in motion, a kind of heat suffuses him. He experiences something like tunnel vision.

Inside, he scans the mailboxes. A few letters are visible behind the grille in hers. He opens the door with his key and runs up the stairs—turning at landings, climbing, turning, climbing, until he is there, at the top floor. It is midnight, and the building is silent. He slips the key into the lock, turns and pushes. The door will not open. He has forgotten the police lock, the iron bar she'd had installed before she left—with a separate locking mechanism. He doesn't have that key. He leans against the door for a moment, and the faint scent of the room inside reaches him. He is dizzy with the scent, and the door suddenly enrages him. The scent is inside, and he must get inside.

He pounds his shoulder against the glossy black wood in a steady rhythm, putting all his weight against it. The door shakes in its hinges, but he can feel the solidity of the iron bar in the center. There is not an iota of movement in the bar. He moves back in the hallway—halfway to the rear apartment—runs forward, raises his right leg, and kicks the central panel of the door. A terrific crash, but the door does not yield. He continues to run and kick, in a frenzy, until he starts falling down.

Out of breath, he sits on the stairs to the roof and looks at Judy's door. He cannot believe there is no way to get it open. The wood is cracked in several places. Finally, as his breathing slows, he gives up. The iron bar will never move.

Slowly, swirling like smoke, an idea emerges. He turns and looks up the stairs, into the darkness. After a moment he stands up, mounts the stairs, opens the hatch, and climbs out onto the roof. The air cools him—he is drenched with sweat. Purple sky. Stars. He crosses the flat part of the roof to the front of the building, where it suddenly drops off in a steep slope—a Rapunzel roof, tiled with overlapping slate. There is a masonry ridge, perhaps an inch high, at the bottom edge, fifteen feet down. He moves sideways until he comes to a place he estimates lies directly above the dormer window. He gets down on his belly and carefully slides his legs over onto the tiles, lowering more and more of himself onto the steep incline, testing to see if he can control his downward motion. Sufficient control seems possible, and, very slowly, he releases his grip on the roof and begins to slide. His face presses against the slate, and he can feel the sweat from his cheek on the slate. From somewhere off toward Amsterdam Avenue comes the sound of a siren.

He descends blindly and stops when his toes touch the ridge. Beyond the ridge, there is empty space and a clear drop to the sidewalk, but he is unafraid. He remains motionless for several moments, and his noisy brain falls still. He is no longer drunk. A profound calm prevails, a sense of peacefulness—as sweet, to him, as water to some traveler in the desert. Carefully, he slides down sideways until his entire body lies along the ridge. He raises his head and looks at the deserted street below—the pools of light under the street lamps, the tops of the parked cars, the square patterns of the cracks in the sidewalk—and there is a cleanness and orderliness to things. He becomes aware that there is a reality that lies behind the appearance of the world, a pure reality he has never sensed before, and the knowledge fills him with gratitude.

He moves his head farther out and looks for the dormer window. There it is. He had thought to hang on to the edge of the roof and swing himself down and into the window. In his mind, it had been a perfectly straightforward procedure. In his mind, he had known he could do anything—anything he was capable of imagining. But now, as he looks at the dormer window—too far away, full of tricky angles—he sees that the plan is impossible. He immediately discards the plan, as if he had been caught up in a story that ended abruptly. He no longer has any interest in getting into the apartment.

Moving slowly and carefully, as calm in his soul as the calmness in the great purple sky above him, he retreats. Using the friction of his arms and legs, of his damp palms and the sides of his shoes, he inches his way up the sloping roof. He reaches the top of the building.

Once inside, he closes the roof door behind him and descends rapidly. He passes the door to the apartment without a glance.

As his children are born, Sean begins to write a book about his past. At first he is ebullient, possessed by gaiety. He doesn't remember much—his childhood all jumbled, without chronology. There are only isolated scenes, places, sights and sounds, moods, in no apparent order. It seems a small thing to write down these floating memories, to play with them at a distance. It seems like fun.

His children, simply by coming into the world, have got him started. As the work gets difficult, the fact of his children sustains him in some roundabout fashion. His gaiety changes to a mood of taut attentiveness, as the past he had trivialized with his amnesia begins, with tantalizing slowness, to reveal itself. He knows hard work for the first time in his life, and he is grateful. Soon he finds himself in a kind of trance; after hours of writing he will look down at a page or two with a sense of awe, because the work is better than anything he could reasonably have expected of himself. He will live this way for four years. In his mind, his writing, his ability to write at all, is connected to his children.

He develops a habit of going into their room late at night. Blue light from the street lamp outside angles through the large windows to spill on the waxed wooden floor. Philip is three, sleeping on his side, his small hand holding a rubber frog. Sean crosses the room and looks at John, aged two. Behind delicate eyelids, his eyes move in a dream. Sean goes to a spot equidistant from both beds and sits down on the floor, his legs folded. He stares at the pale-blue bars of light on the floor and listens. He hears the children breathe. When they move, he hears them move.

His mind clears. After half an hour he gets up, adjusts their blankets, and goes to bed.

At a small dinner party with his wife, in Manhattan, he becomes aware that the host and hostess are tense and abstracted. The hostess apologizes and explains that she should have cancelled the dinner. There had been a tragedy that afternoon. The young couple living directly above, on the eighth floor, had left a window open, and their baby girl had somehow pulled herself up and fallen through to her death.

"You're white as a ghost," his wife says as they leave the table. "Sean, you're trembling!"

They forgo coffee, with apologies, and go home immediately. Sean drives fast, parks by a hydrant, and runs up the stoop into the house.

"It's OK, it's OK," his wife says.

He nods to the sitter in the living room and keeps on going, up the stairs, to the children's room. They are asleep, safe in their beds.

"We have to get guardrails," he says, going to the windows, locking them. "Bars—those things—whatever they are."

"Yes. We will," his wife whispers. "OK."

"All the windows. Front and back."

"Yes, yes. Don't wake them, now."

That night he must sleep in their room.

Sean lies full length in the oversize bathtub, hot water to his chin. When he comes home from work (he writes in a small office a mile away), he almost always takes a bath. Philip and John push the door open and rush, stark naked, to the tub. They're about to be put to bed, but they've escaped. Sean doesn't move. Philip's head and shoulders are visible, while John, shorter, shows only his head. Their faces are solemn. Sean stares into their clear, intelligent eyes—so near—and waits, showing no expression, so as to draw the moment out. The sight of them is a profound refreshment.

"Do it, Daddy," Philip says.

"Do what?"

"The noise. When you wash your face."

Sean rises to a sitting position. He washes his face, and then rinses by bending forward and lifting cupped handfuls of water. He simultaneously blows and moans into the handfuls of water, making a satisfying noise. The boys smile. The drama of Daddy-in-the-bath fascinates them. They can't get enough of it.

Sean reaches out and lifts first one and then the other over the edge and into the tub. His hands encompass their small chests, and he can feel the life in them. The boys laugh and splash about, slippery as pink seals fresh from the womb. They hang on his neck and slide over his chest.

His wife comes in and pulls them up, into towels. They go off to bed. Later, in the kitchen, she says, "I wish you wouldn't do that."

"What?"

"In the bath like that."

He is nonplussed. "Good heavens. Why not?"

"It could scare them."

"But they love it!"

"It's icky."

"Icky," he repeats. He goes to the refrigerator for some ice. He can feel the anger starting, his face beginning to flush. He makes a drink and goes into the living room. The anger mounts as he hears the sounds of her working in the kitchen, making dinner. Abruptly, he puts down his drink, goes into the hall, down the stairs, and out the front door. He spends the evening in a bar frequented by writers and returns home drunk at three in the morning.

A few years later, Sean drives home from the office. He has worked late, missed dinner. He thinks about his boys, and begins to weep. He pulls off the expressway and parks in the darkness by the docks. It occurs to him that he is in bad trouble. The weeping has come out of nowhere, to overwhelm him, like some exotic physical reflex, and it could as well have happened on the street or in a restaurant. There is more pressure in him than he can control, or even gauge, his pretenses to the contrary notwithstanding. As he calms down, he allows himself to face the fact that his wife has begun to prepare for the end: a whisper of discreet activity—ice-skating with a male friend on weekends, veiled references to an unknown future, a certain coyness around the house. When he goes, he will have to leave the children. He starts the car, and the boys are in his mind; he feels the weight of their souls in his mind.

He unlocks the front door of the house, hangs his coat in the closet, and climbs the stairs. Silence. A fire burns in the fireplace in the empty living room. The kitchen and dining room are empty. He moves along the landing and starts up the second flight of stairs.

"Daddy." Philip is out of sight in his bedroom, but his voice is clear, his tone direct, as if they'd been talking together, as if they were in the middle of a conversation.

"I'm coming." Sean wonders why the house is so quiet. His wife must be up in the attic. John must be asleep.

"Why were you crying?" Philip asks.

Sean stops at the top of the stairs. His first thought is not how the boy knows but if the knowledge has scared him. He goes into the room, and there is Philip, wide awake, kneeling at the foot of his bed, an expectant look on his face.

"Hi." Sean can see the boy is not alarmed. Curious, focused, but not scared.

"Why?" the boy asks. He is six years old.

"Grownups cry sometimes, you know. It's OK."

The boy takes it in, still waiting.

"I'm not sure," Sean says. "It's complicated. Probably a lot of things. But it's OK. I feel better now."

"That's good."

Sean senses the boy's relief. He sits down on the floor. "How did you know I was crying?" He has never felt as close to another human being as he does at this moment. His tone is deliberately casual.

The boy starts to answer, his intelligent face eager, animated. Sean watches the clearly marked stages: First, Philip draws a breath to begin speaking. He is confident. Second, he searches for language to frame what he knows, but, to his puzzlement, it isn't there. Third, he realizes he can't answer the question. He stares into the middle distance for several moments. Sean waits, but he has seen it all in the boy's face.

"I don't know," the boy says. "I just knew."

"I understand."

After a while the boy gives a sudden large yawn, and gets under the covers. Sean goes downstairs.

The time arrives when he must tell the boys he is going away. Philip is eight, and John almost seven. They go up into the attic playroom. Sean masks the storm in his heart and explains that no one in the family is at fault. He has no choice—he must leave, and not live in the house anymore. As he says this, the boys glance quickly at each other—almost furtively—and Sean feels a special sharp, mysterious pang.

Twelve years later, Sean stands on line at Gate 6 in Boston's Logan Airport, waiting to check in for Eastern's 7:45 A.M. flight to Philadelphia. He is gray-haired, a bit thick around the middle, wears reading glasses low on his nose, and walks, as he moves closer to the desk, with a slight limp, from a cartilage operation on his right knee. He wears a dark suit and a trenchcoat, and carries a soft canvas overnight bag hanging from his shoulder.

"Morning." The attendant is a black woman with whom he has checked in every Monday morning for the last two years. "It's nowhere near full," she says. "I'll upgrade you now." Sean commutes weekly between the two cities, and the airline has provided him with a special card. When first class is not full, he gets a first-class seat at no extra charge. She hands him his boarding pass, and he nods as he moves away.

He sits down and waits for the boarding call. Businessmen surround him, two military officers, three stewardesses, a student carrying a book bag from the university in Boston where Sean teaches. He doesn't recognize the student but watches him abstractedly. Philip and John are that age now. Sean recalls that when his boys entered college, in

Washington and Chicago, he found himself easing up on his own students in Boston, softening his style despite himself.

The flight is called. He surrenders his ticket and moves down the enclosed walkway to the open door of the plane. The stewardess recognizes him and takes his coat. He settles down in seat 2-A and accepts a cup of coffee. The ritual is familiar and reassuring. Sean is at ease.

It had not always been thus. When he'd begun commuting, Sean was tense in the air. It had been difficult for him to look out the window without a flash of panic. In his fear, he was abnormally sensitive to the other passengers—controlling his anger at loud conversations, conscious of any intrusion, however minute, into the space allotted to him. Expansive people irritated him the most. He could not abide the way they threw their elbows about, or thoughtlessly stretched their legs, or clumsily bumped into his seat. He found himself hating the other passengers, cataloguing their faults like a miser counting money. But eventually, as he got used to flying, he began to recognize the oddness, the almost pathological oddness of his hatred, and it went away. Only on very rough flights did it recur.

Now he can gaze down through miles of empty space without fear. He wonders why, and concludes that both his former fear of heights and his present lack of fear are inexplicable. The stewardess brings breakfast, and his right knee cracks painfully as he adjusts his position.

The tenth summer of Sunday softball. The game Sean helped to organize had become a tradition in the town of Siasconset. Philip and John began as small boys and grew to young men playing the infield. Sean's second wife had taken pictures from the start, and the effect was that of time-lapse photography—a collapsed history in which the father grew older, the sons grew taller and stronger, and everyone else stayed more or less the same. Sean stood on the mound with a one-run lead, runner at first, and two outs. The batter was Gino, a power hitter. Sean threw an inside pitch and watched Gino's hips come around, watched the bat come around, and heard the snap of solid contact. The ball disappeared in speed toward third base. Sean turned to see John frozen in the air, impossibly high off the ground, feet together, toes pointed down, his legs and torso perfectly aligned in a smooth curve, a continuous brushstroke, his long arm pointing straight up at full extension, and there, nestled deep in the pocket of his glove, the white ball. Sean gave a shout of joy, dimly aware of pain in his knee, shouting all the way down as he fell, twisting, utterly happy, numb with pleasure.

The stewardess clears away his breakfast. Below, New York City slips past. He finds the old neighborhood, even the street, but he can't make out the house where his first wife still lives. They have retained good relations, and talk on the phone every month or so. His second, younger wife approves of the first, and vice versa. Sean is absurdly proud of this.

"Do you ever dream about me?" he had once asked her on the phone. "I mean, do I ever appear in your dreams?"

Slightly taken aback, she had laughed nervously. "No. What an odd question."

"I only ask because you crop up in mine. What is it—eleven years now, twelve? You still show up now and then."

The plane lands smoothly at the Philadelphia airport. Looping his bag over his shoulder, Sean is out the door, through the building, and into a cab.

"Downtown. The Drexler Building."

In his late forties, to his amazement, and through a process he never completely understood, the board of the Drexler Foundation had asked him to direct that part of their organization which gave money to the arts. It is work he enjoys.

He pays the driver and stares up at the Drexler Building—seventy stories of glass reflecting the clouds, the sky. Pushing through the big revolving door, he crosses the lobby, quickening his step as he sees the express elevator ready to leave. He jumps through just as the doors close behind him, pushes the button for the sixty-fifth floor, and turns.

For a split second he is disoriented. Philip, his older son, stands before him on the other side of the elevator, facing front. Sean's heart lurches, and then he sees that it is a young man of Philip's age, size, and general appearance, delivering a large envelope to Glidden & Glidden, on sixty-four. For a moment the two ideas overlap—the idea of Philip and the idea of the young man—and in that moment time seems to slow down. It is as if Sean had seen his son across a supernatural barrier—as if he, Sean, were a ghost haunting the elevator, able to see the real body of his son but unable to be seen by him. An almost unbearable sadness comes over him. As he emerges from this illusion, he knows full well that his son is hundreds of miles away at college, and yet he finds within himself a pressure of love for the young man so great it is all he can do to remain silent. The elevator ascends, and Sean regains control of himself. Now he can see the young man clearly—alert, a little edgy, clear blue eyes, a bit of acne.

"I hate elevators," the young man says, his eyes fixed on the lights above the door indicating the floors.

"I'm not crazy about them, but it beats walking."

The elevator approaches sixty-four, but then the lights go out, the emergency light comes on, and it stops between sixty-three and sixty-four. A slight bump downward. Sean grabs the rail involuntarily. Under the flat white light of the emergency bulb, the young man is pale, gaunt-looking.

"Oh my God," he says.

They fall a few feet more.

The young man presses himself into a corner. His eyes are wild.

Sean is utterly calm.

"Oh God oh God oh God." The young man's voice begins to rise.

"This has happened to me several times," Sean lies. "In Chicago. Once in Baltimore. The elevators have brakes, non-electrical, separate from all the other systems, which automatically engage if the elevator exceeds a certain speed." This, he thinks, is the truth. "Do you understand what I'm saying?"

The young man's mouth is open, as if to scream. He looks in all directions, finally at Sean.

"It can't fall. It can't. Do you understand?"

"Yes." The young man swallows hard.

"We're perfectly safe."

Sean watches the young man as several minutes go by. He remains silent, remembering his own panic in airplanes, his own need for privacy on those occasions, guessing that the boy feels likewise. After another minute, however, he can see the fear rising again in the young man's face. Sean shrugs off his bag and crosses the space between them.

"Listen," he says quietly, "it's going to be OK."

The young man is breathing fast. He stares at Sean without seeing him. Sean reaches out and takes the young man's head in his hands.

"I want you to listen to me, now. We are quite safe. Focus on me, now. I know we are safe, and if you focus on me *you* will know we are safe." The young man sees him now. He moves his head slightly in Sean's hands.

"Hypnotism," he whispers.

"No, for Christ's sake, it isn't hypnotism," Sean says. "We're going to stay like this until the lights come on. We're going to stay like this until the door opens, or they come get us, or whatever." Sean can feel the young man begin to calm down. He holds the boy's head gently and stares into his eyes. "Good. That's good."

After a while the lights come on, the elevator rises, and the doors open. The boy jumps out. "Come on, come on!" he cries.

Sean smiles. "This is sixty-four. I'm going to sixty-five."

The young man moves forward, but the door closes. The elevator goes up one floor, and Sean gets out.

That night, as he lies in bed waiting for sleep, Sean goes over the entire incident in his mind. He laughs aloud, remembering the young man's expression when he realized Sean was going to stay in the elevator.

Then he remembers the day in 1942 when his father showed up unexpectedly, took him home from school, washed the windows, and carried him out on the windowsill. He remembers looking down at the cracks in the sidewalk. Here, in the darkness, he can see the cracks in the sidewalk from more than forty years ago. He feels no fear—only a sense of astonishment.

E. L. DOCTOROW

Willi

One spring day I walked in the meadow behind the barn and felt rising around me the exhalations of the field, the moist sweetness of the grasses, and I imagined the earth's soul lifting to the warmth of the sun and mingling me in some divine embrace. There was such brilliant conviction in the colors of the golden hay meadow, the blue sky, that I could not help laughing. I threw myself down in the grass and spread my arms. I fell at once into a trance and yet remained incredibly aware, so that whatever I opened my eyes to look at I did not merely see but felt as its existence. Such states come naturally to children. I was reso-nant with the hum of the universe, I was made indistinguishable from the world in a great bonding of natural revelation. I saw the drowse of gnats weaving between the grasses and leaving infinitesimally fine threads of shimmering net, so highly textured that the breath of the soil below lifted it in gentle billows. Minute crawling life on the stalks of hay made colossal odyssey, journeys of a lifetime, before my eyes. Yet there was no thought of miracle, of the miracle of microscopic sentience. The scale of the universe was not pertinent, and the smallest indications of energy were in proportion to the sun, which lay like an Egyptian eye between the stalks, and lit them as it lights the earth, by halves. The hay had fallen under me so that my own body's outline was patterned on the field, the outspread legs and arms, the fingers, and I was aware of my being as the arbitrary shape of an agency that had chosen to make me in this manner as a means of communicating with me. The very idea of a head and limbs and a body was substantive only as an act of communica-tion, and I felt myself in the prickle of the flattened grass, and the sense of imposition was now enormous, a prodding, a lifting of this part of the world that was for some reason my momentary responsibility, that was giving me possession of itself. And I rose and seemed to ride on the planes of the sun, which I felt in fine striations, alternated with thin lines of the earth's moist essences. And invisibled by my revelation, I reached the barn and examined the face of it, standing with my face in the painted whiteness of its glare as a dog or a cat stands nose to a door until someone comes and lets it out. And I moved along the white barn wall, sidestepping until I came to the window which was a simple square without glass, and could only be felt by the geometrical coolness of its volume of inner air, for it was black within. And there I stood, as if in the mouth of a vacuum, and felt the insubstantial being of the sun meadow pulled past me into the barn, like a torrential implosion of light into darkness and life into death, and I myself too disintegrated in that force and was sucked like the chaff of the field in that roaring. Yet I stood where I was. And in quite normal spatial relationship with my surroundings felt the sun's quiet warmth on my back and the coolness of the cool barn on my face. And the windy universal roar in my ears had narrowed and refined itself to a recognizable frequency, that of a woman's pulsating song in the act of love, the gasp and note and gasp and note of an ecstatic score. I listened. And pressed upon by the sun, as if it were a hand on the back of my neck, I moved my face into the portal of the cool darkness, and no longer blinded by the sunlight, my eyes saw on the straw and in the dung my mother, denuded, in a pose of utmost degradation, a body, a reddened headless body, the head enshrouded in her clothing, everything turned inside out, as if blown out by the wind, all order, truth, and reason, and this defiled mama played violently upon and being made to sing her defilement. How can I describe what I felt! I felt I deserved to see this! I felt it was my triumph, but I felt monstrously betrayed. I felt drained suddenly of the strength to stand. I turned my back and slid down the wall to a sitting position under the window. My heart in my chest banged in sickened measure of her cries. I wanted to kill him, this killer of my mother who was killing her. I wanted to leap through the window and drive a pitchfork into his back, but I wanted him to be killing her, I wanted him to be killing her for me. I wanted to be him. I lay on the ground, and with my arms over my head and my hands clasped and my ankles locked, I rolled down the slope behind the barn, through the grass and the crop of hay. I flattened the hay like a mechanical cylinder of irrepressible force rolling fast and faster over rocks, through rivulets, across furrows and over hummocks of the uneven imperfect flawed irregular earth, the sun flashing in my closed eyes in diurnal emergency, as if time and the planet had gone out of control. As it has. (I am recalling these things now, a man older than my father when he died, and to whom a woman of my mother's age when all this happened is a young woman barely half my age. What an incredible achievement of fantasy is the scientific mind! We posit an empirical world, yet how can I be here at this desk in this room—and not be here? If memory is a matter of the stimulation of so many cells of the brain, the greater the stimulus—remorse, the recognition of fate—the more powerfully complete becomes the sensation of the memory until there is transfer, as in a time machine, and the memory is in the ontological sense another reality.) Papa, I see you now in the universe of your own making. I walk the polished floorboards of your house and seat myself at your dining table. I feel the tassels of the tablecloth on the tops of my bare knees. The light of the candelabra shines on your smiling mouth of big teeth. I notice the bulge of your neck produced by your shirt collar. Your pink scalp is visible through the close-cropped German-style haircut. I see your head raised in conversation and your white plump hand of consummate gesture making its point to your wife at the other end of the table. Mama is so attentive. The candle flame burns in her eyes and I imagine the fever there, but she is quite calm and seriously engrossed by what you say. Her long neck, very white, is hung with a thin chain from which depends on the darkness of her modest dress a cream-colored cameo, the carved profile of another fine lady of another time. In her neck a soft slow pulse beats. Her small hands are folded and the bones of her wrists emerge from the touch of lace at her cuffs. She is smiling at you in your loving proprietorship, proud of you, pleased to be yours, and the mistress of this house, and the mother of this boy. Of my tutor across the table from me who idly twirls the stem of his wineglass and glances at her, she is barely aware. Her eyes are for her husband. I think now Papa her feelings in this moment are sincere. I know now each moment has its belief and what we call treachery is the belief of each moment, the wish for it to be as it seems to be. It is possible in joy to love the person you have betrayed and to be refreshed in your love for him, it is entirely possible. Love renews all faces and customs and ideals and leaves the bars of the prison shining. But how could a boy know that? I ran to my room and waited for someone to follow me. Whoever dared to enter my room, I would attack—would pummel. I wanted it to be her, I wanted her to come to me, to hug me and to hold my head and kiss me on the lips as she liked to do, I wanted her to make those wordless sounds of comfort as she held me to her when I was hurt or unhappy, and when she did that I would beat her with my fists, beat her to the floor, and see her raise her hands helplessly in terror as I beat her and kicked her and jumped upon her and drove the breath from her body. But it was my tutor who, sometime later, opened the door, looked in with his hand upon the knob, smiled, said a few words, and wished me good night. He closed the door and I heard him walk up the steps to the next floor, where he had his rooms. Ledig was his name. He was a Christian. I had looked but could not find in his face any sign of smugness or leering pride or cruelty. There was nothing coarse about him, nothing that could possibly give me offense. He was barely twenty. I even thought I saw in his eyes a measure of torment. He was habitually melancholic anyway, and during my lessons his mind often wandered and he would gaze out the window and sigh. He was as much a schoolboy as his pupil. So there was every reason to refrain from judgment, to let time pass, to think, to gain understanding. Nobody knew that I knew. I had that choice. But did I? They had made my position intolerable. I was given double vision, the kind that comes with a terrible blow. I found I could not have anything to do with my kind sweet considerate mother. I found I could not bear the gentle pedagogics of my tutor. How, in that rural isolation, could I be expected to go on? I had no friends, I was not permitted to play with the children of the peasants who worked for us. I had only this trinity of Mother and Tutor and Father, this unholy trinity of deception and ignorance who had excommunicated me from my life at the age of thirteen. This of course in the calendar of traditional Judaism is the year a boy enjoys his initiation into manhood.

Meanwhile my father was going about the triumph of his life, running a farm according to the most modern principles of scientific management, astonishing his peasants and angering the other farmers in the region with his success. The sun brought up his crops, the Galician Agricultural Society gave him an award for the quality of his milk, and he lived in the state of abiding satisfaction given to individuals who are more than a match for the life they have chosen for themselves. I had incorporated him into the universe of giant powers that I, a boy, experienced in the changes of the seasons. I watched bulls bred to cows, watched mares foal, I saw life come from the egg and the multiplicative wonders of mudholes and ponds, the jell and slime of life shimmering in gravid expectation. Everywhere I looked, life sprang from something not life, insects unfolded from sacs on the surface of still waters and were instantly on the prowl for their dinner, everything that came into being knew at once what to do and did it unastonished that it was what it was, unimpressed by where it was, the great earth heaving up its bloodied newborns from every pore, every cell, bearing the variousness of itself from every conceivable substance which it contained in itself, sprouting life that flew or waved in the wind or blew from the mountains or stuck to the damp black underside of rocks, or swam or suckled or bellowed or silently separated in two. I placed my father in all of this as the owner and manager. He lived in the universe of giant powers by understanding it and making it serve him, using the daily sun for his crops and breeding what naturally bred, and so I distinguished him in it as the god-eye in the kingdom, the intelligence that brought order and gave everything its value. He loved me and I can still feel my pleasure in making him laugh, and I might not be deceiving myself when I remember the feel on my infant hand of his unshaved cheek, the winy smell of his breath, the tobacco smoke in his thick wavy hair, or his mock-wondering look of foolish happiness during our play together. He had close-set eyes, the color of dark grapes, that opened wide in our games. He would laugh like a horse and show large white teeth. He was a strong man, stocky and powerful—the constitution I inherited—and he had emerged as an orphan from the alleys of cosmopolitan Eastern

Europe, like Darwin's amphibians from the sea, and made himself a landowner, a husband and father. He was a Jew who spoke no Yiddish and a farmer raised in the city. I was not allowed to play with village children, or to go to their crude schools. We lived alone, isolated on our estate, neither Jew nor Christian, neither friend nor petitioner of the Austro-Hungarians, but in the pride of the self-constructed self. To this day I don't know how he arranged it or what hungering rage had caused him to deny every classification society imposes and to live as an anomaly, tied to no past in a world which, as it happened, had no future. But I am in awe that he did it. Because he stood up in his life he was exposed to the swords of Mongol horsemen, the scythes of peasants in revolution, the lowered brows of monstrous bankers and the cruciform gestures of prelates. His arrogance threatened him with the cumulative power of all of European history which was ready to take his head, nail it to a pole and turn him into one of the scarecrows in his fields, arms held stiffly out toward life. But when the moment came for this transformation, it was accomplished quite easily, by a word from his son. I was the agency of his downfall. Ancestry and myth, culture, history and time were ironically composed in the shape of his own boy.

I watched her for several days. I remembered the rash of passion on her flesh. I was so ashamed of myself that I felt continuously ill, and it was the vaguest, most diffuse nausea, nausea of the blood, nausea of the bone. In bed at night I found it difficult breathing, and terrible waves of fever broke over me and left me parched in my terror. I couldn't purge from my mind the image of her overthrown body, the broad whitenesses, her shoed feet in the air; I made her scream ecstatically every night in my dreams and awoke one dawn in my own sap. That was the crisis that toppled me, for in fear of being found out by the maid and by my mother, for fear of being found out by them all as the archcriminal of my dreams, I ran to him, I went to him for absolution, I confessed and put myself at his mercy. Papa, I said. He was down by the kennels mating a pair of vizslas. He used this breed to hunt. He had rigged some sort of harness for the bitch so that she could not bolt, a kind of pillory, and she was putting up a terrible howl, and though her tail showed her amenable, she moved her rump away from the proddings of the erect male, who mounted and pumped and missed and mounted again and couldn't hold her still. My father was banging the fist of his right hand into the palm of his left. Put it to her, he shouted, come on, get it in there, give it to her. Then the male had success and the mating began, the female standing there quietly now, sweat dripping off her chops, an occasional groan escaping from her. And then the male came, and stood front paws on her back, his tongue lolling as he panted, and they waited as dogs do for the detumescence. My father knelt beside them and soothed them with quiet words. Good dogs, he said, good dogs. You must guard them at this time, he said to me, they try to uncouple too early and hurt themselves. Papa, I said. He turned and looked at me over his shoulder as he knelt beside the dogs, and I saw his happiness, and the glory of him in his workpants tucked into a black pair of riding boots and his shirt open at the collar and the black hair of his chest curled as high as the throat, and I said, Papa, they should be named Mama and Ledig. And then I turned so quickly I do not even remember his face changing, I did not even wait to see if he understood me, I turned and ran, but I am sure of this—he never called after me.

There was a sun room in our house, a kind of conservatory with a glass outer wall and slanted ceiling of green glass framed in steel. It was a very luxurious appointment in that region, and it was my mother's favorite place to be. She had filled it with plants and books, and she liked to lie on a chaise in this room and read and smoke cigarettes. I found her there, as I knew I would, and I gazed at her with wonder and fascination because I knew her fate. She was incredibly beautiful, with her dark hair parted in the center and tied behind her in a bun, and her small hands, and the lovely fullness of her chin, the indications under her chin of some fattening, like a quality of indolence in her character. But a man would not dwell on this as on her neck, so lovely and slim, or the high modestly dressed bosom. A man would not want to see signs of the future. Since she was my mother it had never occurred to me how many years younger she was than my father. He had married her out of the gymnasium; she was the eldest of four daughters and her parents had been eager to settle her in prosperous welfare, which is what a mature man offers. It is not that the parents are unaware of the erotic component for the man in this sort of marriage. They are fully aware of it. Rectitude, propriety, are always very practical. I gazed at her in wonder and awe. I blushed. What? she said. She put her book down and smiled and held out her arms. What, Willi, what is it? I fell into her arms and began to sob and she held me and my tears wet the dark dress she wore. She held my head and whispered, What, Willi, what did you do to yourself, poor Willi? Then, aware that my sobs had become breathless and hysterical, she held me at arm's length—tears and snot were dribbling from me—and her eyes widened in genuine alarm.

That night I heard from the bedroom the shocking exciting sounds of her undoing. I have heard such terrible sounds of blows upon a body in Berlin after the war, Freikorps hoodlums in the streets attacking whores they had dragged from the brothel and tearing the clothes from their bodies and beating them to the cobblestones. I sat up in bed, hardly able to breathe, terrified, but feeling undeniable arousal. Give it to her, I muttered, banging my fist in my palm. Give it to her. But then I could bear it no longer and ran into their room and stood between them, lifting my screaming mother from the bed, holding her in my arms, shouting at my father to stop, to stop. But he reached around me and grabbed her hair with one hand and punched her face with the other. I was enraged, I pushed her back and jumped at him, pummeling him, shouting that I would kill him. This was in Galicia in the year 1910. All of it was to be destroyed anyway, even without me.

ANDRE DUBUS

The Fat Girl

Her name was Louise. Once when she was sixteen a boy kissed her at a barbecue; he was drunk and he jammed his tongue into her mouth and ran his hands up and down her hips. Her father kissed her often. He was thin and kind and she could see in his eyes when he looked at her the lights of love and pity.

It started when Louise was nine. You must start watching what you eat, her mother would say. I can see you have my metabolism. Louise also had her mother's pale blond hair. Her mother was slim and pretty, carried herself erectly, and ate very little. The two of them would eat bare lunches, while her older brother ate sandwiches and potato chips, and then her mother would sit smoking while Louise eyed the bread box, the pantry, the refrigerator. Wasn't that good, her mother would say. In five years you'll be in high school and if you're fat the boys won't like you; they won't ask you out. Boys were as far away as five years, and she would go to her room and wait for nearly an hour until she knew her mother was no longer thinking of her, then she would creep into the kitchen and, listening to her mother talking on the phone, or her footsteps upstairs, she would open the bread box, the pantry, the jar of peanut butter. She would put the sandwich under her shirt and go outside or to the bathroom to eat it.

Her father was a lawyer and made a lot of money and came home looking pale and happy. Martinis put color back in his face, and at dinner he talked to his wife and two children. Oh give her a potato, he would say to Louise's mother. She's a growing girl. Her mother's voice then became tense: If she has a potato she shouldn't have dessert. She should have both, her father would say, and he would reach over and touch Louise's cheek or hand or arm.

In high school she had two girlfriends and at night and on weekends they rode in a car or went to movies. In movies she was fascinated by fat actresses. She wondered why they were fat. She knew why she was fat: she was fat because she was Louise. Because God had made her that way. Because she wasn't like her friends Joan and Marjorie, who drank milk shakes after school and were all bones and tight skin. But what about those actresses, with their talents, with their broad and profound faces? Did they eat as heedlessly as Bishop Humphries and his wife who sometimes came to dinner and, as Louise's mother said, gorged between amenities? Or did they try to lose weight, did they go about hungry and angry and thinking of food? She thought of them eating lean meats and salads with friends, and then going home and building strange large sandwiches with French bread. But mostly she believed they did not go through these failures; they were fat because they chose to be. And she was certain of something else too: she could see it in their faces: they did not eat secretly. Which she did: her creeping to the kitchen when she was nine became, in high school, a ritual of deceit and pleasure. She was a furtive eater of sweets. Even her two friends did not know her secret.

Joan was thin, gangling, and flat-chested; she was attractive enough and all she needed was someone to take a second look at her face, but the school was large and there were pretty girls in every classroom and walking all the corridors, so no one ever needed to take a second look at Joan. Marjorie was thin too, an intense, heavy-smoking girl with brittle laughter. She was very intelligent, and with boys she was shy because she knew she made them uncomfortable, and because she was smarter than they were and so could not understand or could not believe the levels they lived on. She was to have a nervous breakdown before earning her Ph.D. in philosophy at the University of California, where she met and married a physicist and discovered within herself an untrammelled passion: she made love with her husband on the couch, the carpet, in the bathtub, and on the washing machine. By that time much had happened to her and she never thought of Louise. Joan would finally stop growing and begin moving with grace and confidence. In college she would have two lovers and then several more during the six years she spent in Boston before marrying a middle-aged editor who had two sons in their early teens, who drank too much, who was tenderly, boyishly grateful for her love, and whose wife had been killed while rock-climbing in New Hampshire with her lover. She would not think of Louise either, except in an earlier time, when lovers were still new to her and she was ecstatically surprised each time one of them loved her and, sometimes at night, lying in a man's arms, she would tell how in high school no one dated her, she had been thin and plain (she would still believe that: that she had been plain; it had never been true) and so had been forced into the weekend and nighttime company of a neurotic smart girl and a shy fat girl. She would say this with self-pity exaggerated by Scotch and her need to be more deeply loved by the man who held her.

She never eats, Joan and Marjorie said of Louise. They ate lunch with her at school, watched her refusing potatoes, ravioli, fried fish. Sometimes she got through the cafeteria line with only a salad. That is how they would remember her: a girl whose hapless body was destined to be fat. No one saw the sandwiches she made and took to her room when she came home from school. No one saw the store of Milky Ways, Butterfingers, Almond Joys, and Hersheys far back on her closet shelf, behind the stuffed animals of her childhood. She was not a hypocrite. When she was out of the house she truly believed she was dieting; she forgot about the candy, as a man speaking into his office dictaphone may forget the lewd photographs hidden in an old shoe in his closet. At other times, away from home, she thought of the waiting candy with near lust. One night driving home from a movie, Marjorie said: "You're lucky you don't smoke; it's in*cred*ible what I go through to hide it from my parents." Louise turned to her a smile which was elusive and mysterious; she yearned to be home in bed, eating chocolate in the dark. She did not need to smoke; she already had a vice that was insular and destructive.

She brought it with her to college. She thought she would leave it behind. A move from one place to another, a new room without the haunted closet shelf, would do for her what she could not do for herself. She packed her large dresses and went. For two weeks she was busy with registration, with shyness, with classes; then she began to feel at home. Her room was no longer like a motel. Its walls had stopped watching her, she felt they were her friends, and she gave them her secret. Away from her mother, she did not have to be as elaborate; she kept the candy in her drawer now.

The school was in Massachusetts, a girls' school. When she chose it, when she and her father and mother talked about it in the evenings, everyone so carefully avoided the word boys that sometimes the conversations seemed to be about nothing but boys. There are no boys there, the neuter words said; you will not have to contend with that. In her father's eyes were pity and encouragement; in her mother's was disappointment, and her voice was crisp. They spoke of courses, of small classes where Louise would get more attention. She imagined herself in those small classes; she saw herself as a teacher would see her, as the other girls would; she would get no attention.

The girls at the school were from wealthy families, but most of them wore the uniform of another class: blue jeans and work shirts, and many wore overalls. Louise bought some overalls, washed them until the dark blue faded, and wore them to classes. In the cafeteria she ate as she had in high school, not to lose weight nor even to sustain her lie, but because eating lightly in public had become as habitual as good manners. Everyone had to take gym, and in the locker room with the other girls, and wearing shorts on the volleyball and badminton courts, she hated her body. She liked her body most when she was unaware of it: in bed at night, as sleep gently took her out of her day, out of herself. And she liked parts of her body. She liked her brown eyes and sometimes looked at them in the mirror: they were not shallow eyes, she thought; they were indeed windows of a tender soul, a good heart. She liked her lips and nose, and her chin, finely shaped between her wide and sagging cheeks. Most of all she liked her long pale blond hair, she liked washing and drying it and lying naked on her bed, smelling of shampoo, and feeling the soft hair at her neck and shoulders and back.

Her friend at college was Carrie, who was thin and wore thick glasses and often at night she cried in Louise's room. She did not know why she was crying. She was crying, she said, because she was unhappy. She could say no more. Louise said she was unhappy too, and Carrie moved in with her. One night Carrie talked for hours, sadly and bitterly, about her parents and what they did to each other. When she finished she hugged Louise and they went to bed. Then in the dark Carrie spoke across the room: "Louise? I just wanted to tell you. One night last week I woke up and smelled chocolate. You were eating chocolate, in your bed. I wish you'd eat it in front of me, Louise, whenever you feel like it."

Stiffened in her bed, Louise could think of nothing to say. In the silence she was afraid Carrie would think she was asleep and would tell her again in the morning or tomorrow night. Finally she said okay. Then after a moment she told Carrie if she ever wanted any she could feel free to help herself; the candy was in the top drawer. Then she said thank you.

They were roommates for four years and in the summers they exchanged letters. Each fall they greeted with embraces, laughter, tears, and moved into their old room, which had been stripped and cleansed of them for the summer. Neither girl enjoyed summer. Carrie did not like being at home because her parents did not love each other. Louise lived in a small city in Louisiana. She did not like summer because she had lost touch with Joan and Marjorie; they saw each other, but it was not the same. She liked being with her father but with no one else. The flicker of disappointment in her mother's eyes at the airport was a vanguard of the army of relatives and acquaintances who awaited her: they would see her on the streets, in stores, at the country club, in her home, and in theirs; in the first moments of greeting, their eyes would tell her she was still fat Louise, who had been fat as long as they could remember, who had gone to college and returned as fat as ever. Then their eyes dismissed her, and she longed for school and Carrie, and she wrote letters to her friend. But that saddened her too. It wasn't simply that Carrie was her only friend, and when they finished college they might never see each other again. It was that her existence in the world was so divided; it had begun when she was a child creeping to the kitchen; now that division was much sharper, and her friendship with Carrie seemed disproportionate and perilous. The world she was destined to live in had nothing to do with the intimate nights in their room at school.

In the summer before their senior year, Carrie fell in love. She wrote to Louise about him, but she did not write much, and this hurt Louise more than if Carrie had shown the joy her writing tried to conceal. That fall they returned to their room; they were still close and warm, Carrie still needed Louise's ears and heart at night as she spoke of her parents and her recurring malaise whose source the two friends never discovered. But on most weekends Carrie left, and caught a bus to Boston where her boyfriend studied music. During the week she often spoke hesitantly of sex; she was not sure if she liked it. But Louise, eating candy and listening, did not know whether Carrie was telling the truth or whether, as in her letters of the past summer, Carrie was keeping from her those delights she may never experience.

Then one Sunday night when Carrie had just returned from Boston and was unpacking her overnight bag, she looked at Louise and said: "I was thinking about you. On the bus coming home tonight." Looking at Carrie's concerned, determined face, Louise prepared herself for humiliation. "I was thinking about when we graduate. What you're going to do. What's to become of you. I want you to be loved the way I love you. Louise, if I help you, *really* help you, will you go on a diet?"

Louise entered a period of her life she would remember always, the way some people remember having endured poverty. Her diet did not begin the next day. Carrie told her to eat on Monday as though it were the last day of her life. So for the first time since grammar school Louise went into a school cafeteria and ate everything she wanted. At breakfast and lunch and dinner she glanced around the table to see if the other girls noticed the food on her tray. They did not. She felt there was a lesson in this, but it lay beyond her grasp. That night in their room she ate the four remaining candy bars. During the day Carrie rented a small refrigerator, bought an electric skillet, an electric broiler, and bathroom scales.

On Tuesday morning Louise stood on the scales, and Carrie wrote in her notebook: *October 14: 184 lbs.* Then she made Louise a cup of black coffee and scrambled one egg and sat with her while she ate. When Carrie went to the dining room for breakfast, Louise walked about the campus for thirty minutes. That was part of the plan. The campus was pretty, on its lawns grew at least one of every tree native to New England, and in the warm morning sun Louise felt a new hope. At noon they met in their room, and Carrie broiled her a piece of hamburger and served it with lettuce. Then while Carrie ate in the dining room Louise walked again. She was weak with hunger and she felt queasy. During her afternoon classes she was nervous and tense, and she chewed her pencil and tapped her heels on the floor and tightened her calves. When she returned to her room late that afternoon, she was so glad to see Carrie that she embraced her; she had felt she could not bear another minute of hunger, but now with Carrie she knew she could make it at least through tonight. Then she would sleep and face tomorrow when it came. Carrie broiled her a steak and served it with lettuce. Louise studied while Carrie ate dinner, then they went for a walk.

That was her ritual and her diet for the rest of the year, Carrie alternating fish and chicken breasts with the steaks for dinner, and every day was nearly as bad as the first. In the evenings she was irritable. In all her life she had never been afflicted by ill temper and she looked upon it now as a demon which, along with hunger, was taking possession of her soul. Often she spoke sharply to Carrie. One night during their after-dinner walk Carrie talked sadly of night, of how darkness made her more aware of herself, and at night she did not know why she was in college, why she studied, why she was walking the earth with other people. They were standing on a wooden foot bridge, looking down at a dark pond. Carrie kept talking; perhaps soon she would cry. Suddenly Louise said: "I'm sick of lettuce. I never want to see a piece of lettuce for the rest of my life. I hate it. We shouldn't even buy it, it's immoral."

Carrie was quiet. Louise glanced at her, and the pain and irritation in Carrie's face soothed her. Then she was ashamed. Before she could say she was sorry, Carrie turned to her and said gently: "I know. I know how terrible it is."

Carrie did all the shopping, telling Louise she knew how hard it was to go into a supermarket when you were hungry. And Louise was always hungry. She drank diet soft drinks and started smoking Carrie's cigarettes, learned to enjoy inhaling, thought of cancer and emphysema but they were as far away as those boys her mother had talked about when she was nine. By Thanksgiving she was smoking over a pack a day and her weight in Carrie's notebook was one hundred and sixty-two pounds. Carrie was afraid if Louise went home at Thanksgiving she would lapse from the diet, so Louise spent the vacation with Carrie, in Philadelphia. Carrie wrote her family about the diet, and told Louise that she had. On the phone to Philadelphia, Louise said: "I feel like a bedwetter. When I was a little girl I had a friend who used to come spend the night and Mother would put a rubber sheet on the bed and we all pretended there wasn't a rubber sheet and that she hadn't wet the bed. Even me, and I slept with her." At Thanksgiving dinner she lowered her eyes as Carrie's father put two slices of white meat on her plate and passed it to her over the bowls of steaming food.

When she went home at Christmas she weighed a hundred and fifty-five pounds; at the airport her mother marveled. Her father laughed and hugged her and said: "But now there's less of you to love." He was troubled by her smoking but only mentioned it once; he told her she was beautiful and, as always, his eyes bathed her with love. During the long vacation her mother cooked for her as Carrie had, and Louise returned to school weighing a hundred and forty-six pounds.

Flying north on the plane she warmly recalled the surprised and congratulatory eyes of her relatives and acquaintances. She had not seen Joan or Marjorie. She thought of returning home in May, weighing the hundred and fifteen pounds which Carrie had in October set as their goal. Looking toward the stoic days ahead, she felt strong. She thought of those hungry days of fall and early winter (and now: she was hungry now: with almost a frown, almost a brusque shake of the head, she refused peanuts from the stewardess): those first weeks of the diet when she was the pawn of an irascibility which still, conditioned to her ritual as she was, could at any moment take command of her. She thought of the nights of trying to sleep while her stomach growled. She thought of her addiction to cigarettes. She thought of the people at school: not one teacher, not one girl, had spoken to her about her loss of weight, not even about her absence from meals. And without warning her spirit collapsed. She did not feel strong, she did not feel she was committed to and within reach of achieving a valuable goal. She felt that somehow she had lost more than pounds of fat; that some time during her dieting she had lost herself too. She tried to remember what it had felt like to be Louise before she had started living on meat and fish, as an unhappy adult may look sadly in the memory of childhood for lost virtues and hopes. She looked down at the earth far below, and it seemed to her that her soul, like her body aboard the plane, was in some rootless flight. She neither knew its destination nor where it had departed from; it was on some passage she could not even define.

During the next few weeks she lost weight more slowly and once for eight days Carrie's daily recording stayed at a hundred and thirty-six. Louise woke in the morning thinking of one hundred and thirty-six and then she stood on the scales and they echoed her. She became obsessed with that number, and there wasn't a day when she didn't say it aloud, and through the days and nights the number stayed in her mind, and if a teacher had spoken those digits in a classroom she would have opened her mouth to speak. What if that's me, she said to Carrie. I mean what if a hundred and thirty-six is my real weight and I just can't lose anymore. Walking hand-in-hand with her despair was a longing for this to be true, and that longing angered her and wearied her, and every day she was gloomy. On the ninth day she weighed a hundred and thirty-five and a half pounds. She was not relieved; she thought bitterly of the months ahead, the shedding of the last twenty and a half pounds.

On Easter Sunday, which she spent at Carrie's, she weighed one hundred and twenty pounds, and she ate one slice of glazed pineapple with her ham and lettuce. She did not enjoy it: she felt she was being friendly with a recalcitrant enemy who had once tried to destroy her.

Carrie's parents were laudative. She liked them and she wished they would touch sometimes, and look at each other when they spoke. She guessed they would divorce when Carrie left home, and she vowed that her own marriage would be one of affection and tenderness. She could think about that now: marriage. At school she had read in a Boston paper that this summer the cicadas would come out of their seventeen-year hibernation on Cape Cod, for a month they would mate and then die, leaving their young to burrow into the ground where they would stay for seventeen years. That's me, she had said to Carrie. Only my hibernation lasted twenty-one years.

Often her mother asked in letters and on the phone about the diet, but Louise answered vaguely. When she flew home in late May she weighed a hundred and thirteen pounds, and at the airport her mother cried and hugged her and said again and again: You're so *beautiful*. Her father blushed and bought her a martini. For days her relatives and acquaintances congratulated her, and the applause in their eyes lasted the entire summer, and she loved their eyes, and swam in the country club pool, the first time she had done this since she was a child.

She lived at home and ate the way her mother did and every morning she weighed herself on the scales in her bathroom. Her mother liked to take her shopping and buy her dresses and they put her old ones in the Goodwill box at the shopping center; Louise thought of them existing on the body of a poor woman whose cheap meals kept her fat. Louise's mother had a photographer come to the house, and Louise posed on the couch and standing beneath a live oak and sitting in a wicker lawn chair next to an azalea bush. The new clothes and the photographer made her feel she was going to another country or becoming a citizen of a new one. In the fall she took a job of no consequence, to give herself something to do.

Also in the fall a young lawyer joined her father's firm, he came one night to dinner, and they started seeing each other. He was the first man outside her family to kiss her since the barbecue when she was sixteen. Louise celebrated Thanksgiving not with rice dressing and candied sweet potatoes and mince meat and pumpkin pies, but by giving Richard her virginity which she realized, at the very last moment of its existence, she had embarked on giving him over thirteen months ago, on that Tuesday in October when Carrie had made her a cup of black coffee and scrambled one egg. She wrote this to Carrie, who replied happily by return mail. She also, through glance and smile and innuendo, tried to tell her mother too. But finally she controlled that impulse, because Richard felt guilty about making love with the daughter of his partner and friend. In the spring they married. The wedding was a large one, in the Episcopal church, and Carrie flew from Boston to be maid of honor. Her parents had recently separated and she was living with the musician and was still victim of her unpredictable malaise. It overcame her on the night before the wedding, so Louise was up with her until past three and woke next morning from a sleep so heavy that she did not want to leave it.

Richard was a lean, tall, energetic man with the metabolism of a pencil sharpener. Louise fed him everything he wanted. He liked Italian food and she got recipes from her mother and watched him eating spaghetti with the sauce she had only tasted, and ravioli and lasagna, while she ate antipasto with her chianti. He made a lot of money and borrowed more and they bought a house whose lawn sloped down to the shore of a lake; they had a wharf and a boathouse, and Richard bought a boat and they took friends waterskiing. Richard bought her a car and they spent his vacations in Mexico, Canada, the Bahamas, and in the fifth year of their marriage they went to Europe and, according to their plan, she conceived a child in Paris. On the plane back, as she looked out the window and beyond the sparkling sea and saw her country, she felt that it was waiting for her, as her home by the lake was, and her parents, and her good friends who rode in the boat and waterskied; she thought of the accumulated warmth and pelf of her marriage, and how by slimming her body she had bought into the pleasures of the nation. She felt cunning, and she smiled to herself, and took Richard's hand.

But these moments of triumph were sparse. On most days she went about her routine of leisure with a sense of certainty about herself that came merely from not thinking. But there were times, with her friends, or with Richard, or alone in the house, when she was suddenly assaulted by the feeling that she had taken the wrong train and arrived at a place where no one knew her, and where she ought not to be. Often, in bed with Richard, she talked of being fat: "I was the one who started the friendship with Carrie, I chose her, I started the conversations. When I understood that she was my friend I understood something else: I had chosen her for the same reason I'd chosen Joan and Marjorie. They were all thin. I was always thinking about what people saw when they looked at me and I didn't want them to see two fat girls. When I was alone I didn't mind being fat but then I'd have to leave the house again and then I didn't want to look like me. But at home I didn't mind except when I was getting dressed to go out of the house and when Mother looked at me. But I stopped looking at her when she looked at me. And in college I felt good with Carrie; there weren't any boys and I didn't have any other friends and so when I wasn't with Carrie I thought about her and I tried to ignore the other people around me, I tried to make them not exist. A lot of the time I could do that. It was strange, and I felt like a spy."

If Richard was bored by her repetition he pretended not to be. But she knew the story meant very little to him. She could have been telling him of a childhood illness, or wearing braces, or a broken heart at sixteen. He could not see her as she was when she was fat. She felt as though she were trying to tell a foreign lover about her life in the United States, and if only she could command the language he would know and love all of her and she would feel complete. Some of the acquaintances of her childhood were her friends now, and even they did not seem to remember her when she was fat.

Now her body was growing again, and when she put on a maternity dress for the first time she shivered with fear. Richard did not smoke and he asked her, in a voice just short of demand, to stop during her pregnancy. She did. She ate carrots and celery instead of smoking, and at cocktail parties she tried to eat nothing, but after her first drink she ate nuts and cheese and crackers and dips. Always at these parties Richard had talked with his friends and she had rarely spoken to him until they drove home. But now when he noticed her at the hors d'oeuvres table he crossed the room and, smiling, led her back to his group. His smile and his hand on her arm told her he was doing his clumsy, husbandly best to help her through a time of female mystery.

She was gaining weight but she told herself it was only the baby, and would leave with its birth. But at other times she knew quite clearly that she was losing the discipline she had fought so hard to gain during her last year with Carrie. She was hungry now as she had been in college, and she ate between meals and after dinner and tried to eat only carrots and celery, but she grew to hate them, and her desire for sweets was as vicious as it had been long ago. At home she ate bread and jam and when she shopped for groceries she bought a candy bar and ate it driving home and put the wrapper in her purse and then in the garbage can under the sink. Her cheeks had filled out, there was loose flesh under her chin, her arms and legs were plump, and her mother was concerned. So was Richard. One night when she brought pie and milk to the living room where they were watching television, he said: "You already had a piece. At dinner."

She did not look at him.

"You're gaining weight. It's not all water, either. It's fat. It'll be summertime. You'll want to get into your bathing suit."

The pie was cherry. She looked at it as her fork cut through it; she speared the piece and rubbed it in the red juice on the plate before lifting it to her mouth.

"You never used to eat pie," he said. "I just think you ought to watch it a bit. It's going to be tough on you this summer."

In her seventh month, with a delight reminiscent of climbing the stairs to Richard's apartment before they were married, she returned to her world of secret gratification. She began hiding candy in her underwear drawer. She ate it during the day and at night while Richard slept, and at breakfast she was distracted, waiting for him to leave.

She gave birth to a son, brought him home, and nursed both him and her appetites. During this time of celibacy she enjoyed her body through her son's mouth; while he suckled she stroked his small head and back. She was hiding candy but she did not conceal her other indulgences: she was smoking again but still she ate between meals, and at dinner she ate what Richard did, and coldly he watched her, he grew petulant, and when the date marking the end of their celibacy came they let it pass. Often in the afternoons her mother visited and scolded her and Louise sat looking at the baby and said nothing until finally, to end it, she promised to diet. When her mother and father came for dinners, her father kissed her and held the baby and her mother said nothing about Louise's body, and her voice was tense. Returning from work in the evenings Richard looked at a soiled plate and glass on the table beside her chair as if detecting traces of infidelity, and at every dinner they fought.

"Look at you," he said. "Lasagna, for God's sake. When are you going to start? It's not simply that you haven't lost any weight. You're gaining. I can see it. I can feel it when you get in bed. Pretty soon you'll weigh more than I do and I'll be sleeping on a trampoline."

"You never touch me anymore."

"I don't want to touch you. Why should I? Have you *looked* at yourself?"

"You're cruel," she said. "I never knew how cruel you were."

She ate, watching him. He did not look at her. Glaring at his plate, he worked with fork and knife like a hurried man at a lunch counter.

"I bet you didn't either," she said.

That night when he was asleep she took a Milky Way to the bathroom. For a while she stood eating in the dark, then she turned on the light. Chewing, she looked at herself in the mirror; she looked at her eyes and hair. Then she stood on the scales and looking at the numbers between her feet, one hundred and sixty-two, she remembered when she had weighed a hundred and thirty-six pounds for eight days. Her memory of those eight days was fond and amusing, as though she were recalling an Easter egg hunt when she was six. She stepped off the scales and pushed them under the lavatory and did not stand on them again.

It was summer and she bought loose dresses and when Richard took friends out on the boat she did not wear a bathing suit or shorts; her friends gave her mischievous glances, and Richard did not look at her. She stopped riding on the boat. She told them she wanted to stay with the baby, and she sat inside holding him until she heard the boat leave the wharf. Then she took him to the front lawn and walked with him in the shade of the trees and talked to him about the blue jays and mockingbirds and cardinals she saw on their branches. Sometimes she stopped and watched the boat out on the lake and the friend skiing behind it.

Every day Richard quarreled, and because his rage went no further than her weight and shape, she felt excluded from it, and she remained calm within layers of flesh and spirit, and watched his frustration, his impotence. He truly believed they were arguing about her weight. She knew better: she knew that beneath the argument lay the question of who Richard was. She thought of him smiling at the wheel of his boat, and long ago courting his slender girl, the daughter of his partner and friend. She thought of Carrie telling her of smelling chocolate in the dark and, after that, watching her eat it night after night. She smiled at Richard, teasing his anger.

He is angry now. He stands in the center of the living room, raging at her, and he wakes the baby. Beneath Richard's voice she hears the soft crying, feels it in her heart, and quietly she rises from her chair and goes upstairs to the child's room and takes him from the crib. She brings him to the living room and sits holding him in her lap, pressing him gently against the folds of fat at her waist. Now Richard is pleading with her. Louise thinks tenderly of Carrie broiling meat and fish in their room, and walking with her in the evenings. She wonders if Carrie still has the malaise. Perhaps she will come for a visit. In Louise's arms now the boy sleeps.

"I'll help you," Richard says. "I'll eat the same things you eat."

But his face does not approach the compassion and determination and love she had seen in Carrie's during what she now recognizes as the worst year of her life. She can remember nothing about that year except hunger, and the meals in her room. She is hungry now. When she puts the boy to bed she will get a candy bar from her room. She will eat it here, in front of Richard. This room will be hers soon. She considers the possibilities: all these rooms and the lawn where she can do whatever she wishes. She knows he will leave soon. It has been in his eyes all summer. She stands, using one hand to pull herself out of the chair. She carries the boy to his crib, feels him against her large breasts, feels that his sleeping body touches her soul. With a surge of vindication and relief she holds him. Then she kisses his forehead and places him in the crib. She goes to the bedroom and in the dark takes a bar of candy from her drawer. Slowly she descends the stairs. She knows Richard is waiting but she feels his departure so happily that, when she enters the living room, unwrapping the candy, she is surprised to see him standing there.

STANLEY ELKIN

A Poetics for Bullies

I'm Push the bully, and what I hate are new kids and sissies, dumb kids and smart, rich kids, poor kids, kids who wear glasses, talk funny, show off, patrol boys and wise guys and kids who pass pencils and water the plants—and cripples, *especially* cripples. I love nobody loved.

One time I was pushing this red-haired kid (I'm a pusher, no hitter, no belter; an aggressor of marginal violence, I hate *real* force) and his mother stuck her head out the window and shouted something I've never forgotten. *"Push,"* she yelled. *"You, Push.* You pick on him because you wish you had his red hair!" It's true; I *did* wish I had his red hair. I wish I were tall, or fat, or thin. I wish I had different eyes, different hands, a mother in the supermarket. I wish I were a man, a small boy, a girl in the choir. I'm a coveter, a Boston Blackie of the heart, casing the world. Endlessly I covet and case. (Do you know what makes me cry? The Declaration of Independence. "All men are created equal." That's beautiful.)

If you're a bully like me, you use your head. Toughness isn't enough. You beat them up, they report you. Then where are you? I'm not even particularly strong. (I used to be strong. I used to do exercise, work out, but strength implicates you, and often isn't an advantage anyway—read the judo ads. Besides, your big bullies aren't bullies at all—they're *athletes*. With them, beating guys up is a sport.) But what I lose in size and strength I make up in courage. I'm very brave. That's a lie about bullies being cowards underneath. If you're a coward, get out of the business.

I'm best at torment.

A kid has a toy bow, toy arrows. "Let Push look," I tell him.

He's suspicious, he knows me. "Go way, Push," he says, this mama-warned Push doubter.

"Come on," I say, "come on."

"No, Push. I can't. My mother said I can't."

I raise my arms, I spread them. I'm a bird—slow, powerful, easy, free. I move my head offering profile like something beaked. I'm the Thunderbird. "In the school where I go I have a teacher who teaches me magic," I say. "Arnold Salamancy, give Push your arrows. Give him one, he gives back two. Push is the God of the Neighborhood."

"Go way, Push," the kid says, uncertain.

"Right," Push says, himself again. "Right. I'll disappear. First the fingers." My fingers ball to fists. "My forearms next." They jackknife into my upper arms. "The arms." Quick as bird-blink they snap behind my back, fit between the shoulder blades like a small knapsack. (I am double-jointed, protean.) "My head," I say.

"No, Push," the kid says, terrified. I shudder and everything comes back, falls into place from the stem of self like a shaken puppet.

"The arrow, the arrow. Two where was one." He hands me an arrow.

"Trouble, trouble, double rubble!" I snap it and give back the pieces.

Well, sure. There *is* no magic. If there were I would learn it. I would find out the words, the slow turns and strange passes, drain the bloods and get the herbs, do the fires like a vestal. I would look for the main chants. *Then* I'd change things. *Push* would!

But there's only casuistical trick. Sleight-of-mouth, the bully's poetics. You know the formulas:

"Did you ever see a match burn twice?" you ask. Strike. Extinguish. Jab his flesh with the hot stub.

"Play 'Gestapo'?"

"How do you play?"

"What's your name?"

"It's Morton."

I slap him. "You're lying.

"Adam and Eve and Pinch Me Hard went down to the lake for a swim. Adam and Eve fell in. Who was left?"

"Pinch Me Hard."

I do.

Physical puns, conundrums. Push the punisher, the conundrummer! But there has to be more than tricks in a bag of tricks.

I don't know what it is. Sometimes I think *I'm* the only new kid. In a room, the school, the playground, the neighborhood, I get the feeling I've just moved in, no one knows me. You know what I like? To stand in crowds. To wait with them at the airport to meet a plane. Someone asks what time it is. I'm the first to answer. Or at the ballpark when the vendor comes. He passes the hot dog down the long row. I want *my* hands on it, too. On the dollar going up, the change coming down.

I am ingenious, I am patient.

A kid is going downtown on the elevated train. He's got his little suit on, his shoes are shined, he wears a cap. This is a kid going to the travel bureaus, the foreign tourist offices to get brochures, maps, pictures of the mountains for a unit at his school—a kid looking for extra credit. I follow him. He comes out of the Italian Tourist Information Center. His arms are full. I move from my place at the window. I follow for two blocks and bump into him as he steps from a curb. It's a *collision*— The pamphlets fall from his arms. Pretending confusion, I walk on his paper Florence. I grind my heel in his Riviera. I climb Vesuvius and sack his Rome and dance on the Isle of Capri.

The Industrial Museum is a good place to find children. I cut somebody's five- or six-year-old kid brother out of the herd of eleven- and twelve-year-olds he's come with. *"Quick,"* I say. I pull him along the corridors, up the stairs, through the halls, down to a mezzanine landing. Breathless, I pause for a minute. "I've got some gum. Do you want a stick?" He nods; I stick him. I rush him into an auditorium and abandon him. He'll be lost for hours.

I sidle up to a kid at the movies. "You smacked my brother," I tell him. "After the show—I'll be outside."

I break up games. I hold the ball above my head. "You want it? Take it."

I go into barber shops. There's a kid waiting. "I'm next," I tell him, "understand?"

One day Eugene Kraft rang my bell. Eugene is afraid of me, so he helps me. He's fifteen and there's something wrong with his saliva glands and he drools. His chin is always chapped. I tell him he has to drink a lot because he loses so much water.

"Push? Push," he says. He's wiping his chin with his tissues. "Push, there's this kid—"

"Better get a glass of water, Eugene."

"No, Push, no fooling, there's this new kid—he just moved in. You've got to see this kid."

"Eugene, get some water, please. You're drying up. I've never seen you so bad. There are deserts in you, Eugene."

"All right, Push, but then you've got to see—"

"Swallow, Eugene. You better swallow."

He gulps hard.

"Push, this is a kid and a half. Wait, you'll see."

"I'm very concerned about you, Eugene. You're dying of thirst, Eugene. Come into the kitchen with me."

I push him through the door. He's very excited. I've never seen him so excited. He talks at me over his shoulder, his mouth flooding, his teeth like the little stone pebbles at the bottom of a fishbowl. "He's got this sport coat, with a patch over the heart. Like a king, Push. No kidding."

"Be careful of the carpet, Eugene."

I turn on the taps in the sink. I mix in hot water. "Use your tissues, Eugene. Wipe your chin."

He wipes himself and puts the Kleenex in his pocket. All of Eugene's pockets bulge. He looks, with his bulging pockets, like a clumsy smuggler.

"Wipe, Eugene. Swallow, you're drowning."

"He's got this funny accent—you could die." Excited, he tamps at his mouth like a diner, a tubercular.

"Drink some water, Eugene."

"No, Push. I'm not thirsty—really."

"Don't be foolish, kid. That's because your mouth's so wet. Inside where it counts you're drying up. It stands to reason. Drink some water."

"He has this crazy haircut."

"*Drink*," I command. I shake him. *"Drink!"*

"Push, I've got no glass. Give me a glass at least."

"I can't do that, Eugene. You've got a terrible sickness. How could I let you use our drinking glasses? Lean under the tap and open your mouth."

He knows he'll have to do it, that I won't listen to him until he does. He bends into the sink.

"Push, it's *hot,*" he complains. The water splashes into his nose, it gets on his glasses and for a moment his eyes are magnified, enormous. He pulls away and scrapes his forehead on the faucet.

"Eugene, you touched it. Watch out, please. You're too close to the tap. Lean your head deeper into the sink."

"It's *hot*, Push."

"Warm water evaporates better. With your affliction you've got to evaporate fluids before they get into your glands."

He feeds again from the tap.

"Do you think that's enough?" I ask after a while.

"I do, Push, I really do," he says. He is breathless.

"Eugene," I say seriously, "I think you'd better get yourself a canteen."

"A canteen, Push?"

"That's right. Then you'll always have water when you need it. Get one of those Boy Scout models. The two-quart kind with a canvas strap."

"But you hate the Boy Scouts, Push."

"They make very good canteens, Eugene. *And wear it!* I never want to see you without it. Buy it today."

"All right, Push."

"Promise!"

"All right, Push."

"Say it out."

He made the formal promise that I like to hear.

"Well, then," I said, "let's go see this new kid of yours."

He took me to the schoolyard. "Wait," he said, "you'll see." He skipped ahead.

"Eugene," I said, calling him back. "Let's understand something. No matter what this new kid is like, nothing changes as far as you and I are concerned."

"Aw, Push," he said.

"Nothing, Eugene. I mean it. You don't get out from under me."

"Sure, Push, I know that."

There were some kids in the far corner of the yard, sitting on the ground, leaning up against the wire fence. Bats and gloves and balls lay scattered around them. (It was where they told dirty jokes. Sometimes I'd come by during the little kids' recess and tell them all about what their daddies do to their mommies.)

"There. See? Do you see him?" Eugene, despite himself, seemed hoarse.

"Be quiet," I said, checking him, freezing as a hunter might. I stared.

He was a *prince*, I tell you.

He was tall, tall, even sitting down. His long legs comfortable in expensive wool, the trousers of a boy who had been on ships, jets; who owned a horse, perhaps; who knew Latin—what *didn't* he know?— somebody made up, like a kid in a play with a beautiful mother and a handsome father; who took his breakfast from a sideboard, and picked, even at fourteen and fifteen and sixteen, his mail from a silver plate. He would have hobbies—stamps, stars, things lovely dead. He wore a sport coat, brown as wood, thick as heavy bark. The buttons were leather buds. His shoes seemed carved from horses' saddles, gunstocks. His clothes had once grown in nature. *What it must feel like inside those clothes,* I thought.

I looked at his face, his clear skin, and guessed at the bones, white as beached wood. His eyes had skies in them. His yellow hair swirled on his head like a crayoned sun.

"Look, look at him," Eugene said. "The sissy. Get him, Push."

He was talking to them and I moved closer to hear his voice. It was clear, beautiful, but faintly foreign—like herb-seasoned meat.

When he saw me he paused, smiling. He waved. The others didn't look at me.

"Hello there," he called. "Come over if you'd like. I've been telling the boys about tigers."

"Tigers," I said.

"Give him the 'match burn twice,' Push," Eugene whispered.

"Tigers, is it?" I said. "What do you know about tigers?" My voice was high.

"The 'match burn twice,' Push."

"Not so much as a Master *Tugjah.* I was telling the boys. In India there are men of high caste—*Tugjahs,* they're called. I was apprenticed to one once in the Southern Plains and might perhaps have earned my mastership, but the Red Chinese attacked the northern frontier and . . . well, let's just say I had to leave. At any rate, these *Tugjahs* are as intimate with the tiger as you are with dogs. I don't mean they keep them as pets. The relationship goes deeper. Your dog is a service animal, as is your elephant."

"Did you ever see a match burn twice?" I asked suddenly.

"Why no, can you do that? Is it a special match you use?"

"No," Eugene said, "it's an ordinary match. He used an ordinary match."

"Can you do it with one of mine, do you think?"

He took a matchbook from his pocket and handed it to me. The cover was exactly the material of his jacket, and in the center was a patch with a coat-of-arms identical to the one he wore over his heart.

I held the matchbook for a moment and then gave it back to him. "I don't feel like it," I said.

"Then some other time, perhaps," he said.

Eugene whispered to me. "His accent, Push, his funny *accent.*"

"Some other time, perhaps," I said. I am a good mimic. I can duplicate a particular kid's lisp, his stutter, a thickness in his throat. There were two or three here whom I had brought close to tears by holding up my mirror to their voices. I can parody their limps, their waddles, their girlish runs, their clumsy jumps. I can throw as they throw, catch as they catch. I looked around. "Some other time, perhaps," I said again. No one would look at me.

"I'm *so* sorry," the new one said, "we don't know each other's names. You are?"

"I'm so sorry," I said. "You are?"

He seemed puzzled. Then he looked sad, disappointed. No one said anything.

"It don't sound the same," Eugene whispered.

It was true. I sounded nothing like him. I could imitate only defects, only flaws.

A kid giggled.

"Shh," the prince said. He put one finger to his lips.

"Look at that," Eugene said under his breath. "He's a sissy."

He had begun to talk to them again. I squatted, a few feet away. I ran gravel through my loose fists, one bowl in an hourglass feeding another.

He spoke of jungles, of deserts. He told of ancient trade routes traveled by strange beasts. He described lost cities and a lake deeper than the deepest level of the sea. There was a story about a boy who had been captured by bandits. A woman in the story—it wasn't clear whether she was the boy's mother—had been tortured. His eyes clouded for a moment when he came to this part and he had to pause before continuing. Then he told how the boy escaped—it was cleverly done—and found help, mountain tribesmen riding elephants. The elephants charged the cave in which the mo—*the woman*—was still a prisoner. It might have collapsed and killed her, but one old bull rushed in and, shielding her with his body, took the weight of the crashing rocks. Your elephant is a service animal.

I let a piece of gravel rest on my thumb and flicked it in a high arc above his head. Some of the others who had seen me stared, but the boy kept on talking. Gradually I reduced the range, allowing the chunks of gravel to come closer to his head.

"You see?" Eugene said quietly. "He's afraid. He pretends not to notice."

The arcs continued to diminish. The gravel went faster, straighter. No one was listening to him now, but he kept talking.

"—of magic," he said, "what occidentals call 'a witch doctor.' There are spices that induce these effects. The *Bogdovii* was actually able to stimulate the growth of rocks with the powder. The Dutch traders were ready to go to war for the formula. Well, you can see what it could mean for the Low Countries. Without accessible quarries they've never been able to construct a permanent system of dikes. But with the *Bogdovii's* powder"—he reached out and casually caught the speeding chip as if it had been a Ping-Pong ball—"they could turn a grain of sand into a pebble, use the pebbles to grow stones, the stones to grow rocks. This little piece of gravel, for example, could be changed into a mountain." He dipped his thumb into his palm as I had and balanced the gravel on his nail. He flicked it; it rose from his nail like a missile, and climbed an impossible arc. It disappeared. "The *Bogdovii* never revealed how it was done."

I stood up. Eugene tried to follow me.

"Listen," he said, "you'll get him."

"Swallow," I told him. "Swallow, you pig!"

I have lived my life in pursuit of the vulnerable: Push the chink seeker, wheeler dealer in the flawed cement of the personality, a collapse maker. But what isn't vulnerable, *who* isn't? There is that which is unspeakable, so I speak it, that which is unthinkable, which I think. Me and the devil, we do God's dirty work, after all.

I went home after I left him. I turned once at the gate, and the boys were around him still. The useless Eugene had moved closer. *He* made room for him against the fence.

I ran into Frank the fat boy. He made a move to cross the street, but I had seen him and he went through a clumsy retractive motion. I could tell he thought I would get him for that, but I moved by, indifferent to a grossness in which I had once delighted. As I passed he seemed puzzled, a little hurt, a little—this was astonishing—guilty. *Sure* guilty. Why *not* guilty? The forgiven tire of their exemption. Nothing could ever be forgiven, and I forgave nothing. I held them to the mark. Who else cared about the fatties, about the dummies and slobs and clowns, about the gimps and squares and oafs and fools the kids with a mouthful of mush, all those shut-ins of the mind and heart, all those losers? Frank the fat boy knew, and passed me shyly. His wide, fat body, stiffened, forced jokishly martial when he saw me, had already become flaccid as he moved by, had already made one more forgiven surrender. Who cared?

The streets were full of failure. Let them. Let them be. There was a paragon, a paragon lose. What could he be doing here, why had he come, what did he want? It was impossible that this hero from India and everywhere had made his home here; that he lived, as Frank the fat boy did, as Eugene did, as *I* did, in an apartment; that he shared our lives.

In the afternoon I looked for Eugene. He was in the park, in a tree. There was a book in his lap. He leaned against the thick trunk.

"Eugene," I called up to him.

"Push, they're closed. It's Sunday, Push. The stores are closed. I looked for the canteen. The stores are closed."

"Where is he?"

"Who, Push? What do you want, Push?"

"Him. Your pal. The prince. Where? Tell me, Eugene, or I'll shake you out of that tree. I'll burn you down. I swear it. Where is he?"

"No, Push. I was wrong about that guy. He's nice. He's really nice. Push, he told me about a doctor who could help me. Leave him alone, Push."

"Where, Eugene? *Where?* I count to three."

Eugene shrugged and came down the tree.

I found the name Eugene gave me—funny, foreign—over the bell in the outer hall. The buzzer sounded and I pushed open the door. I stood inside and looked up the carpeted stairs, the angled banisters.

"What is it?" She sounded old, worried.

"The new kid," I called, "the new kid."

"It's for you," I heard her say.

"Yes?" His voice, the one I couldn't mimic. I mounted the first stair. I leaned back against the wall and looked up through the high, boxy banister poles. It was like standing inside a pipe organ.

"Yes?"

From where I stood at the bottom of the stairs I could see only a boot. He was wearing boots.

"Yes? What is it, please?"

"You," I roared. "Glass of fashion, model of form, it's me! It's Push the bully!"

I heard his soft, rapid footsteps coming down the stairs—a springy, spongy urgency. He jingled, the bastard. He had coins—I could see them: rough, golden, imperfectly round; raised, massively gowned goddesses, their heads fingered smooth, their arms gone—and keys to strange boxes, thick doors. I saw his boots. I backed away.

"I brought you down," I said.

"Be quiet, please. There's a woman who's ill. A boy who must study. There's a man with bad bones. An old man needs sleep."

"He'll get it," I said.

"We'll go outside," he said.

"No. Do you live here? What do you do? Will you be in our school? Were you telling the truth?"

"Shh. Please. You're very excited."

"Tell me your name," I said. It could be my campaign, I thought. His *name*. Scratched in new sidewalk, chalked onto walls, written on papers dropped in the street. To leave it behind like so many clues, to give him a fame, to take it away, to slash and cross out, to erase and to smear—my kid's witchcraft. "Tell me your name."

"It's John," he said softly.

"What?"

"It's John."

"John what? Come on now. I'm Push the bully."

"John Williams," he said.

"John Williams? John Williams? Only that? Only John Williams?" He smiled.

"Who's that on the bell? The name on the box?"

"She needs me," he said.

"Cut it out."

"I help her," he said.

"You stop that."

"There's a man that's in pain. A woman who's old. A husband that's worried. A wife that despairs."

"You're the bully," I said. "Your John Williams is a service animal," I yelled in the hall.

He turned and began to climb the stairs. His calves bloomed in their leather sheathing.

"Lover," I whispered to him.

He turned to me at the landing. He shook his head sadly.

"We'll see," I said.

"We'll see what we'll see," he said.

That night I painted his name on the side of the gymnasium in enormous letters. In the morning it was still there, but it wasn't what I meant. There was nothing incantatory in the huge letters, no scream, no curse. I had never traveled with a gang, there had been no together-ness in my tearing, but this thing on the wall seemed the act of vandals, the low production of ruffians. When you looked at it you were surprised they had gotten the spelling right.

Astonishingly, it was allowed to remain. And each day there was something more celebrational in the giant name, something of in-creased hospitality, lavish welcome. John Williams might have been a football hero, or someone back from the kidnapers. Finally I had to take it off myself.

Something had changed.

Eugene was not wearing his canteen. Boys didn't break off their conversations when I came up to them. One afternoon a girl winked at me. (Push has never picked on girls. *Their* submissiveness is part of their nature. They are ornamental. Don't get me wrong, please. There is a way in which they function as part of the landscape, like flowers at a funeral. They have a strange cheerfulness. They are the organizers of pep rallies and dances. They put out the Year Book. They are *born* Gray Ladies. I can't bully them.)

John Williams was in the school, but except for brief glimpses in the hall I never saw him. Teachers would repeat the things he had said in their other classes. They read from his papers. In the gym the coach described plays he had made, set shots he had taken. Everyone talked about him, and girls made a reference to him a sort of love signal. If it was suggested that he had smiled at one of them, the girl referred to would blush or, what was worse, look aloofly mysterious. *(Then* I could have punished her, *then* I could.) Gradually his name began to appear on all their notebooks, in the margins of their texts. (It annoyed me to remember what *I* had done on the wall.) The big canvas books, with their careful, elaborate J's and W's, took on the appearance of ancient, illuminated fables. It was the unconscious embroidery of love, hope's bright doodle. Even the administration was aware of him. In Assembly the principal announced that John Williams had broken all existing records in the school's charity drives. She had never seen good citizenship like his before, she said.

It's one thing to live with a bully, another to live with a hero.

Everyone's hatred I understand, no one's love; everyone's grievance, no one's content.

I saw Mimmer. Mimmer should have graduated years ago. I saw Mimmer the dummy.

"Mimmer," I said, "you're in his class."

"He's very smart."

"Yes, but is it fair? You work harder. I've seen you study. You spend hours. Nothing comes. He was born knowing. You could have used just a little of what he's got so much of. It's not fair."

"He's very clever. It's wonderful," Mimmer says.

Slud is crippled. He wears a shoe with a built-up heel to balance himself.

"Ah, Slud," I say, "I've seen him run."

"He has beaten the horses in the park. It's very beautiful," Slud says.

"He's handsome, isn't he, Clob?" Clob looks contagious, radioactive. He has severe acne. He is ugly *under* his acne.

"He gets the girls," Clob says.

He gets *everything*, I think. But I'm alone in my envy, awash in my lust. It's as if I were a prophet to the deaf. Schnooks, schnooks, I want to scream, dopes and settlers. What good does his smile do you, of what use is his good heart?

The other day I did something stupid. I went to the cafeteria and shoved a boy out of the way and took his place in the line. It was foolish, but their fear is almost all gone and I felt I had to show the flag. The boy only grinned and let me pass. Then someone called my name. It was *him*. I turned to face him. "Push," he said, "you forgot your silver." He handed it to a girl in front of him and she gave it to the boy in front of her and it came to me down the long line.

I plot, I scheme. Snares, I think; tricks and traps. I remember the old days when there were ways to snap fingers, crush toes, ways to pull noses, twist heads and punch arms—the old-timey Flinch Law I used to impose, the gone bully magic of deceit. But nothing works against him, I think. How does he know so much? He is bully-prepared, that one, not to be trusted.

It is worse and worse.

In the cafeteria he eats with Frank. "You don't want those potatoes," he tells him. "Not the ice cream, Frank. One sandwich, remember. You lost three pounds last week." The fat boy smiles his fat love at him. John Williams puts his arm around him. He seems to squeeze him thin.

He's helping Mimmer to study. He goes over his lessons and teaches him tricks, short cuts. "I want you up there with me on the Honor Roll, Mimmer."

I see him with Slud the cripple. They go to the gym. I watch from the balcony. "Let's develop those arms, my friend." They work out with weights. Slud's muscles grow, they bloom from his bones.

I lean over the rail. I shout down, "He can bend iron bars. Can he pedal a bike? Can he walk on rough ground? Can he climb up a hill? Can he wait on a line? Can he dance with a girl? Can he go up a ladder or jump from a chair?"

Beneath me the rapt Slud sits on a bench and raises a weight. He holds it at arm's length, level with his chest. He moves it high, higher. It rises above his shoulders, his throat, his head. He bends back his neck to see what he's done. If the weight should fall now it would crush his throat. I stare down into his smile.

I see Eugene in the halls. I stop him. "Eugene, what's he done for you?" I ask. He smiles—he never did this—and I see his mouth's flood. "High tide," I say with satisfaction.

Williams has introduced Clob to a girl. They have double-dated.

A week ago John Williams came to my house to see me! I wouldn't let him in.

"Please open the door, Push. I'd like to chat with you. Will you open the door? Push? I think we ought to talk. I think I can help you to be happier."

I was furious. I didn't know what to say to him. "I don't want to be happier. Go way." It was what little kids used to say to me.

"*Please* let me help you."

"*Please* let me—" I begin to echo. "Please let me alone."

"We ought to be friends, Push."

"No deals." I am choking, I am close to tears. What can I do? *What?* I want to kill him.

I double-lock the door and retreat to my room. He is still out there. I have tried to live my life so that I could keep always the lamb from my door.

He has gone too far this time; and I think sadly, I will have to fight him, I will have to fight him. Push pushed. I think sadly of the pain. Push pushed. I will have to fight him. Not to preserve honor but its opposite. Each time I see him I will have to fight him. And then I think—*of course*. And *I* smile. He has done *me* a favor. I know it at once. If he fights me he fails. He fails if he fights me. *Push pushed pushes!* It's physics! Natural law! I know he'll beat me, but I won't prepare, I won't train, I won't use the tricks I know. It's strength against strength, and my strength is as the strength of ten because my jaw is glass! *He doesn't know everything, not everything he doesn't.* And I think, I could go out now, he's still there, I could hit him in the hall, but I think, No, I want them to see, I want *them* to see!

The next day I am very excited. I look for Williams. He's not in the halls. I miss him in the cafeteria. Afterward I look for him in the school-yard where I first saw him. (He has them organized now. He teaches them games of Tibet, games of Japan; he gets them to play lost sports of the dead.) He does not disappoint me. He is there in the yard, a circle around him, a ring of the loyal.

I join the ring. I shove in between two kids I have known. They try to change places; they murmur and fret.

Williams sees me and waves. His smile could grow flowers. "Boys," he says, "boys, make room for Push. Join hands, boys." They welcome me to the circle. One takes my hand, then another. I give to each calmly.

I wait. *He doesn't know everything.*

"Boys," he begins, "today we're going to learn a game that the knights of the lords and kings of old France used to play in another century. Now you may not realize it, boys, because today when we think of a knight we think, too, of his fine charger, but the fact is that a horse was a rare animal—not a domestic European animal at all, but Asian. In western Europe, for example, there was no such thing as a workhorse until the eighth century. Your horse was just too expensive to be put to heavy labor in the fields. (This explains, incidentally, the prevalence of famine in western Europe, whereas famine is unrecorded in Asia until the ninth century, when Euro-Asian horse trading was at its height.) It wasn't only expensive to purchase a horse, it was expensive to keep one. A cheap fodder wasn't developed in Europe until the tenth century. Then, of course, when you consider the terrific risks that the warrior horse of a knight naturally had to run, you begin to appreciate how expensive it would have been for the lord—unless he was extremely rich—to provide all his knights with horses. He'd want to make pretty certain that the knights who got them knew how to handle a horse. (Only your knights errant—an elite, crack corps—ever had horses. We don't realize that most knights were *home* knights; *chevalier chez* they were called.)

"This game, then, was devised to let the lord, or king, see which of his knights had the skill and strength in his hands to control a horse. Without moving your feet, you must try to jerk the one next to you off balance. Each man has two opponents, so it's very difficult. If a man falls, or if his knee touches the ground, he's out. The circle is diminished but must close up again immediately. Now, once for practice only—"

"Just a minute," I interrupt.

"Yes, Push?"

I leave the circle and walk forward and hit him as hard as I can in the face.

He stumbles backward. The boys groan. He recovers. He rubs his jaw and smiles. I think he is going to let me hit him again. I am prepared for this. He knows what I'm up to and will use his passivity. Either way I win, but I am determined he shall hit me. I am ready to kick him, but as my foot comes up he grabs my ankle and turns it forcefully. I spin in the air. He lets go and I fall heavily on my back. I am surprised at how easy it was, but am content if they understand. I get up and am walking away, but there is an arm on my shoulder. He pulls me around roughly. He hits me.

"Sic semper tyrannus," he exults.

"Where's your other cheek?" I ask, falling backward.

"One cheek for tyrants," he shouts. He pounces on me and raises his fist and I cringe. His anger is terrific. I do not want to be hit again.

"You see? You see?" I scream at the kids, but I have lost the train of my former reasoning. I have in no way beaten him. I can't remember now what I had intended.

He lowers his fist and gets off my chest and they cheer. "Hurrah," they yell. "Hurrah, hurrah." The word seems funny to me.

He offers his hand when I try to rise. It is so difficult to know what to do. Oh God, it is so difficult to know which gesture is the right one. I don't even know this. He knows everything, and I don't even know this. I am a fool on the ground, one hand behind me pushing up, the other not yet extended but itching in the palm where the need is. It is better to give than receive, surely. It is best not to need at all.

Appalled, guessing what I miss, I rise alone.

"Friends?" he asks. He offers to shake.

"Take it, Push." It's Eugene's voice.

"Go ahead, Push." Slud limps forward.

"Push, hatred's so ugly," Clob says, his face shining.

"You'll feel better, Push," Frank, thinner, taller, urges softly.

"Push, don't be foolish," Mimmer says.

I shake my head. I may be wrong. I am probably wrong. All I know at last is what feels good. "Nothing doing," I growl. "No deals." I begin to talk, to spray my hatred at them. They are not an easy target even now. "Only your knights errant—your crack corps—ever have horses. Slud may dance and Clob may kiss but they'll never be good at it. *Push is no service animal.* No. No. Can you hear that, Williams? There isn't any magic, but your no is still stronger than your yes, and distrust is where I put my faith." I turn to the boys. "What have you settled for? Only your knights errant ever have horses. *What have you settled for?* Will Mimmer do sums in his head? How do you like your lousy hunger, thin boy? Slud, you can break me but you can't catch me. And Clob will never shave without pain, and ugly, let me tell you, is *still* in the eye of the beholder!"

John Williams mourns for me. He grieves his gamy grief. No one has everything—not even John Williams. He doesn't have *me*. He'll never have me, I think. If my life were only to deny him that, it would almost be enough. I could do his voice now if I wanted. His corruption began when he lost me. "You," I shout, rubbing it in, *"indulger,* dispense me no dispensations. Push the bully hates your heart!"

"Shut him up, somebody," Eugene cries. His saliva spills from his mouth when he speaks.

"Swallow! *Pig, swallow!"*

He rushes toward me.

Suddenly I raise my arms and he stops. I feel a power in me. I am Push, Push the bully, God of the Neighborhood, its incarnation of envy and jealousy and need. I vie, strive, emulate, compete, a contender in every event there is. I didn't make myself. I probably can't save myself, but maybe that's the only need I don't have. I taste my lack and that's how I win—by having nothing to lose. It's not good enough! I want and I want and I will die wanting, but first I will have something. This time I will have something. I say it aloud. "This time I will have something." I step toward them. The power makes me dizzy. It is enormous. They feel it. They back away. They crouch in the shadow of my outstretched wings. It isn't deceit this time but the real magic at last, the genuine thing: the cabala of my hate, of my irreconcilableness.

Logic is nothing. Desire is stronger.

I move toward Eugene. *"I will have something,"* I roar.

"Stand back," he shrieks, "I'll spit in your eye."

"I will have something. I will have terror. I will have drought. I bring the dearth. Famine's contagious. Also is thirst. Privation, privation, barrenness, void. I dry up your glands, I poison your well."

He is choking, gasping, chewing furiously. He opens his mouth. It is dry. His throat is parched. There is sand on his tongue.

They moan. They are terrified, but they move up to see. We are thrown together. Slud, Frank, Clob, Mimmer, the others, John Williams, myself. I will not be reconciled, or halve my hate. *It's* what I have, all I can keep. My bully's sour solace. It's enough, I'll make do.

I can't stand them near me. I move against them. I shove them away. I force them off. I press them, thrust them aside. *I push through.*

RICHARD FORD

Rock Springs

Edna and I had started down from Kalispell heading for Tampa–St. Pete, where I still had some friends from the old glory days who wouldn't turn me in to the police. I had managed to scrape with the law in Kalispell over several bad checks—which is a prison crime in Montana. And I knew Edna was already looking at her cards and thinking about a move, since it wasn't the first time I'd been in law scrapes in my life. She herself had already had her own troubles, losing her kids and keeping her ex-husband, Danny, from breaking in her house and stealing her things while she was at work, which was really why I had moved in in the first place, that and needing to give my little daughter, Cheryl, a better shake in things.

I don't know what was between Edna and me, just beached by the same tides when you got down to it. Though love has been built on frailer ground than that, as I well know. And when I came in the house that afternoon, I just asked her if she wanted to go to Florida with me, leave things where they sat, and she said, "Why not? My datebook's not that full."

Edna and I had been a pair eight months, more or less man and wife, some of which time I had been out of work, and some when I'd worked at the dog track as a lead-out and could help with the rent and talk sense to Danny when he came around. Danny was afraid of me because Edna had told him I'd been in prison in Florida for killing a man once, though that wasn't true. I had once been in jail in Tallahassee for stealing tires and had gotten into a fight on the county farm where a man had lost his eye. But I hadn't done the hurting, and Edna just wanted the story worse than it was so Danny wouldn't act crazy and make her have to take her kids back, since she had made a good adjustment to not having them, and I already had Cheryl with me. I'm not a violent person and would never put a man's eye out, much less kill someone. My former wife, Helen, would come all the way from Waikiki Beach to testify to that. We never had violence, and I believe in crossing the street to stay out of trouble's way. Though Danny didn't know that.

But we were half down through Wyoming, going toward I-80 and feeling good about things, when the oil light flashed on in the car I'd stolen, a sign I knew to be a bad one.

I'd gotten us a good car, a cranberry Mercedes I'd stolen out of an ophthalmologist's lot in Whitefish, Montana. I stole it because I thought it would be comfortable over a long haul, because I thought it got good mileage, which it didn't, and because I'd never had a good car in my life, just old Chevy junkers and used trucks back from when I was a kid swamping citrus with Cubans.

The car made us all high that day. I ran the windows up and down, and Edna told us some jokes and made faces. She could be lively. Her features would light up like a beacon and you could see her beauty, which wasn't ordinary. It all made me giddy, and I drove clean down to Bozeman, then straight on through the park to Jackson Hole. I rented us the bridal suite in the Quality Court in Jackson and left Cheryl and her little dog, Duke, sleeping while Edna and I drove to a rib barn and drank beer and laughed till after midnight.

It felt like a whole new beginning for us, bad memories left behind and a new horizon to build on. I got so worked up, I had a tattoo done on my arm that said FAMOUS TIMES, and Edna bought a Bailey hat with an Indian feather band and a little turquoise-and-silver bracelet for Cheryl, and we made love on the seat of the car in the Quality Court parking lot just as the sun was burning up on the Snake River, and everything seemed then like the end of the rainbow.

It was that very enthusiasm, in fact, that made me keep the car one day longer instead of driving it into the river and stealing another one, like I should have done and *had* done before.

Where the car went bad there wasn't a town in sight or even a house, just some low mountains maybe fifty miles away or maybe a hundred, a barbed-wire fence in both directions, hardpan prairie, and some hawks sailing through the evening air seizing insects.

I got out to look at the motor, and Edna got out with Cheryl and the dog to let them have a pee by the car. I checked the water and checked the oil stick, and both of them said perfect.

"What's that light mean, Earl?" Edna said. She had come and stood by the car with her hat on. She was just sizing things up for herself.

"We shouldn't run it," I said. "Something's not right in the oil."

She looked around at Cheryl and Little Duke, who were peeing on the hardtop side by side like two little dolls, then out at the mountains, which were becoming black and lost in the distance. "What're we doing?" she said. She wasn't worried yet, but she wanted to know what I was thinking about.

"Let me try it again," I said.

"That's a good idea," she said, and we all got back in the car.

When I turned the motor over, it started right away and the red light stayed off and there weren't any noises to make you think something was wrong. I let it idle a minute, then pushed the accelerator down and watched the red bulb. But there wasn't any light on, and I started wondering if maybe I hadn't dreamed I saw it, or that it had been the sun catching an angle off the window chrome, or maybe I was scared of something and didn't know it.

"What's the matter with it, Daddy?" Cheryl said from the back seat. I looked back at her, and she had on her turquoise bracelet and Edna's hat set back on the back of her head and that little black-and-white Heinz dog on her lap. She looked like a little cowgirl in the movies.

"Nothing, honey, everything's fine now," I said.

"Little Duke tinkled where I tinkled," Cheryl said, and laughed.

"You're two of a kind," Edna said, not looking back. Edna was usually good with Cheryl, but I knew she was tired now. We hadn't had much sleep, and she had a tendency to get cranky when she didn't sleep. "We oughta ditch this damn car first chance we get," she said.

"What's the first chance we got?" I said, because I knew she'd been at the map.

"Rock Springs, Wyoming," Edna said with conviction. "Thirty miles down this road."

She pointed out ahead. I had wanted all along to drive the car into Florida like a big success story. But I knew Edna was right about it, that we shouldn't take crazy chances. I had kept thinking of it as my car and not the ophthalmologist's, and that was how you got caught in these things.

"Then my belief is we ought to go to Rock Springs and negotiate ourselves a new car," I said. I wanted to stay upbeat, like everything was panning out right.

"That's a great idea," Edna said, and she leaned over and kissed me hard on the mouth.

"That's a great idea," Cheryl said. "Let's pull on out of here right now."

The sunset that day I remember as being the prettiest I'd ever seen. Just as it touched the rim of the horizon, it all at once fired the air into jewels and red sequins the precise likes of which I had never seen before and haven't seen since. The West has it all over everywhere for sunsets, even Florida, where it's supposedly flat but where half the time trees block your view.

"It's cocktail hour," Edna said after we'd driven awhile. "We ought to have a drink and celebrate something." She felt better thinking we were going to get rid of the car. It certainly had dark troubles and was something you'd want to put behind you.

Edna had out a whiskey bottle and some plastic cups and was measuring levels on the glove-box lid. She liked drinking, and she liked drinking in the car, which was something you got used to in Montana, where it wasn't against the law, where, though, strangely enough, a bad check would land you in Deer Lodge Prison for a year.

"Did I ever tell you I once had a monkey?" Edna said, setting my drink on the dashboard where I could reach it when I was ready. Her spirits were already picked up. She was like that, up one minute and down the next.

"I don't think you ever did tell me that," I said. "Where were you then?"

"Missoula," she said. She put her bare feet on the dash and rested the cup on her breasts. "I was waitressing at the Amvets. It was before I met you. Some guy came in one day with a monkey. A spider monkey. And I said, just to be joking, 'I'll roll you for that monkey.' And the guy said, 'Just one roll?' And I said, 'Sure.' He put the monkey down on the bar, picked up the cup, and rolled out boxcars. I picked it up and rolled out three fives. And I just stood there looking at the guy. He was just some guy passing through, I guess a vet. He got a strange look on his face—I'm sure not as strange as the one I had—but he looked kind of sad and surprised and satisfied all at once. I said, 'We can roll again.' But he said, 'No, I never roll twice for anything.' And he sat and drank a beer and talked about one thing and another for a while, about nuclear war and building a stronghold somewhere up in the Bitterroot, whatever it was, while I just watched the monkey, wondering what I was going to do with it when the guy left. And pretty soon he got up and said, 'Well, good-bye, Chipper'; that was this monkey's name, of course. And then he left before I could say anything. And the monkey just sat on the bar all that night. I don't know what made me think of that, Earl. Just something weird. I'm letting my mind wander."

"That's perfectly fine," I said. I took a drink of my drink. "I'd never own a monkey," I said after a minute. "They're too nasty. I'm sure Cheryl would like a monkey, though, wouldn't you, honey?" Cheryl was down on the seat playing with Little Duke. She used to talk about monkeys all the time then. "What'd you ever do with that monkey?" I said, watching the speedometer. We were having to go slower now because the red light kept fluttering on. And all I could do to keep it off was go slower. We were going maybe thirty-five and it was an hour before dark, and I was hoping Rock Springs wasn't far away.

"You really want to know?" Edna said. She gave me a quick, sharp glance, then looked back at the empty desert as if she was brooding over it.

"Sure," I said. I was still upbeat. I figured *I* could worry about breaking down and let other people be happy for a change.

"I kept it a week," she said. She seemed gloomy all of a sudden, as if she saw some aspect of the story she had never seen before. "I took it home and back and forth to the Amvets on my shifts. And it didn't cause any trouble. I fixed a chair up for it to sit on, back of the bar, and people liked it. It made a nice little clicking noise. We changed its name to Mary because the bartender figured out it was a girl. Though I was never really comfortable with it at home. I felt like it watched me too much. Then one day a guy came in, some guy who'd been in Vietnam, still wore a fatigue coat. And he said to me, 'Don't you know that a monkey'll kill you? It's got more strength in its fingers than you got in your whole body.' He said people had been killed in Vietnam by monkeys, bunches of them marauding while you were asleep, killing you and covering you with leaves. I didn't believe a word of it, except that when I got home and got undressed I started looking over across the room at Mary on her chair in the dark watching me. And I got the creeps. And after a while I got up and went out to the car, got a length of clothesline wire, and came back in and wired her to the doorknob through her little silver collar, and went back and tried to sleep. And I guess I must've slept the sleep of the dead—though I don't remember it —because when I got up I found Mary had tipped off her chair back and hanged herself on the wire line. I'd made it too short."

Edna seemed badly affected by that story and slid low in the seat so she couldn't see out over the dash. "Isn't that a shameful story, Earl, what happened to that poor little monkey?"

"I see a town! I see a town!" Cheryl started yelling from the back seat, and right up Little Duke started yapping and the whole car fell into a racket. And sure enough she had seen something I hadn't, which was Rock Springs, Wyoming, at the bottom of a long hill, a little glowing jewel in the desert with I-80 running on the north side and the black desert spread out behind.

"That's it, honey," I said. "That's where we're going. You saw it first."

"We're hungry," Cheryl said. "Little Duke wants some fish, and I want spaghetti." She put her arms around my neck and hugged me.

"Then you'll just get it," I said. "You can have anything you want. And so can Edna and so can Little Duke." I looked over at Edna, smiling, but she was staring at me with eyes that were fierce with anger. "What's wrong?" I said.

"Don't you care anything about that awful thing that happened to me?" she said. Her mouth was drawn tight, and her eyes kept cutting back at Cheryl and Little Duke, as if they had been tormenting her.

"Of course I do," I said. "I thought that was an awful thing." I didn't want her to be unhappy. We were almost there, and pretty soon we could sit down and have a real meal without thinking somebody might be hurting us.

"You want to know what I did with that monkey?" Edna said.

"Sure I do," I said.

She said, "I put her in a green garbage bag, put it in the trunk of my car, drove to the dump, and threw her in the trash." She was staring at me darkly, as if the story meant something to her that was real important but that only she could see and that the rest of the world was a fool for.

"Well, that's horrible," I said. "But I don't see what else you could do. You didn't mean to kill it. You'd have done it differently if you had. And then you had to get rid of it, and I don't know what else you could have done. Throwing it away might seem unsympathetic to somebody, probably, but not to me. Sometimes that's all you can do, and you can't worry about what somebody else thinks." I tried to smile at her, but the red light was staying on if I pushed the accelerator at all, and I was trying to gauge if we could coast to Rock Springs before the car gave out completely. I looked at Edna again. "What else can I say?" I said.

"Nothing," she said, and stared back at the dark highway. "I should've known that's what you'd think. You've got a character that leaves something out, Earl. I've known that a long time."

"And yet here you are," I said. "And you're not doing so bad. Things could be a lot worse. At least we're all together here."

"Things could always be worse," Edna said. "You could go to the electric chair tomorrow."

"That's right," I said. "And somewhere somebody probably will. Only it won't be you."

"I'm hungry," said Cheryl. "When're we gonna eat? Let's find a motel. I'm tired of this. Little Duke's tired of it too."

Where the car stopped rolling was some distance from the town, though you could see the clear outline of the interstate in the dark with Rock Springs lighting up the sky behind. You could hear the big tractors hitting the spacers in the overpass, revving up for the climb to the mountains.

I shut off the lights.

"What're we going to do now?" Edna said irritably, giving me a bitter look.

"I'm figuring it," I said. "It won't be hard, whatever it is. You won't have to do anything."

"I'd hope not," she said, and looked the other way.

Across the road and across a dry wash a hundred yards was what looked like a huge mobile-home town, with a factory or a refinery of some kind lit up behind it and in full swing. There were lights on in a lot of the mobile homes, and there were cars moving along an access road that ended near the freeway overpass a mile the other way. The lights in the mobile homes seemed friendly to me, and I knew right then what I should do.

"Get out," I said, and opened the door.

"Are we walking?" Edna said.

"We're pushing," I said.

"I'm not pushing," Edna said, and reached up and locked her door.

"All right," I said. "Then you just steer."

"You pushing us to Rock Springs, are you, Earl? It doesn't look like it's more than about three miles," Edna said.

"I'll push," Cheryl said from the back.

"No, hon. Daddy'll push. You just get out with Little Duke and move out of the way."

Edna gave me a threatening look, just as if I'd tried to hit her. But when I got out she slid into my seat and took the wheel, staring angrily ahead straight into the cottonwood scrub.

"Edna can't drive that car," Cheryl said from out in the dark. "She'll run it in the ditch."

"Yes, she can, hon. Edna can drive it as good as I can. Probably better."

"No, she can't," Cheryl said. "No, she can't either." And I thought she was about to cry, but she didn't.

I told Edna to keep the ignition on so it wouldn't lock up and to steer into the cottonwoods with the parking lights on so she could see. And when I started, she steered it straight off into the trees, and I kept pushing until we were twenty yards into the cover and the tires sank in the soft sand and nothing at all could be seen from the road.

"Now where are we?" she said, sitting at the wheel. Her voice was tired and hard, and I knew she could have put a good meal to use. She had a sweet nature, and I recognized that this wasn't her fault but mine. Only I wished she could be more hopeful.

"You stay right here, and I'll go over to that trailer park and call us a cab," I said.

"What cab?" Edna said, her mouth wrinkled as if she'd never heard anything like that in her life.

"There'll be cabs," I said, and tried to smile at her. "There's cabs everywhere."

"What're you going to tell him when he gets here? Our stolen car broke down and we need a ride to where we can steal another one? That'll be a big hit, Earl."

"I'll talk," I said. "You just listen to the radio for ten minutes and then walk on out to the shoulder like nothing was suspicious. And you and Cheryl act nice. She doesn't need to know about this car."

"Like we're not suspicious enough already, right?" Edna looked up at me out of the lighted car. "You don't think right, did you know that, Earl? You think the world's stupid and you're smart. But that's not how it is. I feel sorry for you. You might've *been* something, but things just went crazy someplace."

I had a thought about poor Danny. He was a vet and crazy as a shithouse mouse, and I was glad he wasn't in for all this. "Just get the baby in the car," I said, trying to be patient. "I'm hungry like you are."

"I'm tired of this," Edna said. "I wish I'd stayed in Montana."

"Then you can go back in the morning," I said. "I'll buy the ticket and put you on the bus. But not till then."

"Just get on with it, Earl," she said, slumping down in the seat, turning off the parking lights with one foot and the radio on with the other.

The mobile-home community was as big as any I'd ever seen. It was attached in some way to the plant that was lighted up behind it, because I could see a car once in a while leave one of the trailer streets, turn in the direction of the plant, then go slowly into it. Everything in the plant was white, and you could see that all the trailers were painted white and looked exactly alike. A deep hum came out of the plant, and I thought as I got closer that it wouldn't be a location I'd ever want to work in.

I went right to the first trailer where there was a light and knocked on the metal door. Kids' toys were lying in the gravel around the little wood steps, and I could hear talking on TV that suddenly went off. I heard a woman's voice talking, and then the door opened wide.

A large Negro woman with a wide, friendly face stood in the doorway. She smiled at me and moved forward as if she was going to come out, but she stopped at the top step. There was a little Negro boy behind her peeping out from behind her legs, watching me with his eyes half closed. The trailer had that feeling that no one else was inside, which was a feeling I knew something about.

"I'm sorry to intrude," I said. "But I've run up on a little bad luck tonight. My name's Earl Middleton."

The woman looked at me, then out into the night toward the freeway as if what I had said was something she was going to be able to see. "What kind of bad luck?" she said, looking down at me again.

"My car broke down out on the highway," I said. "I can't fix it myself, and I wondered if I could use your phone to call for help."

The woman smiled down at me knowingly. "We can't live without cars, can we?"

"That's the honest truth," I said.

"They're like our hearts," she said firmly, her face shining in the little bulb light that burned beside the door. "Where's your car situated?"

I turned and looked over into the dark, but I couldn't see anything because of where we'd put it. "It's over there," I said. "You can't see it in the dark."

"Who all's with you now," the woman said. "Have you got your wife with you?"

"She's with my little girl and our dog in the car," I said. "My daughter's asleep or I would have brought them."

"They shouldn't be left in the dark by themselves," the woman said, and frowned. "There's too much unsavoriness out there."

"The best I can do is hurry back," I said. I tried to look sincere, since everything except Cheryl being asleep and Edna being my wife was the truth. The truth is meant to serve you if you'll let it, and I wanted it to serve me. "I'll pay for the phone call," I said. "If you'll bring the phone to the door I'll call from right here."

The woman looked at me again as if she was searching for a truth of her own, then back out into the night. She was maybe in her sixties, but I couldn't say for sure. "You're not going to rob me, are you, Mr. Middleton?" she said, and smiled like it was a joke between us.

"Not tonight," I said, and smiled a genuine smile. "I'm not up to it tonight. Maybe another time."

"Then I guess Terrel and I can let you use our phone with Daddy not here, can't we, Terrel? This is my grandson, Terrel Junior, Mr. Middleton." She put her hand on the boy's head and looked down at him. "Terrel won't talk. Though if he did he'd tell you to use our phone. He's a sweet boy." She opened the screen for me to come in.

The trailer was a big one with a new rug and a new couch and a living room that expanded to give the space of a real house. Something good and sweet was cooking in the kitchen, and the trailer felt like it was somebody's comfortable new home instead of just temporary. I've lived in trailers, but they were just snail backs with one room and no toilet, and they always felt cramped and unhappy—though I've thought maybe it might've been me that was unhappy in them.

There was a big Sony TV and a lot of kids' toys scattered on the floor. I recognized a Greyhound bus I'd gotten for Cheryl. The phone was beside a new leather recliner, and the Negro woman pointed for me to sit down and call and gave me the phone book. Terrel began fingering his toys, and the woman sat on the couch while I called, watching me and smiling.

There were three listings for cab companies, all with one number different. I called the numbers in order and didn't get an answer until the last one, which answered with the name of the second company. I said I was on the highway beyond the interstate and that my wife and family needed to be taken to town and I would arrange for a tow later. While I was giving the location, I looked up the name of a tow service to tell the driver in case he asked.

When I hung up, the Negro woman was sitting looking at me with the same look she had been staring with into the dark, a look that seemed to want truth. She was smiling, though. Something pleased her and I reminded her of it.

"This is a very nice home," I said, resting in the recliner, which felt like the driver's seat of the Mercedes and where I'd have been happy to stay.

"This isn't *our* house, Mr. Middleton," the Negro woman said. "The company owns these. They give them to us for nothing. We have our own home in Rockford, Illinois."

"That's wonderful," I said.

"It's never wonderful when you have to be away from home, Mr. Middleton, though we're only here three months, and it'll be easier when Terrel Junior begins his special school. You see, our son was killed in the war, and his wife ran off without Terrel Junior. Though you shouldn't worry. He can't understand us. His little feelings can't be hurt." The woman folded her hands in her lap and smiled in a satisfied way. She was an attractive woman and had on a blue-and-pink floral dress that made her seem bigger than she could've been, just the right woman to sit on the couch she was sitting on. She was good nature's picture, and I was glad she could be, with her little brain-damaged boy, living in a place where no one in his right mind would want to live a minute. "Where do *you* live, Mr. Middleton?" she said politely, smiling in the same sympathetic way.

"My family and I are in transit," I said. "I'm an ophthalmologist, and we're moving back to Florida, where I'm from. I'm setting up practice in some little town where it's warm year-round. I haven't decided where."

"Florida's a wonderful place," the woman said. "I think Terrel would like it there."

"Could I ask you something?" I said.

"You certainly may," the woman said. Terrel had begun pushing his Greyhound across the front of the TV screen, making a scratch that no one watching the set could miss. "Stop that, Terrel Junior," the woman said quietly. But Terrel kept pushing his bus on the glass, and she smiled at me again as if we both understood something sad. Except I knew Cheryl would never damage a television set. She had respect for nice things, and I was sorry for the lady that Terrel didn't. "What did you want to ask?" the woman said.

"What goes on in that plant or whatever it is back there beyond these trailers, where all the lights are on?"

"Gold," the woman said, and smiled.

"It's what?" I said.

"Gold," the Negro woman said, smiling as she had for almost all the time I'd been there. "It's a gold mine."

"They're mining gold back there?" I said, pointing.

"Every night and every day," she said, smiling in a pleased way.

"Does your husband work there?" I said.

"He's the assayer," she said. "He controls the quality. He works three months a year, and we live the rest of the time at home in Rockford. We've waited a long time for this. We've been happy to have our grand-son, but I won't say I'll be sorry to have him go. We're ready to start our lives over." She smiled broadly at me and then at Terrel, who was giving her a spiteful look from the floor. "You said you had a daughter," the Negro woman said. "And what's her name?"

"Irma Cheryl," I said. "She's named for my mother."

"That's nice," she said. "And she's healthy, too. I can see it in your face." She looked at Terrel Junior with pity.

"I guess I'm lucky," I said.

"So far you are," she said. "But children bring you grief, the same way they bring you joy. We were unhappy for a long time before my husband got his job in the gold mine. Now, when Terrel starts to school, we'll be kids again." She stood up. "You might miss your cab, Mr. Middleton," she said, walking toward the door, though not to be forcing me out. She was too polite. "If *we* can't see your car, the cab surely won't be able to."

"That's true," I said, and got up off the recliner, where I'd been so comfortable. "None of us have eaten yet, and your food makes me know how hungry we probably all are."

"There are fine restaurants in town, and you'll find them," the Negro woman said. "I'm sorry you didn't meet my husband. He's a wonderful man. He's everything to me."

"Tell him I appreciate the phone," I said. "You saved me."

"You weren't hard to save," the woman said. "Saving people is what we were all put on earth to do. I just passed you on to whatever's coming to you."

"Let's hope it's good," I said, stepping back into the dark.

"I'll be hoping, Mr. Middleton. Terrel and I will both be hoping."

I waved to her as I walked out into the darkness toward the car where it was hidden in the night.

The cab had already arrived when I got there. I could see its little red and green roof lights all the way across the dry wash, and it made me worry that Edna was already saying something to get us in trouble, something about the car or where we'd come from, something that would cast suspicion on us. I thought, then, how I never planned things well enough. There was always a gap between my plan and what happened, and I only responded to things as they came along and hoped I wouldn't get in trouble. I was an offender in the law's eyes. But I always *thought* differently, as if I weren't an offender and had no intention of being one, which was the truth. But as I read on a napkin once, between the idea and the act a whole kingdom lies. And I had a hard time with my acts, which were oftentimes offender's acts, and my ideas, which were as good as the gold they mined there where the bright lights were blazing.

"We're waiting for you, Daddy," Cheryl said when I crossed the road. "The taxicab's already here."

"I see, hon," I said, and gave Cheryl a big hug. The cabdriver was sitting in the driver's seat having a smoke with the lights on inside. Edna was leaning against the back of the cab between the taillights, wearing her Bailey hat. "What'd you tell him?" I said when I got close.

"Nothin'," she said. "What's there to tell?"

"Did he see the car?"

She glanced over in the direction of the trees where we had hid the Mercedes. Nothing was visible in the darkness, though I could hear Little Duke combing around in the underbrush tracking something, his little collar tinkling. "Where're we going?" she said. "I'm so hungry I could pass out."

"Edna's in a terrible mood," Cheryl said. "She already snapped at me."

"We're tired, honey," I said. "So try to be nicer."

"She's never nice," Cheryl said.

"Run go get Little Duke," I said. "And hurry back."

"I guess *my* questions come last here, right?" Edna said.

I put my arm around her. "That's not true," I said.

"Did you find somebody over there in the trailers you'd rather stay with? You were gone long enough."

"That's not a thing to say," I said. "I was just trying to make things look right, so we don't get put in jail."

"So *you* don't, you mean," Edna said and laughed a little laugh I didn't like hearing.

"That's right. So I don't," I said. "I'd be the one in Dutch." I stared out at the big, lighted assemblage of white buildings and white lights beyond the trailer community, plumes of white smoke escaping up into the heartless Wyoming sky, the whole company of buildings looking like some unbelievable castle, humming away in a distorted dream. "You know what all those buildings are there?" I said to Edna, who hadn't moved and who didn't really seem to care if she ever moved anymore ever.

"No. But I can't say it matters, 'cause it isn't a motel and it isn't a restaurant," she said.

"It's a gold mine," I said, staring at the gold mine, which, I knew now from walking to the trailer, was a greater distance from us than it seemed, though it seemed huge and near, up against the cold sky. I thought there should've been a wall around it with guards instead of just the lights and no fence. It seemed as if anyone could go in and take what they wanted, just the way I had gone up to that woman's trailer and used the telephone, though that obviously wasn't true.

Edna began to laugh then. Not the mean laugh I didn't like, but a laugh that had something caring behind it, a full laugh that enjoyed a joke, a laugh she was laughing the first time I laid eyes on her, in Missoula in the Eastgate bar in 1979, a laugh we used to laugh together when Cheryl was still with her mother and I was working steady at the track and not stealing cars or passing bogus checks to merchants. A better time all around. And for some reason it made me laugh just hearing her, and we both stood there behind the cab in the dark, laughing at the gold mine in the desert, me with my arm around her and Cheryl out rustling up Little Duke and the cabdriver smoking in the cab and our stolen Mercedes-Benz, which I'd had such hopes for in Florida, stuck up to its axle in sand, where I'd never get to see it again.

"I always wondered what a gold mine would look like when I saw it," Edna said, still laughing, wiping a tear from her eye.

"Me too," I said. "I was always curious about it."

"We're a couple of fools, ain't we, Earl?" she said, unable to quit laughing completely. "We're two of a kind."

"It might be a good sign, though," I said.

"How could it be?" she said. "It's not our gold mine. There aren't any drive-up windows." She was still laughing.

"We've seen it," I said, pointing. "That's it right there. It may mean we're getting closer. Some people never see it at all."

"In a pig's eye, Earl," she said. "You and me see it in a pig's eye."

And she turned and got into the cab to go.

The cabdriver didn't ask anything about our car or where it was, to mean he'd noticed something queer. All of which made me feel like we had made a clean break from the car and couldn't be connected with it until it was too late, if ever. The driver told us a lot about Rock Springs while he drove, that because of the gold mine a lot of people had moved there in just six months, people from all over, including New York, and that most of them lived out in the trailers. Prostitutes from New York City, who he called "B-girls," had come into town, he said, on the prosperity tide, and Cadillacs with New York plates cruised the little streets every night, full of Negroes with big hats who ran the women. He told us that everybody who got in his cab now wanted to know where the women were, and when he got our call he almost didn't come because some of the trailers were brothels operated by the mine for engineers and computer people away from home. He said he got tired of running back and forth out there just for vile business. He said that *60 Minutes* had even done a program about Rock Springs and that a blowup had resulted in Cheyenne, though nothing could be done unless the prosperity left town. "It's prosperity's fruit," the driver said. "I'd rather be poor, which is lucky for me."

He said all the motels were sky-high, but since we were a family he could show us a nice one that was affordable. But I told him we wanted a first-rate place where they took animals, and the money didn't matter because we had had a hard day and wanted to finish on a high note. I also knew that it was in the little nowhere places that the police look for you and find you. People I'd known were always being arrested in cheap hotels and tourist courts with names you'd never heard of before. Never in Holiday Inns or Travelodges.

I asked him to drive us to the middle of town and back out again so Cheryl could see the train station, and while we were there I saw a pink Cadillac with New York plates and a TV aerial being driven slowly by a Negro in a big hat down a narrow street where there were just bars and a Chinese restaurant. It was an odd sight, nothing you could ever expect.

"There's your pure criminal element," the cabdriver said, and seemed sad. "I'm sorry for people like you to see a thing like that. We've got a nice town here, but there're some that want to ruin it for everybody. There used to be a way to deal with trash and criminals, but those days are gone forever."

"You said it," Edna said.

"You shouldn't let it get *you* down," I said to the cabdriver. "There's more of you than them. And there always will be. You're the best advertisement this town has. I know Cheryl will remember you and not *that* man, won't you, honey?" But Cheryl was asleep by then, holding Little Duke in her arms on the taxi seat.

The driver took us to the Ramada Inn on the interstate, not far from where we'd broken down. I had a small pain of regret as we drove under the Ramada awning that we hadn't driven up in a cranberry-colored Mercedes but instead in a beat-up old Chrysler taxi driven by an old man full of complaints. Though I knew it was for the best. We were better off without that car, better, really, in any other car but that one, where the signs had turned bad.

I registered under another name and paid for the room in cash so there wouldn't be any questions. On the line where it said "Representing" I wrote "ophthalmologist" and put "M.D." after the name. It had a nice look to it, even though it wasn't my name.

When we got to the room, which was in the back where I'd asked for it, I put Cheryl on one of the beds and Little Duke beside her so they'd sleep. She'd missed dinner, but it only meant she'd be hungry in the morning, when she could have anything she wanted. A few missed meals don't make a kid bad. I'd missed a lot of them myself and haven't turned out completely bad.

"Let's have some fried chicken," I said to Edna when she came out of the bathroom. "They have good fried chicken at the Ramadas, and I noticed the buffet was still up. Cheryl can stay right here, where it's safe, till we're back."

"I guess I'm not hungry anymore," Edna said. She stood at the window staring out into the dark. I could see out the window past her some yellowish foggy glow in the sky. For a moment I thought it was the gold mine out in the distance lighting the night, though it was only the interstate.

"We could order up," I said. "Whatever you want. There's a menu on the phone book. You could just have a salad."

"You go ahead," she said. "I've lost my hungry spirit." She sat on the bed beside Cheryl and Little Duke and looked at them in a sweet way and put her hand on Cheryl's cheek just as if she'd had a fever. "Sweet little girl," she said. "Everybody loves you."

"What do you want to do?" I said. "I'd like to eat. Maybe *I'll* order up some chicken."

"Why don't you do that?" she said. "It's your favorite." And she smiled at me from the bed.

I sat on the other bed and dialed room service. I asked for chicken, garden salad, potato, and a roll, plus a piece of hot apple pie and ice tea. I realized I hadn't eaten all day. When I put down the phone I saw that Edna was watching me, not in a hateful way or a loving way, just in a way that seemed to say she didn't understand something and was going to ask me about it.

"When did watching me get so entertaining?" I said, and smiled at her. I was trying to be friendly. I knew how tired she must be. It was after nine o'clock.

"I was just thinking how much I hated being in a motel without a car that was mine to drive. Isn't that funny? I started feeling like that last night when that purple car wasn't mine. That purple car just gave me the willies, I guess, Earl."

"One of those cars *outside* is yours," I said. "Just stand right there and pick it out."

"I know," she said. "But that's different, isn't it?" She reached and got her blue Bailey hat, put it on her head, and set it way back like Dale Evans. She looked sweet. "I used to like to go to motels, you know," she said. "There's something secret about them and free—I was never paying, of course. But you felt safe from everything and free to do what you wanted because you'd made the decision to be there and paid that price, and all the rest was the good part. Fucking and everything, you know." She smiled at me in a good-natured way.

"Isn't that the way this is?" I said. I was sitting on the bed, watching her, not knowing what to expect her to say next.

"I don't guess it is, Earl," she said, and stared out the window. "I'm thirty-two and I'm going to have to give up on motels. I can't keep that fantasy going anymore."

"Don't you like this place?" I said, and looked around at the room. I appreciated the modern paintings and the lowboy bureau and the big TV. It seemed like a plenty nice enough place to me, considering where we'd been already.

"No, I don't," Edna said with real conviction. "There's no use in my getting mad at you about it. It isn't your fault. You do the best you can for everybody. But every trip teaches you something. And I've learned I need to give up on motels before some bad thing happens to me. I'm sorry."

"What does that mean?" I said, because I really didn't know what she had in mind to do, though I should've guessed.

"I guess I'll take that ticket you mentioned," she said, and got up and faced the window. "Tomorrow's soon enough. We haven't got a car to take me anyhow."

"Well, that's a fine thing," I said, sitting on the bed, feeling like I was in a shock. I wanted to say something to her, to argue with her, but I couldn't think what to say that seemed right. I didn't want to be mad at her, but it made me mad.

"You've got a right to be mad at me, Earl," she said, "but I don't think you can really blame me." She turned around and faced me and sat on the windowsill, her hands on her knees. Someone knocked on the door. I just yelled for them to set the tray down and put it on the bill.

"I guess I *do* blame you," I said. I was angry. I thought about how I could have disappeared into that trailer community and hadn't, had come back to keep things going, had tried to take control of things for everybody when they looked bad.

"Don't. I wish you wouldn't," Edna said, and smiled at me like she wanted me to hug her. "Anybody ought to have their choice in things if they can. Don't you believe that, Earl? Here I am out here in the desert where I don't know anything, in a stolen car, in a motel room under an assumed name, with no money of my own, a kid that's not mine, and the law after me. And I have a choice to get out of all of it by getting on a bus. What would you do? I know exactly what you'd do."

"You think you do," I said. But I didn't want to get into an argument about it and tell her all I could've done and didn't do. Because it wouldn't have done any good. When you get to the point of arguing, you're past the point of changing anybody's mind, even though it's supposed to be the other way, and maybe for some classes of people it is, just never mine.

Edna smiled at me and came across the room and put her arms around me where I was sitting on the bed. Cheryl rolled over and looked at us and smiled, then closed her eyes, and the room was quiet. I was beginning to think of Rock Springs in a way I knew I would always think of it, a lowdown city full of crimes and whores and disappointments, a place where a woman left me, instead of a place where I got things on the straight track once and for all, a place I saw a gold mine.

"Eat your chicken, Earl," Edna said. "Then we can go to bed. I'm tired, but I'd like to make love to you anyway. None of this is a matter of not loving you, you know that."

*   *   *

Sometime late in the night, after Edna was asleep, I got up and walked outside into the parking lot. It could've been anytime because there was still the light from the interstate frosting the low sky and the big red Ramada sign humming motionlessly in the night and no light at all in the east to indicate it might be morning. The lot was full of cars all nosed in, most of them with suitcases strapped to their roofs and their trunks weighed down with belongings the people were taking someplace, to a new home or a vacation resort in the mountains. I had laid in bed a long time after Edna was asleep, watching the Atlanta Braves on cable television, trying to get my mind off how I'd feel when I saw that bus pull away the next day, and how I'd feel when I turned around and there stood Cheryl and Little Duke and no one to see about them but me alone, and that the first thing I had to do was get hold of some automobile and get the plates switched, then get them some breakfast and get us all on the road to Florida, all in the space of probably two hours, since that Mercedes would certainly look less hid in the daytime than the night, and word travels fast. I've always taken care of Cheryl myself as long as I've had her with me. None of the women ever did; most of them didn't even seem to like her, though they took care of me in a way so that I could take care of her. And I knew that once Edna left, all that was going to get harder. Though what I wanted most to do was not think about it just for a little while, try to let my mind go limp so it could be strong for the rest of what there was. I thought that the difference between a successful life and an unsuccessful one, between me at that moment and all the people who owned the cars that were nosed into their proper places in the lot, maybe between me and that woman out in the trailers by the gold mine, was how well you were able to put things like this out of your mind and not be bothered by them, and maybe, too, by how many troubles like this one you had to face in a lifetime. Through luck or design they had all faced fewer troubles, and by their own characters, they forgot them faster. And that's what I wanted for me. Fewer troubles, fewer memories of trouble.

I walked over to a car, a Pontiac with Ohio tags, one of the ones with bundles and suitcases strapped to the top and a lot more in the trunk, by the way it was riding. I looked inside the driver's window. There were maps and paperback books and sunglasses and the little plastic holders for cans that hang on the window wells. And in the back there were kids' toys and some pillows and a cat box with a cat sitting in it staring up at me like I was the face of the moon. It all looked familiar to me, the very same things I would have in my car if I had a car. Nothing seemed surprising, nothing different. Though I had a funny sensation at that moment and turned and looked up at the windows along the back of the Ramada Inn. All were dark except two. Mine and another one. And I wondered, because it seemed funny, what would you think a man was doing if you saw him in the middle of the night looking in the windows of cars in the parking lot of the Ramada Inn? Would you think he was trying to get his head cleared? Would you think he was trying to get ready for a day when trouble would come down on him? Would you think his girlfriend was leaving him? Would you think he had a daughter? Would you think he was anybody like you?

TESS GALLAGHER

The Lover of Horses

They say my great-grandfather was a gypsy, but the most popular explanation for his behavior was that he was a drunk. How else could the women have kept up the scourge of his memory all these years, had they not had the usual malady of our family to blame? Probably he was both, a gypsy and a drunk.

Still, I have reason to believe the gypsy in him had more to do with the turn his life took than his drinking. I used to argue with my mother about this, even though most of the information I have about my great-grandfather came from my mother, who got it from her mother. A drunk, I kept telling her, would have had no initiative. He simply would have gone down with his failures and have had nothing to show for it. But my great-grandfather had eleven children, surely a sign of industry, and he was a lover of horses. He had so many horses he was what people called "horse poor."

I did not learn, until I traveled to where my family originated at Collenamore in the West of Ireland, that my great-grandfather had most likely been a "whisperer," a breed of men among the gypsies who were said to possess the power of talking sense into horses. These men had no fear of even the most malicious and dangerous horses. In fact, they would often take the wild animal into a closed stall in order to perform their skills.

Whether a certain intimacy was needed or whether the whisperers simply wanted to protect their secret conversations with horses is not known. One thing was certain—that such men gained power over horses by whispering. What they whispered no one knew. But the effectiveness of their methods was renowned, and anyone for counties around who had an unruly horse could send for a whisperer and be sure that the horse would take to heart whatever was said and reform his behavior from that day forth.

By all accounts, my great-grandfather was like a huge stallion himself, and when he went into a field where a herd of horses was grazing, the horses would suddenly lift their heads and call to him. Then his bearded mouth would move, and though he was making sounds that could have been words, which no horse would have had reason to understand, the horses would want to hear; and one by one they would move toward him across the open space of the field. He could turn his back and walk down the road, and they would follow him. He was probably drunk, my mother said, because he was swaying and mumbling all the while. Sometimes he would stop dead-still in the road and the horses would press up against him and raise and lower their heads as he moved his lips. But because these things were only seen from a distance, and because they have eroded in the telling, it is now impossible to know whether my great-grandfather said anything of importance to the horses. Or even if it was his whispering that had brought about their good behavior. Nor was it clear when he left them in some barnyard as suddenly as he'd come to them, whether they had arrived at some new understanding of the difficult and complex relationship between men and horses.

Only the aberrations of my great-grandfather's relationship with horses have survived—as when he would bathe in the river with his favorite horse or when, as my grandmother told my mother, he insisted on conceiving his ninth child in the stall of a bay mare named Redwing. Not until I was grown and going through the family Bible, did I discover that my grandmother had been this ninth child, and so must have known something about the matter.

These oddities in behavior lead me to believe that when my great-grandfather, at the age of fifty-two, abandoned his wife and family to join a circus that was passing through the area, it was not simply drunken bravado, nor even the understandable wish to escape family obligations. I believe the gypsy in him finally got the upper hand, and it led to such a remarkable happening that no one in the family has so far been willing to admit it: not the obvious transgression—that he had run away to join the circus—but that he was in all likelihood a man who had been stolen by a horse.

This is not an easy view to sustain in the society we live in. But I have not come to it frivolously, and have some basis for my belief. For although I have heard the story of my great-grandfather's defection time and again since childhood, the one image that prevails in all versions is that of a dappled gray stallion that had been trained to dance a variation of the mazurka. So impressive was this animal that he mesmerized crowds with his sliding step-and-hop to the side through the complicated figures of the dance, which he performed, not in the way of Lippizaners—with other horses and their riders—but riderless and with the men of the circus company as his partners.

It is known that my great-grandfather became one of these dancers. After that he was reputed, in my mother's words, to have gone "completely to ruin." The fact that he walked from the house with only the clothes on his back, leaving behind his own beloved horses (twenty-nine of them to be exact), further supports my idea that a powerful force must have held sway over him, something more profound than the miseries of drink or the harsh imaginings of his abandoned wife.

Not even the fact that seven years later he returned and knocked on his wife's door asking to be taken back could exonerate him from what he had done, even though his wife did take him in and looked after him until he died some years later. But the detail that no one takes note of in the account is that when my great-grandfather returned, he was carrying a saddle blanket and the black plumes from the headgear of one of the circus horses. This passes by even my mother as simply a sign of the ridiculousness of my great-grandfather's plight—for after all, he was homeless and heading for old age as a "good for nothing drunk" and "a fool for horses."

No one has bothered to conjecture what these curious emblems, saddle blanket and plumes, must have meant to my great-grandfather. But he hung them over the foot of his bed—"like a fool" my mother said. And sometimes when he got very drunk he would take up the blanket and, wrapping it like a shawl over his shoulders, he would grasp the plumes. Then he would dance the mazurka. He did not dance in the living room, but took himself out into the field, where the horses stood at attention and watched as if suddenly experiencing the smell of the sea or a change of wind in the valley. "Drunks don't care what they do," my mother would say as she finished her story about my great-grandfather. "Talking to a drunk is like talking to a stump."

Ever since my great-grandfather's outbreaks of gypsy-necessity, members of my family have been stolen by things—by mad ambitions, by musical instruments, by otherwise harmless pursuits ranging from mushroom hunting to childbearing or, as was my father's case, by the more easily recognized and popular obsession with card playing. To some extent, I still think it was failure of imagination in this respect that brought about his diminished prospects in the life of our family.

But even my mother had been powerless against the attraction of a man so convincingly driven. When she met him at a birthday dance held at the country house of one of her young friends, she asked him what he did for his living. My father pointed to a deck of cards in his shirt pocket and said, "I play cards." But love is such as it is, and although my mother was otherwise a deadly practical woman, it seemed she could fall in love with no man but my father.

So it is possible that the propensity to be stolen is somewhat contagious when ordinary people come into contact with people such as my father. Though my mother loved him at the time of the marriage, she soon began to behave as if she had been stolen from a more fruitful and upright life that she was always imagining might have been hers.

My father's card playing was accompanied, to no one's surprise, by bouts of drinking. The only thing that may have saved our family from a life of poverty was the fact that my father seldom gambled with money. Such were his charm and powers of persuasion that he was able to convince other players to accept his notes on everything from the fish he intended to catch next season to the sale of his daughter's hair.

I know about this last wager because I remember the day he came to me with a pair of scissors and said it was time to cut my hair. Two snips and it was done. But what I cannot forget is the way he wept onto the backs of his hands and held the braids together like a broken noose from which a life had suddenly slipped. I was thirteen at the time and my hair had never been cut. It was his pride and joy that I had such hair. But for me it was only a burdensome difference between me and my classmates, so I was glad to be rid of it. What anyone else could have wanted with my long, shiny braids is still a mystery to me.

When my father was seventy-three he fell ill and the doctors gave him only a few weeks to live. My father was convinced that his illness had come on him because he'd hit a particularly bad losing streak at cards. He had lost heavily the previous month, and items of value, mostly belonging to my mother, had disappeared from the house. He developed the strange idea that if he could win at cards he could cheat the prediction of the doctors and live at least into his eighties.

By this time I had moved away from home and made a life for myself in an attempt to follow the reasonable dictates of my mother, who had counseled her children severely against all manner of rash ambition and foolhardiness. Her entreaties were leveled especially in my direction since I had shown a suspect enthusiasm for a certain pony when I was around the age of five. And it is true I felt I had lost a dear friend when my mother saw to it that the neighbors who owned this pony moved it to pasture elsewhere.

But there were other signs that I might wander off into unpredictable pursuits. The most telling of these was that I refused to speak aloud to anyone until the age of eleven. I whispered everything, as if my mind were a repository of secrets that could only be divulged in this intimate manner. If anyone asked me a question, I was always polite about answering, but I had to do it by putting my mouth near the head of my inquisitor and using only my breath and lips to make my reply.

My teachers put my whispering down to shyness and made special accommodations for me. When it came time for recitations I would accompany the teacher into the cloakroom and there whisper to her the memorized verses or the speech I was to have prepared. God knows, I might have continued on like this into the present if my mother hadn't plotted with some neighborhood boys to put burrs in my long hair. She knew by other signs that I had a terrible temper, and she was counting on that to deliver me into the world where people shouted and railed at one another and talked in an audible fashion about things both common and sacred.

When the boys shut me into a shed, according to plan, there was nothing for me to do but to cry out for help and to curse them in a torrent of words I had only heard used by adults. When my mother heard this she rejoiced, thinking that at last she had broken the treacherous hold of the past over me—of my great-grandfather's gypsy blood and the fear that against all her efforts I might be stolen away, as she had been, and as my father had, by some as yet unforseen predilection. Had I not already experienced the consequences of such a life in our household, I doubt she would have been successful, but the advantages of an ordinary existence among people of a less volatile nature had begun to appeal to me.

It was strange, then, that after all the care my mother had taken for me in this regard, when my father's illness came on him, my mother brought her appeal to me. "Can you do something?" she wrote, in her cramped, left-handed scrawl. "He's been drinking and playing cards for three days and nights. I am at my wit's end. Come home at once."

Somehow I knew this was a message addressed to the very part of me that most baffled and frightened my mother—the part that belonged exclusively to my father and his family's inexplicable manias.

When I arrived home my father was not there.

"He's at the tavern. In the back room," my mother said. "He hasn't eaten for days. And if he's slept, he hasn't done it here."

I made up a strong broth, and as I poured the steaming liquid into a Thermos I heard myself utter syllables and other vestiges of language that I could not reproduce if I wanted to. "What do you mean by that?" my mother demanded, as if a demon had leapt out of me. "What did you say?" I didn't—I couldn't—answer her. But suddenly I felt that an unsuspected network of sympathies and distant connections had begun to reveal itself to me in my father's behalf.

There is a saying that when lovers have need of moonlight, it is there. So it seemed, as I made my way through the deserted town toward the tavern and card room, that all nature had been given notice of my father's predicament, and that the response I was waiting for would not be far off.

But when I arrived at the tavern and had talked my way past the barman and into the card room itself, I saw that my father had an enormous pile of blue chips at his elbow. Several players had fallen out to watch, heavy-lidded and smoking their cigarettes like weary gangsters. Others were slumped on folding chairs near the coffee urn with its empty "Pay Here" Styrofoam cup.

My father's cap was pushed to the back of his head so that his forehead shone in the dim light, and he grinned over his cigarette at me with the

serious preoccupation of a child who has no intention of obeying anyone. And why should he, I thought, as I sat down just behind him and
loosened the stopper on the Thermos. The five or six players still at the
table casually appraised my presence to see if it had tipped the scales of
their luck in an even more unfavorable direction. Then they tossed
their cards aside, drew fresh cards, or folded.

In the center of the table were more blue chips, and poking out from
my father's coat pocket I recognized the promissory slips he must have
redeemed, for he leaned to me without taking his eyes from his cards
and in a low voice said, "I'm having a hell of a good time. The time of my
life."

He was winning. His face seemed ravaged by the effort, but he was
clearly playing on a level that had carried the game far beyond the
realm of mere card playing and everyone seemed to know it. The
dealer cocked an eyebrow as I poured broth into the plastic Thermos
cup and handed it to my father who slurped from it noisily, then set it
down.

"Tell the old kettle she's got to put up with me a few more years," he
said, and lit up a fresh cigarette. His eyes as he looked at me, however,
seemed over-brilliant, as if doubt, despite all his efforts, had gained a
permanent seat at his table. I squeezed his shoulder and kissed him
hurriedly on his forehead. The men kept their eyes down and, as I
paused at the door, there was a shifting of chairs and a clearing of
throats. Just outside the room I nearly collided with the barman who
was carrying in a fresh round of beer. His heavy jowls waggled as he
recovered himself and looked hard at me over the icy bottles. Then he
disappeared into the card room with his provisions.

I took the long way home, finding pleasure in the fact that at this hour
all the stoplights had switched on to a flashing-yellow caution cycle.
Even the teenagers who usually cruised the town had gone home or to
more secluded spots. *Doubt,* I kept thinking as I drove with my father's
face before me, that's the real thief. And I knew my mother had
brought me home because of it, because she knew that once again a
member of our family was about to be stolen.

Two more days and nights I ministered to my father at the card room.
I would never stay long because I had the fear that I might spoil his luck.
But many unspoken tendernesses passed between us in those brief
appearances as he accepted the nourishment I offered, or when he
looked up and handed me his beer bottle to take a swig from—a ritual
we'd shared since my childhood.

My father continued to win—to the amazement of the local barflies
who poked their faces in and out of the card room and gave the dwindling three or four stalwarts who remained at the table a commiserating
shake of their heads. There had never been a winning streak like it in
the history of the tavern, and indeed, we heard later that the man who

owned the card room and tavern had to sell out and open a fruit stand on the edge of town as a result of my father's extraordinary good luck.

Twice during this period my mother urged the doctor to order my father home. She was sure my father would, at some fateful moment, risk the entire winnings in some mad rush toward oblivion. But his doctor spoke of a new "gaming therapy" for the terminally ill, based on my father's surge of energies in the pursuit of his gambling. Little did he know that my father was, by that stage, oblivious to even his winning, he had gone so far into exhaustion.

Luckily for my father, the hour came when, for lack of players, the game folded. Two old friends drove him home and helped him down from the pickup. They paused in the driveway, one on either side of him, letting him steady himself. When the card playing had ended there had been nothing for my father to do but to get drunk.

My mother and I watched from the window as the men steered my father toward the hydrangea bush at the side of the house where he relieved himself with perfect precision on one mammoth blossom. Then they hoisted him up the stairs and into the entryway. My mother and I took over from there.

"Give 'em hell, boys," my father shouted after the men, concluding some conversation he was having with himself.

"You betcha," the driver called back, laughing. Then he climbed with his companion into the cab of his truck and roared away.

Tied around my father's waist was a cloth sack full of bills and coins that flapped and jingled against his knees as we bore his weight between us up the next flight of stairs and into the living room. There we deposited him on the couch where he took up residence, refusing to sleep in his bed—for fear, my mother claimed, that death would know where to find him. But I preferred to think he enjoyed the rhythms of the household; from where he lay at the center of the house he could overhear all conversations that took place and add his opinions when he felt like it.

My mother was so stricken by the signs of his further decline that she did everything he asked, instead of arguing with him or simply refusing. Instead of taking his winnings straight to the bank so as not to miss a day's interest, she washed an old goldfish bowl and dumped all the money into it, most of it in twenty-dollar bills. Then she placed it on the coffee table near his head so he could run his hand through it at will, or let his visitors do the same.

"Money feels good on your elbow," he would say to them. "I played them under the table for that. Yes, sir, take a feel of that!" Then he would lean back on his pillows and tell my mother to bring his guests a shot of whiskey. "Make sure she fills my glass up," he'd say to me so that my mother was certain to overhear. And my mother, who'd never allowed a bottle of whiskey to be brought into her house before now, would look at me as if the two of us were more than any woman should have to bear.

"If you'd only brought him home from that card room," she said again and again. "Maybe it wouldn't have come to this."

This included the fact that my father had radically altered his diet. He lived only on greens. If it was green he would eat it. By my mother's reckoning, the reason for his change of diet was that if he stopped eating what he usually ate, death would think it wasn't him and go look for somebody else.

Another request my father made was asking my mother to sweep the doorway after anyone came in or went out.

"To make sure death wasn't on their heels; to make sure death didn't slip in as they left." This was my mother's reasoning. But my father didn't give any reasons. Nor did he tell us finally why he wanted all the furniture moved out of the room except for the couch where he lay. And the money, they could take that away too.

But soon his strength began to ebb, and more and more family and friends crowded into the vacant room to pass the time with him, to laugh at stories remembered from his childhood or from his nights as a young man at the country dances when he and his older brother would work all day in the cotton fields, hop a freight train to town and dance all night. Then they would have to walk home, getting there just at day-break in time to go straight to work again in the cotton fields.

"We were like bulls then," my father would say in a burst of the old vigor, then close his eyes suddenly as if he hadn't said anything at all.

As long as he spoke to us, the inevitability of his condition seemed easier to bear. But when, at the last, he simply opened his mouth for food or stared silently toward the far wall, no one knew what to do with themselves.

My own part in that uncertain time came to me accidentally. I found myself in the yard sitting on a stone bench under a little cedar tree my father loved because he liked to sit there and stare at the ocean. The tree whispered, he said. He said it had a way of knowing what your troubles were. Suddenly a craving came over me. I wanted a cigarette, even though I don't smoke, hate smoking, in fact. I was sitting where my father had sat, and to smoke seemed a part of some rightness that had begun to work its way within me. I went into the house and bummed a pack of cigarettes from my brother. For the rest of the morning I sat under the cedar tree and smoked. My thoughts drifted with its shiftings and murmurings, and it struck me what a wonderful thing nature is because it knows the value of silence, the innuendos of silence and what they could mean for a word-bound creature such as I was.

I passed the rest of the day in a trance of silences, moving from place to place, revisiting the sites I knew my father loved—the "dragon tree," a hemlock that stood at the far end of the orchard, so named for how the wind tossed its triangular head; the rose arbor where he and my mother had courted; the little marina where I sat in his fishing boat and dutifully smoked the hated cigarettes, flinging them one by one into the brackish water.

I was waiting to know what to do for him, he who would soon be a piece of useless matter of no more consequence than the cigarette butts that floated and washed against the side of his boat. I could feel some action accumulating in me through the steadiness of water raising and lowering the boat, through the sad petal-fall of roses in the arbor and the tossing of the dragon tree.

That night when I walked from the house I was full of purpose. I headed toward the little cedar tree. Without stopping to question the necessity of what I was doing, I began to break off the boughs I could reach and to pile them on the ground.

"What are you doing?" my brother's children wanted to know, crowding around me as if I might be inventing some new game for them.

"What does it look like?" I said.

"Pulling limbs off the tree," the oldest said. Then they dashed away in a pack under the orchard trees, giggling and shrieking.

As I pulled the boughs from the trunk I felt a painful permission as when two silences, tired of holding back, give over to each other some shared regret. I made my bed on the boughs and resolved to spend the night there in the yard, under the stars, with the hiss of the ocean in my ear, and the maimed cedar tree standing over me like a gift torn out of its wrappings.

My brothers, their wives and my sister had now begun their nightly vigil near my father, taking turns at staying awake. The windows were open for the breeze and I heard my mother trying to answer the question of why I was sleeping outside on the ground—"like a damned fool" I knew they wanted to add.

"She doesn't want to be here when death comes for him," my mother said, with an air of clairvoyance she had developed from a lifetime with my father. "They're too much alike," she said.

The ritual of night games played by the children went on and on long past their bedtimes. Inside the house, the kerosene lantern, saved from my father's childhood home, had been lit—another of his strange requests during the time before his silence. He liked the shadows it made and the sweet smell of the kerosene. I watched the darkness as the shapes of my brothers and sister passed near it, gigantic and misshapen where they bent or raised themselves or crossed the room.

Out on the water the wind had come up. In the orchard the children were spinning around in a circle, faster and faster until they were giddy and reeling with speed and darkness. Then they would stop, rest a moment, taking quick ecstatic breaths before plunging again into the opposite direction, swirling around and around in the circle until the excitement could rise no higher, their laughter and cries brimming over, then scattering as they flung one another by the arms or chased each other toward the house as if their lives depended on it.

I lay awake for a long while after their footsteps had died away and the car doors had slammed over the goodbyes of the children being taken home to bed and the last of the others had been bedded down in the house while the adults went on waiting.

It was important to be out there alone and close to the ground. The pungent smell of the cedar boughs was around me, rising up in the crisp night air toward the tree, whose turnings and swayings had altered, as they had to, in order to accompany the changes about to overtake my father and me. I thought of my great-grandfather bathing with his horse in the river, and of my father who had just passed through the longest period in his life without the clean feel of cards falling through his hands as he shuffled or dealt them. He was too weak now even to hold a cigarette; there was a burn mark on the hardwood floor where his last cigarette had fallen. His winnings were safely in the bank and the luck that was to have saved him had gone back to that place luck goes to when it is finished with us.

So this is what it comes to, I thought, and listened to the wind as it mixed gradually with the memory of children's voices that still seemed to rise and fall in the orchard. There was a soft crooning of syllables that was satisfying to my ears, but ultimately useless and absurd. Then it came to me that I was the author of those unwieldy sounds, and that my lips had begun to work of themselves.

In a raw pulsing of language I could not account for, I lay awake through the long night and spoke to my father as one might speak to an ocean or the wind, letting him know by that threadbare accompaniment that the vastness he was about to enter had its rhythms in me also. And that he was not forsaken. And that I was letting him go. That so far I had denied the disreputable world of dancers and drunkards, gamblers and lovers of horses to which I most surely belonged. But from that night forward I vowed to be filled with the first unsavory desire that would have me. To plunge myself into the heart of my life and be ruthlessly lost forever.

JOHN GARDNER

Redemption

One day in April—a clear, blue day when there were crocuses in bloom —Jack Hawthorne ran over and killed his brother, David. Even at the last moment he could have prevented his brother's death by slamming on the tractor brakes, easily in reach for all the shortness of his legs; but he was unable to think, or, rather, thought unclearly, and so watched it happen, as he would again and again watch it happen in his mind, with nearly undiminished intensity and clarity, all his life. The younger brother was riding, as both of them knew he should not have been, on the cultipacker, a two-ton implement lumbering behind the tractor, crushing new-plowed ground. Jack was twelve, his brother, David, seven. The scream came not from David, who never got a sound out, but from their five-year-old sister, who was riding on the fender of the tractor, looking back. When Jack turned to look, the huge iron wheels had reached his brother's pelvis. He kept driving, reacting as he would to a half-crushed farm animal, and imagining, in the same stab of thought, that perhaps his brother would survive. Blood poured from David's mouth.

Their father was nearly destroyed by it. Sometimes Jack would find him lying on the cow-barn floor, crying, unable to stand up. Dale Hawthorne, the father, was a sensitive, intelligent man, by nature a dreamer. It showed in old photographs, his smile coded, his eyes on the horizon. He loved all his children and would not consciously have been able to hate his son even if Jack had indeed been, as he thought himself, his brother's murderer. But he could not help sometimes seeming to blame his son, though consciously he blamed only his own unwisdom and—so far as his belief held firm—God. Dale Hawthorne's mind swung violently at this time, reversing itself almost hour by hour, from desperate faith to the most savage, black-hearted atheism. Every sickly calf, every sow that ate her litter, was a new, sure proof that the religion he'd followed all his life was a lie. Yet skeletons were orderly, as were, he thought, the stars. He was unable to decide, one moment full of rage at God's injustice, the next moment wracked by doubt of His existence.

Though he was not ordinarily a man who smoked, he would sometimes sit up all night now, or move restlessly, hurriedly, from room to room, chain-smoking Lucky Strikes. Or he would ride away on his huge, darkly thundering Harley-Davidson 80, trying to forget, morbidly dwelling on what he'd meant to put behind him—how David had once laughed, cake in his fists; how he'd once patched a chair with precocious skill—or Dale Hawthorne would think, for the hundredth time, about suicide, hunting in mixed fear and anger for some reason not to miss the next turn, fly off to the right of the next iron bridge onto the moonlit gray rocks and black water below—discovering, invariably, no reason but the damage his suicide would do to his wife and the children remaining.

Sometimes he would forget for a while by abandoning reason and responsibility for love affairs. Jack's father was at this time still young, still handsome, well-known for the poetry he recited at local churches or for English classes or meetings of the Grange—recited, to loud applause (he had poems of all kinds, both serious and comic), for thrashing crews, old men at the V.A. Hospital, even the tough, flint-eyed orphans at the Children's Home. He was a celebrity, in fact, as much Romantic poet-hero as his time and western New York State could afford—and beyond all that, he was now so full of pain and unassuageable guilt that women's hearts flew to him unbidden. He became, with all his soul and without cynical intent—though fleeing all law, or what he'd once thought law—a hunter of women, trading off his sorrow for the sorrows of wearied, unfulfilled country wives. At times he would be gone from the farm for days, abandoning the work to Jack and whoever was available to help—some neighbor or older cousin or one of Jack's uncles. No one complained, at least not openly. A stranger might have condemned him, but no one in the family did, certainly not Jack, not even Jack's mother, though her sorrow was increased. Dale Hawthorne had always been, before the accident, a faithful man, one of the most fair-minded, genial farmers in the country. No one asked that, changed as he was, he do more, for the moment, than survive.

As for Jack's mother, though she'd been, before the accident, a cheerful woman—one who laughed often and loved telling stories, sometimes sang anthems in bandanna and blackface before her husband recited poems—she cried now, nights, and did only as much as she had strength to do—so sapped by grief that she could barely move her arms. She comforted Jack and his sister, Phoebe—herself as well—by embracing them vehemently whenever new waves of guilt swept in, by constant reassurance and extravagant praise, frequent mention of how proud some relative would be—once, for instance, over a drawing of his sister's, "Oh, Phoebe, if only your great-aunt Lucy could see this!" Great-aunt Lucy had been famous, among the family and friends, for her paintings of families of lions. And Jack's mother forced on his sister and himself comforts more permanent: piano and, for Jack, French-horn lessons, school and church activities, above all an endless, exhausting ritual of chores. Because she had, at thirty-four, considerable strength of character—except that, these days, she was always eating—and because, also, she was a woman of strong religious faith, a woman who, in her years of church work and teaching at the high school, had made scores of close, for the most part equally religious, friends, with whom she regularly corresponded, her letters, then theirs, half filling the mailbox at the foot of the hill and cluttering every table, desk, and niche in the large old house—friends who now frequently visited or phoned— she was able to move step by step past disaster and in the end keep her family from wreck. She said very little to her children about her troubles. In fact, except for the crying behind her closed door, she kept her feelings strictly secret.

But for all his mother and her friends could do for him—for all his father's older brothers could do, or, when he was there, his father himself—the damage to young Jack Hawthorne took a long while healing. Working the farm, plowing, cultipacking, disking, dragging, he had plenty of time to think—plenty of time for the accident to replay, with the solidity of real time repeated, in his mind, his whole body flinching from the image as it came, his voice leaping up independent of him, as if a shout could perhaps drive the memory back into its cave. Maneuvering the tractor over sloping, rocky fields, dust whorling out like smoke behind him or, when he turned into the wind, falling like soot until his skin was black and his hair as thick and stiff as old clothes in an attic— the circles of foothills every day turning greener, the late-spring wind flowing endless and sweet with the smell of coming rain—he had all the time in the world to cry and swear bitterly at himself, standing up to drive, as his father often did, Jack's sore hands clamped tight to the steering wheel, his shoes unsteady on the bucking axlebeam—for stones lay everywhere, yellowed in the sunlight, a field of misshapen skulls. He'd never loved his brother, he raged out loud, never loved anyone as well as he should have. He was incapable of love, he told himself, striking the steering wheel. He was inherently bad, a spiritual defective. He was evil.

So he raged and grew increasingly ashamed of his raging, reminded by the lengthening shadows across the field of the theatricality in all he did, his most terrible sorrow mere sorrow on a stage, the very thunderclaps above—dark blue, rushing sky, birds crazily wheeling—mere opera set, proper lighting for his rant. At once he would hush himself, lower his rear end to the tractor seat, lock every muscle to the stillness of a statue, and drive on, solitary, blinded by tears; yet even now it was theater, not life—mere ghastly posturing, as in that story of his father's, how Lord Byron once tried to get Shelley's skull to make a drinking cup. Tears no longer came, though the storm went on building. Jack rode on, alone with the indifferent, murderous machinery in the widening ten-acre field.

When the storm at last hit, he'd been driven up the lane like a dog in flight, lashed by gusty rain, chased across the tracks to the tractor shed and from there to the kitchen, full of food smells from his mother's work and Phoebe's, sometimes the work of two or three friends who'd stopped by to look in on the family. Jack kept aloof, repelled by their bright, melodious chatter and absentminded humming, indignant at their pretense that all was well. "My, how you've grown!" the old friend or fellow teacher from high school would say, and to his mother, "My, what big *hands* he has, Betty!" He would glare at his little sister, Phoebe, his sole ally, already half traitor—she would bite her lips, squinting, concentrating harder on the mixing bowl and beaters; she was forever making cakes—and he would retreat as soon as possible to the evening chores.

He had always told himself stories to pass the time when driving the tractor, endlessly looping back and forth, around and around, fitting the land for spring planting. He told them to himself aloud, taking all parts in the dialogue, gesturing, making faces, discarding dignity, here where no one could see or overhear him, half a mile from the nearest house. Once all his stories had been of sexual conquest or of heroic battle with escaped convicts from the Attica Prison or kidnappers who, unbe-knownst to anyone, had built a small shack where they kept their captives, female and beautiful, in the lush, swampy woods beside the field. Now, after the accident, his subject matter changed. His fantasies came to be all of self-sacrifice, pitiful stories in which he redeemed his life by throwing it away to save others more worthwhile. To friends and officials of his fantasy, especially to heroines—a girl named Margaret, at school, or his cousin Linda—he would confess his worthlessness at pain-ful length, naming all his faults, granting himself no quarter. For a time this helped, but the lie was too obvious, the manipulation of shame to buy love, and in the end despair bled all color from his fantasies. The foulness of his nature became clearer and clearer in his mind until, like his father, he began to toy—dully but in morbid earnest now—with the idea of suicide. His chest would fill with anguish, as if he were dreaming some nightmare wide awake, or bleeding internally, and his arms and legs would grow shaky with weakness, until he had to stop and get down from the tractor and sit for a few minutes, his eyes fixed on some comforting object, for instance a dark, smooth stone.

Even from his father and his father's brothers, who sometimes helped with the chores, he kept aloof. His father and uncles were not talkative men. Except for his father's comic poems, they never told jokes, though they liked hearing them; and because they had lived there all their lives and knew every soul in the county by name, nothing much surprised them or, if it did, roused them to mention it. Their wives might gossip, filling the big kitchen with their pealing laughter or righteous indignation, but the men for the most part merely smiled or compressed their lips and shook their heads. At the G.L.F. feedstore, occasionally, eating an ice cream while they waited for their grist, they would speak of the weather or the Democrats; but in the barn, except for "Jackie, shift that milker, will you?" or "You can carry this up to the milk house now," they said nothing. They were all tall, square men with deeply cleft chins and creases on their foreheads and muscular jowls; all Presbyterians, sometimes deacons, sometimes elders; and they were all gentle-hearted, decent men who looked lost in thought, especially Jack's father, though on occasion they'd abruptly frown or mutter, or speak a few words to a cow, or a cat, or a swallow. It was natural that Jack, working with such men, should keep to himself, throwing down ensilage from the pitch-dark, sweet-ripe crater of the silo or hay bales from the mow, dumping oats in front of the cows' noses, or—taking the long-handled, blunt wooden scraper from the whitewashed wall—pushing manure into the gutters.

He felt more community with the cows than with his uncles or, when he was there, his father. Stretched out flat between the two rows of stanchions, waiting for the cows to be finished with their silage so he could drive them out to pasture, he would listen to their chewing in the dark, close barn, a sound as soothing, as infinitely restful, as waves along a shore, and would feel their surprisingly warm, scented breath, their bovine quiet, and for a while would find that his anxiety had left him. With the cows, the barn cats, the half-sleeping dog, he could forget and feel at home, feel that life was pleasant. He felt the same when walking up the long, fenced lane at the first light of sunrise—his shoes and pants legs sopping wet with dew, his ears full of birdcalls—going to bring in the herd from the upper pasture. Sometimes on the way he would step off the deep, crooked cow path to pick cherries or red raspberries, brighter than jewels in the morning light. They were sweeter then than at any other time, and as he approached, clouds of sparrows would explode into flight from the branches, whirring off to safety. The whole countryside was sweet, early in the morning—newly cultivated corn to his left; to his right, alfalfa and, beyond that, wheat. He felt at one with it all. It was what life ought to be, what he'd once believed it was.

But he could not make such feelings last. *No,* he thought bitterly on one such morning, throwing stones at the dull, indifferent cows, driving them down the lane. However he might hate himself and all his race, a cow was no better, or a field of wheat. Time and again he'd been driven half crazy, angry enough to kill, by the stupidity of cows when they'd pushed through a fence and—for all his shouting, for all the indignant barking of the dog—they could no longer locate the gap they themselves had made. And no better to be grain, smashed flat by the first rainy wind. So, fists clenched, he raged inside his mind, grinding his teeth to drive out thought, at war with the universe. He remembered his father, erect, eyes flashing, speaking Mark Antony's angry condemnation from the stage at the Grange. His father had seemed to him, that night, a creature set apart. His extended arm, pointing, was the terrible warning of a god. And now, from nowhere, the black memory of his brother's death rushed over him again, mindless and inexorable as a wind or wave, the huge cultipacker lifting—only an inch or so—as it climbed toward the shoulders, then sank on the cheek, flattening the skull—and he heard, more real than the morning, his sister's scream.

One day in August, a year and a half after the accident, they were combining oats—Jack and two neighbors and two of his cousins—when Phoebe came out, as she did every day, to bring lunch to those who worked in the field. Their father had been gone, this time, for nearly three weeks, and since he'd left at the height of the harvest season, no one was sure he would return, though as usual they kept silent about it. Jack sat alone in the shade of an elm, apart from the others. It was a habit they'd come to accept as they accepted, so far as he knew, his father's ways. Phoebe brought the basket from the shade where the others had settled to the shade here on Jack's side, farther from the bright, stubbled field.

"It's chicken," she said, and smiled, kneeling.

The basket was nearly as large as she was—Phoebe was seven—but she seemed to see nothing unreasonable in her having to lug it up the hill from the house. Her face was flushed, and drops of perspiration stood out along her hairline, but her smile was not only uncomplaining but positively cheerful. The trip to the field was an escape from housework, he understood; even so, her happiness offended him.

"Chicken," he said, and looked down glumly at his hard, tanned arms black with oat-dust. Phoebe smiled on, her mind far away, as it seemed to him, and like a child playing house she took a dishtowel from the basket, spread it on the grass, then set out wax-paper packages of chicken, rolls, celery, and salt, and finally a small plastic Thermos, army green.

She looked up at him now. "I brought you a Thermos all for yourself because you always sit alone."

He softened a little without meaning to. "Thanks," he said.

She looked down again, and for all his self-absorption he was touched, noticing that she bowed her head in the way a much older girl might do, troubled by thought, though her not quite clean, dimpled hands were a child's. He saw that there was something she wanted to say and, to forestall it, brushed flying ants from the top of the Thermos, unscrewed the cap, and poured himself iced tea. When he drank, the tea was so cold it brought a momentary pain to his forehead and made him aware once more of the grating chaff under his collar, blackening all his exposed skin, gritty around his eyes—aware, too, of the breezeless, insect-filled heat beyond the shade of the elm. Behind him, just at the rim of his hearing, one of the neighbors laughed at some remark from the younger of his cousins. Jack drained the cup, brooding on his aching muscles. Even in the shade his body felt baked dry.

"Jack," his sister said, "did you want to say grace?"

"Not really," he said, and glanced at her.

He saw that she was looking at his face in alarm, her mouth slightly opened, eyes wide, growing wider, and though he didn't know why, his heart gave a jump. "I already said it," he mumbled. "Just not out loud."

"Oh," she said, then smiled.

When everyone had finished eating she put the empty papers, the jug, and the smaller Thermos in the basket, grinned at them all and said good-bye—whatever had bothered her was forgotten as soon as that—and, leaning far over, balancing the lightened but still-awkward basket, started across the stubble for the house. As he cranked the tractor she turned around to look back at them and wave. He nodded and, as if embarrassed, touched his straw hat.

Not till he was doing the chores that night did he grasp what her look of alarm had meant. If he wouldn't say grace, then perhaps there was no heaven. Their father would never get well, and David was dead. He squatted, drained of all strength again, staring at the hoof of the cow he'd been stripping, preparing her for the milker, and thought of his absent father. He saw the motorcycle roaring down a twisting mountain road, the clatter of the engine ringing like harsh music against shale. If what he felt was hatred, it was a terrible, desperate envy, too; his father all alone, uncompromised, violent, cut off as if by centuries from the warmth, chatter, and smells of the kitchen, the dimness of stained glass where he, Jack, sat every Sunday between his mother and sister, looking toward the pulpit where in the old days his father had sometimes read the lesson, soft-voiced but aloof from the timid-eyed flock, Christ's sheep.

Something blocked the light coming in through the cowbarn window from the west, and he turned his head, glancing up.

"You all right there, Jackie?" his uncle Walt said, bent forward, near-sightedly peering across the gutter.

He nodded and quickly wiped his wrist across his cheeks. He moved his hands once more to the cow's warm teats.

A few nights later, when he went in from chores, the door between the kitchen and living room was closed, and the house was unnaturally quiet. He stood a moment listening, still holding the milk pail, absently fitting the heel of one boot into the bootjack and tugging until the boot slipped off. He pried off the other, then walked to the icebox in his stocking feet, opened the door, carried the pitcher to the table, and filled it from the pail. When he'd slid the pitcher into the icebox again and closed the door, he went without a sound, though not meaning to be stealthy, toward the living room. Now, beyond the closed door, he heard voices, his sister and mother, then one of his aunts. He pushed the door open and looked in, about to speak.

Though the room was dim, no light but the small one among the pictures on the piano, he saw his father at once, kneeling by the davenport with his face on his mother's lap. Phoebe was on the davenport beside their mother, hugging her and him, Phoebe's cheeks stained, like her mother's, with tears. Around them, as if reverently drawn back, Uncle Walt, Aunt Ruth, and their two children sat watching, leaning forward with shining eyes. His father's head, bald down the center, glowed, and he had his glasses off.

"Jackie," his aunt called sharply, "come in. It's all over. Your dad's come home."

He would have fled, but his knees had no strength in them and his chest was wild, churning as if with terror. He clung to the doorknob, grotesquely smiling—so he saw himself. His father raised his head. "Jackie," he said, and was unable to say more, all at once sobbing like a baby.

"Hi, Dad," he brought out, and somehow managed to go to him and get down on his knees beside him and put his arm around his back. He felt dizzy now, nauseated, and he was crying like his father. "I hate you," he whispered too softly for any of them to hear.

His father stayed. He worked long days, in control once more, though occasionally he smoked, pacing in his room nights, or rode off on his motorcycle for an hour or two, and seldom smiled. Nevertheless, in a month he was again reciting poetry for schools and churches and the Grange, and sometimes reading Scripture from the pulpit Sunday mornings. Jack, sitting rigid, hands over his face, was bitterly ashamed of those poems and recitations from the Bible. His father's eyes no longer flashed, he no longer had the style of an actor. Even his gestures were submissive, as pliant as the grass. Though tears ran down Jack Hawthorne's face—no one would deny that his father was still effective, reading carefully, lest his voice should break. "Tomorrow's Bridge" and "This Too Will Pass"—Jack scorned the poems' opinions, scorned the way his father spoke directly to each listener, as if each were some new woman, his father some mere suffering sheep among sheep, and scorned the way Phoebe and his mother looked on smiling, furtively weeping, heads lifted. Sometimes his father would recite a poem that

Jack himself had written, in the days when he'd tried to write poetry, a comic limerick or some maudlin piece about a boy on a hill. Though it was meant as a compliment, Jack's heart would swell with rage; yet he kept silent, more private than before. At night he'd go out to the cavernous haymow or up into the orchard and practice his French horn. One of these days, he told himself, they'd wake up and find him gone.

He used the horn more and more now to escape their herding warmth. Those around him were conscious enough of what was happening—his parents and Phoebe, his uncles, aunts, and cousins, his mother's many friends. But there was nothing they could do. "That horn's his whole world," his mother often said, smiling but clasping her hands together. Soon he was playing third horn with the Batavia Civic Orchestra, though he refused to play in church or when company came. He began to ride the Bluebus to Rochester, Saturdays, to take lessons from Arcady Yegudkin, "the General," at the Eastman School of Music.

Yegudkin was seventy. He'd played principal horn in the orchestra of Czar Nikolai and at the time of the Revolution had escaped, with his wife, in a dramatic way. At the time of the purge of Kerenskyites, the Bolsheviks had loaded Yegudkin and his wife, along with hundreds more, onto railroad flatcars, reportedly to carry them to Siberia. In a desolate place, machine guns opened fire on the people on the flatcars, then soldiers pushed the bodies into a ravine, and the train moved on. The soldiers were not careful to see that everyone was dead. Perhaps they did not relish their work; in any case, they must have believed that, in a place so remote, a wounded survivor would have no chance against wolves and cold weather. The General and his wife were among the few who lived, he virtually unmarked, she horribly crippled. Local peasants nursed the few survivors back to health, and in time the Yegudkins escaped to Europe. There Yegudkin played horn with all the great orchestras and received such praise—so he claimed, spreading out his clippings—as no other master of French horn had received in all history. He would beam as he said it, his Tartar eyes flashing, and his smile was like a thrown-down gauntlet.

He was a barrel-shaped, solidly muscular man, hard as a boulder for all his age. His hair and mustache were as black as coal except for touches of silver, especially where it grew, with majestic indifference to ordinary taste, from his cavernous nostrils and large, dusty-looking ears. The sides of his mustache were carefully curled, in the fashion once favored by Russian dandies, and he was one of the last men in Rochester, New York, to wear spats. He wore formal black suits, a huge black overcoat, and a black fedora. His wife, who came with him and sat on the long maple bench outside his door, never reading or knitting or doing anything at all except that sometimes she would speak unintelligibly to a student—Yegudkin's wife, shriveled and twisted, watched him as if worshipfully, hanging on his words. She looked at least twice the old man's age. Her hair was snow white and she wore lumpy black shoes and long black shapeless dresses. The two of them would come, every Saturday morning, down the long marble hallway of the second floor of Killburn Hall, the General erect and imperious, like some sharp-eyed old Slavonic king, moving slowly, waiting for the old woman who crept beside him, gray claws on his coat sleeve, and seeing Jack Hawthorne seated on the bench, his books and French horn in its tattered black case on the floor beside him, the General would extend his left arm and boom, "Goot mworning!"

Jack, rising, would say, "Morning, sir."

"You have met my wife?" the old man would say then, bowing and taking the cigar from his mouth. He asked it each Saturday.

"Yes, sir. How do you do?"

The old man was too deaf to play in orchestras anymore. "What's the difference?" he said. "Every symphony in America, they got Yegudkins. I have teach them all. Who teach you this? *The General!*" He would smile, chin lifted, triumphant, and salute the ceiling.

He would sit in the chair beside Jack's and would sing, with violent gestures and a great upward leap of the belly to knock out the high B's and C's—*Tee! Tee!*—as Jack read through Kopprasch, Gallay, and Kling, and when it was time to give Jack's lip a rest, the General would speak earnestly, with the same energy he put into his singing, of the United States and his beloved Russia that he would nevermore see. The world was at that time filled with Russophobes. Yegudkin, whenever he read a paper, would be so enraged he could barely contain himself. "In all my age," he often said, furiously gesturing with his black cigar, "if the Russians would come to this country of America, I would take up a rifle and shot at them—*boof!* But the newspapers telling you lies, all lies! You think them dumb fools, these Russians? You think they are big, fat bush-overs?" He spoke of mile-long parades of weaponry, spoke of Russian cunning, spoke with great scorn, a sudden booming laugh, of Napoleon. Jack agreed with a nod to whatever the General said. Nevertheless, the old man roared on, taking great pleasure in his rage, it seemed, some-times talking like a rabid communist, sometimes like a fascist, some-times like a citizen helplessly caught between mindless, grinding forces, vast, idiot herds. The truth was, he hated both Russians and Americans about equally, cared only for music, his students and, possibly, his wife. In his pockets, in scorn of the opinions of fools, he carried condoms, dirty pictures, and grimy, wadded-up dollar bills.

One day a new horn he'd ordered from Germany, an Alexander, ar-rived at his office—a horn he'd gotten for a graduate student. The old man unwrapped and assembled it, the graduate student looking on—a shy young man, blond, in a limp gray sweater—and the glint in the

General's eye was like madness or at any rate lust, perhaps gluttony. When the horn was ready he went to the desk where he kept his clippings, his tools for the cleaning and repair of French horns, his cigars, photographs, and medals from the Czar, and pulled open a wide, shallow drawer. It contained perhaps a hundred mouthpieces, of all sizes and materials, from raw brass to lucite, silver, and gold, from the shallowest possible cup to the deepest. He selected one, fitted it into the horn, pressed the rim of the bell into the right side of his large belly— the horn seemed now as much a part of him as his arm or leg—clicked the shining keys to get the feel of them, then played. In that large, cork-lined room, it was as if, suddenly, a creature from some other universe had appeared, some realm where feelings become birds and dark sky, and spirit is more solid than stone. The sound was not so much loud as large, too large for a hundred French horns, it seemed. He began to play now not single notes but, to Jack's astonishment, chords—two notes at a time, then three. He began to play runs. As if charged with life independent of the man, the horn sound fluttered and flew crazily, like an enormous trapped hawk hunting frantically for escape. It flew to the bottom of the lower register, the foundation concert F, and crashed below it, and on down and down, as if the horn in Yegudkin's hands had no bottom, then suddenly changed its mind and flew upward in a split-second run to the horn's top E, dropped back to the middle and then ran once more, more fiercely at the E, and this time burst through it and fluttered, manic, in the trumpet range, then lightly dropped back into its own home range and, abruptly, in the middle of a note, stopped. The room still rang, shimmered like a vision.

"Good horn," said Yegudkin, and held the horn toward the graduate student, who sat, hands clamped on his knees, as if in a daze.

Jack Hawthorne stared at the instrument suspended in space and at his teacher's hairy hands. Before stopping to think, he said, "You think I'll ever play like that?"

Yegudkin laughed loudly, his black eyes widening, and it seemed that he grew larger, beatific and demonic at once, like the music; overwhelming. "Play like *me?*" he exclaimed.

Jack blinked, startled by the bluntness of the thing, the terrible lack of malice, and the truth of it. His face tingled and his legs went weak, as if the life were rushing out of them. He longed to be away from there, far away, safe. Perhaps Yegudkin sensed it. He turned gruff, sending away the graduate student, then finishing up the lesson. He said nothing, today, of the stupidity of mankind. When the lesson was over he saw Jack to the door and bid him good-bye with a brief half-smile that was perhaps not for Jack at all but for the creature on the bench. "Next Saturday?" he said, as if there might be some doubt.

Jack nodded, blushing.

At the door opening on the street he began to breathe more easily, though he was weeping. He set down the horn case to brush away his tears. The sidewalk was crowded—dazed-looking Saturday-morning shoppers herding along irritably, meekly, through painfully bright light. Again he brushed tears away. He'd been late for his bus. Then the crowd opened for him and, with the horn cradled under his right arm, his music under his left, he plunged in, starting home.

GAIL GODWIN

Dream Children

The worst thing. Such a terrible thing to happen to a young woman. It's a wonder she didn't go mad.

As she went about her errands, a cheerful, neat young woman, a wife, wearing pants with permanent creases and safari jackets and high-necked sweaters that folded chastely just below the line of the small gold hoops she wore in her ears, she imagined people saying this, or thinking it to themselves. But nobody knew. Nobody knew anything, other than that she and her husband had moved here a year ago, as so many couples were moving farther away from the city, the husband commuting, or staying in town during the week—as hers did. There was nobody here, in this quaint, unspoiled village, nestled in the foothills of the mountains, who could have looked at her and guessed that anything out of the ordinary, predictable, auspicious spectrum of things that happen to bright, attractive young women had happened to her. She always returned her books to the local library on time; she bought liquor at the local liquor store only on Friday, before she went to meet her husband's bus from the city. He was something in television, a producer? So many ambitious young couples moving to this Dutch farming village, found in 1690, to restore ruined fieldstone houses and plant herb gardens and keep their own horses and discover the relief of finding oneself insignificant in Nature for the first time!

A terrible thing. So freakish. If you read it in a story or saw it on TV, you'd say no, this sort of thing could never happen in an American hospital.

DePuy, who owned the old Patroon farm adjacent to her land, frequently glimpsed her racing her horse in the early morning, when the mists still lay on the fields, sometimes just before the sun came up and there was a frost on everything. "One woodchuck hole and she and that stallion will both have to be put out of their misery," he told his wife. "She's too reckless. I'll bet you her old man doesn't know she goes streaking to hell across the fields like that." Mrs. DePuy nodded, silent, and went about her business. She, too, watched that other woman ride, a woman not much younger than herself, but with an aura of romance— of tragedy, perhaps. The way she looked: like those heroines in English novels who ride off their bad tempers and unrequited love affairs, clenching their thighs against the flanks of spirited horses with murderous red eyes. Mrs. DePuy, who had ridden since the age of three, recognized something beyond recklessness in that elegant young woman, in her crisp checked shirts and her dove-gray jodhpurs. *She has nothing to fear anymore,* thought the farmer's wife, with sure feminine instinct; she both envied and pitied her. "What she needs is children," remarked DePuy.

"A Dry Sack, a Remy Martin, and . . . let's see, a half-gallon of the Chablis, and I think I'd better take a Scotch . . . and the Mouton-Cadet . . . and maybe a dry vermouth." Mrs. Frye, another farmer's wife, who runs the liquor store, asks if her husband is bringing company for the weekend. "He sure is; we couldn't drink all that by ourselves," and the young woman laughs, her lovely teeth exposed, her small gold earrings quivering in the light. "You know, I saw his name—on the television the other night," says Mrs. Frye. "It was at the beginning of that new comedy show, the one with the woman who used to be on another show with her husband and little girl, only they divorced, you know the one?" "Of course I do. It's one of my husband's shows. I'll tell him you watched it." Mrs. Frye puts the bottles in an empty box, carefully inserting wedges of cardboard between them. Through the window of her store she sees her customer's pert bottle-green car, some sort of little foreign car with the engine running, filled with groceries and weekend parcels, and that big silver-blue dog sitting up in the front seat just like a human being. "I think that kind of thing is so sad," says Mrs. Frye; "families breaking up, poor little children having to divide their loyalties." "I couldn't agree more," replies the young woman, nodding gravely. Such a personable, polite girl! "Are you sure you can carry that, dear? I can get Earl from the back. . . ." But the girl has it hoisted on her shoulder in a flash, is airily maneuvering between unopened cartons stacked in the aisle, in her pretty boots. Her perfume lingers in Mrs. Frye's store for a half-hour after she has driven away.

After dinner, her husband and his friends drank brandy. She lay in front of the fire, stroking the dog, and listening to Victoria Darrow, the news commentator, in person. A few minutes ago, they had all watched Victoria on TV. "That's right; thirty-nine!" Victoria now whispered to her. "What? That's kind of you. I'm photogenic, thank God, or I'd have been put out to pasture long before. . . . I look five, maybe seven years younger on the screen . . . but the point I'm getting at is, I went to this doctor and he said, 'If you want to do this thing, you'd better go home today and get started.' He told me—did you know this? Did you know that a woman is born with all the eggs she'll ever have, and when she gets to my age, the ones that are left have been rattling around so long they're a little shopworn; then every time you fly you get an extra dose of radioactivity, so those poor eggs. He told me when a woman over forty comes into his office pregnant, his heart sinks; that's why he quit practicing obstetrics, he said; he could still remember the screams of a woman whose baby he delivered . . . she was having natural child-birth and she kept saying, 'Why won't you let me see it, I insist on seeing it,' and so he had to, and he says he can still hear her screaming."

"Oh, what was—what was wrong with it?"

But she never got the answer. Her husband, white around the lips, was standing over Victoria ominously, offering the Remy Martin bottle. "Vicky, let me pour you some more," he said. And to his wife, "I think Blue Boy needs to go out."

"Yes, yes, of course. Please excuse me, Victoria. I'll just be . . ."

Her husband followed her to the kitchen, his hand on the back of her neck. "Are you okay? That stupid yammering bitch. She and her twenty-six-year-old lover! I wish I'd never brought them, but she's been hinting around the studio for weeks."

"But I like them, I like having them. I'm fine. Please go back. I'll take the dog out and come back. Please . . ."

"All right. If you're sure you're okay." He backed away, hands dangling at his sides. A handsome man, wearing a pink shirt with Guatema-lan embroidery. Thick black hair and a face rather boyish, but cunning. Last weekend she had sat beside him, alone in this house, just the two of them, and watched him on television: a documentary, in several parts, in which TV "examines itself." There was his double, sitting in an armchair in his executive office, coolly replying to the questions of Victoria Darrow. *"Do you personally watch all the programs you produce, Mr. McNair?"* She watched the man on the screen, how he moved his lips when he spoke, but kept the rest of his face, his body perfectly still. Funny, she had never noticed this before. He managed to say that he did and did not watch all the programs he produced.

Now, in the kitchen, she looked at him backing away, a little like a renegade in one of his own shows—a desperate man, perhaps, who had just killed somebody and is backing away, hands dangling loosely at his sides, Mr. McNair, her husband. That man on the screen. Once a lover above her in bed. That friend who held her hand in the hospital. One hand in hers, the other holding the stopwatch. For a brief instant, all the images coalesce and she feels something again. But once outside, under the galaxies of autumn-sharp stars, the intelligent dog at her heels like some smart gray ghost, she is glad to be free of all that. She walks quickly over the damp grass to the barn, to look in on her horse. She under-stands something: her husband, Victoria Darrow lead double lives that seem perfectly normal to them. But if she told her husband that she, too, is in two lives, he would become alarmed; he would sell this house and make her move back to the city where he could keep an eye on her welfare.

She is discovering people like herself, down through the centuries, all over the world. She scours books with titles like *The Timeless Moment, The Sleeping Prophet, Between Two Worlds, Silent Union: A Record of Unwilled Communication;* collecting evidence, weaving a sort of underworld net of colleagues around her.

A rainy fall day. Too wet to ride. The silver dog asleep beside her in her special alcove, a padded window seat filled with pillows and books. She is looking down on the fields of dried lithrium, and the fir trees beyond, and the mountains gauzy with fog and rain, thinking, in a kind of terror and ecstasy, about all these connections. A book lies face down on her lap. She has just read the following:

> Theodore Dreiser and his friend John Cowper Powys had been dining at Dreiser's place on West Fifty Seventh Street. As Powys made ready to leave and catch his train to the little town up the Hudson, where he was then living, he told Dreiser, "I'll appear before you here, later in the evening."
>
> Dreiser laughed. "Are you going to turn yourself into a ghost, or have you a spare key?" he asked. Powys said he would return "in some form," he didn't know exactly what kind.
>
> After his friend left, Dreiser sat up and read for two hours. Then he looked up and saw Powys standing in the doorway to the living room. It was Powys' features, his tall stature, even the loose tweed garments which he wore. Dreiser rose at once and strode toward the figure, saying, "Well, John, you kept your word. Come on in and tell me how you did it." But the figure vanished when Dreiser came within three feet of it.
>
> Dreiser then went to the telephone and called Powys' house in the country. Powys answered. Dreiser told him what had happened and Powys said, "I told you I'd be there and you oughtn't to be surprised." But he refused to discuss how he had done it, if, indeed, he knew how.

"But don't you get frightened, up here all by yourself, alone with all these creaky sounds?" asked Victoria, the next morning.

"No, I guess I'm used to them," she replied, breaking eggs into a bowl. "I know what each one means. The wood expanding and contracting . . . the wind getting caught between the shutter and the latch . . .

Sometimes small animals get lost in the stone walls and scratch around till they find their way out . . . or die."

"Ugh. But don't you imagine things? I would, in a house like this. How old? That's almost three hundred years of lived lives, people suffering and shouting and making love and giving birth, under this roof. . . . You'd think there'd be a few ghosts around."

"I don't know," said her hostess blandly. "I haven't heard any. But of course, I have Blue Boy, so I don't get scared." She whisked the eggs, unable to face Victoria. She and her husband had lain awake last night, embarrassed at the sounds coming from the next room. No ghostly moans, those. "Why can't that bitch control herself, or at least lower her voice," he said angrily. He stroked his wife's arm, both of them pretending not to remember. She had bled for an entire year afterward, until the doctor said they would have to remove everything. "I'm empty," she had said when her husband had tried again, after she was healed. "I'm sorry, I just don't feel anything." Now they lay tenderly together on these weekends, like childhood friends, like effigies on a lovers' tomb, their mutual sorrow like a sword between them. She assumed he had another life, or lives, in town. As she had here. Nobody is just one person, she had learned.

"I'm sure I would imagine things," said Victoria. "I would see things and hear things inside my head much worse than an ordinary murderer or rapist."

The wind caught in the shutter latch . . . a small animal dislodging pieces of fieldstone in its terror, sending them tumbling down the inner walls, from attic to cellar . . . a sound like a child rattling a jar full of marbles, or small stones . . .

"I have so little imagination," she said humbly, warming the butter in the omelet pan. She could feel Victoria Darrow's professional curiosity waning from her dull country life, focusing elsewhere.

Cunning!

As a child of nine, she had gone through a phase of walking in her sleep. One summer night, they found her bed empty, and after an hour's hysterical search they had found her in her nightgown, curled up on the flagstones beside the fishpond. She woke, baffled, in her father's tense clutch, the stars all over the sky, her mother repeating over and over again to the night at large, "Oh, my God, she could have drowned!" They took her to a child psychiatrist, a pretty Austrian woman who spoke to her with the same vocabulary she used on grownups, putting the child instantly at ease. "It is not at all uncommon what you did. I have known so many children who take little night journeys from their beds, and then they awaken and don't know what all the fuss is about! Usually these journeys are quite harmless, because children are surrounded by a magical reality that keeps them safe. Yes, the race of

children possesses magically sagacious powers! But the grownups, they
tend to forget how it once was for them. They worry, they are afraid of
so many things. You do not want your mother and father, who love you
so anxiously, to live in fear of you going to live with the fishes." She had
giggled at the thought. The woman's steady gray-green eyes were
trained on her carefully, suspending her in a kind of bubble. Then she
had rejoined her parents, a dutiful "child" again, holding a hand up to
each of them. The night journeys had stopped.

A thunderstorm one night last spring. Blue Boy whining in his insulated
house below the garage. She had lain there, strangely elated by the
nearness of the thunderclaps that tore at the sky, followed by instanta-
neous flashes of jagged light. Wondering shouldn't she go down and let
the dog in; he hated storms. Then dozing off again . . .
    She woke. The storm had stopped. The dark air was quiet. Something
had changed, some small thing—what? She had to think hard before she
found it: the hall light, which she kept burning during the weeknights
when she was there alone, had gone out. She reached over and switched
the button on her bedside lamp. Nothing. A tree must have fallen and
hit a wire, causing the power to go off. This often happened here. No
problem. The dog had stopped crying. She felt herself sinking into a
delicious, deep reverie, the kind that sometimes came just before morning, as if her being broke slowly into tiny pieces and spread itself over
the world. It was a feeling she had not known until she had lived by
herself in this house: this weightless though conscious state in which she
lay, as if in a warm bath, and yet was able to send her thoughts anywhere, as if her mind contained the entire world.
    And as she floated in this silent world, transparent and buoyed upon
the dream layers of the mind, she heard a small rattling sound, like
pebbles being shaken in a jar. The sound came distinctly from the guest
room, a room so chosen by her husband and herself because it was the
farthest room from their bedroom on this floor. It lay above what had
been the old side of the house, built seventy-five years before the new
side, which was completed in 1753. There was a bed in it, and a chair,
and some plants in the window. Sometimes on weekends when she
could not sleep, she went and read there, or meditated, to keep from
waking her husband. It was not the room where Victoria Darrow and
her young lover would sleep the following fall, because she would say
quietly to her husband, "No . . . not that room. I—I've made up the
bed in the other room." "What?" he would want to know. "The one
next to ours? Right under our noses?"
    She did not lie long listening to this sound before she understood it
was one she had never heard in the house before. It had a peculiar
regularity to its rhythm; there was nothing accidental about it, nothing
influenced by the wind, or the nerves of some lost animal. *K-chunk,*

k-chunk, k-chunk, it went. At intervals of exactly a half-minute apart. She still remembered how to time such things, such intervals. She was as good as any stopwatch when it came to timing certain intervals.

K-chunk, k-chunk, k-chunk. That determined regularity. Something willed, something poignantly repeated, as though the repetition was a means of consoling someone in the dark. Her skin began to prickle. Often, lying in such states of weightless reverie, she had practiced the trick of sending herself abroad, into rooms of the house, out into the night to check on Blue Boy, over to the barn to look in on her horse, who slept standing up. Once she had heard a rather frightening noise, as if someone in the basement had turned on a faucet, and so she forced herself to "go down," floating down two sets of stairs into the darkness, only to discover what she had known all the time: the hookup system between the hot-water tank and the pump, which sounded like someone turning on the water.

Now she went through the palpable, prickly darkness, without lights, down the chilly hall in her sleeveless gown, into the guest room. Although there was no light, not even a moon shining through the window, she could make out the shape of the bed and then the chair, the spider plants on the window, and a small dark shape in one corner, on the floor, which she and her husband had painted a light yellow.

K-chunk, k-chunk, k-chunk. The shape moved with the noise.

Now she knew what they meant, that "someone's hair stood on end." It was true. As she forced herself across the borders of a place she had never been, she felt, distinctly, every single hair on her head raise itself a millimeter or so from her scalp.

She knelt down and discovered him. He was kneeling, a little cold and scared, shaking a small jar filled with some kind of pebbles. (She later found out, in a subsequent visit, that they were small colored shells, of a triangular shape, called coquinas: she found them in a picture in a child's nature book at the library.) He was wearing pajamas a little too big for him, obviously hand-me-downs, and he was exactly two years older than the only time she had ever held him in her arms.

The two of them knelt in the corner of the room, taking each other in. His large eyes were the same as before: dark and unblinking. He held the small jar close to him, watching her. He was not afraid, but she knew better than to move too close.

She knelt, the tears streaming down her cheeks, but she made no sound, her eyes fastened on that small form. And then the hall light came on silently, as well as the lamp beside her bed, and with wet cheeks and pounding heart she could not be sure whether or not she had actually been out of the room.

But what did it matter, on the level where they had met? He traveled so much farther than she to reach that room. *("Yes, the race of children possesses magically sagacious powers!")*

She and her husband sat together on the flowered chintz sofa, watching the last of the series in which TV purportedly examined itself. She said, "Did you ever think that the whole thing is really a miracle? I mean, here we sit, eighty miles away from your studios, and we turn on a little machine and there is Victoria, speaking to us as clearly as she did last weekend when she was in this very room. Why, it's magic, it's time travel and space travel right in front of our eyes, but because it's been 'discovered,' because the world understands that it's only little dots that transmit Victoria electrically to us, it's *all right*. We can bear it. Don't you sometimes wonder about all the miracles that haven't been officially approved yet? I mean, who knows, maybe in a hundred years everybody will take it for granted that they can send an image of themselves around in space by some perfectly natural means available to us now. I mean, when you think about it, what *is* space? What *is* time? Where do the so-called boundaries of each of us begin and end? Can anyone explain it?"

He was drinking Scotch and thinking how they had decided not to renew Victoria Darrow's contract. Somewhere on the edges of his mind hovered an anxious, growing certainty about his wife. At the local grocery store this morning, when he went to pick up a carton of milk and the paper, he had stopped to chat with DePuy. "I don't mean to interfere, but she doesn't know those fields," said the farmer. "Last year we had to shoot a mare, stumbled into one of those holes. . . . It's madness, the way she rides."

And look at her now, her face so pale and shining, speaking of miracles and space travel, almost on the verge of tears. . . .

And last night, his first night up from the city, he had wandered through the house, trying to drink himself into this slower weekend pace, and he had come across a pile of her books, stacked in the alcove where, it was obvious, she lay for hours, escaping into science fiction, and the occult.

Now his own face appeared on the screen. "I want to be fair," he was telling Victoria Darrow. "I want to be objective. . . . Violence has always been part of the human makeup. I don't like it any more than you do, but there it is. I think it's more a question of whether we want to face things as they are or escape into fantasies of how we would like them to be."

Beside him, his wife uttered a sudden bell-like laugh.

(". . . *It's madness, the way she rides.*")

He did want to be fair, objective. She had told him again and again that she liked her life here. And he—well, he had to admit he liked his own present setup.

"I am a pragmatist," he was telling Victoria Darrow on the screen. He decided to speak to his wife about her riding and leave her alone about the books. She had the right to some escape, if anyone did. But the titles: *Marvelous Manifestations, The Mind Travellers, A Doctor Looks at Spiritualism, The Other Side* . . . Something revolted in him, he couldn't help it; he felt an actual physical revulsion at this kind of thinking. Still it was better than some other escapes. His friend Barnett, the actor, who said at night he went from room to room, after his wife was asleep, collecting empty glasses. ("Once I found one by the Water Pik, a second on the ledge beside the tub, a third on the back of the john, and a fourth on the floor beside the john. . . .")

He looked sideways at his wife, who was absorbed, it seemed, in watching him on the screen. Her face was tense, alert, animated. She did not look mad. She wore slim gray pants and a loose-knit pullover made of some silvery material, like a knight's chain mail. The lines of her profile were clear and silvery themselves, somehow sexless and pure, like a child's profile. He no longer felt lust when he looked at her, only a sad determination to protect her. He had a mistress in town, whom he loved, but he had explained, right from the beginning, that he considered himself married for the rest of his life. He told this woman the whole story. "And I am implicated in it. I could never leave her." An intelligent, sensitive woman, she had actually wept and said, "Of course not."

He always wore the same pajamas, a shade too big, but always clean. Obviously washed again and again in a machine that went through its cycles frequently. She imagined his "other mother," a harassed woman with several children, short on money, on time, on dreams—all the things she herself had too much of. The family lived, she believed, somewhere in Florida, probably on the west coast. She had worked that out from the little coquina shells: their bright colors, even in moonlight shining through a small window with spider plants in it. His face and arms had been suntanned early in the spring and late into the autumn. They never spoke or touched. She was not sure how much of this he understood. She tried and failed to remember where she herself had gone, in those little night journeys to the fishpond. Perhaps he never remembered afterward, when he woke up, clutching his jar, in a roomful of brothers and sisters. Or with a worried mother or father come to collect him, asleep by the sea. Once she had a very clear dream of the whole family, living in a trailer, with palm trees. But that was a dream; she recognized its difference in quality from those truly magic times when, through his own childish powers, he somehow found a will strong enough, or innocent enough, to project himself upon her still-floating consciousness, as clearly and as believably as her own husband's image on the screen.

There had been six of those times in six months. She dared to look forward to more. So unafraid he was. The last time was the day after

Victoria Darrow and her young lover and her own good husband had returned to the city. She had gone farther with the child than ever before. On a starry-clear, cold September Monday, she had coaxed him down the stairs and out of the house with her. He held to the banisters, a child unused to stairs, and yet she knew there was no danger; he floated in his own dream with her. She took him to see Blue Boy. Who disappointed her by whining and backing away in fear. And then to the barn to see the horse. Who perked up his ears and looked interested. There was no touching, of course, no touching or speaking. Later she wondered if horses, then, were more magical than dogs. If dogs were more "realistic." She was glad the family was poor, the mother harassed. They could not afford any expensive child psychiatrist who would hypnotize him out of his night journeys.

He loved her. She knew that. Even if he never remembered her in his other life.

"At last I was beginning to understand what Teilhard de Chardin meant when he said that man's true home is the mind. I understood that when the mystics tell us that the mind is a place, they *don't mean it as a metaphor.* I found these new powers developed with practice. I had to detach myself from my ordinary physical personality. The intelligent part of me had to remain wide awake, and move down into this world of thoughts, dreams and memories. After several such journeyings I understood something else: dream and reality aren't competitors, but reciprocal sources of consciousness." This she read in a "respectable book," by a "respectable man," a scientist, alive and living in England, only a few years older than herself. She looked down at the dog, sleeping on the rug. His lean silvery body actually ran as he slept! Suddenly his muzzle lifted, the savage teeth snapped. Where was he "really" now? Did the dream rabbit in his jaws know it was a dream? There was much to think about, between her trips to the nursery.

Would the boy grow, would she see his body slowly emerging from its child's shape, the arms and legs lengthening, the face thinning out into a man's—like a certain advertisement for bread she had seen on TV where a child grows up, in less than a half-minute of sponsor time, right before the viewer's eyes. Would he grow into a man, grow a beard . . . outgrow the nursery region of his mind where they had been able to meet?

And yet, some daylight part of his mind must have retained an image of her from that single daylight time they had looked into each other's eyes.

The worst thing, such an awful thing to happen to a young woman . . . She was having this natural childbirth, you see, her husband in the delivery room with her, and the pains were coming a half-minute apart, and the doctor had just said, "This is going to be a breeze, Mrs. McNair," and they never knew exactly what went wrong, but all of a sudden the pains stopped and they had to go in after the baby without even time to give her a saddle block or any sort of anesthetic. . . . They must have practically had to tear it out of her . . . the husband fainted. The baby was born dead, and they gave her a heavy sedative to put her out all night.

When she woke the next morning, before she had time to remember what had happened, a nurse suddenly entered the room and laid a baby in her arms. "Here's your little boy," she said cheerfully, and the woman thought, with a profound, religious relief, *So that other nightmare was a dream,* and she had the child at her breast feeding him before the nurse realized her mistake and rushed back into the room, but they had to knock the poor woman out with more sedatives before she would let the child go. She was screaming and so was the little baby and they clung to each other till she passed out.

They would have let the nurse go, only it wasn't entirely her fault. The hospital was having a strike at the time; some of the nurses were outside picketing and this nurse had been working straight through for forty-eight hours, and when she was questioned afterward she said she had just mixed up the rooms, and yet, she said, when she had seen the woman and the baby clinging to each other like that, she had undergone a sort of revelation in her almost hallucinatory exhaustion: the nurse said she saw that all children and mothers were interchangeable, that nobody could own anybody or anything, any more than you could own an idea that happened to be passing through the air and caught on your mind, or any more than you owned the rosebush that grew in your back yard. There were only mothers and children, she realized; though, afterward, the realization faded.

It was the kind of freakish thing that happens once in a million times, and it's a wonder the poor woman kept her sanity.

In the intervals, longer than those measured by any stopwatch, she waited for him. In what the world accepted as "time," she shopped for groceries, for clothes; she read; she waved from her bottle-green car to Mrs. Frye, trimming the hedge in front of the liquor store, to Mrs. DePuy, hanging out her children's pajamas in the back yard of the old Patroon farm. She rode her horse through the fields of the waning season, letting him have his head; she rode like the wind, a happy, happy woman. She rode faster than fear because she was a woman in a dream, a woman anxiously awaiting her child's sleep. The stallion's hoofs pounded the earth. Oiling his tractor, DePuy resented the foolish woman and almost wished for a woodchuck hole to break that arrogant ride. Wished deep in a violent level of himself he never knew he had. For he was a kind, distracted father and husband, a practical, hard-working man who would never descend deeply into himself. Her body, skimming through time, felt weightless to the horse.

Was she a woman riding a horse and dreaming she was a mother who anxiously awaited her child's sleep; or was she a mother dreaming of herself as a free spirit who could ride her horse like the wind because she had nothing to fear?

I am a happy woman, that's all I know. Who can explain such things?

Lawrence Sargent Hall

The Ledge

On Christmas morning before sunup the fisherman embraced his warm wife and left his close bed. She did not want him to go. It was Christmas morning. He was a big, raw man, with too much strength, whose delight in winter was to hunt the sea ducks that flew in to feed by the outer ledges, bare at low tide.

As his bare feet touched the cold floor and the frosty air struck his nude flesh, he might have changed his mind in the dark of this special day. It was a home day, which made it seem natural to think of the outer ledges merely as some place he had shot ducks in the past. But he had promised his son, thirteen, and his nephew, fifteen, who came from inland. That was why he had given them his present of an automatic shotgun each the night before, on Christmas Eve. Rough man though he was known to be, and no spoiler of boys, he kept his promises when he understood what they meant. And to the boys, as to him, home meant where you came for rest after you had had your Christmas fill of action and excitement.

His legs astride, his arms raised, the fisherman stretched as high as he could in the dim privacy of his bedroom. Above the snug murmur of his wife's protest he heard the wind in the pines and knew it was easterly as the boys had hoped and he had surmised the night before. Conditions would be ideal, and when they were, anybody ought to take advantage of them. The birds would be flying. The boys would get a man's sport their first time outside on the ledges.

His son at thirteen, small but steady and experienced, was fierce to grow up in hunting, to graduate from sheltered waters and the blinds along the shores of the inner bay. His nephew at fifteen, an overgrown farm boy, had a farm boy's love of the sea, though he could not swim a stroke and was often sick in choppy weather. That was the reason his father, the fisherman's brother, was a farmer and chose to sleep in on the holiday morning at his brother's house. Many of the ones the farmer had grown up with were regularly seasick and could not swim, but they were unafraid of the water. They could not have dreamed of being anything but fishermen. The fisherman himself could swim like a seal and was never sick, and he would sooner die than be anything else.

He dressed in the cold and dark, and woke the boys gruffly. They tumbled out of bed, their instincts instantly awake while their thoughts still fumbled slumbrously. The fisherman's wife in the adjacent bedroom heard them apparently trying to find their clothes, mumbling sleepily and happily to each other, while her husband went down to the hot kitchen to fry eggs—sunny-side up, she knew, because that was how they all liked them.

Always in winter she hated to have them go outside, the weather was so treacherous and there were so few others out in case of trouble. To the fisherman these were no more than woman's fears, to be taken for granted and laughed off. When they were first married, they fought miserably every fall because she was after him constantly to put his boat up until spring. The fishing was all outside in winter, and though prices were high the storms made the rate of attrition high on gear. Nevertheless he did well. So she could do nothing with him.

People thought him a hard man, and gave him the reputation of being all out for himself because he was inclined to brag and be disdainful. If it was true, and his own brother was one of those who strongly felt it was, they lived better than others, and his brother had small right to criticize. There had been times when in her loneliness she had yearned to leave him for another man. But it would have been dangerous. So over the years she had learned to shut her mind to his hard-driving, and take what comfort she might from his unsympathetic competence. Only once or twice, perhaps, had she gone so far as to dwell guiltily on what it would be like to be a widow.

The thought that her boy, possibly because he was small, would not be insensitive like his father, and the rattle of dishes and smell of frying bacon downstairs in the kitchen shut off from the rest of the chilly house, restored the cozy feeling she had had before she was alone in bed. She heard them after a while go out and shut the back door.

Under her window she heard the snow grind dryly beneath their boots, and her husband's sharp, exasperated commands to the boys. She shivered slightly in the envelope of her own warmth. She listened to the noise of her son and nephew talking elatedly. Twice she caught the glimmer of their lights on the white ceiling above the window as they went down the path to the shore. There would be frost on the skiff and freezing suds at the water's edge. She herself used to go gunning when she was younger; now, it seemed to her, anyone going out like that on Christmas morning had to be incurably male. They would none of them think about her until they returned and piled the birds they had shot on top of the sink for her to dress.

Ripping into the quiet pre-dawn cold she heard the hot snarl of the outboard taking them out to the boat. It died as abruptly as it had burst into life. Two or three or four or five minutes later the big engine broke into a warm reassuring roar. He had the best of equipment, and he kept it in the best of condition. She closed her eyes. It would not be too long before the others would be up for Christmas. The summer drone of the exhaust deepened. Then gradually it faded in the wind until it was lost at sea, or she slept.

The engine had started immediately in spite of the temperature. This put the fisherman in a good mood. He was proud of his boat. Together he and the two boys heaved the skiff and outboard onto the stern and secured it athwartships. His son went forward along the deck, iridescent in the ray of the light the nephew shone through the windshield, and cast the mooring pennant loose into darkness. The fisherman swung to starboard, glanced at his compass, and headed seaward down the obscure bay.

There would be just enough visibility by the time they reached the headland to navigate the crooked channel between the islands. It was the only nasty stretch of water. The fisherman had done it often in fog or at night—he always swore he could go anywhere in the bay blindfolded—but there was no sense in taking chances if you didn't have to. From the mouth of the channel he could lay a straight course for Brown Cow Island, anchor the boat out of sight behind it, and from the skiff set their tollers off Devil's Hump three hundred yards to seaward. By then the tide would be clearing the ledge and they could land and be ready to shoot around half-tide.

It was early, it was Christmas, and it was farther out than most hunters cared to go in this season of the closing year, so that he felt sure no one would be taking possession ahead of them. He had shot thousands of ducks there in his day. The Hump was by far the best hunting. Only thing was you had to plan for the right conditions because you didn't have too much time. About four hours was all, and you had to get it before three in the afternoon when the birds left and went out to sea ahead of nightfall.

They had it figured exactly right for today. The ledge would not be going under until after the gunning was over, and they would be home for supper in good season. With a little luck the boys would have a skiffload of birds to show for their first time outside. Well beyond the legal limit, which was no matter. You took what you could get in this life, or the next man made out and you didn't.

The fisherman had never failed to make out gunning from Devil's Hump. And this trip, he had a hunch, would be above the ordinary. The westerly wind would come up just stiff enough, the tide was right, and it was going to storm by tomorrow morning so the birds would be moving. Things were perfect.

The old fierceness was in his bones. Keeping a weather eye to the murk out front and a hand on the wheel, he reached over and cuffed both boys playfully as they stood together close to the heat of the exhaust pipe running up through the center of the house. They poked back at him and shouted above the drumming engine, making bets as they always did on who would shoot the most birds. This trip they had the thrill of new guns, the best money could buy, and a man's hunting ground. The black retriever wagged at them and barked. He was too old and arthritic to be allowed in December water, but he was jaunty anyway at being brought along.

Groping in his pocket for his pipe, the fisherman suddenly had his high spirits rocked by the discovery that he had left his tobacco at home. He swore. Anticipation of a day out with nothing to smoke made him incredulous. He searched his clothes, and then he searched them again, unable to believe the tobacco was not somewhere. When the boys inquired what was wrong he spoke angrily to them, blaming them for being in some devious way at fault. They were instantly crestfallen and willing to put back after the tobacco, though they could appreciate what it meant only through his irritation. But he bitterly refused. That would throw everything out of phase. He was a man who did things the way he set out to do.

He clamped his pipe between his teeth, and twice more during the next few minutes he ransacked his clothes in disbelief. He was no stoic. For one relaxed moment he considered putting about gunning some-where nearer home. Instead he held his course and sucked the empty pipe, consoling himself with the reflection that at least he had whiskey enough if it got too uncomfortable on the ledge. Peremptorily he made the boys check to make certain the bottle was really in the knapsack with the lunches where he thought he had taken care to put it. When they reassured him, he despised his fate a little less.

The fisherman's judgment was as usual accurate. By the time they were abreast of the headland there was sufficient light so that he could wind his way among the reefs without slackening speed. At last he turned his bow toward open ocean, and as the winter dawn filtered upward through long layers of smoky cloud on the eastern rim his spirits rose again with it.

He opened the throttle, steadied on his course, and settled down to the two-hour run. The wind was stronger but seemed less cold coming from the sea. The boys had withdrawn from the fisherman and were talking together while they watched the sky through the windows. The boat churned solidly through a light chop, flinging spray off her flaring bow. Astern the headland thinned rapidly till it lay like a blackened sill on the gray water. No other boats were abroad.

The boys fondled their new guns, sighted along the barrels, worked the mechanisms, compared notes, boasted, and gave each other contra-dictory advice. The fisherman got their attention once and pointed at the horizon. They peered through the windows and saw what looked like a black scum floating on top of gently agitated water. It wheeled and tilted, rippled, curled, then rose, strung itself out and became a huge raft of ducks escaping over the sea. A good sign.

The boys rushed out and leaned over the washboards in the wind and spray to see the flock curl below the horizon. Then they went and hovered around the hot engine, bewailing their lot. If only they had been already out and waiting. Maybe these ducks would be crazy enough to return later and be slaughtered. Ducks were known to be foolish.

In due course and right on schedule they anchored at mid-morning in the lee of Brown Cow Island. They put the skiff overboard and loaded it with guns, knapsacks, and tollers. The boys showed their eagerness by being clumsy. The fisherman showed his in bad temper and abuse which they silently accepted in the absorbed tolerance of being boys. No doubt they laid it to lack of tobacco.

By outboard they rounded the island and pointed due east in the direction of a ridge of foam which could be seen whitening the surface three hundred yards away. They set the decoys in a broad, straddling vee opening wide into the ocean. The fisherman warned them not to get their hands wet, and when they did he made them carry on with red and painful fingers, in order to teach them. Once they got their numbed fingers inside their oilskins and hugged their warm crotches. In the meantime the fisherman had turned the skiff toward the patch of foam where as if by magic, like a black glossy rib of earth, the ledge had broken through the belly of the sea.

Carefully they inhabited their slippery nub of the North American continent, while the unresting Atlantic swelled and swirled as it had for eons round the indomitable edges. They hauled the skiff after them, established themselves as comfortably as they could in a shallow sump on top, lay on their sides a foot or so above the water, and waited, guns in hand.

In time the fisherman took a Thermos bottle from the knapsack and they drank steaming coffee, and waited for the nodding decoys to lure in the first flight to the rock. Eventually the boys got hungry and restless. The fisherman let them open the picnic lunch and eat one sandwich apiece, which they both shared with the dog. Having no tobacco the fisherman himself would not eat.

Actually the day was relatively mild, and they were warm enough at present in their woollen clothes and socks underneath oilskins and hip boots. After a while, however, the boys began to feel cramped. Their nerves were agonized by inactivity. The nephew complained and was severely told by the fisherman—who pointed to the dog, crouched unmoving except for his white-rimmed eyes—that part of doing a man's hunting was learning how to wait. But he was beginning to have misgivings of his own. This could be one of those days where all the right conditions masked an incalculable flaw.

If the fisherman had been alone, as he often was, stopping off when the necessary coincidence of tide and time occurred on his way home from hauling trawls, and had plenty of tobacco, he would not have fidgeted. The boys' being nervous made him nervous. He growled at them again. When it came it was likely to come all at once, and then in a few moments be over. He warned them not to slack off, never to slack off, to be always ready. Under his rebuke they kept their tortured peace, though they could not help shifting and twisting until he lost what patience he had left and bullied them into lying still. A duck could see an eyelid twitch. If the dog could go without moving so could they.

"Here it comes!" the fisherman said tersely at last.

The boys quivered with quick relief. The flock came in downwind, quartering slightly, myriad, black, and swift.

"Beautiful—" breathed the fisherman's son.

"All right," said the fisherman, intense and precise. "Aim at singles in the thickest part of the flock. Wait for me to fire and then don't stop shooting till your gun's empty." He rolled up onto his left elbow and spread his legs to brace himself. The flock bore down, arrowy and vibrant, then a hundred yards beyond the decoys it veered off.

"They're going away!" the boys cried, sighting in.

"Not yet!" snapped the fisherman. "They're coming round."

The flock changed shape, folded over itself, and drove into the wind in a tight arc. "Thousands—" the boys hissed through their teeth. All at once a whistling storm of black and white broke over the decoys.

"Now!" the fisherman shouted. "Perfect!" And he opened fire at the flock just as it hung suspended in momentary chaos above the tollers. The three pulled at their triggers and the birds splashed into the water, until the last report went off unheard, the last smoking shell flew unheeded over their shoulders, and the last of the routed flock scattered diminishing, diminishing, diminishing in every direction.

Exultantly the boys dropped their guns, jumped up and scrambled for the skiff.

"I'll handle that skiff!" the fisherman shouted at them. They stopped. Gripping the painter and balancing himself he eased the skiff into the water stern first and held the bow hard against the side of the rock shelf the skiff had rested on. "You stay here," he said to his nephew. "No sense in all three of us going in the boat."

The boy on the reef gazed at the gray water rising and falling hypnotically along the glistening edge. It had dropped about a foot since their arrival. "I want to go with you," he said in a sullen tone, his eyes on the streaming eddies.

"You want to do what I tell you if you want to gun with me," answered the fisherman harshly. The boy couldn't swim, and he wasn't going to have him climbing in and out of the skiff any more than necessary. Besides, he was too big.

The fisherman took his son in the skiff and cruised round and round among the decoys picking up dead birds. Meanwhile the other boy stared unmoving after them from the highest part of the ledge. Before they had quite finished gathering the dead birds, the fishermen cut the outboard and dropped to his knees in the skiff. "Down!" he yelled. "Get down!" About a dozen birds came tolling in. "Shoot—shoot!" his son hollered from the bottom of the boat to the boy on the ledge.

The dog, who had been running back and forth whining, sank to his belly, his muzzle on his forepaws. But the boy on the ledge never stirred. The ducks took late alarm at the skiff, swerved aside and into the air, passing with a whirr no more than fifty feet over the head of the boy, who remained on the ledge like a statue, without his gun, watching the two crouching in the boat.

The fisherman's son climbed onto the ledge and held the painter. The bottom of the skiff was covered with feathery black and white bodies with feet upturned and necks lolling. He was jubilant. "We got twenty-seven!" he told his cousin. "How's that? Nine apiece. Boy—" he added, "what a cool Christmas!"

The fisherman pulled the skiff onto its shelf and all three went and lay down again in anticipation of the next flight. The son, reloading, patted his gun affectionately. "I'm going to get me ten next time," he said. Then he asked his cousin, "Whatsamatter—didn't you see the strays?"

"Yeah," the boy said.

"How come you didn't shoot at 'em?"

"Didn't feel like it," replied the boy, still with a trace of sullenness.

"You stupid or something?" The fisherman's son was astounded. "What a highlander!" But the fisherman, though he said nothing, knew that the older boy had had an attack of ledge fever.

"Cripes!" his son kept at it. "I'd at least of tried."

"Shut up," the fisherman finally told him, "and leave him be."

At slack water three more flocks came in, one right after the other, and when it was over, the skiff was half full of clean, dead birds. During the subsequent lull they broke out the lunch and ate it all and finished the hot coffee. For a while the fisherman sucked away on his cold pipe. Then he had himself a swig of whiskey.

The boys passed the time contentedly jabbering about who shot the most—there were ninety-two all told—which of their friends they would show the biggest ones to, how many each could eat at a meal provided they didn't have to eat any vegetables. Now and then they heard sporadic distant gunfire on the mainland, at its nearest point about two miles to the north. Once far off they saw a fishing boat making in the direction of home.

At length the fisherman got a hand inside his oilskins and produced his watch.

"Do we have to go now?" asked his son.

"Not just yet," he replied. "Pretty soon." Everything had been perfect. As good as he had ever had it. Because he was getting tired of the boys' chatter he got up, heavily in his hip boots, and stretched. The tide had turned and was coming in, the sky was more ashen, and the wind had freshened enough so that whitecaps were beginning to blossom. It would be a good hour before they had to leave the ledge and pick up the tollers. However, he guessed they would leave a little early. On account of the rising wind he doubted there would be much more shooting. He stepped carefully along the back of the ledge, to work his kinks out. It was also getting a little colder.

The whiskey had begun to warm him, but he was unprepared for the sudden blaze that flashed upward inside him from belly to head. He was standing looking at the shelf where the skiff was. Only the foolish skiff was not there!

For the second time that day the fisherman felt the deep vacuity of disbelief. He gaped, seeing nothing but the flat shelf of rock. He whirled, started toward the boys, slipped, recovered himself, fetched a complete circle, and stared at the unimaginably empty shelf. Its emptiness made him feel as if everything he had done that day so far, his life so far, he had dreamed. What could have happened? The tide was still nearly a foot below. There had been no sea to speak of. The skiff could hardly have slid off by itself. For the life of him, consciously careful as he inveterately was, he could not now remember hauling it up the last time. Perhaps in the heat of hunting, he had left it to the boy. Perhaps he could not remember which was the last time.

"Christ—" he exclaimed loudly, without realizing it because he was so entranced by the invisible event.

"What's wrong, Dad?" asked his son, getting to his feet.

The fisherman went blind with uncontainable rage. "Get back down there where you belong!" he screamed. He scarcely noticed the boy sink back in amazement. In a frenzy he ran along the ledge thinking the skiff might have been drawn up at another place, though he knew better. There was no other place.

He stumbled, half falling, back to the boys who were gawking at him in consternation, as though he had gone insane. "Goddamn it!" he yelled savagely, grabbing both of them and yanking them to their knees. "Get on your feet!"

"What's wrong?" his son repeated in a stifled voice.

"Never mind what's wrong," he snarled. "Look for the skiff—it's adrift!" When they peered around he gripped their shoulders, brutally facing them about. "Downwind—" He slammed his fist against his thigh. "Jesus!" he cried, struck to madness by their stupidity.

At last he sighted the skiff himself, magically bobbing along the grim sea like a toller, a quarter of a mile to leeward on a direct course for home. The impulse to strip himself naked was succeeded instantly by a queer calm. He simply sat down on the ledge and forgot everything except the marvelous mystery.

As his awareness partially returned he glanced toward the boys. They were still observing the skiff speechlessly. Then he was gazing into the clear young eyes of his son.

"Dad," asked the boy steadily, "what do we do now?"

That brought the fisherman upright. "The first thing we have to do," he heard himself saying with infinite tenderness as if he were making love, "is think."

"Could you swim it?" asked his son.

He shook his head and smiled at them. They smiled quickly back, too quickly. "A hundred yards maybe, in this water. I wish I could," he added. It was the most intimate and pitiful thing he had ever said. He walked in circles round them, trying to break the stall his mind was left in.

He gauged the level of the water. To the eye it was quite stationary, six inches from the shelf at this second. The fisherman did not have to mark it on the side of the rock against the passing of time to prove to his reason that it was rising, always rising. Already it was over the brink of reason, beyond the margins of thought—a senseless measurement. No sense to it.

All his life the fisherman had tried to lick the element of time, by getting up earlier and going to bed later, owning a faster boat, planning more than the day would hold, and tackling just one other job before the deadline fell. If, as on rare occasions he had the grand illusion, he ever really had beaten the game, he would need to call on all his reserves of practice and cunning now.

He sized up the scant but unforgivable three hundred yards to Brown Cow Island. Another hundred yards behind it his boat rode at anchor, where, had he been aboard, he could have cut in a fathometer to plumb the profound and occult seas, or a ship-to-shore radio on which in an interminably short time he would have heard his wife's voice talking to him over the air about homecoming.

"Couldn't we wave something so somebody would see us?" his nephew suggested.

The fisherman spun round. "Load your guns!" he ordered. They loaded as if the air had suddenly gone frantic with birds. "I'll fire once and count to five. Then you fire. Count to five. That way they won't just think it's only somebody gunning ducks. We'll keep doing that."

"We've only got just two-and-a-half boxes left," said his son.

The fisherman nodded, understanding that from beginning to end their situation was purely mathematical, like the ticking of the alarm clock in his silent bedroom. Then he fired. The dog, who had been keeping watch over the decoys, leaped forward and yelped in confusion. They all counted off, fired the first five rounds by threes, and reloaded. The fisherman scanned first the horizon, then the contracting borders of the ledge, which was the sole place the water appeared to be climbing. Soon it would be over the shelf.

They counted off and fired the second five rounds. "We'll hold off awhile on the last one," the fisherman told the boys. He sat down and pondered what a trivial thing was a skiff. This one he and the boy had knocked together in a day. Was a gun, manufactured for killing.

His son tallied up the remaining shells, grouping them symmetrically in threes on the rock when the wet box fell apart. "Two short," he announced. They reloaded and laid the guns on their knees.

Behind thickening clouds they could not see the sun going down. The water, coming up, was growing blacker. The fisherman thought he might have told his wife they would be home before dark since it was Christmas day. He realized he had forgotten about its being any particular day. The tide would not be high until two hours after sunset. When they did not get in by nightfall, and could not be raised by radio, she might send somebody to hunt for them right away. He rejected this arithmetic immediately, with a sickening shock, recollecting it was a two-and-a-half-hour run at best. Then it occurred to him that she might send somebody on the mainland who was nearer. She would think he had engine trouble.

He rose and searched the shoreline, barely visible. Then his glance dropped to the toy shoreline at the edges of the reef. The shrinking ledge, so sinister from a boat, grew dearer minute by minute as though the whole wide world he gazed on from horizon to horizon balanced on its contracting rim. He checked the water level and found the shelf awash.

Some of what went through his mind the fisherman told to the boys. They accepted it without comment. If he caught their eyes they looked away to spare him or because they were not yet old enough to face what they saw. Mostly they watched the rising water. The fisherman was unable to initiate a word of encouragement. He wanted one of them to ask him whether somebody would reach them ahead of the tide. He would have found it possible to say yes. But they did not inquire.

The fisherman was not sure how much, at their age, they were able to imagine. Both of them had seen from the docks drowned bodies put ashore out of boats. Sometimes they grasped things, and sometimes not. He supposed they might be longing for the comfort of their mothers, and was astonished, as much as he was capable of any astonishment except the supreme one, to discover himself wishing he had not left his wife's dark, close, naked bed that morning.

"Is it time to shoot now?" asked his nephew.

"Pretty soon," he said, as if he were putting off making good on a promise. "Not yet."

His own boy cried softly for a brief moment, like a man, his face averted in an effort neither to give nor show pain.

"Before school starts," the fisherman said, wonderfully detached, "we'll go to town and I'll buy you boys anything you want."

With great difficulty, in a dull tone as though he did not in the least desire it, his son said after a pause, "I'd like one of those new thirty-horse outboards."

"All right," said the fisherman. And to his nephew, "How about you?"

The nephew shook his head desolately. "I don't want anything," he said.

After another pause the fisherman's son said, "Yes he does, Dad. He wants one too."

"All right—" the fisherman said again, and said no more.

The dog whined in uncertainty and licked the boys' faces where they sat together. Each threw an arm over his back and hugged him. Three strays flew in and sat companionably down among the stiff-necked decoys. The dog crouched, obedient to his training. The boys observed them listlessly. Presently, sensing something untoward, the ducks took off, splashing the wave tops with feet and wingtips, into the dusky waste.

The sea began to make up in the mountain wind, and the wind bore a new and deathly chill. The fisherman, scouring the somber, dwindling shadow of the mainland for a sign, hoped it would not snow. But it did. First a few flakes, then a flurry, then storming past horizontally. The fisherman took one long, bewildered look at Brown Cow Island three hundred yards dead to leeward, and got to his feet.

Then it shut in, as if what was happening on the ledge was too private even for the last wan light of the expiring day.

"Last round," the fisherman said austerely.

The boys rose and shouldered their tacit guns. The fisherman fired into the flying snow. He counted methodically to five. His son fired and counted. His nephew. All three fired and counted. Four rounds.

"You've got one left, Dad," his son said.

The fisherman hesitated another second, then he fired the final shell. Its pathetic report, like the spat of a popgun, whipped away on the wind and was instantly blanketed in falling snow.

Night fell all in a moment to meet the ascending sea. They were now barely able to make one another out through driving snowflakes, dim as ghosts in their yellow oilskins. The fisherman heard a sea break and glanced down where his feet were. They seemed to be wound in a snowy sheet. Gently he took the boys by the shoulders and pushed them in front of him, feeling with his feet along the shallow sump to the place where it triangulated into a sharp crevice at the highest point of the ledge. "Face ahead," he told them. "Put the guns down."

"I'd like to hold mine, Dad," begged his son.

"Put it down," said the fisherman. "The tide won't hurt it. Now brace your feet against both sides and stay there."

They felt the dog, who was pitch black, running up and down in perplexity between their straddled legs. "Dad," said his son, "what about the pooch?"

If he had called the dog by name it would have been too personal. The fisherman would have wept. As it was he had all he could do to keep from laughing. He bent his knees, and when he touched the dog hoisted him under one arm. The dog's belly was soaking wet.

So they waited, marooned in their consciousness, surrounded by a monstrous tidal space which was slowly, slowly closing them out. In this space the periwinkle beneath the fisherman's boots was king. While hovering airborne in his mind he had an inward glimpse of his house as curiously separate, like a June mirage.

Snow, rocks, seas, wind the fisherman had lived by all his life. Now he thought he had never comprehended what they were, and he hated them. Though they had not changed. He was deadly chilled. He set out to ask the boys if they were cold. There was no sense. He thought of the whiskey, and sidled backward, still holding the awkward dog, till he located the bottle under water with his toe. He picked it up squeamishly as though afraid of getting his sleeve wet, worked his way forward and bent over his son. "Drink it," he said, holding the bottle against the boy's ribs. The boy tipped his head back, drank, coughed hotly, then vomited.

"I can't," he told his father wretchedly.

"Try—try—" the fisherman pleaded, as if it meant the difference between life and death.

The boy obediently drank, and again he vomited hotly. He shook his head against his father's chest and passed the bottle forward to his cousin, who drank and vomited also. Passing the bottle back, the boys dropped it in the frigid water between them.

When the waves reached his knees the fisherman set the warm dog loose and said to his son, "Turn around and get up on my shoulders." The boy obeyed. The fisherman opened his oilskin jacket and twisted his hands behind him through his suspenders, clamping the boy's booted ankles with his elbows.

"What about the dog?" the boy asked.

"He'll make his own way all right," the fisherman said. "He can take the cold water." His knees were trembling. Every instinct shrieked for gymnastics. He ground his teeth and braced like a colossus against the sides of the submerged crevice.

The dog, having lived faithfully as though one of them for eleven years, swam a few minutes in and out around the fisherman's legs, not knowing what was happening, and left them without a whimper. He would swim and swim at random by himself, round and round in the blinding night, and when he had swum routinely through the paralyzing water all he could, he would simply, in one incomprehensible moment, drown. Almost the fisherman, waiting out infinity, envied him his pattern.

Freezing seas swept by, flooding inexorably up and up as the earth sank away imperceptibly beneath them. The boy called out once to his cousin. There was no answer. The fisherman, marveling on a terror without voice, was dumbly glad when the boy did not call again. His own boots were long full of water. With no sensation left in his straddling legs he dared not move them. So long as the seas came sidewide against his hips, and then sidewise against his shoulders, he might balance—no telling how long. The upper half of him was what felt frozen. His legs, disengaged from his nerves and his will, he came to regard quite scientifically. They were the absurd, precarious axis around which reeled the surged universal tumult. The waves would come on; he could not visualize how many tossing reinforcements lurked in the night beyond—inexhaustible numbers, and he wept in supernatural fury at each because it was higher, till he transcended hate and took them, swaying like a convert, one by one as they lunged against him and away aimlessly into their own undisputed, wild realm.

From his hips upward the fisherman stretched to his utmost as a man does whose spirit reaches out of dead sleep. The boy's head, none too high, must be at least seven feet above the ledge. Though growing larger every minute, it was a small light life. The fisherman meant to hold it there, if need be, through a thousand tides.

By and by the boy, slumped on the head of his father, asked, "Is it over your boots, Dad?"

"Not yet," the fisherman said. Then through his teeth he added, "If I fall—kick your boots off—swim for it—downwind—to the island. . . ."

"You . . . ?" the boy finally asked.

The fisherman nodded against the boy's belly. "—Won't see each other," he said.

The boy did for the fisherman the greatest thing that can be done. He may have been too young for perfect terror, but he was old enough to know there were things beyond the power of any man. All he could do he did, trusting his father to do all he could, and asking nothing more.

The fisherman, rocked to his soul by a sea, held his eyes shut upon the interminable night.

"Is it time now?" the boy said.

The fisherman could hardly speak. "Not yet," he said. "Not just yet. . . ."

As the land mass pivoted toward sunlight the day after Christmas, a tiny fleet of small craft converged off shore like iron filings to a magnet. At daybreak they found the skiff floating unscathed off the headland, half full of ducks and snow. The shooting *had* been good, as someone hearing on the mainland the previous afternoon had supposed. Two hours afterward they found the unharmed boat adrift five miles at sea. At high noon they found the fisherman at ebb tide, his right foot jammed cruelly into a glacial crevice of the ledge beside three shotguns, his hands tangled behind him in his suspenders, and under his right elbow a rubber boot with a sock and a live starfish in it. After dragging unlit depths all day for the boys, they towed the fisherman home in his own boat at sundown, and in the frost of evening, mute with discovering purgatory, laid him on his wharf for his wife to see.

She, somehow, standing on the dock as in her frequent dream, gazing at the fisherman pure as crystal on the icy boards, a small rubber boot still frozen under one clenched arm, saw him exaggerated beyond remorse or grief, absolved of his mortality.

BARRY HANNAH

Water Liars

When I am run down and flocked around by the world, I go down to Farte Cove off the Yazoo River and take my beer to the end of the pier where the old liars are still snapping and wheezing at one another. The lineup is always different, because they're always dying out or succumbing to constipation, etc., whereupon they go back to the cabins and wait for a good day when they can come out and lie again, leaning on the rail with coats full of bran cookies. The son of the man the cove was named for is often out there. He pronounces his name Far*tay,* with a great French stress on the last syllable. Otherwise you might laugh at his history or ignore it in favor of the name as it's spelled on the sign.

I'm glad it's not my name.

This poor dignified man has had to explain his nobility to the semiliterate of half of America before he could even begin a decent conversation with them. On the other hand, Farte, Jr., is a great liar himself. He tells about seeing ghost people around the lake and tells big loose ones about the size of the fish those ghosts took out of Farte Cove in years past.

Last year I turned thirty-three years old and, raised a Baptist, I had a sense of being Jesus and coming to something decided in my life— because we all know Jesus was crucified at thirty-three. It had all seemed especially important, what you do in this year, and holy with meaning.

On the morning after my birthday party, during which I and my wife almost drowned in vodka cocktails, we both woke up to the making of a truth session about the lovers we'd had before we met each other. I had a mildly exciting and usual history, and she had about the same, which surprised me. For ten years she'd sworn I was the first. I could not believe her history was exactly equal with mine. It hurt me to think that in the era when there were supposed to be virgins she had allowed anyone but *me,* and so on.

I was dazed and exhilarated by this information for several weeks. Finally, it drove me crazy, and I came out to Farte Cove to rest, under the pretense of a fishing week with my chum Wyatt.

I'm still figuring out why I couldn't handle it.

My sense of the past is vivid and slow. I hear every sign and see every shadow. The movement of every limb in every passionate event occupies my mind. I have a prurience on the grand scale. It makes no sense that I should be angry about happenings before she and I ever saw each other. Yet I feel an impotent homicidal urge in the matter of her lovers. She has excused my episodes as the course of things, though she has a vivid memory too. But there is a blurred nostalgia women have that men don't.

You could not believe how handsome and delicate my wife is naked.

I was driven wild by the bodies that had trespassed her twelve and thirteen years ago.

My vacation at Farte Cove wasn't like that easy little bit you get as a rich New Yorker. My finances weren't in great shape; to be true, they were about in ruin, and I left the house knowing my wife would have to answer the phone to hold off, for instance, the phone company itself. Everybody wanted money and I didn't have any.

I was going to take the next week in the house while she went away, watch our three kids and all the rest. When you both teach part-time in the high schools, the income can be slow in summer.

No poor-mouthing here. I don't want anybody's pity. I just want to explain. I've got good hopes of a job over at Alabama next year. Then I'll get myself among higher-paid liars, that's all.

Sidney Farte was out there prevaricating away at the end of the pier when Wyatt and I got there Friday evening. The old faces I recognized; a few new harkening idlers I didn't.

"Now, Doctor Mooney, he not only saw the ghost of Lily, he says he had intercourse with her. Said it was involuntary. Before he knew what he was doing, he was on her making cadence and all their clothes blown away off in the trees around the shore. She turned into a wax candle right under him."

"Intercourse," said an old-timer, breathing heavy. He sat up on the rail. It was a word of high danger to his old mind. He said it with a long disgust, glad, I guess, he was not involved.

"MacIntire, a Presbyterian preacher, I seen him come out here with his son-and-law, anchor near the bridge, and pull up fifty or more white perch big as small pumpkins. You know what they was using for bait?"

"What?" asked another geezer.

"*Nuthin.* Caught on the bare hook. It was Gawd made them fish bite," said Sidney Farte, going at it good.

"Naw. There be a season they bite a bare hook. Gawd didn't have to've done that," said another old guy, with a fringe of red hair and a racy Florida shirt.

"Nother night," said Sidney Farte, "I saw the ghost of Yazoo hisself with my pa, who's dead. A Indian king with four deer around him."

The old boys seemed to be used to this one. Nobody said anything. They ignored Sidney.

"Tell you what," said a well-built small old boy. "That was somethin when we come down here and had to chase that whole high-school party off the end of this pier, them drunken children. They was smokin dope and two-thirds a them nekid swimmin in the water. Good hunnerd of em. From your so-called *good* high school. What you think's happnin at the bad ones?"

I dropped my beer and grew suddenly sick. Wyatt asked me what was wrong. I could see my wife in 1960 in the group of high-schoolers she must have had. My jealousy went out into the stars of the night above me. I could not bear the roving carelessness of teen-agers, their judgeless tangling of wanting and bodies. But I was the worst back then. In the mad days back then, I dragged the panties off girls I hated and talked badly about them once the sun came up.

"Worst time in my life," said a new, younger man, maybe sixty but with the face of a man who had surrendered, "me and Woody was fishing. Had a lantern. It was about eleven. We was catching a few fish but rowed on into that little cove over there near town. We heard all these sounds, like they was ghosts. We was scared. We thought it might be the Yazoo hisself. We known of some fellows the Yazoo had killed to death just from fright. It was the over the sounds of what was normal human sighin and amoanin. It was big unhuman sounds. We just stood still in the boat. Ain't nuthin else us to do. For thirty minutes."

"An what was it?" said the old geezer, letting himself off the rail.

"We had a big flashlight. There came up this rustlin in the brush and I beamed it over there. The two of em makin the sounds get up with half they clothes on. It was my own daughter Charlotte and an older guy I didn't even know with a mustache. My *own* daughter, and them sounds over the water scarin us like ghosts."

"My Gawd, that's awful," said the old geezer by the rail. "Is that the truth? I wouldn't've told that. That's terrible."

Sidney Farte was really upset.

"This ain't the place!" he said. "Tell your kind of story somewhere else."

The old man who'd told his story was calm and fixed to his place. He'd told the truth. The crowd on the pier was outraged and discomfited. He wasn't one of them. But he stood his place. He had a distressed pride. You could see he had never recovered from the thing he'd told about.

I told Wyatt to bring the old man back to the cabin. He was out here away from his wife the same as me and Wyatt. Just an older guy with a big hurting bosom. He wore a suit and the only way you'd know he was on vacation was he'd removed his tie. He didn't know where the bait house was. He didn't know what to do on vacation at all. But he got drunk with us and I can tell you he and I went out the next morning with our poles, Wyatt driving the motorboat, fishing for white perch in the cove near the town. And we were kindred.

We were both crucified by the truth.

MARK HELPRIN

Letters from the
Samantha

These letters were recovered in good condition from the vault of the sunken *Samantha*, an iron-hulled sailing ship of one thousand tons, built in Scotland in 1879 and wrecked during the First World War in the Persian Gulf off Basra.

20 August, 1909, 20° 14′ 18″ S,
43° 51′ 57″ E
Off Madagascar

DEAR SIR:

Many years have passed since I joined the Green Star Line. You may note in your records and logs, if not, indeed, by memory, the complete absence of disciplinary action against me. During my command, the *Samantha* has been a trim ship on time. Though my subordinates sometimes complain, they are grateful, no doubt, for my firm rule and tidiness. It saves the ship in storms, keeps them healthy, and provides good training—even though they will be masters of steamships.

No other vessel of this line has been as punctual or well run. Even today we are a week ahead and our Madagascar wood will reach Alexandria early. Bound for London, the crew are happy, and though we sail the Mozambique Channel, they act as if we had just caught sight of Margate. There are no problems on this ship. But I must in conscience report an irregular incident for which I am ready to take full blame.

Half a day out of Androka, we came upon a sea so blue and casual that its waters seemed fit to drink. Though the wind was slight and we made poor time, we were elated by perfect climate and painter's colors, for off the starboard side Madagascar rose as green and tranquil as a well-watered palm, its mountains engraved by thrashing freshwater streams which beat down to the coast. A sweet upwelling breeze blew steadily from shore and confounded our square sails. Twenty minutes after noon, the lookout sighted a tornado on land. In the ship's glass I saw it, horrifying and enormous. Though at a great distance, its column appeared as thick as a massive tree on an islet in an atoll, and stretched at least 70 degrees upward from the horizon.

I have seen these pipes of windy fleece before. If there is sea nearby, they rush to it. So did this. When it became not red and black from soil and debris but silver and green from the water it drew, I began to tighten ship. Were the typhoon to have struck us directly, no preparation would have saved us. But what a shame to be swamped by high waves, or to be dismasted by beaten sea and wind. Hatches were battened as if for storm, minor sails furled, and the mainsail driven down half.

It moved back and forth over the sea in illegible patterning, as if tacking to changing winds. To our dismay, the distance narrowed. We were afraid, though every man on deck wanted to see it, to feel it, perhaps to ride its thick swirling waters a hundred times higher than our mast—higher than the peaks inland. I confess that I have wished to be completely taken up by such a thing, to be lifted into the clouds, arms and legs pinned in the stream. The attraction is much like that of phosphorescent seas, when glowing light and smooth swell are dangerously magnetic even for hardened masters of good ships. I have wanted to surrender to plum-colored seas, to know what one might find there naked and alone. But I have not, and will not.

Finally, we began to run rough water. The column was so high that we bent our heads to see its height, and the sound was greater than any engine, causing masts and spars to resonate like cords. Waves broke over the prow. Wind pushed us on, and the curl of the sea rushed to fill the depression of the waters. No more than half a mile off the starboard bow, the column veered to the west, crossing our path to head for Africa as rapidly as an express. Within minutes, we could not even see it.

As it crossed our bows, I veered in the direction from which it had come. It seemed to communicate a decisiveness of course, and here I took opportunity to evade. In doing so we came close to land. This was dangerous not only for the presence of reefs and shoals but because of the scattered debris. Trees as tall as masts and much thicker, roots sucked clean, lay in puzzlement upon the surface. Brush and vines were everywhere. The water was reddish brown from earth which had fallen from the cone. We were meticulously careful in piloting through this fresh salad, as a good ram against a solid limb would have been the end. Our cargo is hardwoods, and would have sunk us like granite. I myself straddled the sprit stays, pushing aside small logs with a boat hook and calling out trim to the wheel.

Nearly clear, we came upon a clump of tangled vegetation. I could not believe my eyes, for floating upon it was a large monkey, bolt upright and dignified. I sighted him first, though the lookout called soon after. On impulse, I set trim for the wavy mat and, as we smashed onto it, offered the monkey an end of the boat hook. When he seized it I was almost pulled in, for his weight is nearly equal to mine. I observed that he had large teeth, which appeared both white and sharp. He came close, and then took to the lines until he sat high on the topgallant. As he passed, his foot cuffed my shoulder and I could smell him.

My ship is a clean ship. I regretted immediately my gesture with the hook. We do not need the mysterious defecations of such a creature, or the threat of him in the rigging at night. But we could not capture him to throw him back into the sea and, even had we collared him, might not have been able to get him overboard without danger to ourselves. We are now many miles off the coast. It is dark, and he sits high off the deck. The night watch is afraid and requests that I fell him with my rifle. They have seen his sharp teeth, which he displays with much screaming and gesticulating when they near him in the rigging. I think he is merely afraid, and I cannot bring myself to shoot him. I realize that no animals are allowed on board and have often had to enforce this rule when coming upon a parrot or cat hidden belowdecks where some captains do not go. But this creature we have today removed from the sea is like a man, and he has ridden the typhoon. Perhaps we will pass a headland and throw him overboard on a log. He must eventually descend for want of food. Then we will have our way. I will report further when the matter is resolved, and assure you that I regret this breach of regulations.

Yours & etc.,
SAMSON LOW
Master, S/V SAMANTHA

23 August, 1909, 10° 43′ 3″ S,
49° 5′ 27″ E
South of the Seychelles

DEAR SIR:

We have passed the Channel and are heading north-northeast, hoping to ride the summer monsoon. It is shamefully hot, though the breeze is less humid than usual. Today two men dropped from the heat but they resumed work by evening. Because we are on a homeward tack, morale is at its best, or rather would be were it not for that damned ape in the rigging. He has not come down, and we have left behind his island and its last headland. He will have to have descended by the time we breach passage between Ras Asir and Jazirat Abd al-Kuri. The mate has suggested that there we throw him into the sea on a raft, which the carpenter has already set about building. He has embarked upon this with my permission, since there is little else for him to do. It has been almost an overly serene voyage and the typhoon caused no damage.

The raft he designed is very clever and has become a popular subject of discussion. It is about six feet by three feet, constructed of spare pine dunnage we were about to cast away when the typhoon was sighted. On each side is an outrigger for stability in the swell. In the center is a box, in which is a seat. Flanking this box are several smaller ones for fruit, biscuit, and a bucket of fresh water, in case the creature should drift a long time on the sea. This probably will not be so; the currents off Ras Asir drive for the beach, and we have noted that dunnage is quickly thrown upon the strand. Nevertheless, the crew have added their own touch—a standard distress flag flying from a ten-foot switch. They do not know, but I will order it replaced by a banner of another color, so that a hapless ship will not endanger itself to rescue a speechless monkey.

The crew have divided into two factions—those who wish to have the monkey shot, and those who would wait for him to descend and then put him in his boat. I am with the latter, since I would be the huntsman, and have already mentioned my lack of enthusiasm for this. A delegation of the first faction protested. They claimed that the second faction comprised those who stayed on deck, that the creature endangered balance in the rigging, and that he produced an uncanny effect in his screeching and bellicose silhouettes, which from below are humorous but which at close range, they said, are disconcerting and terrifying.

Since I had not seen him for longer than a moment and wanted to verify their complaint, I went up. Though sixty years of age, I did not use the bosun's chair, and detest those masters who do. It is pharaonic, and smacks of days in my father's youth when he saw with his own eyes gentlemen in sedan chairs carried about the city. The sight of twenty men laboring to hoist a ship's rotund captain is simply Egyptian, and I will not have it. Seventy feet off the deck, a giddy height to which I have not ascended in years, I came even with the ape. The ship was passing a boisterous sea and had at least a twenty-degree roll, which flung the two of us from side to side like pendula.

I am not a naturalist, nor have we on board a book of zoology, so the most I can do is to describe him. He is almost my height (nearly five feet ten inches) and appears to be sturdily built. Feet and hands are human in appearance except that they have a bulbous, skew, arthritic look common to monkeys. He is muscular and covered with fine reddish-brown hair. One can see the whiteness of his tendons when he stretches an arm or leg. I have mentioned the sharp, dazzling white teeth, set in rows like a trap, canine and pointed. His face is curiously delicate, and covered with orange hair leading to a snow-white crown of fur. My breath nearly failed when I looked into his eyes, for they are a bright, penetrating blue.

At first, he began to scream and swing as if he would come at me. If he had, I would have fared badly. The sailors fear him, for there is no man on board with half his strength, no man on the sea with a tenth his agility in the ropes, and if there is a man with the glacierlike pinnacled teeth, then he must be in a Scandinavian or Eastern European circus, for there they are fond of such things. To my surprise, he stopped his pantomime and, with a gentle and quizzical tilt of the head, looked me straight in the eyes. I had been sure that as a man I could answer his gaze as if from infallibility, and I calmly looked back. But he had me. His eyes unset me, so that I nearly shook. From that moment, he has not threatened or bared his teeth, but merely rests near the top of the foremast. The crew have attributed his conversion to my special power. This is flattering, though not entirely, as it assumes my ability to commune with an ape. Little do they suspect that it is I and not the monkey who have been converted, although to what I do not know. I am still thoroughly ashamed of my indiscretion and the trouble arising from it. We will get him and put him adrift off Ras Asir.

This evening, the cook grilled up some beef. I had him thoroughly vent the galley and use a great many herbs. The aroma was maddening. I sat in near-hypnotic ease in a canvas chair on the quarterdeck, a glass of wine in hand, as the heat fell to a cool breeze. We are all sunburnt and have been working hard, as the ape silently watches, to trim regularly and catch the best winds. We are almost in the full swift of the monsoon, and shortly will ride it in all its speed. It was wonderful to sit on deck and smell the herb-laden meat. The sea itself must have been jealous. I had several men ready with cargo net and pikes, certain that he would come down. We stared up at him as if he were the horizon, waiting. He smelled the food and agitated back and forth. Though he fretted, he did not descend. Even when we ate we saw him shunting to and fro on a yardarm. We left a dish for him away from us but he did not venture to seize it. If he had, we would have seized him.

From his impatience, I predict that tomorrow he will surrender to his stomach. Then we will catch him and this problem will be solved. I truly regret such an irregularity, though it would be worthwhile if he could only tell us how far he was lifted inside the silvered cone, and what it was like.

Yours & etc.,
SAMSON LOW

25 August, 1909, 2° 13′ 10″ N,
51° 15′ 17″ E
Off Mogadishu

DEAR SIR:

Today he came down. After the last correspondence, it occurred to me that he might be vegetarian, and that though he was hungry, the meat had put him off. Therefore, I searched my memory for the most aromatic vegetable dish I know. In your service as a fourth officer, I called at Jaffa port, in Palestine, in January of 1873. We went up to Sfat, a holy town high in the hills, full of Jews and Arabs, quiet and mystical. There were so many come into that freezing velvet dome of stars that all hostelries were full. I and several others paid a small sum for private lodging and board. At two in the morning, after we had returned from Mt. Jermak, the Arabs made a hot lively fire from bundles of dry cypress twigs, and in a great square iron pan heated local oil and herbs, in which they fried thick sections of potato. I have never eaten so well. Perhaps it was our hunger, the cold, the silence, being high in the mountains at Sfat, where air is like ether and all souls change. Today I made the cook follow that old receipt.

We had been in the monsoon for several hours, and the air was littered with silver sparks—apparitions of heat from a glittering afternoon. Though the sun was low, iron decks could not be tread. In the rigging, he appeared nearly finished, limp and slouching, an arm hanging without energy, his back bent. We put potatoes in a dish on the forecastle. He descended slowly, finally touching deck lightly and ambling to the bows like a spider, all limbs brushing the planks. He ate his fill, and we threw the net over him. We had expected a ferocious struggle, but his posture and expression were so peaceful that I ordered the net removed. Sailors stood ready with pikes, but he stayed in place. Then I approached him and extended my hand as if to a child.

In imitation, he put out his arm, looking much less fearsome. Without a show of teeth, in his tired state, crouched on all fours to half our heights, he was no more frightening than a hound. I led him to the stern and back again while the crew cheered and laughed. Then the mate took him, and then the entire hierarchy of the ship, down to the cabin boys, who are smaller than he and seemed to interest him the most. By dark, he had strolled with every member of the crew and was miraculously tame. But I remembered his teeth, and had him chained to his little boat.

He was comfortable there, surrounded by fruit and water (which he ate and drank methodically) and sitting on a throne of sorts, with half a dozen courtiers eager to look in his eyes and hold his obliging wrist. Mine is not the only London post in which he will be mentioned. Those who can write are describing him with great zeal. I have seen some of these letters. He has been portrayed as a "mad baboon," a "man-eating gorilla of horrible colors, muscled but as bright as a bird," a "pygmy man set down on the sea by miracle and typhoon," and as all manner of Latin names, each different from the others and incorrectly spelled.

Depending on the bend of the monsoon and whether it continues to run strongly, we will pass Ras Asir in three days. I thought of casting him off early but was implored to wait for the Cape. I relented, and in doing so was made to understand why those in command must stay by rules. I am sure, however, that my authority is not truly diminished, and when the ape is gone I will again tighten discipline.

I have already had the distress flag replaced by a green banner. It flies over the creature on his throne. Though in splendor, he is in chains and in three days' time will be on the sea once more.

Yours & etc.,
SAMSON LOW

28 August, 1909, 12° 4' 39" N,
50° 1' 2" E
North of Ras Asir

DEAR SIR:

A most alarming incident has occurred. I must report, though it is among the worst episodes of my command. This morning, I arose, expecting to put the ape over the side as we rounded Ras Asir at about eleven. (The winds have been consistently excellent and a northward breeze veering off the monsoon has propelled us as steadily as an engine.) Going out on deck, I discovered that his boat was nowhere to be seen. At first, I thought that the mate had already disposed of him, and was disappointed that we were far from the coast. Then, to my shock, I saw him sitting unmanacled atop the main cargo hatch.

I screamed at the mate, demanding to know what had happened to the throne (as it had come to be called). He replied that it had gone overboard during the twelve-to-four watch. I stormed below and got that watch out in a hurry. Though sleepy-eyed, they were terrified. I told them that if the guilty one did not come forth I would put them all in irons. My temper was short and I could have struck them down. Two young sailors, as frightened as if they were surrendering themselves to die, admitted that they had thrown it over. They said they did not want to see the ape put to drift.

They are in irons until we make Suez. Their names are Mulcahy and Esper, and their pay is docked until they are freed. As we rounded the Cape, cutting close in (for the waters there are deep), we could see that though the creature would have been immediately cast up on shore, the shore itself was barren and inhospitable, and surely he would have died there. My Admiralty chart does not detail the inland topography of this area and shows only a yellow tongue marked "Africa" thrusting into the Gulf of Aden.

I can throw him overboard now or later. I do not want to do it. I brought him on board in the first place. There is nothing with which to fashion another raft. We have many tons of wood below, but not a cubic foot of it is lighter than water. The wind is good and we are making for the Bab al-Mandab, where we will pass late tomorrow afternoon—after that, the frustrating run up the Red Sea to the Canal.

The mate suggests that we sell him to the Egyptians. But I am reluctant to make port with this in mind, as it would be a victory for the two in chains and in the eyes of many others. And we are not animal traders. If he leaves us at sea the effects of his presence will be invalidated, we will touch land with discipline restored, and I will have the option of destroying these letters, though everything here has been entered in short form in the log. I have ordered him not to be fed, but they cast him scraps. I must get back my proper hold on the ship.

Yours & etc.,
SAMSON LOW

30 August, 1909, 15° 49′ 30″ N,
41° 5′ 32″ E
Red Sea off Massawa

DEAR SIR:

I have been felled by an attack of headaches. Never before has this happened. There is pressure in my skull enough to burst it. I cannot keep my balance; my eyes roam and I am drunk with pain. For the weary tack up the Red Sea I have entrusted the mate with temporary command, retiring to my cabin with the excuse of heat prostration. I have been in the Red Sea time and again but have never felt apprehension that death would follow its heat. We have always managed. To the east, the mountains of the Hijaz are so dry and forbidding that I have seen sailors look away in fright.

The ape has begun to suffer from the heat. He is listless and ignored. His novelty has worn off (with the heat as it is) and no one pays him any attention. He will not go belowdecks but spends most of the day under the canvas sun shield, chewing slowly, though there is nothing in his mouth. It is hot there—the light so white and uncompromising it sears the eyes. I have freed his champions from irons and restored their pay. By this act I have won over the crew and caused the factions to disappear. No one thinks about the ape. But I dare not risk a recurrence of bad feeling and have decided to cast him into the sea. Where we found him, a strong seaward current would have carried him to the open ocean. Here, at least, he can make the shore, although it is the most barren coast on earth. But who would have thought he might survive the typhoon? He has been living beyond his time. To be picked up and whirled at incomprehensible speed, carried for miles above the earth where no man has ever been, and thrown into the sea is a death sentence. If he survived that, perhaps he can survive Arabian desert.

His expression is neither sad nor fierce. He looks like an old man, neutral to the world. In the last two days he has become the target of provocation and physical blows. I have ordered this stopped, but a sailor will sometimes throw a nail or a piece of wood at him. We shall soon be rid of him.

Yesterday we came alongside another British ship, the *Stonepool*, of the Dutch Express Line. On seeing the ape, they were envious. What is it, their captain asked, amazed at its coloring. I replied that he was a Madagascar ape we had fished from the sea, and I offered him to them, saying he was as tame as a dog. At first, they wanted him. The crew cried out for his acceptance, but the captain demurred, shaking his head and looking into my eyes as if he were laughing at me. "Damn!" I said, and went below without even a salute at parting.

My head aches. I must stop. At first light tomorrow, I will toss him back.

Yours & etc.,
SAMSON LOW

3 September, 1909
Suez

DEAR SIR:

The morning before last I went on deck at dawn. The ape was sitting on the main hatch, his eyes upon me from the moment I saw him. I walked over to him and extended my arm, which he would not take in his customary manner. I seized his wrist, which he withdrew. However, as he did this I laid hold of the other wrist, and pulled him off the hatch. He did not bare his teeth. He began to scream. Awakened by this, most of the crew stood in the companionways or on deck, silently observing.

He was hard to drag, but I towed him to the rail. When I took his other arm to hoist him over, he bared his teeth with a frightening shriek. Everyone was again terrified. The teeth must be six inches long.

He came at me with those teeth, and I could do nothing but throttle him. With my hands on his throat, his arms were free. He grasped my side. I felt the pads of his hands against my ribs. I had to tolerate that awful sensation to keep hold of his throat. No man aboard came close. He shrieked and moaned. His eyes reddened. My response was to tighten my hold, to end the horror. I gripped so hard that my own teeth were bared and I made sounds similar to his. He put his hands around my neck as if to strangle me back, but I had already taken the inside position and, despite his great strength, lessened the power of his grip merely by lifting my arms against his. Nevertheless he choked me. But I had a great head start. We held this position for long minutes, sweating, until his arms dropped and his body convulsed. In rage, I threw him by the neck into the sea, where he quickly sank.

Some of the crew have begun to talk about him as if he were about to be canonized. Others see him as evil. I assembled them as the coasts began to close on Suez and the top of the sea was white and still. I made my views clear, for in years of command and in a life on the sea I have learned much. I felt confident of what I told them.

He is not a symbol. He stands neither for innocence nor for evil. There is no parable and no lesson in his coming and going. I was neither right nor wrong in bringing him aboard (though it was indeed incorrect) or in what I later did. We must get on with the ship's business. He does not stand for a man or men. He stands for nothing. He was an ape, simian and lean, half sensible. He came on board, and now he is gone.

Yours & etc.,
SAMSON LOW

URSULA K. LE GUIN

Ile Forest

"Surely," said the young doctor, "there are unpardonable crimes! Murder can't go unpunished."

The senior partner shook his head. "There are unpardonable people, perhaps; but crimes . . . they depend . . ."

"On what? To take a human life—that's absolute. Self-defense aside, of course. The sacredness of human life—"

"Is nothing the law can judge of," the older man said dryly. "I have a murder in the family, as a matter of fact. Two murders." And, gazing mostly at the fire, he told his story.

My first practice was up north in the Valone. I went there with my sister in 1902. Even then it was a drab place. The old estates had sold out to the beet-root plantations, and collieries spread a murk on the hills to the south and west. It was just a big, dull plain; only at the east end of it, Valone Alte, did you get any sense of being in the mountains. On the first day I drove to Valone Alte I noticed a grove of trees; the trees in the valley had all been cut down. There were birches turning gold, and a house behind them, and behind it a stand of huge old oaks, turning dim red and brown; it was October. It was beautiful. When my sister and I drove out on Sunday I went that way, and she said in her drowsy way that it was like the castle in the fairy tale, the castle of silver in a forest of gold. I had several patients in Valone Alte, and always drove that road. In winter when the leaves were down you could see the old house; in spring you could hear the cuckoos calling, and in summer the mourning-doves. I didn't know if anyone lived there. I never asked.

The year went round; I didn't have all the practice I'd hoped for, but Poma, my sister Pomona, was good at making ends meet, for all she looked so sleepy and serene. So we got on. One evening I came in and found a call had been left from a place called Ile on the Valone Alte road. I asked Minna, the housekeeper, where it was.

"Why, in Ile Forest," she said, as if there was a forest the size of Siberia there. "Past the old mill."

"The castle of silver," Poma said, smiling. I set right off. I was curious. You know how it is, when you've built up your fancies about a place, and then suddenly are called to go into it. The old trees stood round, the windows of the house reflected the last red of the west. As I tied up my horse, a man came out to meet me.

He didn't come out of any fairy tale. He was about forty and had that hatchet face you see up north, hard as flint. He took me straight in. The house was unlit; he carried a kerosene lamp. What I could see of the rooms looked bare, empty. No carpets, nothing. The upstairs room we came to had no rug either; bed, table, a few chairs; but a roaring hot fire in the hearth. It helps to have a forest, when you need firewood.

The patient was the owner of the forest, Ileskar. Pneumonia. And he was a fighter. I was there on and off for seventy hours, and he never drew a breath in all that time that wasn't an act of pure willpower. The third night, I had a woman in labor in Mesoval, but I left her to the midwife. I was young, you know, and I said to myself that babies come into the world every day, but it's not every day a brave man leaves it. He fought; and I tried to help him. At dawn the fever went down abruptly, the way it does now with these new drugs, but it wasn't any drug; he'd fought, and won. I drove home in a kind of exaltation, in a white windy sunrise.

And I dropped in daily while he convalesced. He drew me, the place drew me. That last night, it had been one of those nights you have only when you're young—whole nights, from sunset to sunrise, when life and death are present with you, and outside the windows there's the forest, and the winter, and the dark.

I say "forest" just as Minna did, meaning that stand of a few hundred trees. It had been a forest once. It had covered all Valone Alte, and so had the Ileskar properties. For a century and a half it had all gone down and down; nothing left now but the grove, and the house, and a share in the Kravay plantations, enough to keep one Ileskar alive. And Martin, the hatchet-faced fellow, his servant technically, though they shared the work and ate together. Martin was a strange fellow, jealous, devoted to Ileskar. I felt that devotion as an actual force, not sexual, but possessive, defensive. It did not puzzle me too much. There was something about Galven Ileskar that made it seem quite natural. Natural to admire him, and to protect him.

I got his story from Minna, mostly; her mother had worked for his mother. The father had spent what was left to spend, and then died of the pleurisy. Galven went into the army at twenty; at thirty he married, retired as a captain, and came back to Ile. After about three years his wife deserted him, ran away with a man from Brailava. And about that I learned a little from Galven himself. He was grateful to me for my visits;

I suppose it was plain that I wanted his friendship. He felt he should not withhold himself. I'd rambled on about Poma and myself, so he felt obliged to tell me about his marriage. "She was very weak," he said. He had a gentle, husky voice. "I took her weakness for sweetness. A mistake. But it wasn't her fault. A mistake. You know she left me, with another man."

I nodded, very embarrassed.

"I saw him whip a horse blind once," Galven said, in the same thoughtful, painful way. "Stand and whip its eyes till they were open sores. When I got there he'd just finished. He gave a big sigh of satisfaction, as if he'd just gotten up from dinner. It was his own horse. I didn't do anything. Told him to get off the place, clear out. Not enough. . . ."

"You and your—wife are divorced, then?"

"Yes," he said, and then he looked across the room at Martin, who was building up the fire. Martin nodded, and Galven said, "Yes," again. He was only a week or so convalescent, he looked tired; it was a bit strange, but I already knew he was a strange fellow. He said, "I'm sorry. I've forgotten how to talk to civilized people."

It was really painful to have him apologizing to me, and so I just went on with the first thing that came to mind about Poma and myself and old Minna and my patients, and presently I wound up asking if I might bring Poma sometime when I came out to Ile. "She's admired the place so much when we drive past."

"It would be a great pleasure to me," Galven said. "But you'll let me get on my feet again, first? And it is a bit of a wolf's den, you know. . . ."

I was deaf. "She wouldn't notice that," I said. "Her own room's like a thicket, scarves and shawls and little bottles and books and hairpins, she never puts anything away. She never gets her buttons into the right buttonholes, and she leaves everything around behind her, sort of like a ship's wake." I wasn't exaggerating. Poma loved soft clothes and gauzy things, and wherever she'd been there was a veil dripping off a chair arm, or a scarf fluttering on a rosebush, or some creamy fluffy thing dropped by the door, as if she were some sort of little animal that left bits of its fur around, the way rabbits leave white plumes on the briars in the early morning in the fields. When she'd lost a scarf and left her neck bare she'd catch up any sort of kerchief, and I'd ask her what she had on her shoulders now, the hearth rug? and she'd smile her sweet, embarrassed, lazy smile. She was a sweet one, my little sister. I got a bit of a shock when I told her I'd take her out to Ile one of these days. "No," she said, like that.

"Why not?" I was chagrined. I'd talked a lot about Ileskar, and she had seemed interested.

"He doesn't want women and strangers around," she said. "Let the poor fellow be."

"Nonsense. He's very lonely, and doesn't know how to break out of it."

"Then you're just what he needs," she said, with a smile. I insisted—I was bent on doing Galven good, you see—and finally she said, "I have queer ideas about that place, Gil. When you talk about him, I keep thinking of the forest. The old forest, I mean, the way it must have been. A great, dim place, with glades no one ever sees, and places people have known but forgotten, and wild animals roaming in it. A place you get lost in. I think I'll stay home and tend my roses."

I suppose I said something about "feminine illogic," and the rest. Anyhow, I trampled on, and she gave in to me. To yield was her grace, as not to yield was Galven's. No day had been set for our visit, and that reassured her. In fact it was a couple of months before she went to Ile.

I remember the wide, heavy, February sky hanging over the valley as we drove there. The house looked naked in that winter light among bare trees. You saw the shingles off the roof, the uncurtained windows, the weedy driveways. I had spent an uneasy night, dreaming that I was trying to track somebody, some little animal it seemed, through the woods, and never finding it.

Martin wasn't about. Galven put up our pony and brought us into the house. He was wearing old officer's trousers with the stripe taken off, an old coat and a coarse woollen muffler. I had never noticed, till I looked through Poma's eyes, how poor he was. Compared with him, we were wealthy: we had our coats, our coals, our cart and pony, our little treasures and possessions. He had an empty house.

He or Martin had felled one of the oaks to feed the enormous fireplace downstairs. The chairs we sat in were from his room upstairs. We were cold, we were stiff. Galven's good manners were frozen. I asked where Martin was. "Hunting," Galven said, expressionless.

"Do you hunt, Mr. Ileskar?" Poma asked. Her voice was easy, her face looked rosy in the firelight. Galven looked at her and thawed. "I used to go over to the marshes for duck, when my wife was alive," he said. "There aren't many birds left, but I liked it, wading out in the marshes as the sun came up."

"Just the thing for a bad chest," I said, "take it up again by all means." All at once we were all relaxed. Galven got to tell us hunting stories that had been passed down in his family—tales of boar hunting; there'd been no wild boar in the Valone for a hundred years. And that sent us to the tales that old villagers like Minna could still tell you in those days; Poma was fascinated with them, and Galven told her one, a kind of crude, weird epic of avalanches and ax-armed heroes which must have come down from hut to hut, over the centuries, from the high mountains above the valley. He spoke well, in his dry, soft voice, and we listened well, there by the fire, with drafts and shadows at our back. I tried to write that tale down once, and found I could remember only fragments, all the poetry of it gone; but I heard Poma tell it to her children once, word for word as Galven told it that afternoon in Ile.

As we drove away from the place I thought I saw Martin come out of the forest toward the house, but it was too dark to be sure.

At supper Poma asked, "His wife is dead?"

"Divorced."

She poured some tea and dreamed over it awhile.

"Martin was avoiding us," I said.

"Disapproves of my coming there."

"He's a dour one all right. But you did like Galven?"

Poma nodded and presently, as if by afterthought, smiled. And soon she drifted off to her room, leaving a filmy pink scarf clinging to her chair by a thread.

After a few weeks Galven called on us. I was flattered, and startled. I had never imagined him away from Ile, standing like anybody else in our six-by-six parlor. He had got himself a horse, in Mesoval. He was tremendously pleased and serious, explaining to us how it was a really fine mare, but old and overridden, and how you went about "bringing back" a ruined horse. "When she's fit again, perhaps you'd like to ride her, Miss Pomona," he said, for my sister had mentioned that she loved riding. "She's very gentle."

Pomona accepted at once; she never could resist a ride—"It's my laziness," she always said, "the horse does the work, and I just sit there."

While Galven was there, Minna kept peering through the crack of the door. After he'd gone she treated us with the first inkling of respect she'd shown us yet. We'd moved up a notch in the world. I took advantage of it to ask her about the man from Brailava.

"He used to come to hunt. Mr. Ileskar used to entertain, those days. Not like in his father's day, but still, there'd be ladies and gentlemen come. That one come for the hunting. They say he beat his horse blind and then had an awful quarrel with Mr. Ileskar about it and was sent off. But he come back, I guess, and made a fool of Mr. Ileskar after all."

So it was true about the horse. I hadn't been sure. Galven did not lie, but I had a notion that in his loneliness he had not kept a firm hold on the varieties, the distinctions, of truth. I don't know what gave me that impression, other than his having said once or twice that his wife was dead; and she was, for him, if not for others. At any rate Minna's grin displeased me—her silly respect for Ileskar as "a gentleman," and disrespect for him as a man. I said so. She shrugged her wide shoulders. "Well, doctor, then tell me why he didn't up and follow 'em? Why'd he let the fellow just walk off with his wife?"

She had a point there.

"She wasn't worth his chasing after," I said. Minna shrugged again, and no wonder. By her code, and Galven's, that was not how pride worked.

In fact it was inconceivable that he had simply given in. I had seen him fight a worse enemy than an adulterer. . . . Had Martin somehow interfered? Martin was a strong Christian; he had a different code. But strong as he might be he could not have held Galven back from anything Galven willed to do. It was all very curious, and I brooded over it at odd moments all that spring. It was the *passiveness* of Galven's behavior that I simply could not fit in to the proud, direct, intransigent man I thought I knew. Some step was missing.

I took Poma out several times to ride at Ile that spring; the winter had left her a bit run down, and I prescribed the exercise. That gave Galven great pleasure. It was a long time since he'd felt himself of use to another human being. Come June he got a second horse, when his money from the Kravay plantations came in; it was called Martin's horse, and Martin rode it when he went to Mesoval, but Galven rode it when Poma came to ride the old black mare. They were a funny pair, Galven every inch the cavalryman on the big rawboned roan, Poma lazy and smiling, sidesaddle on the fat old mare. All summer he'd ride down on Sunday afternoon leading the mare, pick up Poma, and they'd ride out all afternoon. She came in bright-eyed from these rides, wind-flushed, and I laid it to the outdoor exercise—oh, there's no fool like a young doctor!

There came an evening of August, the evening of a hot day. I'd been on an obstetrics call, five hours, premature twins, stillborn, and I came home about six and lay down in my room. I was worn out. The stillbirth, the sickly heavy heat, the sky gray with coal smoke over the flat, dull plain, it all pulled me down. Lying there I heard horses' hooves on the road, soft on the dust, and after a while I heard Galven's and Pomona's voices. They were in the little rose plot under my window. She was saying, "I don't know, Galven."

"You cannot come there," he said.

If she answered, I could not hear her.

"When the roof leaks there," he said, "it leaks. We nail old shingles over the hole. It takes money to roof a house like that. I have no money. I have no profession. I was brought up not to have a profession. My kind of people have land, not money. I don't have land. I have an empty house. And it's where I live, it's what I am, Pomona. I can't leave it. But you can't live there. There is nothing there. Nothing."

"There's yourself," she said, or I think that's what she said; she spoke very low.

"It comes to the same thing."

"Why?"

There was a long pause. "I don't know," he said. "I started out all right. It was coming back, maybe. Bringing her back to that house. I tried it, I tried to give Ile to her. It is what I am. But it wasn't any good, it isn't any good, it's no use, Pomona!" That was said in anguish, and she answered only with his name. After that I couldn't hear what they said, only the murmur of their voices, unnerved and tender. Even in the shame of listening it was a wonderful thing to hear, that tenderness. And still I was afraid, I felt the sickness, the weariness I had felt that afternoon bringing the dead to birth. It was impossible that my sister should love Galven Ileskar. It wasn't that he was poor, it wasn't that he chose to live in a half-ruined house at the end of nowhere; that was his heritage, that was his right. Singular men lead singular lives. And Poma had the right to choose all that, if she loved him. It wasn't that that made it impossible. It was the missing step. It was something more profoundly lacking, lacking in Galven. There was a gap, a forgotten place, a break in his humanity. He was not quite my brother, as I had thought all men were. He was a stranger, from a different land.

That night I kept looking at Poma; she was a beautiful girl, as soft as sunlight. I damned myself for not ever having looked at her, for not having been a decent brother to her, taking her somewhere, anywhere, into company, where she'd have found a dozen men ready to love her and marry her. Instead, I had taken her to Ile.

"I've been thinking," I said next morning at breakfast. "I'm fed up with this place. I'm ready to try Brailava." I thought I was being subtle, till I saw the terror in her eyes.

"Are you?" she said weakly.

"All we'll ever do here is scrape by. It's not fair to you, Poma. I'm writing Cohen to ask him to look out for a partnership for me in the city."

"Shouldn't you wait a while longer?"

"Not here. It gets us nowhere."

She nodded, and left me as soon as she could. She didn't leave a scarf or handkerchief behind, not a trace. She hid in her room all day. I had only a couple of calls to make. God, that was a long day!

I was watering the roses after supper, and she came to me there, where she and Galven had talked the night before. "Gil," she said, "I want to talk with you."

"Your skirt's caught on the rosebush."

"Unhook me, I can't reach it."

I broke the thorn and freed her.

"I'm in love with Galven," she said.

"Oh I see," said I.

"We talked it over. He feels we can't marry; he's too poor. I wanted you to know about it, though. So you'd understand why I don't want to leave the Valone."

I was wordless, or rather words strangled me. Finally I got some out— "You mean you want to stay here, even though—?"

"Yes. At least I can see him."

She was awake, my sleeping beauty. He had waked her; he had given her what she lacked, and what few men could have given her: the sense of peril, which is the root of love. Now she needed what she had always had and never needed, her serenity, her strength. I stared at her and finally said, "You mean to live with him?"

She turned white, dead white. "I would if he asked me," she said. "Do you think he'd do that?" She was furious, and I was floored. I stood there with the watering can and apologized—"Poma, I'm sorry, I didn't mean to— But what are you going to *do?*"

"I don't know," she said, still angry.

"You mean you just intend to go on living here, and he there, and—" She already had me at the point of telling her to marry him. I got angry in my turn. "All right," I said, "I'll go speak to him."

"What about?" she said, defensive of him at once.

"About what he intends to do! If he wants to marry you, surely he can find some kind of work?"

"He has tried," she said. "He wasn't brought up to work. And he has been ill, you know."

Her dignity, her vulnerable dignity, went to my heart. "Oh Poma, I know that! And you know that I respect him, that I love him; he was my friend first, wasn't he? But the illness—what kind of illness?—There are times I don't think I've ever really known him at all—" I could not say any more, for she did not understand me. She was blind to the dark places in the forest, or they were all bright to her. She feared for him; but she did not fear him at all.

And so I rode off that evening to Ile.

Galven was not there. Martin said he had taken out the mare to exercise her. Martin was cleaning harness in the stable by lantern light and moonlight, and I talked with him there while I waited for Galven to come back. Moonlight enlarged the woods of Ile; the birches and the house looked silver, the oaks were a wall of black. Martin came to the stable door with me for a smoke. I looked at his face in the moonlight, and I thought I could trust him, if only he'd trust me.

"Martin, I want to ask you something. I have good reason for asking it."

He sucked at his pipe, and waited.

"Do you consider Galven to be sane?"

He was silent; sucked at his pipe, grinned a little. "Sane?" he said. "I'm not one to judge. I chose to live here too."

"Listen, Martin, you know that I'm his friend. But he and my sister, they're in love, they talk of marrying. I'm the only one to look after her. I want to know more about—" I hesitated and finally said, "About his first marriage."

Martin was looking out into the yard, his light eyes full of moonlight. "No need to stir that up, doctor. But you ought to take your sister away."

"Why?"

No answer.

"I have a right to know."

"Look at him?" Martin broke out, fierce, turning on me. "Look at him! You know him well enough, though you'll never know what he was, what he should have been. What's done is done, there's no mending it, let him be. What would she do, here, when he went into his black mood? I've lived day after day in this house with him when he never spoke a word, and there was nothing you could do for him, nothing. Is that for a young girl to live with? He's not fit to live with people. He's not sane, if you want. Take her away from here!"

It was not wholly jealousy, but it was not logic, either, that led his argument. Galven had argued against himself in the same way last night. I was sure Galven had had no "black mood" since he had known Poma. The blackness lay further behind.

"Did he divorce his wife, Martin?"

"She's dead."

"You know that for a fact?"

Martin nodded.

"All right; if she's dead, that story's closed. All I can do is speak to him."

"You won't do that!"

It wasn't either question or threat so much as it was terror, real terror in his voice. I was clinging to common sense by now desperately, clutching at the straw. "Somebody's got to face reality," I said angrily. "If they marry they've got to have something to live on—"

"To live on, to live on, that's not what it's about! He can't marry anybody. Get her out of here!"

"Why?"

"All right, you asked if he was sane, I'll answer you. No. No, he isn't sane. He's done something he doesn't know about, he doesn't remember, if she comes here it will happen again, how do I know it won't happen again!"

I felt very dizzy, there in the night wind under the high dark and silver of the trees. I finally said in a whisper, "His wife?"

No answer.

"For the love of God, Martin!"

"All right," the man whispered. "Listen. He came on them in the woods. There, back in the oaks." He pointed to the great trees standing somber under moonlight. "He'd been out hunting. It was the day after he'd sent off the man from Brailava, told him get out and never come back. And she was in a rage with him for it, they'd quarreled half the night, and he went off to the marshes before dawn. He came back early and he found them there, he took a short cut through the woods, he found them there in broad daylight in the forest. And he shot her point-blank and clubbed the man with his rifle, beat his brains out. I heard the shot, so close to the house, I came out and found them. I took him home. There were a couple of other men staying here, I sent them away, I told them she'd run off. That night he tried to kill himself, I had to watch him, I had to tie him up." Martin's voice shook and broke again and again. "For weeks he never said a word, he was like a dumb animal, I had to lock him in. And it wore off but it would come back on him, I had to watch him night and day. It wasn't her, it wasn't that he'd come on them that way like dogs in heat, it was that he'd killed them, that's what broke him. He came out of it, he began to act like himself again, but only when he'd forgotten that. He forgot it. He doesn't remember it. He doesn't know it. I told him the same story, they'd run off, gone abroad, and he believed it. He believes it now. Now, now will you bring your sister here?"

All I could say at first was, "Martin, I'm sorry, I'm sorry." Then, pulling myself together, "They—what did you do?"

"They're where they died. Do you want to dig them up and make sure?" he said in a cracked, savage voice. "There in the forest. Go ahead, here, here's the manure shovel, it's what I dug a hole for them with. You're a doctor, you won't believe Galven could do that to a man, there wasn't anything left of the head but—but—" Martin put his face into his hands suddenly and rocked back and forth, crouching down on his heels, crouching and rocking and sobbing.

I said what I could to him, but all he could say to me was, "If I could just forget it, the way he has!"

When he began to get himself under control again, I left, not waiting for Galven. Not waiting, I say—I was running from him. I wanted to be out from under the shadow of those trees. I kept the pony at a trot all the way home, glad of the empty road and the wash of moonlight over the wide valley. And I came into our house out of breath and shaking; and found Galven Ileskar standing there, by the fire, alone.

"Where's my sister?" I yelled, and he stared in bewilderment. "Upstairs," he stammered, and I went up the stairs four at a time. There she was in her room, sitting on her bed, among all the pretty odds and ends and bits and tatters that she never put away. She had been crying. "Gil!" she said, with the same bewildered look. "What's wrong?"

"Nothing—I don't know," and I backed out, leaving her scared to death, poor girl. But she waited up there while I came back down to Galven; that's what they'd arranged, the custom of the times, you know, the men were to talk the matter over.

He said the same thing: "What's wrong, Gil?" And what was I to say? There he stood, tense and gallant, with his clear eyes, my friend, ready to tell me he loved my sister and had found some kind of job and would stand by her all his life, and was I supposed to say, "Yes, there's something wrong, Galven Ileskar," and tell him what it was? Oh, there was something wrong, all right, but it was a deeper wrong, and an older one, than any he had done. Was I to give in to it?

"Galven," I said, "Poma's spoken to me. I don't know what to say. I can't forbid you to marry, but I can't—I can't—" And I stuck; I couldn't speak; Martin's tears blinded me.

"Nothing could make me hurt her," he said very quietly, as if making a promise. I don't know whether he understood me; I don't know whether, as Martin believed, he did not know what he had done. In a way it did not matter. The pain and the guilt of it were in him, then and always. That he knew, knew from end to end, and endured without complaint.

Well, that wasn't quite the end of it. It should have been, but what he could endure, I couldn't, and finally, against every impulse of mercy, I told Poma what Martin had told me. I couldn't let her walk into the forest undefended. She listened to me, and as I spoke I knew I'd lost her. She believed me, all right. God help her, I think she knew before I told her!—not the facts, but the truth. But my telling her forced her to take sides. And she did. She said she'd stay with Ileskar. They were married in October.

The doctor cleared his throat, and gazed a long time at the fire, not noticing his junior partner's impatience.

"Well?" the young man burst out at last like a firecracker—"What happened?"

"What happened? Why, nothing much happened. They lived on at Ile. Galven had got himself a job as an overseer for Kravay; after a couple of years he did pretty well at it. They had a son and a daughter. Galven died when he was fifty; pneumonia again, his heart couldn't take it. My sister's still at Ile. I haven't seen her for a couple of years, I hope to spend Christmas there. . . . Oh, but the reason I told you all this. You said there are unpardonable crimes. And I agree that murder ought to be one. And yet, among all men, it was the murderer whom I loved, who turned out in fact to be my brother. . . . Do you see what I mean?"

BERNARD MALAMUD

The Magic Barrel

Not long ago there lived in uptown New York, in a small almost meager room, though crowded with books, Leo Finkle, a rabbinical student in the Yeshiva University. Finkle, after six years of study, was to be ordained in June and had been advised by an acquaintance that he might find it easier to win himself a congregation if he were married. Since he had no present prospects of marriage, after two tormented days of turning it over in his mind, he called in Pinye Salzman, a marriage broker whose two-line advertisement he had read in the *Forward*.

The matchmaker appeared one night out of the dark fourth-floor hallway of the graystone rooming house where Finkle lived, grasping a black, strapped portfolio that had been worn thin with use. Salzman, who had been long in the business, was of slight but dignified build, wearing an old hat, and an overcoat too short and tight for him. He smelled frankly of fish, which he loved to eat, and although he was missing a few teeth, his presence was not displeasing, because of an amiable manner curiously contrasted with mournful eyes. His voice, his lips, his wisp of beard, his bony fingers were animated, but give him a moment of repose and his mild blue eyes revealed a depth of sadness, a characteristic that put Leo a little at ease although the situation, for him, was inherently tense.

He at once informed Salzman why he had asked him to come, explaining that his home was in Cleveland, and that but for his parents, who had married comparatively late in life, he was alone in the world. He had for six years devoted himself almost entirely to his studies, as a result of which, understandably, he had found himself without time for a social life and the company of young women. Therefore he thought it the better part of trial and error—of embarrassing fumbling—to call in an experienced person to advise him on these matters. He remarked in passing that the function of the marriage broker was ancient and honorable, highly approved in the Jewish community, because it made practical the necessary without hindering joy. Moreover, his own parents had been brought together by a matchmaker. They had made, if not a financially profitable marriage—since neither had possessed any worldly goods to speak of—at least a successful one in the sense of their everlasting devotion to each other. Salzman listened in embarrassed surprise, sensing a sort of apology. Later, however, he experienced a glow of pride in his work, an emotion that had left him years ago, and he heartily approved of Finkle.

The two went to their business. Leo had led Salzman to the only clear place in the room, a table near a window that overlooked the lamp-lit city. He seated himself at the matchmaker's side but facing him, attempting by an act of will to suppress the unpleasant tickle in his throat. Salzman eagerly unstrapped his portfolio and removed a loose rubber band from a thin packet of much-handled cards. As he flipped through them, a gesture and sound that physically hurt Leo, the student pretended not to see and gazed steadfastly out the window. Although it was still February, winter was on its last legs, signs of which he had for the first time in years begun to notice. He now observed the round white moon, moving high in the sky through a cloud menagerie, and watched with half-open mouth as it penetrated a huge hen, and dropped out of her like an egg laying itself. Salzman, though pretending through eyeglasses he had just slipped on to be engaged in scanning the writing on the cards, stole occasional glances at the young man's distinguished face, noting with pleasure the long, severe scholar's nose, brown eyes heavy with learning, sensitive yet ascetic lips, and a certain almost hollow quality of the dark cheeks. He gazed around at shelves upon shelves of books and let out a soft, contented sigh.

When Leo's eyes fell upon the cards, he counted six spread out in Salzman's hand.

"So few?" he asked in disappointment.

"You wouldn't believe me how much cards I got in my office," Salzman replied. "The drawers are already filled to the top, so I keep them now in a barrel, but is every girl good for a new rabbi?"

Leo blushed at this, regretting all he had revealed of himself in a curriculum vitae he had sent to Salzman. He had thought it best to acquaint him with his strict standards and specifications, but in having done so, felt he had told the marriage broker more than was absolutely necessary.

He hesitantly inquired, "Do you keep photographs of your clients on file?"

"First comes family, amount of dowry, also what kind promises," Salzman replied, unbuttoning his tight coat and settling himself in the chair. "After comes pictures, rabbi."

"Call me Mr. Finkle. I'm not yet a rabbi."

Salzman said he would, but instead called him doctor, which he changed to rabbi when Leo was not listening too attentively.

Salzman adjusted his horn-rimmed spectacles, gently cleared his throat and read in an eager voice the contents of the top card:

"Sophie P. Twenty-four years. Widow one year. No children. Educated high school and two years college. Father promises eight thousand dollars. Has wonderful wholesale business. Also real estate. On the mother's side comes teachers, also one actor. Well known on Second Avenue."

Leo gazed up in surprise. "Did you say a widow?"

"A widow don't mean spoiled, rabbi. She lived with her husband maybe four months. He was a sick boy she made a mistake to marry him."

"Marrying a widow has never entered my mind."

"This is because you have no experience. A widow, especially if she is young and healthy like this girl, is a wonderful person to marry. She will be thankful to you the rest of her life. Believe me, if I was looking now for a bride, I would marry a widow."

Leo reflected, then shook his head.

Salzman hunched his shoulders in an almost imperceptible gesture of disappointment. He placed the card down on the wooden table and began to read another:

"Lily H. High school teacher. Regular. Not a substitute. Has savings and new Dodge car. Lived in Paris one year. Father is successful dentist thirty-five years. Interested in professional man. Well Americanized family. Wonderful opportunity.

"I knew her personally," said Salzman. "I wish you could see this girl. She is a doll. Also very intelligent. All day you could talk to her about books and theyater and what not. She also knows current events."

"I don't believe you mentioned her age?"

"Her age?" Salzman said, raising his brows. "Her age is thirty-two years."

Leo said after a while, "I'm afraid that seems a little too old."

Salzman let out a laugh. "So how old are you, rabbi?"

"Twenty-seven."

"So what is the difference, tell me, between twenty-seven and thirty-two? My own wife is seven years older than me. So what did I suffer?—Nothing. If Rothschild's a daughter wants to marry you, would you say on account her age, no?"

"Yes," Leo said dryly.

Salzman shook off the no in the yes. "Five years don't mean a thing. I give you my word that when you will live with her for one week you will forget her age. What does it mean five years—that she lived more and knows more than somebody who is younger? On this girl, God bless her, years are not wasted. Each one that it comes makes better the bargain."

"What subject does she teach in high school?"

"Languages. If you heard the way she speaks French, you will think it is music. I am in the business twenty-five years, and I recommend her with my whole heart. Believe me, I know what I'm talking, rabbi."

"What's on the next card?" Leo said abruptly.

Salzman reluctantly turned up the third card:

"Ruth K. Nineteen years. Honor student. Father offers thirteen thousand cash to the right bridegroom. He is a medical doctor. Stomach specialist with marvelous practice. Brother-in-law owns own garment business. Particular people."

Salzman looked as if he had read his trump card.

"Did you say nineteen?" Leo asked with interest.

"On the dot."

"Is she attractive?" He blushed. "Pretty?"

Salzman kissed his fingertips. "A little doll. On this I give you my word. Let me call the father tonight and you will see what means pretty."

But Leo was troubled. "You're sure she's that young?"

"This I am positive. The father will show you the birth certificate."

"Are you positive there isn't something wrong with her?" Leo insisted.

"Who says there is wrong?"

"I don't understand why an American girl her age should go to a marriage broker."

A smile spread over Salzman's face.

"So for the same reason you went, she comes."

Leo flushed. "I am pressed for time."

Salzman, realizing he had been tactless, quickly explained. "The father came, not her. He wants she should have the best, so he looks around himself. When we will locate the right boy he will introduce him and encourage. This makes a better marriage than if a young girl without experience takes for herself. I don't have to tell you this."

"But don't you think this young girl believes in love?" Leo spoke uneasily.

Salzman was about to guffaw but caught himself and said soberly, "Love comes with the right person, not before."

Leo parted dry lips but did not speak. Noticing that Salzman had snatched a glance at the next card, he cleverly asked, "How is her health?"

"Perfect," Salzman said, breathing with difficulty. "Of course, she is a little lame on her right foot from an auto accident that it happened to her when she was twelve years, but nobody notices on account she is so brilliant and also beautiful."

Leo got up heavily and went to the window. He felt curiously bitter and upbraided himself for having called in the marriage broker. Finally, he shook his head.

"Why not?" Salzman persisted, the pitch of his voice rising.

"Because I detest stomach specialists."

"So what do you care what is his business? After you marry her do you need him? Who says he must come every Friday night in your house?"

Ashamed of the way the talk was going, Leo dismissed Salzman, who went home with heavy, melancholy eyes.

Though he had felt only relief at the marriage broker's departure, Leo was in low spirits the next day. He explained it as arising from Salzman's failure to produce a suitable bride for him. He did not care for his type of clientele. But when Leo found himself hesitating whether to seek out another matchmaker, one more polished than Pinye, he wondered if it could be—his protestations to the contrary, and although he honored his father and mother—that he did not, in essence, care for the matchmaking institution? This thought he quickly put out of mind yet found himself still upset. All day he ran around in the woods—missed an important appointment, forgot to give out his laundry, walked out of a Broadway cafeteria without paying and had to run back with the ticket in his hand; had even not recognized his landlady in the street when she passed with a friend and courteously called out, "A good evening to you, Doctor Finkle." By nightfall, however, he had regained sufficient calm to sink his nose into a book and there found peace from his thoughts.

Almost at once there came a knock on the door. Before Leo could say enter, Salzman, commercial cupid, was standing in the room. His face was gray and meager, his expression hungry, and he looked as if he would expire on his feet. Yet the marriage broker managed, by some trick of the muscles, to display a broad smile.

"So good evening. I am invited?"

Leo nodded, disturbed to see him again, yet unwilling to ask the man to leave.

Beaming still, Salzman laid his portfolio on the table. "Rabbi, I got for you tonight good news."

"I've asked you not to call me rabbi. I'm still a student."

"Your worries are finished. I have for you a first-class bride."

"Leave me in peace concerning this subject." Leo pretended lack of interest.

"The world will dance at your wedding."

"Please, Mr. Salzman, no more."

"But first must come back my strength," Salzman said weakly. He fumbled with the portfolio straps and took out of the leather case an oily paper bag, from which he extracted a hard, seeded roll and a small, smoked white fish. With a quick motion of his hand he stripped the fish out of its skin and began ravenously to chew. "All day in a rush," he muttered.

Leo watched him eat.

"A sliced tomato you have maybe?" Salzman hesitantly inquired.

"No."

The marriage broker shut his eyes and ate. When he had finished he carefully cleaned up the crumbs and rolled up the remains of the fish, in the paper bag. His spectacled eyes roamed the room until he discovered, amid some piles of books, a one-burner gas stove. Lifting his hat he humbly asked, "A glass tea you got, rabbi?"

Conscience-stricken, Leo rose and brewed the tea. He served it with a chunk of lemon and two cubes of lump sugar, delighting Salzman.

After he had drunk his tea, Salzman's strength and good spirits were restored.

"So tell me, rabbi," he said amiably, "you considered some more the three clients I mentioned yesterday?"

"There was no need to consider."

"Why not?"

"None of them suits me."

"What then suits you?"

Leo let it pass because he could give only a confused answer.

Without waiting for a reply, Salzman asked, "You remember this girl I talked to you—the high school teacher?"

"Age thirty-two?"

But, surprisingly, Salzman's face lit in a smile. "Age twenty-nine."

Leo shot him a look. "Reduced from thirty-two?"

"A mistake," Salzman avowed. "I talked today with the dentist. He took me to his safety deposit box and showed me the birth certificate. She was twenty-nine years last August. They made her a party in the mountains where she went for her vacation. When her father spoke to me the first time I forgot to write the age and I told you thirty-two, but now I remember this was a different client, a widow."

"The same one you told me about? I thought she was twenty-four?"

"A different. Am I responsible that the world is filled with widows?"

"No, but I'm not interested in them, nor for that matter, in school teachers."

Salzman pulled his clasped hands to his breast. Looking at the ceiling he devoutly exclaimed, "Yiddishe kinder, what can I say to somebody that he is not interested in high school teachers? So what then you are interested?"

Leo flushed but controlled himself.

"In what else will you be interested," Salzman went on, "if you not interested in this fine girl that she speaks four languages and has personally in the bank ten thousand dollars? Also her father guarantees further twelve thousand. Also she has a new car, wonderful clothes, talks on all subjects, and she will give you a first-class home and children. How near do we come in our life to paradise?"

"If she's so wonderful, why hasn't she married ten years ago?"

"Why?" said Salzman with a heavy laugh. "—Why? Because she is *partikiler*. This is why. She wants the *best*."

Leo was silent, amused at how he had entangled himself. But Salzman had aroused his interest in Lily H., and he began seriously to consider calling on her. When the marriage broker observed how intently Leo's mind was at work on the facts he had supplied, he felt certain they would soon come to an agreement.

Late Saturday afternoon, conscious of Salzman, Leo Finkle walked with Lily Hirschorn along Riverside Drive. He walked briskly and erectly, wearing with distinction the black fedora he had that morning taken with trepidation out of the dusty hat box on his closet shelf, and the heavy black Saturday coat he had thoroughly whisked clean. Leo also owned a walking stick, a present from a distant relative, but quickly put temptation aside and did not use it. Lily, petite and not unpretty, had on something signifying the approach of spring. She was au courant, animatedly, with all sorts of subjects, and he weighed her words and found her surprisingly sound—score another for Salzman, whom he uneasily sensed to be somewhere around, hiding perhaps high in a tree along the street, flashing the lady signals with a pocket mirror; or perhaps a cloven-hoofed Pan, piping nuptial ditties as he danced his invisible way before them, strewing wild buds on the walk and purple grapes in their path, symbolizing fruit of a union, though there was of course still none.

Lily startled Leo by remarking, "I was thinking of Mr. Salzman, a curious figure, wouldn't you say?"

Not certain what to answer, he nodded.

She bravely went on, blushing, "I for one am grateful for his introducing us. Aren't you?"

He courteously replied, "I am."

"I mean," she said with a little laugh—and it was all in good taste, or at least gave the effect of being not in bad—"do you mind that we came together so?"

He was not displeased with her honesty, recognizing that she meant to set the relationship aright, and understanding that it took a certain amount of experience in life, and courage, to want to do it quite that way. One had to have some sort of past to make that kind of beginning.

He said that he did not mind. Salzman's function was traditional and honorable—valuable for what it might achieve, which, he pointed out, was frequently nothing.

Lily agreed with a sigh. They walked on for a while and she said after a long silence, again with a nervous laugh, "Would you mind if I asked you something a little bit personal? Frankly, I find the subject fascinating." Although Leo shrugged, she went on half embarrassedly, "How was it that you came to your calling? I mean was it a sudden passionate inspiration?"

Leo, after a time, slowly replied, "I was always interested in the Law."

"You saw revealed in it the presence of the Highest?"

He nodded and changed the subject. "I understand that you spent a little time in Paris, Miss Hirschorn?"

"Oh, did Mr. Salzman tell you, Rabbi Finkle?" Leo winced but she went on, "It was ages ago and almost forgotten. I remember I had to return for my sister's wedding."

And Lily would not be put off. "When," she asked in a trembly voice, "did you become enamored of God?"

He stared at her. Then it came to him that she was talking not about Leo Finkle, but of a total stranger, some mystical figure, perhaps even passionate prophet that Salzman had dreamed up for her—no relation to the living or dead. Leo trembled with rage and weakness. The trickster had obviously sold her a bill of goods, just as he had him, who'd expected to become acquainted with a young lady of twenty-nine, only to behold, the moment he laid eyes upon her strained and anxious face, a woman past thirty-five and aging rapidly. Only his self-control had kept him this long in her presence.

"I am not," he said gravely, "a talented religious person," and in seeking words to go on, found himself possessed by shame and fear. "I think," he said in a strained manner, "that I came to God not because I loved Him, but because I did not."

This confession he spoke harshly because its unexpectedness shook him.

Lily wilted. Leo saw a profusion of loaves of bread go flying like ducks high over his head, not unlike the winged loaves by which he had counted himself to sleep last night. Mercifully, then, it snowed, which he would not put past Salzman's machinations.

He was infuriated with the marriage broker and swore he would throw him out of the room the minute he reappeared. But Salzman did not come that night, and when Leo's anger had subsided, an unaccountable despair grew in its place. At first he thought this was caused by his disappointment in Lily, but before long it became evident that he had involved himself with Salzman without a true knowledge of his own intent. He gradually realized—with an emptiness that seized him with six hands—that he had called in the broker to find him a bride because he was incapable of doing it himself. This terrifying insight he had derived as a result of his meeting and conversation with Lily Hirschorn. Her probing questions had somehow irritated him into revealing—to himself more than her—the true nature of his relationship to God, and from that it had come upon him, with shocking force, that apart from his parents, he had never loved anyone. Or perhaps it went the other way, that he did not love God so well as he might, because he had not loved man. It seemed to Leo that his whole life stood starkly revealed and he saw himself for the first time as he truly was—unloved and loveless. This bitter but somehow not fully unexpected revelation brought him to a point of panic, controlled only by extraordinary effort. He covered his face with his hands and cried.

The week that followed was the worst of his life. He did not eat and lost weight. His beard darkened and grew ragged. He stopped attending seminars and almost never opened a book. He seriously considered leaving the Yeshiva, although he was deeply troubled at the thought of the loss of all his years of study—saw them like pages torn from a book, strewn over the city—and at the devastating effect of this decision upon his parents. But he had lived without knowledge of himself, and never in the Five Books and all the Commentaries—mea culpa—had the truth been revealed to him. He did not know where to turn, and in all this desolating loneliness there was no *to whom*, although he often thought of Lily but not once could bring himself to go downstairs and make the call. He became touchy and irritable, especially with his landlady, who asked him all manner of personal questions; on the other hand, sensing his own disagreeableness, he waylaid her on the stairs and apologized abjectly, until mortified, she ran from him. Out of this, however, he drew the consolation that he was a Jew and that a Jew suffered. But gradually, as the long and terrible week drew to a close, he regained his composure and some idea of purpose in life: to go on as planned. Although he was imperfect, the ideal was not. As for his quest of a bride, the thought of continuing afflicted him with anxiety and heartburn, yet perhaps with this new knowledge of himself he would be more successful than in the past. Perhaps love would now come to him and a bride to that love. And for this sanctified seeking who needed a Salzman?

The marriage broker, a skeleton with haunted eyes, returned that very night. He looked, withal, the picture of frustrated expectancy—as if he had steadfastly waited the week at Miss Lily Hirschorn's side for a telephone call that never came.

Casually coughing, Salzman came immediately to the point: "So how did you like her?"

Leo's anger rose and he could not refrain from chiding the matchmaker: "Why did you lie to me, Salzman?"

Salzman's pale face went dead white, the world had snowed on him.

"Did you not state that she was twenty-nine?" Leo insisted.

"I give you my word—"

"She was thirty-five, if a day. *At least* thirty-five."

"Of this don't be too sure. Her father told me—"

"Never mind. The worst of it was that you lied to her."

"How did I lie to her, tell me?"

"You told her things about me that weren't true. You made me out to be more, consequently less than I am. She had in mind a totally different person, a sort of semimystical Wonder Rabbi."

"All I said, you was a religious man."

"I can imagine."

Salzman sighed. "This is my weakness that I have," he confessed. "My wife says to me I shouldn't be a salesman, but when I have two fine people that they would be wonderful to be married, I am so happy that I talk too much." He smiled wanly. "This is why Salzman is a poor man."

Leo's anger left him. "Well, Salzman, I'm afraid that's all."

The marriage broker fastened hungry eyes on him.

"You don't want any more a bride?"

"I do," said Leo, "but I have decided to seek her in a different way. I am no longer interested in an arranged marriage. To be frank, I now admit the necessity of premarital love. That is, I want to be in love with the one I marry."

"Love?" said Salzman, astounded. After a moment he remarked, "For us, our love is our life, not for the ladies. In the ghetto they—"

"I know, I know," said Leo. "I've thought of it often. Love, I have said to myself, should be a by-product of living and worship rather than its own end. Yet for myself I find it necessary to establish the level of my need and fulfill it."

Salzman shrugged but answered, "Listen, rabbi, if you want love, this I can find for you also. I have such beautiful clients that you will love them the minute your eyes will see them."

Leo smiled unhappily. "I'm afraid you don't understand."

But Salzman hastily unstrapped his portfolio and withdrew a manila packet from it.

"Pictures," he said, quickly laying the envelope on the table.

Leo called after him to take the pictures away, but as if on the wings of the wind, Salzman had disappeared.

March came. Leo had returned to his regular routine. Although he felt not quite himself yet—lacked energy—he was making plans for a more active social life. Of course it would cost something, but he was an expert in cutting corners; and when there were no corners left he would make circles rounder. All the while Salzman's pictures had lain on the table, gathering dust. Occasionally as Leo sat studying, or enjoying a cup of tea, his eyes fell on the manila envelope, but he never opened it.

The days went by and no social life to speak of developed with a member of the opposite sex—it was difficult, given the circumstances of his situation. One morning Leo toiled up the stairs to his room and stared out the window at the city. Although the day was bright his view of it was dark. For some time he watched the people in the street below hurrying along and then turned with a heavy heart to his little room. On the table was the packet. With a sudden relentless gesture he tore it open. For a half-hour he stood by the table in a state of excitement, examining the photographs of the ladies Salzman had included. Finally, with a deep sigh he put them down. There were six, of varying degrees of attractiveness, but look at them long enough and they all became Lily

Hirschorn: all past their prime, all starved behind bright smiles, not a true personality in the lot. Life, despite their frantic yoohooings, had passed them by; they were pictures in a briefcase that stank of fish. After a while, however, as Leo attempted to return the photographs into the envelope, he found in it another, a snapshot of the type taken by a machine for a quarter. He gazed at it a moment and let out a cry.

Her face deeply moved him. Why, he could at first not say. It gave him the impression of youth—spring flowers, yet age—a sense of having been used to the bone, wasted; this came from the eyes, which were hauntingly familiar, yet absolutely strange. He had a vivid impression that he had met her before, but try as he might he could not place her although he could almost recall her name, as if he had read it in her own handwriting. No, this couldn't be; he would have remembered her. It was not, he affirmed, that she had an extraordinary beauty—no, though her face was attractive enough; it was that *something* about her moved him. Feature for feature, even some of the ladies of the photographs could do better; but she leaped forth to his heart—had *lived,* or wanted to—more than just wanted, perhaps regretted how she had lived—had somehow deeply suffered: it could be seen in the depths of those reluctant eyes, and from the way the light enclosed and shone from her, and within her, opening realms of possibility: this was her own. Her he desired. His head ached and eyes narrowed with the intensity of his gazing, then as if an obscure fog had blown up in the mind, he experienced fear of her and was aware that he had received an impression, somehow, of evil. He shuddered, saying softly, it is thus with us all. Leo brewed some tea in a small pot and sat sipping it without sugar, to calm himself. But before he had finished drinking, again with excitement he examined the face and found it good: good for Leo Finkle. Only such a one could understand him and help him seek whatever he was seeking. She might, perhaps, love him. How she had happened to be among the discards in Salzman's barrel he could never guess, but he knew he must urgently go find her.

Leo rushed downstairs, grabbed up the Bronx telephone book, and searched for Salzman's home address. He was not listed, nor was his office. Neither was he in the Manhattan book. But Leo remembered having written down the address on a slip of paper after he had read Salzman's advertisement in the "personals" column of the *Forward.* He ran up to his room and tore through his papers, without luck. It was exasperating. Just when he needed the matchmaker he was nowhere to be found. Fortunately Leo remembered to look in his wallet. There on a card he found his name written and a Bronx address. No phone number was listed, the reason—Leo now recalled—he had originally communicated with Salzman by letter. He got on his coat, put a hat on over his skullcap and hurried to the subway station. All the way to the far end of the Bronx he sat on the edge of his seat. He was more than once tempted to take out the picture and see if the girl's face was as he remembered it, but he refrained, allowing the snapshot to remain in his inside coat pocket, content to have her so close. When the train pulled into the station he was waiting at the door and bolted out. He quickly located the street Salzman had advertised.

The building he sought was less than a block from the subway, but it was not an office building, nor even a loft, nor a store in which one could rent office space. It was a very old tenement house. Leo found Salzman's name in pencil on a soiled tag under the bell and climbed three dark flights to his apartment. When he knocked, the door was opened by a thin, asthmatic, gray-haired woman, in felt slippers.

"Yes?" she said, expecting nothing. She listened without listening. He could have sworn he had seen her, too, before but he knew it was an illusion.

"Salzman—does he live here? Pinye Salzman," he said, "the match-maker?"

She stared at him a long minute. "Of course."

He felt embarrassed. "Is he in?"

"No." Her mouth, though left open, offered nothing more.

"The matter is urgent. Can you tell me where his office is?"

"In the air." She pointed upward.

"You mean he has no office?" Leo asked.

"In his socks."

He peered into the apartment. It was sunless and dingy, one large room divided by a half-open curtain, beyond which he could see a sagging metal bed. The near side of a room was crowded with rickety chairs, old bureaus, a three-legged table, racks of cooking utensils, and all the apparatus of a kitchen. But there was no sign of Salzman or his magic barrel, probably also a figment of the imagination. An odor of frying fish made Leo weak to the knees.

"Where is he?" he insisted. "I've got to see your husband."

At length she answered, "So who knows where he is? Every time he thinks a new thought he runs to a different place. Go home, he will find you."

"Tell him Leo Finkle."

She gave no sign she had heard.

He walked downstairs, depressed.

But Salzman, breathless, stood waiting at his door.

Leo was astounded and overjoyed. "How did you get here before me?"

"I rushed."

"Come inside."

They entered. Leo fixed tea, and a sardine sandwich for Salzman. As they were drinking he reached behind him for the packet of pictures and handed them to the marriage broker.

Salzman put down his glass and said expectantly, "You found somebody you like?"

"Not among these."

The marriage broker turned away.

"Here is the one I want." Leo held forth the snapshot.

Salzman slipped on his glasses and took the picture into his trembling hand. He turned ghastly and let out a groan.

"What's the matter?" cried Leo.

"Excuse me. Was an accident this picture. She isn't for you."

Salzman frantically shoved the manila packet into his portfolio. He thrust the snapshot into his pocket and fled down the stairs.

Leo, after momentary paralysis, gave chase and cornered the marriage broker in the vestibule. The landlady made hysterical outcries but neither of them listened.

"Give me back the picture, Salzman."

"No." The pain in his eyes was terrible.

"Tell me who she is then."

"This I can't tell you. Excuse me."

He made to depart, but Leo, forgetting himself, seized the matchmaker by his tight coat and shook him frenziedly.

"Please," sighed Salzman. *"Please."*

Leo ashamedly let him go. "Tell me who she is," he begged. "It's very important for me to know."

"She is not for you. She is a wild one—wild, without shame. This is not a bride for a rabbi."

"What do you mean wild?"

"Like an animal. Like a dog. For her to be poor was a sin. This is why to me she is dead now."

"In God's name, what do you mean?"

"Her I can't introduce to you," Salzman cried.

"Why are you so excited?"

"Why, he asks," Salzman said, bursting into tears. "This is my baby, my Stella, she should burn in hell."

Leo hurried up to bed and hid under the covers. Under the covers he thought his life through. Although he soon fell asleep he could not sleep her out of his mind. He woke, beating his breast. Though he prayed to be rid of her, his prayers went unanswered. Through days of torment he endlessly struggled not to love her; fearing success, he escaped it. He then concluded to convert her to goodness, himself to God. The idea alternately nauseated and exalted him.

He perhaps did not know that he had come to a final decision until he encountered Salzman in a Broadway cafeteria. He was sitting alone at a rear table, sucking the bony remains of a fish. The marriage broker appeared haggard, and transparent to the point of vanishing.

Salzman looked up at first without recognizing him. Leo had grown a pointed beard and his eyes were weighted with wisdom.

"Salzman," he said, "love has at last come to my heart."

"Who can love from a picture?" mocked the marriage broker.

"It is not impossible."

"If you can love her, then you can love anybody. Let me show you some new clients that they just sent me their photographs. One is a little doll."

"Just her I want," Leo murmured.

"Don't be a fool, doctor. Don't bother with her."

"Put me in touch with her, Salzman," Leo said humbly. "Perhaps I can be of service."

Salzman had stopped eating and Leo understood with emotion that it was now arranged.

Leaving the cafeteria, he was, however, afflicted by a tormenting suspicion that Salzman had planned it all to happen this way. Leo was informed by letter that she would meet him on a certain corner, and she was there one spring night, waiting under a street lamp. He appeared, carrying a small bouquet of violets and rosebuds. Stella stood by the lamppost, smoking. She wore white with red shoes, which fitted his expectations, although in a troubled moment he had imagined the dress red, and only the shoes white. She waited uneasily and shyly. From afar he saw that her eyes—clearly her father's—were filled with desperate innocence. He pictured, in her, his own redemption. Violins and lit candles revolved in the sky. Leo ran forward with flowers outthrust.

Around the corner, Salzman, leaning against a wall, chanted prayers for the dead.

BOBBIE ANN MASON

Shiloh

Leroy Moffitt's wife, Norma Jean, is working on her pectorals. She lifts three-pound dumbbells to warm up, then progresses to a twenty-pound barbell. Standing with her legs apart, she reminds Leroy of Wonder Woman.

"I'd give anything if I could just get these muscles to where they're real hard," says Norma Jean. "Feel this arm. It's not as hard as the other one."

"That's 'cause you're right-handed," says Leroy, dodging as she swings the barbell in an arc.

"Do you think so?"

"Sure."

Leroy is a truckdriver. He injured his leg in a highway accident four months ago, and his physical therapy, which involves weights and a pulley, prompted Norma Jean to try building herself up. Now she is attending a body-building class. Leroy has been collecting temporary disability since his tractor-trailer jackknifed in Missouri, badly twisting his left leg in its socket. He has a steel pin in his hip. He will probably not be able to drive his rig again. It sits in the backyard, like a gigantic bird that has flown home to roost. Leroy has been home in Kentucky for three months, and his leg is almost healed, but the accident frightened him and he does not want to drive any more long hauls. He is not sure what to do next. In the meantime, he makes things from craft kits. He started by building a miniature log cabin from notched Popsicle sticks. He varnished it and placed it on the TV set, where it remains. It reminds him of a rustic Nativity scene. Then he tried string art (sailing ships on black velvet), a macramé owl kit, a snap-together B-17 Flying Fortress, and a lamp made out of a model truck, with a light fixture screwed in the top of the cab. At first the kits were diversions, something to kill time, but now he is thinking about building a full-scale log house from a kit. It would be considerably cheaper than building a regular house, and besides, Leroy has grown to appreciate how things are put together. He has begun to realize that in all the years he was on the road he never took time to examine anything. He was always flying past scenery.

"They won't let you build a log cabin in any of the new subdivisions," Norma Jean tells him.

"They will if I tell them it's for you," he says, teasing her. Ever since they were married, he has promised Norma Jean he would build her a new home one day. They have always rented, and the house they live in is small and nondescript. It does not even feel like a home, Leroy realizes now.

Norma Jean works at the Rexall drugstore, and she has acquired an amazing amount of information about cosmetics. When she explains to Leroy the three stages of complexion care, involving creams, toners, and moisturizers, he thinks happily of other petroleum products—axle grease, diesel fuel. This is a connection between him and Norma Jean. Since he has been home, he has felt unusually tender about his wife and guilty over his long absences. But he can't tell what she feels about him. Norma Jean has never complained about his traveling; she has never made hurt remarks, like calling his truck a "widow-maker." He is reasonably certain she has been faithful to him, but he wishes she would celebrate his permanent homecoming more happily. Norma Jean is often startled to find Leroy at home, and he thinks she seems a little disappointed about it. Perhaps he reminds her too much of the early days of their marriage, before he went on the road. They had a child who died as an infant, years ago. They never speak about their memories of Randy, which have almost faded, but now that Leroy is home all the time, they sometimes feel awkward around each other, and Leroy wonders if one of them should mention the child. He has the feeling that they are waking up out of a dream together—that they must create a new marriage, start afresh. They are lucky they are still married. Leroy has read that for most people losing a child destroys the marriage —or else he heard this on *Donahue*. He can't always remember where he learns things anymore.

At Christmas, Leroy bought an electric organ for Norma Jean. She used to play the piano when she was in high school. "It don't leave you," she told him once. "It's like riding a bicycle."

The new instrument had so many keys and buttons that she was bewildered by it at first. She touched the keys tentatively, pushed some buttons, then pecked out "Chopsticks." It came out in an amplified fox-trot rhythm, with marimba sounds.

"It's an orchestra!" she cried.

The organ had a pecan-look finish and eighteen preset chords, with optional flute, violin, trumpet, clarinet, and banjo accompaniments. Norma Jean mastered the organ almost immediately. At first she played Christmas songs. Then she bought *The Sixties Songbook* and learned every tune in it, adding variations to each with the rows of brightly colored buttons.

"I didn't like these old songs back then," she said. "But I have this crazy feeling I missed something."

"You didn't miss a thing," said Leroy.

Leroy likes to lie on the couch and smoke a joint and listen to Norma Jean play "Can't Take My Eyes Off You" and "I'll Be Back." He is back again. After fifteen years on the road, he is finally settling down with the woman he loves. She is still pretty. Her skin is flawless. Her frosted curls resemble pencil trimmings.

Now that Leroy has come home to stay, he notices how much the town has changed. Subdivisions are spreading across western Kentucky like an oil slick. The sign at the edge of town says "Pop: 11,500"—only seven hundred more than it said twenty years before. Leroy can't figure out who is living in all the new houses. The farmers who used to gather around the courthouse square on Saturday afternoons to play checkers and spit tobacco juice have gone. It has been years since Leroy has thought about the farmers, and they have disappeared without his noticing.

Leroy meets a kid named Stevie Hamilton in the parking lot at the new shopping center. While they pretend to be strangers meeting over a stalled car, Stevie tosses an ounce of marijuana under the front seat of Leroy's car. Stevie is wearing orange jogging shoes and a T-shirt that says CHATTAHOOCHEE SUPER-RAT. His father is a prominent doctor who lives in one of the expensive subdivisions in a new white-columned brick house that looks like a funeral parlor. In the phone book under his name there is a separate number, with the listing "Teenagers."

"Where do you get this stuff?" asks Leroy. "From your pappy?"

"That's for me to know and you to find out," Stevie says. He is slit-eyed and skinny.

"What else you got?"

"What you interested in?"

"Nothing special. Just wondered."

Leroy used to take speed on the road. Now he has to go slowly. He needs to be mellow. He leans back against the car and says, "I'm aiming to build me a log house, soon as I get time. My wife, though, I don't think she likes the idea."

"Well, let me know when you want me again," Stevie says. He has a cigarette in his cupped palm, as though sheltering it from the wind. He takes a long drag, then stomps it on the asphalt and slouches away.

Stevie's father was two years ahead of Leroy in high school. Leroy is thirty-four. He married Norma Jean when they were both eighteen, and their child Randy was born a few months later, but he died at the age of four months and three days. He would be about Stevie's age now.

Norma Jean and Leroy were at the drive-in, watching a double feature *(Dr. Strangelove* and *Lover Come Back)*, and the baby was sleeping in the back seat. When the first movie ended, the baby was dead. It was the sudden infant death syndrome. Leroy remembers handing Randy to a nurse at the emergency room, as though he were offering her a large doll as a present. A dead baby feels like a sack of flour. "It just happens sometimes," said the doctor, in what Leroy always recalls as a nonchalant tone. Leroy can hardly remember the child anymore, but he still sees vividly a scene from *Dr. Strangelove* in which the President of the United States was talking in a folksy voice on the hot line to the Soviet premier about the bomber accidentally headed toward Russia. He was in the War Room, and the world map was lit up. Leroy remembers Norma Jean standing catatonically beside him in the hospital and himself thinking: Who is this strange girl? He had forgotten who she was. Now scientists are saying that crib death is caused by a virus. Nobody knows anything, Leroy thinks. The answers are always changing.

When Leroy gets home from the shopping center, Norma Jean's mother, Mabel Beasley, is there. Until this year, Leroy has not realized how much time she spends with Norma Jean. When she visits, she inspects the closets and then the plants, informing Norma Jean when a plant is droopy or yellow. Mabel calls the plants "flowers," although there are never any blooms. She always notices if Norma Jean's laundry is piling up. Mabel is a short, overweight woman whose tight, brown-dyed curls look more like a wig than the actual wig she sometimes wears. Today she has brought Norma Jean an off-white dust ruffle she made for the bed; Mabel works in a custom-upholstery shop.

"This is the tenth one I made this year," Mabel says. "I got started and couldn't stop."

"It's real pretty," says Norma Jean.

"Now we can hide things under the bed," says Leroy, who gets along with his mother-in-law primarily by joking with her. Mabel has never really forgiven him for disgracing her by getting Norma Jean pregnant. When the baby died, she said that fate was mocking her.

"What's that thing?" Mabel says to Leroy in a loud voice, pointing to a tangle of yarn on a piece of canvas.

Leroy holds it up for Mabel to see. "It's my needlepoint," he explains. "This is a *Star Trek* pillow cover."

"That's what a woman would do," says Mabel. "Great day in the morning!"

"All the big football players on TV do it," he says.

"Why, Leroy, you're always trying to fool me. I don't believe you for one minute. You don't know what to do with yourself—that's the whole trouble. Sewing!"

"I'm aiming to build us a log house," says Leroy. "Soon as my plans come."

"Like *heck* you are," says Norma Jean. She takes Leroy's needlepoint and shoves it into a drawer. "You have to find a job first. Nobody can afford to build now anyway."

Mabel straightens her girdle and says, "I still think before you get tied down y'all ought to take a little run to Shiloh."

"One of these days, Mama," Norma Jean says impatiently.

Mabel is talking about Shiloh, Tennessee. For the past few years, she has been urging Leroy and Norma Jean to visit the Civil War battle-ground there. Mabel went there on her honeymoon—the only real trip she ever took. Her husband died of a perforated ulcer when Norma Jean was ten, but Mabel, who was accepted into the United Daughters of the Confederacy in 1975, is still preoccupied with going back to Shiloh.

"I've been to kingdom come and back in that truck out yonder," Leroy says to Mabel, "but we never yet set foot in that battleground. Ain't that something? How did I miss it?"

"It's not even that far," Mabel says.

After Mabel leaves, Norma Jean reads to Leroy from a list she has made. "Things you could do," she announces. "You could get a job as a guard at Union Carbide, where they'd let you set on a stool. You could get on at the lumberyard. You could do a little carpenter work, if you want to build so bad. You could—"

"I can't do something where I'd have to stand up all day."

"You ought to try standing up all day behind a cosmetics counter. It's amazing that I have strong feet, coming from two parents that never had strong feet at all." At the moment Norma Jean is holding on to the kitchen counter, raising her knees one at a time as she talks. She is wearing two-pound ankle weights.

"Don't worry," says Leroy. "I'll do something."

"You could truck calves to slaughter for somebody. You wouldn't have to drive any big old truck for that."

"I'm going to build you this house," says Leroy. "I want to make you a real home."

"I don't want to live in any log cabin."

"It's not a cabin. It's a house."

"I don't care. It looks like a cabin."

"You and me together could lift those logs. It's just like lifting weights."

Norma Jean doesn't answer. Under her breath, she is counting. Now she is marching through the kitchen. She is doing goose steps.

Before his accident, when Leroy came home he used to stay in the house with Norma Jean, watching TV in bed and playing cards. She would cook fried chicken, picnic ham, chocolate pies—all his favorites.

Now he is home alone much of the time. In the mornings, Norma Jean disappears, leaving a cooling place in the bed. She eats a cereal called Body Buddies, and she leaves the bowl on the table, with the soggy tan balls floating in a milk puddle. He sees things about Norma Jean that he never realized before. When she chops onions, she stares off into a corner, as if she can't bear to look. She puts on her house slippers almost precisely at nine o'clock every evening and nudges her jogging shoes under the couch. She saves bread heels for the birds. Leroy watches the birds at the feeder. He notices the peculiar way goldfinches fly past the window. They close their wings, then fall, then spread their wings to catch and lift themselves. He wonders if they close their eyes when they fall. Norma Jean closes her eyes when they are in bed. She wants the lights turned out. Even then, he is sure she closes her eyes.

He goes for long drives around town. He tends to drive a car rather carelessly. Power steering and an automatic shift make a car feel so small and inconsequential that his body is hardly involved in the driving process. His injured leg stretches out comfortably. Once or twice he has almost hit something, but even the prospect of an accident seems minor in a car. He cruises the new subdivisions, feeling like a criminal rehearsing for a robbery. Norma Jean is probably right about a log house being inappropriate here in the new subdivisions. All the houses look grand and complicated. They depress him.

One day when Leroy comes home from a drive he finds Norma Jean in tears. She is in the kitchen making a potato and mushroom-soup casserole, with grated-cheese topping. She is crying because her mother caught her smoking.

"I didn't hear her coming. I was standing here puffing away pretty as you please," Norma Jean says, wiping her eyes.

"I knew it would happen sooner or later," says Leroy, putting his arm around her.

"She don't know the meaning of the word 'knock,' " says Norma Jean. "It's a wonder she hadn't caught me years ago."

"Think of it this way," Leroy says. "What if she caught me with a joint?"

"You better not let her!" Norma Jean shrieks. "I'm warning you, Leroy Moffitt!"

"I'm just kidding. Here, play me a tune. That'll help you relax."

Norma Jean puts the casserole in the oven and sets the timer. Then she plays a ragtime tune, with horns and banjo, as Leroy lights up a joint and lies on the couch, laughing to himself about Mabel's catching him at it. He thinks of Stevie Hamilton—a doctor's son pushing grass. Everything is funny. The whole town seems crazy and small. He is reminded of Virgil Mathis, a boastful policeman Leroy used to shoot pool with. Virgil recently led a drug bust in a back room at a bowling alley, where he seized ten thousand dollars' worth of marijuana. The newspaper had a picture of him holding up the bags of grass and grinning widely. Right now, Leroy can imagine Virgil breaking down the door and arresting him with a lungful of smoke. Virgil would probably have been alerted to the scene because of all the racket Norma Jean is making. Now she sounds like a hard-rock band. Norma Jean is terrific. When she switches to a Latin-rhythm version of "Sunshine Superman," Leroy hums along. Norma Jean's foot goes up and down, up and down.

"Well, what do you think?" Leroy says, when Norma Jean pauses to search through her music.

"What do I think about what?"

His mind had gone blank. Then he says, "I'll sell my rig and build us a house." That wasn't what he wanted to say. He wanted to know what she thought—what she *really* thought—about them.

"Don't start in on that again," says Norma Jean. She begins playing "Who'll Be the Next in Line?"

Leroy used to tell hitchhikers his whole life story—about his travels, his hometown, the baby. He would end with a question: "Well, what do you think?" It was just a rhetorical question. In time, he had the feeling that he'd been telling the same story over and over to the same hitchhikers. He quit talking to hitchhikers when he realized how his voice sounded—whining and self-pitying, like some teenage-tragedy song. Now Leroy has the sudden impulse to tell Norma Jean about himself, as if he had just met her. They have known each other so long they have forgotten a lot about each other. They could become reacquainted. But when the oven timer goes off and she runs to the kitchen, he forgets why he wants to do this.

The next day, Mabel drops by. It is Saturday and Norma Jean is cleaning. Leroy is studying the plans of his log house, which have finally come in the mail. He has them spread out on the table—big sheets of stiff blue paper, with diagrams and numbers printed in white. While Norma Jean runs the vacuum, Mabel drinks coffee. She sets her coffee cup on a blueprint.

"I'm just waiting for time to pass," she says to Leroy, drumming her fingers on the table.

As soon as Norma Jean switches off the vacuum, Mabel says in a loud voice, "Did you hear about the datsun dog that killed the baby?"

Norma Jean says, "The word is 'dachshund.' "

"They put the dog on trial. It chewed the baby's legs off. The mother was in the next room all the time." She raises her voice. "They thought it was neglect."

Norma Jean is holding her ears. Leroy manages to open the refrigerator and get some Diet Pepsi to offer Mabel. Mabel still has some coffee and she waves away the Pepsi.

"Datsuns are like that," Mabel says. "They're jealous dogs. They'll tear a place to pieces if you don't keep an eye on them."

"You better watch out what you're saying, Mabel," says Leroy.

"Well, facts is facts."

Leroy looks out the window at his rig. It is like a huge piece of furniture gathering dust in the backyard. Pretty soon it will be an antique. He hears the vacuum cleaner. Norma Jean seems to be cleaning the living room rug again.

Later, she says to Leroy, "She just said that about the baby because she caught me smoking. She's trying to pay me back."

"What are you talking about?" Leroy says, nervously shuffling blueprints.

"You know good and well," Norma Jean says. She is sitting in a kitchen chair with her feet up and her arms wrapped around her knees. She looks small and helpless. She says, "The very idea, her bringing up a subject like that! Saying it was neglect."

"She didn't mean that," Leroy says.

"She might not have *thought* she meant it. She always says things like that. You don't know how she goes on."

"But she didn't really mean it. She was just talking."

Leroy opens a king-sized bottle of beer and pours it into two glasses, dividing it carefully. He hands a glass to Norma Jean and she takes it from him mechanically. For a long time, they sit by the kitchen window watching the birds at the feeder.

Something is happening. Norma Jean is going to night school. She has graduated from her six-week body-building course and now she is taking an adult-education course in composition at Paducah Community College. She spends her evenings outlining paragraphs.

"First you have a topic sentence," she explains to Leroy. "Then you divide it up. Your secondary topic has to be connected to your primary topic."

To Leroy, this sounds intimidating. "I never was any good in English," he says.

"It makes a lot of sense."

"What are you doing this for, anyhow?"

She shrugs. "It's something to do." She stands up and lifts her dumbbells a few times.

"Driving a rig, nobody cared about my English."

"I'm not criticizing your English."

Norma Jean used to say, "If I lose ten minutes' sleep, I just drag all day." Now she stays up late, writing compositions. She got a B on her first paper—a how-to theme on soup-based casseroles. Recently Norma Jean has been cooking unusual foods—tacos, lasagna, Bombay chicken. She doesn't play the organ anymore, though her second paper was called "Why Music Is Important to Me." She sits at the kitchen table, concentrating on her outlines, while Leroy plays with his log house plans, practicing with a set of Lincoln Logs. The thought of getting a truckload of notched, numbered logs scares him, and he wants to be prepared. As he and Norma Jean work together at the kitchen table, Leroy has the hopeful thought that they are sharing something, but he knows he is a fool to think this. Norma Jean is miles away. He knows he is going to lose her. Like Mabel, he is just waiting for time to pass.

One day, Mabel is there before Norma Jean gets home from work, and Leroy finds himself confiding in her. Mabel, he realizes, must know Norma Jean better than he does.

"I don't know what's got into that girl," Mabel says. "She used to go to bed with the chickens. Now you say she's up all hours. Plus her a-smoking. I like to died."

"I want to make her this beautiful home," Leroy says, indicating the Lincoln Logs. "I don't think she even wants it. Maybe she was happier with me gone."

"She don't know what to make of you, coming home like this."

"Is that it?"

Mabel takes the roof off his Lincoln Log cabin. "You couldn't get *me* in a log cabin," she says. "I was raised in one. It's no picnic, let me tell you."

"They're different now," says Leroy.

"I tell you what," Mabel says, smiling oddly at Leroy.

"What?"

"Take her on down to Shiloh. Y'all need to get out together, stir a little. Her brain's all balled up over them books."

Leroy can see traces of Norma Jean's features in her mother's face. Mabel's worn face has the texture of crinkled cotton, but suddenly she looks pretty. It occurs to Leroy that Mabel has been hinting all along that she wants them to take her with them to Shiloh.

"Let's all go to Shiloh," he says. "You and me and her. Come Sunday."

Mabel throws up her hand in protest. "Oh, no, not me. Young folks want to be by theirselves."

When Norma Jean comes in with groceries, Leroy says excitedly, "Your mama here's been dying to go to Shiloh for thirty-five years. It's about time we went, don't you think?"

"I'm not going to butt in on anybody's second honeymoon," Mabel says.

"Who's going on a honeymoon, for Christ's sake?" Norma Jeans says loudly.

"I never raised no daughter of mine to talk that-a-way," Mabel says.

"You ain't seen nothing yet," says Norma Jean. She starts putting away boxes and cans, slamming cabinet doors.

"There's a log cabin at Shiloh," Mabel says. "It was there during the battle. There's bullet holes in it."

"When are you going to *shut up* about Shiloh, Mama?" asks Norma Jean.

"I always thought Shiloh was the prettiest place, so full of history," Mabel goes on. "I just hoped y'all could see it once before I die, so you could tell me about it." Later, she whispers to Leroy, "You do what I said. A little change is what she needs."

"Your name means 'the king,' " Norma Jean says to Leroy that evening. He is trying to get her to go to Shiloh, and she is reading a book about another century.

"Well, I reckon I ought to be right proud."

"I guess so."

"Am I still king around here?"

Norma Jean flexes her biceps and feels them for hardness. "I'm not fooling around with anybody, if that's what you mean," she says.

"Would you tell me if you were?"

"I don't know."

"What does *your* name mean?"

"It was Marilyn Monroe's real name."

"No kidding!"

"Norma comes from the Normans. They were invaders," she says. She closes her book and looks hard at Leroy. "I'll go to Shiloh with you if you'll stop staring at me."

On Sunday, Norma Jean packs a picnic and they go to Shiloh. To Leroy's relief, Mabel says she does not want to come with them. Norma Jean drives, and Leroy, sitting beside her, feels like some boring hitchhiker she has picked up. He tries some conversation, but she answers him in monosyllables. At Shiloh, she drives aimlessly through the park, past bluffs and trails and steep ravines. Shiloh is an immense place, and Leroy cannot see it as a battleground. It is not what he expected. He thought it would look like a golf course. Monuments are everywhere, showing through the thick clusters of trees. Norma Jean passes the log cabin Mabel mentioned. It is surrounded by tourists looking for bullet holes.

"That's not the kind of log house I've got in mind," says Leroy apologetically.

"I know *that*."

"This is a pretty place. Your mama was right."

"It's OK," says Norma Jean. "Well, we've seen it. I hope she's satisfied."

They burst out laughing together.

At the park museum, a movie on Shiloh is shown every half hour, but they decide that they don't want to see it. They buy a souvenir Confederate flag for Mabel, and then they find a picnic spot near the cemetery.

Norma Jean has brought a picnic cooler, with pimiento sandwiches, soft drinks, and Yodels. Leroy eats a sandwich and then smokes a joint, hiding it behind the picnic cooler. Norma Jean has quit smoking altogether. She is picking cake crumbs from the cellophane wrapper, like a fussy bird.

Leroy says, "So the boys in gray ended up in Corinth. The Union soldiers zapped 'em finally. April 7, 1862."

They both know that he doesn't know any history. He is just talking about some of the historical plaques they have read. He feels awkward, like a boy on a date with an older girl. They are still just making conversation.

"Corinth is where Mama eloped to," says Norma Jean.

They sit in silence and stare at the cemetery for the Union dead and, beyond, at a tall cluster of trees. Campers are parked nearby, bumper to bumper, and small children in bright clothing are cavorting and squealing. Norma Jean wads up the cake wrapper and squeezes it tightly in her hand. Without looking at Leroy, she says, "I want to leave you."

Leroy takes a bottle of Coke out of the cooler and flips off the cap. He holds the bottle poised near his mouth but cannot remember to take a drink. Finally he says, "No, you don't."

"Yes, I do."

"I won't let you."

"You can't stop me."

"Don't do me that way."

Leroy knows Norma Jean will have her own way. "Didn't I promise to be home from now on?" he says.

"In some ways, a woman prefers a man who wanders," says Norma Jean. "That sounds crazy, I know."

"You're not crazy."

Leroy remembers to drink from his Coke. Then he says, "Yes, you *are* crazy. You and me could start all over again. Right back at the beginning."

"We *have* started all over again," says Norma Jean. "And this is how it turned out."

"What did I do wrong?"

"Nothing."

"Is this one of those women's lib things?" Leroy asks.

"Don't be funny."

The cemetery, a green slope dotted with white markers, looks like a subdivision site. Leroy is trying to comprehend that his marriage is breaking up, but for some reason he is wondering about white slabs in a graveyard.

"Everything was fine till Mama caught me smoking," says Norma Jean, standing up. "That set something off."

"What are you talking about?"

"She won't leave me alone—*you* won't leave me alone." Norma Jean seems to be crying, but she is looking away from him. "I feel eighteen again. I can't face that all over again." She starts walking away. "No, it *wasn't* fine. I don't know what I'm saying. Forget it."

Leroy takes a lungful of smoke and closes his eyes as Norma Jean's words sink in. He tries to focus on the fact that thirty-five hundred soldiers died on the grounds around him. He can only think of that war as a board game with plastic soldiers. Leroy almost smiles, as he compares the Confederates' daring attack on the Union camps and Virgil Mathis's raid on the bowling alley. General Grant, drunk and furious, shoved the Southerners back to Corinth, where Mabel and Jet Beasley were married years later, when Mabel was still thin and good-looking. The next day, Mabel and Jet visited the battleground, and then Norma Jean was born, and then she married Leroy and they had a baby, which they lost, and now Leroy and Norma Jean are here at the same battleground. Leroy knows he is leaving out a lot. He is leaving out the insides of history. History was always just names and dates to him. It occurs to him that building a house out of logs is similarly empty—too simple. And the real inner workings of a marriage, like most of history, have escaped him. Now he sees that building a log house is the dumbest idea he could have had. It was clumsy of him to think Norma Jean would want a log house. It was a crazy idea. He'll have to think of something else, quickly. He will wad the blueprints into tight balls and fling them into the lake. Then he'll get moving again. He opens his eyes. Norma Jean has moved away and is walking through the cemetery, following a serpentine brick path.

Leroy gets up to follow his wife, but his good leg is asleep and his bad leg still hurts him. Norma Jean is far away, walking rapidly toward the bluff by the river, and he tries to hobble toward her. Some children run past him, screaming noisily. Norma Jean has reached the bluff, and she is looking out over the Tennessee River. Now she turns toward Leroy and waves her arms. Is she beckoning to him? She seems to be doing an exercise for her chest muscles. The sky is unusually pale—the color of the dust ruffle Mabel made for their bed.

James Alan McPherson

The Story of a Scar

Since Dr. Wayland was late and there were no recent newsmagazines in the waiting room, I turned to the other patient and said: "As a concerned person, and as your brother, I ask you, without meaning to offend, how did you get that scar on the side of your face?"

The woman seemed insulted. Her brown eyes, which before had been wandering vacuously about the room, narrowed suddenly and sparked humbling reprimands at me. She took a draw on her cigarette, puckered her lips, and blew a healthy stream of smoke toward my face. It was a mean action, deliberately irreverent and cold. The long curving scar on the left side of her face darkened. "I ask *you*," she said, "as a nosy person with no connections in your family, how come your nose is all bandaged up?"

It was a fair question, considering the possible returns on its answer. Dr. Wayland would remove the bandages as soon as he came in. I would not be asked again. A man lacking permanence must advertise. "An accident of passion," I told her. "I smashed it against the headboard of my bed while engaged in the act of love."

Here she laughed, but not without intimating, through heavy, broken chuckles, some respect for my candor and the delicate cause of my affliction. This I could tell from the way the hardness mellowed in her voice. Her appetites were whetted. She looked me up and down, almost approvingly, and laughed some more. This was a robust woman, with firm round legs and considerable chest. I am small. She laughed her appreciation. Finally, she lifted a brown palm to her face, wiping away tears. "You *cain't* be no married man," she observed. "A wife ain't worth *that* much."

I nodded.

"I knowed it," she said. "The best mens don't git married. They do they fishin' in goldfish bowls."

"I am no adulterer," I cautioned her. "I find companionship wherever I can."

She quieted me by throwing out her arm in a suggestion of offended modesty. She scraped the cigarette on the white tile beneath her foot. "You don't have to tell me a thing," she said. "I know mens goin' and comin'. There ain't a-one of you I'd trust to take my grandmama to Sunday school." Here she paused, seemingly lost in some morbid reflection, her eyes wandering across the room to Dr. Wayland's frosted glass door. The solemnity of the waiting room reclaimed us. We inhaled the antiseptic fumes that wafted from the inner office. We breathed deeply together, watching the door, waiting. "Not a-one," my companion said softly, her dark eyes wet.

The scar still fascinated me. It was a wicked black mark that ran from her brow down over her left eyelid, skirting her nose but curving over and through both lips before ending almost exactly in the center of her chin. The scar was thick and black and crisscrossed with a network of old stitch patterns, as if some meticulous madman had first attempted to carve a perfect half-circle in her flesh, and then decided to embellish his handiwork. It was so grotesque a mark that one had the feeling it was the art of no human hand and could be peeled off like so much soiled putty. But this was a surgeon's office and the scar was real. It was as real as the honey-blond wig she wore, as real as her purple pantsuit. I studied her approvingly. Such women have a natural leaning toward the abstract expression of themselves. Their styles have private meanings, advertise secret distillations of their souls. Their figures, and their disfigurations, make meaningful statements. Subjectively, this woman was the true sister of the man who knows how to look while driving a purple Cadillac. Such craftsmen must be approached with subtlety if they are to be deciphered. "I've never seen a scar quite like that one," I began, glancing at my watch. Any minute Dr. Wayland would arrive and take off my bandages, removing me permanently from access to her sympathies. "Do you mind talking about what happened?"

"I *knowed* you'd git back around to that," she answered, her brown eyes cruel and level with mine. "Black guys like you with them funny eyeglasses are a real trip. You got to know everything. You sit in corners and watch people." She brushed her face, then wiped her palm on the leg of her pantsuit. "I read you the minute you walk in here."

"As your brother . . ." I began.

"How can you be my brother when your mama's a man?" she said. We both laughed.

"I was pretty once," she began, sniffing heavily. "When I was sixteen my mama's preacher was set to leave his wife and his pulpit and run off with me to *Dee*troit City. Even with this scar and all the weight I done put on, you can still see what I had." She paused. *"Cain't* you?" she asked significantly.

I nodded quickly, looking into her big body for the miniature of what she was.

From this gesture she took assurance. "I was twenty when it happen," she went on. "I had me a good job in the post office, down to the Tenth Street branch. I was a sharp dresser, too, and I had me my choice of mens: big ones, puny ones, old mens, married mens, even D. B. Ferris, my shift supervisor, was after me on the sly—don't let these white mens fool you. He offered to take me off the primaries and turn me on to a desk job in hand-stampin' or damaged mail. But I had my pride. I told him I rather work the facin' table, *every shift,* than put myself in his debt. I shook my finger in his face and said, 'You ain't foolin' me, with your *sly self!* I know where the *wild goose went;* and if you don't start havin' some *respect* for black women, he go'n come *back!*' So then he turn red in the face and put me on the facin' table. Every shift. What could I do? You ain't got no rights in the post office, no matter what lies the government tries to tell you. But I was makin' good money, dressin' bad, and I didn't want to start no trouble for myself. Besides, in them days there was a bunch of good people workin' my shift: Leroy Boggs, Red Bone, 'Big Boy' Tyson, Freddy May . . ."

"What about that scar?" I interrupted her tiresome ramblings. "Which one of them cut you?"

Her face flashed a wall of brown fire. "This here's *my* story!" she muttered, eyeing me up and down with suspicion. "You dudes cain't stand to hear the whole of anything. You want everything broke down in little pieces." And she waved a knowing brown finger. "That's how come you got your nose all busted up. There's some things you have to take your time about."

Again I glanced at my watch, but was careful to nod silent agreement with her wisdom. "It was my boyfriend that caused it," she continued in a slower, more cautious tone. "And the more I look at you the more I can see you just like him. He had that same way of sittin' with his legs crossed, squeezin' his sex juices up to his brains. His name was Billy Crawford, and he worked the parcel-post window down to the Tenth Street branch. He was nine years older than me and was goin' to school nights on the GI Bill. I was twenty when I met him durin' lunch break down in the swing room. He was sittin' at a table against the wall, by hisself, eatin' a cheese sandwich with his nose in a goddamn book. I didn't know any better then. I sat down by him. He looked up at me and say, 'Water seeks its own level, and people do, too. You are not one of the riffraff or else you would of sit with them good-timers and bullshitters 'cross the room. Welcome to my table.' By riffraff he meant all them other dudes and girls from the back room, who believed in havin' a little fun playin' cards and such durin' lunch hour. I thought what he said was kind of funny, and so I laughed. But I should of knowed better. He give me a cheese sandwich and started right off preachin' at me about the lowlife in the back room. Billy couldn't stand none of 'em. He hated the way they dressed, the way they talked, and the way they carried on durin' work hours. He said if all them tried to be like him and advanced themselfs, the Negro wouldn't have no problems. He'd point out Eugene Wells or Red Bone or Crazy Sammy Michaels and tell me, 'People like them think they can homestead in the post office. They think these primaries will need human hands for another twenty years. But you just watch the Jews and Puerto Ricans that pass through here. *They* know what's goin' on. I bet you don't see none of them settin' up their beds under these tables. They tryin' to improve themselfs and get out of here, just like me.' Then he smile and held out his hand. 'And since I see you're a smart girl that keeps a cold eye and some distance on these bums, welcome to the club. My name's Billy Crawford.'

"To tell you the truth, I liked him. He was different from all the jive-talkers and finger-poppers I knew. I liked him because he wasn't ashamed to wear a white shirt and a black tie. I liked the way he always knew just what he was gonna do next. I liked him because none of the other dudes could stand him, and he didn't seem to care. On our first date he took me out to a place where the white waiters didn't git mad when they saw us comin'. That's the kind of style he had. He knew how to order wine with funny names, the kind you don't never see on billboards. He held open doors for me, told me not to order rice with gravy over it or soda water with my meal. I didn't mind him helpin' me. He was a funny dude in a lot of ways: his left leg was shot up in the war and he limped sometimes, but it looked like he was struttin'. He would stare down anybody that watched him walkin'. He told me he had cut his wife loose after he got out of the army, and he told me about some of the games she had run on him. Billy didn't trust women. He said they all was after a workin' man's money, but he said that I was different. He said he could tell I was a God-fearin' woman and my mama had raised me right, and he was gonna improve my mind. In those days I didn't have no objections. Billy was fond of sayin', 'You met me at the right time in your life.'

"But Red Bone, my co-worker, saw what was goin' down and began to take a strong interest in the affair. Red was the kind of strong-minded sister that mens just like to give in to. She was one of them big yellow gals, with red hair and a loud rap that could put a man in his place by just soundin' on him. She like to wade through the mail room, elbowin' dudes aside and sayin', 'You don't wanna mess with *me*, fool! I'll *destroy* you! Anyway, you ain't nothin' but a dirty thought I had when I was three years old!' But if she liked you she could be warm and soft, like a mama. 'Listen,' she kept tellin' me, 'that Billy Crawford is a potential punk. The more I watch him, the less man I see. Every time we downstairs havin' fun I catch his eyeballs rollin' over us from behind them goddamn books! There ain't a rhythm in his body, and the only muscles he exercises is his eyes.'

"That kind of talk hurt me some, especially comin' from her. But I know it's the way of some women to bad-mouth a man they want for themselfs. And what woman don't want a steady man and a good provider?—which is what Billy was. Usually, when they start downgradin' a steady man, you can be sure they up to somethin' else besides lookin' out after you. So I told her, 'Billy don't have no bad habits.' I told her, 'He's a hard worker, he don't drink, smoke, nor run around, and he's gonna git a *college* degree.' But that didn't impress Red. I was never able to figure it out, but she had something in for Billy. Maybe it was his attitude; maybe it was the little ways he let everybody know that he was just passin' through; maybe it was because Red had broke every man she ever had and had never seen a man with no handholes on him. Because that Billy Crawford was a strong man. He worked the day shift, and could of been a supervisor in three or four years if he wanted to crawl a little and grease a few palms; but he did his work, quiet-like, pulled what overtime he could, and went to class three nights a week. On his day off he'd study and maybe take me out for a drink after I got off. Once or twice a week he might let me stay over at his place, but most of the time he'd take me home to my Aunt Alvene's, where I was roomin' in those days, before twelve o'clock.

"To tell the truth, I didn't really miss the partyin' and the dancin' and the good-timin' until Red and some of the others started avoidin' me. Down in the swing room durin' lunch hour, for example, they wouldn't wave for me to come over and join a card game. Or when Leroy Boggs went around to the folks on the floor of the mail room, collectin' money for a party, he wouldn't even ask me to put a few dollars in the pot. He'd just smile at me in a cold way and say to somebody loud enough for me to hear, 'No, sir; ain't no way you can git quality folk to come out to a Saturday night fish fry.'

"Red squared with me when I asked her what was goin' down. She told me, 'People sayin' you been wearin' a high hat since you started goin' with the professor. The talk is you been throwin' around big words and developin' a strut just like his. Now I don't believe these reports, being your friend and sister, but I do think you oughta watch your step. I remember what my grandmama used to tell me: "It don't make no difference how well you fox-trot if everybody else is dancin' the two-step." Besides, that Billy Crawford is a potential punk, and you gonna be one lonely girl when somebody finally turns him out. Use your mind, girl, and stop bein' silly. Everybody is watchin' you!'

"I didn't say nothin', but what Red said started me to thinkin' harder than I had ever thought before. Billy had been droppin' strong hints that we might git married after he got his degree, in two or three years. He was plannin' on being a high school teacher. But outside of being married to a teacher, what was I go'n git out of it? Even if we did git

married, I was likely to be stuck right there in the post office with no
friends. And if he didn't marry me, or if he was a punk like Red believed, then I was a real dummy for givin' up my good times and my
best days for a dude that wasn't go'n do nothin' for me. I didn't make up
my mind right then, but I begin to watch Billy Crawford with a different kind of eye. I'd just turn around at certain times and catch him in his
routines: readin', workin', eatin', runnin' his mouth about the same
things all the time. Pretty soon I didn't have to watch him to know what
he was doin'. He was more regular than Monday mornings. That's when
a woman begins to tip. It ain't never a decision, but somethin' in you
starts to lean over and practice what you gonna say whenever another
man bumps into you at the right time. Some women, especially married
ones, like to tell lies to their new boyfriends; if the husband is a hard
worker and a good provider, they'll tell the boyfriend that he's mean to
them and ain't no good when it comes to sex; and if he's good with sex,
they'll say he's a cold dude that's not concerned with the problems of
the world like she is, or that they got married too young. Me, I believe in
tellin' the truth: that Billy Crawford was too good for most of the
women in this world, me included. He deserved better, so I started
lookin' round for somebody on my own level.

"About this time a sweet-talkin' young dude was transferred to our
branch from the 39th Street substation. The grapevine said it was because he was makin' woman trouble over there and caused too many
fights. I could see why. He dressed like he was settin' fashions every day;
wore special-made bell-bottoms with so much flare they looked like
they was starched. He wore two diamond rings on the little finger of his
left hand that flashed while he was throwin' mail, and a gold tooth that
sparkled all the time. His name was Teddy Johnson, but they called him
'Eldorado' because that was the kind of hog he drove. He was involved
in numbers and other hustles and used the post office job for a front. He
was a strong talker, a easy walker, that dude was a *woman* stalker! I have
to give him credit. He was the last *true* son of the Great McDaddy—"

"Sister," I said quickly, overwhelmed suddenly by the burden of
insight. "I *know* the man of whom you speak. There is no time for this
gutter-patter and indirection. Please, for my sake and for your own,
avoid stuffing the shoes of the small with mythic homilies. This man was
a bum, a hustler and a small-time punk. He broke up your romance with
Billy, then he lived off you, cheated on you, and cut you when you
confronted him." So pathetic and gross seemed her elevation of the
fellow that I abandoned all sense of caution. "Is your mind so *dead,*" I
continued, "did his switchblade slice so *deep,* do you have so little
respect for yourself, or at least for the idea of *proportion* in this sad
world, that you'd sit here and *praise* this brute!?"

She lit a second cigarette. Then, dropping the match to the floor, she
seemed to shudder, to struggle in contention with herself. I sat straight

on the blue plastic couch, waiting. Across the room the frosted glass door creaked, as if about to open; but when I looked, I saw no telling shadow behind it. My companion crossed her legs and held back her head, blowing two thoughtful streams of smoke from her broad nose. I watched her nervously, recognizing the evidence of past destructiveness, yet fearing the imminent occurrence of more. But it was not her temper or the potential strength of her fleshy arms that I feared. Finally she sighed, her face relaxed, and she wet her lips with the tip of her tongue. "You know everything," she said in a soft tone, much unlike her own. "A black mama birthed you, let you suck her titty, cleaned your dirty drawers, and you still look at us through paper and movie plots." She paused, then continued in an even softer and more controlled voice. "Would you believe me if I said that Teddy Johnson loved me, that this scar is to him what a weddin' ring is to another man? Would you believe that he was a better man than Billy?"

I shook my head in firm disbelief.

She seemed to smile to herself, although the scar, when she grimaced, made the expression more like a painful frown. "Then would you believe that I was the cause of Billy Crawford goin' crazy and not gettin' his college degree?"

I nodded affirmation.

"Why?" she asked.

"Because," I answered, "from all I know already, that would seem to be the most likely consequence. I would expect the man to have been destroyed by the pressures placed on him. And, although you are my sister and a woman who has already suffered greatly, I must condemn you and your roughneck friends for this destruction of a man's ambitions."

Her hardened eyes measured my face. She breathed heavily, seeming to grow larger and rounder on the red chair. "My brother," she began in an icy tone, "is as far from what you are as I am from being patient." Now her voice became deep and full, as if aided suddenly by some intricately controlled wellspring of pain. Something aristocratic and old and frighteningly wise seemed to have awakened in her face. "Now this is the way it happened," she fired at me, her eyes wide and rolling. "I want you to *write* it on whatever part of your brain that ain't already covered with page print. I want you to *remember* it every time you stare at a scarred-up sister on the street, and *choke* on it before you can work up spit to condemn her. I was *faithful* to that Billy Crawford. As faithful as a woman could be to a man that don't ever let up or lean back and stop worryin' about where he's gonna be ten years from last week. Life is to be *lived*, not traded on like *dollars!* . . . All that time I was goin' with him, my feets itched to dance, my ears hollered to hear somethin' besides that whine in his voice, my body wanted to press up against somethin' besides that facin' table. I was young and pretty; and what woman don't want to enjoy what she got while she got it? Look around sometime: there ain't *no mens,* young nor old, chasin' *no older womens,* no matter how pretty they *used to be!* But Billy Crawford couldn't see nothin' besides them *goddamn books* in front of his face. And what the Jews and Puerto Ricans was doin'. Whatever else Teddy Johnson was, he was a dude that knowed how to live. He wasn't out to *destroy* life, you can believe *that!* Sure I listened to his rap. Sure I give him the come-on. With Billy workin' right up front and watchin' everything, Teddy was the only dude on the floor that would talk to me. Teddy would say, 'A girl that's got what you got needs a man that have what I have.' And that ain't all he said, either!

"Red Bone tried to push me closer to him, but I am not a sneaky person and didn't pay her no mind. She'd say, 'Girl, I think you and Eldorado ought to git it on. There ain't a better lookin' dude workin' in the post office. Besides, you ain't goin' *nowheres* with that professor Billy Crawford. And if *you* scared to tell him to lean up off you, I'll do it *myself,* bein' as I am your sister and the one with your interest in mind.' But I said to her, 'Don't do me no favors. No matter what you think of Billy, I am no sneaky woman. I'll handle my own affairs.' Red just grin and look me straight in the eye and grin some more. I already told you she was the kind of strong-minded sister that could look right down into you. Nobody but a woman would understand what she was lookin' at.

"Now Billy wasn't no dummy durin' all this time. Though he worked the parcel-post window up front, from time to time durin' the day he'd walk back in the mail room and check out what was goin' down. Or else he'd sit back and listen to the gossip durin' lunch hour, down in the swing room. He must of seen Teddy Johnson hangin' round me, and I know he seen Teddy give me the glad-eye a few times. Billy didn't say nothin' for a long time, but one day he pointed to Teddy and told me, 'See that fellow over there? He's a bloodletter. There's some people with a talent for stoppin' bleedin' by just being around, and there's others that start it the same way. When you see that greasy smile of his you can bet it's soon gonna be a bad day for somebody, if they ain't careful. That kind of fellow's been walkin' free for too long.' He looked at me with that tight mouth and them cold brown eyes of his. He said, 'You know what I mean?' I said I didn't. He said, 'I hope you don't ever have to find out.'

"It was D. B. Ferris, my shift supervisor, that set up things. He's the same dude I told you about, the one that was gonna give me the happy hand. We never saw much of him in the mail room, although he was kinda friendly with Red Bone. D. B. Ferris was always up on the ramps behind one of the wall slits, checkin' out everything that went down on the floor and tryin' to catch somebody snitchin' a letter. There ain't no tellin' how much he knew about private things goin' on. About this time he up and transferred three or four of us, the ones with no seniority, to the night shift. There was me, Red, and Leroy Boggs. When Billy found out he tried to talk D. B. Ferris into keepin' me on the same shift as his, but Ferris come to me and I told him I didn't mind. And I didn't. I told him I was tired of bein' watched by him and everybody else. D. B. Ferris looked up toward the front where Billy was workin' and smiled that old smile of his. Later, when Billy asked me what I said, I told him there wasn't no use tryin' to fight the government. 'That's true,' he told me— and I thought I saw some meanness in his eyes—'but there are some other things you can fight,' he said. At that time my head was kinda light, and I didn't catch what he meant.

"About my second day on the night shift, Teddy Johnson began workin' overtime. He didn't need the money and didn't like to work nohow, but some nights around ten or eleven, when we clocked out for lunch and sat around in the swing room, in would strut Teddy. Billy would be in school or at home. Usually, I'd be sittin' with Red and she'd tell me things while Teddy was walkin' over. 'Girl, it *must* be love to make a dude like Eldorado work overtime. *He* needs to work like *I* need to be a Catholic.' Then Teddy would sit down and she'd commence to play over us like her life depended on gittin' us together. She'd say, 'Let's go over to my place this mornin' when we clock out. I got some bacon and eggs and a bottle of Scotch.' Teddy would laugh and look in my eyes and say, 'Red, we don't wanna cause no trouble for this here fine young thing, who I hear is engaged to a college man.' Then I'd laugh with them and look at Teddy and wouldn't say nothin' much to nobody.

"Word must of gotten back to Billy soon after that. He didn't say nothin' at first, but I could see a change in his attitude. All this time I was tryin' to git up the guts to tell Billy I was thinkin' about breaking off, but I just couldn't. It wasn't that I thought he needed me; I just knew he was the kind of dude that doesn't let a girl decide when somethin' is over. Bein' as much like Billy as you are, you must understand what I'm tryin' to say. On one of my nights off, when we went out to a movie, he asked, 'What time did you get in this mornin'?' I said, 'Five-thirty, same as always.' But I was lyin'. Red and me had stopped for breakfast on the way home. Billy said, 'I called you at six-thirty this morning, and your Aunt Alvene said you was still out.' I told him, 'She must of been too sleepy to look in my room.' He didn't say more on the subject, but later that evenin', after the movie, he said, 'I was in the war for two years. It made me a disciplined man, and I hope I don't ever have to lose my temper.' I didn't say nothin', but the cold way he said it was like a window shade flappin' up from in front of his true nature, and I was scared.

"It was three years ago this September twenty-second that the thing happened. It was five-thirty in the mornin'. We had clocked out at four-forty-five, but Red had brought a bottle of Scotch to work, and we was

down in the swing room drinkin' a little with our coffee, just to relax. I'll
tell you the truth: Teddy Johnson was there, too. He had come down just
to give us a ride home. I'll never forget that day as long as I live. Teddy
was dressed in a pink silk shirt with black ruffles on the sleeves, the kind
that was so popular a few years ago. He was wearin' shiny black bell-
bottoms that hugged his little hips like a second coat of skin, and looked
like pure silk when he walked. He sat across from me, flashin' those
diamond rings every time he poured more Scotch in our cups. Red was
sittin' back with a smile on her face, watchin' us like a cat that had just
ate.

"I was sittin' with my back to the door and didn't know anything,
until I saw something change in Red's face. I still see it in my sleep at
night. Her face seemed to light up and git scared and happy at the same
time. She was lookin' behind me, over my shoulder, with all the smart-
ness in the world burnin' in her eyes. I turned around. Billy Crawford
was standin' right behind me with his hands close to his sides. He wore a
white shirt and a thin black tie, and his mouth was tight like a little slit.
He said, 'It's time for you to go home,' with that voice of his that was too
cold to be called just mean. I sat there lookin' up at him. Red's voice was
even colder. She said to me, 'You gonna let him order you around like
that?' I didn't say nothin'. Red said to Teddy, 'Ain't *you* got something to
say about this?' Teddy stood up slow and swelled out his chest. He said,
'Yeah. I got somethin' to say,' looking hard at Billy. But Billy just kept
lookin' down at me. 'Let's go,' he said. 'What you got to say?' Red Bone
said to Teddy. Teddy said to me, 'Why don't *you* tell the dude, baby?'
But I didn't say nothin'. Billy shifted his eyes to Teddy and said, 'I got
nothing against you. You ain't real, so you don't matter. You been strut-
ting the streets too long, but that ain't my business. So keep out of this.'
Then he looked down at me again. 'Let's go,' he said. I looked up at the
way his lips curled and wanted to cry and hit him at the same time. I felt
like a trigger bein' pulled. Then I heard Red sayin', 'Why don't you go
back to bed with them *goddamn books, punk!* And leave decent folks
alone!' For the first time Billy glanced over at her. His mouth twitched.
But then he looked at me again. 'This here's the *last time* I'm asking,' he
said. That's when I exploded and started to jump up. 'I ain't goin'
nowhere!' I screamed. The last plain thing I remember was tryin' to git
to his face, but it seemed to turn all bright and silvery and hot, and then
I couldn't see nothin' no more.

"They told me later that he sliced me so fast there wasn't time for
nobody to act. By the time Teddy jumped across the table I was down,
and Billy had stabbed me again in the side. Then him and Teddy tussled
over the knife, while me and Red screamed and screamed. Then Teddy
went down holdin' his belly, and Billy was comin' after me again, when
some of the dudes from the freight dock ran in and grabbed him. They
say it took three of them to drag him off me, and all the time they was

pullin' him away he kept slashin' out at me with that knife. It seemed like all the walls was screamin' and I was floatin' in water, and I thought I was dead and in hell, because I felt hot and prickly all over, and I could hear some woman's voice that might of been mine screamin' over and over, 'You devil! . . . You *devil!*' "

She lit a third cigarette. She blew a relieving cloud of smoke downward. The thin white haze billowed about her purple legs, dissipated, and vanished. A terrifying fog of silence and sickness crept into the small room, and there was no longer the smell of medicine. I dared not steal a glance at my watch, although by this time Dr. Wayland was agonizingly late. I had heard it all, and now I waited. Finally her eyes fixed on the frosted glass door. She wet her lips again and, in a much slower and pained voice, said, "This here's the third doctor I been to see. The first one stitched me up like a turkey and left this scar. The second one refused to touch me." She paused and wet her lips again. "This man fixed your nose for you," she said softly. "Do you think he could do somethin' about this scar?"

I searched the end table next to my couch for a newsmagazine, carefully avoiding her face. "Dr. Wayland is a skilled man," I told her. "Whenever he's not late. I think he may be able to do something for you."

She sighed heavily and seemed to tremble. "I don't expect no miracle or nothin'," she said. "If he could just fix the part around my eye I wouldn't expect nothin' else. People say the rest don't look too bad."

I clutched a random magazine and did not answer. Nor did I look at her. The flesh around my nose began to itch, and I looked toward the inner office door with the most extreme irritation building in me. At that moment it seemed a shadow began to form behind the frosted glass, signaling perhaps the approach of someone. I resolved to put aside all notions of civility and go into the office before her, as was my right. The shadow behind the door darkened, but vanished just as suddenly. And then I remembered the most important question, without which the entire exchange would have been wasted. I turned to the woman, now drawn together in the red plastic chair, as if struggling to sleep in a cold bed. "Sister," I said, careful to maintain a casual air. "Sister . . . what is your name?"

LEONARD MICHAELS

Murderers

When my uncle Moe dropped dead of a heart attack I became expert in the subway system. With a nickel I'd get to Queens, twist and zoom to Coney Island, twist again toward the George Washington Bridge—beyond which was darkness. I wanted proximity to darkness, strangeness. Who doesn't? The poor in spirit, the ignorant and frightened. My family came from Poland, then never went any place until they had heart attacks. The consummation of years in one neighborhood: a black Cadillac, corpse inside. We should have buried Uncle Moe where he shuffled away his life, in the kitchen or toilet, under the linoleum, near the coffee pot. Anyhow, they were dropping on Henry Street and Cherry Street. Blue lips. The previous winter it was cousin Charlie, forty-five years old. Moe, Charlie, Sam, Adele—family meant a punch in the chest, fire in the arm. I didn't want to wait for it. I went to Harlem, the Polo Grounds, Far Rockaway, thousands of miles on nickels, mainly underground. Tenements watched me go, day after day, fingering nickels. One afternoon I stopped to grind my heel against the curb. Melvin and Arnold Bloom appeared, then Harold Cohen. Melvin said, "You step in dog shit?" Grinding was my answer. Harold Cohen said, "The rabbi is home. I saw him on Market Street. He was walking fast." Oily Arnold, eleven years old, began to urge: "Let's go up to our roof." The decision waited for me. I considered the roof, the view of industrial Brooklyn, the Battery, ships in the river, bridges, towers, and the rabbi's apartment. "All right," I said. We didn't giggle or look to one another for moral signals. We were running.

The blinds were up and curtains pulled, giving sunlight, wind, birds to the rabbi's apartment—a magnificent metropolitan view. The rabbi and his wife never took it, but in the light and air of summer afternoons, in the eye of gull and pigeon, they were joyous. A bearded young man, and his young pink wife, sacramentally bald. Beard and Baldy, with everything to see, looked at each other. From a water tank on the opposite roof, higher than their windows, we looked at them. In psychoanalysis this is "The Primal Scene." To achieve the primal scene we crossed a ledge six inches wide. A half-inch indentation in the brick gave us fingerholds. We dragged bellies and groins against the brick face to a steel ladder. It went up the side of the building, bolted into brick, and up the side of the water tank to a slanted tin roof which caught the afternoon sun. We sat on that roof like angels, shot through with light, derealized in brilliance. Our sneakers sucked hot slanted metal. Palms and fingers pressed to bone on nailheads.

The Brooklyn Navy Yard with destroyers and aircraft carriers, the Statue of Liberty putting the sky to the torch, the dull remote skyscrapers of Wall Street, and the Empire State Building were among the wonders we dominated. Our view of the holy man and his wife, on their living-room couch and floor, on the bed in their bedroom, could not be improved. Unless we got closer. But fifty feet across the air was right. We heard their phonograph and watched them dancing. We couldn't hear the gratifications or see pimples. We smelled nothing. We didn't want to touch.

For a while I watched them. Then I gazed beyond into shimmering nullity, gray, blue, and green murmuring over rooftops and towers. I had watched them before. I could tantalize myself with this brief ocular perversion, the general cleansing nihil of a view. This was the beginning of philosophy. I indulged in ambience, in space like eons. So what if my uncle Moe was dead? I was philosophical and luxurious. I didn't even have to look at the rabbi and his wife. After all, how many times had we dissolved stickball games when the rabbi came home? How many times had we risked shameful discovery, scrambling up the ladder, exposed to their windows—if they looked. We risked life itself to achieve this eminence. I looked at the rabbi and his wife.

Today she was a blonde. Bald didn't mean no wigs. She had ten wigs, ten colors, fifty styles. She looked different, the same, and very good. A human theme in which nothing begat anything and was gorgeous. To me she was the world's lesson. Aryan yellow slipped through pins about her ears. An olive complexion mediated yellow hair and Arabic black eyes. Could one care what she really looked like? What was *really?* The minute you wondered, she looked like something else, in another wig, another style. Without the wigs she was a baldy-bean lady. Today she was a blonde. Not blonde. *A* blonde. The phonograph blared and her deep loops flowed Tommy Dorsey, Benny Goodman, and then the thing itself, Choo-Choo Lopez. Rumba! One, two-three. One, two-three. The rabbi stepped away to delight in blond imagination. Twirling and individual, he stepped away snapping fingers, going high and light on his toes. A short bearded man, balls afling, cock shuddering like a springboard. Rumba! One, two-three. *Olé! Vaya,* Choo-Choo!

I was on my way to spend some time in Cuba.
Stopped off at Miami Beach, la-la.
Oh, what a rumba they teach, la-la.
Way down in Miami Beach,
Oh, what a chroombah they teach, la-la.
Way-down-in-Miami-Beach.

She, on the other hand, was somewhat reserved. A shift in one lush hip was total rumba. He was Mr. Life. She was dancing. He was a naked man. She was what she was in the garment of her soft, essential self. He was snapping, clapping, hopping to the beat. The beat lived in her visible music, her lovely self. Except for the wig. Also a watchband that desecrated her wrist. But it gave her a bit of the whorish. She never took it off.

Harold Cohen began a cocktail-mixer motion, masturbating with two fists. Seeing him at such hard futile work, braced only by sneakers, was terrifying. But I grinned. Out of terror, I twisted an encouraging face. Melvin Bloom kept one hand on the tin. The other knuckled the rumba numbers into the back of my head. Nodding like a defective, little Arnold Bloom chewed his lip and squealed as the rabbi and his wife smacked together. The rabbi clapped her buttocks, fingers buried in the cleft. They stood only on his legs. His back arched, knees bent, thighs thick with thrust, up, up, up. Her legs wrapped his hips, ankles crossed, hooked for constriction. "Oi, oi, oi," she cried, wig flashing left, right, tossing the Brooklyn Navy Yard, the Statue of Liberty, and the Empire State Building to hell. Arnold squealed oi, squealing rubber. His sneaker heels stabbed tin to stop his slide. Melvin said, "Idiot." Arnold's ring hooked a nailhead and the ring and ring finger remained. The hand, the arm, the rest of him, were gone.

We rumbled down the ladder. "Oi, oi, oi," she yelled. In a freak of ecstasy her eyes had rolled and caught us. The rabbi drilled to her quick and she had us. "OI, OI," she yelled above congas going clop, doom-doom, clop, doom-doom on the way to Cuba. The rabbi flew to the window, a red mouth opening in his beard: "Murderers." He couldn't know what he said. Melvin Bloom was crying. My fingers were tearing, bleeding into brick. Harold Cohen, like an adding machine, gibbered the name of God. We moved down the ledge quickly as we dared. Bongos went tocka-ti-tocka, tocka-ti-tocka. The rabbi screamed, "MEL-VIN BLOOM, PHILLIP LIEBOWITZ, HAROLD COHEN, MELVIN BLOOM," as if our names, screamed this way, naming us where we hung, smashed us into brick.

Nothing was discussed.

The rabbi used his connections, arrangements were made. We were sent to a camp in New Jersey. We hiked and played volleyball. One day, apropos of nothing, Melvin came to me and said little Arnold had been made of gold and he, Melvin, of shit. I appreciated the sentiment, but to my mind they were both made of shit. Harold Cohen never again spoke to either of us. The counselors in the camp were World War II veterans, introspective men. Some carried shrapnel in their bodies. One had a metal plate in his head. Whatever you said to them they seemed to be thinking of something else, even when they answered. But step out of line and a plastic lanyard whistled burning notice across your ass.

At night, lying in the bunkhouse, I listened to owls. I'd never before heard that sound, the sound of darkness, blooming, opening inside you like a mouth.

ARTHUR MILLER

The Misfits

Wind blew down from the mountains for two nights, pinning them to their little camp on the desert floor. Around the fire on the grand plateau between the two mountain ranges, they were the only moving things. But awakening now with the first pink of dawn they heard the hush of a windless morning. Quickly the sky flared with true dawn like damp paper catching fire, and the shroud of darkness slipped off the little plane and the truck standing a few yards away.

As soon as they had eaten breakfast they took their accustomed positions. Perce Howland went to the tail, ready to unlash the ropes, Gay Langland stood near the propeller, and both watched the pilot, Guido Racanelli, loading his shotgun pistol and stowing it under the seat in the cockpit. He looked thoughtful, even troubled, zipping up the front of his ripped leather jacket. "Sumbitch valve is rattling," he complained.

"It's better than wages, Guido," Perce called from the tail.

"Hell it is if I get flattened up there," Guido said.

"You know them canyons," Gay Langland said.

"Gay, it don't mean a damn thing what the wind does down here. Up there's where it counts." He thumbed toward the mountains behind them. "I'm ten feet from rocks at the bottom of a dive; the wind smacks you down then and you never pull up again."

They saw he was serious so they said nothing. Guido stood still for a moment, studying the peaks in the distance, his hard, melon cheeks browned by wind, the white goggle marks around his eyes turning him into some fat jungle bird. At last he said, "Oh, hell with it. We'll get the sumbitches." He climbed into the cockpit calling to Gay, "Turn her over!"

Perce Howland quickly freed the tail and then the wing tips and Gay hurried to the propeller, swung the blade down and hopped back. A puff of white smoke floated up from the engine ports.

"Goddamn car gas," Guido muttered. They were buying low octane to save money. Then he called, "Go again, Gay-boy; ignition on!" Gay reached up and pulled the propeller down and jumped back. The engine said its "Chaahh!" and the fuselage shuddered and the propeller turned into a wheel in the golden air. The little, stiff-backed plane tumbled toward the open desert, bumping along over the sage clumps and crunching whitened skeletons of winter-killed cattle, growing smaller as it shouldered its way over the broken ground, until its nose turned upward and space opened between the doughnut tires and the desert, and it turned and flew back over the heads of Gay and Perce. Guido waved down, a stranger now, fiercely goggled and wrapped in leather. The plane flew away, losing itself against the orange and purple mountains which vaulted from the desert to hide from the cowboys' eyes the wild animals they wanted for themselves.

They had at least two hours before the plane would fly out of the mountains, driving the horses before it, so they washed the plates and the cups and stored them in the aluminum grub box. If Guido did find horses, they would break camp and return to Bowie tonight, so they packed up their bedrolls with sailors' tidiness and laid them neatly side by side on the ground. Six great truck tires, each with a rope coiled within, lay on the open truck bed. Gay Langland looked them over and touched them with his hand, trying to think if there was anything they were leaving behind. Serious as he was he looked a little amused, even slightly surprised. He was forty-six years old but his ears still stuck out like a little boy's and his hair lay in swirls from the pressure of his hat. After two days and nights of lying around he was eager to be going and doing and he savored the pleasurable delay of this final inspection.

Perce Howland watched, his face dreamy and soft with his early-morning somnambulist's stare. He stood and moved, bent over the tires and straightened himself as effortlessly as wheat, as though he had been created full-grown and dressed as he now was, hipless and twenty-two, in his snug dungarees and tight plaid shirt and broad-brimmed hat pushed back on his blond head. Now Gay got into the cab and started the engine and Perce slid into the seat beside him. A thin border collie leaped in after him. "You nearly forgot Belle," he said to Gay. The dog snuggled down behind Gay's feet and they started off.

Thirty miles ahead stood the lava mountains which were the northern border of this desert, the bed of a bowl seven thousand feet in the air, a place no one ever saw excepting a few cowboys searching for strays. People in Bowie, sixty miles away, did not know of this place.

Now that they were on the move, following the two-track trail through the sage, they felt between them the comfort of purpose and their isolation. It was getting warm now. Perce slumped in his seat, blinking as though he would go to sleep, and the older man smoked a cigarette and let his body flow from side to side with the pitching of the truck. There was a moving cloud of dust in the distance, and Gay said,

"Antelope," and Perce tipped his hat back and looked. "Must be doin' sixty," he said, and Gay said, "More."

After a while Perce said, "We better get over to Largo by tomorrow if we're gonna get into that rodeo. They's gonna be a crowd trying to sign up for that one."

"We'll drive down in the morning," Gay said.

"Like to win some money. I just wish I get me a good horse down there."

"They be glad to fix you up. You're known pretty good around here now."

Perce tucked his thumbs into his belt so his fingers could touch his prize, the engraved belt buckle with his name spelled out under the raised figure of the bucking horse. He had been coming down from Nevada since he was sixteen, picking up money at the local rodeos, but this trip had been different. Sometime, somewhere in the past weeks, he had lost the desire to go back home.

They rode in silence. Gay had to hold the gearshift lever in high or it would slip out into neutral when they hit a bump. The transmission fork was worn out, he knew, and the front tires were going, too. He dropped one hand to his pants pocket and felt the four silver dollars he had left from the ten Roslyn had given him.

As though he had read Gay's mind, Perce said, "Roslyn would've liked it up here. She'd liked to have seen that antelope, I bet."

Through the corner of his eye Gay watched the younger man, who was looking ahead with a little grin on his face. "Yeah. She's a damned good sport, old Roslyn." He watched Perce for any sign of guile.

"Only educated women I ever knew before was back home near Teachers College," Perce said. "I was learning them to ride for a while, and I used to think, hell, education's everything. But when I saw the husbands they got married to, why I don't give them much credit. And they just as soon climb on a man as tell him good morning."

"Just because a woman's educated don't mean much. Woman's a woman," Gay said. The image of his wife came into his mind. For a moment he wondered if she was still living with the same man.

"You divorced?" Perce asked.

"No. I never bothered with it," Gay said. It surprised him how Perce said just what was on his mind sometimes. "How'd you know I was thinking of that?" he asked, grinning with embarrassment.

"Hell, I didn't know," Perce said.

"You're always doin' that. I think of somethin' and you say it."

"That's funny," Perce said.

They rode on in silence. They were nearing the middle of the desert where they would turn east. Gay was driving faster now, holding on to the gearshift lever to keep it from springing into neutral. The time was coming soon when he would need about fifty dollars or sell the truck, because it would be useless without repairs. Without a truck and without a horse he would be down to what was in his pocket.

Perce spoke out of the silence. "If I don't win Saturday, I'm gonna have to do something for money."

"Goddamn, you always say what's in my mind."

Perce laughed. His face looked very young and pink. "Why?"

"I was just now thinkin'," Gay said, "what I'm gonna do for money."

"Well, Roslyn give you some," Perce said.

He said it innocently, and Gay knew it was innocent, and yet he felt angry blood moving into his neck. Something had happened in these five weeks since he'd met Perce and let him come home to Roslyn's house to sleep, and Gay did not know for sure what it was. Roslyn had taken to calling Perce cute, and now and again she would bend over and kiss him on the back of the neck when he was sitting in the living-room chair, drinking with them.

Not that that meant anything in itself because he'd known eastern women before, and it was just their way. What he wondered at was Perce's hardly noticing what she did to him. Sometimes it was like he'd already had her and could ignore her the way a man will who knows he's boss. Gay sensed the bottom of his life falling if it turned out Roslyn had really been loving this boy beside him. It had happened to him once before, but this frightened him even more and he did not know exactly why. Not that he couldn't do without her. There wasn't anybody or anything he couldn't do without. He had been all his life like Perce Howland, a man moving on or ready to. Only when he had discovered his wife with a stranger in a parked car did he understand that he had never had a stake to which he'd been pleasantly tethered.

He had not seen her or his children for years, and only rarely thought about any of them. Any more than his father had thought of him very much after the day he had gotten on his pony, when he was fourteen, to go to town from the ranch, and had kept going into Montana and stayed there for three years. He lived in his country and his father did and it was the same endless range wherever he went and it connected him sufficiently with his father and his wife and his children. All might turn up sometime in some town or at some rodeo where he might happen to look over his shoulder and see his daughter or one of his sons, or they might never turn up. He had neither left anyone nor not-left as long as they were all alive on these ranges, for everything here was always beyond the furthest shot of vision and far away, and mostly he had worked alone or with one or two men between distant mountains anyway.

He drove steadily across the grand plateau, and he felt he was going to be afraid. He was not afraid now, but something new was opening up inside him. He had somehow passed the kidding point: he had to work again and earn his way as he always had before he met Roslyn. Not that he didn't work for her, but it wasn't the same. Driving her car, repairing her house, running errands wasn't what you'd call work. Still it was too. Yet it wasn't either. He grew tired of thinking about it.

In the distance now he could see the shimmering wall of heat rising from the clay flatland they wanted to get to—a beige waste as bare and hard as pavement, a prehistoric lake bed thirty miles long by seventeen miles wide couched between two mountain ranges, where a man might drive a car at a hundred miles an hour with his hands off the wheel and never hit anything at all.

When they had rolled a few hundred yards onto the clay lake bed, Gay pulled up and shut off the engine. The air was still, in a dead, sunlit silence. Opening his door, he could hear a squeak in the hinge he had never noticed before. When they walked around out here they could hear their shirts rasping against their backs and the brush of a sleeve against their trousers. They looked back toward the mountains at whose feet they had camped and scanned the ridges for Guido's plane.

Perce Howland said, "I sure hope they's five up in there."

"Guido spotted five last week, he said."

"He said he wasn't sure if one wasn't only a colt."

Gay let himself keep silence. He felt he was going to argue with Perce. "How long you think you'll be stayin' around here?" he asked.

"Don't know," Perce said, and spat over the side of the truck. "I'm gettin' a little tired of this, though."

"Well, it's better than wages."

"Hell, yes. Anything's better than wages."

Gay's eyes crinkled. "You're a real misfit, boy."

"That suits me fine," Perce said. They often had this conversation and savored it. "Better than workin' for some goddamn cow outfit buckarooin' so somebody else can buy gas for his Cadillac."

"Damn right," Gay said.

"Hell, Gay, you are the most misfitted man I ever saw and you done all right."

"I got no complaints," Gay said.

"I don't want nothin' and I don't want to want nothin'."

"That's the way, boy."

Gay felt closer to him again and he was glad for it. He kept his eyes on the ridges far away. The sun felt good on his shoulders. "I think he's havin' trouble with them sumbitches up in there."

Perce stared out at the ridges. "Ain't two hours yet." Then he turned to Gay. "These mountains must be cleaned out by now, ain't they."

"Just about," Gay said. "Just a couple small herds left."

"What you goin' to do when you got these cleaned out?"

"Might go north, I think. Supposed to be some big herds in around Thighbone Mountain and that range up in there."

"How far's that?"

"North about a hundred miles. If I can get Guido interested."

Perce smiled. "He don't like movin' around much, does he?"

"He's just misfitted like us," Gay said. "He don't want nothin'." Then he added, "They wanted him for an airline pilot flyin' up into Montana and back. Good pay too."

"Wouldn't do it, huh?"

"Not Guido," Gay said, grinning. "Might not like some of the passengers, he told them."

Both men laughed and Perce shook his head in tickled admiration for Guido. Then he said, "They wanted me take over the riding academy up home. Just stand around and see the customers get satisfied and put them girls off and on."

He fell silent. Gay knew the rest. It was the same story. It brought him closer to Perce and it was what he had liked about him in the first place. He had come on Perce in a bar where the boy was buying drinks for everybody with his rodeo winnings, and his hair still clotted with blood from a bucking horse's kick an hour earlier. Roslyn had offered to get a doctor for him and he had said, "Thank you, kindly. But if you're bad hurt you gonna die and the doctor can't do nothin', and if you ain't bad hurt you get better anyway without no doctor."

Now it suddenly came upon Gay that Perce must have known Roslyn before they had met in the bar. He stared at the boy's straight profile. "Want to come up north with me if I go?" he asked.

Perce thought a moment. "Think I'll stay around here. Not much rodeoin' up north."

"I might find a pilot up there if Guido won't come. And Roslyn drive us up in her car."

Perce turned to him, a little surprised. "Would she go up there?"

"Sure. She's a damn good sport," Gay said. He watched Perce's eyes, which had turned interested and warm.

Perce said, "Well, maybe; except to tell you the truth, Gay, I never feel comfortable takin' these horses."

"Somebody's goin' to take them if we don't."

"I know," Perce said. He turned to watch the far ridges again. "Just seems to me they belong up there."

"They ain't doin' nothin' up there but eatin' out good cattle range. The cow outfits shoot them down if they see them."

"I know," Perce said.

There was silence. Neither bug nor lizard nor rabbit moved on the great basin around them. Gay said, "I'd a soon sell them for riding horses, but they ain't big enough. And the freight's more than they're worth. You saw them—they ain't nothin' but skinny horses."

"I just don't know if I'd want to see like a hundred of them goin' for chicken feed, though. I don't mind like five or six, but a hundred's a lot of horses. I don't know."

Gay thought. "Well, if it ain't this it's wages. Around here anyway." He was speaking of himself and explaining himself.

They heard the shotgun off in the sky somewhere and they stopped moving. Gay slid out of the tire in which he had been lounging and off the truck. He went to the cab and brought out a pair of binoculars, blew dust off the lenses, mounted the truck and, with his elbows propped on his knees, he focused on the far mountains.

"See anything?" Perce asked.

"He's still in the pass, I guess," Gay said.

They sat still, watching the empty sky over the pass. The sun was making them perspire now and Gay wiped his wet eyebrows with the back of one hand. They heard the shotgun again. Gay spoke without lowering the glasses: "He's probably blasting them out of some corner."

"I see him," Perce said quickly. "I see him glintin', I see the plane."

It angered Gay that Perce had seen it first without glasses. In the glasses Gay could see the plane clearly now. The plane was flying out of the pass, circling back and disappearing into the pass again. "He's got them in the pass now. Just goin' back in for them."

Now Gay could see moving specks on the ground where the pass opened onto the desert table. "I see them," he said. "One, two, three, four. Four and a colt."

"We gonna take the colt?" Perce asked.

"Hell, can't take the mare without the colt."

Gay handed him the glasses. "Take a look."

Gay went forward to the cab and opened its door. His dog lay shivering on the floor under the pedals. He snapped his fingers and she leaped down to the ground and stood there, quivering as though the ground had hidden explosives everywhere. He climbed back onto the truck and sat on a tire beside Perce, who was looking through the glasses.

"He's divin' down on them. God, they sure can run."

"Let's have a look," Gay said.

The plane was dropping down from the arc of its climb and as the roaring motor flew over them they lifted their heads and galloped faster. They had been running now for over an hour and would slow down when the plane had to climb after a dive and the motor's noise grew quieter. As Guido climbed again Gay and Perce heard a shot, distant and harmless, and the shot sped the horses on as the plane took time to climb, bank, and turn. Then as the horses slowed to a trot the plane dived down over their backs again and their heads shot up and they galloped until the engine's roar receded. The sky was clear and lightly blue and only the little plane swung back and forth across the desert like the glinting tip of a magic wand, and the horses came on toward the vast striped clay bed where the truck was parked, and at its edge they halted.

The two men waited for the horses to reach the edge of the lake bed when Guido would land the plane and they would take off with the truck.

"They see the heat waves," Gay said, looking through the glasses. The plane dived down on them and they scattered but would not go forward onto the unknowable territory from the cooler, sage-dotted desert behind them. The men on the truck heard the shotgun again. Now the horses broke their formation and leaped onto the lake bed, all heading in different directions, but only trotting, exploring the ground under their feet and the strange, superheated air in their nostrils. Gradually, as the plane wound around the sky to dive again, the horses closed ranks and slowly galloped shoulder to shoulder out onto the borderless waste, the colt a length behind with its nose nearly touching the mare's long tail.

"That's a big mare," Perce said. His eyes were still dreamy and his face was calm, but his skin had reddened.

"She's a bigger mare than usual up there, ya," Gay said. Both men knew the mustang herds lived in total isolation and that inbreeding had reduced them to the size of large ponies. The herd swerved now and they could see the stallion. He was smaller than the mare, but still larger than any they had brought down before. The other two horses were small, the way mustangs ought to be.

The plane was hurrying down for a landing now. Gay and Perce Howland got to their feet and each reached into a tire behind him and drew out a coil of rope whose ends hung in a loop. They glanced out and saw Guido taxiing toward them and they strapped themselves to stanchions sticking up from the truck bed and stood waiting for him. He cut the engine twenty yards away and leaped out of the open cockpit before the plane had halted, its right wing tilted down, as always, because of the weak starboard shock absorber. He trotted over to the truck, lifting his goggles off and stuffing them into his torn jacket pocket. His face was puffed with preoccupation. He jumped into the cab of the truck and the collie dog jumped in after him and sat on the floor, quivering. He started the truck and they roared across the flat clay.

The herd was standing still in a small clot of dots more than two miles off. The truck rolled smoothly past sixty. Gay on the right front corner of the truck bed and Perce on the left pulled their hats down to their eyebrows against the rush of air and hefted the looped ropes which the wind was threatening to coil and foul in their palms. Guido knew that Gay was a good roper and that Perce was unsure, so he headed for the herd's left in order to come up to them on Gay's side of the truck if he could. This whole method of mustanging—the truck, the tires attached to ropes and the plane—was his idea, and once again he felt the joy of having thought of it all. It had awakened him to life after a year's hibernation. His wife dying in childbirth had been like a gigantic and insane ocean wave rising out of a calm sea, and it had left him stranded in his cousin's house in Bowie, suddenly a bachelor after eleven married years. Only this had broken the silence of the world for him, this roaring across the lake bed with his left boot ready over the brake pedal should the truck start to overturn on a sudden swerve.

The horses, at a standstill now, were staring at the oncoming truck, and the men saw that this herd was beautiful.

A wet spring had rounded them out, and they shone in the sunlight. The mare was almost black and the stallion and the two others were deeply brown. The colt was curly-coated and had a gray sheen. The stallion dipped his head suddenly and turned his back on the truck and galloped. The others turned and clattered after him, with the colt running alongside the mare. Guido pressed down on the gas and the truck surged forward, whining. They were a few yards behind the animals now and they could see the bottoms of their hoofs, fresh hoofs that made a gentle tacking clatter because they had never been shod. The truck was coming abreast of the mare now and beside her the others galloped, slim-legged and wet after running almost two hours.

As the truck drew alongside the mare and Gay began twirling his loop above his head, the whole herd wheeled away to the right and Guido jammed the gas pedal down and swung with them, but the truck tilted violently so he slowed down and fell behind them a few yards until they would straighten out and move ahead again. At the edge of their strength they wheeled like circus horses, almost tamely in their terror, and suddenly Guido saw a breadth between the stallion and the two browns and he sped in between, cutting the mare off at the left with her colt. Now the horses stretched, the clatter quickened. Their hind legs flew straight back and their necks stretched low and forward. Gay whirled his loop over his head and the truck came up alongside the stallion whose lungs were screaming with exhaustion and Gay flung the noose. It fell on the stallion's head and, with a whipping of the lead, Gay made it slip down over his neck. The horse swerved away to the right and stretched the rope until the tire was pulled off the truck bed and dragged along the hard clay. The three men watched from the slowing truck as the stallion, with startled eyes, pulled the giant tire for a few yards, then reared up with his forelegs in the air and came down facing the tire and trying to back away from it. Then he stood there, heaving, his hind legs dancing in an arc from right to left and back again as he shook his head in the remorseless noose.

As soon as he was sure the stallion was secure, Guido turned sharply left toward the mare and the colt which were trotting idly together by themselves in the distance. The two browns were already disappearing toward the north, but they would halt soon because they were tired, while the mare might continue back into her familiar hills where the truck could not follow. He straightened the truck and jammed down the gas pedal. In a minute he drew up on her left side because the colt was running on her right. She was very heavy, he saw, and he wondered now if she was a mustang at all. Then through his right window he saw the loop flying out and down over her head, and he saw her head fly up and then she fell back. He turned to the right, braking with his left boot, and he saw her dragging a tire and coming to a halt, with the free colt watching her and trotting beside her very close. Then he headed straight ahead across the flat toward two specks which rapidly enlarged until they became the two browns which were at a standstill and watching the oncoming truck. He came in between them and they galloped; Perce on the left roped one and Gay roped the other almost at the same time. And Guido leaned his head out of his window and yelled up at Perce. "Good boy!" he hollered, and Perce let himself return an excited grin, although there seemed to be some trouble in his eyes.

Guido made an easy half circle and headed back to the mare and the colt and slowed to a halt twenty yards away and got out of the cab.

The three men approached the mare. She had never seen a man and her eyes were wide in fear. Her rib cage stretched and collapsed very rapidly and there was a trickle of blood coming out of her nostrils. She had a heavy, dark brown mane and her tail nearly touched the ground. The colt with dumb eyes shifted about on its silly bent legs trying to keep the mare between itself and the men, and the mare kept shifting her rump to shield the colt from them.

They wanted now to move the noose higher up on the mare's neck because it had fallen on her from the rear and was tight around the middle of her neck where it could choke her if she kept pulling against the weight of the tire. Gay was the best roper, so Perce and Guido stood by as he twirled a noose over his head, then let it fall open softly, just behind the forefeet of the mare. They waited for a moment, then approached her and she backed a step. Then Gay pulled sharply on the rope and her forefeet were tied together. With another rope Gay lassoed her hind feet and she swayed and fell to the ground on her side. Her body swelled and contracted, but she seemed resigned. The colt stretched its nose to her tail and stood there as the men came to the mare and spoke quietly to her, and Guido bent down and opened the noose and slipped it up under her jaw. They inspected her for a brand, but she was clean.

"Never see a horse that size up here," Gay said to Guido.

Perce said, "She's no mustang. Might even be standardbred." He looked to Guido for confirmation.

Guido sat on his heels and opened the mare's mouth and the other two looked in with him. "She's fifteen if she's a day," Gay said. "She wouldn't be around much longer anyway."

"Ya, she's old." Perce's eyes were filled with thought.

Guido stood up and the three went back to the truck, and drove across the lake bed to the stallion.

"Ain't a bad-lookin' horse," Perce said.

He was standing still, heaving for breath. His head was down, holding the rope taut, and he was looking at them with deep brown eyes that were like the lenses of enormous binoculars. Gay got his rope ready. "He ain't nothin' but a misfit," he said. "You couldn't run cattle with him; he's too small to breed and too old to cut."

"He is small," Perce conceded. "Got a nice neck though."

"Oh, they're nice-*lookin'* horses, some of them," Guido said. "What the hell you goin' to do with them, though?"

Gay twirled the loop over his head and they spread out around the stallion. "They're just old misfit horses, that's all," he said, and he flung the rope behind the stallion's forelegs and the horse backed a step and he drew the rope and the noose bit into the horse's fetlocks drawing them together, and he swayed but he would not fall. "Take hold here," Gay called to Perce, who ran around the horse and took the rope from him and held it taut. Then Gay went back to the truck, got another rope, returned to the rear of the horse and looped his hind legs. But the stallion would not fall. Guido stepped closer to push him over, but he swung his head and showed his teeth and Guido stepped back. "Pull him down!" Guido yelled to Gay and Perce, and they jerked their ropes to trip the stallion, but he righted himself and stood there, bound by the head to the tire and by his feet to the two ropes which the men held. Then Guido hurried over to Perce and took the rope from him and walked with it toward the rear of the horse and pulled hard. The stallion's forefeet slipped back and he came down on his knees and his nose struck the clay ground and he snorted as he struck, but he would not topple over and stayed there on his knees as though he were bowing to something, with his nose propping up his head against the ground and his sharp bursts of breath blowing up dust in little clouds under his nostrils. Now Guido gave the rope back to young Perce Howland who held it taut and he came up alongside the stallion's neck and laid his hands on the side of the neck and pushed and the horse fell over onto his flank and lay there and, like the mare, when he felt the ground against his body he seemed to let himself out and for the first time his eyes blinked and his breath came now in sighs and no longer fiercely. Guido shifted the noose up under his jaw, and they opened the ropes around his hoofs and when he felt his legs free he first raised his head curiously and then clattered up and stood there looking at them, from one to the other, blood dripping from his nostrils and a stain of deep red on both dusty knees.

Then the men moved without hurrying to the truck and Gay stored his two extra ropes and got behind the wheel with Guido beside him, and Perce climbed onto the back of the truck and lay down facing the sky and made a pillow with his palms.

Gay headed the truck south toward the plane. Guido was slowly catching his breath and now he lighted a cigarette, puffed it and rubbed his left hand into his bare scalp. He sat gazing out the windshield and the side window. "I'm sleepy," he said.

"What you reckon?" Gay asked.

"What you?" Guido said.

"That mare might be six hundred pounds."

"I'd say about that, Gay."

"About four hundred apiece for the browns and a little more for the stallion. What's that come to?"

"Nineteen hundred, maybe two thousand," Guido said.

They fell silent figuring the money. Two thousand pounds at six cents a pound came to a hundred and twenty dollars. The colt might make it a few dollars more, but not much. Figuring the gas for the plane and the truck, and twelve dollars for their groceries, they came to the figure of a hundred dollars for the three of them. Guido would get forty-five, since he had used his plane, and Gay would get thirty-five, including the use of his truck, and Perce Howland, if he agreed, as he undoubtedly would, had the remaining twenty.

"We should've watered them the last time," Gay said. "They can pick up a lot of weight if you let them water."

"Yeah, let's be sure to do that," Guido said.

They knew they would as likely as not forget to water the horses before they unloaded them at the dealer's lot in Bowie. They would be in a hurry to unload and be free of them, free to pitch and roll with time in the bars or asleep in Roslyn's house or making a try in some rodeo. Once they had figured their shares they stopped thinking of money, and they divided it and even argued about it only because it was the custom of men. They had not come up here for the money.

Gay stopped the truck beside the plane. Guido opened his door and said, "See you in town. Let's get the other truck tomorrow morning."

"Perce wants to go over to Largo and sign up for the rodeo tomorrow," Gay said. "Tell ya—we'll go in and get the truck and come back here this afternoon maybe. Maybe we bring them in tonight."

"All right, if you want to. I'll see you boys tomorrow," Guido said, and he got out and stopped for a moment to talk to Perce. "Perce?"

Perce propped himself up on one elbow and looked down at him. Guido smiled. "You sleeping?"

"I was about to."

"We figure about a hundred dollars clear. Twenty all right for you?"

"Ya, twenty's all right," Perce said. He hardly seemed to be listening.

"See you in town," Guido said, and turned on his bandy legs and waddled off to the plane where Gay was already standing with his hands on the propeller blade. Guido got in and Gay swung the blade down and the engine started immediately. Guido gunned the plane and she trundled off and into the sky and the two men on the ground watched her as she flew toward the mountains and away.

Now Gay returned to the truck and said, "Twenty all right?" And he said this because he thought Perce looked hurt.

"Heh? Ya, twenty's all right," Perce answered. Then he let himself down and stood beside the truck and wet the ground while Gay waited for him. Then Perce got into the cab and they drove off.

Perce agreed to come back this afternoon with Gay in the larger truck and load the horses, although as they drove across the lake bed in silence they both knew, gradually, that they would wait until morning, because they were tired now and would be more tired later. The mare and her colt stood between them and the sage desert toward which they were heading. Perce stared out the window at the mare and he saw that she was watching them, apprehensively but not in real alarm, and the colt was lying upright on the clay. Perce looked long at the colt as they approached and he thought about it waiting there beside the mare, unbound and free to go off, and he said to Gay, "Ever hear of a colt leave a mare?"

"Not that one," Gay said. "He ain't goin' nowhere."

Perce laid his head back and closed his eyes. His tobacco swelled out his left cheek and he let it soak there.

Now the truck left the clay lake bed and it pitched and rolled over the sage clumps. They would return to their camp and pick up their bedrolls.

"Think I'll go back to Roslyn's tonight," Gay said.

"Okay," Perce said and did not open his eyes.

"We can pick them up in the morning, then take you to Largo."

"Okay," Perce said.

Gay thought about Roslyn. She would probably razz them about all the work they had done for a few dollars, saying they were too dumb to figure in their labor time and other hidden expenses. To hear her sometimes they hadn't made any profit at all. "Roslyn going to feel sorry for the colt," Gay said, "so might as well not mention it."

Perce opened his eyes and looked out at the mountains. "Hell, she feeds that dog of hers canned dog food, doesn't she?"

Gay felt closer to Perce again and he smiled. "Sure does."

"Well, what's she think is in the can?"

"She knows what's in it."

"There's wild horses in the can," Perce said, as though it was part of an angry argument with himself.

They were silent for a while.

"You comin' back to Roslyn's with me or you gonna stay in town?"

"I'd just as soon go back with you."

"Okay," Gay said. He felt good about going into her cabin now. There would be her books on the shelves he had built for her, and they would have some drinks, and Perce would fall asleep on the couch and they would go into the bedroom together. He liked to come back to her after he had worked, more than when he had only driven her here and there or just stayed around her place. He liked his own money in his pocket when he came to her. And he tried harder to visualize how it would be with her and he thought of himself being forty-seven soon, and then nearing fifty. She would go back east one day, maybe this year, maybe next. He wondered again when he would begin turning gray and he set his jaw against the idea of himself gray and an old man.

Perce spoke, sitting up in his seat. "I want to phone my mother. Damn, I haven't called her all year." He sounded angry. He stared out the window at the mountains. He had the memory of how the colt looked and he felt an almost violent wish for it to be gone when they returned. Then he said, "I got to get to Largo tomorrow and register."

"We'll go," Gay said, sensing the boy's unaccountable irritation.

"I could use a good win," he said. He thought of five hundred dollars now, and of the many times he had won five hundred dollars. "You know something, Gay? I'm never goin' to amount to a damn thing." Then, suddenly he laughed. He laughed without restraint for a moment and then laid his head back and closed his eyes.

"I told you that first time I met you, didn't I?" Gay grinned. He felt a bravery between them now, and he was relieved to see that Perce was grinning. He felt the mood coming on for some drinks at Roslyn's.

"That colt won't bring two dollars anyway," Perce said. "What you say we just left him there?"

"Why, you know he'd just follow the truck right into town."

After they had driven for fifteen minutes without speaking, Gay said he wanted to go north very soon for the hundreds of horses that were supposed to be in the mountains there. But Perce had fallen fast asleep beside him. Gay wanted to talk about that expedition because as they rolled onto the highway from the desert he began to visualize Roslyn razzing them again, and it was clear to him that he had somehow failed to settle anything for himself; he had put in three days for thirty-five dollars and there would be no way to explain it so it made sense and it would be embarrassing. And yet he knew that it had all been the way it ought to be even if he could never explain it to her or anyone else. He reached out and nudged Perce, who opened his eyes and lolled his head over to face him. "You comin' up to Thighbone with me, ain't you?"

"Okay," Perce said, and went back to sleep.

Gay felt more peaceful now the younger man would not be leaving him. There was a future again, something to head for.

The sun shone hot on the beige plain all day. Neither fly nor bug nor snake ventured out on the waste to molest the four horses tethered there, or the colt. They had run nearly two hours at a gallop and as the afternoon settled upon them they pawed the hard ground for water, but there was none. Toward evening the wind came up and they backed into it and faced the mountains from which they had come. From time to time the stallion caught the scent of the pastures up there and he started to walk toward the vaulted fields in which he had grazed, but the tire bent his neck around and after a few steps he would turn to face it and leap into the air with his forelegs striking at the sky and then he would come down and be still again. With the deep blue darkness the wind blew faster, tossing their manes and flinging their long tails in between their legs. The cold of night raised the colt onto its legs and it stood close to the mare for warmth. Facing the southern range five horses blinked under the green glow of the risen moon and they closed their eyes and slept. The colt settled again on the hard ground and lay under the mare. In the high hollows of the mountains the grass they had cropped this morning straightened in the darkness. On the lusher swards which were still damp with the rains of spring their hoofprints had begun to disappear. When the first pink glow of another morning lit the sky, the colt stood up and, as it had done at every dawn, it walked waywardly for water. The mare shifted warningly and her bone hoofs ticked the clay. The colt turned its head and returned to her and stood at her side with vacant eyes, its nostrils sniffing the warming air.

JOYCE CAROL OATES

Where Are You Going, Where Have You Been?

FOR BOB DYLAN

Her name was Connie. She was fifteen and she had a quick, nervous giggling habit of craning her neck to glance into mirrors or checking other people's faces to make sure her own was all right. Her mother, who noticed everything and knew everything and who hadn't much reason any longer to look at her own face, always scolded Connie about it. "Stop gawking at yourself. Who are you? You think you're so pretty?" she would say. Connie would raise her eyebrows at these familiar old complaints and look right through her mother, into a shadowy vision of herself as she was right at that moment: she knew she was pretty and that was everything. Her mother had been pretty once too, if you could believe those old snapshots in the album, but now her looks were gone and that was why she was always after Connie.

"Why don't you keep your room clean like your sister? How've you got your hair fixed—what the hell stinks? Hair spray? You don't see your sister using that junk."

Her sister June was twenty-four and still lived at home. She was a secretary in the high school Connie attended, and if that wasn't bad enough—with her in the same building—she was so plain and chunky and steady that Connie had to hear her praised all the time by her mother and her mother's sisters. June did this, June did that, she saved money and helped clean the house and cooked and Connie couldn't do a thing, her mind was all filled with trashy daydreams. Their father was away at work most of the time and when he came home he wanted supper and he read the newspaper at supper and after supper he went to bed. He didn't bother talking much to them, but around his bent head Connie's mother kept picking at her until Connie wished her mother was dead and she herself was dead and it was all over. "She makes me want to throw up sometimes," she complained to her friends. She had a high, breathless, amused voice that made everything she said sound a little forced, whether it was sincere or not.

There was one good thing: June went places with girlfriends of hers, girls who were just as plain and steady as she, and so when Connie wanted to do that her mother had no objections. The father of Connie's best girlfriend drove the girls the three miles to town and left them at a shopping plaza so they could walk through the stores or go to a movie, and when he came to pick them up again at eleven he never bothered to ask what they had done.

They must have been familiar sights, walking around the shopping plaza in their shorts and flat ballerina slippers that always scuffed on the sidewalk, with charm bracelets jingling on their thin wrists; they would lean together to whisper and laugh secretly if someone passed who amused or interested them. Connie had long dark blond hair that drew anyone's eye to it, and she wore part of it pulled up on her head and puffed out and the rest of it she let fall down her back. She wore a pullover jersey blouse that looked one way when she was at home and another way when she was away from home. Everything about her had two sides to it, one for home and one for anywhere that was not home: her walk, which could be childlike and bobbing, or languid enough to make anyone think she was hearing music in her head; her mouth, which was pale and smirking most of the time, but bright and pink on these evenings out; her laugh, which was cynical and drawling at home —"Ha, ha, very funny,"—but high-pitched and nervous anywhere else, like the jingling of the charms on her bracelet.

Sometimes they did go shopping or to a movie, but sometimes they went across the highway, ducking fast across the busy road, to a drive-in restaurant where older kids hung out. The restaurant was shaped like a big bottle, though squatter than a real bottle, and on its cap was a revolving figure of a grinning boy holding a hamburger aloft. One night in midsummer they ran across, breathless with daring, and right away someone leaned out a car window and invited them over, but it was just a boy from high school they didn't like. It made them feel good to be able to ignore him. They went up through the maze of parked and cruising cars to the bright-lit, fly-infested restaurant, their faces pleased and expectant as if they were entering a sacred building that loomed up out of the night to give them what haven and blessing they yearned for. They sat at the counter and crossed their legs at the ankles, their thin shoulders rigid with excitement, and listened to the music that made everything so good: the music was always in the background, like music at a church service; it was something to depend upon.

A boy named Eddie came in to talk with them. He sat backwards on his stool, turning himself jerkily around in semicircles and then stopping and turning back again, and after a while he asked Connie if she would like something to eat. She said she would and so she tapped her friend's arm on her way out—her friend pulled her face up into a brave, droll look—and Connie said she would meet her at eleven, across the way. "I just hate to leave her like that," Connie said earnestly, but the boy said that she wouldn't be alone for long. So they went out to his car, and on the way Connie couldn't help but let her eyes wander over the windshields and faces all around her, her face gleaming with a joy that had nothing to do with Eddie or even this place; it might have been the music. She drew her shoulders up and sucked in her breath with the pure pleasure of being alive, and just at that moment she happened to glance at a face just a few feet away from hers. It was a boy with shaggy black hair, in a convertible jalopy painted gold. He stared at her and then his lips widened into a grin. Connie slit her eyes at him and turned away, but she couldn't help glancing back and there he was, still watching her. He wagged a finger and laughed and said, "Gonna get you, baby," and Connie turned away again without Eddie noticing anything.

She spent three hours with him, at the restaurant where they ate hamburgers and drank Cokes in wax cups that were always sweating, and then down an alley a mile or so away, and when he left her off at five to eleven only the movie house was still open at the plaza. Her girlfriend was there, talking with a boy. When Connie came up, the two girls smiled at each other and Connie said, "How was the movie?" and the girl said, "*You* should know." They rode off with the girl's father, sleepy and pleased, and Connie couldn't help but look back at the darkened shopping plaza with its big empty parking lot and its signs that were faded and ghostly now, and over at the drive-in restaurant where cars were still circling tirelessly. She couldn't hear the music at this distance.

Next morning June asked her how the movie was and Connie said, "So-so."

She and that girl and occasionally another girl went out several times a week, and the rest of the time Connie spent around the house—it was summer vacation—getting in her mother's way and thinking, dreaming about the boys she met. But all the boys fell back and dissolved into a single face that was not even a face but an idea, a feeling, mixed up with the urgent insistent pounding of the music and the humid night air of July. Connie's mother kept dragging her back to the daylight by finding things for her to do or saying suddenly, "What's this about the Pettinger girl?"

And Connie would say nervously, "Oh, her. That dope." She always drew thick clear lines between herself and such girls, and her mother was simple and kind enough to believe it. Her mother was so simple, Connie thought, that it was maybe cruel to fool her so much. Her mother went scuffling around the house in old bedroom slippers and complained over the telephone to one sister about the other, then the other called up and the two of them complained about the third one. If June's name was mentioned her mother's tone was approving, and if Connie's name was mentioned it was disapproving. This did not really mean she disliked Connie, and actually Connie thought that her mother preferred her to June just because she was prettier, but the two of them kept up a pretense of exasperation, a sense that they were tugging and struggling over something of little value to either of them. Sometimes, over coffee, they were almost friends, but something would come up— some vexation that was like a fly buzzing suddenly around their heads— and their faces went hard with contempt.

One Sunday Connie got up at eleven—none of them bothered with church—and washed her hair so that it could dry all day long in the sun. Her parents and sister were going to a barbecue at an aunt's house and Connie said no, she wasn't interested, rolling her eyes to let her mother know just what she thought of it. "Stay home alone then," her mother said sharply. Connie sat out back in a lawn chair and watched them drive away, her father quiet and bald, hunched around so that he could back the car out, her mother with a look that was still angry and not at all softened through the windshield, and in the back seat poor old June, all dressed up as if she didn't know what a barbecue was, with all the running yelling kids and the flies. Connie sat with her eyes closed in the sun, dreaming and dazed with the warmth about her as if this were a kind of love, the caresses of love, and her mind slipped over onto thoughts of the boy she had been with the night before and how nice he had been, how sweet it always was, not the way someone like June would suppose but sweet, gentle, the way it was in movies and promised in songs; and when she opened her eyes she hardly knew where she was, the back yard ran off into weeds and a fencelike line of trees and behind it the sky was perfectly blue and still. The asbestos "ranch house" that was now three years old startled her—it looked small. She shook her head as if to get awake.

It was too hot. She went inside the house and turned on the radio to drown out the quiet. She sat on the edge of her bed, barefoot, and listened for an hour and a half, to a program called XYZ Sunday Jamboree, record after record of hard, fast, shrieking songs she sang along with, interspersed by exclamations from "Bobby King": "An' look here, you girls at Napoleon's—Son and Charley want you to pay real close attention to this song coming up!"

And Connie paid close attention herself, bathed in a glow of slow-pulsed joy that seemed to rise mysteriously out of the music itself and lay languidly about the airless little room, breathed in and breathed out with each gentle rise and fall of her chest.

After a while she heard a car coming up the drive. She sat up at once, startled, because it couldn't be her father so soon. The gravel kept crunching all the way in from the road—the driveway was long—and Connie ran to the window. It was a car she didn't know. It was an open jalopy, painted a bright gold that caught the sunlight opaquely. Her heart began to pound and her fingers snatched at her hair, checking it, and she whispered, "Christ, Christ," wondering how she looked. The car came to a stop at the side door and the horn sounded four short taps, as if this were a signal Connie knew.

She went into the kitchen and approached the door slowly, then hung out the screen door, her bare toes curling down off the step. There were two boys in the car and now she recognized the driver: he had shaggy, shabby black hair that looked crazy as a wig and he was grinning at her.

"I ain't late, am I?" he said.

"Who the hell do you think you are?" Connie said.

"Toldja I'd be out, didn't I?"

"I don't even know who you are."

She spoke sullenly, careful to show no interest or pleasure, and he spoke in a fast, bright monotone. Connie looked past him to the other boy, taking her time. He had fair brown hair, with a lock that fell onto his forehead. His sideburns gave him a fierce, embarrassed look, but so far he hadn't even bothered to glance at her. Both boys wore sunglasses. The driver's glasses were metallic and mirrored everything in miniature.

"You wanta come for a ride?" he said.

Connie smirked and let her hair fall loose over one shoulder.

"Don'tcha like my car? New paint job," he said. "Hey."

"What?"

"You're cute."

She pretended to fidget, chasing flies away from the door.

"Don'tcha believe me, or what?" he said.

"Look, I don't even know who you are," Connie said in disgust.

"Hey, Ellie's got a radio, see. Mine broke down." He lifted his friend's arm and showed her the little transistor radio the boy was holding, and now Connie began to hear the music. It was the same program that was playing inside the house.

"Bobby King?" she said.

"I listen to him all the time. I think he's great."

"He's kind of great," Connie said reluctantly.

"Listen, that guy's *great*. He knows where the action is."

Connie blushed a little, because the glasses made it impossible for her to see just what this boy was looking at. She couldn't decide if she liked him or if he was a jerk, and so she dawdled in the doorway and wouldn't come down or go back inside. She said, "What's all that stuff painted on your car?"

"Can'tcha read it?" He opened the door very carefully, as if he were afraid it might fall off. He slid out just as carefully, planting his feet firmly on the ground, the tiny metallic world in his glasses slowing down like gelatin hardening, and in the midst of it Connie's bright green blouse. "This here is my name, to begin with," he said. ARNOLD FRIEND was written in tarlike black letters on the side, with a drawing of a round, grinning face that reminded Connie of a pumpkin, except it wore sunglasses. "I wanta introduce myself. I'm Arnold Friend and that's my real name and I'm gonna be your friend, honey, and inside the car's Ellie Oscar, he's kinda shy." Ellie brought his transistor radio up to his shoulder and balanced it there. "Now, these numbers are a secret code, honey," Arnold Friend explained. He read off the numbers 33, 19, 17 and raised his eyebrows at her to see what she thought of that, but she didn't think much of it. The left rear fender had been smashed and around it was written, on the gleaming gold background: DONE BY CRAZY WOMAN DRIVER. Connie had to laugh at that. Arnold Friend was pleased at her laughter and looked up at her. "Around the other side's a lot more—you wanta come and see them?"

"No."

"Why not?"

"Why should I?"

"Don'tcha wanta see what's on the car? Don'tcha wanta go for a ride?"

"I don't know."

"Why not?"

"I got things to do."

"Like what?"

"Things."

He laughed as if she had said something funny. He slapped his thighs. He was standing in a strange way, leaning back against the car as if he were balancing himself. He wasn't tall, only an inch or so taller than she would be if she came down to him. Connie liked the way he was dressed, which was the way all of them dressed: tight faded jeans stuffed into black, scuffed boots, a belt that pulled his waist in and showed how lean he was, and a white pullover shirt that was a little soiled and showed the hard small muscles of his arms and shoulders. He looked as if he probably did hard work, lifting and carrying things. Even his neck looked muscular. And his face was a familiar face, somehow; the jaw and chin and cheeks slightly darkened because he hadn't shaved for a day or two, and the nose long and hawklike, sniffing as if she were a treat he was going to gobble up and it was all a joke.

"Connie, you ain't telling the truth. This is your day set aside for a ride with me and you know it," he said, still laughing. The way he straightened and recovered from his fit of laughing showed that it had been all fake.

"How do you know what my name is?" she said suspiciously.

"It's Connie."

"Maybe and maybe not."

"I know my Connie," he said, wagging his finger. Now she remembered him even better, back at the restaurant, and her cheeks warmed at the thought of how she had sucked in her breath just at the moment she passed him—how she must have looked to him. And he had remembered her. "Ellie and I come out here especially for you," he said. "Ellie can sit in back. How about it?"

"Where?"

"Where what?"

"Where're we going?"

He looked at her. He took off the sunglasses and she saw how pale the skin around his eyes was, like holes that were not in shadow but instead in light. His eyes were like chips of broken glass that catch the light in an amiable way. He smiled. It was as if the idea of going for a ride somewhere, to someplace, was a new idea to him.

"Just for a ride, Connie sweetheart."

"I never said my name was Connie," she said.

"But I know what it is. I know your name and all about you, lots of things," Arnold Friend said. He had not moved yet but stood still leaning back against the side of his jalopy. "I took a special interest in you, such a pretty girl, and found out all about you—like I know your parents and sister are gone somewheres and I know where and how long they're going to be gone, and I know who you were with last night, and your best girlfriend's name is Betty. Right?"

He spoke in a simple lilting voice, exactly as if he were reciting the words to a song. His smile assured her that everything was fine. In the car Ellie turned up the volume on his radio and did not bother to look around at them.

"Ellie can sit in the back seat," Arnold Friend said. He indicated his friend with a casual jerk of his chin, as if Ellie did not count and she should not bother with him.

"How'd you find out all that stuff?" Connie said.

"Listen: Betty Schultz and Tony Fitch and Jimmy Pettinger and Nancy Pettinger," he said in a chant. "Raymond Stanley and Bob Hutter—"

"Do you know all those kids?"

"I know everybody."

"Look, you're kidding. You're not from around here."

"Sure."

"But—how come we never saw you before?"

"Sure you saw me before," he said. He looked down at his boots, as if he were a little offended. "You just don't remember."

"I guess I'd remember you," Connie said.

"Yeah?" He looked up at this, beaming. He was pleased. He began to mark time with the music from Ellie's radio, tapping his fists lightly together. Connie looked away from his smile to the car, which was painted so bright it almost hurt her eyes to look at it. She looked at that name, ARNOLD FRIEND. And up at the front fender was an expression that was familiar—MAN THE FLYING SAUCERS. It was an expression kids had used the year before but didn't use this year. She looked at it for a while as if the words meant something to her that she did not yet know.

"What're you thinking about? Huh?" Arnold Friend demanded. "Not worried about your hair blowing around in the car, are you?"

"No."

"Think I maybe can't drive good?"

"How do I know?"

"You're a hard girl to handle. How come?" he said. "Don't you know I'm your friend? Didn't you see me put my sign in the air when you walked by?"

"What sign?"

"My sign." And he drew an X in the air, leaning out toward her. They were maybe ten feet apart. After his hand fell back to his side the X was still in the air, almost visible. Connie let the screen door close and stood perfectly still inside it, listening to the music from her radio and the boy's blend together. She stared at Arnold Friend. He stood there so stiffly relaxed, pretending to be relaxed, with one hand idly on the door handle as if he were keeping himself up that way and had no intention of ever moving again. She recognized most things about him, the tight jeans that showed his thighs and buttocks and the greasy leather boots and the tight shirt, and even that slippery friendly smile of his, that sleepy dreamy smile that all the boys used to get across ideas they didn't want to put into words. She recognized all this and also the sing-song way he talked, slightly mocking, kidding, but serious and a little melancholy, and she recognized the way he tapped one fist against the other in homage to the perpetual music behind him. But all these things did not come together.

She said suddenly, "Hey, how old are you?"

His smiled faded. She could see then that he wasn't a kid, he was much older—thirty, maybe more. At this knowledge her heart began to pound faster.

"That's a crazy thing to ask. Can'tcha see I'm your own age?"

"Like hell you are."

"Or maybe a coupla years older. I'm eighteen."

"Eighteen?" she said doubtfully.

He grinned to reassure her and lines appeared at the corners of his mouth. His teeth were big and white. He grinned so broadly his eyes became slits and she saw how thick the lashes were, thick and black as if painted with a black tarlike material. Then, abruptly, he seemed to become embarrassed and looked over his shoulder at Ellie. *"Him,* he's crazy," he said. "Ain't he a riot? He's a nut, a real character." Ellie was still listening to the music. His sunglasses told nothing about what he was thinking. He wore a bright orange shirt unbuttoned halfway to show his chest, which was a pale, bluish chest and not muscular like Arnold Friend's. His shirt collar was turned up all around and the very tips of the collar pointed out past his chin as if they were protecting him. He was pressing the transistor radio up against his ear and sat there in a kind of daze, right in the sun.

"He's kinda strange," Connie said.

"Hey, she says you're kinda strange! Kinda strange!" Arnold Friend cried. He pounded on the car to get Ellie's attention. Ellie turned for the first time and Connie saw with shock that he wasn't a kid either—he had a fair, hairless face, cheeks reddened slightly as if the veins grew too close to the surface of his skin, the face of a forty-year-old baby. Connie felt a wave of dizziness rise in her at this sight and she stared at him as if waiting for something to change the shock of the moment, make it all right again. Ellie's lips kept shaping words, mumbling along with the words blasting in his ear.

"Maybe you two better go away," Connie said faintly.

"What? How come?" Arnold Friend cried. "We come out here to take you for a ride. It's Sunday." He had the voice of the man on the radio now. It was the same voice, Connie thought. "Don'tcha know it's Sunday all day? And honey, no matter who you were with last night, today you're with Arnold Friend and don't you forget it! Maybe you better step out here," he said, and this last was in a different voice. It was a little flatter, as if the heat was finally getting to him.

"No. I got things to do."

"Hey."

"You two better leave."

"We ain't leaving until you come with us."

"Like hell I am—"

"Connie, don't fool around with me. I mean—I mean, don't fool *around,*" he said, shaking his head. He laughed incredulously. He placed his sunglasses on top of his head, carefully, as if he were indeed wearing a wig, and brought the stems down behind his ears. Connie stared at him, another wave of dizziness and fear rising in her so that for a moment he wasn't even in focus but was just a blur standing there against his gold car, and she had the idea that he had driven up the driveway all right but had come from nowhere before that and belonged nowhere and that everything about him and even about the music that was so familiar to her was only half real.

"If my father comes and sees you—"

"He ain't coming. He's at a barbecue."

"How do you know that?"

"Aunt Tillie's. Right now they're—uh—they're drinking. Sitting around," he said vaguely, squinting as if he were staring all the way to town and over to Aunt Tillie's back yard. Then the vision seemed to get clear and he nodded energetically. "Yeah. Sitting around. There's your sister in a blue dress, huh? And high heels, the poor sad bitch—nothing like you, sweetheart! And your mother's helping some fat woman with the corn, they're cleaning the corn—husking the corn—"

"What fat woman?" Connie cried.

"How do I know what fat woman, I don't know every goddamn fat woman in the world!" Arnold Friend laughed.

"Oh, that's Mrs. Hornsby. . . . Who invited her?" Connie said. She felt a little lightheaded. Her breath was coming quickly.

"She's too fat. I don't like them fat. I like them the way you are, honey," he said, smiling sleepily at her. They stared at each other for a while through the screen door. He said softly, "Now, what you're going to do is this: you're going to come out that door. You're going to sit up front with me and Ellie's going to sit in the back, the hell with Ellie, right? This isn't Ellie's date. You're my date. I'm your lover, honey."

"What? You're crazy—"

"Yes. I'm your lover. You don't know what that is but you will," he said. "I know that too. I know all about you. But look: it's real nice and you couldn't ask for nobody better than me, or more polite. I always keep my word. I'll tell you how it is, I'm always nice at first, the first time. I'll hold you so tight you won't think you have to try to get away or pretend anything because you'll know you can't. And I'll come inside you where it's all secret and you'll give in to me and you'll love me—"

"Shut up! You're crazy!" Connie said. She backed away from the door. She put her hands up against her ears as if she'd heard something terrible, something not meant for her. "People don't talk like that, you're crazy," she muttered. Her heart was almost too big now for her chest and its pumping made sweat break out all over her. She looked out to see Arnold Friend pause and then take a step toward the porch, lurching. He almost fell. But, like a clever drunken man, he managed to catch his balance. He wobbled in his high boots and grabbed hold of one of the porch posts.

"Honey?" he said. "You still listening?"

"Get the hell out of here!"

"Be nice, honey. Listen."

"I'm going to call the police—"

He wobbled again and out of the side of his mouth came a fast spat curse, an aside not meant for her to hear. But even this "Christ!" sounded forced. Then he began to smile again. She watched this smile come, awkward as if he were smiling from inside a mask. His whole face was a mask, she thought wildly, tanned down to his throat but then running out as if he had plastered makeup on his face but had forgotten about his throat.

"Honey—? Listen, here's how it is. I always tell the truth and I promise you this: I ain't coming in that house after you."

"You better not! I'm going to call the police if you—if you don't—"

"Honey," he said, talking right through her voice, "honey. I'm not coming in there but you are coming out here. You know why?"

She was panting. The kitchen looked like a place she had never seen before, some room she had run inside but that wasn't good enough, wasn't going to help her. The kitchen window had never had a curtain, after three years, and there were dishes in the sink for her to do— probably—and if you ran your hand across the table you'd probably feel something stick there.

"You listening, honey? Hey?"

"—going to call the police—"

"Soon as you touch the phone I don't need to keep my promise and can come inside. You won't want that."

She rushed forward and tried to lock the door. Her fingers were shaking. "But why lock it," Arnold Friend said gently, talking right into her face. "It's just a screen door. It's just nothing." One of his boots was at a strange angle, as if his foot wasn't in it. It pointed out to the left, bent at the ankle. "I mean, anybody can break through a screen door and glass and wood and iron or anything else if he needs to, anybody at all, and specially Arnold Friend. If the place got lit up with a fire, honey, you'd come runnin' out into my arms, right into my arms an' safe at home—like you knew I was your lover and'd stopped fooling around. I don't mind a nice shy girl but I don't like no fooling around." Part of those words were spoken with a slight rhythmic lilt, and Connie some- how recognized them—the echo of a song from last year, about a girl rushing into her boyfriend's arms and coming home again—

Connie stood barefoot on the linoleum floor, staring at him. "What do you want?" she whispered.

"I want you," he said.

"What?"

"Seen you that night and thought, that's the one, yes sir. I never needed to look anymore."

"But my father's coming back. He's coming to get me. I had to wash my hair first—" She spoke in a dry, rapid voice, hardly raising it for him to hear.

"No, your daddy is not coming and yes, you had to wash your hair and you washed it for me. It's nice and shining and all for me. I thank you, sweetheart," he said with a mock bow, but again he almost lost his balance. He had to bend and adjust his boots. Evidently his feet did not go all the way down; the boots must have been stuffed with something so that he would seem taller. Connie stared out at him and behind him at Ellie in the car, who seemed to be looking off toward Connie's right, into nothing. This Ellie said, pulling the words out of the air one after another as if he were just discovering them, "You want me to pull out the phone?"

"Shut your mouth and keep it shut," Arnold Friend said, his face red from bending over or maybe from embarrassment because Connie had seen his boots. "This ain't none of your business."

"What—what are you doing? What do you want?" Connie said. "If I call the police they'll get you, they'll arrest you—"

"Promise was not to come in unless you touch that phone, and I'll keep that promise," he said. He resumed his erect position and tried to force his shoulders back. He sounded like a hero in a movie, declaring something important. But he spoke too loudly and it was as if he were speaking to someone behind Connie. "I ain't made plans for coming in that house where I don't belong but just for you to come out to me, the way you should. Don't you know who I am?"

"You're crazy," she whispered. She backed away from the door but did not want to go into another part of the house, as if this would give him permission to come through the door. "What do you . . . you're crazy, you. . . ."

"Huh? What're you saying, honey?"

Her eyes darted everywhere in the kitchen. She could not remember what it was, this room.

"This is how it is, honey: you come out and we'll drive away, have a nice ride. But if you don't come out we're gonna wait till your people come home and then they're all going to get it."

"You want that telephone pulled out?" Ellie said. He held the radio away from his ear and grimaced, as if without the radio the air was too much for him.

"I toldja shut up, Ellie," Arnold Friend said, "you're deaf, get a hearing aid, right? Fix yourself up. This little girl's no trouble and's gonna be nice to me, so Ellie keep to yourself, this ain't your date—right? Don't hem in on me, don't hog, don't crush, don't bird dog, don't trail me," he said in a rapid, meaningless voice, as if he were running through all the expressions he'd learned but was no longer sure which of them was in style, then rushing on to new ones, making them up with his eyes closed. "Don't crawl under my fence, don't squeeze in my chipmunk hole, don't sniff my glue, suck my popsicle, keep your own greasy fingers on yourself!" He shaded his eyes and peered in at Connie, who was backed against the kitchen table. "Don't mind him, honey, he's just a creep. He's a dope. Right? I'm the boy for you and like I said, you come out here nice like a lady and give me your hand, and nobody else gets hurt, I mean, your nice old bald-headed daddy and your mummy and your sister in her high heels. Because listen: why bring them in this?"

"Leave me alone," Connie whispered.

"Hey, you know that old woman down the road, the one with the chickens and stuff—you know her?"

"She's dead!"

"Dead? What? You know her?" Arnold Friend said.

"She's dead—"

"Don't you like her?"

"She's dead—she's—she isn't here anymore—"

"But don't you like her, I mean, you got something against her? Some grudge or something?" Then his voice dipped as if he were conscious of a rudeness. He touched the sunglasses perched up on top of his head as if to make sure they were still there. "Now, you be a good girl."

"What are you going to do?"

"Just two things, or maybe three," Arnold Friend said. "But I promise it won't last long and you'll like me the way you get to like people you're close to. You will. It's all over for you here, so come on out. You don't want your people in any trouble, do you?"

She turned and bumped against a chair or something, hurting her leg, but she ran into the back room and picked up the telephone. Something roared in her ear, a tiny roaring, and she was so sick with fear that she could do nothing but listen to it—the telephone was clammy and very heavy and her fingers groped down to the dial but were too weak to touch it. She began to scream into the phone, into the roaring. She cried out, she cried for her mother, she felt her breath start jerking back and forth in her lungs as if it were something Arnold Friend was stabbing her with again and again with no tenderness. A noisy sorrowful wailing rose all about her and she was locked inside it the way she was locked inside this house.

After a while she could hear again. She was sitting on the floor with her wet back against the wall.

Arnold Friend was saying from the door, "That's a good girl. Put the phone back."

She kicked the phone away from her.

"No, honey. Pick it up. Put it back right."

She picked it up and put it back. The dial tone stopped.

"That's a good girl. Now, you come outside."

She was hollow with what had been fear but what was now just an emptiness. All that screaming had blasted it out of her. She sat, one leg cramped under her, and deep inside her brain was something like a pinpoint of light that kept going and would not let her relax. She thought, I'm not going to see my mother again. She thought, I'm not going to sleep in my bed again. Her bright green blouse was all wet.

Arnold Friend said, in a gentle-loud voice that was like a stage voice, "The place where you came from ain't there anymore, and where you had in mind to go is cancelled out. This place you are now—inside your daddy's house—is nothing but a cardboard box I can knock down any time. You know that and always did know it. You hear me?"

She thought, I have got to think. I have got to know what to do.

"We'll go out to a nice field, out in the country here where it smells so nice and it's sunny," Arnold Friend said. "I'll have my arms tight around you so you won't need to try to get away and I'll show you what love is like, what it does. The hell with this house! It looks solid all right," he said. He ran his fingernail down the screen and the noise did not make Connie shiver, as it would have the day before. "Now, put your hand on your heart, honey. Feel that? That feels solid too but we know better. Be nice to me, be sweet like you can because what else is there for a girl like you but to be sweet and pretty and give in?—and get away before her people get back?"

She felt her pounding heart. Her hand seemed to enclose it. She thought for the first time in her life that it was nothing that was hers, that belonged to her, but just a pounding, living thing inside this body that wasn't really hers either.

"You don't want them to get hurt," Arnold Friend went on. "Now, get up, honey. Get up all by yourself."

She stood.

"Now, turn this way. That's right. Come over here to me.—Ellie, put that away, didn't I tell you? You dope. You miserable creepy dope," Arnold Friend said. His words were not angry but only part of an incantation. The incantation was kindly. "Now, come out through the kitchen to me, honey, and let's see a smile, try it, you're a brave, sweet little girl and now they're eating corn and hot dogs cooked to bursting over an outdoor fire, and they don't know one thing about you and never did and honey, you're better than them because not a one of them would have done this for you."

Connie felt the linoleum under her feet; it was cool. She brushed her hair back out of her eyes. Arnold Friend let go of the post tentatively and opened his arms for her, his elbows pointing in toward each other and his wrists limp, to show that this was an embarrassed embrace and a little mocking, he didn't want to make her self-conscious.

She put out her hand against the screen. She watched herself push the door slowly open as if she were back safe somewhere in the other doorway, watching this body and this head of long hair moving out into the sunlight where Arnold Friend waited.

"My sweet little blue-eyed girl," he said in a half-sung sigh that had nothing to do with her brown eyes but was taken up just the same by the vast sunlit reaches of the land behind him and on all sides of him—so much land that Connie had never seen before and did not recognize except to know that she was going to it.

FLANNERY O'CONNOR

A Good Man Is Hard to Find

The grandmother didn't want to go to Florida. She wanted to visit some of her connections in east Tennessee and she was seizing at every chance to change Bailey's mind. Bailey was the son she lived with, her only boy. He was sitting on the edge of his chair at the table, bent over the orange sports section of the *Journal*. "Now look here, Bailey," she said, "see here, read this," and she stood with one hand on her thin hip and the other rattling the newspaper at his bald head. "Here this fellow that calls himself The Misfit is aloose from the Federal Pen and headed toward Florida and you read here what it says he did to these people. Just you read it. I wouldn't take my children in any direction with a criminal like that aloose in it. I couldn't answer to my conscience if I did."

Bailey didn't look up from his reading so she wheeled around then and faced the children's mother, a young woman in slacks, whose face was as broad and innocent as a cabbage and was tied around with a green head-kerchief that had two points on the top like a rabbit's ears. She was sitting on the sofa, feeding the baby his apricots out of a jar. "The children have been to Florida before," the old lady said. "You all ought to take them somewhere else for a change so they would see different parts of the world and be broad. They never have been to east Tennessee."

The children's mother didn't seem to hear her but the eight-year-old boy, John Wesley, a stocky child with glasses, said, "If you don't want to go to Florida, why dontcha stay at home?" He and the little girl, June Star, were reading the funny papers on the floor.

"She wouldn't stay at home to be queen for a day," June Star said without raising her yellow head.

"Yes and what would you do if this fellow, The Misfit, caught you?" the grandmother asked.

"I'd smack his face," John Wesley said.

"She wouldn't stay at home for a million bucks," June Star said. "Afraid she'd miss something. She has to go everywhere we go."

"All right, Miss," the grandmother said. "Just remember that the next time you want me to curl your hair."

June Star said her hair was naturally curly.

The next morning the grandmother was the first one in the car, ready to go. She had her big black valise that looked like the head of a hippopotamus in one corner, and underneath it she was hiding a basket with Pitty Sing, the cat, in it. She didn't intend for the cat to be left alone in the house for three days because he would miss her too much and she was afraid he might brush against one of the gas burners and accidentally asphyxiate himself. Her son, Bailey, didn't like to arrive at a motel with a cat.

She sat in the middle of the back seat with John Wesley and June Star on either side of her. Bailey and the children's mother and the baby sat in front and they left Atlanta at eight forty-five with the mileage on the car at 55890. The grandmother wrote this down because she thought it would be interesting to say how many miles they had been when they got back. It took them twenty minutes to reach the outskirts of the city.

The old lady settled herself comfortably, removing her white cotton gloves and putting them up with her purse on the shelf in front of the back window. The children's mother still had on slacks and still had her head tied up in a green kerchief, but the grandmother had on a navy blue straw sailor hat with a bunch of white violets on the brim and a navy blue dress with a small white dot in the print. Her collars and cuffs were white organdy trimmed with lace and at her neckline she had pinned a purple spray of cloth violets containing a sachet. In case of an accident, anyone seeing her dead on the highway would know at once that she was a lady.

She said she thought it was going to be a good day for driving, neither too hot nor too cold, and she cautioned Bailey that the speed limit was fifty-five miles an hour and that the patrolmen hid themselves behind billboards and small clumps of trees and sped out after you before you had a chance to slow down. She pointed out interesting details of the scenery: Stone Mountain; the blue granite that in some places came up to both sides of the highway; the brilliant red clay banks slightly streaked with purple; and the various crops that made rows of green lacework on the ground. The trees were full of silver-white sunlight and the meanest of them sparkled. The children were reading comic magazines and their mother had gone back to sleep.

"Let's go through Georgia fast so we won't have to look at it much," John Wesley said.

"If I were a little boy," said the grandmother, "I wouldn't talk about my native state that way. Tennessee has the mountains and Georgia has the hills."

"Tennessee is just a hillbilly dumping ground," John Wesley said, "and Georgia is a lousy state too."

"You said it," June Star said.

"In my time," said the grandmother, folding her thin veined fingers, "children were more respectful of their native states and their parents and everything else. People did right then. Oh look at the cute little pickaninny!" she said and pointed to a Negro child standing in the door of a shack. "Wouldn't that make a picture, now?" she asked and they all turned and looked at the little Negro out of the back window. He waved.

"He didn't have any britches on," June Star said.

"He probably didn't have any," the grandmother explained. "Little niggers in the country don't have things like we do. If I could paint, I'd paint that picture," she said.

The children exchanged comic books.

The grandmother offered to hold the baby and the children's mother passed him over the front seat to her. She set him on her knee and bounced him and told him about the things they were passing. She rolled her eyes and screwed up her mouth and stuck her leathery thin face into his smooth bland one. Occasionally he gave her a faraway smile. They passed a large cotton field with five or six graves fenced in the middle of it, like a small island. "Look at the graveyard!" the grandmother said, pointing it out. "That was the old family burying ground. That belonged to the plantation."

"Where's the plantation?" John Wesley asked.

"Gone With the Wind," said the grandmother. "Ha. Ha."

When the children finished all the comic books they had brought, they opened the lunch and ate it. The grandmother ate a peanut butter sandwich and an olive and would not let the children throw the box and the paper napkins out the window. When there was nothing else to do they played a game by choosing a cloud and making the other two guess what shape it suggested. John Wesley took one the shape of a cow and June Star guessed a cow and John Wesley said, no, an automobile, and June Star said he didn't play fair, and they began to slap each other over the grandmother.

The grandmother said she would tell them a story if they would keep quiet. When she told a story, she rolled her eyes and waved her head and was very dramatic. She said once when she was a maiden lady she had been courted by a Mr. Edgar Atkins Teagarden from Jasper, Georgia. She said he was a very good-looking man and a gentleman and that he brought her a watermelon every Saturday afternoon with his initials cut in it, E. A. T. Well, one Saturday, she said, Mr. Teagarden brought the watermelon and there was nobody at home and he left it on the front porch and returned in his buggy to Jasper, but she never got the watermelon, she said, because a nigger boy ate it when he saw the initials, E. A. T.! This story tickled John Wesley's funny bone and he giggled and giggled but June Star didn't think it was any good. She said she wouldn't marry a man that just brought her a watermelon on Saturday. The grandmother said she would have done well to marry Mr. Teagarden because he was a gentleman and had bought Coca-Cola stock when it first came out and that he had died only a few years ago, a very wealthy man.

They stopped at The Tower for barbecued sandwiches. The Tower was a part stucco and part wood filling station and dance hall set in a clearing outside of Timothy. A fat man named Red Sammy Butts ran it and there were signs stuck here and there on the building and for miles up and down the highway saying, TRY RED SAMMY'S FAMOUS BAR-BECUE. NONE LIKE FAMOUS RED SAMMY'S! RED SAM! THE FAT BOY WITH THE HAPPY LAUGH! A VETERAN! RED SAMMY'S YOUR MAN!

Red Sammy was lying on the bare ground outside The Tower with his head under a truck while a gray monkey about a foot high, chained to a small chinaberry tree, chattered nearby. The monkey sprang back into the tree and got on the highest limb as soon as he saw the children jump out of the car and run toward him.

Inside, The Tower was a long dark room with a counter at one end and tables at the other and dancing space in the middle. They all sat down at a board table next to the nickelodeon and Red Sam's wife, a tall burnt-brown woman with hair and eyes lighter than her skin, came and took their order. The children's mother put a dime in the machine and played "The Tennessee Waltz," and the grandmother said that tune always made her want to dance. She asked Bailey if he would like to dance but he only glared at her. He didn't have a naturally sunny disposition like she did and trips made him nervous. The grandmother's brown eyes were very bright. She swayed her head from side to side and pretended she was dancing in her chair. June Star said play something she could tap to so the children's mother put in another dime and played a fast number and June Star stepped out onto the dance floor and did her tap routine.

"Ain't she cute?" Red Sam's wife said, leaning over the counter. "Would you like to come be my little girl?"

"No I certainly wouldn't," June Star said. "I wouldn't live in a broken-down place like this for a million bucks!" and she ran back to the table.

"Ain't she cute?" the woman repeated, stretching her mouth politely.

"Aren't you ashamed?" hissed the grandmother.

Red Sam came in and told his wife to quit lounging on the counter and hurry up with these people's order. His khaki trousers reached just to his hip bones and his stomach hung over them like a sack of meal swaying under his shirt. He came over and sat down at a table nearby and let out a combination sigh and yodel. "You can't win," he said. "You can't win," and he wiped his sweating red face off with a gray handkerchief. "These days you don't know who to trust," he said. "Ain't that the truth?"

"People are certainly not nice like they used to be," said the grandmother.

"Two fellers come in here last week," Red Sammy said, "driving a Chrysler. It was a old beat-up car but it was a good one and these boys looked all right to me. Said they worked at the mill and you know I let them fellers charge the gas they bought? Now why did I do that?"

"Because you're a good man!" the grandmother said at once.

"Yes'm, I suppose so," Red Sam said as if he were struck with this answer.

His wife brought the orders, carrying the five plates all at once without a tray, two in each hand and one balanced on her arm. "It isn't a soul in this green world of God's that you can trust," she said. "And I don't count nobody out of that, not nobody," she repeated, looking at Red Sammy.

"Did you read about that criminal, The Misfit, that's escaped?" asked the grandmother.

"I wouldn't be a bit surprised if he didn't attact this place right here," said the woman. "If he hears about it being here, I wouldn't be none surprised to see him. If he hears it's two cent in the cash register, I wouldn't be a tall surprised if he . . ."

"That'll do," Red Sam said. "Go bring these people their Co'-Colas," and the woman went off to get the rest of the order.

"A good man is hard to find," Red Sammy said. "Everything is getting terrible. I remember the day you could go off and leave your screen door unlatched. Not no more."

He and the grandmother discussed better times. The old lady said that in her opinion Europe was entirely to blame for the way things were now. She said the way Europe acted you would think we were made of money and Red Sam said it was no use talking about it, she was exactly right. The children ran outside into the white sunlight and looked at the monkey in the lacy chinaberry tree. He was busy catching fleas on himself and biting each one carefully between his teeth as if it were a delicacy.

They drove off again into the hot afternoon. The grandmother took cat naps and woke up every few minutes with her own snoring. Outside of Toombsboro she woke up and recalled an old plantation that she had visited in this neighborhood once when she was a young lady. She said the house had six white columns across the front and that there was an avenue of oaks leading up to it and two little wooden trellis arbors on either side in front where you sat down with your suitor after a stroll in the garden. She recalled exactly which road to turn off to get to it. She knew that Bailey would not be willing to lose any time looking at an old house, but the more she talked about it, the more she wanted to see it once again and find out if the little twin arbors were still standing. "There was a secret panel in this house," she said craftily, not telling the truth but wishing that she were, "and the story went that all the family silver was hidden in it when Sherman came through but it was never found . . ."

"Hey!" John Wesley said. "Let's go see it! We'll find it! We'll poke all the woodwork and find it! Who lives there? Where do you turn off at? Hey Pop, can't we turn off there?"

"We never have seen a house with a secret panel!" June Star shrieked. "Let's go to the house with the secret panel! Hey Pop, can't we go see the house with the secret panel!"

"It's not far from here, I know," the grandmother said. "It wouldn't take over twenty minutes."

Bailey was looking straight ahead. His jaw was as rigid as a horseshoe. "No," he said.

The children began to yell and scream that they wanted to see the house with the secret panel. John Wesley kicked the back of the front seat and June Star hung over her mother's shoulder and whined desperately into her ear that they never had any fun even on their vacation, that they could never do what THEY wanted to do. The baby began to scream and John Wesley kicked the back of the seat so hard that his father could feel the blows in his kidney.

"All right!" he shouted and drew the car to a stop at the side of the road. "Will you all shut up? Will you all just shut up for one second? If you don't shut up, we won't go anywhere."

"It would be very educational for them," the grandmother murmured.

"All right," Bailey said, "but get this: this is the only time we're going to stop for anything like this. This is the one and only time."

"The dirt road that you have to turn down is about a mile back," the grandmother directed. "I marked it when we passed."

"A dirt road," Bailey groaned.

After they had turned around and were headed toward the dirt road, the grandmother recalled other points about the house, the beautiful glass over the front doorway and the candle-lamp in the hall. John Wesley said that the secret panel was probably in the fireplace.

"You can't go inside this house," Bailey said. "You don't know who lives there."

"While you all talk to the people in front, I'll run around behind and get in a window," John Wesley suggested.

"We'll all stay in the car," his mother said.

They turned onto the dirt road and the car raced roughly along in a swirl of pink dust. The grandmother recalled the times when there were no paved roads and thirty miles was a day's journey. The dirt road was hilly and there were sudden washes in it and sharp curves on dangerous embankments. All at once they would be on a hill, looking down over the blue tops of trees for miles around, then the next minute, they would be in a red depression with the dust-coated trees looking down on them.

"This place had better turn up in a minute," Bailey said, "or I'm going to turn around."

The road looked as if no one had traveled on it in months.

"It's not much farther," the grandmother said and just as she said it, a horrible thought came to her. The thought was so embarrassing that she turned red in the face and her eyes dilated and her feet jumped up, upsetting her valise in the corner. The instant the valise moved, the newspaper top she had over the basket under it rose with a snarl and Pitty Sing, the cat, sprang onto Bailey's shoulder.

The children were thrown to the floor and their mother, clutching the baby, was thrown out the door onto the ground; the old lady was thrown into the front seat. The car turned over once and landed right-side-up in a gulch off the side of the road. Bailey remained in the driver's seat with the cat—gray-striped with a broad white face and an orange nose—clinging to his neck like a caterpillar.

As soon as the children saw they could move their arms and legs, they scrambled out of the car, shouting, "We've had an ACCIDENT!" The grandmother was curled up under the dashboard, hoping she was injured so that Bailey's wrath would not come down on her all at once. The horrible thought she had had before the accident was that the house she had remembered so vividly was not in Georgia but in Tennessee.

Bailey removed the cat from his neck with both hands and flung it out the window against the side of a pine tree. Then he got out of the car and started looking for the children's mother. She was sitting against the side of the red gutted ditch, holding the screaming baby, but she only had a cut down her face and a broken shoulder. "We've had an ACCIDENT!" the children screamed in a frenzy of delight.

"But nobody's killed," June Star said with disappointment as the grandmother limped out of the car, her hat still pinned to her head but the broken front brim standing up at a jaunty angle and the violet spray hanging off the side. They all sat down in the ditch, except the children, to recover from the shock. They were all shaking.

"Maybe a car will come along," said the children's mother hoarsely.

"I believe I have injured an organ," said the grandmother, pressing her side, but no one answered her. Bailey's teeth were clattering. He had on a yellow sport shirt with bright blue parrots designed in it and his face was as yellow as the shirt. The grandmother decided that she would not mention that the house was in Tennessee.

The road was about ten feet above and they could see only the tops of the trees on the other side of it. Behind the ditch they were sitting in there were more woods, tall and dark and deep. In a few minutes they saw a car some distance away on top of a hill, coming slowly as if the occupants were watching them. The grandmother stood up and waved both arms dramatically to attract their attention. The car continued to come on slowly, disappeared around a bend and appeared again, moving even slower, on top of the hill they had gone over. It was a big black battered hearselike automobile. There were three men in it.

It came to a stop just over them and for some minutes, the driver looked down with a steady expressionless gaze to where they were sitting, and didn't speak. Then he turned his head and muttered something to the other two and they got out. One was a fat boy in black trousers and a red sweatshirt with a silver stallion embossed on the front of it. He moved around on the right side of them and stood staring, his mouth partly open in a kind of loose grin. The other had on khaki pants and a blue striped coat and a gray hat pulled down very low, hiding most of his face. He came around slowly on the left side. Neither spoke.

The driver got out of the car and stood by the side of it, looking down at them. He was an older man than the other two. His hair was just beginning to gray and he wore silver-rimmed spectacles that gave him a scholarly look. He had a long creased face and didn't have on any shirt or undershirt. He had on blue jeans that were too tight for him and was holding a black hat and a gun. The two boys also had guns.

"We've had an ACCIDENT!" the children screamed.

The grandmother had the peculiar feeling that the bespectacled man was someone she knew. His face was as familiar to her as if she had known him all her life but she could not recall who he was. He moved away from the car and began to come down the embankment, placing his feet carefully so that he wouldn't slip. He had on tan and white shoes and no socks, and his ankles were red and thin. "Good afternoon," he said. "I see you all had you a little spill."

"We turned over twice!" said the grandmother.

"Oncet," he corrected. "We seen it happen. Try their car and see will it run, Hiram," he said quietly to the boy with the gray hat.

"What you got that gun for?" John Wesley asked. "Whatcha gonna do with that gun?"

"Lady," the man said to the children's mother, "would you mind calling them children to sit down by you? Children make me nervous. I want all you all to sit down right together there where you're at."

"What are you telling US what to do for?" June Star asked.

Behind them the line of woods gaped like a dark open mouth. "Come here," said their mother.

"Look here now," Bailey began suddenly, "we're in a predicament! We're in . . ."

The grandmother shrieked. She scrambled to her feet and stood staring. "You're The Misfit!" she said. "I recognized you at once!"

"Yes'm," the man said, smiling slightly as if he were pleased in spite of himself to be known, "but it would have been better for all of you, lady, if you hadn't of reckernized me."

Bailey turned his head sharply and said something to his mother that shocked even the children. The old lady began to cry and The Misfit reddened.

"Lady," he said, "don't you get upset. Sometimes a man says things he don't mean. I don't reckon he meant to talk to you thataway."

"You wouldn't shoot a lady, would you?" the grandmother said and removed a clean handkerchief from her cuff and began to slap at her eyes with it.

The Misfit pointed the toe of his shoe into the ground and made a little hole and then covered it up again. "I would hate to have to," he said.

"Listen," the grandmother almost screamed, "I know you're a good man. You don't look a bit like you have common blood. I know you must come from nice people!"

"Yes mam," he said, "finest people in the world." When he smiled he showed a row of strong white teeth. "God never made a finer woman than my mother and my daddy's heart was pure gold," he said. The boy with the red sweatshirt had come around behind them and was standing with his gun at his hip. The Misfit squatted down on the ground. "Watch them children, Bobby Lee," he said. "You know they make me nervous." He looked at the six of them huddled together in front of him and he seemed to be embarrassed as if he couldn't think of anything to say. "Ain't a cloud in the sky," he remarked, looking up at it. "Don't see no sun but don't see no cloud neither."

"Yes, it's a beautiful day," said the grandmother. "Listen," she said, "you shouldn't call yourself The Misfit because I know you're a good man at heart. I can just look at you and tell."

"Hush!" Bailey yelled. "Hush! Everybody shut up and let me handle this!" He was squatting in the position of a runner about to sprint forward but he didn't move.

"I pre-chate that, lady," The Misfit said and drew a little circle in the ground with the butt of his gun.

"It'll take a half a hour to fix this here car," Hiram called, looking over the raised hood of it.

"Well, first you and Bobby Lee get him and that little boy to step over yonder with you," The Misfit said, pointing to Bailey and John Wesley. "The boys want to ast you something," he said to Bailey. "Would you mind stepping back in them woods there with them?"

"Listen," Bailey began, "we're in a terrible predicament! Nobody realizes what this is," and his voice cracked. His eyes were as blue and intense as the parrots in his shirt and he remained perfectly still.

The grandmother reached up to adjust her hat brim as if she were going to the woods with him but it came off in her hand. She stood staring at it and after a second she let it fall on the ground. Hiram pulled Bailey up by the arm as if he were assisting an old man. John Wesley caught hold of his father's hand and Bobby Lee followed. They went off toward the woods and just as they reached the dark edge, Bailey turned and supporting himself against a gray naked pine trunk, he shouted, "I'll be back in a minute, Mamma, wait on me!"

"Come back this instant!" his mother shrilled but they all disappeared into the woods.

"Bailey Boy!" the grandmother called in a tragic voice but she found she was looking at The Misfit squatting on the ground in front of her. "I just know you're a good man," she said desperately. "You're not a bit common!"

"Nome, I ain't a good man," The Misfit said after a second as if he had considered her statement carefully, "but I ain't the worst in the world neither. My daddy said I was a different breed of dog from my brothers and sisters. 'You know,' Daddy said, 'it's some that can live their whole life out without asking about it and it's others has to know why it is, and this boy is one of the latters. He's going to be into everything!'" He put on his black hat and looked up suddenly and then away deep into the woods as if he were embarrassed again. "I'm sorry I don't have on a shirt before you ladies," he said, hunching his shoulders slightly. "We buried our clothes that we had on when we escaped and we're just making do until we can get better. We borrowed these from some folks we met," he explained.

"That's perfectly all right," the grandmother said. "Maybe Bailey has an extra shirt in his suitcase."

"I'll look and see terrectly," The Misfit said.

"Where are they taking him?" the children's mother screamed.

"Daddy was a card himself," The Misfit said. "You couldn't put anything over on him. He never got in trouble with the Authorities though. Just had the knack of handling them."

"You could be honest too if you'd only try," said the grandmother. "Think how wonderful it would be to settle down and live a comfortable life and not have to think about somebody chasing you all the time."

The Misfit kept scratching in the ground with the butt of his gun as if he were thinking about it. "Yes'm, somebody is always after you," he murmured.

The grandmother noticed how thin his shoulder blades were just behind his hat because she was standing up looking down on him. "Do you ever pray?" she asked.

He shook his head. All she saw was the black hat wiggle between his shoulder blades. "Nome," he said.

There was a pistol shot from the woods, followed closely by another. Then silence. The old lady's head jerked around. She could hear the wind move through the tree tops like a long satisfied insuck of breath. "Bailey Boy!" she called.

"I was a gospel singer for a while," The Misfit said. "I been most everything. Been in the arm service, both land and sea, at home and abroad, been twict married, been an undertaker, been with the railroads, plowed Mother Earth, been in a tornado, seen a man burnt alive oncet," and looked up at the children's mother and the little girl who were sitting close together, their faces white and their eyes glassy; "I even seen a woman flogged," he said.

"Pray, pray," the grandmother began, "pray, pray . . ."

"I never was a bad boy that I remember of," The Misfit said in an almost dreamy voice, "but somewheres along the line I done something wrong and got sent to the penitentiary. I was buried alive," and he looked up and held her attention to him by a steady stare.

"That's when you should have started to pray," she said. "What did you do to get sent to the penitentiary that first time?"

"Turn to the right, it was a wall," The Misfit said, looking up again at the cloudless sky. "Turn to the left, it was a wall. Look up it was a ceiling, look down it was a floor. I forget what I done, lady. I set there and set there, trying to remember what it was I done and I ain't recalled it to this day. Oncet in a while, I would think it was coming to me, but it never come."

"Maybe they put you in by mistake," the old lady said vaguely.

"Nome," he said. "It wasn't no mistake. They had the papers on me."

"You must have stolen something," she said.

The Misfit sneered slightly. "Nobody had nothing I wanted," he said. "It was a head-doctor at the penitentiary said what I had done was kill my daddy but I known that for a lie. My daddy died in nineteen ought nineteen of the epidemic flu and I never had a thing to do with it. He was buried in the Mount Hopewell Baptist churchyard and you can go there and see for yourself."

"If you would pray," the old lady said, "Jesus would help you."

"That's right," The Misfit said.

"Well then, why don't you pray?" she asked trembling with delight suddenly.

"I don't want no hep," he said. "I'm doing all right by myself."

Bobby Lee and Hiram came ambling back from the woods. Bobby Lee was dragging a yellow shirt with bright blue parrots in it.

"Thow me that shirt, Bobby Lee," The Misfit said. The shirt came flying at him and landed on his shoulder and he put it on. The grandmother couldn't name what the shirt reminded her of. "No, lady," The

Misfit said while he was buttoning it up, "I found out the crime don't matter. You can do one thing or you can do another, kill a man or take a tire off his car, because sooner or later you're going to forget what it was you done and just be punished for it."

The children's mother had begun to make heaving noises as if she couldn't get her breath. "Lady," he asked, "would you and that little girl like to step off yonder with Bobby Lee and Hiram and join your husband?"

"Yes, thank you," the mother said faintly. Her left arm dangled helplessly and she was holding the baby, who had gone to sleep, in the other. "Hep that lady up, Hiram," The Misfit said as she struggled to climb out of the ditch, "and Bobby Lee, you hold onto that little girl's hand."

"I don't want to hold hands with him," June Star said. "He reminds me of a pig."

The fat boy blushed and laughed and caught her by the arm and pulled her off into the woods after Hiram and her mother.

Alone with The Misfit, the grandmother found that she had lost her voice. There was not a cloud in the sky nor any sun. There was nothing around her but woods. She wanted to tell him that he must pray. She opened and closed her mouth several times before anything came out. Finally she found herself saying, "Jesus, Jesus," meaning, Jesus will help you, but the way she was saying it, it sounded as if she might be cursing.

"Yes'm," The Misfit said as if he agreed. "Jesus thown everything off balance. It was the same case with Him as with me except He hadn't committed any crime and they could prove I had committed one because they had the papers on me. Of course," he said, "they never shown me my papers. That's why I sign myself now. I said long ago, you get you a signature and sign everything you do and keep a copy of it. Then you'll know what you done and you can hold up the crime to the punishment and see do they match and in the end you'll have something to prove you ain't been treated right. I call myself The Misfit," he said, "because I can't make what all I done wrong fit what all I gone through in punishment."

There was a piercing scream from the woods, followed closely by a pistol report. "Does it seem right to you, lady, that one is punished a heap and another ain't punished at all?"

"Jesus!" the old lady cried. "You've got good blood! I know you wouldn't shoot a lady! I know you come from nice people! Pray! Jesus, you ought not to shoot a lady. I'll give you all the money I've got!"

"Lady," The Misfit said, looking beyond her far into the woods, "there never was a body that give the undertaker a tip."

There were two more pistol reports and the grandmother raised her head like a parched old turkey hen crying for water and called, "Bailey Boy, Bailey Boy!" as if her heart would break.

"Jesus was the only One that ever raised the dead." The Misfit continued, "and He shouldn't have done it. He thrown everything off balance. If He did what He said, then it's nothing for you to do but throw away everything and follow Him, and if He didn't, then it's nothing for you to do but enjoy the few minutes you got left the best way you can—by killing somebody or burning down his house or doing some other meanness to him. No pleasure but meanness," he said and his voice had become almost a snarl.

"Maybe He didn't raise the dead," the old lady mumbled, not knowing what she was saying and feeling so dizzy that she sank down in the ditch with her legs twisted under her.

"I wasn't there so I can't say He didn't," The Misfit said. "I wisht I had of been there," he said, hitting the ground with his fist. "It ain't right I wasn't there because if I had of been there I would of known. Listen lady," he said in a high voice, "if I had of been there I would of known and I wouldn't be like I am now." His voice seemed about to crack and the grandmother's head cleared for an instant. She saw the man's face twisted close to her own as if he were going to cry and she murmured, "Why you're one of my babies. You're one of my own children!" She reached out and touched him on the shoulder. The Misfit sprang back as if a snake had bitten him and shot her three times through the chest. Then he put his gun down on the ground and took off his glasses and began to clean them.

Hiram and Bobby Lee returned from the woods and stood over the ditch, looking down at the grandmother who half sat and half lay in a puddle of blood with her legs crossed under her like a child's and her face smiling up at the cloudless sky.

Without his glasses, The Misfit's eyes were red-rimmed and pale and defenseless-looking. "Take her off and throw her where you thrown the others," he said, picking up the cat that was rubbing itself against his leg.

"She was a talker, wasn't she?" Bobby Lee said, sliding down the ditch with a yodel.

"She would of been a good woman," The Misfit said, "if it had been somebody there to shoot her very minute of her life."

"Some fun!" Bobby Lee said.

"Shut up, Bobby Lee," The Misfit said. "It's no real pleasure in life."

GRACE PALEY

The Used-Boy Raisers

There were two husbands disappointed by eggs.

I don't like them that way either, I said. Make your own eggs. They sighed in unison. One man was livid; one was pallid.

"There isn't a drink around here, is there?" asked Livid.

Never find one here, said Pallid. Don't look; driest damn house. Pallid pushed the eggs away, pain and disgust his escutcheon.

Livid said, Now really, isn't there a drink? Beer? he hoped.

Nothing, said Pallid, who'd been through the pantries, closets, and refrigerators looking for a white shirt.

You're damn right, I said. I buttoned the high button of my powder-blue duster. I reached under the kitchen table for a brown paper bag full of an embroidery which asked God to Bless Our Home.

I was completing this motto for the protection of my sons, who were also Livid's. It is true that some months earlier, from a far place—the British plains in Africa—he had written hospitably to Pallid: I do think they're fine boys, you understand. I love them too, but Faith is their mother and now Faith is your wife. I'm so much away. If you want to think of them as yours, old man, go ahead.

Why, thank you, Pallid had replied, airmail, overwhelmed. Then he implored the boys, when not in use, to play in their own room. He made all efforts to be kind.

Now as we talked of time past and upon us, I pierced the ranch house that nestles in the shade of a cloud and a Norway maple, just under the golden script.

Ha-ha, said Livid, dripping coffee on his pajama pants, you'll never guess whom I met up with, Faith.

Who? I asked.

Saw your old boyfriend Clifford at the Green Coq. He looks well. One thing must be said, he addressed Pallid, she takes good care of her men.

True, said Pallid.

How is he? I asked coolly. What's he doing? I haven't seen him in two years.

Oh, you'll never guess. He's marrying. A darling girl. She was with him. Little tootsies, little round bottom, little tummy—she must be twenty-two, but she looks seventeen. One long yellow braid down her back. A darling girl. Stubby nose, fat little underlip. Her eyes put on in pencil. Shoulders down like a dancer . . . slender neck. Oh, darling, darling.

You certainly observed her, said Pallid.

I have a functioning retina, said Livid. Then he went on. Better watch out, Faith. You'd be surprised, the dear little chicks are hatching out all over the place. All the sunny schoolgirls rolling their big black eyes. I hope you're really settled this time. To me, whatever is under the dam is in another county; however, in my life you remain an important person historically, he said. And that's why I feel justified in warning you. I must warn you. Watch out, sweetheart! he said, leaning forward to whisper harshly and give me a terrible bellyache.

What's all this about? asked Pallid innocently. In the first place, she's settled . . . and then she's still an attractive woman. Look at her.

Oh yes, said Livid, looking. An attractive woman. Magnificent, sometimes.

We were silent for several seconds in honor of that generous remark.

Then Livid said, Yes, magnificent, but I just wanted to warn you, Faith.

He pushed his eggs aside finally and remembered Clifford. A mystery wrapped in an enigma . . . I wonder why he wants to marry.

I don't know, it just ties a man down, I said.

And yet, said Pallid seriously, what would I be without marriage? In luminous recollection—a gay dog, he replied.

At this moment, the boys entered: Richard the horse thief and Tonto the crack shot.

Daddy! they shouted. They touched Livid, tickled him, unbuttoned his pajama top, whistled at the several gray hairs coloring his chest. They tweaked his ear and rubbed his beard the wrong way.

Well, well, he cautioned. How are you boys, have you been well? You look fine. Sturdy. How are your grades? he inquired. He dreamed that they were just up from Eton for the holidays.

I don't go to school, said Tonto. I go to the park.

I'd like to hear the child read, said Livid.

Me. I can read, Daddy, said Richard. I have a book with a hundred pages.

Well, well, said Livid. Get it.

I kindled a fresh pot of coffee. I scrubbed cups and harassed Pallid into opening a sticky jar of damson-plum jam. Very shortly, what could be read, had been, and Livid, knotting the tie strings of his pants vigorously, approached me at the stove. Faith, he admonished, that boy can't read a tinker's damn. Seven years old.

Eight years old, I said.

Yes, said Pallid, who had just remembered the soap cabinet and was rummaging in it for a pint. If they were my sons in actuality as they are in everyday life, I would send them to one of the good parochial schools in the neighborhood where reading is taught. Reading. St. Bartholomew's, St. Bernard's, St. Joseph's.

Livid became deep purple and gasped. Over my dead body, *Merde*, he said in deference to the children. I've said, yes, you may think of the boys as your own, but if I ever hear they've come within an inch of that church, I'll run you through, you bastard. I was fourteen years old when in my own good sense I walked out of that grotto of deception, head up. You sonofabitch, I don't give a damn how *au courant* it is these days, how gracious to be seen under a dome on Sunday. . . . Shit! Hypocrisy. Corruption. Cave dwellers. Idiots. Morons.

Recalling childhood and home, poor Livid writhed in his seat. Pallid listened, head to one side, his brows gathering the onsets of grief.

You know, he said slowly, we iconoclasts . . . we free-thinkers . . . we latter-day masons . . . we idealists . . . we dreamers . . . we are never far from our nervous old mother, the Church. She is never far from us.

Wherever we are, we can hear, no matter how faint, her hourly bells, tolling the countryside, reverberating in the cities, bringing to our civilized minds the passionate deed of Mary. Every hour on the hour we are startled with remembrance of what was done for us. FOR US.

Livid muttered in great pain. Those bastards, oh oh oh, those contemptible, goddamnable bastards. Do we have to do the nineteenth century all over again? All right, he bellowed, facing us all, I'm ready. That Newman!

He turned to me for approval.

You know, I said, this subject has never especially interested me. It's your little dish of lava.

Pallid spoke softly, staring past the arched purple windows of his soul. I myself, although I lost God a long time ago, have never lost faith.

What the hell are you talking about, you moron? roared Livid. I have never lost my love for the wisdom of the Church of the World. When I go to sleep at night, I inadvertently pray. I also do so when I rise. It is not to God, it is to that unifying memory out of childhood. The first words I ever wrote were: What are the sacraments? Faith, can you ever forget your old grandfather intoning Kaddish? It will sound in your ears forever.

Are you kidding? I was furious to be drawn into their conflict. Kaddish? What do I know about Kaddish. Who's dead? You know my opinions perfectly well. I believe in the Diaspora, not only as a fact but a tenet. I'm against Israel on technical grounds. I'm very disappointed that they decided to become a nation in my lifetime. I believe in the Diaspora. After all, they *are* the chosen people. Don't laugh. They really are. But once they're huddled in one little corner of a desert, they're like anyone else: Frenchies, Italians, temporal nationalities. Jews have one hope only—to remain a remnant in the basement of world affairs—no, I mean something else—a splinter in the toe of civilizations, a victim to aggravate the conscience.

Livid and Pallid were astonished at my outburst, since I rarely express my opinion on any serious matter but only live out my destiny, which is to be, until my expiration date, laughingly the servant of man.

I continued. I hear they don't even look like Jews anymore. A bunch of dirt farmers with no time to read.

They're your own people, Pallid accused, dilating in the nostril, clenching his jaw. And they're under the severest attack. This is not the time to revile them.

I had resumed my embroidery. I sighed. My needle was now deep in the clouds which were pearl gray and late afternoon. I am only trying to say that they aren't meant for geographies but for history. They are not supposed to take up space but to continue in time.

They looked at me with such grief that I decided to consider all sides of the matter. I said, Christ probably had all that trouble—now that you mention it—because he knew he was going to gain the whole world but he forgot Jerusalem.

When you married us, said Pallid, and accused me, didn't you forget Jerusalem?

I never forget a thing, I said. Anyway, guess what. I just read somewhere that England is bankrupt. The country is wadded with installment paper.

Livid's hand trembled as he offered Pallid a light. Nonsense, he said. That's not true. Nonsense. The great British Island is the tight little fist of the punching arm of the Commonwealth.

What's true is true, I said, smiling.

Well, I said, since no one stirred, do you think you'll ever get to work today? Either of you?

Oh, my dear, I haven't even seen you and the boys in over a year. It's quite pleasant and cozy here this morning, said Livid.

Yes, isn't it? said Pallid, the surprised host. Besides, it's Saturday.

How do you find the boys? I asked Livid, the progenitor.

American, American, rowdy, uncontrolled. But you look well, Faith. Plumper, but womanly and well.

Very well, said Pallid, pleased.

But the boys, Faith. Shouldn't they be started on something? Just lining up little plastic cowboys. It's silly, really.

They're so young, apologized Pallid, the used-boy raiser.

You'd both better go to work, I suggested, knotting the pearl-gray late-afternoon thread. Please put the dishes in the sink first. Please. I'm sorry about the eggs.

Livid yawned, stretched, peeked at the clock, sighed. Saturday or no, alas, my time is not my own. I've got an appointment downtown in about forty-five minutes, he said.

I do too, said Pallid. I'll join you on the subway.

I'm taking a cab, said Livid.

I'll split it with you, said Pallid.

They left for the bathroom, where they shared things nicely—shaving equipment, washstand, shower, and so forth.

I made the beds and put the aluminum cot away. Livid would find a hotel room by nightfall. I did the dishes and organized the greedy day; dinosaurs in the morning, park in the afternoon, peanut butter in between, and at the end of it all, to reward us for a week of beans endured, a noble rib roast with little onions, dumplings, and pink applesauce.

Faith, I'm going now, Livid called from the hall. I put my shopping list aside and went to collect the boys, who were wandering among the rooms looking for Robin Hood. Go say good-bye to your father, I whispered.

Which one? they asked.

The real father, I said. Richard ran to Livid. They shook hands manfully. Pallid embraced Tonto and was kissed eleven times for his affection.

Good-bye now, Faith, said Livid. Call me if you want anything at all. Anything at all, my dear. Warmly with sweet propriety he kissed my cheek. Ascendant, Pallid kissed me with considerable business behind the ear.

Good-bye, I said to them.

I must admit that they were at last clean and neat, rather attractive, shiny men in their thirties, with the grand affairs of the day ahead of them. Dark night, the search for pleasure and oblivion were well ahead. Good-bye, I said, have a nice day. Good-bye, they said once more, and set off in pride on paths which are not my concern.

JAYNE ANNE PHILLIPS

The Heavenly Animal

Jancy's father always wanted to fix her car. Every time she came home for a visit, he called her at her mother's house and asked about the car with a second sentence.

Well, he'd say, How are you?

Fine, I'm fine.

And how's the car? Have any trouble?

He became incensed if Jancy's mother answered. He slammed the receiver down and broke the connection. They always knew who it was by the stutter of silence, then the violent click. He lived alone in a house ten blocks away.

Often, he would drive by and see Jancy's car before she'd even taken her coat off. He stopped his aging black Ford on the sloping street and honked two tentative blasts. He hadn't come inside her mother's house since the divorce five years ago. He wouldn't even step on the grass of the block-shaped lawn. This time Jancy saw his car from the bathroom window. She cursed and pulled her pants up. She walked outside and the heavy car door swung open. Her father wore a wool hat with a turned-up brim and small gray feather. Jancy loved the feather.

Hi, she said.

Well, hi there. When did you get in?

About five minutes ago.

Have any trouble?

She got into the car. The black interior was very clean and the empty litter bag hung from the radio knob. Jancy thought she could smell its new plastic mingling with the odor of his cigar. She leaned over and kissed him.

Thank god, she thought, he looks better.

He pointed to her car. What the hell did you do to the chrome along the side there? he said.

Trying to park, Jancy said. Got in a tight spot.

Her father shook his head and grimaced. He held the butt of the cigar with his thumb and forefinger. Jancy saw the flat chewed softness of the butt where he held it in his mouth, and the stain on his lips where it touched.

Jesus, Honey, he said.

Can't win them all.

But you got to win some of them, he said. That car's got to last you a long time.

It will, Jancy said. It's a good car. Like a tank. I could drive that car through the fiery pits of hell and come out smelling like a rose.

Well. Everything you do to it takes money to fix. And I just don't have it.

Don't want it fixed, Jancy said. Works fine without the chrome.

He never asked her at first how long she was going to stay. For the past few years she'd come home between school terms. Or from far-flung towns up East, out West. Sometimes during her visits she left to see friends. He would rant close to her face, breathing hard.

Why in God's name would you go to Washington, D.C.? Nothing there but niggers. And what the hell do you want in New York? You're going to wear out your car. You've driven that car thirty thousand miles in one year— Why? What the hell for?

The people I care about are far apart. I don't get many chances to see them.

Jesus Christ, you come home and off you go.

I'll be back in four days.

That's not the goddamn point. You'll get yourself crippled up in a car wreck running around like this. Then where will you be?

Jancy would sigh and feel herself harden.

I won't stay in one place all my life out of fear I'll get crippled if I move, she'd say.

Well I understand that, but *Jesus.*

His breathing would grow quiet. He rubbed his fingers and twisted the gold Masonic ring he wore in place of a wedding band.

Honey, he'd say. You got to *think* of these things.

And they would both sit staring.

Down the street Jancy saw red stop signs and the lawns of churches. Today he was in a good mood. Today he was just glad to see her. And he didn't know she was going to see Michael. Or was she?

What do you think? he said. Do you want to go out for lunch tomorrow? I go down to the Catholic church there, they have a senior citizen's meal. Pretty good food.

Jancy smiled. Do you remember when you stopped buying Listerine, she asked, because you found out a Catholic owned the company?

She could tell he didn't remember, but he grinned.

Hell, he said. Damn Catholics own everything.

He was sixty-seven. Tiny blood vessels in his cheeks had burst. There was that redness in his skin, and the blue of shadows, gauntness of the weight loss a year ago. His skin got softer, his eyelids translucent as crepe. His eyelashes were very short and reddish. The flesh drooped under his heavy brows. As a young man, he'd been almost sloe-eyed. Bedroom eyes, her mother called them. Now his eyes receded in the mysterious colors of his face.

OK, Jancy said. Lunch.

She got out of the car and bent to look in at him through the open window.

Hey, she said. You look pretty snappy in that hat.

Tonight her mother would leave after supper for Ohio. Jancy would be alone in the house and she would stare at the telephone. She tore lettuce while her mother broiled the steaks.

I don't know why you want to drive all the way up there at night, Jancy said. Why don't you leave in the morning?

I can make better time at night, her mother said. And besides, the wedding is in two days. Your aunt wanted me to come last week. It's not every day her only daughter gets married, and since you refuse to go to weddings . . .

She paused. They heard the meat crackle in the oven.

I'm sorry to leave when you've just gotten here. I thought you'd be here two weeks ago, and we'd have some time before I left. But you'll be here when I get back.

Jancy looked intently into the salad bowl.

Jancy? asked her mother. Why are you so late getting here? Why didn't you write?

I was just busy . . . finishing the term, packing, subletting the apartment—

You could have phoned.

I didn't want to. I hate calling long-distance. It makes me feel lost, listening to all that static.

That's ridiculous, her mother said. Let's get this table cleared off. I don't know why you always come in and dump everything on the first available spot.

Because I believe in instant relief, Jancy said.

—books, backpack, maps, your purse—

She reached for the books and Jancy's leather purse fell to the floor. Its contents spilled and rolled. She bent to retrieve the mess before Jancy could stop her, picking up small plastic bottles of pills.

What are these? she said. What are you doing with all these pills?

I cleaned out my medicine cabinet and threw all the bottles in my purse. They're pills I've had for years—

Don't you think you better throw them away? You might forget what you're taking.

They're all labeled, Jancy said.

Her mother glanced down.

Dalmane, she said. What's Dalmane?

A sleeping pill.

Why would you need sleeping pills?

Because I have trouble sleeping. Why do you think?

Since when?

I don't know. A long time. Off and on. Will you cut it out with the third degree?

Why can't you sleep?

Because I dream my mother is relentlessly asking me questions.

It's Michael. Michael's thrown you for a loop.

Jancy threw the bottles in her purse and stood up quickly. No, she said, Or yes. We're both upset right now.

He certainly is. You're lucky to be rid of him.

I don't want to be rid of him.

He'll drive you crazy if you're not careful. He's got a screw loose and you know it.

You liked him, Jancy said. You liked him so much it made me angry.

Yes, I liked him. But not after this whole mess started. Calling you cruel because he couldn't have things his way. If he was so in love it would have lasted. Cruel. There's not a cruel bone in your body.

I should never have told you he said those things.

They were silent. Jancy smelled the meat cooking.

Why shouldn't you tell me? her mother asked quietly. If you can't talk to your mother, who can you talk to?

Oh Christ, Jancy said. Nobody. I'm hungry. Let's eat and change the subject.

They sat down over full plates. There was steak when Jancy or her brothers came home. Their mother saved it for weeks, months, in the freezer. The meat sizzled on Jancy's plate and she tried to eat. She looked up. The lines in her mother's face seemed deeper than before, grown in. And she was so thin, so perfectly groomed. Earrings. Creased pants. Silk scarves. A bath at the same time every morning while the *Today* show played the news. At night she rubbed the calluses off her heels carefully with a pumice stone.

She looked at Jancy. What are you doing tomorrow? she asked.

Having lunch at the Catholic church, Jancy said.

That ought to be good. Canned peaches and weepy mashed potatoes. Your father is something. Of course he doesn't speak to me on the street, but I see him drive by here in that black car. Every day. Watching for one of you to come home.

Jancy said nothing.

He looks terrible, her mother said.

He looks better than he did, said Jancy.

That's not saying much. He looked horrible for months. Thinner and thinner, like a walking death. I'd see him downtown. He went to the pool hall every day, always by himself. He never did have any friends.

He did, Jancy said. He told me. In the war.

I don't know. I didn't meet him till after that, when he was nearly forty. By then he never seemed to belong—

I remember that weekend you went away and he moved out, Jancy said. He never belonged in this house. The house he built had such big rooms.

Did you know that house is for sale again? her mother asked. It's changed hands several times.

I didn't know, Jancy said. Let's not talk about it.

Her mother sighed. All right, she said. Let's talk about washing these dishes. I really have to get started.

Mom, Jancy said, I might call Michael.

What for? He's five states away and that's where he ought to be.

I may go up there.

Oh, Jancy.

I have to. I can't just let it end here.

Her mother was silent. They heard a gentle thunder.

Clouding up, Jancy said. You may have rain. Need help with your bags?

The car's already packed.

Well, Jancy said.

Her mother collected maps, parcels, a large white-ribboned present. Jancy heard her moving around and thought of waking at night in the house her father had built, the house in the country. There would be the cornered light from the bathroom in the hall. Her father would walk slowly past in slippers and robe to adjust the furnace. The motor would kick in and grunt its soft hum several times a night. Half asleep, Jancy knew her father was awake. The furnace. They must have been winter nights.

Can you grab this? her mother asked.

Jancy took the present. I'll walk you out, she said.

No, just give it to me. There, I've got it.

Jancy smiled. Her mother took her hand.

You're gutsy, she said. You'll be OK.

Good, said Jancy. It's always great to be OK.

Give me a hug.

Jancy embraced her. How often did someone hold her? Her hair smelled fragrant and dark.

Jancy left the lights off. She took a sleeping pill and lay down on the living room couch. Rain splattered the windows. She imagined her father standing by the dining room table. When he moved out he had talked to her brothers about guns.

One rifle goes, he'd said. One stays. Which do you want?

Jancy remembered cigarette smoke in the room, how it curled between their faces.

It don't make any difference to me, he said. But this one's the best for rabbit.

He fingered change far down in his trouser pockets. One brother asked the other which he wanted. The other said it didn't matter, didn't matter. Finally the youngest took the gun and climbed the steps to his room. Their father walked into the kitchen, murmuring, It'll kill rabbits and birds. And if you go after deer, just use slugs.

Jancy heard water dripping. How long had it gone on? Rain was coming down the chimney. She got up and closed the flue, mopped up the rain with a towel. The pills didn't work anymore. What would she do all night? She was afraid of this house, afraid of all the houses in this town. After midnight they were silent and blank. They seemed abandoned.

She looked at the telephone. She picked up the receiver.

Michael? she said.

She dialed his number. The receiver clicked and snapped.

What number are you calling please?

He's gone, thought Jancy.

Hello? What number—

Jancy repeated the numerals.

That number has been disconnected. There's a new number. Shall I ring it for you?

The plastic dial of the princess phone was transparent and yellowed with light.

Ma'am? Shall I ring it?

Yes, Jancy said.

No one home.

Jancy took a bottle of whiskey off the shelf. She would drink enough to make her sleep. The rain had stopped and the house was still. Light from streetlamps fell through the windows. Jancy watched the deserted town. Heavy elms loomed over the sidewalks. Limbs of trees rose and fell on a night breeze. Their shadows moved on the lit-up surface of the street.

A black car glided by.

Jancy stepped back from the window. Taillights blinked red as the car turned corners and passed away soundlessly.

She picked up the phone and dialed. She lay in the cramped hallway while the purr of a connection stopped and started. How did it sound there, ringing in the dark? Loud and empty.

Hello?

His voice, soft. When they lived together, he used to stand looking out the window at the alley late at night. He was naked and perfect. He watched the Midwestern alleys roll across eight city blocks paved in old brick. Telephone poles stood weathered and alone. Their drooping wires glistened, humming one note. He gripped the wooden frame of the window and stood looking, centaur, quiet, his flanks whitened in moonlight.

Jancy, he said now. It's you, isn't it.

Jancy wore a skirt and sat in the living room. Her father would pull up outside. She would see him lean to watch the door of the house, his head inclined toward her. His car shining and just washed. His hat. His cigar. His baggy pants bought at the same store downtown for thirty years.

Jancy walked outside to watch for him. She didn't want to jump when the horn sounded. And it suddenly hurt her that her father was always waiting.

Did he know their old house was being sold again? He had contracted the labor and built it himself. He had designed the heating system, radiant heat piped under the floors so the wooden parquet was always warm. He had raised the ceiling of the living room fifteen inches so that the crown of her mother's inherited antique bookcase would fit into it. He was a road builder, but those last few years, when Jancy was a teenager, he'd had a series of bad jobs—selling bulldozers, cars, insurance— After they'd moved he stopped working altogether . . .

The horn sounded suddenly close and shocked her.

Jancy?

Now why did you do that? I'm standing right here, aren't I?

Are you asleep?

No, I just didn't hear you pull up. But you didn't have to blare that horn at me. It's loud enough to wake the dead.

Well, he said, I thought you needed waking, standing there staring into space like a knothead.

Right, said Jancy. She got into the car and he was still smiling. She laughed in spite of herself.

I'm a little early, he said. They don't open at the church till noon. Do you want to go for a drive?

Where to?

We could drive out the falls road, he said.

That would take them past the old house. The hedges and trees would be larger than Jancy could believe, lush with new leaves, and rippling. Her father had planted them all.

I don't think so, said Jancy.

The house is for sale.

I know.

Dumbest thing I ever did was to let your mother talk me into selling that house.

I don't want to hear about my mother.

I'll hate her for the rest of my life for breaking up our family, he said, his breathing grown heavy. He scowled and touched the ridges in the steering wheel.

Jancy leaned back in the seat and watched clouds through the tinted windshield. Remember when you built roads? she asked.

He waited a moment, then looked over at her and pushed his hat back. I built a lot of them around here, he said, but the state don't keep them up anymore. They closed the graveyard road.

He'd taught her how to drive on that road, a narrow unpainted blacktop that wound under train trestles and through the cemetery. He said if she could drive on that road she could drive anywhere. He made her go that way, cutting across a blind curve up the sudden hill of the entrance, past the carved pillars with their lopsided lamps. This way, he'd said, and she'd pulled off onto a gravel path that turned sharply along the crest of a hill. Tombstones were scattered in the lumpy grass. Far below Jancy saw the graveyard road looping west by the river, on through woods to the country towns of Volga and Coalton and Mud Lick.

Stop here, her father directed. He nodded at a patch of ground. There we are, he said, this is where we'll be.

Jancy was sixteen; she'd stared at him and gripped the steering wheel.

All right, he'd said. Back up. Let's see how you do going backward.

Now her father started his black Ford and they passed the clipped lawns of houses. He drove slowly, his cigar in his mouth.

What will they have to eat at the church? Jancy asked.

Oh, he said. They publish a menu in the paper. Meat loaf today. Fifty cents a person over sixty. Not bad food. Cooks used to work up at the junior high. But we don't have to go there. We can go to a restaurant if you want.

No, I'd rather go where you usually go. But are you sure I'm allowed?

Certainly. You're my guest. A dollar for guests.

They pulled into the church parking lot. The doors of the rec center were closed. They sat in the car and waited. Jancy remembered dances held in this building, how she was thirteen and came here to dance with the high school boys. They had danced until they were wet with sweat, then stepped outside into the winter air. Girls stood by the lighted door and shivered while the boys smoked cigarettes, squinting into vaporous trails of smoke rings.

What about your car? asked her father.

What about it?

I'm going to take it up to Smitty's and have him go over it.

No. Doesn't need it. The car is fine. I had it checked—

I've made arrangements with Smitty for today. He's got room and we better—

But the last time he fixed it, one of the sparkplugs flew out while I was driving on the interstate—

Don't you be taking off on Smitty, her father said. He's done us a lot of good work on that car. I'm trying to help you. You don't want my help, why just let me know and I'll bow out anytime.

Jancy sighed. Her father held his hat in his lap and traced the faint lines of the wool plaid with his fingers.

I appreciate your help, she said. But I don't know if Smitty—

He might have made a mistake that one time, her father said. But he usually does real good by us.

Volkswagen buses of old people began to pull up. Drivers opened the double doors of the vans and rolled up a set of mobile steps. Old ladies appeared with their blond canes and black-netted pillbox hats. They stepped out one after another, smiling and peeking about.

Where are the old men? Jancy asked.

I think they die off quicker, her father said. These same old dames have been coming here ever since I have. They just keep moving.

Inside were long rows of Formica tables. Eight or nine elderly people sat at each. There were rows of empty chairs. Women with a cashbox between them sat beside the door. Jancy's father put his arm around Jancy's waist and patted her.

This is my daughter, he said.

Well, isn't she pretty? said one of the cashiers. The other women nodded and smiled.

Jancy signed the guest book. Under "address" she wrote "at large." Her father was waiting at one of the tables. He had pulled a chair out for her and was standing behind it, waiting to seat her. The women were watching them, like the circling nurses that day at the hospital. Her father lay in bed, his arms so thin that his elbows seemed too large.

This is my daughter, he'd said to the nurses. She came all the way from California to see me.

Isn't that nice, they'd said. Is she married?

Hell no, her father had laughed. She's married to me.

Now Jancy felt the chair press up behind her legs and she sat down. Her father took his hat off and nodded at people across the table. She saw that his eyes were alight.

Aren't you going to have to get yourself a summer hat? she asked.

I reckon so, he said. I just can't find one I like.

Behind the waist-high counter, Jancy saw the fat cooks spooning peaches onto plates from metal cans. They were big women, their hair netted in silver nets, faces round and flushed from the ovens. They passed out cafeteria trays premolded for portions.

I used to eat out of those trays in grade school, Jancy said. Are they going to make us sing "God Is Great"?

No, her father said. But go ahead if it makes you feel better.

He chuckled. The last time they'd eaten together was last December. Michael had come home with Jancy and they'd gone out to lunch with her father at the Elks Club. Afterward he had held Michael's coat for him and eased it onto his shoulders. He'd never done that for anyone but his sons. Later he'd asked her, Are you going to marry this man?

Jancy? Aren't you going to eat? Her father was leaning close to her, pointing at her plate.

What? Oh. I ate a big breakfast. Here, you eat the rest of mine.

You should eat, said her father. Your face looks thin. Have you lost weight?

Maybe a little.

You run around too much. If you'd stay in one place for a while you'd gain a little weight and look better.

Jancy picked up her fork and put it down. Her father had always made her uneasy. He went into rages, especially in the car. If he couldn't pass or the car in front slowed suddenly for a turn, he'd turn red and curse—Goddammit, you son of a bitch, he'd say. That's right, you chucklehead—That word "chucklehead" was his utmost brand of contempt. He said it stressing the first syllable, fuming like a mad bull.

Jancy? You finished? Ready to go?

Her father pushed his plate away and sat watching her, touching the rim of his empty glass with a finger. She couldn't answer him. She knew that she would leave to see Michael. When she told her father, he would shake his head and stammer as he tried to talk. She got up and started for the door.

Jancy's father burned a coal fire past mid-May. He picked up a poker and stabbed at white embers clinging to the grate. Flakes of ash drifted into the room.

How long will you be up there? he asked.

I don't know, she said.

Christ Almighty. What are you doing? If this thing between you and him is over, just forget it. Why go chasing up there after him? Let him come here, he knows where you are.

I don't have a place for him to stay.

Why couldn't he stay up at the house with you and your mother?

Because we don't want to stay with my mother.

He clenched his fists and glowered into the fire. He shook his head.

I know you're an adult, he said. But goddammit, Jancy, it's not right. I don't care what you say. It's not right and it won't come to no good.

It already *has* come to good, Jancy said. She looked at him until he broke their gaze.

Why don't you give it up? he said. Give it up and marry him.

Give what up?

All this running around you're doing. Jesus, Honey, you can't do this all your life. Aren't you twenty-five this summer? I won't be here forever. What's going to happen to you?

I don't know, Jancy said. How can I know?

He leaned forward, elbows on knees, and clasped his hands. You need a family, he said. No one will ever help you but your family.

Maybe not, said Jancy.

She thought of the drive. Moving up the East Coast to Michael. She would arrive and sit in the car, waiting to stop trembling, waiting for twelve hours of hot road and radio talk to go away. She would want Michael so much and she would be afraid to go into the house.

She looked up at her father.

I have to do this, she said.

What time are you leaving?

Five A.M.

Does your mother know you're going?

I told her I might.

Well. Come down by and we'll hose off the car.

No, you don't need to get up that early.

I'm always awake by then, he said.

Her father was sitting outside on the porch swing as she drove up. He motioned her to pull into the yard under the buckeye tree. The sky had begun to lighten. The stars were gone. The air was chill, misted. He wore a woolen shirt and the hat with the feather nearly hidden in the brim. Before Jancy could get out of the car he picked up the garden hose and twisted the brass nozzle. Water streamed over the windshield. Jancy watched his wavering form as the water broke and runneled. He held the cigar between his teeth and sprayed the bumpers, the headlights, the long sides of the car. He sprayed each tire, walking, revolving, his hand on his hip, the hat pulled low. His face was gentle and gaunt. He would get sicker. Jancy touched her eyes, her mouth. A resignation welled up like tears. He was there and then he was made of moving lines as water flew into the glass. The water stopped slowly.

Jancy got out of the car and they stood looking up at a sky toned the coral of flesh.

It's a long way, he said. You'll get there while it's light?

Yes, Jancy said. Don't worry.

The car sat dripping and poised.

It looks good, Jancy said. I'm taking off in style.

She got in and rolled the window down. Her father came close.

Turn the motor on, he said, then nodded, satisfied at the growl of the engine. Above them the buckeye spread out green and heavy.

When are the buckeyes ripe? Jancy asked.

Not till August.

Can you eat them?

Nope, her father laughed. Buckeyes don't do a thing, don't have a use in the world.

He bent down and kissed her.

Take your time, he said. Go easy.

She drove fast the first few hours. The sun looked like the moon, dim, layered over. Morning fog burned off slowly. Maryland mountains were thick and dipped in pockets of fog. Woods stretched on both sides of the road. Sometimes from an overpass Jancy saw straggled neon lights still burning in a small town. No cars on the highway; she was alone, she ate up the empty ribbon of the road.

She drove up over a rise and suddenly, looming out of the mist, the deer was there. She saw the sexual lines of its head and long neck. It moved into her, lifted like a flying horse. She swerved. The arching body hit the fender with a final thud and bounced again, hard, into the side of the car. Jancy looked through the rearview mirror and saw the splayed form skidding back along the berm of the road, bouncing twice in slow motion, twirling and stopping.

The road seemed to close like a tunnel. The look of the deer's head, the beginning arch of the body, was all around Jancy. She seemed to see through the image into the tunneling road. She heard, close to her ear, the soft whuff of the large head bent over grass, tearing the long grass with its teeth.

She pulled off the road. I should go back and see what I've done, she thought. She turned the motor off. She felt she was still moving, and the road shifted into three levels. Wet grass of the road banks was lush. The road shimmered; one plane of it tilted and moved sideways into the other. Jancy gripped the vinyl seat of the car. She was sinking. The door wouldn't open and she slid across to get out the other side. She stood up in the cool air and there was total silence. Jancy tried to walk. The earth and the asphalt were spongy. She moved around the car and saw first the moonish curve of the dented fender. The door was crumpled where the deer had bounced back and slammed into her. Jancy imagined its flanks, the hard mounds of its rump. The sheen of it. She staggered and stepped back. The sudden cushion of the grass surprised her and she fell. She saw then the sweep of short hairs glistening along the length of the car. The door handle was packed and smeared with golden feces.

There was really nowhere to go.

Once it was Christmas Day. They were driving from home, from the house her father had built in the country. A deer jumped the road in front of them, clearing the snow, the pavement, the fences of the fields, in two bounds. Beyond its arc the hills rumpled in snow. The narrow

road wound through white meadows, across the creek, and on. Her
father was driving. Her brothers had shining play pistols with leather
holsters. Her mother wore clip-on earrings of tiny wreaths. They were
all dressed in new clothes, and they moved down the road through the
trees.

David Quammen

Walking Out

As the train rocked dead at Livingston he saw the man, in a worn khaki shirt with button flaps buttoned, arms crossed. The boy's hand sprang up by reflex, and his face broke into a smile. The man smiled back gravely, and nodded. He did not otherwise move. The boy turned from the window and, with the awesome deliberateness of a fat child harboring reluctance, began struggling to pull down his bag. His father would wait on the platform. First sight of him had reminded the boy that nothing was simple enough now for hurrying.

They drove in the old open Willys toward the cabin beyond town. The windshield of the Willys was up, but the fine cold sharp rain came into their faces, and the boy could not raise his eyes to look at the road. He wore a rain parka his father had handed him at the station. The man, protected by only the khaki, held his lips strung in a firm silent line that seemed more grin than wince. Riding through town in the cold rain, open topped and jaunty, getting drenched as though by necessity, was —the boy understood vaguely—somehow in the spirit of this season.

"We have a moose tag," his father shouted.

The boy said nothing. He refused to care what it meant, that they had a moose tag.

"I've got one picked out. A bull. I've stalked him for two weeks. Up in the Crazies. When we get to the cabin, we'll build a good roaring fire." With only the charade of a pause, he added, "Your mother." It was said like a question. The boy waited. "How is she?"

"All right, I guess." Over the jeep's howl, with the wind stealing his voice, the boy too had to shout.

"Are you friends with her?"

"I guess so."

"Is she still a beautiful lady?"

"I don't know. I guess so. I don't know that."

"You must know that. Is she starting to get wrinkled like me? Does she seem worried and sad? Or is she just still a fine beautiful lady? You must know that."

"She's still a beautiful lady, I guess."

"Did she tell you any messages for me?"

"She said . . . she said I should give you her love," the boy lied, impulsively and clumsily. He was at once embarrassed that he had done it.

"Oh," his father said. "Thank you, David."

They reached the cabin on a mile of dirt road winding through meadow to a spruce grove. Inside, the boy was enwrapped in the strong syncretic smell of all seasonal mountain cabins: pine resin and insect repellent and a mustiness suggesting damp bathing trunks stored in a drawer. There were yellow pine floors and rope-work throw rugs and a bead curtain to the bedroom and a cast-iron cook stove with none of the lids or handles missing and a pump in the kitchen sink and old issues of *Field and Stream,* and on the mantel above where a fire now finally burned was a picture of the boy's grandfather, the railroad telegrapher, who had once owned the cabin. The boy's father cooked a dinner of fried ham, and though the boy did not like ham he had expected his father to cook canned stew or Spam, so he said nothing. His father asked him about school and the boy talked and his father seemed to be interested. Warm and dry, the boy began to feel safe from his own anguish. Then his father said:

"We'll leave tomorrow around ten."

Last year on the boy's visit they had hunted birds. They had lived in the cabin for six nights, and each day they had hunted pheasant in the wheat stubble, or blue grouse in the woods, or ducks along the irrigation slews. The boy had been wet and cold and miserable at times, but each evening they returned to the cabin and to the boy's suitcase of dry clothes. They had eaten hot food cooked on a stove, and had smelled the cabin smell, and had slept together in a bed. In six days of hunting, the boy had not managed to kill a single bird. Yet last year he had known that, at least once a day, he would be comfortable, if not happy. This year his father planned that he should not even be comfortable. He had said in his last letter to Evergreen Park, before the boy left Chicago but when it was too late for him not to leave, that he would take the boy camping in the mountains, after big game. He had pretended to believe that the boy would be glad.

The Willys was loaded and moving by ten minutes to ten. For three hours they drove, through Big Timber, and then north on the highway, and then back west again on a logging road that took them winding and bouncing higher into the mountains. Thick cottony streaks of white cloud hung in among the mountaintop trees, light and dense dollops against the bulking sharp dark olive, as though in a black-and-white photograph. They followed the gravel road for an hour, and the boy thought they would soon have a flat tire or break an axle. If they had a flat, the boy knew, his father would only change it and drive on until they had the second, farther from the highway. Finally they crossed a creek and his father plunged the Willys off into a bed of weeds.

His father said, "Here."

The boy said, "Where?"

"Up that little drainage. At the head of the creek."

"How far is it?"

"Two or three miles."

"Is that where you saw the moose?"

"No. That's where I saw the sheepman's hut. The moose is farther. On top."

"Are we going to sleep in a hut? I thought we were going to sleep in a tent."

"No. Why should we carry a tent up there when we have a perfectly good hut?"

The boy couldn't answer that question. He thought now that this might be the time when he would cry. He had known it was coming.

"I don't much want to sleep in a hut," he said, and his voice broke with the simple honesty of it, and his eyes glazed. He held his mouth tight against the trembling.

As though something had broken in him too, the boy's father laid his forehead down on the steering wheel, against his knuckles. For a moment he remained bowed, breathing exhaustedly. But he looked up again before speaking.

"Well, we don't have to, David."

The boy said nothing.

"It's an old sheepman's hut made of logs, and it's near where we're going to hunt and we can fix it dry and good. I thought you might like that. I thought it might be more fun than a tent. But we don't have to do it. We can drive back to Big Timber and buy a tent, or we can drive back to the cabin and hunt birds, like last year. Whatever you want to do. You have to forgive me the kind of ideas I get. I hope you will. We don't have to do anything that you don't want to do."

"No," the boy said. "I want to."

"Are you sure?"

"No," the boy said. "But I just want to."

They bushwhacked along the creek, treading a thick soft mixture of moss and humus and needles, climbing upward through brush. Then the brush thinned and they were ascending an open creek bottom, thirty yards wide, darkened by fir and cedar. Farther, and they struck a trail, which led them upward along the creek. Farther still, and the trail received a branch, then another, then forked.

"Who made this trail? Did the sheepman?"

"No," his father said. "Deer and elk."

Gradually the creek's little canyon narrowed, steep wooded shoulders funneling closer on each side. For a while the game trails forked and converged like a maze, but soon again there were only two branches, and finally one, heavily worn. It dodged through alder and willow, skirting tangles of browned raspberry, so that the boy and his father could never see more than twenty feet ahead. When they stopped to rest, the boy's father unstrapped the .270 from his pack and loaded it.

"We have to be careful now," he explained. "We may surprise a bear."

Under the cedars, the creek bottom held a cool dampness that seemed to be stored from one winter to the next. The boy began at once to feel chilled. He put on his jacket, and they continued climbing. Soon he was sweating again in the cold.

On a small flat where the alder drew back from the creek, the hut was built into one bank of the canyon, with the sod of the hillside lapping out over its roof. The door was a low dark opening. Forty or fifty years ago, the boy's father explained, this hut had been built and used by a Basque shepherd. At that time there had been many Basques in Montana, and they had run sheep all across this ridge of the Crazies. His father forgot to explain what a Basque was, and the boy didn't remind him.

They built a fire. His father had brought sirloin steaks and an onion for dinner, and the boy was happy with him about that. As they ate, it grew dark, but the boy and his father had stocked a large comforting pile of naked deadfall. In the darkness, by firelight, his father made chocolate pudding. The pudding had been his father's surprise. The boy sat on a piece of canvas and added logs to the fire while his father drank coffee. Sparks rose on the heat and the boy watched them climb toward the cedar limbs and the black pools of sky. The pudding did not set.

"Do you remember your grandfather, David?"

"Yes," the boy said, and wished it were true. He remembered a funeral when he was three.

"Your grandfather brought me up on this mountain when I was seventeen. That was the last year he hunted." The boy knew what sort of thoughts his father was having. But he knew also that his own home was in Evergreen Park, and that he was another man's boy now, with another man's name, though this indeed was his father. "Your grandfather was fifty years older than me."

The boy said nothing.

"And I'm thirty-four years older than you."

"And I'm only eleven," the boy cautioned him.

"Yes," said his father. "And someday you'll have a son and you'll be forty years older than him, and you'll want so badly for him to know who you are that you could cry."

The boy was embarrassed.

"And that's called the cycle of life's infinite wisdom," his father said, and laughed at himself unpleasantly.

"What did he die of?" the boy asked, desperate to escape the focus of his father's rumination.

"He was eighty-seven then. Christ. He was tired." The boy's father went silent. Then he shook his head, and poured himself the remaining coffee.

Through that night the boy was never quite warm. He slept on his side with his knees drawn up, and this was uncomfortable but his body seemed to demand it for warmth. The hard cold mountain earth pressed upward through the mat of fir boughs his father had laid, and drew heat from the boy's body like a pallet of leeches. He clutched the bedroll around his neck and folded the empty part at the bottom back under his legs. Once he woke to a noise. Though his father was sleeping between him and the door of the hut, for a while the boy lay awake, listening worriedly, and then woke again on his back to realize time had passed. He heard droplets begin to hit the canvas his father had spread over the sod roof of the hut. But he remained dry.

He rose to the smell of a fire. The tarp was rigid with sleet and frost. The firewood and the knapsacks were frosted. It was that gray time of dawn before any blue and, through the branches above, the boy was unable to tell whether the sky was murky or clear. Delicate sheet ice hung on everything, but there was no wetness. The rain seemed to have been hushed by the cold.

"What time is it?"

"Early yet."

"How early?" The boy was thinking about the cold at home as he waited outside on 96th Street for his school bus. That was the cruelest moment of his day, but it seemed a benign and familiar part of him compared to this.

"Early. I don't have a watch. What difference does it make, David?"

"Not any."

After breakfast they began walking up the valley. His father had the .270, and the boy carried an old Winchester .30–30, with open sights. The walking was not hard, and with this gentle exercise in the cold morning the boy soon felt fresh and fine. Now I'm hunting for moose with my father, he told himself. That's just what I'm doing. Few boys in Evergreen Park had ever been moose hunting with their fathers in Montana, he knew. I'm doing it now, the boy told himself.

Reaching the lip of a high meadow, a mile above the shepherd's hut, they had not seen so much as a magpie.

Before them, across hundreds of yards, opened a smooth lake of tall lifeless grass, browned by September drought and killed by the frosts and beginning to rot with November's rain. The creek was here a deep quiet channel of smooth curves overhung by the grass, with a dark surface like heavy oil. When they had come fifty yards into the meadow, his father turned and pointed out to the boy a large ponderosa pine with a forked crown that marked the head of their creek valley. He showed the boy a small aspen grove midway across the meadow, toward which they were aligning themselves.

"Near the far woods is a beaver pond. The moose waters there. We can wait in the aspens and watch the whole meadow without being seen. If he doesn't come, we'll go up another canyon, and check again on the way back."

For an hour, and another, they waited. The boy sat with his hands in his jacket pockets, bunching the jacket tighter around him, and his buttocks drew cold moisture from the ground. His father squatted on his heels like a country man, rising periodically to inspect the meadow in all directions. Finally he stood up; he fixed his stare on the distant fringe of woods and, like a retriever, did not move. He said, "David."

The boy stood beside him. His father placed a hand on the boy's shoulder. The boy saw a large dark form rolling toward them like a great slug in the grass.

"Is it the moose?"

"No," said his father. "That is a grizzly bear, David. An old male grizzly."

The boy was impressed. He sensed an aura of power and terror and authority about the husky shape, even at two hundred yards.

"Are we going to shoot him?"

"No."

"Why not?"

"We don't have a permit," his father whispered. "And because we don't want to."

The bear plowed on toward the beaver pond for a while, then stopped. It froze in the grass and seemed to be listening. The boy's father added: "That's not hunting for the meat. That's hunting for the fear. I don't need the fear. I've got enough in my life already."

The bear turned and moiled off quickly through the grass. It disappeared back into the far woods.

"He heard us."

"Maybe," the boy's father said. "Let's go have a look at that beaver pond."

A sleek furred carcass lay low in the water, swollen grotesquely with putrescence and coated with glistening blowflies. Four days, the boy's father guessed. The moose had been shot at least eighteen times with a .22 pistol. One of its eyes had been shot out; it had been shot twice in the jaw; and both quarters on the side that lay upward were ruined with shots. Standing up to his knees in the sump, the boy's father took the trouble of counting the holes, and probing one of the slugs out with his knife. That only made him angrier. He flung the lead away.

For the next three hours, with his father withdrawn into a solitary and characteristic bitterness, the boy felt abandoned. He did not understand why a moose would be slaughtered with a light pistol and left to rot. His father did not bother to explain; like the bear, he seemed to understand it as well as he needed to. They walked on, but they did not really hunt.

They left the meadow for more pine, and now tamarack, naked tamarack, the yellow needles nearly all down and going ginger where they coated the trail. The boy and his father hiked along a level path into another canyon, this one vast at the mouth and narrowing between high ridges of bare rock. They crossed and recrossed the shepherd's creek, which in this canyon was a tumbling free-stone brook. Following five yards behind his father, watching the cold, unapproachable rage that shaped the line of the man's shoulders, the boy was miserably uneasy because his father had grown so distant and quiet. They climbed over deadfalls blocking the trail, skirted one boulder large as a cabin, and blundered into a garden of nettles that stung them fiercely through their trousers. They saw fresh elk scat, and they saw bear, diarrhetic with late berries. The boy's father eventually grew bored with brooding, and showed the boy how to stalk. Before dusk that day they had shot an elk.

An open and gently sloped hillside, almost a meadow, ran for a quarter mile in quaking aspen, none over fifteen feet tall. The elk was above. The boy's father had the boy brace his gun in the notch of an aspen and take the first shot. The boy missed. The elk reeled and bolted down and his father killed it before it made cover. It was a five-point bull. They dressed the elk out and dragged it down to the cover of large pines, near the stream, where they would quarter it tomorrow, and then they returned under twilight to the hut.

That night even the fetal position could not keep the boy warm. He shivered wakefully for hours. He was glad that the following day, though full of walking and butchery and oppressive burdens, would be their last in the woods. He heard nothing. When he woke, through the door of the hut he saw whiteness like bone.

Six inches had fallen, and it was still snowing. The boy stood about in the campsite, amazed. When it snowed three inches in Evergreen Park, the boy would wake before dawn to the hiss of sand trucks and the ratchet of chains. Here there had been no warning. The boy was not much colder than he had been yesterday, and the transformation of the woods seemed mysterious and benign and somehow comic. He thought of Christmas. Then his father barked at him.

His father's mood had also changed, but in a different way; he seemed serious and hurried. As he wiped the breakfast pots clean with snow, he gave the boy orders for other chores. They left camp with two empty pack frames, both rifles, and a handsaw and rope. The boy soon understood why his father felt pressure of time: it took them an hour to climb the mile to the meadow. The snow continued. They did not rest until they reached the aspens.

"I had half a mind at breakfast to let the bull lie and pack us straight down out of here," his father admitted. "Probably smarter and less trouble in the long run. I could have come back on snowshoes next week. But by then it might be three feet deep and starting to drift. We can get two quarters out today. That will make it easier for me later." The boy was surprised by two things: that his father would be so wary in the face of a gentle snowfall and that he himself would have felt disappointed to be taken out of the woods that morning. The air of the meadow teemed with white.

"If it stops soon, we're fine," said his father.

It continued.

The path up the far canyon was hard climbing in eight inches of snow. The boy fell once, filling his collar and sleeves, and the gun-sight put a small gouge in his chin. But he was not discouraged. That night they would be warm and dry at the cabin. A half mile on and he came up beside his father, who had stopped to stare down at dark splashes of blood.

Heavy tracks and a dragging belly mark led up to the scramble of deepening red, and away. The tracks were nine inches long and showed claws. The boy's father knelt. As the boy watched, one shining maroon splotch the size of a saucer sank slowly beyond sight into the snow. The blood was warm.

Inspecting the tracks carefully, his father said, "She's got a cub with her."

"What happened?"

"Just a kill. Seems to have been a bird. That's too much blood for a grouse, but I don't see signs of any four-footed creature. Maybe a turkey." He frowned thoughtfully. "A turkey without feathers. I don't know. What I dislike is coming up on her with a cub." He drove a round into the chamber of the .270.

Trailing red smears, the tracks preceded them. Within fifty feet they found the body. It was half-buried. The top of its head had been shorn away, and the cub's brains had been licked out.

His father said "Christ," and plunged off the trail. He snapped at the boy to follow closely.

They made a wide crescent through brush and struck back after a quarter mile. His father slogged ahead in the snow, stopping often to stand holding his gun ready and glancing around while the boy caught up and passed him. The boy was confused. He knew his father was worried, but he did not feel any danger himself. They met the trail again, and went on to the aspen hillside before his father allowed them to rest. The boy spat on the snow. His lungs ached badly.

"Why did she do that?"

"She didn't. Another bear got her cub. A male. Maybe the one we saw yesterday. Then she fought him for the body, and she won. We didn't miss them by much. She may even have been watching. Nothing could put her in a worse frame of mind."

He added: "If we so much as see her, I want you to pick the nearest big tree and start climbing. Don't stop till you're twenty feet off the ground. I'll stay down and decide whether we have to shoot her. Is your rifle cocked?"

"No."

"Cock it, and put on the safety. She may be a black bear and black bears can climb. If she comes up after you, lean down and stick your gun in her mouth and fire. You can't miss."

He cocked the Winchester, as his father had said.

They angled downhill to the stream, and on to the mound of their dead elk. Snow filtered down steadily in purposeful silence. The boy was thirsty. It could not be much below freezing, he was aware, because with the exercise his bare hands were comfortable, even sweating between the fingers.

"Can I get a drink?"

"Yes. Be careful you don't wet your feet. And don't wander anywhere. We're going to get this done quickly."

He walked the few yards, ducked through the brush at streamside, and knelt in the snow to drink. The water was painful to his sinuses and bitterly cold on his hands. Standing again, he noticed an animal body ahead near the stream bank. For a moment he felt sure it was another dead cub. During that moment his father called:

"David! Get up here right now!"

The boy meant to call back. First he stepped closer to turn the cub with his foot. The touch brought it alive. It rose suddenly with a high squealing growl and whirled its head like a snake and snapped. The boy shrieked. The cub had his right hand in its jaws. It would not release.

It thrashed senselessly, working its teeth deeper and tearing flesh with each movement. The boy felt no pain. He knew his hand was being damaged and that realization terrified him and he was desperate to get the hand back before it was ruined. But he was helpless. He sensed the same curious terror racking the cub that he felt in himself, and he screamed at the cub almost reasoningly to let him go. His screams scared the cub more. Its head snatched back and forth. The boy did not think to shout for his father. He did not see him or hear him coming.

His father moved at full stride in a slowed laboring run through the snow, saying nothing and holding the rifle he did not use, crossed the last six feet still gathering speed, and brought his right boot up into the cub's belly. That kick seemed to lift the cub clear of the snow. It opened its jaws to another shrill piggish squeal, and the boy felt dull relief on his hand, as though his father had pressed open the blades of a spring trap with his foot. The cub tumbled once and disappeared over the stream bank, then surfaced downstream, squalling and paddling. The boy looked at his hand and was horrified. He still had no pain, but the hand was unrecognizable. His fingers had been peeled down through the palm like flaps on a banana. Glands at the sides of his jaw threatened that he would vomit, and he might have stood stupidly watching the hand bleed if his father had not grabbed him.

He snatched the boy by the arm and dragged him toward a tree without even looking at the boy's hand. The boy jerked back in angry resistance as though he had been struck. He screamed at his father. He screamed that his hand was cut, believing his father did not know, and as he screamed he began to cry. He began to feel hot throbbing pain. He began to worry about the blood he was losing. He could imagine his blood melting red holes in the snow behind him and he did not want to look. He did not want to do anything until he had taken care of his hand. At that instant he hated his father. But his father was stronger. He all but carried the boy to a tree.

He lifted the boy. In a voice that was quiet and hurried and very unlike the harsh grip with which he had taken the boy's arm, he said:

"Grab hold and climb up a few branches as best you can. Sit on a limb and hold tight and clamp the hand under your other armpit, if you can do that. I'll be right back to you. Hold tight because you're going to get dizzy." The boy groped desperately for a branch. His father supported him from beneath, and waited. The boy clambered. His feet scraped at the trunk. Then he was in the tree. Bark flakes and resin were stuck to the raw naked meat of his right hand. His father said:

"Now here, take this. Hurry."

The boy never knew whether his father himself had been frightened enough to forget for that moment about the boy's hand, or whether his father was still thinking quite clearly. His father may have expected that much. By the merciless clarity of his own standards, he may have expected that the boy should be able to hold on to a tree, and a wound, and a rifle, all with one hand. He extended the stock of the Winchester toward the boy.

The boy wanted to say something, but his tears and his fright would not let him gather a breath. He shuddered, and could not speak. "David," his father urged. The boy reached for the stock and faltered and clutched at the trunk with his good arm. He was crying and gasping, and he wanted to speak. He was afraid he would fall out of the tree. He released his grip once again, and felt himself tip. His father extended the gun higher, holding the barrel. The boy swung out his injured hand, spraying his father's face with blood. He reached and he tried to close torn dangling fingers around the stock and he pulled the trigger.

The bullet entered low on his father's thigh and shattered the knee and traveled down the shin bone and into the ground through his father's heel.

His father fell, and the rifle fell with him. He lay in the snow without moving. The boy thought he was dead. Then the boy saw him grope for the rifle. He found it and rolled onto his stomach, taking aim at the sow grizzly. Forty feet up the hill, towering on hind legs, she canted her head to one side, indecisive. When the cub pulled itself up a snowbank from the stream, she coughed at it sternly. The cub trotted straight to her with its head low. She knocked it off its feet with a huge paw, and it yelped. Then she turned quickly. The cub followed.

The woods were silent. The gunshot still echoed awesomely back to the boy but it was an echo of memory, not sound. He felt nothing. He saw his father's body stretched on the snow and he did not really believe he was where he was. He did not want to move: he wanted to wake. He sat in the tree and waited. The snow fell as gracefully as before.

His father rolled onto his back. The boy saw him raise himself to a sitting position and look down at the leg and betray no expression, and then slump back. He blinked slowly and lifted his eyes to meet the boy's eyes. The boy waited. He expected his father to speak. He expected his father to say *Shinny down using your elbows and knees and get the first-aid kit and boil water and phone the doctor. The number is taped to the dial.* His father stared. The boy could see the flicker of thoughts behind his father's eyes. His father said nothing. He raised his arms slowly and crossed them over his face, as though to nap in the sun.

The boy jumped. He landed hard on his feet and fell onto his back. He stood over his father. His hand dripped quietly onto the snow. He was afraid that his father was deciding to die. He wanted to beg him to reconsider. The boy had never before seen his father hopeless. He was afraid.

But he was no longer afraid of his father.

Then his father uncovered his face and said, "Let me see it."

They bandaged the boy's hand with a sleeve cut from the other arm of his shirt. His father wrapped the hand firmly and split the sleeve end with his deer knife and tied it neatly in two places. The boy now felt searing pain in his torn palm, and his stomach lifted when he thought of the damage, but at least he did not have to look at it. Quickly the plaid flannel bandage began to soak through maroon. They cut a sleeve from his father's shirt to tie over the wound in his thigh. They raised the trouser leg to see the long swelling bruise down the calf where he was hemorrhaging into the bullet's tunnel. Only then did his father realize that he was bleeding also from the heel. The boy took off his father's boot and placed a half-clean handkerchief on the insole where the bullet had exited, as his father instructed him. Then his father laced the boot on again tightly. The boy helped his father to stand. His father tried a step, then collapsed in the snow with a blasphemous howl of pain. They had not known that the knee was shattered.

The boy watched his father's chest heave with the forced sighs of suffocating frustration, and heard the air wheeze through his nostrils. His father relaxed himself with the breathing, and seemed to be thinking. He said,

"You can find your way back to the hut."

The boy held his own breath and did not move.

"You can, can't you?"

"But I'm not. I'm not going alone. I'm only going with you."

"All right, David, listen carefully," his father said. "We don't have to worry about freezing. I'm not worried about either of us freezing to death. No one is going to freeze in the woods in November, if he looks after himself. Not even in Montana. It just isn't that cold. I have matches and I have a fresh elk. And I don't think this weather is going to get any worse. It may be raining again by morning. What I'm concerned about is the bleeding. If I spend too much time and effort trying to walk out of here, I could bleed to death.

"I think your hand is going to be all right. It's a bad wound, but the doctors will be able to fix it as good as new. I can see that. I promise you that. You'll be bleeding some too, but if you take care of that hand it won't bleed any more walking than if you were standing still. Then you'll be at the doctor's tonight. But if I try to walk out on this leg it's going to bleed and keep bleeding and I'll lose too much blood. So I'm staying here and bundling up warm and you're walking out to get help. I'm sorry about this. It's what we have to do.

"You can't possibly get lost. You'll just follow this trail straight down the canyon the way we came up, and then you'll come to the meadow. Point yourself toward the big pine tree with the forked crown. When you get to that tree you'll find the creek again. You may not be able to see it, but make yourself quiet and listen for it. You'll hear it. Follow that down off the mountain and past the hut till you get to the jeep."

He struggled a hand into his pocket. "You've never driven a car, have you?"

The boy's lips were pinched. Muscles in his cheeks ached from clenching his jaws. He shook his head.

"You can do it. It isn't difficult." His father held up a single key and began telling the boy how to start the jeep, how to work the clutch, how to find reverse and then first and then second. As his father described the positions on the floor shift the boy raised his swaddled right hand. His father stopped. He rubbed at his eye sockets, like a man waking.

"Of course," he said. "All right. You'll have to help me."

Using the saw with his left hand, the boy cut a small forked aspen. His father showed the boy where to trim it so that the fork would reach just to his armpit. Then they lifted him to his feet. But the crutch was useless on a steep hillside of deep grass and snow. His father leaned over the boy's shoulders and they fought the slope for an hour.

When the boy stepped in a hole and they fell, his father made no exclamation of pain. The boy wondered whether his father's knee hurt as badly as his own hand. He suspected it hurt worse. He said nothing about his hand, though several times in their climb it was twisted or crushed. They reached the trail. The snow had not stopped, and their tracks were veiled. His father said:

"We need one of the guns. I forgot. It's my fault. But you'll have to go back down and get it."

The boy could not find the tree against which his father said he had leaned the .270, so he went toward the stream and looked for blood. He saw none. The imprint of his father's body was already softened beneath an inch of fresh silence. He scooped his good hand through the snowy depression and was startled by cool slimy blood, smearing his fingers like phlegm. Nearby he found the Winchester.

"The lucky one," his father said. "That's all right. Here." He snapped open the breach and a shell flew and he caught it in the air. He glanced dourly at the casing, then cast it aside in the snow. He held the gun out for the boy to see, and with his thumb let the hammer down one notch.

"Remember?" he said. "The safety."

The boy knew he was supposed to feel great shame, but he felt little. His father could no longer hurt him as he once could, because the boy was coming to understand him. His father could not help himself. He did not want the boy to feel contemptible, but he needed him to, because of the loneliness and the bitterness and the boy's mother; and he could not help himself.

After another hour they had barely traversed the aspen hillside. Pushing the crutch away in angry frustration, his father sat in the snow. The boy did not know whether he was thinking carefully of how they might get him out, or still laboring with the choice against despair. The light had wilted to something more like moonlight than afternoon. The sweep of snow had gone gray, depthless, flat, and the sky warned sullenly of night. The boy grew restless. Then it was decided. His father hung himself piggyback over the boy's shoulders, holding the rifle. The boy supported him with elbows crooked under his father's knees. The boy was tall for eleven years old, and heavy. The boy's father weighed 164 pounds.

The boy walked.

He moved as slowly as drifting snow: a step, then time, then another step. The burden at first seemed to him overwhelming. He did not think he would be able to carry his father far.

He took the first few paces expecting to fall. He did not fall, so he kept walking. His arms and shoulders were not exhausted as quickly as he had thought they would be, so he kept walking. Shuffling ahead in the deep powder was like carrying one end of an oak bureau up stairs. But for a surprisingly long time the burden did not grow any worse. He found balance. He found rhythm. He was moving.

Dark blurred the woods, but the snow was luminous. He could see the trail well. He walked.

"How are you, David? How are you holding up?"

"All right."

"We'll stop for a while and let you rest. You can set me down here." The boy kept walking. He moved so ponderously, it seemed after each step that he had stopped. But he kept walking.

"You can set me down. Don't you want to rest?"

The boy did not answer. He wished that his father would not make him talk. At the start he had gulped for air. Now he was breathing low and regularly. He was watching his thighs slice through the snow. He did not want to be disturbed. After a moment he said, "No."

He walked. He came to the cub, shrouded beneath new snow, and he did not see it, and fell over it. His face was smashed deep into the snow by his father's weight. He could not move. But he could breathe. He rested. When he felt his father's thigh roll across his right hand, he remembered the wound. He was lucky his arms had been pinned to his sides, or the hand might have taken the force of their fall. As he waited for his father to roll himself clear, the boy noticed the change in temperature. His sweat chilled him quickly. He began shivering.

His father had again fallen in silence. The boy knew that he would not call out or even mention the pain in his leg. The boy realized that he did not want to mention his hand. The blood soaking the outside of his flannel bandage had grown sticky. He did not want to think of the alien tangle of flesh and tendons and bones wrapped inside. There was pain, but he kept the pain at a distance. It was not *his* hand anymore. He was not counting on ever having it back. If he was resolved about that, then the pain was not his either. It was merely pain of which he was aware. His good hand was numb.

"We'll rest now."

"I'm not tired," the boy said. "I'm just getting cold."

"We'll rest," said his father. "I'm tired."

Under his father's knee, the boy noticed, was a cavity in the snow, already melted away by fresh blood. The dark flannel around his father's thigh did not appear sticky. It gleamed.

His father instructed the boy how to open the cub with the deer knife. His father stood on one leg against a deadfall, holding the Winchester ready, and glanced around on all sides as he spoke. The boy used his left hand and both his knees. He punctured the cub low in the belly, to a soft squirting sound, and sliced upward easily. He did not gut the cub. He merely cut out a large square of belly meat. He handed it to his father, in exchange for the rifle.

His father peeled off the hide and left the fat. He sawed the meat in half. One piece he rolled up and put in his jacket pocket. The other he divided again. He gave the boy a square thick with glistening raw fat.

"Eat it. The fat too. Especially the fat. We'll cook the rest farther on. I don't want to build a fire here and taunt Momma."

The meat was chewy. The boy did not find it disgusting. He was hungry.

His father sat back on the ground and unlaced the boot from his good foot. Before the boy understood what he was doing, he had relaced the boot. He was holding a damp wool sock.

"Give me your left hand." The boy held out his good hand, and his father pulled the sock down over it. "It's getting a lot colder. And we need that hand."

"What about yours? We need your hands too. I'll give you my—"

"No, you won't. We need your feet more than anything. It's all right. I'll put mine inside your shirt."

He lifted his father, and they went on. The boy walked.

He moved steadily through cold darkness. Soon he was sweating again, down his ribs and inside his boots. Only his hands and ears felt as though crushed in a cold metal vise. But his father was shuddering. The boy stopped.

His father did not put down his legs. The boy stood on the trail and waited. Slowly he released his wrist holds. His father's thighs slumped. The boy was careful about the wounded leg. His father's grip over the boy's neck did not loosen. His fingers were cold against the boy's bare skin.

"Are we at the hut?"

"No. We're not even to the meadow."

"Why did you stop?" his father asked.

"It's so cold. You're shivering. Can we build a fire?"

"Yes," his father said hazily. "We'll rest. What time is it?"

"We don't know," the boy said. "We don't have a watch."

The boy gathered small deadwood. His father used the Winchester stock to scoop snow away from a boulder, and they placed the fire at the boulder's base. His father broke up pine twigs and fumbled dry toilet paper from his breast pocket and arranged the wood, but by then his fingers were shaking too badly to strike a match. The boy lit the fire. The boy stamped down the snow, as his father instructed, to make a small ovenlike recess before the fire boulder. He cut fir boughs to floor the recess. He added more deadwood. Beyond the invisible clouds there seemed to be part of a moon.

"It stopped snowing," the boy said.

"Why?"

The boy did not speak. His father's voice had sounded unnatural. After a moment his father said:

"Yes, indeed. It stopped."

They roasted pieces of cub meat skewered on a green stick. Dripping fat made the fire spatter and flare. The meat was scorched on the outside and raw within. It tasted as good as any meat the boy had ever eaten. They burned their palates on hot fat. The second stick smoldered through before they had noticed, and that batch of meat fell in the fire. The boy's father cursed once and reached into the flame for it and dropped it and clawed it out, and then put his hand in the snow. He did not look at the blistered fingers. They ate. The boy saw that both his father's hands had gone clumsy and almost useless.

The boy went for more wood. He found a bleached deadfall not far off the trail, but with one arm he could only break up and carry small loads. They lay down in the recess together like spoons, the boy nearer the fire. They pulled fir boughs into place above them, resting across the snow. They pressed close together. The boy's father was shivering spastically now, and he clenched the boy in a fierce hug. The boy put his father's hands back inside his own shirt. The boy slept. He woke when the fire faded and added more wood and slept. He woke again and tended the fire and changed places with his father and slept. He slept less soundly with his father between him and the fire. He woke again when his father began to vomit.

The boy was terrified. His father wrenched with sudden vomiting that brought up cub meat and yellow liquid and blood and sprayed them across the snow by the grayish-red glow of the fire and emptied his stomach dry and then would not release him. He heaved on pathetically. The boy pleaded to be told what was wrong. His father could not or would not answer. The spasms seized him at the stomach and twisted the rest of his body taut in ugly jerks. Between the attacks he breathed with a wet rumbling sound deep in his chest, and did not speak. When the vomiting subsided, his breathing stretched itself out into long bubbling sighs, then shallow gasps, then more liquidy sighs. His breath caught and froth rose in his throat and into his mouth and he gagged on it and began vomiting again. The boy thought his father would choke. He knelt beside him and held him and cried. He could not see his father's face well and he did not want to look closely while the sounds that were coming from inside his father's body seemed so unhuman. The boy had never been more frightened. He wept for himself, and for his father. He knew from the noises and movements that his father must die. He did not think his father could ever be human again.

When his father was quiet, he went for more wood. He broke limbs from the deadfall with fanatic persistence and brought them back in bundles and built the fire up bigger. He nestled his father close to it and held him from behind. He did not sleep, though he was not awake. He waited. Finally he opened his eyes on the beginnings of dawn. His father sat up and began to spit.

"One more load of wood and you keep me warm from behind and then we'll go."

The boy obeyed. He was surprised that his father could speak. He thought it strange now that his father was so concerned for himself and so little concerned for the boy. His father had not even asked how he was.

The boy lifted his father, and walked.

Sometime while dawn was completing itself, the snow had resumed. It did not filter down soundlessly. It came on a slight wind at the boy's back, blowing down the canyon. He felt as though he were tumbling forward with the snow into a long vertical shaft. He tumbled slowly. His father's body protected the boy's back from being chilled by the wind. They were both soaked through their clothes. His father was soon shuddering again.

The boy walked. Muscles down the back of his neck were sore from yesterday. His arms ached, and his shoulders and thighs, but his neck hurt him most. He bent his head forward against the weight and the pain, and he watched his legs surge through the snow. At his stomach he felt the dull ache of hunger, not as an appetite but as an affliction. He thought of the jeep. He walked.

He recognized the edge of the meadow but through the snow-laden wind he could not see the cluster of aspens. The snow became deeper where he left the wooded trail. The direction of the wind was now variable, sometimes driving snow into his face, sometimes whipping across him from the right. The grass and snow dragged at his thighs, and he moved by stumbling forward and then catching himself back. Twice he stepped into small overhung fingerlets of the stream, and fell violently, shocking the air from his lungs and once nearly spraining an ankle. Farther out into the meadow, he saw the aspens. They were a hundred yards off to his right. He did not turn directly toward them. He was afraid of crossing more hidden creeks on the intervening ground. He was not certain now whether the main channel was between him and the aspen grove or behind him to the left. He tried to project from the canyon trail to the aspens and on to the forked pine on the far side of the meadow, along what he remembered as almost a straight line. He pointed himself toward the far edge, where the pine should have been. He could not see a forked crown. He could not even see trees. He could see only a vague darker corona above the curve of white. He walked.

He passed the aspens and left them behind. He stopped several times with the wind rasping against him in the open meadow, and rested. He did not set his father down. His father was trembling uncontrollably. He had not spoken for a long time. The boy wanted badly to reach the far side of the meadow. His socks were soaked and his boots and cuffs were glazed with ice. The wind was chafing his face and making him dizzy. His thighs felt as if they had been bruised with a club. The boy wanted to give up and set his father down and whimper that this had gotten to be very unfair; and he wanted to reach the far trees. He did not doubt which he would do. He walked.

He saw trees. Raising his head painfully, he squinted against the rushing flakes. He did not see the forked crown. He went on, and stopped again, and craned his neck, and squinted. He scanned a wide angle of pines, back and forth. He did not see it. He turned his body and his burden to look back. The snow blew across the meadow and seemed, whichever way he turned, to be streaking into his face. He pinched his eyes tighter. He could still see the aspens. But he could not judge where the canyon trail met the meadow. He did not know from just where he had come. He looked again at the aspens, and then ahead to the pines. He considered the problem carefully. He was irritated that the forked ponderosa did not show itself yet, but not worried. He was forced to estimate. He estimated, and went on in that direction.

When he saw a forked pine it was far off to the left of his course. He turned and marched toward it gratefully. As he came nearer, he bent his head up to look. He stopped. The boy was not sure that this was the right tree. Nothing about it looked different, except the thick cakes of snow weighting its limbs, and nothing about it looked especially familiar. He had seen thousands of pine trees in the last few days. This was one like the others. It definitely had a forked crown. He entered the woods at its base.

He had vaguely expected to join a trail. There was no trail. After two hundred yards he was still picking his way among trees and deadfalls and brush. He remembered the shepherd's creek that fell off the lip of the meadow and led down the first canyon. He turned and retraced his tracks to the forked pine.

He looked for the creek. He did not see it anywhere near the tree. He made himself quiet, and listened. He heard nothing but wind, and his father's tremulous breathing.

"Where is the creek?"

His father did not respond. The boy bounced gently up and down, hoping to jar him alert.

"Where is the creek? I can't find it."

"What?"

"We crossed the meadow and I found the tree but I can't find the creek. I need you to help."

"The compass is in my pocket," his father said.

He lowered his father into the snow. He found the compass in his father's breast pocket, and opened the flap, and held it level. The boy noticed with a flinch that his right thigh was smeared with fresh blood. For an instant he thought he had a new wound. Then he realized that the blood was his father's. The compass needle quieted.

"What do I do?"

His father did not respond. The boy asked again. His father said nothing. He sat in the snow and shivered.

The boy left his father and made random arcs within sight of the forked tree until he found a creek. They followed it onward along the flat and then where it gradually began sloping away. The boy did not see what else he could do. He knew that this was the wrong creek. He hoped that it would flow into the shepherd's creek, or at least bring them out on the same road where they had left the jeep. He was very tired. He did not want to stop. He did not care anymore about being warm. He wanted only to reach the jeep, and to save his father's life.

He wondered whether his father would love him more generously for having done it. He wondered whether his father would ever forgive him for having done it.

If he failed, his father could never again make him feel shame, the boy thought naively. So he did not worry about failing. He did not worry about dying. His hand was not bleeding, and he felt strong. The creek swung off and down to the left. He followed it, knowing that he was lost. He did not want to reverse himself. He knew that turning back would make him feel confused and desperate and frightened. As long as he was following some pathway, walking, going down, he felt strong.

That afternoon he killed a grouse. He knocked it off a low branch with a heavy short stick that he threw like a boomerang. The grouse fell in the snow and floundered and the boy ran up and plunged on it. He felt it thrashing against his chest. He reached in and it nipped him and he caught it by the neck and squeezed and wrenched mercilessly until long after it stopped writhing. He cleaned it as he had seen his father clean grouse and built a small fire with matches from his father's breast pocket and seared the grouse on a stick. He fed his father. His father could not chew. The boy chewed mouthfuls of grouse, and took the chewed gobbets in his hand, and put them into his father's mouth. His father could swallow. His father could no longer speak.

The boy walked. He thought of his mother in Evergreen Park, and at once he felt queasy and weak. He thought of his mother's face and her voice as she was told that her son was lost in the woods in Montana with a damaged hand that would never be right, and with his father, who had been shot and was unconscious and dying. He pictured his mother receiving the news that her son might die himself, unless he could carry his father out of the woods and find his way to the jeep. He saw her face change. He heard her voice. The boy had to stop. He was crying. He could not control the shape of his mouth. He was not crying with true sorrow, as he had in the night when he held his father and thought his father would die; he was crying in sentimental self-pity. He sensed the difference. Still he cried.

He must not think of his mother, the boy realized. Thinking of her could only weaken him. If she knew where he was, what he had to do, she could only make it impossible for him to do it. He was lucky that she knew nothing, the boy thought.

No one knew what the boy was doing, or what he had yet to do. Even the boy's father no longer knew. The boy was lucky. No one was watching, no one knew, and he was free to be capable.

The boy imagined himself alone at his father's grave. The grave was open. His father's casket had already been lowered. The boy stood at the foot in his black Christmas suit, and his hands were crossed at his groin, and he was not crying. Men with shovels stood back from the grave, waiting for the boy's order for them to begin filling it. The boy felt a horrible swelling sense of joy. The men watched him, and he stared down into the hole. He knew it was a lie. If his father died, the boy's mother would rush out to Livingston and have him buried and stand at the grave in a black dress and veil squeezing the boy to her side like he was a child. There was nothing the boy could do about that. All the more reason he must keep walking.

Then she would tow the boy back with her to Evergreen Park. And he would be standing on 96th Street in the morning dark before his father's cold body had even begun to grow alien and decayed in the buried box. She would drag him back, and there would be nothing the boy could do. And he realized that if he returned with his mother after the burial, he would never again see the cabin outside Livingston. He would have no more summers and no more Novembers anywhere but in Evergreen Park.

The cabin now seemed to be at the center of the boy's life. It seemed to stand halfway between this snowbound creek valley and the train station in Chicago. It would be his cabin soon.

The boy knew nothing about his father's will, and he had never been told that legal ownership of the cabin was destined for him. Legal ownership did not matter. The cabin might be owned by his mother, or sold to pay for his father's debts, or taken away by the state, but it would still be the boy's cabin. It could only forever belong to him. His father had been telling him *Here, this is yours. Prepare to receive it.* The boy had sensed that much. But he had been threatened, and unwilling. The boy realized now that he might be resting warm in the cabin in a matter of hours, or he might never see it again. He could appreciate the justice of that. He walked.

He thought of his father as though his father were far away from him. He saw himself in the black suit at the grave, and he heard his father speak to him from aside: *That's good. Now raise your eyes and tell them in a man's voice to begin shoveling. Then turn away and walk slowly back down the hill. Be sure you don't cry. That's good.* The boy stopped. He felt his glands quiver, full of new tears. He knew that it was a lie. His father would never be there to congratulate him. His father would never know how well the boy had done.

He took deep breaths. He settled himself. Yes, his father would know somehow, the boy believed. His father had known all along. His father knew.

He built the recess just as they had the night before, except this time he found flat space between a stone back and a large fallen cottonwood trunk. He scooped out the snow, he laid boughs, and he made a fire against each reflector. At first the bed was quite warm. Then the melt from the fires began to run down and collect in the middle, forming a puddle of wet boughs under them. The boy got up and carved runnels across the packed snow to drain the fires. He went back to sleep and slept warm, holding his father. He rose again each half hour to feed the fires.

The snow stopped in the night, and did not resume. The woods seemed to grow quieter, settling, sighing beneath the new weight. What was going to come had come.

The boy grew tired of breaking deadwood and began walking again before dawn and walked for five more hours. He did not try to kill the grouse that he saw because he did not want to spend time cleaning and cooking it. He was hurrying now. He drank from the creek. At one point he found small black insects like winged ants crawling in great numbers across the snow near the creek. He stopped to pinch up and eat thirty or forty of them. They were tasteless. He did not bother to feed any to his father. He felt he had come a long way down the mountain. He thought he was reaching the level now where there might be roads. He followed the creek, which had received other branches and grown to a stream. The ground was flattening again and the drainage was widening, opening to daylight. As he carried his father, his head ached. He had stopped noticing most of his other pains. About noon of that day he came to the fence.

It startled him. He glanced around, his pulse drumming suddenly, preparing himself at once to see the long empty sweep of snow and broken fence posts and thinking of Basque shepherds fifty years gone. He saw the cabin and the smoke. He relaxed, trembling helplessly into laughter. He relaxed, and was unable to move. Then he cried, still laughing. He cried shamelessly with relief and dull joy and wonder, for as long as he wanted. He held his father, and cried. But he set his father down and washed his own face with snow before he went to the door.

He crossed the lot walking slowly, carrying his father. He did not now feel tired.

The young woman's face was drawn down in shock and revealed at first nothing of friendliness.

"We had a jeep parked somewhere, but I can't find it," the boy said. "This is my father."

They would not talk to him. They stripped him and put him before the fire wrapped in blankets and started tea and made him wait. He wanted to talk. He wished they would ask him a lot of questions. But they went about quickly and quietly, making things warm. His father was in the bedroom.

The man with the face full of dark beard had telephoned for a doctor. He went back into the bedroom with more blankets, and stayed. His wife went from room to room with hot tea. She rubbed the boy's naked shoulders through the blanket, and held a cup to his mouth, but she would not talk to him. He did not know what to say to her, and he could not move his lips very well. But he wished she would ask him some questions. He was restless, thawing in silence before the hearth.

He thought about going back to their own cabin soon. In his mind he gave the bearded man directions to take him and his father home. It wasn't far. It would not require much of the man's time. They would thank him, and give him an elk steak. Later he and his father would come back for the jeep. He could keep his father warm at the cabin as well as they were doing here, the boy knew.

While the woman was in the bedroom, the boy overheard the bearded man raise his voice:

"He what?"

"He carried him out," the woman whispered.

"What do you mean, carried him?"

"Carried him. On his back. I saw."

"Carried him from where?"

"Where it happened. Somewhere on Sheep Creek, maybe."

"Eight miles?"

"I know."

"Eight miles? How could he do that?"

"I don't know. I suppose he couldn't. But he did."

The doctor arrived in half an hour, as the boy was just starting to shiver. The doctor went into the bedroom and stayed five minutes. The woman poured the boy more tea and knelt beside him and hugged him around the shoulders.

When the doctor came out, he examined the boy without speaking. The boy wished the doctor would ask him some questions, but he was afraid he might be shivering too hard to answer in a man's voice. While the doctor touched him and probed him and took his temperature, the boy looked the doctor directly in the eye, as though to show him he was really all right.

The doctor said:

"David, your father is dead. He has been dead for a long time. Probably since yesterday."

"I know that," the boy said.

PHILIP ROTH

The Conversion
of the Jews

"You're a real one for opening your mouth in the first place," Itzie said. "What do you open your mouth all the time for?"

"I didn't bring it up, Itz, I didn't," Ozzie said.

"What do you care about Jesus Christ for anyway?"

"I didn't bring up Jesus Christ. He did. I didn't even know what he was talking about. Jesus is historical, he kept saying. Jesus is historical." Ozzie mimicked the monumental voice of Rabbi Binder.

"Jesus was a person that lived like you and me," Ozzie continued. "That's what Binder said—"

"Yeah? . . . So what! What do I give two cents whether he lived or not. And what do you gotta open your mouth!" Itzie Lieberman favored closed-mouthedness, especially when it came to Ozzie Freedman's questions. Mrs. Freedman had to see Rabbi Binder twice before about Ozzie's questions and this Wednesday at four thirty would be the third time. Itzie preferred to keep *his* mother in the kitchen; he settled for behind-the-back subtleties such as gestures, faces, snarls and other less delicate barnyard noises.

"He was a real person, Jesus, but he wasn't like God, and we don't believe he is God." Slowly, Ozzie was explaining Rabbi Binder's position to Itzie, who had been absent from Hebrew School the previous afternoon.

"The Catholics," Itzie said helpfully, "they believe in Jesus Christ, that he's God." Itzie Lieberman used "the Catholics" in its broadest sense—to include the Protestants.

Ozzie received Itzie's remark with a tiny head bob, as though it were a footnote, and went on. "His mother was Mary, and his father probably was Joseph," Ozzie said. "But the New Testament says his real father was God."

"His *real* father?"

"Yeah," Ozzie said, "that's the big thing, his father's supposed to be God."

"Bull."

"That's what Rabbi Binder says, that it's impossible—"

"Sure it's impossible. That stuff's all bull. To have a baby you gotta get laid," Itzie theologized. "Mary hadda get laid."

"That's what Binder says: 'The only way a woman can have a baby is to have intercourse with a man.' "

"He said *that*, Ozz?" For a moment it appeared that Itzie had put the theological question aside. "He said that, intercourse?" A little curled smile shaped itself in the lower half of Itzie's face like a pink mustache. "What you guys do, Ozz, you laugh or something?"

"I raised my hand."

"Yeah? Whatja say?"

"That's when I asked the question."

Itzie's face lit up. "Whatja ask about—intercourse?"

"No, I asked the question about God, how if He could create the heaven and earth in six days, and make all the animals and the fish and the light in six days—the light especially, that's what always gets me, that He could make the light. Making fish and animals, that's pretty good—"

"That's damn good." Itzie's appreciation was honest but unimaginative: it was as though God had just pitched a one-hitter.

"But making light . . . I mean when you think about it, it's really something," Ozzie said. "Anyway, I asked Binder if He could make all that in six days, and He could *pick* the six days He wanted right out of nowhere, why couldn't He let a woman have a baby without having intercourse."

"You said intercourse, Ozz, to Binder?"

"Yeah."

"Right in class?"

"Yeah."

Itzie smacked the side of his head.

"I mean, no kidding around," Ozzie said, "that'd really be nothing. After all that other stuff, that'd practically be nothing."

Itzie considered a moment. "What'd Binder say?"

"He started all over again explaining how Jesus was historical and how he lived like you and me but he wasn't God. So I said I under*stood* that. What I wanted to know was different."

What Ozzie wanted to know was always different. The first time he had wanted to know how Rabbi Binder could call the Jews "The Chosen People" if the Declaration of Independence claimed all men to be created equal. Rabbi Binder tried to distinguish for him between political equality and spiritual legitimacy, but what Ozzie wanted to know, he insisted vehemently, was different. That was the first time his mother had to come.

Then there was the plane crash. Fifty-eight people had been killed in a plane crash at La Guardia. In studying a casualty list in the newspaper his mother had discovered among the list of those dead eight Jewish names (his grandmother had nine but she counted Miller as a Jewish name); because of the eight she said the plane crash was "a tragedy." During free-discussion time on Wednesday Ozzie had brought to Rabbi Binder's attention this matter of "some of his relations" always picking out the Jewish names. Rabbi Binder had begun to explain cultural unity and some other things when Ozzie stood up at his seat and said that what he wanted to know was different. Rabbi Binder insisted that he sit down and it was then that Ozzie shouted that he wished all fifty-eight were Jews. That was the second time his mother came.

"And he kept explaining about Jesus being historical, and so I kept asking him. No kidding, Itz, he was trying to make me look stupid."

"So what he finally do?"

"Finally he starts screaming that I was deliberately simpleminded and a wise guy, and that my mother had to come, and this was the last time. And that I'd never get bar mitzvahed if he could help it. Then, Itz, then he starts talking in that voice like a statue, real slow and deep, and he says that I better think over what I said about the Lord. He told me to go to his office and think it over." Ozzie leaned his body towards Itzie. "Itz, I thought it over for a solid hour, and now I'm convinced God could do it."

Ozzie had planned to confess his latest transgression to his mother as soon as she came home from work. But it was a Friday night in November and already dark, and when Mrs. Freedman came through the door she tossed off her coat, kissed Ozzie quickly on the face, and went to the kitchen table to light the three yellow candles, two for the Sabbath and one for Ozzie's father.

When his mother lit the candles she would move her two arms slowly toward her, dragging them through the air, as though persuading people whose minds were half made up. And her eyes would get glassy with tears. Even when his father was alive Ozzie remembered that her eyes had gotten glassy, so it didn't have anything to do with his dying. It had something to do with lighting the candles.

As she touched the flaming match to the unlit wick of a Sabbath candle, the phone rang, and Ozzie, standing only a foot from it, plucked it off the receiver and held it muffled to his chest. When his mother lit candles Ozzie felt there should be no noise; even breathing, if you could manage it, should be softened. Ozzie pressed the phone to his breast and watched his mother dragging whatever she was dragging, and he felt his own eyes get glassy. His mother was a round, tired, gray-haired penguin of a woman whose gray skin had begun to feel the tug of gravity and the weight of her own history. Even when she was dressed up she didn't look like a chosen person. But when she lit candles she looked like something better; like a woman who knew momentarily that God could do anything.

After a few mysterious minutes she was finished. Ozzie hung up the phone and walked to the kitchen table where she was beginning to lay the two places for the four-course Sabbath meal. He told her that she would have to see Rabbi Binder next Wednesday at four thirty, and then he told her why. For the first time in their life together she hit Ozzie across the face with her hand.

All through the chopped liver and chicken soup part of the dinner Ozzie cried; he didn't have any appetite for the rest.

On Wednesday, in the largest of the three basement classrooms of the synagogue, Rabbi Marvin Binder, a tall, handsome, broad-shouldered man of thirty with thick strong-fibered black hair, removed his watch from his pocket and saw that it was four o'clock. At the rear of the room Yakov Blotnik, the seventy-one-year-old custodian, slowly polished the large window, mumbling to himself, unaware that it was four o'clock or six o'clock, Monday or Wednesday. To most of the students Yakov Blotnik's mumbling, along with his brown curly beard, scythe nose, and two heel-trailing black cats, made of him an object of wonder, a foreigner, a relic, toward whom they were alternately fearful and disrespectful. To Ozzie the mumbling had always seemed a monotonous, curious prayer; what made it curious was that old Blotnik had been mumbling so steadily for so many years, Ozzie suspected he had memorized the prayers and forgotten all about God.

"It is now free-discussion time," Rabbi Binder said. "Feel free to talk about any Jewish matter at all—religion, family, politics, sports—"

There was silence. It was a gusty, clouded November afternoon and it did not seem as though there ever was or could be a thing called baseball. So nobody this week said a word about that hero from the past, Hank Greenberg—which limited free discussion considerably.

And the soul-battering Ozzie Freedman had just received from Rabbi Binder had imposed its limitation. When it was Ozzie's turn to read aloud from the Hebrew book the rabbi had asked him petulantly why he didn't read more rapidly. He was showing no progress. Ozzie said he could read faster but that if he did he was sure not to understand what he was reading. Nevertheless, at the rabbi's repeated suggestion Ozzie tried, and showed a great talent, but in the midst of a long passage he stopped short and said he didn't understand a word he was reading, and started in again at a drag-footed pace. Then came the soul-battering.

Consequently when free-discussion time rolled around none of the students felt too free. The rabbi's invitation was answered only by the mumbling of feeble old Blotnik.

"Isn't there anything at all you would like to discuss?" Rabbi Binder asked again, looking at his watch. "No questions or comments?"

There was a small grumble from the third row. The rabbi requested that Ozzie rise and give the rest of the class the advantage of his thought.

Ozzie rose. "I forget it now," he said, and sat down in his place.

Rabbi Binder advanced a seat toward Ozzie and poised himself on the edge of the desk. It was Itzie's desk and the rabbi's frame only a dagger's-length away from his face snapped him to sitting attention.

"Stand up again, Oscar," Rabbi Binder said calmly, "and try to assemble your thoughts."

Ozzie stood up. All his classmates turned in their seats and watched as he gave an unconvincing scratch to his forehead.

"I can't assemble any," he announced, and plunked himself down.

"Stand up!" Rabbi Binder advanced from Itzie's desk to the one directly in front of Ozzie; when the rabbinical back was turned Itzie gave it five-fingers off the tip of his nose, causing a small titter in the room. Rabbi Binder was too absorbed in squelching Ozzie's nonsense once and for all to bother with titters. "Stand up, Oscar. What's your question about?"

Ozzie pulled a word out of the air. It was the handiest word. "Religion."

"Oh, now you remember?"

"Yes."

"What is it?"

Trapped, Ozzie blurted the first thing that came to him. "Why can't He make anything He wants to make!"

As Rabbi Binder prepared an answer, a final answer, Itzie, ten feet behind him, raised one finger on his left hand, gestured it meaningfully toward the rabbi's back, and brought the house down.

Binder twisted quickly to see what had happened and in the midst of the commotion Ozzie shouted into the rabbi's back what he couldn't have shouted to his face. It was a loud, toneless sound that had the timbre of something stored inside for about six days.

"You don't know! You don't know anything about God!"

The rabbi spun back toward Ozzie. "What?"

"You don't know—you don't—"

"Apologize, Oscar, apologize!" It was a threat.

"You don't—"

Rabbi Binder's hand flicked out at Ozzie's cheek. Perhaps it had only been meant to clamp the boy's mouth shut, but Ozzie ducked and the palm caught him squarely on the nose.

The blood came in a short, red spurt on to Ozzie's shirt front.

The next moment was all confusion. Ozzie screamed, "You bastard, you bastard!" and broke for the classroom door. Rabbi Binder lurched a step backward, as though his own blood had started flowing violently in the opposite direction, then gave a clumsy lurch forward and bolted out the door after Ozzie. The class followed after the rabbi's huge blue-suited back, and before old Blotnik could turn from his window, the room was empty and everyone was headed full speed up the three flights leading to the roof.

If one should compare the light of day to the life of man: sunrise to birth; sunset—the dropping down over the edge—to death; then as Ozzie Freedman wiggled through the trapdoor of the synagogue roof, his feet kicking backward bronco-style at Rabbi Binder's outstretched arms—at that moment the day was fifty years old. As a rule, fifty or fifty-five reflects accurately the age of late afternoons in November, for it is in that month, during those hours, that one's awareness of light seems no longer a matter of seeing, but of hearing: light begins clicking away. In fact, as Ozzie locked shut the trapdoor in the rabbi's face, the sharp click of the bolt into the lock might momentarily have been mistaken for the sound of the heavier gray that had just throbbed through the sky.

With all his weight Ozzie kneeled on the locked door; any instant he was certain that Rabbi Binder's shoulder would fling it open, splintering the wood into shrapnel and catapulting his body into the sky. But the door did not move and below him he heard only the rumble of feet, first loud then dim, like thunder rolling away.

A question shot through his brain. "Can this be *me?*" For a thirteen-year-old who had just labeled his religious leader a bastard, twice, it was not an improper question. Louder and louder the question came to him —"Is it me? Is it me?"—until he discovered himself no longer kneeling, but racing crazily toward the edge of the roof, his eyes crying, his throat screaming, and his arms flying everywhichway as though not his own.

"Is it me? Is it me ME ME ME ME! It has to be me—but is it!"

It is the question a thief must ask himself the night he jimmies open his first window, and it is said to be the question with which bridegrooms quiz themselves before the altar.

In the few wild seconds it took Ozzie's body to propel him to the edge of the roof, his self-examination began to grow fuzzy. Gazing down at the street, he became confused as to the problem beneath the question: was it, is-it-me-who-called-Binder-a-bastard? or, is-it-me-prancing-around-on-the-roof? However, the scene below settled all, for there is an instant in any action when whether it is you or somebody else is academic. The thief crams the money in his pockets and scoots out the window. The bridegroom signs the hotel register for two. And the boy on the roof finds a streetful of people gaping at him, necks stretched backward, faces up, as though he were the ceiling of the Hayden Planetarium. Suddenly you know it's you.

"Oscar! Oscar Freedman!" A voice rose from the center of the crowd, a voice that, could it have been seen, would have looked like the writing on scroll. "Oscar Freedman, get down from there. Immediately!" Rabbi

Binder was pointing one arm stiffly up at him; and at the end of that arm, one finger aimed menacingly. It was the attitude of a dictator, but one—the eyes confessed all—whose personal valet had spit neatly in his face.

Ozzie didn't answer. Only for a blink's length did he look toward Rabbi Binder. Instead his eyes began to fit together the world beneath him, to sort out people from places, friends from enemies, participants from spectators. In little jagged starlike clusters his friends stood around Rabbi Binder, who was still pointing. The topmost point on a star compounded not of angels but of five adolescent boys was Itzie. What a world it was, with those stars below, Rabbi Binder below . . . Ozzie, who a moment earlier hadn't been able to control his own body, started to feel the meaning of the word control: he felt Peace and he felt Power.

"Oscar Freedman, I'll give you three to come down."

Few dictators give their subjects three to do anything; but, as always, Rabbi Binder only looked dictatorial.

"Are you ready, Oscar?"

Ozzie nodded his head yes, although he had no intention in the world —the lower one or the celestial one he'd just entered—of coming down even if Rabbi Binder should give him a million.

"All right then," said Rabbi Binder. He ran a hand through his black Samson hair as though it were the gesture prescribed for uttering the first digit. Then, with his other hand cutting a circle out of the small piece of sky around him, he spoke. "One!"

There was no thunder. On the contrary, at that moment, as though "one" was the cue for which he had been waiting, the world's least thunderous person appeared on the synagogue steps. He did not so much come out the synagogue door as lean out, onto the darkening air. He clutched at the doorknob with one hand and looked up at the roof.

"Oy!"

Yakov Blotnik's old mind hobbled slowly, as if on crutches, and though he couldn't decide precisely what the boy was doing on the roof, he knew it wasn't good—that is, it wasn't-good-for-the-Jews. For Yakov Blotnik life had fractionated itself simply: things were either good-for-the-Jews or no-good-for-the-Jews.

He smacked his free hand to his in-sucked cheek, gently. "Oy, Gut!" And then quickly as he was able, he jacked down his head and surveyed the street. There was Rabbi Binder (like a man at an auction with only three dollars in his pocket, he had just delivered a shaky "Two!"); there were the students, and that was all. So far it-wasn't-so-bad-for-the-Jews. But the boy had to come down immediately, before anybody saw. The problem: how to get the boy off the roof?

Anybody who has ever had a cat on the roof knows how to get him down. You call the fire department. Or first you call the operator and you ask her for the fire department. And the next thing there is great jamming of brakes and clanging of bells and shouting of instructions. And then the cat is off the roof. You do the same thing to get a boy off the roof.

That is, you do the same thing if you are Yakov Blotnik and you once had a cat on the roof.

When the engines, all four of them, arrived, Rabbi Binder had four times given Ozzie the count of three. The big hook-and-ladder swung around the corner and one of the firemen leaped from it, plunging headlong toward the yellow fire hydrant in front of the synagogue. With a huge wrench he began to unscrew the top nozzle. Rabbi Binder raced over to him and pulled at his shoulder.

"There's no fire . . ."

The fireman mumbled back over his shoulder and, heatedly, continued working at the nozzle.

"But there's no fire, there's no fire . . ." Binder shouted. When the fireman mumbled again, the rabbi grasped his face with both his hands and pointed it up at the roof.

To Ozzie it looked as though Rabbi Binder was trying to tug the fireman's head out of his body, like a cork from a bottle. He had to giggle at the picture they made: it was a family portrait—rabbi in black skullcap, fireman in red fire hat, and the little yellow hydrant squatting beside like a kid brother, bareheaded. From the edge of the roof Ozzie waved at the portrait, a one-handed, flapping, mocking wave; in doing it his right foot slipped from under him. Rabbi Binder covered his eyes with his hands.

Firemen work fast. Before Ozzie had even regained his balance, a big, round, yellowed net was being held on the synagogue lawn. The firemen who held it looked up at Ozzie with stern, feelingless faces.

One of the firemen turned his head toward Rabbi Binder. "What, is the kid nuts or something?"

Rabbi Binder unpeeled his hands from his eyes, slowly, painfully, as if they were tape. Then he checked: nothing on the sidewalk, no dents in the net.

"Is he gonna jump, or what?" the fireman shouted.

In a voice not at all like a statue, Rabbi Binder finally answered. "Yes, yes, I think so . . . He's been threatening to . . ."

Threatening to? Why, the reason he was on the roof, Ozzie remembered, was to get away; he hadn't even thought about jumping. He had just run to get away, and the truth was that he hadn't really headed for the roof as much as he'd been chased there.

"What's his name, the kid?"

"Freedman," Rabbi Binder answered. "Oscar Freedman."

The fireman looked up at Ozzie. "What is it with you, Oscar? You gonna jump, or what?"

Ozzie did not answer. Frankly, the question had just arisen.

"Look, Oscar, if you're gonna jump, jump—and if you're not gonna jump, don't jump. But don't waste our time, willya?"

Ozzie looked at the fireman and then at Rabbi Binder. He wanted to see Rabbi Binder cover his eyes one more time.

"I'm going to jump."

And then he scampered around the edge of the roof to the corner, where there was no net below, and he flapped his arms at his sides, swishing the air and smacking his palms to his trousers on the downbeat. He began screaming like some kind of engine, "Wheeeee . . . wheeeeee," and leaning way out over the edge with the upper half of his body. The firemen whipped around to cover the ground with the net. Rabbi Binder mumbled a few words to Somebody and covered his eyes. Everything happened quickly, jerkily, as in a silent movie. The crowd, which had arrived with the fire engines, gave out a long, Fourth-of-July fireworks oooh-aahhh. In the excitement no one had paid the crowd much heed, except, of course, Yakov Blotnik, who swung from the doorknob counting heads. "Fier und tsvansik . . . finf und tsvant-sik . . . Oy, Gut!" It wasn't like this with the cat.

Rabbi Binder peeked through his fingers, checked the sidewalk and net. Empty. But there was Ozzie racing to the other corner. The firemen raced with him but were unable to keep up. Whenever Ozzie wanted to he might jump and splatter himself upon the sidewalk, and by the time the firemen scooted to the spot all they could do with their net would be to cover the mess.

"Wheeeee . . . wheeeee . . ."

"Hey, Oscar," the winded fireman yelled, "What the hell is this, a game or something?"

"Wheeeee . . . wheeeee . . ."

"Hey, Oscar—"

But he was off now to the other corner, flapping his wings fiercely. Rabbi Binder couldn't take it any longer—the fire engines from nowhere, the screaming suicidal boy, the net. He fell to his knees, exhausted, and with his hands curled together in front of his chest like a little dome, he pleaded, "Oscar, stop it, Oscar. Don't jump, Oscar. Please come down . . . Please don't jump."

And further back in the crowd a single voice, a single young voice, shouted a lone word to the boy on the roof.

"Jump!"

It was Itzie. Ozzie momentarily stopped flapping.

"Go ahead, Ozz—jump!" Itzie broke off his point of the star and courageously, with the inspiration not of a wise-guy but of a disciple, stood alone. "Jump, Ozz, jump!"

Still on his knees, his hands still curled, Rabbi Binder twisted his body back. He looked at Itzie, then, agonizingly, back to Ozzie.

"OSCAR, DON'T JUMP! PLEASE, DON'T JUMP . . . please please . . ."

"Jump!" This time it wasn't Itzie but another point of the star. By the time Mrs. Freedman arrived to keep her four-thirty appointment with Rabbi Binder, the whole little upside down heaven was shouting and pleading for Ozzie to jump, and Rabbi Binder no longer was pleading with him not to jump, but was crying into the dome of his hands.

Understandably Mrs. Freedman couldn't figure out what her son was doing on the roof. So she asked.

"Ozzie, my Ozzie, what are you doing? My Ozzie, what is it?"

Ozzie stopped wheeeeeing and slowed his arms down to a cruising flap, the kind birds use in soft winds, but he did not answer. He stood against the low, clouded, darkening sky—light clicked down swiftly now, as on a small gear—flapping softly and gazing down at the small bundle of a woman who was his mother.

"What are you doing, Ozzie?" She turned toward the kneeling Rabbi Binder and rushed so close that only a paper-thickness of dusk lay between her stomach and his shoulders.

"What is my baby doing?"

Rabbi Binder gaped up at her but he too was mute. All that moved was the dome of his hands; it shook back and forth like a weak pulse.

"Rabbi, get him down! He'll kill himself. Get him down, my only baby . . ."

"I can't," Rabbi Binder said, "I can't . . ." and he turned his handsome head toward the crowd of boys behind him. "It's them. Listen to them."

And for the first time Mrs. Freedman saw the crowd of boys, and she heard what they were yelling.

"He's doing it for them. He won't listen to me. It's them." Rabbi Binder spoke like one in a trance.

"For them?"

"Yes."

"Why for them?"

"They want him to . . ."

Mrs. Freedman raised her two arms upward as though she were conducting the sky. "For them he's doing it!" And then in a gesture older than pyramids, older than prophets and floods, her arms came slapping down to her sides. "A martyr I have. Look!" She tilted her head to the roof. Ozzie was still flapping softly. "My martyr."

"Oscar, come down, *please,*" Rabbi Binder groaned.

In a startlingly even voice Mrs. Freedman called to the boy on the roof. "Ozzie, come down, Ozzie. Don't be a martyr, my baby."

As though it were a litany, Rabbi Binder repeated her words. "Don't be a martyr, my baby. Don't be a martyr."

"Gawhead, Ozz—*be* a Martin!" It was Itzie. "Be a Martin, be a Martin," and all the voices joined in singing for Martindom, whatever *it* was. "Be a Martin, be a Martin . . ."

Somehow when you're on a roof the darker it gets the less you can hear. All Ozzie knew was that two groups wanted two new things: his friends were spirited and musical about what they wanted; his mother and the rabbi were even-toned, chanting, about what they didn't want. The rabbi's voice was without tears now and so was his mother's.

The big net stared up at Ozzie like a sightless eye. The big, clouded sky pushed down. From beneath it looked like a gray corrugated board. Suddenly, looking up into that unsympathetic sky, Ozzie realized all the strangeness of what these people, his friends, were asking: they wanted him to jump, to kill himself; they were singing about it now—it made them that happy. And there was an even greater strangeness: Rabbi Binder was on his knees, trembling. If there was a question to be asked now it was not "Is it me?" but rather "Is it us? . . . Is it us?"

Being on the roof, it turned out, was a serious thing. If he jumped would the singing become dancing? Would it? What would jumping stop? Yearningly, Ozzie wished he could rip open the sky, plunge his hands through, and pull out the sun; and on the sun, like a coin, would be stamped JUMP or DON'T JUMP.

Ozzie's knees rocked and sagged a little under him as though they were setting him for a dive. His arms tightened, stiffened, froze, from shoulders to fingernails. He felt as if each part of his body were going to vote as to whether he should kill himself or not—and each part as though it were independent of *him*.

The light took an unexpected click down and the new darkness, like a gag, hushed the friends singing for this and the mother and rabbi chanting for that.

Ozzie stopped counting votes, and in a curiously high voice, like one who wasn't prepared for speech, he spoke.

"Mamma?"

"Yes, Oscar."

"Mamma, get down on your knees, like Rabbi Binder."

"Oscar—"

"Get down on your knees," he said, "or I'll jump."

Ozzie heard a whimper, then a quick rustling, and when he looked down where his mother had stood he saw the top of a head and beneath that a circle of dress. She was kneeling beside Rabbi Binder.

He spoke again. "Everybody kneel." There was the sound of everybody kneeling.

Ozzie looked around. With one hand he pointed toward the synagogue entrance. "Make *him* kneel."

There was a noise, not of kneeling, but of body-and-cloth stretching. Ozzie could hear Rabbi Binder saying in a gruff whisper, ". . . or he'll *kill* himself," and when next he looked there was Yakov Blotnik off the doorknob and for the first time in his life upon his knees in the Gentile posture of prayer.

As for the firemen—it is not as difficult as one might imagine to hold a net taut while you are kneeling.

Ozzie looked around again; and then he called to Rabbi Binder.

"Rabbi?"

"Yes, Oscar."

"Rabbi Binder, do you believe in God?"

"Yes."

"Do you believe God can do Anything?" Ozzie leaned his head out into the darkness. "Anything?"

"Oscar, I think—"

"Tell me you believe God can do Anything."

There was a second's hesitation. Then: "God can do Anything."

"Tell me you believe God can make a child without intercourse."

"He can."

"Tell me!"

"God," Rabbi Binder admitted, "can make a child without intercourse."

"Mamma, you tell me."

"God can make a child without intercourse," his mother said.

"Make *him* tell me." There was no doubt who *him* was.

In a few moments Ozzie heard an old comical voice say something to the increasing darkness about God.

Next, Ozzie made everybody say it. And then he made them all say they believed in Jesus Christ—first one at a time, then all together.

When the catechizing was through it was the beginning of evening. From the street it sounded as if the boy on the roof might have sighed.

"Ozzie?" A woman's voice dared to speak. "You'll come down now?"

There was no answer, but the woman waited, and when a voice finally did speak it was thin and crying, and exhausted as that of an old man who had just finished pulling the bells.

"Mamma, don't you see—you shouldn't hit me. He shouldn't hit me. You shouldn't hit me about God, Mamma. You should never hit anybody about God—"

"Ozzie, please come down now."

"Promise me, promise me you'll never hit anybody about God."

He had asked only his mother, but for some reason everyone kneeling in the street promised he would never hit anybody about God.

Once again there was silence.

"I can come down now, Mamma," the boy on the roof finally said. He turned his head both ways as though checking the traffic lights. "Now I can come down . . ."

And he did, right into the center of the yellow net that glowed in the evening's edge like an overgrown halo.

JAMES SALTER

Akhnilo

It was late August. In the harbor the boats lay still, not the slightest stirring of their masts, not the softest clink of a sheave. The restaurants had long since closed. An occasional car, headlights glaring, came over the bridge from North Haven or turned down Main Street, past the lighted telephone booths with their smashed receivers. On the highway the discotheques were emptying. It was after three.

In the darkness Fenn awakened. He thought he had heard something, a slight sound, like the creak of a spring, the one on the screen door in the kitchen. He lay there in the heat. His wife was sleeping quietly. He waited. The house was unlocked though there had been many robberies and worse nearer the city. He heard a faint thump. He did not move. Several minutes passed. Without making a sound he got up and went carefully to the narrow doorway where some stairs descended to the kitchen. He stood there. Silence. Another thump and a moan. It was Birdman falling to another place on the floor.

Outside, the trees were like black reflections. The stars were hidden. The only galaxies were the insect voices that filled the night. He stared from the open window. He was still not sure if he had heard anything. The leaves of the immense beech that overhung the rear porch were close enough to touch. For what seemed a long time he examined the shadowy area around the trunk. The stillness of everything made him feel visible but also strangely receptive. His eyes drifted from one thing to another behind the house, the pale Corinthian columns of the arbor next door, the mysterious hedge, the garage with its rotting sills. Nothing.

Eddie Fenn was a carpenter though he'd gone to Dartmouth and majored in history. Most of the time he worked alone. He was thirty-four. He had thinning hair and a shy smile. Not much to say. There was something quenched in him. When he was younger it was believed to be some sort of talent, but he had never really set out in life, he had stayed close to shore. His wife, who was tall and nearsighted, was from

Connecticut. Her father had been a banker. *Of Greenwich and Havana*
the announcement in the papers had said—he'd managed the branch of
a New York bank there when she was a child. That was in the days when
Havana was a legend and millionaires committed suicide after smoking
a last cigar.

Years had passed. Fenn gazed out at the night. It seemed he was the
only listener to an infinite sea of cries. Its vastness awed him. He
thought of all that lay concealed behind it, the desperate acts, the
longings, the fatal surprises. That afternoon he had seen a robin picking
at something near the edge of the grass, seizing it, throwing it in the air,
seizing it again: a toad, its small, stunned legs fanned out. The bird
threw it again. In ravenous burrows the blind shrews hunted cease-
lessly, the pointed tongues of reptiles were testing the air, there was the
crunch of abdomens, the passivity of the trapped, the soft throes of
mating. We live in slaughter like the ancient kings, he thought. His
daughters were asleep down the hall. Nothing is safe except for an hour.

As he stood there the sound seemed to change, he did not know how.
It seemed to separate as if permitting something to come forth from it,
something glittering and remote. He tried to identify what he was
hearing as gradually the cricket, cicada, no, it was something else,
something feverish and strange, became more clear. The more intently
he listened, the more elusive it was. He was afraid to move for fear of
losing it. He heard the soft call of an owl. The darkness of the trees
which was absolute seemed to loosen, and through it that single, shrill
note.

Unseen the night had opened. The sky was revealing itself, the stars
shining faintly. The town was sleeping, abandoned sidewalks, silent
lawns. Far off among some pines was the gable of a barn. It was coming
from there. He still could not identify it. He needed to be closer, to go
downstairs and out the door, but that way he might lose it, it might
become silent, aware.

He had a disturbing thought, he was unable to dislodge it: it *was*
aware. Quivering there, repeating and repeating itself above the rest, it
seemed to be coming only to him. The rhythm was not constant. It
hurried, hesitated, went on. It was less and less an instinctive cry and
more a kind of signal, a code, not anything he had heard before, not a
collection of long and short impulses but something more intricate, in a
way almost like speech. The idea frightened him. The words, if that was
what they were, were piercing and thin but the awareness of them
made him tremble as if they were the combination to a vault.

Beneath the window lay the roof of the porch. It sloped gently. He
stood there, perfectly still, as if lost in thought. His heart was rattling.
The roof seemed wide as a street. He would have to go out on it hoping
he was unseen, moving silently, without abruptness, pausing to see if
there was a change in the sound to which he was now acutely sensitive.

The darkness would not protect him. He would be entering a night of countless networks, shifting eyes. He was not sure if he should do it, if he dared. A drop of sweat broke free and ran quickly down his bare side. Tirelessly the call continued. His hands were trembling.

Unfastening the screen, he lowered it carefully and leaned it against the house. He was moving quietly, like a serpent, across the faded green roofing. He looked down. The ground seemed distant. He would have to hang from the roof and drop, light as a spider. The peak of the barn was still visible. He was moving toward the lodestar, he could feel it. It was almost as if he were falling. The act was dizzying, irreversible. It was taking him where nothing he possessed would protect him, taking him barefoot, alone.

Fenn felt a thrill go through him. He was going to be redeemed. His life had not turned out as he expected but he still thought of himself as special, as belonging to no one. In fact he thought of failure as romantic. It had almost been his goal. He carved birds, or he had. The tools and partially shaped blocks of wood were on a table in the basement. He had, at one time, almost become a naturalist. Something in him, his silence, his willingness to be apart, was adapted to that. Instead he began to build furniture with a friend who had some money, but the business failed. He was drinking. One morning he woke up lying by the car in the worn ruts of the driveway, the old woman who lived across the street warning away her dog. He went inside before his children saw him. He was very close, the doctor told him frankly, to being an alcoholic. The words astonished him. That was long ago. His family had saved him, but not without cost.

He paused. The earth was firm and dry. He went toward the hedge and across the neighbor's driveway. The tone that was transfixing him was clearer. Following it he passed behind houses he hardly recognized from the back, through neglected yards where cans and rubbish were hidden in dark grass, past empty sheds he had never seen. The ground began to slope gently down, he was nearing the barn. He could hear the voice, *his* voice, pouring overhead. It was coming from somewhere in the ghostly wooden triangle rising like the face of a distant mountain brought unexpectedly close by a turn of the road. He moved towards it slowly, with the fear of an explorer. Above him he could hear the thin stream trilling. Terrified by its closeness he stood still.

At first, he later remembered, it meant nothing, it was too glistening, too pure. It kept pouring out, more and more demonic. He could not identify, he could never repeat, he could not even describe the sound. It had enlarged, it was pushing everything else aside. He stopped trying to comprehend it and instead allowed it to run through him, to invade him like a chant. Slowly, like a pattern that changes its appearance as one stares at it and begins to shift into another dimension, inexplicably the sound altered and exposed its real core. He began to recognize it. It *was* words. They had no meaning, no antecedents, but they were unmistakably a language, the first ever heard from an order vaster and more dense than our own. Above, in the whitish surface, desperate, calling, was the nameless pioneer.

In a kind of ecstasy he stepped closer. Instantly he realized it was wrong. The sound hesitated. He closed his eyes in anguish but too late, it faltered and then stopped. He felt stupid, shamed. He moved back a little, helplessly. All about him the voices clattered. The night was filled with them. He turned this way and that hoping to find it, but the thing he had heard was gone.

It was late. The first pale cast had come to the sky. He was standing near the barn with the fragments of a dream one must struggle to remember: four words, distinct and inimitable, that he had made out. Protecting them, concentrating on them with all his strength, he began to carry them back. The cries of the insects seemed louder. He was afraid something would happen, a dog would bark, a light go on in a bedroom and he would be distracted, he would lose his hold. He had to get back without seeing anything, without hearing anything, without thinking. He was repeating the words to himself as he went, his lips moving steadily. He hardly dared breathe. He could see the house. It had turned gray. The windows were dark. He had to get to it. The sound of the night creatures seemed to swell in torment and rage, but he was beyond that. He was escaping. He had gone an immense distance, he was coming to the hedge. The porch was not far away. He stood on the railing, the eave of the roof within reach. The rain gutter was firm, he pulled himself up. The crumbling green asphalt was warm beneath his feet. One leg over the sill, then the other. He was safe. He stepped back from the window instinctively. He had done it. Outside, the light seemed faint and historic. A spectral dawn began to come through the trees.

Suddenly he heard the floor creak. Someone was there, a figure in the soft light drained of color. It was his wife, he was stunned by the image of her holding a cotton robe about her, her face made plain by sleep. He made a gesture as if to warn her off.

"What is it? What's wrong?" she whispered.

He backed away making vague movements with his hands. His head was sideways, like a horse. He was moving backward. One eye was on her.

"What is it?" she said, alarmed. "What happened?"

No, he pleaded, shaking his head. A word had dropped away. No, no. It was fluttering apart like something in the sea. He was reaching blindly for it.

Her arm went around him. He pulled away abruptly. He closed his eyes.

"Darling, what is it?" He was troubled, she knew. He had never really gotten over his difficulty. He often woke at night, she would find him sitting in the kitchen, his face looking tired and old. "Come to bed," she invited.

His eyes were closed tightly. His hands were over his ears.

"Are you all right?" she said.

Beneath her devotion it was dissolving, the words were spilling away. He began to turn around frantically.

"What is it, what is it?" she cried.

The light was coming everywhere, pouring across the lawn. The sacred whispers were vanishing. He could not spare a moment. Hands clapped to his head he ran into the hall searching for a pencil while she ran after, begging him to tell her what was wrong. They were fading, there was just one left, worthless without the others and yet of infinite value. As he scribbled the table shook. A picture quivered on the wall. His wife, her hair held back with one hand, was peering at what he had written. Her face was close to it.

"What is that?"

Dena, in her nightgown, had appeared in a doorway awakened by the noise.

"What is it?" she asked.

"Help me," her mother cried.

"Daddy, what happened?"

Their hands were reaching for him. In the glass of the picture a brilliant square of blue and green was trembling, the luminous foliage of the trees. The countless voices were receding, turning into silence.

"What is it, what is it?" his wife pleaded.

"Daddy, please!"

He shook his head. He was nearly weeping as he tried to pull away. Suddenly he slumped to the floor and sat there and for Dena they had begun again the phase she remembered from the years she was first in school when unhappiness filled the house and slamming doors and her father clumsy with affection came into their room at night to tell them stories and fell asleep at the foot of her bed.

JOHN UPDIKE

The Christian Roommates

Orson Ziegler came straight to Harvard from the small South Dakota town where his father was the doctor. Orson, at eighteen, was half an inch under six feet tall, with a weight of 164 and an IQ of 152. His eczematous cheeks and vaguely irritated squint—as if his face had been for too long transected by the sight of a level horizon—masked a definite self-confidence. As the doctor's son, he had always mattered in the town. In his high school he had been class president, valedictorian, and captain of the football and baseball teams. (The captain of the basketball team had been Lester Spotted Elk, a full-blooded Chippewa with dirty fingernails and brilliant teeth, a smoker, a drinker, a discipline problem, and the only boy Orson ever had met who was better than he at anything that mattered.) Orson was the first native of his town to go to Harvard, and would probably be the last, at least until his son was of age. His future was firm in his mind: the pre-med course here, medical school either at Harvard, Penn, or Yale, and then back to South Dakota, where he had his wife already selected and claimed and primed to wait. Two nights before he left for Harvard, he had taken her virginity. She had cried, and he had felt foolish, having, somehow, failed. It had been his virginity, too. Orson was sane, sane enough to know that he had lots to learn, and to be, within limits, willing. Harvard processes thousands of such boys and restores them to the world with little apparent damage. Presumably because he was from west of the Mississippi and a Protestant Christian (Methodist), the authorities had given him as a freshman roommate a self-converted Episcopalian from Oregon.

When Orson arrived at Harvard on the morning of Registration Day, bleary and stiff from the series of airplane rides that had begun fourteen hours before, his roommate was already installed. "H. Palamountain" was floridly inscribed in the upper of the two name slots on the door of Room 14. The bed by the window had been slept in, and the desk by the window was neatly loaded with books. Standing sleepless inside the door, inertly clinging to his two heavy suitcases, Orson was conscious of another presence in the room without being able to locate it; optically and mentally, he focused with a slight slowness.

The roommate was sitting on the floor, barefoot, before a small spinning wheel. He jumped up nimbly. Orson's first impression was of the wiry quickness that almost magically brought close to his face the thick-lipped, pop-eyed face of the other boy. He was a head shorter than Orson, and wore, above his bare feet, pegged sky-blue slacks, a lumberjack shirt whose throat was dashingly stuffed with a silk foulard, and a white cap such as Orson had seen before only in photographs of Pandit Nehru. Dropping a suitcase, Orson offered his hand. Instead of taking it, the roommate touched his palms together, bowed his head, and murmured something Orson didn't catch. Then he gracefully swept off the white cap, revealing a narrow crest of curly blond hair that stood up like a rooster's comb. "I am Henry Palamountain." His voice, clear and colorless in the way of West Coast voices, suggested a radio announcer. His handshake was metallically firm and seemed to have a pinch of malice in it. Like Orson, he wore glasses. The thick lenses emphasized the hyperthyroid bulge of his eyes and their fishy, searching expression.

"Orson Ziegler," Orson said.

"I know."

Orson felt a need to add something adequately solemn, standing as they were on the verge of a kind of marriage. "Well, Henry"—he lamely lowered the other suitcase to the floor—"I guess we'll be seeing a lot of each other."

"You may call me Hub," the roommate said. "Most people do. However, call me Henry if you insist. I don't wish to diminish your dreadful freedom. You may not wish to call me anything at all. Already I've made three hopeless enemies in the dormitory."

Every sentence in this smoothly enunciated speech bothered Orson, beginning with the first. He himself had never been given a nickname; it was the one honor his classmates had withheld from him. In his adolescence he had coined nicknames for himself—Orrie, Ziggy—and tried to insinuate them into popular usage, without success. And what was meant by "dreadful freedom"? It sounded sarcastic. And why might he not wish to call him anything at all? And how had the roommate had the time to make enemies? Orson asked irritably, "How long have you *been* here?"

"Eight days." Henry concluded every statement with a strange little pucker of his lips, a kind of satisfied silent click, as if to say, "And what do you think of *that?*"

Orson felt that he had been sized up as someone easy to startle. But he slid helplessly into the straight-man role that, like the second-best bed, had been reserved for him. "That *long?*"

"Yes. I was totally alone until the day before yesterday. You see, I hitchhiked."

"From *Oregon?*"

"Yes. And I wished to allow time enough for any contingency. In case I was robbed, I had sewed a fifty-dollar bill inside my shirt. As it turned out, I made smooth connections all the way. I had painted a large cardboard sign saying 'Harvard.' You should try it sometime. One meets some very interesting Harvard graduates."

"Didn't your parents worry?"

"Of course. My parents are divorced. My father was furious. He wanted me to fly. I told him to give the plane fare to the Indian Relief Fund. He never gives a penny to charity. And, of course, I'm old. I'm twenty."

"You've been in the Army?"

Henry lifted his hands and staggered back as if from a blow. He put the back of his hand to his brow, whimpered "Never," shuddered, straightened up smartly, and saluted. "In fact, the Portland draft board is after me right now." With a preening tug of his two agile hands— which did look, Orson realized, old: bony and veined and red-tipped, like a woman's—he broadened his foulard. "They refuse to recognize any conscientious objectors except Quakers and Mennonites. My bishop agrees with them. They offered me an out if I'd say I was willing to work in a hospital, but I explained that this released a man for combat duty and if it came to that I'd just as soon carry a gun. I'm an excellent shot. I mind killing only on principle."

The Korean War had begun that summer, and Orson, who had been nagged by a suspicion that his duty was to enlist, bristled at such blithe pacifism. He squinted and asked, "What *have* you been doing for two years, then?"

"Working in a plywood mill. As a gluer. The actual gluing is done by machines, but they become swamped in their own glue now and then. It's a kind of excessive introspection—you've read *Hamlet?*"

"Just *Macbeth* and *The Merchant of Venice.*"

"Yes. Anyway. They have to be cleaned with solvent. One wears long rubber gloves up to one's elbows. It's very soothing work. The inside of a gluer is an excellent place for revolving Greek quotations in your head. I memorized nearly the whole of the *Phaedo* that way." He gestured toward his desk, and Orson saw that many of the books were green Loeb editions of Plato and Aristotle, in Greek. Their spines were worn; they looked read and reread. For the first time, the thought of being at Harvard frightened him. Orson had been standing between his suitcases and now he moved to unpack. "Have you left me a bureau?"

"Of course. The better one." Henry jumped on the bed that had not been slept in and bounced up and down as if it were a trampoline. "And I've given you the bed with the better mattress," he said, still bouncing, "and the desk that doesn't have the glare from the window."

"Thanks," Orson said.

Henry was quick to notice his tone. "Would you rather have my bed? My desk?" He jumped from the bed and dashed to his desk and scooped a stack of books from it.

Orson had to touch him to stop him, and was startled by the tense muscularity of the arm he touched. "Don't be silly," he said. "They're exactly alike."

Henry replaced his books. "I don't want any bitterness," he said, "or immature squabbling. As the older man, it's my responsibility to yield. Here. I'll give you the shirt off my back." And he began to peel off his lumberjack shirt, leaving the foulard dramatically knotted around his naked throat. He wore no undershirt.

Having won from Orson a facial expression that Orson himself could not see, Henry smiled and rebuttoned the shirt. "Do you mind my name being in the upper slot on the door? I'll remove it. I apologize. I did it without realizing how sensitive you would be."

Perhaps it was all a kind of humor. Orson tried to make a joke. He pointed and asked, "Do I get a spinning wheel, too?"

"Oh, *that.*" Henry hopped backward on one bare foot and became rather shy. "That's an experiment. I ordered it from Calcutta. I spin for a half hour a day, after Yoga."

"You do Yoga, too?"

"Just some of the elementary positions. My ankles can't take more than five minutes of the Lotus yet."

"And you say you have a bishop."

The roommate glanced up with a glint of fresh interest. "Say. You listen, don't you? Yes. I consider myself an Anglican Christian Platonist strongly influenced by Gandhi." He touched his palms before his chest, bowed, straightened, and giggled. "My bishop hates me," he said. "The one in Oregon, who wants me to be a soldier. I've introduced myself to the bishop here and I don't think he likes me, either. For that matter, I've antagonized my adviser. I told him I had no intention of fulfilling the science requirement."

"For God's sake, why *not?*"

"You don't really want to know."

Orson felt this rebuff as a small test of strength. "Not really," he agreed.

"I consider science a demonic illusion of human hubris. Its phantasmal nature is proved by its constant revision. I asked him, 'Why should I waste an entire fourth of my study time, time that could be spent with Plato, mastering a mass of hypotheses that will be obsolete by the time I graduate?'"

"My Lord, Henry," Orson exclaimed, indignantly defending the millions of lives saved by medical science, "you can't be serious!"

"Please. Hub. I may be difficult for you, and I think it would help if you were to call me by my name. Now let's talk about you. Your father is a doctor, you received all As in high school—I received rather mediocre grades myself—and you've come to Harvard because you believe it affords a cosmopolitan Eastern environment that will be valuable to you after spending your entire life in a small provincial town."

"Who the hell told you all this?" The recital of his application statement made Orson blush. He already felt much older than the boy who had written it.

"University Hall," Henry said. "I went over and asked to see your folder. They didn't want to let me at first, but I explained that if they were going to give me a roommate, after I had specifically requested to live alone, I had a right to information about you, so I could minimize possible friction."

"And they *let* you?"

"Of course. People without convictions have no powers of resistance." His mouth made its little satisfied click, and Orson was goaded to ask, "Why did *you* come to Harvard?"

"Two reasons." He ticked them off on two fingers. "Raphael Demos and Werner Jaeger."

Orson did not know these names, but he suspected that "Friends of yours?" was a stupid question, once it was out of his mouth.

But Henry nodded. "I've introduced myself to Demos. A charming old scholar, with a beautiful young wife."

"You mean you just went to his house and pushed yourself *in?*" Orson heard his own voice grow shrill; his voice, rather high and unstable, was one of the things about himself that he liked least.

Henry blinked, and looked unexpectedly vulnerable, so slender and bravely dressed, his ugly, yellowish, flat-nailed feet naked on the floor, which was uncarpeted and painted black. "That isn't how I would describe it. I went as a pilgrim. He seemed pleased to talk to me." He spoke carefully, and his mouth abstained from clicking.

That he could hurt his roommate's feelings—that this jaunty apparition had feelings—disconcerted Orson more deeply than any of the surprises he had been deliberately offered. As quickly as he had popped up, Henry dropped to the floor, as if through a trapdoor in the plane of conversation. He resumed spinning. The method apparently called for one thread to be wound around the big toe of a foot and to be kept taut by a kind of absentminded pedal motion. While engaged in this, he seemed hermetically sealed inside one of the gluing machines that had incubated his garbled philosophy. Unpacking, Orson was slowed and snagged by a complicated mood of discomfort. He tried to remember how his mother had arranged his bureau drawers at home—socks and underwear in one, shirts and handkerchiefs in another. Home seemed infinitely far from him, and he was dizzily conscious of a great depth of space beneath his feet, as if the blackness of the floor were the color of an abyss. The spinning wheel steadily chuckled. Orson's buzz of unease circled and settled on his roommate, who, it was clear, had thought earnestly about profound matters, matters that Orson, busy as he had been with the practical business of being a good student, had hardly considered. It was also clear that Henry had thought unintelligently. This unintelligence ("I received rather mediocre grades myself") was more of a menace than a comfort. Bent above the bureau drawers, Orson felt cramped in his mind, able neither to stand erect in whole-hearted contempt nor to lie down in honest admiration. His mood was complicated by the repugnance his roommate's physical presence aroused in him. An almost morbidly clean boy, Orson was haunted by glue, and a tacky ambience resisted every motion of his unpacking.

The silence between the roommates continued until a great bell rang ponderously. The sound was near and yet far, like a heartbeat within the bosom of time, and it seemed to bring with it into the room the muffling foliation of the trees in the Yard, which to Orson's prairie-honed eyes had looked tropically tall and lush; the walls of the room vibrated with leaf shadows, and many minute presences—dust motes, traffic sounds, or angels of whom several could dance on the head of a pin—thronged the air and made it difficult to breathe. The stairways of the dormitory rumbled. Boys dressed in jackets and neckties crowded the doorway and entered the room, laughing and calling "Hub. Hey, Hub."

"Get up off the floor, dad."

"Jesus, Hub, put your shoes on."

"Pee-*yew.*"

"And take off that seductive sarong around your neck."

"Consider the lilies, Hub. They toil not, neither do they spin, and yet I say unto you that Solomon in all his glory was not arrayed like one of these."

"Amen, brothers!"

"Fitch, you should be a preacher."

They were all strangers to Orson. Hub stood and smoothly performed introductions.

In a few days, Orson had sorted them out. That jostling conglomerate, so apparently secure and homogeneous, broke down, under habitual exposure, into double individuals: roommates. There were Silverstein and Koshland, Dawson and Kern, Young and Carter, Petersen and Fitch.

Silverstein and Koshland, who lived in the room overhead, were Jews from New York City. All Orson knew about non-biblical Jews was that they were a sad race, full of music, shrewdness, and woe. But Silverstein and Koshland were always clowning, always wisecracking. They played bridge and poker and chess and Go and went to the movies in Boston and drank coffee in the luncheonettes around the Square. They came from the "gifted" high schools of the Bronx and Brooklyn respectively, and treated Cambridge as if it were another borough. Most of what the freshman year sought to teach them they seemed to know already. As winter approached, Koshland went out for basketball, and he and his teammates made the floor above bounce to the thump and rattle of scrimmages with a tennis ball and a wastebasket. One afternoon, a section of ceiling collapsed on Orson's bed.

Next door, in Room 12, Dawson and Kern wanted to be writers. Dawson was from Ohio and Kern from Pennsylvania. Dawson had a sulky, slouching bearing, a certain puppyish facial eagerness, and a terrible temper. He was a disciple of Anderson and Hemingway and himself wrote as austerely as a newspaper. He had been raised as an atheist, and no one in the dormitory incited his temper more often than Hub. Orson, feeling that he and Dawson came from opposite edges of that great psychological realm called the Midwest, liked him. He felt less at ease with Kern, who seemed Eastern and subtly vicious. A farm boy driven by an unnatural sophistication, riddled with nervous ailments ranging from conjunctivitis to hemorrhoids, Kern smoked and talked incessantly. He and Dawson maintained between them a battery of running jokes. At night Orson could hear them on the other side of the wall keeping each other awake with improvised parodies and musical comedies based on their teachers, their courses, or their fellow-freshmen. One midnight, Orson distinctly heard Dawson sing, "My name is Orson Ziegler, I come from South Dakota." There was a pause, then Kern sang back, "I tend to be a niggler, and masturbate by quota."

Across the hall, in 15, lived Young and Carter, Negroes. Carter was from Detroit and very black, very clipped in speech, very well dressed, and apt to collapse, at the jab of a rightly angled joke, into a spastic giggling fit that left his cheeks gleaming with tears; Kern was expert at breaking Carter up. Young was a lean, malt-pale colored boy from North Carolina, here on a national scholarship, out of his depth, homesick, and cold. Kern called him Br'er Possum. He slept all day and at night sat on his bed playing the mouthpiece of a trumpet to himself. At first, he had played the full horn in the afternoon, flooding the dormitory and its green envelope of trees with golden, tremulous versions of languorous tunes like "Sentimental Journey" and "The Tennessee Waltz." It had been nice. But Young's somber sense of tact—a slavish drive toward self-effacement that the shock of Harvard had awakened in him—soon cancelled these harmless performances. He took to hiding from the sun, and at night the furtive spitting sound from across the hall seemed to Orson, as he struggled into sleep, music drowning in shame. Carter always referred to his roommate as "Jonathan," mouthing the syllables fastidiously, as if he were pronouncing the name of a remote being he had just learned about, like Rochefoucauld or Demosthenes.

Cattycorner up the hall, in unlucky 13, Petersen and Fitch kept a

strange household. Both were tall, narrow-shouldered, and broad-bot-
tomed; physiques aside, it was hard to see what they had in common, or
why Harvard had put them together. Fitch, with dark staring eyes and
the flat full cranium of Frankenstein's monster, was a child prodigy from
Maine, choked with philosophy, wild with ideas, and pregnant with the
seeds of the nervous breakdown he was to have, eventually, in April.
Petersen was an amiable Swede with a transparent skin that revealed
blue veins in his nose. For several summers he had worked as a reporter
for the Duluth *Herald*. He had all the newsman's tricks: the side-of-the-
mouth quip, the nip of whiskey, the hat on the back of the head, the
habit of throwing still-burning cigarettes onto the floor. He did not
seem quite to know why he was at Harvard, and in fact did not return at
the end of the freshman year. But, while these two drifted toward their
respective failures, they made a strangely well-suited couple. Each was
strong where the other was helpless. Fitch was so uncoordinated and
unorganized he could not even type; he would lie on his bed in pajamas,
writhing and grimacing, and dictate a tangled humanities paper, twice
the requested length and mostly about books that had not been as-
signed, while Petersen, typing with a hectic two-finger system, would
obligingly turn this chaotic monologue into "copy." His patience
verged on the maternal. When Fitch appeared for a meal wearing a
coat and tie, the joke ran in the dormitory that Petersen had dressed
him. In return, Fitch gave Petersen ideas out of the superabundance
painfully cramming his big flat head. Petersen had absolutely no ideas;
he could neither compare, contrast, nor criticize St. Augustine and
Marcus Aurelius. Perhaps having seen, so young, so many corpses and
fires and policemen and prostitutes had prematurely blighted his mind.
At any rate, mothering Fitch gave him something practical to do, and
Orson envied them.

He envied all the roommates, whatever the bond between them—
geography, race, ambition, physical size—for between himself and Hub
Palamountain he could see no link except forced cohabitation. Not that
living with Hub was superficially unpleasant. Hub was tidy, industrious,
and ostentatiously considerate. He rose at seven, prayed, did Yoga,
spun, and was off to breakfast, often not to be seen again until the end of
the day. He went to sleep, generally, at eleven sharp. If there was noise
in the room, he would insert rubber plugs in his ears, put a black mask
over his eyes, and go to sleep anyway. During the day, he kept a
rigorous round of appointments: he audited two courses in addition to
taking four, he wrestled three times a week for his physical-training
requirement, he wangled tea invitations from Demos and Jaeger and
the Bishop of Massachusetts, he attended free evening lectures and
readings, he associated himself with Phillips Brooks House and spent
two afternoons a week supervising slum boys in a Roxbury redevelop-
ment house. In addition, he had begun to take piano lessons in Brook-

line. Many days, Orson saw him only at meals in the Union, where the dormitory neighbors, in those first fall months when their acquaintance was crisp and young and differing interests had not yet scattered them, tended to regroup around a long table. In these months there was often a debate about the subject posed under their eyes: Hub's vegetarianism. There he would sit, his tray heaped high with a steaming double helping of squash and lima beams, while Fitch would try to locate the exact point at which vegetarianism became inconsistent. "You eat eggs," he said.

"Yes," Hub said.

"You realize that every egg, from the chicken's point of reference, is a newborn baby?"

"But in fact it is not unless it has been fertilized by a rooster."

"But suppose," Fitch pursued, "as sometimes happens—which I happen to know, from working in my uncle's henhouse in Maine—an egg that *should* be sterile has in fact been fertilized and contains an embryo?"

"If I see it, I naturally don't eat that particular egg," Hub said, his lips making that satisfied concluding snap.

Fitch pounced triumphantly, spilling a fork to the floor with a lurch of his hand. "But *why?* The hen feels the same pain on being parted from an egg whether sterile or fertile. The embryo is unconscious—a vegetable. As a vegetarian, you should eat it with special relish." He tipped back in his chair so hard he had to grab the table edge to keep from toppling over.

"It seems to me," Dawson said, frowning darkly—these discussions, clogging some twist of his ego, often spilled him into a vile temper—"that psychoanalysis of hens is hardly relevant."

"On the contrary," Kern said lightly, clearing his throat and narrowing his pink, infected eyes, "it seems to me that there, in the tiny, dim mind of the hen—the minimal mind, as it were—is where the tragedy of the universe achieves a pinpoint focus. Picture the emotional life of a hen. What does she know of companionship? A flock of pecking, harsh-voiced gossips. Of shelter? A few dung-bespattered slats. Of food? Some flecks of mash and grit insolently tossed on the ground. Of love? The casual assault of a polygamous cock—cock in the biblical sense. Then, into this heartless world, there suddenly arrives, as if by magic, an egg. An egg of her own. An egg, it must seem to her, that she and God have made. How she must cherish it, its beautiful baldness, its gentle luster, its firm yet somehow fragile, softly swaying weight."

Carter had broken up. He bent above his tray, his eyes tight shut, his dark face contorted joyfully. "Puhleese," he gasped at last. "You're making my stomach hurt."

"Ah, Carter," Kern said loftily, "if that were only the worst of it. For then, one day, while the innocent hen sits cradling this strange, faceless, oval child, its little weight swaying softly in her wings"—he glanced hopefully at Carter, but the colored boy bit his lower lip and withstood the jab—"an enormous man, smelling of beer and manure, comes and tears the egg from her grasp. And why? Because *he*"—Kern pointed, arm fully extended, across the table, so that his index finger, orange with nicotine, almost touched Hub's nose—"*he*, Saint Henry Palamountain, wants more eggs to eat. 'More eggs!' he cries voraciously, so that brutal steers and faithless pigs can continue to menace the children of American mothers!"

Dawson slammed his silver down, got up from the table, and slouched out of the dining room. Kern blushed. In the silence, Petersen put a folded slice of roast beef in his mouth and said, chewing, "Jesus, Hub, if somebody else kills the animals you might as well eat 'em. They don't give a damn anymore."

"You understand nothing," Hub said simply.

"Hey, Hub," Silverstein called down from the far end of the table. "What's the word on milk? Don't calves drink milk? Maybe you're taking milk out of some calf's mouth."

Orson felt impelled to speak. "*No,*" he said, and his voice seemed to have burst, its pitch was so unsteady and excited. "As anybody except somebody from New York would know, milch cows have weaned their calves. What I wonder about, Hub, is your shoes. You wear leather shoes."

"I do." The gaiety left Hub's defense of himself. His lips became prim.

"Leather is the skin of a steer."

"But the animal has already been slaughtered."

"You sound like Petersen. Your purchase of leather goods—what about your wallet and belt, for that matter?—encourages the slaughter. You're as much of a murderer as the rest of us. More of one—because you think about it."

Hub folded his hands carefully in front of him, propping them, almost in prayer, on the table edge. His voice became like that of a radio announcer, but an announcer rapidly, softly describing the home stretch of a race. "My belt, I believe, is a form of plastic. My wallet was given to me by my mother years ago, before I became a vegetarian. Please remember that I ate meat for eighteen years and I still have an appetite for it. If there were any other concentrated source of protein, I would not eat eggs. Some vegetarians do not. On the other hand, some vegetarians eat fish and take liver extract. I would not do this. Shoes are a problem. There is a firm in Chicago that makes non-leather shoes for extreme vegetarians, but they're very expensive and not comfortable. I once ordered a pair. They killed my feet. Leather, you see, 'breathes' in a way no synthetic substitute does. My feet are tender; I have compromised. I apologize. For that matter, when I play the piano I encourage the slaughter of elephants, and in brushing my teeth, which I must do faithfully because a vegetable diet is so heavy in carbohydrates, I use a brush of pig bristles. I am covered with blood, and pray daily for forgiveness." He took up his fork and resumed eating the mound of squash.

Orson was amazed; he had been impelled to speak by a kind of sympathy, and Hub had answered as if he alone were an enemy. He tried to defend himself. "There are perfectly wearable shoes," he said, "made out of canvas, with crepe-rubber soles."

"I'll look into them," Hub said. "They sound a little sporty to me."

Laughter swept the table and ended the subject. After lunch Orson walked to the library with the beginnings of indigestion; a backwash of emotion was upsetting his stomach. There was a growing confusion inside him he could not resolve. He resented being associated with Hub, and yet felt attacked when Hub was attacked. It seemed to him that Hub deserved credit for putting his beliefs into practice, and that people like Fitch and Kern, in mocking, merely belittled themselves. Yet Hub smiled at their criticism, took it as a game, and fought back in earnest only at Orson, forcing him into a false position. Why? Was it because in being also a Christian he alone qualified for serious rebuke? But Carter went to church, wearing a blue pin-striped suit with a monogrammed handkerchief peaked in the breast pocket, every Sunday; Petersen was a nominal Presbyterian; Orson had once seen Kern sneaking out of Mem Chapel; and even Koshland observed his holidays, by cutting classes and skipping lunch. Why, therefore, Orson asked himself, should Hub pick on him? And why should he care? He had no real respect for Hub. Hub's handwriting was childishly large and careful and his first set of hour exams, even in the course on Plato and Aristotle, had yielded a batch of C's. Orson resented being condescended to by an intellectual inferior. The knowledge that at the table he had come off second best galled him like an unfair grade. His situation with Hub became in his head a diagram in which all his intentions curved off at right angles and his strengths inversely tapered into nothing. Behind the diagram hung the tuck of complacence in Hub's lips, the fishy impudence of his eyes, and the keenly irksome shape and tint of his hands and feet. These images—Hub disembodied—Orson carried with him into the library, back and forth to classes, and along the congested streets around the Square; now and then the glaze of an eye or the flat yellowish nail of a big toe welled up distinctly through the pages of a book and, greatly magnified, slid with Orson into the unconsciousness of sleep. Nevertheless, he surprised himself, sitting one February afternoon in Room 12 with Dawson and Kern, by blurting, "I hate him." He considered what he had said, liked the taste of it, and repeated, "I hate the bastard. I've never hated anybody before in my life." His voice cracked and his eyes warmed with abortive tears.

They had all returned from Christmas vacation to plunge into the weird limbo of reading period and the novel ordeal of midyear exams. This was a dormitory, by and large, of public-school graduates, who feel the strain of Harvard most in their freshman year. The private-school boys, launched by little Harvards like Exeter and Groton, tend to glide through this year and to run aground later on strange reefs, foundering in alcohol, or sinking into dandified apathy. But the institution demands of each man, before it releases him, a wrenching sacrifice of ballast. At Christmas, Orson's mother thought he looked haggard, and set about fattening him up. On the other hand, he was struck by how much his father had aged and shrunk. Orson spent his first days home listening to the mindless music on the radio, hours of it, and driving through farmland on narrow straight roads already banked bright with plowed snow. The South Dakota sky had never looked so open, so clean; he had never realized before that the high dry sun that made even sub-zero days feel warm at noon was a local phenomenon. He made love to his girl again, and again she cried. He said to her he blamed himself, for ineptitude; but in his heart he blamed her. She was not helping him. Back in Cambridge, it was raining, raining in January, and the entryway of the Coop was full of gray footprints and wet bicycles and Radcliffe girls in slickers and sneakers. Hub had stayed here, alone in their room, and had celebrated Christmas with a fast.

In the monotonous, almost hallucinatory month of rereading, outlining, and memorizing, Orson perceived how little he knew, how stupid he was, how unnatural all learning is, and how futile. Harvard rewarded him with three A's and a B. Hub pulled out two B's and two C's. Kern, Dawson, and Silverstein did well; Petersen, Koshland, and Carter got mediocre grades; Fitch flunked one subject, and Young flunked three. The pale Negro slunk in and out of the dorm as if he were diseased and marked for destruction; he became, while still among them, a rumor. The suppressed whistling of the trumpet mouthpiece was no longer heard. Silverstein and Koshland and the basketball crowd adopted Carter and took him to movies in Boston three or four times a week.

After exams, in the heart of the Cambridge winter, there is a grateful pause. New courses are selected, and even the full-year courses, heading into their second half, sometimes put on, like a new hat, a fresh professor. The days quietly lengthen; there is a snowstorm or two; the swimming and squash teams lend the sports pages of the *Crimson* an unaccustomed note of victory. A kind of foreshadow of spring falls bluely on the snow. The elms are seen to be shaped like fountains. The discs of snow pressed by boots into the sidewalk by Albiani's seem large precious coins; the brick buildings, the arched gates, the archaic lecterns, and the barny mansions along Brattle Street dawn upon the freshman as a heritage he temporarily possesses. The thumb-worn spines of his now familiar textbooks seem proof of a certain knowingness, and the strap of the green book bag tugs at his wrist like a living falcon. The letters from home dwindle in importance. The hours open up. There is more time. Experiments are made. Courtships begin. Conversations go on and on; and an almost rapacious desire for mutual discovery possesses acquaintances. It was in this atmosphere, then, that Orson made his confession.

Dawson turned his head away as if the words had menaced him personally. Kern blinked, lit a cigarette, and asked, "What don't you like about him?"

"Well"—Orson shifted his weight uncomfortably in the black but graceful, shapely but hard Harvard chair—"it's little things. Whenever he gets a notice from the Portland draft board, he tears it up without opening it and scatters it out the window."

"And you're afraid that this incriminates you as an accessory and they'll put you in jail?"

"No—I don't know. It seems exaggerated. He exaggerates everything. You should see how he prays."

"How do you know how he prays?"

"He shows me. Every morning, he gets down on his knees and *throws* himself across the bed, his face in the blanket, his arms way out." He showed them.

"God," Dawson said. "That's marvelous. It's medieval. It's more than medieval. It's Counter-Reformation."

"I mean," Orson said, grimacing in realization of how deeply he had betrayed Hub, "I pray, too, but I don't make a show of myself."

A frown clotted Dawson's expression, and passed.

"He's a saint," Kern said.

"He's *not,*" Orson said. "He's not intelligent. I'm taking Chem 1 with him, and he's worse than a child with the math. And those Greek books he keeps on his desk, they look worn because he bought them second-hand."

"Saints don't have to be intelligent," Kern said. "What saints have to have is energy. Hub has it."

"Look how he wrestles," Dawson said.

"I doubt if he wrestles very *well,*" Orson said. "He didn't make the freshman team. I'm sure if we heard him play the piano, it'd be awful."

"You seem to miss the point," Kern said, eyes closed, "of what Hub's all about."

"I know goddamn well what he thinks he's all about," Orson said, "but it's fake. It doesn't go. All this vegetarianism and love of the starving Indian—he's really a terribly cold bastard. I think he's about the coldest person I've ever met in my life."

"I don't think Orson thinks that, do you?" Kern asked Dawson.

"No," Dawson said, and his puppyish smile cleared his cloudy face. "That's not what Orson the Parson thinks."

Kern squirmed. "Is it Orson the Parson, or Orson the Person?"

"I think Hub is the nub," Dawson said.

"Or the rub," Kern added, and both burst into grinding laughter. Orson felt he was being sacrificed to the precarious peace the two roommates kept between themselves, and left, superficially insulted but secretly flattered to have been given, at last, a nickname of sorts: Orson the Parson.

Several nights later they went to hear Carl Sandburg read in New Lecture Hall—the four adjacent roommates, plus Fitch. To avoid sitting next to Hub, who aggressively led them into a row of seats, Orson delayed, and so sat the farthest away from the girl Hub sat directly behind. Orson noticed her immediately; she had a lavish mane of coppery red hair which hung down loose over the back of her seat. The color of it, and the abundance, reminded him, all at once, of horses, earth, sun, wheat, and home. From Orson's angle she was nearly in profile; her face was small, with a tilted shadowy cheekbone and a pale prominent ear. Toward the pallor of her profile he felt an orgasmic surge; she seemed suspended in the crowd and was floating, a crest of whiteness, toward him. She turned away. Hub had leaned forward and was saying something into her other ear. Fitch overheard it, and gleefully relayed it to Dawson who whispered to Kern and Orson, *"Hub said to the girl, 'You have beautiful hair.'"*

Several times during the reading, Hub leaned forward to add something more into her ear, each time springing spurts of choked laughter from Fitch, Dawson, and Kern. Meanwhile, Sandburg, his white bangs as straight and shiny as a doll's wig of artificial fiber, incanted above the lectern and quaintly strummed a guitar. Afterward, Hub walked with the girl into the outdoors. From a distance Orson saw her white face turn and crumple into a laugh. Hub returned to his friends with the complacent nick in the corner of his mouth deepened, in the darkness, to a gash.

It was not the next day, or the next week, but within the month that Hub brought back to the room a heap of red hair. Orson found it lying like a disastrous corpse on a newspaper spread on his bed. "Hub, what the hell is this?"

Hub was on the floor playing with his spinning wheel. "Hair."

"Human hair?"

"Of course."

"Whose?"

"A girl's."

"What happened?" The question sounded strange; Orson meant to ask, "What girl's?"

Hub answered as if he had asked that question. "It's a girl I met at the Sandburg reading; you don't know her."

"This is *her* hair?"

"Yes. I asked her for it. She said she was planning to cut it all off this spring anyway."

Orson stood stunned above the bed, gripped by an urge to bury his face and hands in the hair. "You've been *seeing* her?" This effeminate stridence in his voice: he despised it and only Hub brought it out.

"A little. My schedule doesn't allow for much social life, but my adviser has recommended that I relax now and then."

"You take her to movies?"

"Once in a while. She pays her admission, of course."

"Of *course.*"

Hub took him up on his tone. "Please remember I'm here on my savings alone. I have refused all financial assistance from my father."

"Hub"—the very syllable seemed an expression of pain—"what are you going to do with her hair?"

"Spin it into a rope."

"A *rope?*"

"Yes. It'll be very difficult; her hair is terribly fine."

"And what will you do with the rope?"

"Make a knot of it."

"A *knot?*"

"I think that's the term. I'll coil it and secure it so it can't come undone and give it to her. So she'll always have her hair the way it was when she was nineteen."

"How the hell did you talk this poor girl into it?"

"I didn't talk her into it. I merely offered, and she thought it was a lovely idea. Really, Orson, I don't see why this should offend your bourgeois scruples. Women cut their hair all the time."

"She must think you're insane. She was humoring you."

"As you like. It was a perfectly rational suggestion, and my sanity has never been raised as an issue between us."

"Well, *I* think you're insane. Hub, you're a *nut.*"

Orson left the room and slammed the door, and didn't return until eleven, when Hub was asleep in his eye mask. The heap of hair had been transferred to the floor beside the spinning wheel, and already some strands were entangled with the machine. In time a rope was produced, a braided cord as thick as a woman's little finger, about a foot long, weightless and waxen. The earthy, horsy fire in the hair's color had been quenched in the process. Hub carefully coiled it and with black thread and long pins secured and stiffened the spiral into a disc the size of a small saucer. This he presented to the girl one Friday night. The presentation appeared to satisfy him, for, as far as Orson knew, Hub had no further dates with her. Once in a while Orson passed her in the Yard, and without her hair she scarcely seemed female, her small pale face fringed in curt tufts, her ears looking enormous. He wanted to speak to her; some obscure force of pity, or hope of rescue, impelled him to greet this wan androgyne, but the opening word stuck in his throat. She did not look as if she pitied herself, or knew what had been done to her.

Something magical protected Hub; things deflected from him. The doubt Orson had cast upon his sanity bounced back onto himself. As spring slowly broke, he lost the ability to sleep. Figures and facts churned sluggishly in an insomnious mire. His courses became four parallel puzzles. In mathematics, the crucial transposition upon which the solution pivoted consistently eluded him, vanishing into the chinks between the numbers. The quantities in chemistry became impishly unstable; the unbalanced scales clicked down sharply and the system of interlocked elements that fanned from the lab to the far stars collapsed. In the history survey course, they had reached the Enlightenment, and Orson found himself disturbingly impressed by Voltaire's indictment of God, though the lecturer handled it calmly, as one more dead item of intellectual history, neither true nor false. And in German, which Orson had taken to satisfy his language requirement, the words piled on remorselessly, and the existence of languages other than English, the existence of so many, each so vast, intricate, and opaque, seemed to prove cosmic dementia. He felt his mind, which was always more steady than quick, grow slower and slower. His chair threatened to adhere to him, and he would leap up in panic. Sleepless, stuffed with information he could neither forget nor manipulate, he became prey to obsessive delusions; he became convinced that his girl in South Dakota had taken up with another boy and was making love to him happily, Orson having shouldered the awkwardness and blame of taking her virginity. In the very loops that Emily's ballpoint pen described in her bland letters to him he read the pleased rotundity, the inner fatness of a well-loved woman. He even knew the man. It was Spotted Elk, the black-nailed Chippewa, whose impassive nimbleness had so often mocked Orson on the basketball court, whose terrible ease and speed of reaction had seemed so unjust, and whose defense—he recalled now—Emily had often undertaken. His wife had become a whore, a squaw; the scraggly mute reservation children his father had doctored in the charity clinic became, amid the sliding transparencies of Orson's mind, his own children. In his dreams—or in those limp elisions of imagery which in the absence of sleep passed for dreams—he seemed to be rooming with Spotted Elk, and his roommate, who sometimes wore a mask, invariably had won, by underhanded means, the affection and admiration that were rightfully his. There was a conspiracy. Whenever Orson heard Kern and Dawson laughing on the other side of the wall, he knew it was about him, and about his most secret habits. This ultimate privacy was outrageously invaded; in bed, half-relaxed, he would suddenly see himself bodily involved with Hub's lips, Hub's legs, with Hub's veined, vaguely womanish hands. At first he resisted these visions, tried to erase them; it was like trying to erase ripples on water. He learned to submit to them, to let the attack—for it was an attack, with teeth and sharp acrobatic movements—wash over him, leaving him limp enough to sleep. These dives became the only route to sleep. In the morning he would awake and see Hub sprawled flamboyantly across his bed in prayer, or sitting hunched at his spinning wheel, or, gaudily dressed, tiptoeing to the door and with ostentatious care closing it softly behind him, and he would hate him—hate his appearance, his form, his manner, his pretensions with an avidity of detail he had never known in love. The tiny details of his roommate's physical existence—the wrinkles flickering beside his mouth, the slightly withered look about his hands, the complacently polished creases of his leather shoes—seemed a poisonous food Orson could not stop eating. His eczema worsened alarmingly.

By April, Orson was on the verge of going to the student clinic, which had a department called Mental Health. But at this point Fitch relieved him by having, it seemed, his nervous breakdown for him. For weeks, Fitch had been taking several showers a day. Toward the end he stopped going to classes and was almost constantly naked, except for a towel tucked around his waist. He was trying to complete a humanities paper that was already a month overdue and twenty pages too long. He left the dormitory only to eat and to take more books from the library. One night around nine, Petersen was called to the phone on the second-floor landing. The Watertown police had picked Fitch up as he was struggling through the underbrush on the banks of the Charles four miles away. He claimed he was walking to the West, where he had been told there was enough space to contain God, and proceeded to talk with wild animation to the police chief about the differences and affinities between Kierkegaard and Nietzsche. Hub, ever alert for an opportunity to intrude in the guise of doing good, went to the hall proctor—a spindly and murmurous graduate student of astronomy engaged, under Harlow Shapley, in an endless galaxy count—and volunteered himself as an expert on the case, and even conferred with the infirmary psychologist. Hub's interpretation was that Fitch had been punished for hubris. The psychologist felt the problem was fundamentally Oedipal. Fitch was sent back to Maine. Hub suggested to Orson that now Petersen would need a roommate next year. "I think you and he would hit it off splendidly. You're both materialists."

"I'm *not* a materialist."

Hub lifted his dreadful hands in half-blessing. "Have it your way. I'm determined to minimize friction."

"Dammit, Hub, all the friction between us comes from *you.*"

"How? What do I do? Tell me, and I'll change. I'll give you the shirt off my back." He began to unbutton, and stopped, seeing that the laugh wasn't going to come.

Orson felt weak and empty, and in spite of himself he cringed inwardly, with a helpless affection for his unreal, unreachable friend. "I don't know, Hub," he admitted. "I don't know what it is you're doing to me."

A paste of silence dried in the air between them.

Orson with an effort unstuck himself. "I think you're right, we shouldn't room together next year."

Hub seemed a bit bewildered, but nodded, saying, "I told them in the beginning that I ought to live alone." And his hurt eyes bulging behind their lenses settled into an invulnerable Byzantine stare.

One afternoon in middle May, Orson was sitting stumped at his desk, trying to study. He had taken two exams and had two to go. They stood between him and release like two towering walls of muddy paper. His position seemed extremely precarious: he was unable to retreat and able to advance only along a very thin thread, a high wire of sanity on which he balanced above an abyss of statistics and formulae, his brain a firmament of winking cells. A push would kill him. There was then a hurried pounding up the stairs, and Hub pushed into the room carrying cradled in his arm a metal object the color of a gun and the size of a cat. It had a red tongue. Hub slammed the door behind him, snapped the lock, and dumped the object on Orson's bed. It was the head of a parking meter, sheared from its post. A keen quick pain cut through Orson's groin. "For God's sake," he cried in his contemptible high voice, "what's *that?*"

"It's a parking meter."

"I *know*, I can *see* that. Where the hell did you *get* it?"

"I won't talk to you until you stop being hysterical," Hub said, and crossed to his desk, where Orson had put his mail. He took the top letter, a special delivery from the Portland draft board, and tore it in half. This time, the pain went through Orson's chest. He put his head in his arms on the desk and whirled and groped in the black-red darkness there. His body was frightening him; his nerves listened for a third psychosomatic slash.

There was a rap on the door; from the force of the knock it could only be the police. Hub nimbly dashed to the bed and hid the meter under Orson's pillow. Then he pranced to the door and opened it.

It was Dawson and Kern. "What's up?" Dawson asked, frowning as if the disturbance had been created to annoy him.

"It sounded like Ziegler was being tortured," Kern said.

Orson pointed at Hub and explained, "He's castrated a parking meter!"

"I did not," Hub said. "A car went out of control on Mass. Avenue and hit a parked car, which knocked a meter down. A crowd gathered. The head of the meter was lying in the gutter, so I picked it up and carried it away. I was afraid someone might be tempted to steal it."

"Nobody tried to stop you?" Kern asked.

"Of course not. They were all gathered around the driver of the car."

"Was he hurt?"

"I doubt it. I didn't look."

"You didn't *look!*" Orson cried. "You're a great Samaritan."

"I am not prey," Hub said, "to morbid curiosity."

"Where were the police?" Kern asked.

"They hadn't arrived yet."

Dawson asked, "Well why didn't you wait till a cop arrived and give the meter to him?"

"Why should I give it to an agent of the State? It's no more his than mine."

"But it *is,*" Orson said.

"It was a plain act of Providence that placed it in my hands," Hub said, the corners of his lips dented securely. "I haven't decided yet which charity should receive the money it contains."

Dawson asked, "But isn't that stealing?"

"No more stealing than the State is stealing in making people pay money for space in which to park their own cars."

"Huh," Orson said, getting to his feet. "You give it back or we'll both go to jail." He saw himself ruined, the scarcely commenced career of his life destroyed.

Hub turned serenely. "I'm not afraid. Going to jail under a totalitarian regime is a mark of honor. If you had a conscience, you'd understand."

Petersen and Carter and Silverstein came into the room. Some boys from the lower floors followed them. The story was hilariously retold. The meter was produced from under the pillow and passed around and shaken to demonstrate the weight of pennies it contained. Hub always carried, as a vestige of the lumberjack country he came from, an intricate all-purpose pocket knife. He began to pry open the little money door. Orson came up behind him and got him around the neck with one arm. Hub's body stiffened. He passed the head of the meter and the open knife to Carter, and then Orson experienced sensations of being lifted, of flying, and of lying on the floor, looking up at Hub's face, which was upside down in his vision. He scrambled to his feet and went for him again, rigid with anger and yet, in his heart, happily relaxed; Hub's body was tough and quick and satisfying to grip, though, being a wrestler, he somehow deflected Orson's hands and again lifted and dropped him to the black floor. This time, Orson felt a blow as his coccyx hit the wood; yet even through the pain he perceived, gazing into the heart of this marriage, that Hub was being as gentle with him as he could be. And that he could try in earnest to kill Hub and be in no danger of succeeding was also a comfort. He renewed the attack and again enjoyed the tense defensive skill that made Hub's body a kind of warp in space through which his own body, after an ecstatic instant of contention, was converted to the supine position. He got to his feet and would have gone for Hub the fourth time, but his fellow-freshmen grabbed his arms and held him. He shook them off and without a word returned to his desk and concentrated down into his book, turning the page. The type looked extremely distinct, though it was trembling too hard to be deciphered.

The head of the parking meter stayed in the room for one night. The next day, Hub allowed himself to be persuaded (by the others; Orson had stopped speaking to him) to take it to the Cambridge police headquarters in Central Square. Dawson and Kern tied a ribbon around it, and attached a note: "Please take good care of my baby." None of them, however, had the nerve to go with Hub to the headquarters, though when he came back he said the chief was delighted to get the meter, and had thanked him, and had agreed to donate the pennies to the local orphans' home. In another week, the last exams were over. The freshmen all went home. When they returned in the fall, they were different: sophomores. Petersen and Young did not come back at all. Fitch returned, made up the lost credits, and eventually graduated *magna cum* in History and Lit. He now teaches in a Quaker prep school. Silverstein is a biochemist, Koshland a lawyer. Dawson writes conservative editorials in Cleveland, Kern is in advertising in New York. Carter, as if obliged to join Young in oblivion, disappeared between his junior and senior years. The dormitory neighbors tended to lose sight of each other, though Hub, who had had his case shifted to the Massachusetts jurisdiction, was now and then pictured in the *Crimson,* and once gave an evening lecture, "Why I Am an Episcopalian Pacifist." As the litigation progressed, the Bishop of Massachusetts rather grudgingly vouched for him, and by the time of his final hearing the Korean War was over, and the judge who heard the case ruled that Hub's convictions were sincere, as witnessed by his willingness to go to jail. Hub was rather disappointed at the verdict, since he had prepared a three-year reading list to occupy him in his cell and was intending to memorize all four Gospels in the original Greek. After graduation, he went to Union Theological Seminary, spent several years as the assistant rector of an urban parish in Baltimore, and learned to play the piano well enough to be the background music in a Charles Street cocktail lounge. He insisted on wearing his clerical collar, and as a consequence gave the bar a small celebrity. After a year of overriding people of less strong convictions, he was allowed to go to South Africa, where he worked and preached among the Bantus until the government requested that he leave the country. From there he went to Nigeria, and when last heard from—on a Christmas card, with French salutations and Negro Magi, which arrived, soiled and wrinkled, in South Dakota in February—Hub was in Madagascar, as a "combination missionary, political agitator, and soccer coach." The description struck Orson as probably facetious, and Hub's childish and confident handwriting, with every letter formed individually, afflicted him with some of the old exasperation. Having vowed to answer the card, he mislaid it, uncharacteristically.

Orson didn't speak to Hub for two days after the parking-meter incident. By then, it seemed rather silly, and they finished out the year sitting side by side at their desks as amiably as two cramped passengers who have endured a long bus trip together. When they parted, they shook hands, and Hub would have walked Orson to the subway kiosk except that he had an appointment in the opposite direction. Orson received two A's and two B's on his final exams; for the remaining three years at Harvard, he roomed uneventfully with two other colorless premed students, named Wallace and Neuhauser. After graduation, he married Emily, attended the Yale School of Medicine, and interned in St. Louis. He is now the father of four children and, since the death of his own father, the only doctor in the town. His life has gone much the way he planned it, and he is much the kind of man he intended to be when he was eighteen. He delivers babies, assists the dying, attends the necessary meetings, plays golf, and does good. He is honorable and irritable. If not as much loved as his father, he is perhaps even more respected. In one particular only—a kind of scar he carries without pain and without any clear memory of the amputation—does the man he is differ from the man he assumed he would become. He never prays.

JOY WILLIAMS

The Wedding

Elizabeth always wanted to read fables to her little girl but the child only wanted to hear the story about the little bird who thought a steam shovel was its mother. They would often argue about this. Elizabeth was sick of the story. She particularly disliked the part where the baby bird said, "You are not my mother, you are a *snort*, I want to get out of here!" Elizabeth was thirty and the child was five. At night, at the child's bedtime, Sam would often hear them complaining bitterly to one another. He would preheat the broiler for dinner and freshen his drink and go out and sit on the picnic table. In a little while, the screen door would slam and Elizabeth would come out, shaking her head. The child had frustrated her again. The child would not go to sleep. She was upstairs, wandering around, making "cotton candy" in her bone-china bunny mug. "Cotton candy" was Kleenex sogged in water. Sometimes Elizabeth would tell Sam the story that she had prepared for the child. The people in Elizabeth's fables were always looking for truth or happiness and they were always being given mirrors or lumps of coal. Elizabeth's stories were inhabited by wolves and cart horses and solipsists.

"Please relax," Sam would say.

At eleven o'clock every night, Sam would take a double Scotch on the rocks up to his bedroom.

"Sam," the child called, "have some of my cotton candy. It's delicious."

Elizabeth's child reminded Sam of Hester's little Pearl even though he knew that her father, far from being the "Prince of the Air," was a tax accountant. Elizabeth spoke about him often. He had not shared the 1973 refund with her even though they had filed jointly and half of the year's income had been hers. Apparently the marriage had broken up because she often served hamburgers with baked potatoes instead of French fries. Over the years, astonishment had turned to disapproval and then to true annoyance. The tax accountant told Elizabeth that she didn't know how to do anything right. Elizabeth, in turn, told her accountant that he was always ejaculating prematurely.

"Sam," the child called, "why do you have your hand over your heart?"

"That's my Scotch," Sam said.

Elizabeth was a nervous young woman. She was nervous because she was not married to Sam. This desire to be married again embarrassed her, but she couldn't help it. Sam was married to someone else. Sam was always married to someone.

Sam and Elizabeth met as people usually meet. Suddenly, there was a deceptive light in the darkness. A light that reminded the lonely blackly of the darkness. They met at the wedding dinner of the daughter of a mutual friend. Delicious food was served and many peculiar toasts were given. Sam liked Elizabeth's aura and she liked his too. They danced. Sam had quite a bit to drink. At one point, he thought he saw a red rabbit in the floral centerpiece. It's true, it was Easter week, but he worried about this. They danced again. Sam danced Elizabeth out of the party and into the parking lot. Sam's car was nondescript and tidy except for a bag of melting groceries.

Elizabeth loved the way he kissed. He put his hand on her throat. He lay his tongue deep and quiet inside her mouth. He filled her mouth with the decadent Scotch and cigarette flavor of the tragic middle class. On the other hand, when Sam saw Elizabeth's brightly flowered scanty panties, he thought he'd faint with happiness. He was a sentimentalist.

"I love you," Elizabeth thought she heard him say.

Sam swore that he heard Elizabeth say, "Life is an eccentric privilege."

This worried him but not in time.

They began going out together frequently. Elizabeth promised to always take the baby-sitter home. At first, Elizabeth and Sam attempted to do vile and imaginative things to one another. This was culminated one afternoon when Sam spooned a mound of pineapple-lime Jell-O between Elizabeth's legs and began to eat. At first, of course, Elizabeth was nervous. Then she stopped being nervous and began watching Sam's sweating, good-looking shoulders with real apprehension. Simultaneously, they both gave up. This seemed a good sign. The battle is always between the pleasure principle and the reality principle is it not? Imagination is not what it's cracked up to be. Sam decided to forget the petty, bourgeois rite of eating food out of one another's orifices for a while. He decided to just love Elizabeth instead.

"Did you know that Charles Dickens wanted to marry Little Red Riding Hood?"

"What!" Sam exclaimed, appalled.

"Well, as a child he wanted to marry her," Elizabeth said.

"Oh," Sam said, curiously relieved.

Elizabeth had a house and her little girl. Sam had a house and a car and a Noank sloop. The houses were thirteen hundred miles apart. They spent the winter in Elizabeth's house in the South and they drove up to Sam's house for the summer. The trip took two and one-half days. They had done it twice now. It seemed about the same each time. They argued on the Baltimore Beltway. They bought peaches and cigarettes and fireworks and a ham. The child would often sit on the floor in the front seat and talk into the air-conditioning vent.

"Emergency," she'd say. "Come in please."

On the most recent trip, Sam had called his lawyer from a Hot Shoppe on the New Jersey Turnpike. The lawyer told him that Sam's divorce had become final that morning. This had been Sam's third marriage. He and Annie had seemed very compatible. They tended to each other realistically, with affection and common sense. Then Annie decided to go back to school. She became interested in animal behaviorism. Books accumulated. She was never at home. She was always on field trips, in thickets or on beaches, or visiting some ornithologist in Barnstable. She began keeping voluminous notebooks. Sam came across the most alarming things written in her hand.

> Mantids are cannibalistic and males often literally lose their heads to the females. The result, as far as successful mating is concerned, is beneficial, since the suboesophageal ganglion is frequently removed and with it any inhibition on the copulatory center; the activities of male abdomen are carried out with more vigor than when the body was intact.

"Annie, Annie," Sam had pleaded. "Let's have some people over for drinks. Let's prune the apple tree. Let's bake the orange cake you always made for my birthday."

"I have never made an orange cake in my life," Annie said.

"Annie," Sam said, "don't they have courses in seventeenth-century romantic verse or something?"

"You drink too much," Annie said. "You get quarrelsome every night at nine. Your behavior patterns are severely limited."

Sam clutched his head with his hands.

"Plus you are reducing my ability to respond to meaningful occurrences, Sam."

Sam poured himself another Scotch. He lit a cigarette. He applied a mustache with a piece of picnic charcoal.

"I am Captain Blood," he said. "I want to kiss you."

"When Errol Flynn died, he had the body of a man of ninety," Annie said. "His brain was unrealistic from alcohol."

She had already packed the toast rack and the pewter and rolled up the Oriental rug.

"I am just taking this one Wanda Landowska recording," she said. "That's all I'm taking in the way of records."

Sam, with his charcoal mustache, sat very straight at his end of the table.

"The variations in our life have ceased to be significant," Annie said.

Sam's house was on a hill overlooking a cove. The cove was turning into a saltwater marsh. Sam liked marshes but he thought he had bought property on a deep-water cove where he could take his boat in and out. He wished that he were not involved in the process of his cove turning into a marsh. When he had first bought the place, he was so excited about everything that he had a big dinner party at which he served *soupe de poisson* using only the fish he had caught himself from the cove. He could not, it seems, keep himself from doing this each year. Each year, the *soupe de poisson* did not seem as nice as it had the year before. About a year before Annie left him, she suggested that they should probably stop having that particular dinner party. Sam felt flim-flammed.

When Sam returned to the table in the Hot Shoppe on the New Jersey Turnpike after learning about his divorce, Elizabeth didn't look at him.

"I have been practicing different expressions, none of which seem appropriate," Elizabeth said.

"Well," Sam said.

"I might as well be honest," Elizabeth said.

Sam bit into his egg. He did not feel lean and young and unencumbered.

"In the following sentence, the same word is used in each of the missing spaces, but pronounced differently." Elizabeth's head was bowed. She was reading off the place mat. "Don't look at yours now, Sam," she said, "the answer's on it." She slid his place mat off the table, spilling coffee on his cuff in the process. *"A prominent and————man came into a restaurant at the height of the rush hour. The waitress was ————to serve him immediately as she had————."*

Sam looked at her. She smiled. He looked at the child. The child's eyes were closed and she was moving her thumb around in her mouth as though she were making butter there. Sam paid the bill. The child went to the bathroom. An hour later, just before the Tappan Zee Bridge, Sam said, *"Notable."*

"What?" Elizabeth said.

"*Notable.* That's the word that belongs in all three spaces."

"You looked," Elizabeth said.

"Goddamn it," Sam yelled. "I did not look!"

"I knew this would happen," Elizabeth said. "I knew it was going to be like this."

It is a very hot night. Elizabeth has poison ivy on her wrists. Her wrists are covered with calamine lotion. She has put Saran Wrap over the lotion and secured it with a rubber band. Sam is in love. He smells the wonderfully clean, sun-and-linen smell of Elizabeth and her calamine lotion.

Elizabeth is going to tell a fairy story to the child. Sam tries to convince her that fables are sanctimonious and dully realistic.

"Tell her any one except the 'Frog King,' " Sam whispers.

"Why can't I tell her that one," Elizabeth says. She is worried.

"The toad stands for male sexuality," Sam whispers.

"Oh Sam," she says. "That's so superficial. That's a very superficial analysis of the animal-bridegroom stories."

"I am an animal," Sam growls, biting her softly on the collarbone.

"Oh Sam," she says.

Sam's first wife was very pretty. She had the flattest stomach he had ever seen and very black, very straight hair. He adored her. He was faithful to her. He wrote both their names on the flyleaves of all his books. They were married for six years. They went to Europe. They went to Mexico. In Mexico they lived in a grand room in a simple hotel opposite a square. The trees in the square were pruned in the shape of perfect boxes. Each night, hundreds of birds would come home to the trees. Beside the hotel was the shop of a man who made coffins. So many of the coffins seemed small, for children. Sam's wife grew depressed. She lay in bed for most of the day. She pretended she was dying. She wanted Sam to make love to her and pretend that she was dying. She wanted a baby. She was all mixed up.

Sam suggested that it was the ions in the Mexican air that made her depressed. He kept loving her but it became more and more difficult for them both. She continued to retreat into a landscape of chaos and warring feelings.

Her depression became general. They had been married for almost six years but they were still only twenty-four years old. Often they would go to amusement parks. They liked the bumper cars best. The last time they had gone to the amusement park, Sam had broken his wife's hand when he crashed head-on into her bumper car. They could probably have gotten over the incident had they not been so bitterly miserable at the time.

In the middle of the night, the child rushes down the hall and into Elizabeth and Sam's bedroom.

"Sam," the child cries, "the baseball game! I'm missing the baseball game."

"There is no baseball game," Sam says.

"What's the matter? What's happening!" Elizabeth cries.

"Yes, yes," the child wails. "I'm late, I'm missing it."

"Oh what is it!" Elizabeth cries.

"The child is having an anxiety attack," Sam says.

The child puts her thumb in her mouth and then takes it out again. "I'm only five years old," she says.

"That's right," Elizabeth says. "She's too young for anxiety attacks. It's only a dream." She takes the child back to her room. When she comes back, Sam is sitting up against the pillows, drinking a glass of Scotch.

"Why do you have your hand over your heart?" Elizabeth asks.

"I think it's because it hurts," Sam says.

Elizabeth is trying to stuff another fable into the child. She is determined this time. Sam has just returned from setting the mooring for his sailboat. He is sprawled in a hot bath, listening to the radio.

Elizabeth says, "There were two men wrecked on a desert island and one of them pretended he was home while the other admitted . . ."

"Oh Mummy," the child says.

"I know that one," Sam says from the tub. "They both died."

"This is not a primitive story," Elizabeth says. "Colorless, anticlimactic endings are typical only of primitive stories."

Sam pulls his knees up and slides underneath the water. The water is really blue. Elizabeth had dyed curtains in the tub and stained the porcelain. Blue is Elizabeth's favorite color. Slowly, Sam's house is turning blue. Sam pulls the plug and gets out of the tub. He towels himself off. He puts on a shirt, a tie and a white summer suit. He laces up his sneakers. He slicks back his soaking hair. He goes into the child's room. The lights are out. Elizabeth and the child are looking at each other in the dark. There are fireflies in the room.

"They come in on her clothes," Elizabeth says.

"Will you marry me?" Sam asks.

"I'd love to," she says.

Sam calls his friends up, beginning with Peter, his oldest friend. While they have been out of touch, Peter has become a soft contact lenses king.

"I am getting married," Sam says.

There is a pause, then Peter finally says, "Once more the boat departs."

It is harder to get married than one would think. Sam has forgotten this. For example, what is the tone that should be established for the party? Elizabeth's mother believes that a wedding cake is very necessary. Elizabeth is embarrassed about this.

"I can't think about that, Mother," she says. She puts her mother and the child in charge of the wedding cake. At the child's suggestion, it has a jam center and a sailboat on it.

Elizabeth and Sam decide to get married at the home of a justice of the peace. Her name is Mrs. Custer. Then they will come back to their own house for a party. They invite a lot of people to the party.

"I have taken out 'obey,'" Mrs. Custer says, "but I have left in 'love' and 'cherish.' Some people object to the 'obey.'"

"That's all right," Sam says.

"I could start now," Mrs. Custer says. "But my husband will be coming home soon. If we wait a few moments, he will be here and then he won't interrupt the ceremony."

"That's all right," Sam says.

They stand around. Sam whispers to Elizabeth, "I should pay this woman a little something, but I left my wallet at home."

"That's all right," Elizabeth says.

"Everything's going to be fine," Sam says.

They get married. They drive home. Everyone has arrived, and some of the guests have brought their children. The children run around with Elizabeth's child. One little girl has long red hair and painted green nails.

"I remember you," the child says. "You had a kitty. Why didn't you bring your kitty with you?"

"That kitty bought the chops," the little girl says.

Elizabeth overhears this. "Oh my goodness," she says. She takes her daughter into the bathroom and closes the door.

"There is more than the seeming of things," she says to the child.

"Oh Mummy," the child says, "I just want my nails green like that girl's."

"Elizabeth," Sam calls. "Please come out. The house is full of people. I'm getting drunk. We've been married for one hour and fifteen minutes." He closes his eyes and leans his forehead against the door. Miraculously, he enters. The closed door is not locked. The child escapes by the same entrance, happy to be freed. Sam kisses Elizabeth by the shower stall. He kisses her beside the sink and before the full-length mirror. He kisses her as they stand pressed against the windowsill. Together, in their animistic embrace, they float out the window and circle the house, gazing down at all those who have not found true love, below.

TOBIAS WOLFF

The Liar

My mother read everything except books. Advertisements on buses, entire menus as we ate, billboards; if it had no cover it interested her. So when she found a letter in my drawer that was not addressed to her she read it. "What difference does it make if James has nothing to hide?"— that was her thought. She stuffed the letter in the drawer when she finished it and walked from room to room in the big empty house, talking to herself. She took the letter out and read it again to get the facts straight. Then, without putting on her coat or locking the door, she went down the steps and headed for the church at the end of the street. No matter how angry and confused she might be, she always went to four o'clock Mass and now it was four o'clock.

It was a fine day, blue and cold and still, but Mother walked as though into a strong wind, bent forward at the waist with her feet hurrying behind in short, busy steps. My brother and sisters and I considered this walk of hers funny and we smirked at one another when she crossed in front of us to stir the fire, or water a plant. We didn't let her catch us at it. It would have puzzled her to think that there might be anything amusing about her. Her one concession to the fact of humor was an insincere, startling laugh. Strangers often stared at her.

While Mother waited for the priest, who was late, she prayed. She prayed in a familiar, orderly, firm way: first for her late husband, my father, then for her parents—also dead. She said a quick prayer . . . for my father's parents (just touching base; she had disliked them) and finally for her children in order of their ages, ending with me. Mother did not consider originality a virtue and until my name came up her prayers were exactly the same as on any other day.

But when she came to me she spoke up boldly. "I thought he wasn't going to do it anymore. Murphy said he was cured. What am I supposed to do now?" There was reproach in her tone. Mother put great hope in her notion that I was cured. She regarded my cure as an answer to her prayers and by way of thanksgiving sent a lot of money to the Thomasite

Indian Mission, money she had been saving for a trip to Rome. She felt cheated and she let her feelings be known. When the priest came in Mother slid back on the seat and followed the Mass with concentration. After communion she began to worry again and went straight home without stopping to talk to Frances, the woman who always cornered Mother after Mass to tell about the awful things done to her by Communists, devil-worshippers, and Rosicrucians. Frances watched her go with narrowed eyes.

Once in the house, Mother took the letter from my drawer and brought it into the kitchen. She held it over the stove with her fingernails, looking away so that she would not be drawn into it again, and set it on fire. When it began to burn her fingers she dropped it in the sink and watched it blacken and flutter and close upon itself like a fist. Then she washed it down the drain and called Dr. Murphy.

The letter was to my friend Ralphy in Arizona. He used to live across the street from us but he had moved. Most of the letter was about a tour we, the junior class, had taken of Alcatraz. That was all right. What got Mother was the last paragraph where I said that she had been coughing up blood and the doctors weren't sure what was wrong with her, but that we were hoping for the best.

This wasn't true. Mother took pride in her physical condition, considered herself a horse: "I'm a regular horse," she would reply when people asked about her health. For several years now I had been saying unpleasant things that weren't true and this habit of mine irked Mother greatly, enough to persuade her to send me to Dr. Murphy, in whose office I was sitting when she burned the letter. Dr. Murphy was our family physician and had no training in psychoanalysis but he took an interest in "things of the mind," as he put it. He had treated me for appendicitis and tonsillitis and Mother thought that he could put the truth into me as easily as he took things out of me, a hope Dr. Murphy did not share. He was basically interested in getting me to understand what I did, and lately he had been moving toward the conclusion that I understood what I did as well as I ever would.

Dr. Murphy listened to Mother's account of the letter, and what she had done with it. He was curious about the wording I had used and became irritated when Mother told him she had burned it. "The point is," she said, "he was supposed to be cured and he's not."

"Margaret, I never said he was cured."

"You certainly did. Why else would I have sent over a thousand dollars to the Thomasite Mission?"

"I said that he was responsible. That means that James knows what he's doing, not that he's going to stop doing it."

"I'm sure you said he was cured."

"Never. To say that someone is cured you have to know what health is. With this kind of thing that's impossible. What do you mean by curing James, anyway?"

"You know."

"Tell me anyway."

"Getting him back to reality, what else?"

"Whose reality? Mine or yours?"

"Murphy, what are you talking about? James isn't crazy, he's a liar."

"Well, you have a point there."

"What am I going to do with him?"

"I don't think there's much you can do. Be patient."

"I've been patient."

"If I were you, Margaret, I wouldn't make too much of this. James doesn't steal, does he?"

"Of course not."

"Or beat people up or talk back."

"No."

"Then you have a lot to be thankful for."

"I don't think I can take any more of it. That business about leukemia last summer. And now this."

"Eventually he'll outgrow it, I think."

"Murphy, he's sixteen years old. What if he doesn't outgrow it? What if he just gets better at it?"

Finally Mother saw that she wasn't going to get any satisfaction from Dr. Murphy, who kept reminding her of her blessings. She said something cutting to him and he said something pompous back and she hung up. Dr. Murphy stared at the receiver. "Hello," he said, then replaced it on the cradle. He ran his hand over his head, a habit remaining from a time when he had hair. To show that he was a good sport he often joked about his baldness, but I had the feeling that he regretted it deeply. Looking at me across the desk, he must have wished that he hadn't taken me on. Treating a friend's child was like investing a friend's money.

"I don't have to tell you who that was."

I nodded.

Dr. Murphy pushed his chair back and swiveled it around so he could look out the window behind him, which took up most of the wall. There were still a few sailboats out on the Bay, but they were all making for shore. A woolly gray fog had covered the bridge and was moving in fast. The water seemed calm from this far up, but when I looked closely I could see white flecks everywhere, so it must have been pretty choppy.

"I'm surprised at you," he said. "Leaving something like that lying around for her to find. If you really have to do these things you could at least be kind and do them discreetly. It's not easy for your mother, what with your father dead and all the others somewhere else."

"I know. I didn't mean for her to find it."

"Well." He tapped his pencil against his teeth. He was not convinced professionally, but personally he may have been. "I think you ought to go home now and straighten things out."

"I guess I'd better."

"Tell your mother I might stop by, either tonight or tomorrow. And James—don't underestimate her."

While my father was alive we usually went to Yosemite for three or four days during the summer. My mother would drive and Father would point out places of interest, meadows where boom towns once stood, hanging trees, rivers that were said to flow upstream at certain times. Or he read to us; he had that grown-ups' idea that children love Dickens and Sir Walter Scott. The four of us sat in the back seat with our faces composed, attentive, while our hands and feet pushed, pinched, stomped, goosed, prodded, dug, and kicked.

One night a bear came into our camp just after dinner. Mother had made a tuna casserole and it must have smelled to him like something worth dying for. He came into the camp while we were sitting around the fire and stood swaying back and forth. My brother Michael saw him first and elbowed me, then my sisters saw him and screamed. Mother and Father had their backs to him but Mother must have guessed what it was because she immediately said, "Don't scream like that. You might frighten him and there's no telling what he'll do. We'll just sing and he'll go away."

We sang "Row Row Row Your Boat" but the bear stayed. He circled us several times, rearing up now and then on his hind legs to stick his nose into the air. By the light of the fire I could see his doglike face and watch the muscles roll under his loose skin like rocks in a sack. We sang harder as he circled us, coming closer and closer. "All right," Mother said, "enough's enough." She stood abruptly. The bear stopped moving and watched her. "Beat it," Mother said. The bear sat down and looked from side to side. "Beat it," she said again, and leaned over and picked up a rock.

"Margaret, don't," my father said.

She threw the rock hard and hit the bear in the stomach. Even in the dim light I could see the dust rising from his fur. He grunted and stood to his full height. "See that?" Mother shouted: "He's filthy. Filthy!" One of my sisters giggled. Mother picked up another rock. "Please, Margaret," my father said. Just then the bear turned and shambled away. Mother pitched the rock after him. For the rest of the night he loitered around the camp until he found the tree where we had hung our food. He ate it all. The next day we drove back to the city. We could have bought more supplies in the valley, but Father wanted to go and would not give in to any argument. On the way home he tried to jolly everyone up by making jokes, but Michael and my sisters ignored him and looked stonily out the windows.

Things were never easy between my mother and me, but I didn't underestimate her. She underestimated me. When I was little she suspected me of delicacy, because I didn't like being thrown into the air, and because when I saw her and the others working themselves up for a roughhouse I found somewhere else to be. When they did drag me in I got hurt, a knee in the lip, a bent finger, a bloody nose, and this too Mother seemed to hold against me, as if I arranged my hurts to get out of playing.

Even things I did well got on her nerves. We all loved puns except Mother, who didn't get them, and next to my father I was the best in the family. My specialty was the Swifty—"'You can bring the prisoner down,' said Tom condescendingly." Father encouraged me to perform at dinner, which must have been a trial for outsiders. Mother wasn't sure what was going on, but she didn't like it.

She suspected me in other ways. I couldn't go to the movies without her examining my pockets to make sure I had enough money to pay for the ticket. When I went away to camp she tore my pack apart in front of all the boys who were waiting in the bus outside the house. I would rather have gone without my sleeping bag and a few changes of underwear, which I had forgotten, than be made such a fool of. Her distrust was the thing that made me forgetful.

And she thought I was coldhearted because of what happened the day my father died and later at his funeral. I didn't cry at my father's funeral, and showed signs of boredom during the eulogy, fiddling around with the hymnals. Mother put my hands into my lap and I left them there without moving them as though they were things I was holding for someone else. The effect was ironical and she resented it. We had a sort of reconciliation a few days later after I closed my eyes at school and refused to open them. When several teachers and then the principal failed to persuade me to look at them, or at some reward they claimed to be holding, I was handed over to the school nurse, who tried to pry the lids open and scratched one of them badly. My eye swelled up and I went rigid. The principal panicked and called Mother, who fetched me home. I wouldn't talk to her, or open my eyes, or bend, and they had to lay me on the back seat and when we reached the house Mother had to lift me up the steps one at a time. Then she put me on the couch and played the piano to me all afternoon. Finally I opened my eyes. We hugged each other and I wept. Mother did not really believe my tears, but she was willing to accept them because I had staged them for her benefit.

My lying separated us, too, and the fact that my promises not to lie anymore seemed to mean nothing to me. Often my lies came back to her in embarrassing ways, people stopping her in the street and saying how sorry they were to hear that such and such had happened. No one in the neighborhood enjoyed embarrassing Mother, and these situations stopped occurring once everybody got wise to me. There was no saving her from strangers, though. The summer after Father died I visited my uncle in Redding and when I got back I found to my surprise that Mother had come to meet my bus. I tried to slip away from the gentleman who had sat next to me but I couldn't shake him. When he saw Mother embrace me he came up and presented her with a card and told her to get in touch with him if things got any worse. She gave him his card back and told him to mind his own business. Later, on the way home, she made me repeat what I had said to the man. She shook her head. "It's not fair to people," she said, "telling them things like that. It confuses them." It seemed to me that Mother had confused the man, not I, but I didn't say so. I agreed with her that I shouldn't say such things and promised not to do it again, a promise I broke three hours later in conversation with a woman in the park.

It wasn't only the lies that disturbed Mother; it was their morbidity. This was the real issue between us, as it had been between her and my father. Mother did volunteer work at Children's Hospital and St. Anthony's Dining Hall, collected things for the St. Vincent de Paul Society. She was a lighter of candles. My brother and sisters took after her in this way. My father was a curser of the dark. And he loved to curse the dark. He was never more alive than when he was indignant about something. For this reason the most important act of the day for him was the reading of the evening paper.

Ours was a terrible paper, indifferent to the city that bought it, indifferent to medical discoveries—except for new kinds of gases that made your hands fall off when you sneezed—and indifferent to politics and art. Its business was outrage, horror, gruesome coincidence. When my father sat down in the living room with the paper Mother stayed in the kitchen and kept the children busy, all except me, because I was quiet and could be trusted to amuse myself. I amused myself by watching my father.

He sat with his knees spread, leaning forward, his eyes only inches from the print. As he read he nodded to himself. Sometimes he swore and threw the paper down and paced the room, then picked it up and began again. Over a period of time he developed the habit of reading aloud to me. He always started with the society section, which he called the parasite page. This column began to take on the character of a comic strip or a serial, with the same people showing up from one day to the next, blinking in chiffon, awkwardly holding their drinks for the sake of Peninsula orphans, grinning under sunglasses on the deck of a ski hut in the Sierras. The skiers really got his goat, probably because he couldn't understand them. The activity itself was inconceivable to him. When my sisters went to Lake Tahoe one winter weekend with some friends and came back excited about the beauty of the place, Father calmed them right down. "Snow," he said, "is overrated."

Then the news, or what passed in the paper for news: bodies unearthed in Scotland, former Nazis winning elections, rare animals slaughtered, misers expiring naked in freezing houses upon mattresses stuffed with thousands, millions; marrying priests, divorcing actresses, high-rolling oilmen building fantastic mausoleums in honor of a favorite horse, cannibalism. Through all this my father waded with a fixed and weary smile.

Mother encouraged him to take up causes, to join groups, but he would not. He was uncomfortable with people outside the family. He and my mother rarely went out, and rarely had people in, except on feast days and national holidays. Their guests were always the same, Dr. Murphy and his wife and several others whom they had known since childhood. Most of these people never saw each other outside our house and they didn't have much fun together. Father discharged his obligations as host by teasing everyone about stupid things they had said or done in the past and forcing them to laugh at themselves.

Though Father did not drink, he insisted on mixing cocktails for the guests. He would not serve straight drinks like rum-and-Coke or even Scotch-on-the-rocks, only drinks of his own devising. He gave them lawyerly names like "The Advocate," "The Hanging Judge," "The Ambulance Chaser," "The Mouthpiece," and described their concoction in detail. He told long, complicated stories in a near-whisper, making everyone lean in his direction, and repeated important lines; he also repeated the important lines in the stories my mother told, and corrected her when she got something wrong. When the guests came to the ends of their own stories, he would point out the morals.

Dr. Murphy had several theories about Father, which he used to test on me in the course of our meetings. Dr. Murphy had by this time given up his glasses for contact lenses, and lost weight in the course of fasts which he undertook regularly. Even with his baldness he looked years younger than when he had come to the parties at our house. Certainly he did not look like my father's contemporary, which he was.

One of Dr. Murphy's theories was that Father had exhibited a classic trait of people who had been gifted children by taking an undemanding position in an uninteresting firm. "He was afraid of finding his limits," Dr. Murphy told me: "As long as he kept stamping papers and making out wills, he could go on believing that he didn't *have* limits." Dr. Murphy's fascination with Father made me uneasy, and I felt traitorous listening to him. While he lived, my father would never have submitted himself for analysis; it seemed a betrayal to put him on the couch now that he was dead.

I did enjoy Dr. Murphy's recollections of Father as a child. He told me about something that happened when they were in the Boy Scouts.

Their troop had been on a long hike and Father had fallen behind. Dr. Murphy and the others decided to ambush him as he came down the trail. They hid in the woods on each side and waited. But when Father walked into the trap none of them moved or made a sound and he strolled on without even knowing they were there. "He had the sweetest look on his face," Dr. Murphy said, "listening to the birds, smelling the flowers, just like Ferdinand the Bull." He also told me that my father's drinks tasted like medicine.

While I rode my bicycle home from Dr. Murphy's office Mother fretted. She felt terribly alone but she didn't call anyone because she also felt like a failure. My lying had that effect on her. She took it personally. At such times she did not think of my sisters, one happily married, the other doing brilliantly at Fordham. She did not think of my brother Michael, who had given up college to work with runaway children in Los Angeles. She thought of me. She thought that she had made a mess of her family.

Actually she managed the family well. While my father was dying upstairs she pulled us together. She made lists of chores and gave each of us a fair allowance. Bedtimes were adjusted and she stuck by them. She set regular hours for homework. Each child was made responsible for the next eldest, and I was given a dog. She told us frequently, predictably, that she loved us. At dinner we were each expected to contribute something, and after dinner she played the piano and tried to teach us to sing in harmony, which I could not do. Mother, who was an admirer of the Trapp family, considered this a character defect.

Our life together was more orderly, healthy, while Father was dying than it had been before. He had set us rules to follow, not much different really than the ones Mother gave us after he got sick, but he had administered them in a fickle way. Though we were supposed to get an allowance we always had to ask him for it and then he would give us too much because he enjoyed seeming magnanimous. Sometimes he punished us for no reason, because he was in a bad mood. He was apt to decide, as one of my sisters was going out to a dance, that she had better stay home and do something to improve herself. Or he would sweep us all up on a Wednesday night and take us ice skating.

He changed after he learned about the cancer, and became more calm as the disease spread. He relaxed his teasing way with us, and from time to time it was possible to have a conversation with him which was not about the last thing that had made him angry. He stopped reading the paper and spent time at the window.

He and I became close. He taught me to play poker and sometimes helped me with my homework. But it wasn't his illness that drew us together. The reserve between us had begun to break down after the incident with the bear, during the drive home. Michael and my sisters were furious with him for making us leave early and wouldn't talk to him or look at him. He joked: though it had been a grisly experience we should grin and bear it—and so on. His joking seemed perverse to the others, but not to me. I had seen how terrified he was when the bear came into the camp. He had held himself so still that he had begun to tremble. When Mother started pitching rocks I thought he was going to bolt. I understood—I had been frightened too. The others took it as a lark after they got used to having the bear around, but for Father and me it got worse through the night. I was glad to be out of there, grateful to Father for getting me out. I saw that his jokes were how he held himself together. So I reached out to him with a joke: " 'There's a bear outside,' said Tom intently." The others turned cold looks on me. They thought I was sucking up. But Father smiled.

When I thought of other boys being close to their fathers I thought of them hunting together, tossing a ball back and forth, making birdhouses in the basement, and having long talks about girls, war, careers. Maybe the reason it took us so long to get close was that I had this idea. It kept getting in the way of what we really had, which was a shared fear.

Toward the end Father slept most of the time and I watched him. From below, sometimes, faintly, I heard Mother playing the piano. Occasionally he nodded off in his chair while I was reading to him; his bathrobe would fall open then, and I would see the long new scar on his stomach, red as blood against his white skin. His ribs all showed and his legs were like cables.

I once read in a biography of a great man that he "died well." I assume the writer meant that he kept his pain to himself, did not set off false alarms, and did not too much inconvenience those who were to stay behind. My father died well. His irritability gave way to something else, something like serenity. In the last days he became tender. It was as though he had been rehearsing the scene, that the anger of his life had been a kind of stage fright. He managed his audience—us—with an old trouper's sense of when to clown and when to stand on his dignity. We were all moved, and admired his courage, as he intended we should. He died downstairs in a shaft of late afternoon sunlight on New Year's Day, while I was reading to him. I was alone in the house and didn't know what to do. His body did not frighten me but immediately and sharply I missed my father. It seemed wrong to leave him sitting up and I tried to carry him upstairs to the bedroom but it was too hard, alone. So I called up my friend Ralphy across the street. When he came over and saw what I wanted him for he started crying but I made him help me anyway. A couple of hours later Mother got home and when I told her that Father was dead she ran upstairs, calling his name. A few minutes later she came back down. "Thank God," she said, "at least he died in bed." This seemed important to her and I didn't tell her otherwise. But that night Ralphy's parents called. They were, they said, shocked at what I had done and so was Mother when she heard the story, shocked and furious. Why? Because I had not told her the truth? Or because she had learned the truth, and could not go on believing that Father had died in bed? I really don't know.

"Mother," I said, coming into the living room, "I'm sorry about the letter. I really am."

She was arranging wood in the fireplace and did not look at me or speak for a moment. Finally she finished and straightened up and brushed her hands. She stepped back and looked at the fire she had laid. "That's all right," she said. "Not bad for a consumptive."

"Mother, I'm sorry."

"Sorry? Sorry you wrote it or sorry I found it?"

"I wasn't going to mail it. It was a sort of joke."

"Ha ha." She took up the whisk broom and swept bits of bark into the fireplace, then closed the drapes and settled on the couch. "Sit down," she said. She crossed her legs. "Listen, do I give you advice all the time?"

"Yes."

"I do?"

I nodded.

"Well, that doesn't make any difference. I'm supposed to. I'm your mother. I'm going to give you some more advice, for your own good. You don't have to make all these things up, James. They'll happen anyway." She picked at the hem of her skirt. "Do you understand what I'm saying?"

"I think so."

"You're cheating yourself, that's what I'm trying to tell you. When you get to be my age you won't know anything at all about life. All you'll know is what you've made up."

I thought about that. It seemed logical.

She went on. "I think maybe you need to get out of yourself more. Think more about other people."

The doorbell rang.

"Go see who it is," Mother said. "We'll talk about this later."

It was Dr. Murphy. He and Mother made their apologies and she insisted that he stay for dinner. I went to the kitchen to fetch ice for their drinks, and when I returned they were talking about me. I sat on the sofa and listened. Dr. Murphy was telling Mother not to worry. "James is a good boy," he said. "I've been thinking about my oldest, Terry. He's not really dishonest, you know, but he's not really honest either. I can't seem to reach him. At least James isn't furtive."

"No," Mother said, "he's never been furtive."

Dr. Murphy clasped his hands between his knees and stared at them. "Well, that's Terry. Furtive."

Before we sat down to dinner Mother said grace; Dr. Murphy bowed his head and closed his eyes and crossed himself at the end, though he had lost his faith in college. When he told me that, during one of our meetings, in just those words, I had the picture of a raincoat hanging by itself outside a dining hall. He drank a good deal of wine and persistently turned the conversation to the subject of his relationship with Terry. He admitted that he had come to dislike the boy. Then he mentioned several patients of his by name, some of them known to Mother and me, and said that he disliked them too. He used the word "dislike" with relish, like someone on a diet permitting himself a single potato chip. "I don't know what I've done wrong," he said abruptly, and with reference to no particular thing. "Then again maybe I haven't done anything wrong. I don't know what to think anymore. Nobody does."

"I know what to think," Mother said.

"So does the solipsist. How can you prove to a solipsist that he's not creating the rest of us?"

This was one of Dr. Murphy's favorite riddles, and almost any pretext was sufficient for him to trot it out. He was a child with a card trick.

"Send him to bed without dinner," Mother said. "Let him create that."

Dr. Murphy suddenly turned to me. "Why do you do it?" he asked. It was a pure question, it had no object beyond the satisfaction of his curiosity. Mother looked at me and there was the same curiosity in her face.

"I don't know," I said, and that was the truth.

Dr. Murphy nodded, not because he had anticipated my answer but because he accepted it. "Is it fun?"

"No, it's not fun. I can't explain."

"Why is it all so sad?" Mother asked. "Why all the diseases?"

"Maybe," Dr. Murphy said, "sad things are more interesting."

"Not to me," Mother said.

"Not to me, either," I said. "It just comes out that way."

After dinner Dr. Murphy asked Mother to play the piano. He particularly wanted to sing "Come Home Abbie, the Light's on the Stair."

"That old thing," Mother said. She stood and folded her napkin deliberately and we followed her into the living room. Dr. Murphy stood behind her as she warmed up. Then they sang "Come Home Abbie, the Light's on the Stair," and I watched him stare down at Mother intently, as if he were trying to remember something. Her own eyes were closed. After that they sang "O Magnum Mysterium." They sang it in parts and I regretted that I had no voice, it sounded so good.

"Come on, James," Dr. Murphy said as Mother played the last chords. "These old tunes not good enough for you?"

"He just can't sing," Mother said.

When Dr. Murphy left, Mother lit the fire and made more coffee. She slouched down in the big chair, sticking her legs straight out and moving her feet back and forth. "That was fun," she said.

"Did you and Father ever do things like that?"

"A few times, when we were first going out. I don't think he really enjoyed it. He was like you."

I wondered if Mother and Father had had a good marriage. He admired her and liked to look at her; every night at dinner he had us move the candlesticks slightly to the right and left of center so he could see down the length of the table. And every evening when she set the table she put them in the center again. She didn't seem to miss him very much. But I wouldn't really have known if she did, and anyway I didn't miss him all that much myself, not the way I had. Most of the time I thought about other things.

"James?"

I waited.

"I've been thinking that you might like to go down and stay with Michael for a couple of weeks or so."

"What about school?"

"I'll talk to Father McSorley. He won't mind. Maybe this problem will take care of itself if you start thinking about other people."

"I do."

"I mean helping them, like Michael does. You don't have to go if you don't want to."

"It's fine with me. Really. I'd like to see Michael."

"I'm not trying to get rid of you."

"I know."

Mother stretched, then tucked her feet under her. She sipped noisily at her coffee. "What did that word mean that Murphy used? You know the one?"

"Paranoid? That's where somebody thinks everyone is out to get him. Like that woman who always grabs you after Mass—Frances."

"Not paranoid. Everyone knows what that means. Sol-something."

"Oh. Solipsist. A solipsist is someone who thinks he creates everything around him."

Mother nodded and blew on her coffee, then put it down without drinking from it. "I'd rather be paranoid. Do you really think Frances is?"

"Of course. No question about it."

"I mean really *sick?*"

"That's what paranoid *is*, is being sick. What do you think, Mother?"

"What are you so angry about?"

"I'm not angry." I lowered my voice. "I'm not angry. But you don't believe those stories of hers, do you?"

"Well, no, not exactly. I don't think she knows what she's saying, she just wants someone to listen. She probably lives all by herself in some little room. So she's paranoid. Think of that. And I had no idea. James, we should pray for her. Will you remember to do that?"

I nodded. I thought of Mother singing "O Magnum Mysterium," saying grace, praying with easy confidence, and it came to me that her imagination was superior to mine. She could imagine things as coming together, not falling apart. She looked at me and I shrank; I knew exactly what she was going to say. "Son," she said, "do you know how much I love you?"

The next afternoon I took the bus to Los Angeles. I looked forward to the trip, to the monotony of the road and the empty fields by the roadside. Mother walked with me down the long concourse. The station was crowded and oppressive. "Are you sure this is the right bus?" she asked at the loading platform.

"Yes."

"It looks so old."

"Mother—"

"All right." She pulled me against her and kissed me, then held me an extra second to show that her embrace was sincere, not just like everyone else's, never having realized that everyone else does the same thing. I boarded the bus and we waved at each other until it became embarrassing. Then Mother began checking through her handbag for something. When she had finished I stood and adjusted the luggage over my seat. I sat and we smiled at each other, waved when the driver gunned the engine, shrugged when he got up suddenly to count the passengers, waved again when he resumed his seat. As the bus pulled out my mother and I were looking at each other with plain relief.

I had boarded the wrong bus. This one was bound for Los Angeles but not by the express route. We stopped in San Mateo, Palo Alto, San Jose, Castroville. When we left Castroville it began to rain, hard; my window would not close all the way, and a thin stream of water ran down the wall onto my seat. To keep dry I had to stay away from the wall and lean forward. The rain fell harder. The engine of the bus sounded as though it were coming apart.

In Salinas the man sleeping beside me jumped up but before I had a chance to change seats his place was taken by an enormous woman in a print dress, carrying a shopping bag. She took possession of her seat and spilled over onto half of mine, backing me up to the wall. "That's a storm," she said loudly, then turned and looked at me. "Hungry?" Without waiting for an answer she dipped into her bag and pulled out a piece of chicken and thrust it at me. "Hey, by God," she hooted, "look at him go to town on that drumstick!" A few people turned and smiled. I smiled back around the bone and kept at it. I finished that piece and she handed me another, and then another. Then she started handing out chicken to the people in the seats near us.

Outside of San Luis Obispo the noise from the engine grew suddenly louder and just as suddenly there was no noise at all. The driver pulled off to the side of the road and got out, then got on again dripping wet. A few moments later he announced that the bus had broken down and they were sending another bus to pick us up. Someone asked how long that might take and the driver said he had no idea. "Keep your pants on!" shouted the woman next to me. "Anybody in a hurry to get to L.A. ought to have his head examined."

The wind was blowing hard around the bus, driving sheets of rain against the window on both sides. The bus swayed gently. Outside the light was brown and thick. The woman next to me pumped all the people around us for their itineraries and said whether or not she had ever been where they were from or where they were going. "How about you?" She slapped my knee. "Parents own a chicken ranch? I hope so!" She laughed. I told her I was from San Francisco. "San Francisco, that's where my husband was stationed." She asked me what I did there and I told her I worked with refugees from Tibet.

"Is that right? What do you do with a bunch of Tibetans?"

"Seems like there's plenty of other places they could've gone," said a man in front of us. "Coming across the border like that. We don't go there."

"What do you do with a bunch of Tibetans?" the woman repeated.

"Try to find them jobs, locate housing, listen to their problems."

"You understand that kind of talk?"

"Yes."

"Speak it?"

"Pretty well. I was born and raised in Tibet. My parents were missionaries over there."

Everyone waited.

"They were killed when the Communists took over."

The big woman patted my arm.

"It's all right," I said.

"Why don't you say some of that Tibetan?"

"What would you like to hear?"

"Say 'The cow jumped over the moon.'" She watched me, smiling, and when I finished she looked at the others and shook her head. "That was pretty. Like music. Say some more."

"What?"

"Anything."

They bent toward me. The windows suddenly went blind with rain.

The driver had fallen asleep and was snoring gently to the swaying of the bus. Outside the muddy light flickered to pale yellow, and far off there was thunder. The woman next to me leaned back and closed her eyes and then so did all the others as I sang to them in what was surely an ancient and holy tongue.